THE ST. NICHOLAS ANTHOLOGY

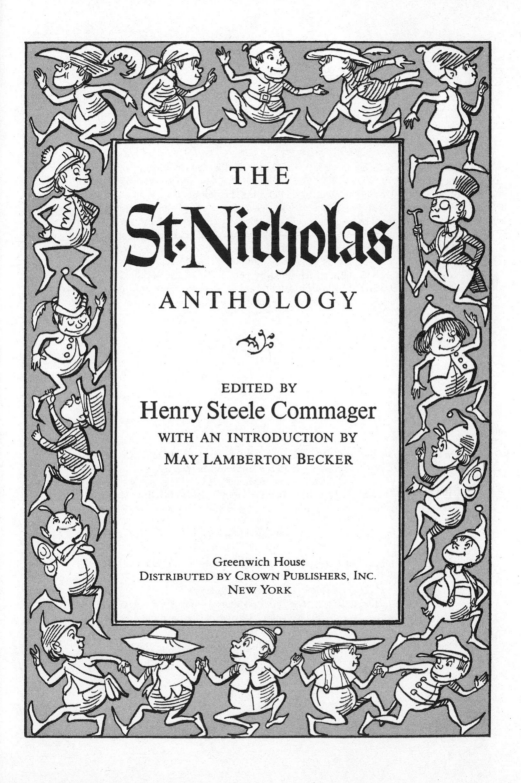

THE
St·Nicholas
ANTHOLOGY

EDITED BY
Henry Steele Commager
WITH AN INTRODUCTION BY
MAY LAMBERTON BECKER

Greenwich House
DISTRIBUTED BY CROWN PUBLISHERS, INC.
NEW YORK

ACKNOWLEDGMENTS: here made for permission to reprint the copyrighted items in this volume.
Copyright, 1909, 1910, 1911, 1912, 1913, 1914, 1915, 1916, 1918, 1919, 1920, 1921, 1923, 1924, 1925, 1926, 1928, 1929, 1930, 1931, 1933, by The Century Co., 1934, 1935, 1937, 1938, 1939, 1940, 1941, 1942, 1943, 1944, 1946, 1947, by D. Appleton-Century Company, Inc.
Reprinted by permission of D. Appleton-Century Company, Inc.
For "Tom Sawyer and His Band" from *The Boy's Life of Mark Twain* by Albert Bigelow Paine. Copyright, 1915, 1916, by Harper & Brothers. Copyright, 1943, 1944, by Louise Paine Moore, Joy Paine Cushman and Frances Paine Wade.
"The Patriots" by Robert S. Hillyer, reprinted by permission of the author, copyright, 1909.
Acknowledgment is also gratefully made to Mr. Edward B. Maguire, representing the latter owners of *St. Nicholas Magazine,* for his courtesy in granting permission to reprint several items.

Library of Congress Cataloging in Publication Data
Main entry under title:
The St. Nicholas anthology.
Originally published: New York : Random House, 1948–1950.
Summary: Contains the "best" of "St. Nicholas," a magazine for boys and girls published at the turn of the century. Includes stories, poems, and original illustrations.
1. Children's literature. [1. Literature—Collections. 2. Short stories] I. Commanger, Henry Steele, 1902– II. St. Nicholas (New York, N.Y.)
PZ5.S785 1983 810'.8'09282 [Fic] 83-11664

ISBN: 0-517-420821

h g f e d c b

A little maid went to a book-store one day
To buy something jolly to read;
  And the queerest old clerk, in the busiest way,
Came forward and sang her the funniest lay,
  At the very top of his speed:

"There 's Chaucer and Spenser and Milton and Pope,
  With Dante and Homer and William Shakspere;
Kipling and Barrie and Anthony Hope;
  Tennyson, Browning, and Sidney Lanier.
There 's Longfellow, Hawthorne, Lowell, and Poe,
  With Petrarch and Plato and Bacon and Gray;
There 's Richardson, Fielding, and Daniel Defoe,
  Cowley and Chatterton, Collins and Gay.
We 've Goethe and Schiller; we 've Heine, Carlisle,
  Kingsley and Bancroft and Howells and Grant;
Beaumont and Fletcher and Madame de Staël,
  Ian Maclaren and Walter Besant.
There 's—"

"Oh, Mr. Clerk," the little maid said,
  "You have really been very kind;
But I can't get all of those names in my head;
But I think I will take from that shelf, instead—
  ST. NICHOLAS, if you don't mind."

MONTROSE J. MOSES

To STEELE and NELL

who helped make it

and to ELISABETH who enjoyed it

CONTENTS

ST. NICHOLAS LEAGUE

RIDDLE BOX

INTRODUCTION

by May Lamberton Becker

IF ANYONE had told the children on our block, the summer that I was ten years old, that some day one of us would be an editor of *St. Nicholas,* we wouldn't have believed a word of it. Mary Mapes Dodge was then the editor; she always had been and always would be, one of the fixed facts in our world: her name was on our magazine and we knew, from her picture, just how she looked. However, I fear we had but a vague idea of what an editor was and certainly no notion of what one did to make a magazine. So far as we were concerned, *St. Nicholas* came to us like anything in nature, like the seasons, like the weather. In summer we knew it would bring us outdoor reading, in September *St. Nicholas* knew we were back in school; when winter's cold had firmly settled in, Thanksgiving stories and directions for homemade presents announced the approach of that great annual event, the Special Christmas Number, a real "visit of St. Nicholas" coming early enough for us to rehearse its entertainments for parlor performance or memorize its verses for the Sunday School tree. You could, and we did, go round the year with our magazine, knowing that, punctual to the day, it would be with us.

Each of us on our block read every word of it. Those who did not subscribe borrowed it from their best friends, and those who did, kept track of each copy lest it should be too often borrowed away and lost. For as soon as the next month's magazine came in, we would put the last one, already showing loving signs of wear, with its predecessors in a pile on top of the bookcase, and when there were enough for a volume our parents would send them off somewhere and back they would come in a Bound Volume, splendid in crimson covers stamped in gold. Then we would read everything in this all over again, and as long as we were children there it would be for rainy days. If you went visiting and caught sight of those crimson covers in a strange bookcase, it wasn't strange any more, for anyone who owned a volume of *St. Nicholas* knew that visiting children would get it out and go to reading.

Well, in time—a long time after—the incredible did come to pass and one of us became an editor of *St. Nicholas.* The window beside my editorial desk was high up in the air, looking out over a skyscraper city very different from the New York of Mary Mapes Dodge. There wasn't a great deal in the room that she would have recognized, but on the other side of my window, extending all the way to the door, was something that would have made her feel, at first sight, instantly and beautifully at home. This was a great black walnut bookcase, in which, rising shelf upon shelf, were every one of those crimson and gold volumes that had been published from the year it began, 1873, to that in which I became literary editor. I never saw a piece of furniture so hard for people to pass. Men and women who came on business would stop short, search the shelves for the year when they used to "take *St. Nicholas*," pull out the time-worn volume and lose themselves in its pages. Famous authors whose first appearance in print had been in the St. Nicholas League for Young Contributors, founded in 1899, would turn to poems that won silver badges or names in its roll of honor. All this you might expect, but what most delighted me was that children as young as I was when first I came under its spell were enchanted by these volumes in just the same way. Whenever they came, they came again: often they brought friends: it was nothing unusual for me, on my way from desk to door, to step carefully around some little person on the floor, surrounded by those big crimson books and lost to the outer world in one of them.

I used to think how wonderful it would be if just the right person should some day go through those volumes as if they were a garden, gathering from it a great bouquet of every sort of its flowers. Of course its serials at once appeared in book form and most of them stayed here indefinitely; many of its verses may be found in the Collected Works of celebrated poets; stories re-told from its pages have been gathered by subject into little volumes, and good reading they used to be. But they couldn't have the special charm of our magazine, which was that it had something about everything, all together in one delicious assortment for us to choose what—and when—we pleased. An anthology like that—what a book it would be!—and, looking at the size of

that bookcase and knowing the riches it contained, how could anyone ever get it done?

So you may imagine my delight when I found that it had actually been done, and that the selection had been made in the right way by Henry Steele Commager. For just as older people couldn't get past that crimson-and-gold bookcase without reading something in it, so people old enough to have children of their own are going to dip into this big book and find their own youth awaiting them. These editors have been young together while they were making these selections, and people who bring it home for their sons and daughters will share more than the book with them. They will share something even sweeter than happiness, which is happiness remembered.

Indeed from the very first and throughout its long life, *St. Nicholas* owed its distinctive character and the success with which this character was maintained to the constant co-operation of youth and maturity. Mrs. Dodge had married young: when her two boys were young and she began to write children's stories she read them whatever she wrote, talked it over with them—and listened to what they said. Eight years after she had written *Hans Brinker*, she was asked by a famous publishing house to create a children's magazine: as editor-in-chief she could do what she pleased with it, provided it would be the best magazine for young folks in the world. So she planned it, named it, and for thirty years conducted it: then she retired and William Fayal Clarke took over: he had been on the editorial staff since the first number, as assistant editor, associate editor and editor-in-chief from 1905 to 1927. Then came others, George F. Thompson, Albert G. Lanier, and all this time young folks who read it kept telling the editor what they thought about it. *St. Nicholas* never offered them anything that did not come up to its high standard. When people who used to take it grew up and had children of their own, they brought home *St. Nicholas* and found it had caught up with the next generation and for all its years, was still new as tomorrow.

Here in these pages you may see what is meant by "the St. Nicholas tradition." This is more than a book. It is a living memory.

PREFACE

by Henry Steele Commager

THE REMEMBRANCE of things past is a fitful affair, but one memory that lingers with me, triumphing over the vicissitudes of time and age, is of the monthly arrival of *St. Nicholas*. There were three of us boys, and as I was the youngest, my turn was naturally last, and I can recall even now (or is it imagination?) the sense of injustice which this stirred in me. We all read *St. Nick* through—the serials first, for we were impatient to know what new adventures befell our heroes and (let me confess) heroines; then the stories, the historical sketches, the League, and even the puzzles. There were other magazines, too—the *Youth's Companion* was a special favorite —but none of them came up to *St. Nick,* none inspired such affection.

All that came to an end, far too soon, as I know now. I left childhood behind me, as even readers of *St. Nicholas* must. But in proper time I married and had children of my own, and found my thoughts reverting once more to *St. Nick*. It was not just sentimentality—I do not say that apologetically, for I do not know why I should be ashamed to confess to sentiment —but a wish that my own children could have something as delightful and exciting as *St. Nicholas*. Alas, poor old *St. Nick* was on its last legs, then, and by the time my boy was old enough for it, it had given up the ghost. Besides, it was the old *St. Nick* that I wanted, not any of your modern magazines, competing desperately and hopelessly with comics, radios, and movies. Fortunately the old *St. Nicholases* were not hard to find, and whenever I ran across those large volumes in their ornate gold and red bindings, I bought them. After a time I had quite an imposing shelf of them. We took them up to the farm, in Vermont, and on rainy days the children would take them down (just as so many children had, in the past) and sprawl on the floor with them, or, better yet, persuade their mother to read from them.

Thus the idea was born of a *St. Nicholas* anthology. It was not just that Steele and Nell enjoyed these volumes, though that was reassuring enough. It was the discovery that their parents enjoyed them, too, and not just vicariously, or as an exercise in nostalgia. *St. Nicholas* held up, through the years! The stories were as good as any that were being written now; the illustrations were incomparably better than any to be found in these decadent days of photography. Why not make a selection of the best of *St. Nicholas*, pictures and all?

I suggested the idea to Mr. Bennett Cerf, whose heart is ever young and gay, and who, as a winner of one of the League's Silver Badges, was no mean St. Nicholaser himself. His approval was prompt and enthusiastic. With characteristic energy he found me a complete set of *St. Nick* from

1873 to 1939, which, to the delight of the whole family, promptly arrived at the house. We had to build new bookshelves for it, and very handsome they were, too, row on row of gaudy red.

There are many ways of compiling an anthology but none, I am sure, as delightful as that which we found. It was understood, from the beginning, that this was to be a family enterprise, and that's what it was. *St. Nick* soon took over the house. One upstairs room had been set aside as a work room, but *St. Nick* flowed irresistibly down the stairs, inundating living room and study; wherever we turned we would stumble on leaning towers of it, and every chair and table was littered with piles of stories torn ruthlessly from their protesting volumes. Evan did the major part of the work—if so vulgar a term can be used for an indulgence so delightful. She read everything, and everything that she liked she passed on to me with her comments, unfailingly sound. I read everything too—well, almost everything; it was not that I mistrusted Evan's judgment, for a moment, but I wanted to see for myself. And besides I wasn't going to miss any of the fun. Those pieces which we agreed upon then went to the children, for the sternest of tests. Steele and Nell (Lisa was too little for anything but the pictures, and the general excitement) read every item, read it and passed it on, with the ruthlessness of childhood. We were, we thought, wonderfully efficient. A card was clipped to every story, and on it the children wrote their verdict. What these verdicts lacked in subtlety, they more than made up in incisiveness. Steele and Nell, I feel, are clearly the ideal book-reviewers for the new generation which wants everything digested into capsule form: their comments were either "terrible," "neat" or "swell."

Sometimes Evan and I were bold enough to differ with them, but on the whole this anthology consists of those stories and articles and poems which wrung from the children the verdict "swell." There are exceptions—particularly in the poetry and the selections from the League, but it can be said that everything in this anthology had the approval of all four of the editors, and that, for nine-tenths of the material, that approval was enthusiastic and unqualified.

For Evan and me, the most flattering part of all this was to find our own judgment so often confirmed by our children. It was not only flattering; it was reassuring. For it suggested (what indeed every reader of *St. Nicholas* knows) that the stories that Miss Dodge and her successors chose can stand the test of time, that for children's literature standards change but little over the years, and that what is really good appeals equally to children and to grown-ups.

Most of the problems which we anticipated somehow took care of themselves. We feared that many of the stories would be dated, the language stilted and archaic, the action tame. We should, of course, have known better; after all *Little Women* delights every generation anew. We feared that there would be grave difficulties in selecting material for one particular age level—the employment of Steele and Nell dictated that at from ten to fourteen —but this fear, too, was unfounded. The best stories already fitted that age level, and where they did not, as with "Rumpty-Dudget's Tower" or the Brownie's poetic adventures, we simply put them in anyway, consoling ourselves with the recollection that a *foolish* consistency was the hobgoblin of little minds. The real problem— the only problem—was to know what to leave out. Had we had our own way this anthology would probably have run to several volumes and in our more ecstatic moments we talked of a Second and Third *St. Nicholas* anthology. But some concession had to be made to practicality, if not to sheer weight, and in the end, with, I must confess, some bitter quarrels and painful repinings, many precious stories were abandoned. What is left is, we think, pure gold.

So here it is, the best of *St. Nick*. Here are the famous names (and what magazine ever boasted more famous names)— Kipling and Howells and Stockton and Lanier and Joel Chandler Harris and Louisa May Alcott and Jack London and Richard Harding Davis and so many others. Here are examples of some of the serials that brought such delight—the Peterkin papers and the adventures of Pinkey Perkins, and the Brownies, and even some of the incomparable Ralph Henry Barbour, though alas there was no space for a complete Barbour book. Here are the poets whose faces were once so familiar to us, from the game of Authors: Longfellow and Whittier and Tennyson and others who came after the Victorian Age but are just as precious, Eugene Field and James Whitcomb Riley. And here, too, are all the familiar illustrations, the wonderful Arthur Rackhams and the brilliant Howard Pyles and the exquisite A. B. Frosts.

No book ever gave more pleasure, in the making, than this. If it gives even a small part of that pleasure to those who read it, I shall be content.

Rye, New York

THE ST. NICHOLAS ANTHOLOGY

A STORY about ANCESTORS

by DOROTHY CANFIELD

JIMMY came to the door of the living-room and stopped short, looking very cross to see that his mother had a caller. He did n't look so cross âs his mother felt, for the caller was an old gentleman whom she had never seen before, who said he was a distant cousin, and who wanted to find out all about their great-grandfathers. He seemed to think they were very important, but Jimmy's mother did n't, and she was wishing very much he would go away and ask somebody else. Jimmy wished so too, from the expression of his face.

Then he wcnt away and his mother heard the typewriter in her study tapping slowly. When he came back, he went into the room, endured being introduced to the old gentleman, and did not squirm too visibly when the caller said that the shape of his head was like that of one of his great uncles'. He had a piece of paper in his hand, and as soon as he could, he laid it on his mother's lap and looked at her hopefully. On it he had written:

dear mother

> will you please tell me a made-to-order stoy about a ironing-bord, a big grandfather clock a bag of pop-corn a bottle of ink a yellow and blak and red stone
>
> good bye mother
> from Jimmy

His mother read it and raised her eyebrows. Jimmy looked at the old gentleman and sighed. It was plain he wished he could do something more than sigh. So did his mother.

"A fine little chap," said the gentleman.

Jimmy shuddered and went away.

But not far. For at the very instant when the old gentleman was saying good-by at the door, Jimmy's mother felt herself clutched from behind.

"Now!" said Jimmy. "Let's beat it."

So they did, off into the pine woods, where they couldn't be seen by any more callers.

But still they could n't seem to get rid of the old gentleman's ideas. Perhaps they had slipped into the story when Jimmy had laid the paper on his mother's lap.

"It's funny," he said, "and you may not like it very well; but this very story is about your great-grandfather and your grand-father."

3

Jimmy looked alarmed.

"But there 's a skunk in it," said his mother.

"Oh, that's all right then," said Jimmy. "Go ahead."

"It began rather a long time ago, maybe forty-five years ago, when my grandfather (that's your great-grandfather) was asked to make an address before a big meeting of teachers down in Massachusetts. He was a very careful man who believed in getting everything ready beforehand, and he started in at once to make ready for this. He had his best suit cleaned, bought himself a fresh necktie, wrote his speech all out, then copied it; more than a week before the day he had spoken to the livery-stable man about driving him to the train. For there were n't many trains a day, forty-five years ago, and to get to his meeting on time, he 'd have to be driven fifteen miles to a junction where he could catch a train going south.

"The morning in September when he was to start was lovely and sunny. He got a beautiful do-up on his necktie, and his coffee was just as he liked it. But right there his good luck stopped, for when he went into his study to get his clean-copied speech, he saw something dreadful. He had left the sheets all spread around, so the ink would dry well, and to hold them down, he had put on them a large oval paper-weight of onyx which somebody had brought him as a present from the Holy Land—the way they do to ministers."

"What 's onyx?" asked Jimmy.

"It 's a shiny sort of stone, red and yellow and black, that 's used for paper-weights," said his mother.

"Oh, yes," said Jimmy; "teacher has one on her desk. I did n't know what its name was. What was the matter with this one?"

"Matter enough. The cat had been playing with it, and had tipped it over against the ink-bottle, and knocked over the ink-

bottle. And all night long the spilled ink had been soaking into the nice, clean, freshly copied pages of Grandfather's speech!

"The cat had tipped it over."

"It was too late to do anything about it, for Patrick, the livery-stable man, had just driven up to the door. There was n't even time to *say* anything about it, although Grandfather had plenty he *could* have said. He just ground his teeth together hard, crammed his hat on over his eyes, and snatched up the rough notes for his speech. They were rather scribbly, and written crisscross of the paper and he had n't wanted to try to read them before an audience; but there wasn't anything else he could do now. He was lucky, in fact, that he had happened to put them on a shelf, and not on the table with his clean copy.

"He felt a little better after an hour's driving, for two reasons. For one, the livery-stable man was rather fresh from Ireland and had a lovely brogue that tickled Grandfather to hear, and he called Grandfather 'Your Reverence,' just like somebody in a story. And then he had turned out with his best outfit, the fast team of trotters, and his elegant new light wagon, the finest in town, with tan-colored velvet cushions and bright red wheels. Grandfather never cared anything about putting on style, but he always liked a good horse, and he did enjoy dusting along the road after those two sorrel spankers, heads up, tails flying, hoofs beating time together like a drummer rattling out a double-quick tattoo. Patrick was proud of them, and every time they went through a village he'd brisk his pair up to their fastest trot. Then he and Grandfather would put their heads together and pretend to be talking and not thinking a thing about their fast horses, although, as a matter of fact, they were very much put out if people did n't turn their heads to look after them as they went spinning through.

"In between villages, where there was n't anybody to see them, they often let the horses walk, and as they began to go down hill into Ransom's ravine, Patrick put the brake on and looked ahead sharply. The road was very rough and stony there, and, after dipping down steeply, led by a narrow bridge across a deep, black crack in the rocks, with a little mountain stream rushing and shouting at the bottom. It was something like a cañon in your geography book, only not so wide and deep. Plenty deep enough, though, for all drivers to want to keep their wits about them when they crossed the bridge.

"They were still a good way from it, when they made out something black and white ahead of them, just going on to the bridge.

" 'That can't be a—' said Patrick, shading his eyes with his hand, for the bushes were thick on each side of the road, just there, and the road was in shadow.

" 'Yes, it is too,' said Grandfather, putting his hand out on the reins in a hurry. 'Don't you go a step nearer till he gets out of the way.'

"Patrick was just as ready to stop as anybody. He had n't been in America very long, but plenty long enough to learn a good deal about skunks.

" 'Are n't they bold!' said Grandfather, surprised to see one right in the middle of the road.

" 'There is n't a thing for *them* to fear,' said Patrick, bitterly.

" 'Look—there 's another, just coming out of the bushes,' said Grandfather.

" 'Two more,' said Patrick, standing up in the wagon, to see better. 'A family of them, your Reverence,' he went on, sitting down hard.

"Sure enough, it was a mother skunk with five young ones, half-grown, about as big as sizable kittens. And they were surely out for a good time. The mother lay down spang in the middle of the road in the soft dust and spread out her legs comfortably, while the young ones began to play, frolicking up and down the bridge and jumping at each other in and out of the bushes.

"Grandfather looked at Patrick. And Patrick looked at Grandfather. Then Grandfather looked at his watch.

" 'Is there any way round?' he asked.

" 'No, your Reverence, not unless you go back ten miles to Bowley's cross-roads. This is the only bridge over the ravine between here and Pentonsville.'

" 'You don't say so!' said Grandfather, rather put out with Patrick.

"They waited a minute or two. Then Grandfather said: 'Come, come, this will never do! Let 's drive up nearer and throw stones at them.'

" 'Never in this world,' said Patrick. 'My wagon cost me seventy-five dollars, and it 's not a nickel it would be worth if we got the creatures' bad feelings stirred up. In fact, we 're a little too near right now to please me.'

" 'Well,' said Grandfather 'I 'll hold

the horses. You go along on foot and throw stones.'

" 'Saving your presence,' said Patrick, 'I had a brother once threw a stone at a skunk. One is enough for one family.'

" 'Nonsense!' said Grandfather; 'it would be perfectly safe from as far as you could throw a stone. Go along with you.'

" 'You never came near my poor brother right after he did it,' said Patrick; 'but, if you like, I 'll hold the horses and you can try it yourself.'

"Now Grandfather could throw a stone as far as the next man, and he did n't really believe that he would come to any harm. But all the same, it would be pretty serious if he did. He had often caught the scent of skunk from half a mile away, and it scared him to think what it might be, close to. Besides, it would n't have to be very bad, to be plenty bad enough to keep him from making his speech. He had a picture of himself standing up on the platform, with ever so slight an odor of skunk floating out from him over the audience. And he knew it would n't do.

" 'No, we 'll wait a while,' he said to Patrick; 'she can't stay there much longer.'

"But she did. The spot just suited her, so soft and quiet, and with plenty of hide-and-seek places for the children. You could see how she was enjoying it. She stretched out one leg and then another, turned over, rolled, sat up and scratched, and then started in to wash herself from head to foot, just like a cat in front of the kitchen stove.

"Grandfather and Patrick gave a groan. And Patrick just gave up. It was plain to see that he could n't think of anything to do but sit there and wait. Grandfather did n't believe in giving up, ever. So he cast around in his mind and hit on an idea.

" 'Maybe we can scare them away by yelling and shouting,' he suggested.

" 'Maybe,' said Patrick, looking uneasy;

'but don't you yell a yell, your Reverence, till I get my team farther away. The very harness would be no good to me if anything should happen.'

"He backed the horses up the road a little and then said: 'Well, we might try it. But not very loud if you please, sir. It might not be to her taste.'

" 'It would n't be any use unless it was loud,' said Grandfather.

" 'It 's not your wagon,' said Patrick, getting angry.

" 'It 's my best suit of clothes,' said Grandfather, angry himself, 'and you have promised to get me to the junction in time for that train.'

" 'Well, here goes,' said Patrick, and he said in rather a loudish voice, 'Get off wid ye! *Whey! Whey!*' the way you 'd talk to a cow in the cabbages.

" 'Oh, you 'll never get anywhere with that sort of business!' said Grandfather, crossly. He stood up in the wagon to get the good of his lungs and drew a deep breath and began to yell like an Indian or a stuck pig, at the top of his voice. He was noted for the loudness of his voice, too. They used to come from all around to get him to address open-air meetings, because he could be heard from so far. He was very cross indeed, by this time, and he let himself go, whooping and howling and bellowing till he was black in the face. He noticed after a while that Patrick was n't helping any, and glanced down to see why. There was Patrick, doubled over the arm of the seat, nearly dead with laughing.

"Grandfather stopped yelling and looked at Patrick coldly. Patrick was ashamed of himself; but he could n't stop.

" 'I can't help it, your Reverence,' he said, giggling and wiping his eyes. 'It 's like as if you were making a speech to the beasts, or preaching them a sermon, and they listening as pleased as any old woman in her pew.'

"As a matter of fact, the skunks had n't objected at all to Grandfather's noise. The mother had turned her head toward him, and two of the young ones had stopped playing, but they showed no signs of thinking his hullabaloo disagreeable. Somebody told Grandfather afterward that skunks are often quite deaf.

"Grandfather was so angry with Patrick and with the skunks and with himself by this time, that I'm sure I don't know what would have happened if at that very minute they had n't seen, far away on the other side of the skunks, a pair of horses come into sight where the road goes over the brow of the hill. Behind the horses was a lumber-wagon, with a canvas cover thrown over some bulky-looking objects. But the load could n't have been heavy, for the horses came along at a good trot. They did, that is, till they came near enough to see the black-and-white animals playing around in the road. Then the driver stopped so short that the wagon almost shoved the horses off their feet from behind.

"Patrick burst out laughing again, and this time Grandfather laughed with him. Not a good loud ha! ha! for he was still hot and angry, but a little grunt of a laugh he could n't keep back. They saw the driver and a little boy in the seat of the lumber-wagon peering down the road, shading their eyes with their hands.

"'ARE—THOSE—SKUNKS?' shouted the man to Grandfather and Patrick. He was so far away that they could only just catch what he said, although he was evidently yelling as loud as he could.

"'AND WHAT ELSE?' yelled Patrick back at him.

"The man stared at the animals harder for a moment, as if to be sure, and then yelled, 'WHY DON'T YOU DO SOMETHING ABOUT IT?'

"'Well, the nerve of him!' said Patrick and Grandfather, so mad at the man they forgot to be mad at each other.

"'DO IT YOURSELF!' shouted Patrick.

"'DO WHAT?' asked the man.

"'For goodness' sake!' said Grandfather, too exasperated to live. Then he raised his voice and shouted, 'THROW SOME STONES AT THEM!'

"'I DASSENT,' yelled back the man; 'GOT SOME VALLYBLE ANTIQUES IN MY WAGON.'

"'GET OUT ON FOOT AND THROW STONES,' shouted Patrick.

"'NOT ON YOUR LIFE!' yelled the man.

"'Some people are too selfish for this world!' said Patrick to Grandfather indignantly. He turned his back, as far as he could, on the skunks and the lumber-wagon and the man and the boy, and lighted his little short pipe. 'We'll just be waiting,' he said to Grandfather, 'for there 's nothing else to do.'

"So they waited. Grandfather held his watch in his hand, watching the second-hand going around faster and faster. The horses stamped and switched their tails against the flies, and tossed their heads till Patrick got out and undid the check-reins.

"Over in the lumber-wagon, Grandfather could see the little boy talking and talking to the man, and he wondered what the child could find to say that took so long. By and by, he saw the little boy get out of the wagon and disappear in the bushes; and a few minutes later, to their great astonishment, he came out of the woods beside the road, where Grandfather and Patrick sat waiting.

"'How 'd you get there?' they asked. 'Is there another bridge over the ravine?'

"'No, but there 's a narrow place where the rocks come pretty close together, and a tree 's fallen across,' he told them. 'I had an idea, and it was too long to yell at you, so I came around to tell you.'

"'Well, what 's your idea?' asked Grandfather, thinking it could n't amount to much.

"The little boy began. 'Old Judge Pell-sew is going to move out West, to live with his married daughter, and before he left he asked my father to take some of his old family relics up to his niece's house in Arlington, and that 's where we are going. It 's mostly a grandfather's clock, and a few chairs.'

" 'Well,' said Grandfather, very short, 'I don't see what that 's got to do with me. I must be at the junction in time for the eleven forty-five train south.'

" 'We live at the junction,' said the little boy, 'so how would this do? We 'll carry the things out into the woods, up the ravine, to the narrow place where I crossed, and you come there to help us get them across, and load them into your wagon. Then your team can turn around and carry the antiques back to Arlington, and we 'll turn around and carry you back to the junction.'

" 'I don't see myself,' said Grandfather, who must have been sixty years old then, 'I don't see myself carrying one end of a grandfather's clock and walking along a fallen tree over a thirty-foot drop.'

" 'Oh, that 'll be all right,' said the little boy. 'One of the things we have is an ironing-board, an extra long one, and we can lay that down for a bridge. Then the last fellow across can pull it over and take it along.'

" 'It might be worth trying,' said Grandfather, doubtfully.

"The little boy put his hands up to his mouth and yelled to his father, ' 'S ALL RIGHT!' and they saw the man get out of the wagon at once and begin to unload the things from the back.

"Patrick tied his horses and they hurried off into the woods after the little boy, for they had n't a minute to lose. The man was already at the narrow place with the ironing-board and two of the chairs. He laid down the board and it was *just* long enough. The little boy had to steady it with his foot as Patrick ran across it and grabbed the two chairs. Then the man rushed back to his wagon and brought the clock along, Grandfather helping carry it across the board. They got it into Patrick's wagon, and set it up in the front seat, and tied it in with the hitch-ropes. They then all tore back to the narrow place and skipped across the ironing-board, all but Patrick, who stooped over to pick it up. But it was heavier than he thought, and slipped right out of his hands and went falling down and down into the ravine.

"*Grandfather helped carry it across the board*"

Patrick looked scared, but the man called to him, 'Never mind! 'T wa'n't one of the antiques!' And then as Patrick nodded, relieved, he added, still shouting over his shoulder as he ran, 'The things are to go to Mrs. Pettingill's, on the West Road.'

" 'I have a brother living on the next farm to there,' Patrick shouted back. 'They 'll get there all right.'

"Grandfather and the man and the little boy piled into the empty lumber-wagon, the horses were turned around double-quick, and off they started, lickety-split. Grandfather knew they never could make it. But the man wanted to show that Patrick was n't the only person to have fast horses, and he kept his on the run for most of the four miles to the junction.

"At that, they 'd have missed the train if it had n't been a little late. They saw it pulling into the station as they came around the turn into the village street, and the man let out a yell at his horses. Down the slope they came, slam-banging along, Grandfather holding to his hat with one hand and to the side of the seat with the other. The conductor of the train thought it was a runaway, and stopped to see what would happen. And that was what saved Grandfather. They slued up in front of the station, the horses lathering white, the wagon swinging over on two wheels, and Grandfather fell out, shouting, 'Hold on! Hold on! Just a minute!' I tell you he could hardly believe it when he actually found himself sitting in the train, taking out his pocket-book, just like any other passenger, to pay for his ticket."

"He must have been feeling just about all right!" commented Jimmy, and rolled over from where he lay on the pine-needles.

His mother looked at him hard and shook her head. Jimmy sat up qickly.

"Great Scott, Mother, it was n't the *wrong train!*"

"No, there was but one south-bound train a day in those days. No, it was the right train all right. But half-way there, he remembered that he had left the notes for his speech in Patrick's wagon when he had made the change."

"For the land of—" Jimmy was horrified. "What did he *do?*"

"He did n't know what to do. And the closer he got to North Adams, the less he knew. He had been asked to tell them something about universities in England, and he had looked up lots of dates and history and statistics and things, and he could n't possibly remember them out of his head. What 's more, he was so shaken up that he could n't seem to think even what was the main part of his speech! Actually, when he stood upon the platform and faced his audience, he had n't thought of a single word to say."

Jimmy looked miserably worried. He forgot the whole middle part of his recitation the last time there was an entertainment at school. So he knew what it was like. He swallowed, in sympathy. "Well—"

"Here is what he did. It came to him, as he looked around the crowd and saw how friendly they seemed. He just started in at the beginning and told them all about what had happened—about the kitten that played with the paper-weight, and his driving so far to get his train, and the skunks and his yelling at them, and what he said, and what Patrick said. He had intended it only as an explanation of why he had n't his speech ready. But do you know, the audience seemed to think there was something funny about it! They got into such gales of laughing that he had to stop two or three times. And when he came to the last part, where he scrambled on the train, they all broke out applauding as if it were the end of a race.

"By that time Grandfather had his nerve back again, and when he told them about leaving his notes he went on, 'So I have n't any speech at all to make. But see here, maybe we can make one together. You must have wanted to know about English universities or you would n't have asked me to talk about them. Suppose you ask me what it was you wanted to know, and I 'll answer your questions?'

"And what do you think! It was the

"He remembered he had left the notes for his speech in Patrick's wagon"

greatest success. Everybody was sort of stirred up about the skunks and was n't afraid to ask questions. And what they asked made Grandfather think of the things he had planned to say, and they had a lovely time. Grandfather used to say that he never spent a better hour with an audience."

"I suppose he could use his notes for another time, too," said Jimmy, lying down again.

"No, he never could find them. When he went back, he asked Patrick about them, of course, but they had n't been seen. Patrick thought they 'd fallen out on the way back. Grandfather put a notice in the newspaper and offered a reward, but nobody ever paid any attention to it."

Jimmy's mother tried to make this sound like the end, but Jimmy cornered her by asking, "Did n't anybody ever find them?"

"Well, yes," she said, "although that part does n't really belong in here. It was queer! Years went by, and Grandfather grew to be an old, old man, who did n't make speeches any more. Then it was his son, my father, your grandfather, who gave the lectures. And one autumn, about twenty-five years after this, he was asked to speak for the Massachusetts teachers. There was n't anything queer about this, for they meet every year and always have to have people lecture them. But while he was still wondering what to talk about, little Alta Brown came up on the front porch, with some old yellow papers in her hand. 'Grandmother says to tell you she thinks these must belong to you,' she said to your grandfather. 'She had a clock-mender tinker up the grandfather's clock yesterday, and he found these in under a sort of false bottom. Grandmother thought it looked like your handwriting.'

"And there were the notes, for Alta's grandmother was the Mrs. Pettingill to whom the old clock had gone. Somehow they 'd been slipped into the clock when it was put in Patrick's wagon. Maybe the man put them there to make sure they did n't blow out, and forgot to say anything about it. Grandfather never thought of asking him. In fact, he did n't know his name and never saw him before or after that day.

"Well, my father was a great joker, and he thought, just for fun, he would tell the audience down in North Adams the story of the speech and then read it to them, twenty-five years behind-time. He thought perhaps it would amuse them. And it did. He happened to speak in the very same hall where Grandfather had been, and the second audience laughed just as hard over those skunks as the first one had. As he talked, an idea came to Father, and when he finished he said, 'It is quite possible that, among the older people here to-day, there may be some one who was present twenty-five years ago. It would be very interesting if so.'

"Then he stopped, and everybody in the audience turned his head around to see if anybody stood up. Father had half expected to see one or two old, old men stand up. But nobody did. Twenty-five years is a long time, after all.

"But right behind him, on the platform, he now heard somebody laughing, and, turning around, saw that it was the young mayor of the city, who was up there to give an address of welcome. He did n't look more than forty years old, and could n't possibly have been a teacher twenty-five years before that. But he now stood up and came forward to the front of the platform. 'I was n't *here*, on that occasion,' he said, while everybody held his breath to hear what he could possibly have to say; 'but I was *there*. I was the little boy who had the idea of using the ironing-board as a bridge.'

"At this, everybody began to laugh again, and some people clapped their hands. But he waved his arms to show them that he had n't finished, and went on: 'And now I 'm going to tell you something which I have never divulged to a soul from that day to this. But before I do, I wish to express a hope that there are plenty of baseball fans in this audience, people who really appreciate the high importance of baseball.'

"Everybody stared. What in the world had baseball to do with that story?

" 'Our town team was going to play the last game of the season that day, and I was crazy to go. But my father was an old-fashioned farmer, who thought that games were all foolishness. So when he said I had

to go up to Arlington with him to help load and unload those darned old antiques, I did n't even dare ask to stay to go to the baseball game. I felt pretty sore and mad about it, you can imagine, and more and more so as our horses trotted along, faster and faster, carrying me farther and farther from the baseball field. Although I knew there was n't the least hope, I kept on hoping, as children will, that something would happen—an earthquake, a flood, or one of the horses dropping dead with heart-failure. But although I knew all about them, and had often played with them when I was visiting the Penrose boys, I never once dreamed that that family of black-and-white cats on the Penrose farm could possibly be of any use in—'

"But he never got any farther. The very minute he said the word 'cats,' somebody in the audience snorted and shouted out a great 'Haw! haw! And then, like forty thousand bunches of firecrackers going off at once, everybody saw what had happened and burst out, just screaming with laughing. The more they laughed, the more they saw how funny it had been, and that made them laugh harder.

"My father laughed the hardest of all. He used to say afterward that they had to laugh twenty-five years' worth, all at once, to make up for the twenty-five years the joke had keep kept dark."

Jimmy and his mother got up and strolled back through the orchard toward the house, Jimmy thinking over the story silently, as he likes to do when there has been a good deal in it. Finally, "You did n't say anything about the bag of pop-corn," he said. "But I suppose he bought that and ate it on the train, going down."

"Yes," said his mother, "I suppose that was where the pop-corn came in."

THE PETERKINS CELEBRATE
THE FOURTH OF JULY

by Lucretia P. Hale

THE DAY began early.

A compact had been made with the little boys the evening before.

They were to be allowed to usher in the glorious day by the blowing of horns exactly at sunrise. But they were to blow them for precisely five minutes only, and no sound of the horns should be heard afterward till the family were down-stairs.

It was thought that a peace might thus be bought by a short though crowded period of noise.

The morning came. Even before the morning, at half-past three o'clock, a terrible blast of the horns aroused the whole family.

Mrs. Peterkin clasped her hands to her head and exclaimed: "I am thankful the lady from Philadelphia is not here!" For she had been invited to stay a week, but had declined to come before the Fourth of July, as she was not well, and her doctor had prescribed quiet.

And the number of the horns was most remarkable! It was as though every cow in the place had arisen and was blowing through both her own horns!

"How many little boys are there? How many have we?" exclaimed Mr. Peterkin, going over their names one by one mechanically, thinking he would do it, as he might count imaginary sheep jumping over a fence, to put himself to sleep. Alas! the counting could not put him to sleep now in such a din.

And how unexpectedly long the five minutes seemed! Elizabeth Eliza was to take out her watch and give the signal for the end of the five minutes and the ceasing of the horns. Why did not the signal come? Why did not Elizabeth Eliza stop them?

And certainly it was long before sunrise; there was no dawn to be seen!

"We will not try this plan again," said Mrs. Peterkin.

"If we live to another Fourth," added Mr. Peterkin, hastening to the door, to inquire into the state of affairs.

Alas! Amanda, by mistake, had waked up the little boys an hour too early. And by another mistake the little boys had invited three or four of their friends to spend the night with them. Mrs. Peterkin had given them permission to have the boys for the whole day, and they understood the day as beginning when they went to bed the night before. This accounted for the number of horns.

It would have been impossible to hear any explanation; but the five minutes were over, and the horns had ceased, and there remained only the noise of a singular leaping of feet, explained perhaps by a possible pillow-fight, that kept the family below partially awake until the bells and cannon made known the dawning of the glorious day—the sunrise, or "the rising of the sons," as Mr. Peterkin jocosely called it when they heard the little boys and their friends clattering down the stairs to begin the outside festivities.

They were bound first for the swamp, for Elizabeth Eliza, at the suggestion of the lady from Philadelphia, had advised them to hang some flags around the pillars of the piazza. Now the little boys knew of a place in the swamp where they had been in the habit of digging for "flag-root," and where they might find plenty of flag flowers. They did bring away all they could, but they were a little out of bloom. The boys were in the midst of nailing up all they had on the pillars of the piazza, when the procession of the Antiques and Horribles passed along. As the procession saw the festive arrangements on the piazza, and the crowd of boys, who cheered them loudly, it stopped to salute the house with some especial strains of greeting.

Poor Mrs. Peterkin! They were directly under her windows! In the few moments of quiet during the boys' absence from the house on their visit to the swamp, she had been trying to find out whether she had a sick-headache, or whether it was all the noise, and she was just deciding it was the sick-headache, but was falling into a light slumber, when the fresh noise outside began.

There were the imitations of the crowing of cocks and braying of donkeys, and the sound of horns, encored and increased by the cheers of the boys. Then began the torpedoes, and the Antiques and Horribles had Chinese crackers also!

And, in despair of sleep, the family came down to breakfast.

Mrs. Peterkin had always been much afraid of fire-works, and had never allowed the boys to bring gunpowder into the house. She was even afraid of torpedoes; they looked so much like sugar-plums, she was sure some of the children would swallow them, and explode before anybody knew it.

She was very timid about other things.

She was not sure even about pea-nuts. Everybody exclaimed over this: "Surely there was no danger in pea-nuts!" But Mrs. Peterkin declared she had been very much alarmed at the Exhibition, and in the crowded corners of the streets in Boston, at the pea-nut stands, where they had machines to roast the pea-nuts. She did not think it was safe. They might go off any time, in the midst of a crowd of people, too!

Mr. Peterkin thought there actually was no danger, and he should be sorry to give up the pea-nut. He thought it an American institution, something really belonging to the Fourth of July. He even confessed to a quiet pleasure in crushing the empty shells with his feet on the sidewalks as he went along the streets.

Agamemnon thought it a simple joy.

In consideration, however, of the fact that they had had no real celebration of the Fourth the last year, Mrs. Peterkin had consented to give over the day, this year, to the amusement of the family as a Centennial celebration. She would prepare herself for a terrible noise—only she did not want any gunpowder brought into the house.

The little boys had begun by firing some torpedoes a few days beforehand, that their mother might be used to the sound, and had selected their horns some week before.

Solomon John had been very busy in inventing some fire-works. As Mrs. Peterkin objected to the use of gunpowder, he found out from the dictionary what the different parts of gunpowder are—saltpeter, charcoal, and sulphur. Charcoal he discovered they had in the wood-house; saltpeter they would find in the cellar, in the beef-barrel; and sulphur they could buy at the apothecary's. He explained to his mother that these materials had never yet exploded in the house, and she was quieted.

Agamemnon, meanwhile, remembered a

recipe he had read somewhere for making a "fulminating paste" of iron filings and powder of brimstone. He had it written down on a piece of paper in his pocket-book. But the iron filings must be finely powdered. This they began upon a day or two before, and, the very afternoon before, laid out some of the paste on the piazza.

Pin-wheels and rockets were contributed by Mr. Peterkin for the evening. According to a programme drawn up by Agamemnon and Solomon John, the reading of the Declaration of Independence was to take place in the morning on the piazza under the flags.

The Bromwiches brought over their flag to hang over the door.

"That is what the lady from Philadelphia meant," explained Elizabeth Eliza.

"She said flags of our country," said the little boys. "We thought she meant 'in the country.'"

Quite a company assembled; but it seemed nobody had a copy of the Declaration of Independence.

Elizabeth Eliza said she could say one line, if they each could add as much. But it proved they all knew the same line that she did, as they began:

"When, in the course of—when, in the course of—when, in the course of human—when, in the course of human events—when, in the course of human events, it becomes—when, in the course of human events, it becomes necessary—when, in the course of human events, it becomes necessary for one people——"

They could not get any farther. Some of the party decided that "one people" was a good place to stop, and the little boys sent off some fresh torpedoes in honor of the people. But Mr. Peterkin was not satisfied. He invited the assembled party to stay until sunset, and meanwhile he would find a copy, and torpedoes were to be saved to be fired off at the close of every sentence.

And now the noon bells rang and the noon bells ceased.

Mrs. Peterkin wanted to ask everybody to dinner. She should have some cold beef. She had let Amanda go, because it was the Fourth, and everybody ought to be free that one day, so she could not have much of a dinner. But when she went to cut her beef, she found Solomon John had taken it to soak, on account of the saltpeter for the fire-works!

Well, they had a pig, so she took a ham, and the boys had bought tamarinds and buns and a cocoa-nut. So the company stayed on, and when the Antiques and Horribles passed again, they were treated to pea-nuts and lemonade.

They sang patriotic songs, they told stories; they fired torpedoes, they frightened the cats with them. It was a warm afternoon; the red poppies were out wide, and the hot sun poured down on the alleyways in the garden. There was a seething sound of a hot day in the buzzing of insects, in the steaming heat that came up from the ground. Some neighboring boys were firing a toy cannon. Every time it went off, Mrs. Peterkin started, and looked to see if one of the little boys was gone. Mr. Peterkin had set out to find a copy of the "Declaration." Agamemnon had disappeared. She had not a moment to decide about her headache. She asked Ann Maria if she were not anxious about the fire-works, and if rockets were not dangerous. They went up, but you were never sure where they came down.

And then came a fresh tumult! All the fire-engines in town rushed toward them, clanging with bells, men and boys yelling! They were out for a practice, and for a Fourth of July show.

Mrs. Peterkin thought the house was on fire, and so did some of the guests. There was great rushing hither and thither. Some thought they would better go home, some thought they would better stay. Mrs. Peterkin hastened into the house to save herself, or see what she could save. Elizabeth Eliza followed her, first proceeding to collect all the pokers and tongs she could find, because they could be thrown out of the window without breaking. She had read of people who had flung looking-glasses out of windows by mistake, in the excitement of the house being on fire, and had carried the pokers and tongs carefully into the garden. There was nothing like being prepared. She always had determined to do the reverse. So with calmness she told Solomon John to take down the looking-glasses. But she met with a difficulty,—there were no pokers and tongs, as they did not use them. They had no open fires; Mrs. Peterkin had been afraid of them. So, Elizabeth Eliza took all the pots and kettles up to the upper windows, ready to be thrown out.

But where was Mrs. Peterkin? Solomon John found she had fled to the attic in terror. He persuaded her to come down, assuring her it was the most unsafe place; but she insisted upon stopping to collect some bags of old pieces, that nobody would think of saving from the general wreck, she said, unless she did. Alas! this was the result of fire-works on Fourth of July! As they came downstairs, they heard the voices of all the company declaring there was no fire—the danger was past. It was long before Mrs. Peterkin could believe it. They told her the fire company was only out for show, and to celebrate the Fourth of July. She thought it already too much celebrated.

Elizabeth Eliza's kettles and pans had come down through the windows with a crash, that had only added to the festivities, the little boys thought.

Mr. Peterkin had been about all this time in search of a copy of the Declaration of Independence. The public library was shut, and he had to go from house to house; but now as the sunset bells and cannon began, he returned with a copy, and read it, to the pealing of the bells and sounding of the cannon. Torpedoes and crackers were fired at every pause. Some sweet-marjoram pots, tin cans filled with crackers which were lighted, went off with great explosions.

At the most exciting moment, near the close of the reading, Agamemnon, with an expression of terror, pulled Solomon John aside.

"I have suddenly remembered where I read about the 'fulminating paste' we made. It was in the preface to 'Woodstock,' and I have been around to borrow the book to read the directions over again, because I was afraid about the 'paste' going off. READ THIS QUICKLY! and tell me, *Where is the fulminating paste?*"

Solomon John was busy winding some covers of paper over a little parcel. It contained chlorate of potash and sulphur mixed. A friend had told him of the composition. The more thicknesses of paper you put around it, the louder it would go off. You must pound it with a hammer. Solomon John felt it must be perfectly safe, as his mother had taken potash for a medicine.

He still held the parcel as he read from Agamemnon's book: "This paste, when it has lain together about twenty-six hours, will *of itself* take fire, and burn all the sulphur away with a blue flame and a bad smell."

"Where is the paste?" repeated Solomon John, in terror.

"We made it just twenty-six hours ago," said Agamemnon.

"We put it on the piazza," exclaimed Solomon John, rapidly recalling the facts, "and it is in front of mother's feet!"

He hastened to snatch the paste away before it should take fire, flinging aside the packet in his hurry. Agamemnon, jumping upon the piazza at the same moment, trod upon the paper parcel, which exploded at once with the shock, and he fell to the ground, while at the same moment the paste "fulminated" into a blue flame directly in front of Mrs. Peterkin!

It was a moment of great confusion. There were cries and screams. The bells were still ringing, the cannon firing, and Mr. Peterkin had just reached the closing words: "Our lives, our fortune, and our sacred honor."

"We are all blown up, as I feared we should be," Mrs. Peterkin at length ventured to say, finding herself in a lilac-bush by the side of the piazza. She scarcely dared to open her eyes to see the scattered limbs about her.

It was so with all. Even Ann Maria Bromwich clutched a pillar of the piazza, with closed eyes.

At length, Mr. Peterkin said, calmly: "Is anybody killed?"

There was no reply. Nobody could tell whether it was because everybody was killed, or because they were too wounded to answer. It was a great while before Mrs. Peterkin ventured to move.

But the little boys soon shouted with joy and cheered the success of Solomon John's fire-works, and hoped he had some more. One of them had his face blackened by an unexpected cracker, and Elizabeth Eliza's muslin dress was burned here and there. But no one was hurt; no one had lost any limbs, though Mrs. Peterkin was sure she had seen some flying in the air. Nobody could understand how, as she had kept her eyes firmly shut.

No greater accident had occurred than the singeing of Solomon John's nose. But there was an unpleasant and terrible odor from the "fulminating paste."

Mrs. Peterkin was extricated from the lilac-bush. No one knew how she got there. Indeed, the thundering noise had stunned everybody. It had roused the neighborhood even more than before. Answering explosions came on every side, and though the sunset light had not faded away, the little boys hastened to send off rockets under cover of the confusion. Solomon John's other fire-works would not go. But all felt he had done enough.

Mrs. Peterkin retreated into the parlor, deciding she really did have a headache. At times she had to come out when a rocket went off, to see if it was one of the little boys. She was exhausted by the adventures of the day, and almost thought it could not have been worse if the boys had been allowed gunpowder. The distracted lady was thankful there was likely to be but one Centennial Fourth in her life-time, and declared she should never more keep anything in the house as dangerous as saltpetered beef, and she should never venture to take another spoonful of potash.

THE SOLDIERING OF BENIAH STIDHAM

by Howard Pyle

WHEN you look at a very old man, it seems hard to imagine that he was ever once a boy, full of sport and mischief like the boys whom we know nowadays.

There is a daguerreotype of Beniah Stidham that was taken about the year 1850. It is the picture of a very, very old man, with a bald, bony forehead, and a face full of wrinkles and furrows. His lips are sucked in between his toothless gums, and his nose is hooked down as though to meet his lean chin beneath.

In the picture he wears a swallow-tailed coat with a rolling collar and with buttons that look like brass. The cuffs of his long, wrinkled coat-sleeves come down almost to the knotted knuckles, and one skinny hand rests upon the top of a hooked cane. It does not seem possible that he could ever have been a boy; but he was—though it was away back in the time of the Revolutionary War.

He was about fifteen years old at the time of the battle of Brandywine—that was in the year 1777. He was then an apprentice in Mr. Connelly's cooper-shops near Brandywine. His father, Amos Stidham, kept a tin-store, and sometimes peddled tinware and buckets down in the lower counties and up through Pennsylvania. At that time Beniah was a big, awkward, loose-jointed, over-grown lad; he shot up like a weed, and his clothes were always too small for him. His hands stuck far out from his sleeves.

They were splay and red, and they were big like his feet. He stuttered when he talked, and everybody laughed at him for it.

Most people thought that he was slack-witted, but he was not; he was only very shy and timid. Sometimes he himself felt that he had as good sense as anybody if he only had a chance to show it.

These things happened in Delaware, which in those days was almost like a part of Pennsylvania.

There was a great deal of excitement in Wilmington at the time of the beginning of the trouble in Boston, the fight at Lexington, and the battle at Bunker Hill. There were enlisted for the war more than twenty young fellows from Wilmington and Brandywine Hundred; they used to drill every evening in a field at the foot of Quaker Hill, where the Meeting house stood and not far from the William Penn Inn. A good many people—especially the boys—used to go in the evening to see

17

them drill. It seemed to Beniah that if he could only go for a soldier he might stand a great deal better chance of getting along than he had in Wilmington, where every one laughed at him and seemed to think that he was lacking in wits.

He had it in his mind a great many times to speak to his father about going for a soldier, but he could not quite find courage to do so, for he felt almost sure that he would be laughed at.

One night he did manage to speak of it, and when he did, it was just as he thought it would be. It was just after supper, and they still sat at table, in the kitchen. He was nervous, and when he began speaking he stuttered more than usual.

"I wo-wo-wo-wo-wish you 'd l-let me go fer a sis-sis-sis-sis-sis-sis-soldier, Father," said he.

His sister Debby burst out laughing.

"A sis-sis-sis-sis-soldier!" she mocked.

"A what!" said Beniah's father. "You a soldier? You would make a pretty soldier,

now, would n't you? Why, you would n't be able to say 'Who goes there?' fer stutterin'!" and then Debby laughed again, and when she saw that it made Beniah angry, she laughed still more.

So Beniah did not go soldiering that time.

After the battle of Brandywine, Lord Howe's fleet of war-ships came up into the Delaware from the Chesapeake Bay, and everybody was anxious and troubled, for there was talk that the enemy would bombard the town. You could see the fleet coming up the bay from the hills back of the town—the sails seemed to cover the water all over; that was in the afternoon, just before supper. That evening a good many people left town, and others sent their china and silver up into the country for safe keeping.

After supper the bellman went through the streets calling a meeting at the Townhall. Captain Stapler was at home at that time and spoke to the people. He told them that there was no danger of the fleet bombarding the town, for the river was two miles away, and the cannon could not carry that far. He showed them that the only way that the enemy could approach the town was up the Christiana River, and that if the citizens would build a redoubt at the head of the marsh the place would be perfectly defended.

The people found a good deal of comfort in what he said; but the next morning the "Roebuck" and "Liverpool" ships of war were seen to be lying, with their tenders and two transports, opposite the town; and once more all the talk was that they were going to bombard.

There was a great deal said that morning at the cooper-shops about all this. Some opined that the ships were certainly going to bombard, but others held that what they would do would be to send a regiment of Hessians up the creek to burn down the town.

During the morning, old Billy Jester came up from Christiana village, and said that the townspeople were building a mud fort down at the Rocks below the Old Swedes' Church, and that they expected two cannon and some soldiers to come down from Fort Mifflin in the afternoon.

This was a great comfort to everybody, for the time.

About eleven o'clock in the morning the enemy suddenly began firing. Boom!—the sudden startling noise sounded dull and heavy, like the falling of some great weight; the windows rattled—boom!—boom!—boom!—and then again, after a little pause,—boom!—boom! There was a little while, a few seconds of breathless listening, and then Tom Pierson, the foreman of the shop, shouted:

"By gum! they're bombarding the town!"

Then he dropped his adze, and ran out of the door without waiting to take his hat. As he ran, there sounded again the same dull, heavy report—boom! boom!

There was no more work in the cooper-shops that day. Beniah ran all the way home. His father was just then away in the lower counties, and Beniah did not know what was going to happen to Debby and his mother. Maybe he would find the house all knocked to pieces with cannon-balls. Boom! boom! sounded the cannon again, and Beniah ran faster and faster, his mouth all dry and clammy with fear and excitement. The streets were full of people hurrying toward the hills. When he got home he found that no harm had happened, but the house was shut and all the doors locked. He met Mrs. Frist, and she told him that his mother and Debby had gone up to Quaker Hill.

He found them there a little while later, but by that time the war-ships had stopped firing, and after a while everybody went back home.

In the afternoon it was known that they had not been firing at the town at all, but at some people who had gone down on the neck to look at them, and whom, no doubt, they took to be militia or something of the kind.

Just before supper it was reported that one of Jonas Stidham's cows had been killed by a cannon-ball. Jonas Stidham was Beniah's uncle, and in the evening he went over to look at the cow. He met several others going on the same errand—two men and three or four boys. There was quite a crowd gathered about the place. The cow lay on its side, with its neck stretched out. There was a great hole in its side, made by the cannon-ball, and there was blood upon the ground. It looked very dreadful, and seemed to bring terrors of war very near; and everybody stood about and talked in low voices.

After he had seen the dead cow, Beniah went down to where they were building the mud fort. They were just putting the cannon into place, and Captain Stapler was drilling a company of young men of the town who had enlisted for its defense. Beniah wished that he was one of them. After the drill was over, Captain Stapler came up to him and said:

"Don't you want to enlist, Beniah?"

Beniah would not have dared to enlist if his father had been at home, but his father was away, and he signed his name to the roll-book!

That was the way that he came to go soldiering.

. . . .

That night Beniah did not go home, for he had to stay with the others who had enlisted. They were quartered at the barn just back of the mud fort. But he sent word by Jimmy Rogers that he was not coming home, because he had enlisted in Captain Stapler's company.

However, Captain Stapler let him go home the next morning for a little while. He found that all the boys knew that he had enlisted, and that he was great among them. He had to tell each one he met all about the matter. They all went along with him—fifteen or twenty of them—and waited in the street outside while he was talking with his family within. His mother had gone out, but his sister Debby was in the kitchen.

"Oh, but you 'll catch it when daddy comes home!" said she.

Beniah pretended not to pay any attention to her.

"When is he coming home?" said he, after a while.

"I don't know, but, mark my words, you 'll catch it when he does come," said Debby.

That night they set pickets along the edge of the marsh, and then Beniah really began to soldier. He took his turn at standing guard about nine o'clock. There was no wind, but the night was very raw and chill. At first Beniah rather liked the excitement of it, but by and by he began to get very cold. He remembered his father's overcoat that hung back of the door in the entry, and he wished he had brought it with him from home; but it was too late to wish for that now. And then it was very lonesome and silent in the darkness of the night. A mist hung all over the marsh, and in the still air the voices of the

men who were working upon the redoubt by lantern-light, and of the volunteers at their quarters in the barn where they had kindled a fire, sounded with perfect clearness and distinctness in the stillness. The tide was coming in, and the water gurgled and rippled in the ditches, where the reeds stood stark and stiff in the gloom. The reed-birds had not yet flown south, and their sleepy "cheep, cheeping" sounded incessantly through the darkness.

The moon was about rising, and the sky, to the east, was lit with a milky paleness. Toward it the marsh stretched away into the distance, the thin tops of the nearer reeds just showing above the white mysterious veil of mist that covered the water. It was all very strange and lonesome, and when Beniah thought of home and how nice it would be to be in his warm bed, he could not help wishing that he had not enlisted. And then he certainly would "catch it" when his father came home, as Debby had said he would. It was not a pleasant prospect.

By and by the moon rose, and at the same time a breeze sprang up. It grew colder than ever, and presently the water began to splash and dash against the river-bank beyond. The veil of mist disappeared, and the water darkled and flashed with broken shadows and sparks of light. Beniah's fingers holding the musket felt numb and dead. He wondered how much longer he would have to stay on guard; he felt as though he had been there a long time already. He crouched down under the lee of the riverbank and in the corner of a fence which stood there to keep the cows off of the marsh.

He had been there maybe five minutes, and was growing very sleepy with the cold, when he suddenly heard a sharp sound, and instantly started wide awake. It was the sound as of an oar striking against the side of a boat. There was something very strange in the sharp rap ringing through the stillness, and whoever had made it had evidently not intended to do so, for the after stillness was unbroken.

Beniah crouched in the fence-corner, listening, breathlessly, intensely. He had forgotten all about being cold and sleepy and miserable. He felt that his heart was beating and leaping unevenly, and his breath came quickly, as though he had been running. Was the enemy coming? What should he do?

He did not move; he only crouched there, trying to hold his breath, and trying to still the beating of his heart with his elbow pressed against his ribs. He was afraid that if there was another sound he might miss hearing it because of his labored breathing and the pulses humming in his ears. He gripped his musket with straining fingers.

There was a pause of perfect stillness. Then suddenly he heard a faint splash as though some one had stepped incautiously into the water. Again there was stillness. Then something moved in the reeds—maybe it was a regiment of Hessians! Beniah crouched lower, and poked his musket through the bars of the fence. What would happen next? He wondered if it was all real—if the enemy was actually coming.

Suddenly the reeds stirred again. Beniah crouched down still lower. Then he saw something slowly rise above the edge of the riverbank, sharp-cut and black against the milky sky. It was the head of a man, and it was surmounted by a tall conical cap—it was the sort of a cap that the British soldiers wore. As Beniah gazed, it seemed to him as though he had now stopped breathing altogether. The head remained there motionless for a while, as though listening; then the body that belonged to it slowly rose as though from the earth, and stood, from the waist up black against the sky.

Beniah tried to say, "Who goes there?" and then he found that what his father had said was true; he could not say the words for stuttering. He was so excited that he could not utter a sound; he would have to shoot without saying, "Who goes there?" There was nothing else to do. He aimed his eye along the barrel of his musket, but it was so dark that he could not see the sights of the gun very well. Should he shoot? He hesitated for an intense second or two—then came a blinding flash of resolve.

He drew the trigger.

Bang!

For a moment he was deafened and bewildered by the report and the blinding flash of light. Then the cloud of pungent gunpowder-smoke drifted away, and his senses came back to him. The head and body were gone from against the sky.

Beniah sprang to his feet and flew back toward the mud fort, yelling he knew not what. It seemed as though the whole night was peopled with enemies. But nobody followed him. Suddenly he stopped in his flight, and stood again listening. Were the British following him? No, they were not. He heard alarmed voices from the fort, and the shouting of the pickets. A strange impulse seized him that he could not resist: he felt that he must go back and see what he had shot. He turned and crept slowly back, step by step, pausing now and then, and listening intently. By and by he came to where the figure had stood, and, craning his neck, peeped cautiously over the riverbank. The moon shone bright on the rippling water in a little open place in the reeds. There was something black lying in the water, and as Beniah continued looking at it, he saw it move with a wallowing splash. Then he ran away shouting and yelling.

. . . .

Captain Stapler thought that an attack

would surely be made, but it was not; and, after a while, he ordered a company from the mud fort out along the river-bank, to see who it was that Beniah had shot. They took a lantern along with them, and Beniah went ahead to show them where it was.

"Yonder 's the place," said he; "and I fu-fired my gi-gi-gi-gi-gun from the fa-fa-fence, ja-just here."

Captain Stapler peered down among the reeds. "By gum!" said he, "he's shot something, sure enough." He went cautiously down the bank; then he stooped over, and soon lifted something that lay in the water. Then there was a groan.

"Come down here, two or three of you!" called out Captain Stapler. "Beniah's actually shot a man, as sure as life!"

A number of the men scrambled down the bank; they lifted the black figure; it groaned again as they did so. They carried it up and laid it down upon the top of the bank. The clothes were very muddy and wet, but the light of the lantern twinkled here and there upon the buttons and braid of a uniform. Captain Stapler bent over the wounded man. "By gracious!" said he, "it 's a Hessian—like enough he 's a spy." Beniah saw that the blood was running over one side of the wet uniform, and he was filled with a sort of terrible triumph. They carried the wounded man to the barn, and Dr. Taylor came and looked at him. The wound was in the neck, and it was not especially dangerous. No doubt the man had been stunned by the ball when it struck him.

The Hessian was a young man. *"Sprechen sie Deutsch?"* asked he, but nobody understood him.

. . . .

The next morning Beniah's father came home. He did not stop to ungear the horse, but drove straight down to the mud fort in his tinware cart. He was very angry.

"What 're you doing here, anyhow?" said he to Beniah; and he caught him by the collar and shook him till Beniah's hat slipped down over one eye. "What 're you doin' here, anyhow—killin' and shootin' and murtherin' folks? You come home with me, Beniah—you come home with me!" and he shook him again.

"He can't go," said Captain Stapler. "You can't take him, Amos. He's enlisted, and he's signed his name upon the rollbook."

"I don't care a rap what he's signed," said Amos. "He hain't goin' to stay here shootin' folks. He 's got to come home along with me, he has." And Beniah went.

Nobody knows what happened after he got home, and Beniah did not tell; but next day he went back to work at the cooper-shops again. All the boys seemed glad to see him, and wanted to know just how he shot the Hessian.

A good many people visited the wounded Hessian down in the barn the day he had been shot. Among others came "Dutch Charlie," the cobbler. He could understand what the Hessian said. He told Captain Stapler that the man was not a spy, but a deserter from the transport-ship in the river. It seemed almost a pity that the man had not been a spy; but, after all, it did not make any great difference in the way people looked on what Beniah Stidham had done; for the fact remained that he was a Hessian. And nobody thought of laughing at Beniah, even when he stuttered in telling how he shot him.

After a while the Hessian got well, and then he started a store in Philadelphia. He did well, and made money, and the queerest part of the whole business was that he married Debby Stidham—in spite of its having been Beniah who shot him in the neck.

This is the story of Beniah Stidham's soldiering. It lasted only two nights and a day, but he got a great deal of glory by it.

"They used to drill every evening"

THE GRIFFIN
AND THE MINOR CANON

by Frank R. Stockton

OVER the great door of an old, old church which stood in a quiet town of a far-away land there was carved in stone the figure of a large griffin. The old-time sculptor had done his work with great care, but the image he had made was not a pleasant one to look at. It had a large head, with enormous open mouth and savage teeth; from its back arose great wings, armed with sharp hooks and prongs; it had stout legs in front, with projecting claws; but there were no legs behind,—the body running out into a long and powerful tail, finished off at the end with a barbed point. This tail was coiled up under him, the end sticking up just back of his wings.

The sculptor, or the people who had ordered this stone figure, had evidently been very much pleased with it, for little copies of it, also in stone, had been placed here and there along the sides of the church, not very far from the ground, so that people could easily look at them, and ponder on their curious forms. There were a great many other sculptures on the outside of this church,—saints, martyrs, grotesque heads of men, beasts, and birds, as well as those of other creatures which can not be named, because nobody knows exactly what they were; but none were so curious and interesting as the great griffin over the door, and the little griffins on the sides of the church.

A long, long distance from the town, in the midst of dreadful wilds scarcely known to man, there dwelt the Griffin whose image had been put up over the church-door. In some way or other, the old-time sculptor had seen him, and afterward, to the best of his memory, had copied his figure in stone. The Griffin had never known this, until, hundreds of years afterward, he heard from a bird, from a wild animal, or in some manner which it is not now easy to find out, that there was a likeness of him on the old church in the distant town. Now, this Griffin had no idea how he looked. He had never seen a mirror, and the streams where he lived were so turbulent and violent that a quiet piece of water, which would reflect the image of any thing looking into it, could not be found. Being, as far as could be ascertained, the very last of his race, he had never seen another griffin. Therefore it was, that, when he heard of this stone image of himself, he became very anxious to know what he looked like, and at last he determined to go to the old church, and see for himself what manner of being he was. So he started off from the dreadful wilds, and flew on and on until he came to the countries inhabited by men, where his appearance in the air created great consternation; but he alighted nowhere, keeping up a steady flight until he reached the suburbs of the town which had his image on its church. Here, late in the afternoon, he

24

alighted in a green meadow by the side of a brook, and stretched himself on the grass to rest. His great wings were tired, for he had not made such a long flight in a century, or more.

The news of his coming spread quickly over the town, and the people, frightened nearly out of their wits by the arrival of so extraordinary a visitor, fled into their houses, and shut themselves up. The Griffin called loudly for some one to come to him, but the more he called, the more afraid the people were to show themselves. At length he saw two laborers hurrying to their homes through the fields, and in a terrible voice he commanded them to stop. Not daring to disobey, the men stood, trembling.

"What is the matter with you all?" cried the Griffin. "Is there not a man in your town who is brave enough to speak to me?"

"I think," said one of the laborers, his voice shaking so that his words could hardly be understood, "that—perhaps— the Minor Canon—would come."

"Go, call him, then!" said the Griffin; "I want to see him."

The Minor Canon, who filled a subordinate position in the old church, had just finished the afternoon services, and was coming out of a side door, with three aged women who had formed the week-day congregation. He was a young man of a kind disposition, and very anxious to do good to the people of the town. Apart from his duties in the church, where he conducted services every week-day, he visited the sick and the poor, counseled and assisted persons who were in trouble, and taught a school composed entirely of the bad children in the town with whom nobody else would have anything to do. Whenever people wanted anything done for them, they always went to the Minor Canon. Thus it was that the laborer thought of the young priest when he found that some one must come and speak to the Griffin.

The Minor Canon had not heard of the strange event, which was known to the whole town except himself and the three old women, and when he was informed of it, and was told that the Griffin had asked to see him, he was greatly amazed, and frightened.

"Me!" he exclaimed. "He has never heard of me! What should he want with *me?*"

"Oh! you must go instantly!" cried the two men. "He is very angry now because he has been kept waiting so long; and nobody knows what will happen if you don't hurry to him."

The poor Minor Canon would rather have had his hand cut off than go out to meet an angry griffin; but he felt that it was his duty to go, for it would be a woful thing if injury should come to the people of the town because he was not brave enough to obey the summons of the Griffin. So, pale and frightened, he started off.

"Well," said the Griffin, as soon as the young man came near, "I am glad to see that there is some one who has the courage to come to me."

The Minor Canon did not feel very courageous, but he bowed his head.

"Is this the town," said Griffin, "where there is a church with a likeness of myself over one of the doors?"

The Minor Canon looked at the frightful figure of the Griffin and saw that it was, without doubt, exactly like the stone image on the church.

"Yes," he said, "you are right."

"Well, then," said the Griffin, "will you take me to it? I wish very much to see it."

The Minor Canon instantly thought that

if the Griffin entered the town without the people knowing what he came for, some of them would probably be frightened to death, and so he sought to gain time to prepare their minds.

"It is growing dark, now," he said, very much afraid, as he spoke, that his words might enrage the Griffin, "and the objects on the front of the church cannot be seen clearly. It will be better to wait until morning, if you wish to get a good view of the stone image of yourself."

"That will suit me very well," said the Griffin. "I see that you are a man of good sense. I am tired, and I will take a nap here on this soft grass, while I cool my tail in the little stream that runs near me. The end of my tail gets red-hot when I am angry or excited, and it is quite warm now. So you may go, but be sure and come early tomorrow morning, and show me the way to the church."

The Minor Canon was glad enough to take his leave, and hurried into the town. In front of the church he found a great many people assembled to hear his report of his interview with the Griffin. When they found that he had not come to spread ruin and devastation, but simply to see his stony likeness on the church, they· showed neither relief nor gratification, but began to upbraid the Minor Canon for consenting to conduct the creature into the town.

"What could I do?" cried the young man. "If I should not bring him he would come himself and, perhaps, end by setting fire to the town with his red-hot tail."

Still the people were not satisfied, and a great many plans were proposed to prevent the Griffin from coming into the town. Some elderly persons urged that the young men should go out and kill him; but the young men scoffed at such a ridiculous idea. Then some one said that it would be a good thing to destroy the stone image

so that the Griffin would have no excuse for entering the town; and this idea was received with such favor that many of the people ran for hammers, chisels, and crowbars, with which to tear down and break up the stone griffin. But the Minor Canon resisted this plan with all the strength of his mind and body. He assured the people that this action would enrage the Griffin beyond measure, for it would be impossible to conceal from him that his image had been destroyed during the night. But the people were so determined to break up the stone griffin that the Minor Canon saw that there was nothing for him to do but to stay there and protect it. All night he walked up and down in front of the church-door, keeping away the men who brought ladders, by which they might mount to the great stone griffin, and knock it to pieces with their hammers and crowbars. After many hours the people were obliged to give up their attempts, and went home to sleep; but the Minor Canon remained at his post till early morning, and then he hurried away to the field where he had left the Griffin.

The monster has just awakened, and rising to his fore-legs and shaking himself, he said that he was ready to go into the town. The Minor Canon, therefore, walked back, the Griffin flying slowly through the air, at a short distance above the head of his guide. Not a person was to be seen in the streets, and they proceded directly to the front of the church, where the Minor Canon pointed out the stone griffin.

The real Griffin settled down in the little square before the church and gazed earnestly at his sculptured likeness. For a long time he looked at it. First he put his head on one side, and then he put it on the other; then he shut his right eye and gazed with his left, after which he shut his left eye and gazed with his right. Then he moved a little to one side and looked at the image, then he moved the other way. After a while he said to the Minor Canon, who had been standing by all this time:

"It is, it must be, an excellent likeness! That breadth between the eyes, that expansive forehead, those massive jaws! I feel that it must resemble me. If there is any fault to find with it, it is that the neck seems a little stiff. But that is nothing. It is an admirable likeness,—admirable!"

The Griffin sat looking at his image all the morning and all the afternoon. The Minor Canon had been afraid to go away and leave him, and had hoped all through the day that he would soon be satisfied with his inspection and fly away home. But by evening the poor young man was utterly exhausted, and felt that he must go away to eat and sleep. He frankly admitted this fact to the Griffin, and asked him if he would not like something to eat. He said this because he felt obliged in politeness to do so, but as soon as he had spoken the words, he was seized with dread lest the monster should demand half a dozen babies, or some tempting repast of that kind.

"Oh, no," said the Griffin, "I never eat between the equinoxes. At the vernal and at the autumnal equinox I take a good meal, and that lasts me for half a year. I am extremely regular in my habits, and do not think it healthful to eat at odd times. But if you need food, go and get it, and I will return to the soft grass where I slept last night and take another nap."

The next day the Griffin came again to the little square before the church, and remained there until evening, steadfastly regarding the stone griffin over the door. The Minor Canon came once or twice to look at him, and the Griffin seemed very glad to see him; but the young clergyman could not stay as he had done before, for he had many duties to perform. Nobody

went to the church, but the people came to the Minor Canon's house, and anxiously asked him how long the Griffin was going to stay.

"I do not know," he answered, "but I think he will soon be satisfied with regarding his stone likeness, and then he will go away."

But the Griffin did not go away. Morning after morning he came to the church, but after a time he did not stay there all day. He seemed to have taken a great fancy to the Minor Canon, and followed him about as he pursued his various avocations. He would wait for him at the side door of the church, for the Minor Canon held services every day, morning and evening, though nobody came now. "If any one *should* come," he said to himself, "I must be found at my post." When the young man came out, the Griffin would accompany him in his visits to the sick and the poor, and would often look into the windows of the school-house where the Minor Canon was teaching his unruly scholars. All the other schools were closed, but the parents of the Minor Canon's scholars forced them to go to school, because they were so bad they could not endure them all day at home,—griffin or no griffin. But it must be said they generally behaved very well when that great monster sat up on his tail and looked through the school-room window.

When it was perceived that the Griffin showed no sign of going away, all the people who were able to do so left the town. The canons and the higher officers of the church had fled away during the first day of the Griffin's visit, leaving behind only the Minor Canon and some of the men who opened the doors and swept the church. All the citizens who could afford it shut up their houses and traveled to distant parts, and only the working people and the poor were left behind. After a while these ventured to go about and attend to their business, for if they did not work they would starve. They were getting a little used to seeing the Griffin, and having been told that he did not eat between equinoxes, they did not feel so much afraid of him as before.

Day by day the Griffin became more and more attached to the Minor Canon. He kept near him a great part of the time, and often spent the night in front of the little house where the young clergyman lived alone. This strange companionship was often burdensome to the Minor Canon; but, on the other hand, he could not deny that he derived a great deal of benefit and instruction from it. The Griffin had lived for hundreds of years, and had seen much; and he told the Minor Canon many wonderful things.

"It is like reading an old book," said the young clergyman to himself; "but how many books I would have had to read before I would have found out what the Griffin has told me about the earth, the air, the water, about minerals, and metals, and growing things, and all the wonders of the world!"

Thus the summer went on, and drew toward its close. And now the people of the town began to be very much troubled again.

"It will not be long," they said, "before the autumnal equinox is here, and then that monster will want to eat. He will be dreadfully hungry, for he has taken so much exercise since his last meal. He will devour our children. Without doubt, he will eat them all. What is to be done?"

To this question no one could give an answer, but all agreed that the Griffin must not be allowed to remain until the approaching equinox. After talking over the matter a great deal, a crowd of the people went to the Minor Canon, at a time when the Griffin was not with him.

"It is all your fault," they said, "that that monster is among us. You brought him here, and you ought to see that he goes away. It is only on your account that he stays here at all, for, although he visits his image every day, he is with you the greater part of the time. If you were not here, he would not stay. It is your duty to go away and then he will follow you, and we shall be free from the dreadful danger which hangs over us."

"Go away!" cried the Minor Canon, greatly grieved at being spoken to in such a way. "Where shall I go? If I go to some other town, shall I not take this trouble there? Have I a right to do that?"

"No," said the people, "you must not go to any other town. There is no town far enough away. You must go to the dreadful wilds where the Griffin lives; and then he will follow you and stay there."

They did not say whether they expected the Minor Canon to stay there also, and he did not ask them anything about it. He bowed his head, and went into his house, to think. The more he thought, the more clear it became to his mind that it was his duty to go away, and thus free the town from the presence of the Griffin.

That evening he packed a leathern bag full of bread and meat, and early the next morning he set out on his journey to the dreadful wilds. It was a long, weary, and doleful journey, especially after he had gone beyond the habitations of men, but the Minor Canon kept on bravely, and never faltered. The way was longer than he had expected, and his provisions soon grew so scanty that he was obliged to eat but a little every day, but he kept up his courage, and pressed on, and, after many days of toilsome travel, he reached the dreadful wilds.

When the Griffin found that the Minor Canon had left the town he seemed sorry, but showed no disposition to go and look for him. After a few days had passed, he became much annoyed, and asked some of the people where the Minor Canon had gone. But, although the citizens had been so anxious that the young clergyman should go to the dreadful wilds, thinking that the Griffin would immediately follow him, they were now afraid to mention the Minor Canon's destination, for the monster seemed angry already, and, if he should suspect their trick he would, doubtless, become very much enraged. So every one said he did not know, and the Griffin wandered

church," he said, "for nobody went there; but it is a pity about the school. I think I will teach it myself until he returns."

It was just about school-time, and the Griffin went inside and pulled the rope which rang the schoolbell. Some of the children who heard the bell ran in to see what was the matter, supposing it to be a joke of some one of their companions; but when they saw the Griffin they stood astonished, and scared.

"Go tell the other scholars," said the monster, "that school is about to open, and that if they are not all here in ten minutes, I shall come after them."

In seven minutes every scholar was in place.

Never was seen such an orderly school. Not a boy or girl moved, or uttered a whisper. The Griffin climbed into the

"The Griffin addressed the scholars"

about disconsolately. One morning he looked into the Minor Canon's schoolhouse, which was always empty now, and thought that it was a shame that everything should suffer on account of the young man's absence.

"It does not matter so much about the

master's seat, his wide wings spread on each side of him, because he could not lean back in his chair while they stuck out behind, and his great tail coiled around, in front of the desk, the barbed end sticking up, ready to tap any boy or girl who might misbehave. The Griffin now addressed the scholars, telling them that he intended to teach them while their master was away. In speaking he endeavored to imitate, as far as possible, the mild and gentle tones of the Minor Canon, but it must be admitted that in this he was not very successful. He had paid a good deal of attention to the studies of the school, and he now determined not to attempt to teach them anything new, but to review them in what they had been studying; so he called up the various classes, and questioned them upon their previous lessons. The children racked their brains to remember what they had learned. They were so afraid of the Griffin's displeasure that they recited as they had never recited before. One of the boys, far down in his class, answered so well that the Griffin was astonished.

"I should think you would be at the head," said he. "I am sure you have never been in the habit of reciting so well. Why is this?"

"Because I did not choose to take the trouble," said the boy, trembling in his boots. He felt obliged to speak the truth, for all the children thought that the great eyes of the Griffin could see right through them, and that he would know when they told a falsehood.

"You ought to be ashamed of yourself," said the Griffin. "Go down to the very tail of the class, and if you are not at the head in two days, I shall know the reason why."

The next afternoon the boy was number one.

It was astonishing how much these children now learned of what they had been studying. It was as if they had been educated over again. The Griffin used no severity toward them, but there was a look about him which made them unwilling to go to bed until they were sure they knew their lessons for the next day.

The Griffin now thought that he ought to visit the sick and the poor; and he began to go about the town for this purpose. The effect upon the sick was miraculous. All, except those who were very ill indeed, jumped from their beds when they heard he was coming, and declared themselves quite well. To those who could not get up, he gave herbs and roots, which none of them had ever before thought of as medicines, but which the Griffin had seen used in various parts of the world; and most of them recovered. But, for all that, they afterward said that, no matter what happened to them, they hoped that they should never again have such a doctor coming to their bed-sides, feeling their pulses and looking at their tongues.

As for the poor, they seemed to have utterly disappeared. All those who had depended upon charity for their daily bread were now at work in some way or other; many of them offering to do odd jobs for their neighbors just for the sake of their meals,—a thing which had been seldom heard of before in the town. The Griffin could find no one who needed his assistance.

The summer had now passed, and the autumnal equinox was rapidly approaching. The citizens were in a state of great alarm and anxiety. The Griffin showed no signs of going away, but seemed to have settled himself permanently among them. In a short time, the day for his semi-annual meal would arrive, and then what would happen? The monster would certainly be very hungry, and would devour all their children.

Now they greatly regretted and lamented that they had sent away the Minor Canon; he was the only one on whom they could have depended in this trouble, for he could talk freely with the Griffin, and so find out what could be done. But it would not do to be inactive. Some step must be taken immediately. A meeting of the citizens was called, and two old men were appointed to go and talk to the Griffin. They were instructed to offer to prepare a splendid dinner for him on equinox day,— one which would entirely satisfy his hunger. They would offer him the fattest mutton, the most tender beef, fish, and game of various sorts, and anything of the kind that he might fancy. If none of these suited, they were to mention that there was an orphan asylum in the next town.

"Anything would be better," said the citizens, "than to have our dear children devoured."

The old men went to the Griffin, but their propositions were not received with favor.

"From what I have seen of the people of this town," said the monster, "I do not think I could relish anything that was ever prepared by them. They appear to be all cowards, and, therefore, mean and selfish. As for eating one of them, old or young, I could n't think of it for a moment. In fact, there was only one creature in the whole place for whom I could have had any appetite, and that is the Minor Canon, who has gone away. He was brave, and good, and honest, and I think I would have relished him."

"Ah!" said one of the old men very politely, "in that case I wish we had not sent him to the dreadful wilds!"

"What!" cried the Griffin. "What do you mean? Explain instantly what you are talking about!"

The old man, terribly frightened at what he had said, was obliged to tell how the Minor Canon had been sent away by the people, in the hope that the Griffin might be induced to follow him.

When the monster heard this, he became furiously angry. He dashed away from the old men and, spreading his wings, flew backward and forward over the town. He was so much excited that his tail became red-hot, and glowed like a meteor against the evening sky. When at last he settled down in the little field where he usually rested, and thrust his tail into the brook, the steam arose like a cloud, and the water of the stream ran hot through the town. The citizens were greatly frightened, and bitterly blamed the old man for telling about the Minor Canon.

"It is plain," they said, "that the Griffin intended at last to go and look for him, and we should have been saved. Now who can tell what misery you have brought upon us."

The Griffin did not remain long in the little field. As soon as his tail was cool he flew to the town-hall and rang the bell. The citizens knew that they were expected to come there, and although they were afraid to go, they were still more afraid to stay away; and they crowded into the hall. The Griffin was on the platform at one end, flapping his wings and walking up and down, and the end of his tail was still so warm that it slightly scorched the boards as he dragged it after him.

When everybody who was able to come was there, the Griffin stood still and addressed the meeting.

"I have had a contemptible opinion of you," he said, "ever since I discovered what cowards you were, but I had no idea that you were so ungrateful, selfish, and cruel, as I now find you to be. Here was your Minor Canon, who labored day and night for your good, and thought of nothing else but how he might benefit you and make you happy; and as soon as you imagine yourselves threatened with a danger,—for well I know you are dreadfully afraid of me,—you send him off, caring not whether he returns or perishes, hoping thereby to save yourselves. Now, I had conceived a great liking for that young man, and had intended, in a day or two, to go and look him up. But I have changed my mind about him. I shall go and find him, but I shall send him back here to live among you, and I intend that he shall enjoy the reward of his labor and his sacrifices. Go, some of you, to the officers of the church, who so cowardly ran away when I first came here, and tell them never to return to this town under penalty of death. And if, when your Minor Canon comes back to you, you do not bow yourselves before him, put him in the highest place among you, and serve and honor him all his life, beware of my terrible vengeance! There were only two good things in this town: the Minor Canon and the stone image of myself over your church-door. One of these you have sent away, and the other I shall carry away myself."

With these words he dismissed the meeting, and it was time, for the end of his tail had become so hot that there was danger of his setting fire to the building.

The next morning, the Griffin came to the church, and tearing the stone image of himself from its fastenings over the great door, he grasped it with his powerful forelegs and flew up into the air. Then, after hovering over the town for a moment, he gave his tail an angry shake and took up his flight to the dreadful wilds. When he reached this desolate region, he set the stone griffin upon a ledge of a rock which rose in front of the dismal cave he called his home. There the image occupied a position somewhat similar to that it had had over the church-door; and the Griffin, panting with the exertion of carrying such an enormous load to so great a distance, lay down upon the ground, and regarded it with much satisfaction. When he felt somewhat rested he went to look for the Minor Canon. He found the young man, weak and half starved, lying under the shadow of a rock. After picking him up and carrying him to his cave, the Griffin flew away to a distant marsh, where he

procured some roots and herbs which he well knew were strengthening and beneficial to man, though he had never tasted them himself. After eating these the Minor Canon was greatly revived, and sat up and listened while the Griffin told him what had happened in the town.

"Do you know," said the monster, when he had finished, "that I have had, and still have, a great liking for you?"

"I am very glad to hear it," said the Minor Canon, with his usual politeness.

"I am not at all sure that you would be," said the Griffin, "if you thoroughly understood the state of the case, but we will not consider that now. If some things were different, other things would be otherwise. I have been so enraged by discovering the manner in which you have been treated that I have determined that you shall at last enjoy the rewards and honors to which you are entitled. Lie down and have a good sleep, and then I will take you back to the town."

As he heard these words, a look of trouble came over the young man's face.

"You need not give yourself any anxiety," said the Griffin, "about my return to the town. I shall not remain there. Now that I have that admirable likeness of myself in front of my cave, where I can sit at my leisure, and gaze upon its noble features and magnificent proportions, I have no wish to see that abode of cowardly and selfish people."

The Minor Canon, relieved from his fears, now lay back, and dropped into a doze; and when he was sound asleep the Griffin took him up, and carried him back to the town. He arrived just before daybreak, and putting the young man gently on the grass in the little field where he himself used to rest, the monster, without having been seen by any of the people, flew back to his home.

When the Minor Canon made his appearance in the morning among the citizens, the enthusiasm and cordiality with which he was received was truly wonderful. He was taken to a house which had been occupied by one of the banished high officers of the place, and every one was anxious to do all that could be done for his health and comfort. The people crowded into the church when he held services, and the three old women who used to be his week-day congregation could not get to the best seats, which they had always been in the habit of taking; and the parents of the bad children determined to reform them at home, in order that he might be spared the trouble of keeping up his former school. The Minor Canon was appointed to the highest office of the old church, and before he died, he became a bishop.

During the first years after his return from the dreadful wilds, the people of the town looked up to him as a man to whom they were bound to do honor and reverence; but they often, also, looked up to the sky to see if there were any signs of the Griffin coming back. However, in the course of time, they learned to honor and reverence their former Minor Canon without the fear of being punished if they did not do so.

But they need never have been afraid of the Griffin. The autumnal equinox day came round, and the monster ate nothing. If he could not have the Minor Canon, he did not care for anything. So, lying down, with his eyes fixed upon the great stone griffin, he gradually declined, and died. It was a good thing for some of the people of the town that they did not know this.

If you should ever visit the old town, you would still see the little griffins on the sides of the church; but the great stone griffin that was over the door is gone.

DADDY JAKE, THE RUNAWAY

by Joel Chandler Harris

CHAPTER I

ONE FINE DAY in September, in the year 1863, there was quite an uproar on the Gaston plantation, in Putnam County, in the State of Georgia. Uncle Jake, the carriage-driver, was missing. He was more than fifty years old, and it was the first time he had been missing since his mistress had been big enough to call him. But he was missing now. Here was his mistress waiting to order the carriage; here was his master fretting and fuming; and here were the two little children, Lucien and Lillian, crying because they did n't know where Uncle Jake was— "Daddy Jake," who had hithertofore seemed always to be within sound of their voices, ready and anxious to amuse them in any and every way.

Then came the news that Daddy Jake has actually run away. This was, indeed, astounding news, and although it was brought by the son of the overseer, none of the Gastons would believe it, least of all Lucien and Lillian. The son of the overseer also brought the further information that Daddy Jake, who had never had an angry word for anybody, had struck the overseer across the head with a hoe-handle, and had then taken to the woods. Dr. Gaston was very angry, indeed, and he told the overseer's son that if anybody was to blame it was his father. Mrs. Gaston, with her eyes full of tears, agreed with her husband, and Lucien and Lillian, when they found that Daddy Jake was really gone, refused to be comforted. Everybody seemed to be dazed. As it was Saturday, and Saturday was a holiday, the negroes stood around their quarters in little groups discussing the wonderful event. Some of them went so far as to say that if Daddy Jake had taken to the woods it was time for the rest of them to follow suit; but this proposition was hooted down by the more sensible among them.

Nevertheless, the excitement on the Gaston plantation ran very high when it was discovered that a negro so trusted and so trustworthy as Daddy Jake had actually run away; and it was not until all the facts were known that the other negroes became reconciled to Daddy Jake's absence. What were the facts? They were very simple, indeed; and yet, many lads and lasses who read this may fail to fully comprehend them.

In the first place, the year in which Daddy Jake became a fugitive was the year 1863, and there was a great deal of doubt and confusion in the South at that time. The Conscription Act and the Impressment Law were in force. Under the one, nearly all the able-bodied men and boys were drafted into the army; and under the other, all the corn and hay and horses that the Confederacy needed were pressed into service. This state of things came near causing a revolt in some of the States, especially in Georgia, where the laws seemed to bear most heavily. Something of this is to be found in the histories of that period, but nothing approaching the real facts has ever been published. After the Conscription Act was passed the planters were compelled to accept the services of such overseers as they could get, and the one whom Dr. Gaston had employed lacked both experience and discretion. He had never been trained to the business. He was the son of a shoemaker, and he became an overseer merely to keep out of the army. A majority of those who made overseeing their business had gone to the war either as volunteers or substitutes, and very few men capable of taking charge of a large plantation were left behind.

At the same time, overseers were a necessity on some of the plantations. Many of the planters were either lawyers or doctors, and these, if they had any practice at all, were compelled to leave their farming interest to the care of agents; there were other planters who had been reared in the belief that an overseer was necessary on a large plantation; so that, for one cause and another, the overseer class was a pretty large one. It was a very respectable class, too; for, under ordinary circumstances, no person who was not known to be trustworthy would be permitted to take charge of the interests of a plantation, for these were as various and as important as those of any other business.

But in 1863 it was a very hard matter to get a trustworthy overseer; and Dr. Gaston, having a large practice as a physician, had hired the first person who applied for the place, without waiting to make any inquiries about either his knowledge or his character; and it turned out that his overseer was not only utterly incompetent, but that he was something of a rowdy besides. An experienced overseer would have known that he was employed, not to excercise con-

trol over the house servants, but to look after the farm-hands; but the new man began business by ordering Daddy Jake to do various things that were not in the line of his duty. Naturally, the old man, who was something of a boss himself, resented this sort of interference. A great many persons were of the opinion that he had been spoiled by kind treatment; but this is doubtful. He had been raised with the white people from a little child, and he was as proud in his way as he was faithful in all ways. Under the circumstances, Daddy Jake did what other confidential servants would have done; he ignored the commands of the new overseer, and went about his business as usual. This led to a quarrel—the overseer doing most of the quarreling. Daddy Jake was on his dignity, and the overseer was angry. Finally, in his fury, he struck the old negro with a strap which he was carrying across his shoulders. The blow was a stinging one, and it was delivered full in Uncle Jake's face. For a moment the old negro was astonished. Then he became furious. Seizing an ax-handle that happened to be close to his hand, he brought it down upon the head of the overseer with full force. There was a tremendous crash as the blow fell, and the overseer went down as if he had been struck by a pile-driver. He gave an awful groan, and trembled a little in his limbs, and then lay perfectly still. Uncle Jake was both dazed and frightened. He would have gone to his master, but he remembered what he had heard about the law. In those days a negro who struck a white man was tried for his life, and if his guilt could be proven, he was either branded with a hot iron and sold to a speculator, or he was hanged.

The certainty of these punishments had no doubt been exaggerated by rumor, but even the rumor was enough to frighten the negroes. Daddy Jake looked at the overseer a moment, and then stooped and felt of him. He was motionless and, apparently, he had ceased to breathe. Then the old negro went to his cabin, gathered up his blanket and clothes, put some provisions in a little bag, and went off into the woods. He seemed to be in no hurry. He walked with his head bent, as if in deep thought. He appeared to understand and appreciate the situation. A short time ago he was the happy and trusted servant of a master and mistress who had rarely given him an unkind word; now he was a fugitive—a runaway. As he passed along by the garden palings he heard two little children playing and prattling on the other side. They were talking about him. He paused and listened.

"Daddy Jake likes me the best," Lucien was saying, "because he tells me stories."

"No," said Lillian, "he likes me the best, cause he tells me all the stories and gives me some ginger-cake, too."

The old negro paused and looked through the fence at the little children, and then he went on his way. But the youngsters saw Daddy Jake, and went running after him.

"Let me go, Uncle Jake!" cried Lucien. "Le' me go, too!" cried Lillian. But Daddy Jake broke into a run and left the children standing in the garden, crying.

"The youngsters saw Daddy Jake, and went running after him"

It was not very long after this before the whole population knew that Daddy Jake had knocked the overseer down and had taken to the woods. In fact, it was only a few minutes, for some of the other negroes had seen him strike the overseer and had seen the overseer fall, and they lost no time in raising the alarm. Fortunately the overseer was not seriously hurt. He had received a blow severe enough to render him unconscious for a few minutes,—but this was all; and he was soon able to describe the fracas to Dr. Gaston, which he did with considerable animation.

"And who told you to order Jake around?" the doctor asked.

"Well, sir, I just thought I had charge of the whole crowd."

"You were very much mistaken, then," said Doctor Gaston, sharply; "and if I had seen you strike Jake with your strap, I should have been tempted to take my buggy whip and give you a dose of your own medicine."

As a matter of fact, Doctor Gaston was very angry, and he lost no time in giving the new overseer what the negroes called his "walking-papers." He paid him up and discharged him on the spot, and it was not many days before everybody on the Gaston plantation knew that the man had fallen into the hands of the Conscription officers of the Confederacy, and that he had been sent on to the front.

At the same time, as Mrs. Gaston herself remarked, this fact, however gratifying it might be, did not bring Daddy Jake back. He was gone, and his absence caused a great deal of trouble on the plantation. It was found that half-a-dozen negroes had to be detailed to do the work which he had voluntarily taken upon himself— one to attend to the carriage-horses, another to look after the cows, another to feed the hogs and sheep, and still others to look after the thousand and one little things to be done about the "big house." But not one of them, nor all of them, filled Daddy Jake's place.

Many and many a time Doctor Gaston walked up and down the veranda wondering where the old negro was, and Mrs. Gaston, sitting in her rocking-chair, looked down the avenue day after day, half expecting to see Daddy Jake make his appearance, hat in hand and with a broad grin on his face. Some of the neighbors, hearing that Uncle Jake had become a fugitive, wanted to get Bill Locke's "track-dogs" and run him down, but Doctor Gaston and his wife would not hear to this. They said that the old negro was n't used to staying in the woods, and that it would n't be long before he would come back home.

Doctor Gaston, although he was much troubled, looked at the matter from a man's point of view. Here was Daddy Jake's home; if he chose to come back, well and good; if he did n't, why, it could n't be helped, and that was an end of the matter. But Mrs. Gaston took a different view. Daddy Jake had been raised with her father; he was an old family-servant; he had known and loved her mother, who was dead; he had nursed Mrs. Gaston herself when she was a baby; in short, he was a fixture in the lady's experience, and his absence worried her not a little. She could not bear to to think that the old negro was out in the woods without food and without shelter. If there was a thunderstorm at night, as there sometimes is in the South during September, she could hardly sleep for thinking about the old negro.

Thinking about him led Mrs. Gaston to talk about him very often, especially to Lucien and Lillian, who had been in the habit of running out to the kitchen while Daddy Jake was eating his supper and begging him to tell a story. So far as they were concerned, his absence was a personal loss. While Uncle Jake was away they were not only deprived of a most agreeable companion, but they could give no excuse for not going to bed. They had no one to amuse them after supper, and, as a consequence, their evenings were very dull. The youngsters submitted to this for several days, expecting that Daddy Jake would return, but in this they were disappointed. They waited and waited for more than a week, and then they began to show their impatience.

"I used to be afraid of runaways," said Lillian one day, "but I 'm not afraid now, 'cause Daddy Jake is a runaway." Lillian was only six years old, but she had her own way of looking at things.

"Pshaw!" exclaimed Lucien, who was nine, and very robust for his age; "I never was afraid of runaways. I know mighty well they would n't hurt me. There was old Uncle Fed; he was a runaway when Papa bought him. Would he hurt anybody?"

"But there might be some bad ones," said Lillian, "and you know Lucinda says Uncle Fed is a real, sure-enough witch."

"Lucinda!" exclaimed Lucien, scornfully. "What does Lucinda know about witches? If one was to be seen she would n't stick her head out of the door to see it. She 'd be scared to death."

"Yes, and so would anybody," said Lillian, with an air of conviction. "I know I would."

"Well, of course,—a little girl," explained Lucien. "Any little girl would be afraid of a witch, but a great big double-fisted woman like Lucinda ought to be ashamed of herself to be afraid of witches, and that, too, when everybody knows there are n't any witches at all, except in the stories."

"Well, I heard Daddy Jake telling about a witch that turned herself into a black cat, and then into a big black wolf," said Lillian.

"Oh, that was in old times," said Lucien, "when the animals used to talk and go on like people. But you never heard Daddy Jake say he saw a witch,—now, did you?"

"No," said Lillian, somewhat doubtfully; "but I heard him talking about them. I hope no witch will catch Daddy Jake."

"Pshaw!" exclaimed Lucien. "Daddy Jake carried his rabbit-foot with him, and you know no witch can bother him as long as he has his rabbit-foot."

"Well," said Lillian, solemnly, "if he's got his rabbit-foot and can keep off the witches all night, he won't come back any more."

"But he *must* come," said Lucien. "I 'm going after him. I 'm going down to the landing to-morrow and I'll take the boat and go down the river and bring him back."

"Oh, may I go too?" asked Lillian.

"Yes," said Lucien loftily, "if you'll help me get some things out of the house and not say anything about what we are going to do."

Lillian was only too glad to pledge herself to secrecy, and the next day found the two children busily preparing for their journey in search of Daddy Jake.

The Gaston plantation lay along the Oconee River in Putnam County, not far from Roach's Ferry. In fact, it lay on both sides of the river, and, as the only method of communication was by means of a bateau, nearly everybody on the plantation knew how to manage the boat. There was not an hour during the day that the bateau was not in use. Lucien and Lillian had been carried across hundreds of times, and they were as much at home in the boat as they were in a buggy. Lucien was too young to row, but he knew how to guide the bateau with a paddle while others used the oars.

This fact gave him confidence, and the result was that the two children quietly made their arrangements to go in search of Daddy Jake. Lucien was the "provider," as he said, and Lillian helped him to carry the things to the boat. They got some meal-sacks, two old quilts, and a good supply of biscuits and meat. Nobody meddled with them, for nobody knew what their plans were, but some of the negroes remarked that they were not only unusually quiet, but very busy—a state of things that is looked upon by those who are acquainted with the ways of children as a very bad sign, indeed.

The two youngsters worked pretty much all day, and they worked hard; so that when night came they were both tired and sleepy. They were tired and sleepy, but they managed to cover their supplies with the meal-sacks, and the morning they were up bright and early. They were up so early, indeed, that they thought it was a very long time until breakfast was ready; and, at last, when the bell rang, they hurried to the table and ate ravenously, as became two travelers about to set out on a voyage of adventure.

It was all they could do to keep their scheme from their mother. Once Lillian was on the point of asking her something about it, but Lucien shook his head, and it was not long before the two youngsters embarked on their journey. After seating Lillian in the bateau, Lucien unfastened the chain from the stake, threw it into the boat, and jumped in himself. Then, as the clumsy affair drifted slowly with the current, he seized one of the paddles, placed the blade against the bank, and pushed the bateau out into the middle of the stream.

It was the beginning of a voyage of adventure, the end of which could not be foretold; but the sun was shining brightly, the mocking-birds were singing in the water-oaks, the blackbirds were whistling blithely in the reeds, and the children were light-hearted and happy. They were going to find Daddy Jake and fetch him back home, and not for a moment did it occur to them that the old negro might have gone in a different direction. It seemed somehow to those on the Gaston plantation that whatever was good, or great, or wonderful had its origin "down the river." Rumor said that the biggest crops were grown in that direction, and that there the negroes were happiest. The river, indeed, seemed to flow to some far-off country where everything was finer and more flourishing. This was the idea of the negroes themselves, and it was natural that Lucien and Lillian should be impressed with the same belief. So they drifted down the river, confident that they would find Daddy Jake. They had no other motive—no other thought. They took no account of the hardships of a voyage such as they had embarked on.

Lazily, almost reluctantly as it seemed, the boat floated down the stream. At first, Lucien was inclined to use the broad oar, but it appeared that when he paddled on one side the clumsy boat tried to turn its head up stream on the other side, and so, after a while, he dropped the oar in the bottom of the boat.

The September sun was sultry that morning, but, obeying some impulse of the current, the boat drifted down the river in the shade of the water-oaks and willows that lined the eastern bank. On the western bank the Gaston plantation lay, and as the boat floated lazily along the little voyagers could hear the field-hands singing as they picked the opening cotton. The song was strangely melodious, though the words were ridiculous.

My dog 's a 'possum dog,
Here, Rattler! here!
He cross de creek upon a log,
Here, Rattler! here!

He run de 'possum up a tree,
Here, Rattler! here!
He good enough fer you an' me,
Here, Rattler! here!

Kaze when it come his fat'nin' time,
Here, Rattler! here!
De 'possum eat de muscadine,
Here, Rattler! here!

He eat till he kin skacely stan',
Here, Rattler! here!
An' den we bake him in de pan,
Here, Rattler! here!

It was to the quaint melody of this song that the boat rocked and drifted along. One of the negroes saw the children and thought he knew them, and he called to them, but received no reply; and this fact was so puzzling that he went back and told the other negroes that there was some mistake about the children. "Ef dey 'd 'a' bin our chillun," he said, "dey'd 'a' hollered back at me, sho'." Whereupon, the field-hands resumed their work and their song, and the boat, gliding southward on the gently undulating current, was soon lost to view.

To the children it seemed to be a very pleasant journey. They had no thought of danger. The river was their familiar friend. They had crossed and recrossed it hundreds of times. They were as contented

"The field-hands were singing as they picked the opening cotton"

in the bateau as they would have been in their mother's room. The weather was warm, but on the river and in the shade of the overhanging trees, the air was cool and refreshing. And after a while the current grew swifter, and the children, dipping their hands in the water, laughed aloud.

Once, indeed, the bateau, in running over a long stretch of shoals, was caught against a rock. An ordinary boat would have foundered, but this boat, clumsy and deep-set, merely obeyed the current. It struck the rock, recoiled, touched it again, and then slowly turned around and pursued its course down the stream. The shoals were noisy but harmless. The water foamed and roared over the rocks, but the current was deep enough to carry the bateau safely down. It was not often that a boat took that course, but Lucien and Lillian had no sense of fear. The roaring and foaming of the water pleased them, and the rushing and whirling of the boat, as it went dashing down the rapids, appeared to be only part of a holiday frolic. After they had passed the shoals, the current became swifter, and the old bateau was swept along at a rapid rate. The trees on the river bank seemed to be running back toward home, and the shadows on the water ran with them.

Sometimes the boat swept through long stretches of meadow and marsh lands, and then the children were delighted to see the sand-pipers and kill-dees running along the margin of the water. The swallows, not yet flown southward, skimmed along the river with quivering wing, and the king-fishers displayed their shining plumage in the sun. Once a moccasin, fat and rusty, frightened by the unexpected appearance of the young voyagers, dropped into the boat; but before Lucien could strike him with the unwieldy oar, he tumbled overboard and disappeared. Then the youngsters ate their dinner. It was a very dry dinner; but they ate it with a relish. The crows, flying lazily over, regarded them curiously.

"I reckon they want some," said Lucien.

"Well, they can't get mine," said Lillian, " 'cause I *jest* about got enough for myself."

They passed a white man who was sitting on the river bank, with his coat off, fishing.

"Where under the sun did you chaps come from?" he cried.

"Up the river," replied Lucien.

"Where in the nation are you going?"

"Down the river."

"Maybe he knows where Daddy Jake is," said Lillian. "Ask him."

"Why, he would n't know Daddy Jake from a side of sole leather," exclaimed Lucien.

By this time the boat had drifted around a bend in the river. The man on the bank took off his hat with his thumb and forefinger, rubbed his head with the other fingers, drove away a swarm of mosquitoes, and muttered, "Well, I'll be switched!" Then he went on with his fishing.

Meanwhile the boat drifted steadily with the current. Sometimes it seemed to the children that the boat stood still, while the banks, the trees, and the fields moved by them like a double panorama. Queer-looking little birds peeped at them from the bushes; fox-squirrels chattered at them from the trees; green frogs greeted them by plunging into the water with a squeak; turtles slid noiselessly off the banks at their approach; a red fox that had come to the river to drink disappeared like a shadow before the sun; and once a great white crane rose in the air, flapping his wings heavily.

Altogether it was a very jolly journey, but after a while Lillian began to get restless.

"Do you reckon Daddy Jake will be in the river when we find him?" she asked.

Lucien himself was becoming somewhat tired, but he was resolved to go right on. Indeed, he could not do otherwise.

"Why, who ever heard of such a thing?" he exclaimed. "What would Daddy Jake be doing in the water?"

"Well, how are we's to find him?"

"Oh, we 'll find him."

"But I want to find him right now," said Lillian, "and I want to see Mamma, and Papa, and my dollies."

"Well," said Lucien, with unconscious humor, "if you don't want to go, you can get out and walk back home." At this, Lillian began to cry.

"Well," said Lucien, "if Daddy Jake was over there in the bushes and was to see you crying because you did n't want to go and find him, he 'd run off into the woods and nobody would see him any more."

Lillian stopped crying at once, and, as the afternoon wore on, both children grew more cheerful; and even when twilight came, and after it the darkness, they were not very much afraid. The loneliness—the sighing of the wind through the trees, the rippling of the water against the sides of the boat, the hooting of the big swamp-owl, the cry of the whippoorwill, and the answer of its cousin, the chuck-will's-widow—all these things would have awed and frightened the children. But, shining steadily in the evening sky, they saw the star they always watched at home. It seemed to be brighter than ever, this familiar star, and they hailed it as a friend and fellow-traveler. They felt that home could n't be so far away, for the star shone in its accustomed place, and this was a great comfort.

After a while the night grew chilly, and then Lucien and Lillian wrapped their quilts about them and cuddled down in the bottom of the boat. Thousands of stars shone overhead, and it seemed to the children that the old bateau, growing tired of its journey, had stopped to rest; but it continued to drift down the river.

CHAPTER II

YOU may be sure there was trouble on the Gaston place when night came and the children did not return. They were missed at dinner-time; but it frequently happened that they went off with some of the plantation wagons, or with some of the field-hands, and so nothing was thought of their absence at noon; but when night fell and all the negroes had returned from their work, and there was still no sign of the children, there was consternation in the big house and trouble all over the plantation. The field-hands, returned from their work, discussed the matter at the doors of their cabins and manifested considerable anxiety.

At first the house-servants were sent scurrying about the place hunting for the truants. Then other negroes were pressed into service, until, finally, every negro on the place was engaged in the search, and torches could be seen bobbing up and down in all parts of the plantation. The negroes called and called, filling the air with their musical halloos, but there was no reply save from the startled birds, or from the dogs, who seemed to take it for granted that everybody was engaged in a grand 'possum hunt and added the strength of their own voices to the general clamor.

While all this was going on, Mrs. Gaston was pacing up and down the long veranda wringing her hands in an agony of grief. There was but one thought in her mind —the *river,* the RIVER! Her husband in the midst of his own grief tried to console her, but he could not. He had almost as much as he could do to control himself, and there was in his own mind—the RIVER!

The search on the plantation and in its vicinity went on until nearly nine o'clock. About that time Big Sam, one of the plough-hands, who was also a famous fisherman, came running to the house with a frightened face.

"Marster," he exclaimed, "de boat gone —she done gone!"

"Oh, I knew it!" exclaimed Mrs. Gaston —"the river, the river!"

"Well!" said Dr. Gaston, "the boat must be found. Blow the horn."

Big Sam seized the dinner-horn and blew a blast that startled the echoes for miles around. The negroes understood this to be a signal to return, and most of them thought that the children had been found, so they came back laughing and singing and went to the big house to see the children.

"Wh'abouts you fine um, marster?" asked the foreman.

"They have n't been found, Jim," said Dr. Gaston. "Big Sam says that the boat is gone from the landing, and that boat must be found to-night."

"Marster," said a negro, coming forward out of the group, "I seed a boat gwine down stream dis mornin'. I wuz way up on de hill—"

"And you did n't come and tell me?" asked Dr. Gaston in a severe tone.

"Well, suh, I hollered at um, an' dey ain't make no answer, an' den it look like ter me 't wuz dem two Ransome boys. Hit mos' drap out'n my min'. An' den you know, suh, our chillun ain't never had no doin's like dat—gittin' in de boat by dey own-alone se'f an' sailin' off dat a-way."

"Well," said Dr. Gaston, "the boat must be found. The children are in it. Where can we get another boat?"

"I got one, suh," said Big Sam.

"Me, too, marster," said another negro.

"Then get them both, and be quick about it!"

"Ah-yi, suh," was the response, and in a moment the group was scattered, and Big Sam could be heard giving orders in a loud and an energetic tone of voice. For once he was in his element. He could be foreman on the Oconee if he could n't in the cotton-patch. He knew every nook and cranny of the river for miles up and down; he had his fish-baskets sunk in many places, and the overhanging limbs of many a tree bore the marks of the lines of his set-hooks. So for once he appointed himself foreman, and took charge of affairs. He and Sandy Bill (so called owing to the peculiar color of his hair) soon had their boats at the landing. The other negroes were assembled there, and the most of them had torches.

"Marster," said Big Sam, "you git in my boat, an' let little Willyum come fer ter hol' de torch. Jesse, you git in dar wid Sandy Bill. Fling a armful er light'ood in bofe boats, boys, kaze we got ter have a light, and dey ain't no tellin' how fur we gwine."

The fat pine was thrown in, everything made ready, and then the boats started. With one sweep of his broad paddle, Big Sam sent his boat into the middle of the stream, and, managed by his strong and willing arms, the clumsy old bateau became a thing of life. Sandy Bill was not far behind him.

The negroes used only one paddle in rowing, and each sat in the stern of his boat, using the rough but effective oar first on one side and then the other.

From a window, Mrs. Gaston watched the boats as they went speeding down the river. By her side was Charity, the cook.

"Is n't it terrible!" she exclaimed, as the

boats passed out of sight. "Oh, what shall
I do?"

" 'T would be mighty bad, Mist'iss, *ef*
dem chillun wuz los'; but dey ain't no
mo' los' dan I is, an' I 'm a-standin' right
yer in de cornder by dish yer cheer."

"Not lost! Why, of course they are lost.
Oh, my darling little children!"

"No 'm, dey ain't no mo' los' dan you is.
Dey tuck dat boat dis mornin', an' dey
went atter ole man Jake—dat's whar dey
er gone. Dey ain't gone nowhar else. Dey
er in dat boat right now; dey may be
asleep, but dey er in dar. Ain't I year um
talkin' yistiddy wid my own years? Ain't
I year dat ar Marse Lucien boy 'low ter
he sister dat he gwine go fetch ole man
Jake back? Ain't I miss a whole can full
er biscuits? Ain't I miss two er dem pies
w'at I lef' out dar in de kitchen? Ain't
I miss a great big hunk er light-bread? An'
who gwine dast ter take um less'n it 's
dem ar chillun? Dey don't fool me, mon.
I 'm one er de oldest rats in de barn—I is
dat!"

Charity's tone was emphatic and energetic. She was so confident that her theory
was the right one that she succeeded in
quieting her mistress somewhat.

"An' mo' 'n dat," she went on, seeing

the effect of her remarks, "dem chillun 'll
come home yer all safe an' soun'. Ef Marster an' dem niggers don't fetch um back,
dey 'll come deyse'f; an' old man Jake 'll
come wid um. You min' w'at I tell you.
You go an' go ter bed, honey, an' don't
pester yo'se'f 'bout dem chillun. I 'll set
up yer in de cornder an' nod, an' keep
my eyes on w'at 's gwine on outside."

But Mrs. Gaston refused to go to bed.
She went to the window, and away down
the river she could see the red light of the
torches projected against the fog. It seemed
as if it were standing still, and the mother's
heart sank within her at the thought. Perhaps they had found the boat—empty!
This and a thousand other cruel suggestions racked her brain.

But the boats were not standing still;
they were moving down the river as rapidly as four of the stoutest arms to be found
in the county could drive them. The pine
torches lit up both banks perfectly. The
negroes rowed in silence a mile or more,
when Big Sam said:

"Marster, kin we sing some?"

"Does it seem to be much of a singing
matter, Sam?" Dr. Gaston asked, grimly.

"No, suh, it don't; but singin' he'ps 'long
might'ly w'en you workin', mo' speshually
ef you er doin' de kind er work whar you
kin sorter hit a lick wid de chune—kinder
keepin' time, like."

Dr. Gaston said nothing, and Big Sam
went on:

" 'Sides dat, marster, we-all useter sing
ter dem chillun, an' dey knows our holler
so well dat I boun' you ef dey wuz ter year
us singin' an' gwine on, dey 'd holler back."

"Well," said Dr. Gaston, struck by the
suggestion, "sing."

"Bill," said Big Sam to the negro in the
other boat, "watch out for me; I'm gwine
away."

"You 'll year fum me w'en you git whar
you gwine," Sandy Bill replied.

With that Big Sam struck up a song. His voice was clear and strong, and he sang with a will.

Oh, Miss Malindy, you er lots too sweet
    for me;
I cannot come to see you
Ontil my time is free—
  Oh, den I 'll come ter see you,
An' take you on my knee.

Oh, Miss Malindy, now don't you go away;
  I cannot come to see you
Ontil some yuther day—
  Oh, den I 'll come ter see you—
Oh, den I 'll come ter stay.

Oh, Miss Malindy, you is my only one;
  I cannot come ter see you
Ontil de day is done—
  Oh, den I 'll come ter see you,
And we 'll have a little fun.

Oh, Miss Malindy, my heart belongs ter
  you;
  I cannot come ter see you
Ontil my work is thoo'.
  Oh, den I 'll come ter see you,
I 'll come in my canoe.

The words of the song, foolish and trivial as they are, do not give the faintest idea of the melody to which it was sung. The other negroes joined in, and the tremulous tenor of little Willyum was especially effective. The deep dark woods on either side seemed to catch up and echo back the plaintive strain. To a spectator on the bank, the scene must have been an uncanny one —the song with its heart-breaking melody, the glistening arms and faces of the two gigantic blacks, the flaring torches, flinging their reflections on the swirling waters, the great gulfs of darkness beyond—all these must have been very impressive. But these things did not occur to those in the boats, least of all to Dr. Gaston. In the minds of all there was but one thought— the children.

The negroes rowed on, keeping time to their songs. Their arms appeared to be as tireless as machinery that has the impulse of steam. Finally Big Sam's boat grounded.

"Hol' on dar, Bill!" he shouted. "Watch out!" He took the torch from the little negro and held it over his head, and then behind him, peering into the darkness beyond. Then he laughed.

"De Lord he'p my soul!" he exclaimed; "I done clean fergit 'bout Moccasin Shoals! Back yo' boat Bill." Suiting the action to the word, he backed his own, and they were soon away from the shoals.

"Now, den," he said to Bill, "git yo' boat in line wid mine, an' hol' yo' paddle in yo' lap." Then the boats, caught by the current, moved toward the shoals, and one after the other touched a rock, turned completely around, and went safely down the rapids, just as the children's boat had done in the forenoon. Once over the shoals, Big Sam and Sandy Bill resumed their oars and their songs, and sent the boats along at a rapid rate.

A man, sitting on the river bank, heard them coming, and put out his torch by covering it with sand. He crouched behind the bushes and watched them go by. After they had passed, he straightened himself, and remarked:

"Well, I 'll be switched!" Then he relighted his torch, and went on with his fishing. It was the same man that Lucien and Lillian had seen.

The boats went on and on. With brief intervals the negroes rowed all night long, but Dr. Gaston found no trace of his children. In sheer desperation, however, he kept on. The sun rose, and the negroes were still rowing. At nine o'clock in the morning the boats entered Ross's mill-pond. This Dr. Gaston knew was the end of his journey. If the boat had drifted into this pond, and been carried over the dam, the children were either drowned or crushed on the rocks below. If their boat had not entered the pond, then they had been rescued the day before by some one living near the river.

It was with a heavy heart that Dr. Gaston landed. And yet there were no signs of a tragedy anywhere near. John Cosby, the miller, fat and hearty, stood in the door of the mill, his arms akimbo, and watched the boats curiously. His children were playing near. A file of geese was marching down to the water, and a flock of pigeons was sailing overhead, taking their morning exercise. Everything seemed to be peaceful and serene. As he passed the dam on his way to the mill, Dr. Gaston saw that there was a heavy head of water, but possibly not enough to carry a large bateau over; still—the children were gone!

The puzzled look on the miller's face disappeared as Dr. Gaston approached. "Well, the gracious goodness!" he exclaimed. "Why, howdy, Doc.—howdy! Why, I 'm right down glad to see you. Whichever an' whichaway did you come?"

"My little children are lost," said Dr. Gaston, shaking the miller's hand. The jolly smile on John Cosby's face disappeared as suddenly as if it had been wiped out with a sponge.

"Well, now, that 's too bad—too bad," he exclaimed, looking at his own rosy-cheeked little ones standing near.

"They were in a bateau," said Dr. Gaston, "and I thought maybe they might have drifted down here and over the mill-dam."

The miller's jolly smile appeared again. "Oh, no, Doc.—no, no! Whichever an' whichaway they went, they never went over that dam. In time of a freshet, the thing might be did; but not now. Oh, no!

Ef it lies betwixt goin' over that dam an' bein' safe, them babies is jest as safe an' soun' as mine is."

"I think," said Dr. Gaston, "that they started out to hunt Jake, my carriage-driver, who has run away."

"Jake run away!" exclaimed Mr. Cosby, growing very red in the face. "Why, the impident scoundull! Hit ain't bin three days sence the ole rascal wuz here. He come an' 'lowed that some of your wagons was a-campin' out about two mile from here, an' he got a bushel of meal, an' said that if you did n't pay me the money down I could take it out in physic. The impident ole scoundull! An' he was jest as 'umble-come-tumble as you please—a-bowin' an' a-scrapin', an' a-howdydoin'.'"

But the old miller's indignation cooled somewhat when Dr. Gaston briefly told him of the incident which caused the old negro to run away.

"Hit sorter sticks in my gizzard," he remarked, "when I hear tell of a nigger hittin' a white man; but I don't blame Jake much."

"And now," said Dr. Gaston, "I want to ask your advice. You are a level-headed man, and I want to know what you think. The children got in the boat, and came down the river. There is no doubt in my mind that they started on a wild-goose chase after Jake; but they are not on the river now, nor is the boat on the river. How do you account for that?"

"Well, Doc., if you want my naked beliefs about it, I 'll give 'em to you, fa 'r an' squar'. It 's my beliefs that them youngsters have run up agin old Jake somewhar up the river, an' that they are jest as safe an' soun' as you is. Them 's my beliefs."

"But what has become of the boat?"

"Well, I 'll tell you. Old Jake is jest as cunning as any other nigger. He took an' took the youngsters out, an' arterwards he drawed the boat out on dry land. He rightly thought there would be pursuit, an' he did n't mean to be ketched."

"Then what would you advise me to do?" asked Dr. Gaston.

The old man scratched his head.

"Well, Doc., I 'm a-talkin' in the dark, but it 's my beliefs them youngsters 'll be at home before you can get there to save your life. Jake may not be there, but if he 's found the boy an' gal, he 'll carry em safe home. Now you mind what I tell you."

Dr. Gaston's anxiety was too great to permit him to put much confidence in the old miller's prediction. What he said seemed reasonable enough, but a thousand terrible doubts had possession of the father's mind. He hardly dared go home without the children. He paced up and down before the mill, a most miserable man. He knew not where to go or what to do.

Mr. Cosby, the miller, watched him awhile and shook his head. "If Doc. don't find them youngsters," he said to himself, "he 'll go plum deestracted." But he said aloud:

"Well, Doc., you an' the niggers must have a breathing-spell. We 'll go up to the house an' see ef we can't find somethin' to eat in the cubberd, an' arterwards, in the time you are restin', we 'll talk about findin' the youngsters. If there 's any need-cessity, I 'll go with you. My son John can run the mill e'en about as good as I can. We 'll go up yan to 'Squire Ross's an' git a horse or two, an' we 'll scour the country on both sides of the river. But you 've got to have a snack of somethin' to eat, an' you 've got to take a rest. Human natur' can't stand the strain."

Torn as he was by grief and anxiety, Dr. Gaston knew this was good advice. He gratefully accepted John Cosby's invitation to breakfast, as well as his offer to aid in the search for the lost children. After Dr. Gaston had eaten, he sat on the miller's porch and tried to collect his thoughts so as to be able to form some plan of search. While the two men were talking, they heard Big Sam burst out laughing. He laughed so loud and heartily that Mr. Cosby grew angry, and went into the back yard to see what the fun was about. In his heart the miller thought the negroes were laughing at the food his wife had set before them, and he was properly indignant.

"Well, well," said he, "what 's this I hear? Two high-fed niggers a-laughin' beca'se their master's little ones are lost and gone! And has it come to this? A purty pass, a mighty purty pass!" Both the negroes grew very serious at this.

"Mars' John, we-all was des projickin' wid one an'er. You know how niggers is w'en dey git nuff ter eat. Dey feel so good dey 'bleege ter holler."

Mr. Cosby sighed, and turned away. "Well," said he, "I hope niggers 's got souls, but I know right p'int-blank that they ain't got no hearts."

Now, what was Big Sam laughing at? He was laughing because he had found out where Lucien and Lillian were. How did he find out? In the simplest manner imaginable. Sandy Bill and Big Sam were sitting in Mr. Cosby's back yard eating their breakfast, while little Willyum was eating his in the kitchen. It was the first time the two older negroes had had an opportunity of talking together since they started from home the day before.

"Sam," said Sandy Bill, "did you see whar de chillun landed w'en we come 'long des a'ter sun-up dis mornin'?"

"Dat I did n't," said Sam, wiping his mouth with the back of his hand—"dat I did n't, an' ef I had I 'd a hollered out ter marster."

"Dat w'at I wuz feared un," said Sandy Bill.

"Feared er what?" asked Big Sam.

"Feared you 'd holler at marster ef you

seed whar dey landed. Dat how come I ter run foul er yo' boat."

"Look yer, nigger man, you ain't done gone 'stracted, is you?"

"Shoo, chile! don't talk ter me 'bout gwine 'stracted. I got ez much sense ez Ole Zip Coon."

"Den why n't you tell marster? Ain't you done see how he troubled in he min'?"

"I know 'im,' said Big Sam. "Dey calls 'im Hudson's cane-brake."

"Now you talkin'," said Sandy Bill. "Well, ef you go dar you 'll fin' right in de middle er dat cane-brake a heap er niggers dat you got 'quaintance wid—Randall Spivey, an' Crazy Sue, an' Cupid Mitchell, an' Isaiah Little—dey er all dar; an' ole man Jake, he dar too."

"I done see dat, en it make me feel bad; but t'er folks got trouble, too, lots wuss'n marster."

"Is dey los' der chillun?"

"Yes—Lord! dey done los' eve'ybody. But marster ain't los' no chillun yit."

"Den wat we doin' way down yer?" asked Big Sam in an angry tone.

"Le'me tell you," said Sandy Bill, laying his hand on Big Sam's shoulder; "le'me tell you. Right cross dar fum whar I run foul er yo' boat is de biggest cane-brake in all creation."

"Look yer, nigger," Sam exclaimed, "how you know?"

"I sent 'im dar. He come by me in de fiel' an' tole me he done kilt de overseer, an' I up an' tell 'im, I did, 'Make fer Hudson's cane-brake,' an dar 's right whar he went."

It was at this point that Big Sam's hearty laughter attracted the attention of Dr. Gaston and Mr. Cosby.

"Now, den," said Sandy Bill, after the miller had rebuked them and returned to the other side of the house, "now, den, ef

I 'd 'a' showed marster whar dem chillun landed, en tole 'im whar dey wuz, he 'd 'a' gone 'cross dar, en seed dem niggers, an' by dis time nex' week ole Bill Locke's nigger-dogs would 'a' done run um all in jail. You know how marster is. He think kaze *he* treat his niggers right dat eve'ybody else treat der'n des dat a-way. But don't you worry 'bout dem chillun."

Was it possible for Sandy Bill to be mistaken?

CHAPTER III

LUCIEN and Lillian, cuddled together in the bottom of their boat, were soon fast asleep. In dreams of home their loneliness and their troubles were all forgotten. Sometimes in the starlight, sometimes in the dark shadows of the overhanging trees, the boat drifted on. At last, toward morning, it was caught in an eddy and carried nearer the bank, where the current was almost imperceptible. Here the clumsy old bateau rocked and swung, sometimes going lazily forward, and then as lazily floating back again.

As the night faded away into the dim gray of morning, the bushes above the boat were thrust softly aside, and a black face looked down upon the children. Then the black face disappeared as suddenly as it came. After a while it appeared again. It was not an attractive face. In the dim light it seemed to look down on the sleeping children with a leer that was almost hideous. It was the face of a woman. Around her head was a faded red handkerchief, tied in a fantastic fashion, and as much of her dress as could be seen was ragged, dirty, and greasy. She was not pleasant to look upon, but the children slept on unconscious of her presence.

Presently the woman came nearer. On the lower bank a freshet had deposited a great heap of sand, which was now dry and soft. The woman sat down on this, hugging her knees with her arms, and gazed at the sleeping children long and earnestly. Then she looked up and down the river, but nothing was to be seen for the fog that lay on the water. She shook her head and muttered:

"Hit 's pizen down yer fer dem babies. Yit how I gwine git um out er dar?"

She caught hold of the boat, turned it around, and, by means of the chain, drew it partially on the sand-bank. Then she lifted Lillian from the boat, wrapping the quilt closer about the child, carried her up the bank, and laid her beneath the trees where no dew had fallen. Returning, she lifted Lucien and placed him beside his sister. But the change aroused him. He raised himself on his elbow and rubbed his eyes. The negro woman, apparently by force of habit, slipped behind a tree.

"Where am I?" Lucien exclaimed, looking around in something of a fright. He caught sight of the frazzled skirt of the woman's dress. "Who is there behind that tree?" he cried.

"Nobody but me, honey—nobody ner nothin' but po' ole Crazy Sue. Don't be skeerd er me. I ain't nigh ez bad ez I looks ter be."

It was now broad daylight, and Lucien could see that the hideous ugliness of the woman was caused by a burn on the side of her face and neck.

"Was n't I in a boat?"

"Yes, honey; I brung you up yer fer ter keep de fog fum pizenin' you."

"I dreamed the Bad Man had me," said Lucien, shivering at the bare recollection.

"No, honey; 't want nobody ner nothin' but po' ole Crazy Sue. De boat down dar on de sandbank, an' yo' little sissy layin' dar soun' asleep. Whar in de name er goodness wuz you-all gwine, honey?" asked Crazy Sue, coming nearer.

"We were going down the river hunting for Daddy Jake. He 's a runaway now. I reckon we 'll find him after a while."

"Is you-all Marse Doc. Gaston' chillun?" asked Crazy Sue, with some show of eagerness.

"Why, of course we are," said Lucien. Crazy Sue's eyes fairly danced with joy. She clasped her hands together and exclaimed:

"Lord, honey, I could shout,—I could des holler and shout; but I ain't gwine do it. You stay right dar by yo' little sissy till I come back; I want ter run an' make somebody feel good. Now, don't you move, honey. Stay right dar."

With that Crazy Sue disappeared in the bushes. Lucien kept very still. In the first place, he was more than half frightened by the strangeness of his surroundings, and, in the second place, he was afraid his little sister would wake and begin to cry. He felt like crying a little himself, for he knew he was many miles from home, and he felt very cold and uncomfortable. Indeed, he felt very lonely and miserable; but just when he was about to cry and call Daddy Jake, he heard voices near him. Crazy Sue came toward him in a half-trot, and behind her—close behind her—was Daddy Jake, his face wreathed in smiles and his eyes swimming in tears. Lucien saw him and rushed toward him, and the old man stooped and hugged the boy to his black bosom.

"Why, honey," he exclaimed, "whar de name er goodness you come f'um? Bless you! ef my eyes wuz sore de sight un you would make um well. How you know whar yo' Daddy Jake is?"

"Me and sister started out to hunt you," said Lucien, whimpering a little, now that he had nothing to whimper for, "and I think you are mighty mean to run off and leave us-all at home."

"Now you talkin', honey," said Daddy

"Lucien saw him and rushed toward him"

Jake, laughing in his old fashion. "I boun' I 'm de meanes' ole nigger in de Nunited State. Yit, ef I 'd 'a' know'd you wuz gwine ter foller me up so close, I 'd 'a' fotch you wid me, dat I would! An dar 's little Missy," he exclaimed, leaning over the little girl, "an' she 's a-sleepin' des ez natchul ez ef she wuz in her bed at home. What I tell you-all?" he went on, turning to a group of negroes that had followed him,—Randall, Cupid, Isaiah, and others,—"What I tell you-all? Ain't I done bin' an' gone an' tole you dat deze chillun wuz de out-doin'est chillun on de top-side er de roun' worl'?"

The negroes—runaways all—laughed and looked pleased, and Crazy Sue fairly danced. They made so much fuss that they woke Lillian, and when she saw Daddy Jake she gave one little cry and leaped in his arms. This made Crazy Sue dance again, and she would have kept it up for a long time, but Randall suggested to Daddy Jake that the boat ought to be hauled ashore and hidden in the bushes. Crazy Sue stayed with the children, while the negro men went after the boat. They hauled it up the bank by the chain, and then they lifted and carried it several hundred yards away from the river, and hid it in the thick bushes and grass.

"Now," said Daddy Jake, when they had returned to where they left the children, "we got ter git away f'um yer. Dey ain't no tellin' w'at gwine ter happen. Ef deze yer chillun kin slip up on us dis away w'at kin a grown man do?"

The old man intended this as a joke, but the others took him at his word, and were moving off. "Wait!" he exclaimed. "De chillun bleeze ter go whar I go. Sue, you pick up little Missy dar, an' I 'll play hoss fer dish yer chap."

Crazy Sue lifted Lillian in her arms, Daddy Jake stooped so that Lucien could climb up on his back, and then all took up their march for the middle of Hudson's

canebrake. Randall brought up the rear in order, as he said, to "stop up de holes."

It was a narrow, slippery, and winding path in which the negroes trod—a path that a white man would have found difficult to follow. It seemed to lead in all directions; but, finally, it stopped on a knoll high and dry above the surrounding swamp. A fire was burning brightly, and the smell of frying meat was in the air. On this knoll the runaway negroes had made their camp, and for safety they could not have selected a better place.

It was not long before Crazy Sue had warmed some breakfast for the children. The negroes had brought the food they found in the boat, and Crazy Sue put some of the biscuits in a tin bucket, hung the bucket on a stick, and held it over the fire. Then she gave them some bacon that had been broiled on a stone, and altogether they made a hearty breakfast.

During the morning most of the negro men stayed in the canebrake, some nodding and some patching their clothes, which were already full of patches. But after dinner, a feast of broiled fish, roasted sweet-potatoes, and ash-cake, they all went away, leaving Crazy Sue to take care of the children. After the men had all gone, the woman sat with her head covered with her arms. She sat thus for a long time. After a while Lucien went to her and put his hand on her shoulder.

"What 's the matter?" he asked.

"Nothin', honey; I wuz des a-settin' yer a-studyin' an' a-studyin'. Lots er times I gits took dat a-way."

"What are you studying about?" said Lucien.

" 'Bout folks. I wuz des a-studyin' 'bout folks, an' 'bout how come I whar I is, w'en I oughter be somers else. W'en I set down dis a-way, I gits dat turrified in de min' dat I can't stay on de groun' sca'cely. Look like I want ter rise up in de elements an' fly."

"What made you run away?" Lucien asked with some curiosity.

"Well, you know, honey," said Crazy Sue, after a pause, "my marster ain't nigh ez good ter his niggers ez yo' pa is ter his'n. 'T ain't dat my marster is any mo' strick, but look like hit fret 'im ef he see one er his niggers settin' down anywheres. Well, one time, long time ago, I had two babies, an' dey wuz twins, an' dey wuz des 'bout ez likely little niggers ez you ever did see. De w'ite folks had me at de house doin' de washin' so I could be where I kin nurse de babies. One time I wuz settin' in my house nursin' un um, an' while I settin' dar I went fast ter sleep. How long I sot dar 'sleep, de Lord only knows, but w'en I woked up, marster wuz stan'in' in de do', watchin' me. He ain't say nothin', yit I knowed dat man wuz mad. He des turn on his heel an' walk away. I let you know I put dem babies down an' hustled out er dat house mighty quick.

"Well, sir, dat night de foreman come 'roun' an' tole me dat I mus' go ter de fiel' de nex' mornin'. Soon ez he say dat, I up an' went ter de big house an' ax marster w'at I gwine do wid de babies ef I went ter de fiel'. He stood an' look at me, he did, an' den he writ a note out er his pocketbook an' tol' me ter han' it ter de overseer. Dat w'at I done dat ve'y night, an' de overseer, he took an' read de note, an' den he up an' say dat I mus' go wid de hoe-han's, way over ter de two-mile place.

"I went, kaze I bleeze ter go; yit all day long, whiles I wuz hoein' I kin year dem babies cryin'. Look like sometimes dey wuz right at me, an' den ag'in look like dey wuz way off yander. I kep' on a-goin' an' I kep' on a-hoein', an' de babies kep' on a-famishin'. Dey des fade away, an' bimeby dey died, bofe un um on de same day. On dat day I had a fit an' fell in de fier, an' dat how come I burnt up so.

"Look like," said the woman, marking on the ground with her bony forefinger—"look like I kin year dem babies cryin' yit, an' dat de reason folks call me Crazy Sue. kaze I kin year um cryin' an' yuther folks can't. I 'm mighty glad dey can't, too, kaze it 'ud break der heart."

"Why did n't you come and tell Papa about it?" said Lucien, indignantly.

"Ah, Lord, honey!" exclaimed Crazy Sue, "yo pa is a mighty good man, an' a mighty good doctor, but he ain't got no medicine w'at could 'a' kyored me an' my marster."

In a little while Daddy Jake put in an appearance, and the children soon forgot Crazy Sue's troubles, and began to think about going home.

"Daddy Jake," said Lucien, "when are you going to take us back home?"

"I want to go right now," said Lillian.

Daddy Jake scratched his head and thought the matter over.

"Dey ain't no use talkin'," said he, "I got ter carry you back an' set you down in sight er de house, but how I gwine do it an' not git kotched? Dat w'at troublin' me."

"Why, Papa ain't mad," said Lucien. "I heard him tell that mean old overseer he had a great mind to take his buggy whip to him for hitting you."

"Ain't dat man dead?" exclaimed Daddy Jake in amazement.

"No, he ain't," said Lucien. "Papa drove him off the place."

"Well, I be blest!" said the old man with a chuckle. "W'at kinder head you reckon dat w'ite man got?—Honey," he went on, growing serious again, "is you *sholy sho* dat man ain't dead?"

"Did n't I see him after you went away? Did n't I hear Papa tell him to go away? Did n't I hear Papa tell Mamma he wished you had broken his neck? Did n't I hear Papa tell Mamma that you were a fool for running away?" Lucien flung these questions at Daddy Jake with an emphasis that left nothing to be desired.

"Well," said Daddy Jake, "dat mus' be so, an' dat bein' de case, we 'll des start in de mornin' and' git home ter supper. We 'll go over yander ter Marse Meredy Ingram's an' borry his carriage an' go home in style. I boun' you, dey 'll all be glad to see us."

Daddy Jake was happy once more. A great burden had been taken from his mind. The other negroes when they came in toward night seemed to be happy, too, because the old man could go back home; and there was not one but would have swapped places with him. Randall was the last to come, and he brought a big fat chicken.

"I wuz comin' 'long cross de woods des now," he said, winking his eye and shaking his head at Daddy Jake, "an', bless gracious, dis chicken flew'd right in my han'. I say ter myse'f, I did, 'Ole lady, you mus' know we got comp'ny at our house,' an' den I clamped down on 'er, an' yer she is. Now, 'bout dark, I 'll take 'er up yander an' make Marse Ingram's cook fry' er brown fer deze chillun, an' I 'll make 'er gimme some milk."

Crazy Sue took the chicken, which had already been killed, wet its feathers thoroughly, rolled it around in the hot embers, and then proceeded to pick and clean it.

Randall's programme was carried out to the letter. Mr. Meredith Ingram's cook fried the chicken for him and put in some hot biscuit for good measure, and the milker gave him some fresh milk, which she said would not be missed.

The children had a good supper, and they would have gone to sleep directly afterward, but the thought of going home with Daddy Jake kept them awake. Randall managed to tell Daddy Jake, out of hearing of the children, that Dr. Gaston and some of his negroes had been seen at Ross's mill that morning.

"Well," said Daddy Jake, "I bleeze ter beat marster home. Ef he go back dar wid out de chillun, my mistiss 'll drap right dead on de flo'." This was his only comment.

Around the fire the negroes laughed and joked, and told their adventures. Lillian felt comfortable and happy, and as for Lucien, he felt himself a hero. He had found Daddy Jake, and now he was going to carry him back home.

Once when there was a lull in the talk, Lillian asked why the frogs made so much fuss.

"I speck it 's kaze dey er mad wid Mr. Rabbit," said Crazy Sue. "Dey er tryin' der best ter drive 'im outen de swamp."

"What are they mad with the Rabbit for?" asked Lucien, thinking there might be a story in the explanation.

"Hit 's one er dem ole-time fusses," said Crazy Sue. "Hit 's most too ole ter talk about."

"Don't you know what the fuss was about?" asked Lucien.

"Well," said Crazy Sue, "one time Mr. Rabbit an' Mr. Coon live close ter one anudder in de same neighborhoods. How dey does now, I ain't a-tellin' you; but in dem times dey want no hard feelin's 'twix' um. Dey des went 'long like two ole cronies. Mr. Rabbit, he wuz a fisherman, and Mr. Coon, he wuz a fisherman——"

"And put 'em in pens," said Lillian, remembering an old rhyme she had heard.

"No, honey, dey ain't no William-Come-Trimbletoe in dis. Mr. Rabbit an' Mr. Coon wuz bofe fishermans, but Mr. Rabbit, he kotch fish, an' Mr. Coon, he fished fer frogs. Mr. Rabbit, he had mighty good luck, an' Mr. Coon, he had mighty bad luck. Mr. Rabbit, he got fat an' slick, an' Mr. Coon, he got po' an' sick.

"Hit went on dis a-way tell one day Mr.

Coon meet Mr. Rabbit in de big road. Dey shook han's dey did, an' den Mr. Coon, he 'low:

" 'Brer Rabbit, whar you git sech a fine chance er fish?'

"Mr. Rabbit laugh an' say: 'I kotch um outen de river, Brer Coon. All I got ter do is ter bait my hook,' sezee.

"Den Mr. Coon shake his head an' 'low: 'Den how come I ain't kin ketch no frogs?'

"Mr. Rabbit sat down in de road an' scratched fer fleas, an' den he 'low: 'Hit 's kaze you done make um all mad, Brer Coon. One time in de dark er de moon, you slipped down ter de branch an' kotch de ole King Frog; an' ever sence dat time, w'enever you er passin' by, you kin year um sing out, fus' one an' den anudder— *Yer he come! Dar he goes! Hit 'im in de eye; hit 'im in de eye! Mash 'im an' smash 'im; mash 'im an' smash 'im!* Yasser, dat w'at dey say. I year um constant, Brer Coon, and dat des w'at dey say.'

"Den Mr. Coon up an' say: "Ef dat de way dey gwine on, how de name er goodness kin I ketch um, Brer Rabbit? I bleeze ter have sump'n ter eat fer me an' my fambly connection.'

"Mr. Rabbit sorter grin in de cornder er his mouf, an' den he say: 'Well, Brer Coon, bein' ez you bin so sociable 'long wid me, an' ain't never showed yo' toofies w'en I pull yo' tail, I 'll des whirl in an' he'p you out.'

"Mr. Coon, he say: 'Thanky, thanky-do, Brer Rabbit.'

"Mr. Rabbit hung his fish on a tree lim', an' say: 'Now, Brer Coon, you bleeze ter do des like I tell you.'

"Mr. Coon 'lowed dat he would ef de Lord spared 'im.

"Den Mr. Rabbit say: 'Now, Brer Coon, you des rack down yander, an' git on de big san'-bar 'twix' de river and de branch. W'en you git dar you mus' stagger like you sick, an' den you mus' whirl roun' an'

roun' an' drap down like you dead. Atter you drap down, you mus' sorter jerk yo' legs once er twice, an' den you mus' lay right still. Ef fly light on yo' nose, let 'im stay dar. Don't move; don't wink yo' eye; don't switch yo' tail. Des lay right dar, an' 't won't be long 'fo' you year fum me. Yit don't you move till I give de word.'

"Mr. Coon, he paced off, he did, an' done des like Mr. Rabbit tol' 'im. He staggered 'roun' on de san'-bank, an' den he drapped down dead. Atter so long a time, Mr. Rabbit come lopin' 'long, an' soon 's he git dar, he squall out, 'Coon dead!' Dis rousted de frogs, an' dey stuck dey heads up fer ter see w'at all de rippit wuz 'bout. One great big green un up an' holler, *W'at de matter? W'at de matter?* He talk like he got a bad col'.

"Mr. Rabbit 'low: 'Coon dead!'

"Frog say: *Don't believe it! Don't believe it!*

" 'N'er frog say: *Yes, he is! Yes, he is!* Little bit er one say: *No, he ain't! No, he ain't!*

"Dey kep' on 'sputin' an' 'sputin', tell bimeby hit look like all de frogs in de neighborhoods wuz dar. Mr. Rabbit look like he ain't a-yearin' ner a-keerin' w'at dey do er say. He sot dar in de san' like he gwine in mournin' fer Mr. Coon. De Frogs kep' gittin' closer an' closer. Mr. Coon, he ain't move. W'en a fly 'd git on 'im, Mr. Rabbit, he 'd bresh 'im off.

"Bimeby he 'low: 'Ef you want ter git 'im outen de way, now 's yo' time, Cousin Frogs. Des whirl in an' bury him deep in de san'.'

"Big ole Frog say: *How we gwine ter do it? How we gwine ter do it?*

"Mr. Rabbit 'low: 'Dig de san' out fum under 'im an' let 'im down in de hole.'

"Den de Frogs dey went ter work sho nuff. Dey mus' 'a' bin a hundred un um, an' dey make dat san' fly, mon. Mr. Coon, he ain't move. De Frogs, dey dig an' scratch in de san' tell atter while dey had a right smart hole, an' Mr. Coon wuz down in dar.

Bimeby big Frog holler: *Dis deep nuff? Dis deep nuff?*

"Mr. Rabbit 'low: 'Kin you jump out?'

"Big Frog say: *Yes, I kin! Yes, I kin!*

"Mr. Rabbit say: 'Den 't ain't deep nuff.'

"Den de Frogs dey dig an' dey dig, tell, bimeby, big Frog say: *Dis deep nuff? Dis deep nuff?*

"Mr. Rabbit 'low: 'Kin you jump out?'

"Big Frog say: *I des kin! I des kin!*

"Mr. Rabbit say: 'Dig it deeper.'

"De Frogs keep on diggin' tell, bimeby,

Crazy Sue gave. Lucien wanted her to tell more stories, but Daddy Jake said it was bedtime; and the children were soon sound asleep.

The next morning Daddy Jake had them up betimes. Crazy Sue took Lillian in her arms, and Daddy Jake took Lucien on his back. As they had gone into the canebrake, so they came out. Randall and some of the other negroes wanted to carry Lillian, but Crazy Sue would n't listen to them. She had brought the little girl in, she said, and she was going to carry her out. Daddy Jake, followed by Crazy Sue, went in the

'Mr. Rabbit squall out, 'coon dead!'"

big Frog holler out: *Dis deep nuff? Dis deep nuff?*

"Mr. Rabbit 'low: 'Kin you jump out?'

"Big Frog say: *No, I can't! No, I can't! Come he'p me! Come he'p me!*

"Mr. Rabbit bust out laughin', and holler out:

"'RISE UP, SANDY, AN' GIT YO' MEAT!' an' Mr. Coon riz."

Lucien and Lillian laughed heartily at this queer story, especially the curious imitation of frogs both big and little that

direction of Mr. Meredith Ingram's house. It was on a hill, more than a mile from the river, and was in a grove of oak-trees. As they were making their way through a plum orchard, not far from the house, Crazy Sue stopped.

"Brer Jake," she said, "dis is all de fur I 'm gwine. I 'm 'mos' too close ter dat house now. You take dis baby an' let dat little man walk. 'T ain't many steps ter whar you gwine." Crazy Sue wrung Daddy Jake's hand, stooped and kissed the children, and with a "God bless you all!"

disappeared in the bushes, and none of the three ever saw her again.

Mr. Meredith Ingram was standing out in his front yard, enjoying a pipe before breakfast. He was talking to himself and laughing when Daddy Jake and the children approached.

"Howdy, Mars' Meredy," said the old negro, taking off his hat and bowing as politely as he could with the child in his arms. Mr. Ingram looked at him through his spectacles and over them.

"Ain't that Gaston's Jake?" he asked, after he had examined the group.

"Yasser," said Daddy Jake, "an' deze is my marster's little chillun."

Mr. Ingram took his pipe out of his mouth.

"Why, what in the world!—Why, what under the sun!—Well, if this does n't beat —why, what in the nation!"—Mr. Ingram failed to find words to express his surprise.

Daddy Jake, however, made haste to tell Mr. Ingram that the little ones had drifted down the river in a boat, that he had found them, and wished to get them home just as quickly as he could.

"My marster bin huntin' fer um, suh," said the old negro, "and I want ter beat him home, kaze ef he go dar widout deze chillun my mistiss 'll be a dead 'oman— she cert'n'y will, suh."

"Well, well, well!" exclaimed Mr. Ingram. "If this don't beat—why, of course, I 'll send them home. I 'll go with 'em myself. Of course I will. Well, if this does n't— George! hitch up the carriage. Fetch out Ben Bolt and Rob Roy, and go and get your breakfast. Jake, you go and help him, and I 'll take these chaps in the house and warm 'em up. Come on, little ones. We 'll have something to eat and then we 'll go right home to Pappy and Mammy." They went in, Mr. Ingram muttering to himself, "Well, if this does n't beat——"

After breakfast Mr. Ingram, the children, Daddy Jake, and George, the driver, were up and away, as the fox-hunters say. Daddy Jake sat on the driver's seat with George, and urged on the horses. They traveled rapidly, and it is well they did, for when they came in sight of the Gaston place, Daddy Jake saw his master entering the avenue that led to the house. The old negro put his hands to his mouth and called so loudly that the horses jumped. Dr. Gaston heard him and stopped, and in a minute more had his children in his arms, and that night there was a happy family in the Gaston house. But nobody was any happier than Daddy Jake.

BUFFALO HUNTING

By Theodore Roosevelt.

WHEN Independence was declared, in 1776, and the United States of America appeared among the powers of the earth, the continent beyond the Alleghanies was one unbroken wilderness; and the buffaloes, the first animals to vanish when the wilderness was settled, roved up to the crests of the mountains which mark the western boundaries of Pennsylvania, Virginia, and the Carolinas. They were plentiful in what are now the States of Ohio, Kentucky, and Tennessee. But by the beginning of the present century they had been driven beyond the Mississippi; and for the next eighty years they formed one of the most distinctive and characteristic features of existence on the great plains. Their numbers were countless —incredible. In vast herds of hundreds of thousands of individuals, they roamed from the Saskatchewan to the Rio Grande and westward to the Rocky Mountains. They furnished all the means of livelihood to the tribes of Horse Indians, and to the curious population of French Metis, or Half-breeds, on the Red River, as well as those dauntless and archtypical wanderers, the white hunters and trappers. Their numbers slowly diminished; but the decrease was very gradual until after the Civil War. They were not destroyed by the settlers, but by the railways and by the skin hunters.

After the ending of the Civil War, the work of constructing transcontinental railway lines was pushed forward with the utmost vigor. These supplied cheap and indispensable, but hitherto wholly lacking, means of transportation to the hunters; and at the same time the demand for buffalo robes and hides became very great, while the enormous numbers of the beasts, and the comparative ease with which they were slaughtered, attracted throngs of adventurers. The result was such a slaughter of big game as the world had never before seen; never before were so many large animals of one species destroyed in so short a time. Several million buffaloes were slain. In fifteen years from the time the destruction fairly began, the great herds were exterminated. In all probability there are not now, all told, a thousand head of wild buffaloes on the American continent; and no herd of a hundred individuals has been in existence since 1884.

The first great break followed the building of the Union Pacific Railway. All the buffaloes of the middle region were then destroyed, and the others were then split into two vast sets of herds, the northern and the southern. The latter were destroyed first, about 1878; the former not until 1883.

57

My own experience with buffaloes was obtained in the latter year, among small bands and scattered individuals, near my ranch on the Little Missouri; I have related it elsewhere. But two of my relatives were more fortunate, and took part in the chase of these lordly beasts when the herds still darkened the prairie as far as the eye could see.

During the first two months of 1877, my brother Elliott, then a lad not seventeen years old, made a buffalo-hunt toward the edge of the Staked Plains in northern Texas. He was thus in at the death of the southern herds, for all, save a few scattering bands, were destroyed within two years of this time.

My brother was with my cousin, John Roosevelt, and they went out on the range with six other adventurers—a German-American, a Scotchman who had been in the Confederate cavalry and afterward in Maximilian's Mexican body-guard, and four Irishmen. It was a party of just such young men as frequently drift to the frontier. All were short of cash, and all were hardy, vigorous fellows eager for excitement and adventure. My brother was much the youngest of the party, and the least experienced; but he was well-grown, strong and healthy, and very fond of boxing, wrestling, running, riding, and shooting; moreover, he had served an apprenticeship in hunting deer and turkeys. Their mess-kit, ammunition, bedding, and provisions were carried in two prairie wagons, each drawn by four horses. In addition to the teams they had six saddle-animals—all of them shaggy, unkempt mustangs. Three or four dogs, setters and half-bred greyhounds, trotted along behind the wagons. Each man took his turn for two days as teamster and cook; and there were always two with the wagons, or camp, as the case might be, while the other six were off hunting, usually in couples. The expedition was

undertaken partly for sport and partly with the hope of profit; for, after purchasing the horses and wagons, none of the party had any money left, and they were forced to rely upon selling skins and hides and, when near the forts, meat.

They started on January 2d, and shaped their course for the head-waters of the Salt Fork of the Brazos, the center of abundance for the great buffalo herds. During the first few days they were in the outskirts of the settled country, and shot only small game—quail and prairie fowl; then they began to kill turkey, deer, and antelope. These they "swapped" for flour and feed, at the ranches or squalid, straggling frontier towns. On several occasions the hunters were lost, spending the night out in the open, or sleeping at a ranch if one was found. Both towns and ranches were filled with rough customers; all of my brother's companions were muscular, hot-headed fellows; and as a consequence they were involved in several savage "free fights," in which, fortunately, nobody was seriously hurt. My brother kept a very brief diary, the entries being fairly startling from their conciseness. A number of times, the mention of their arrival, either at a halting-place, a little village, or a rival buffalo-camp is followed by the laconic remark, "big fight," or "big row"; but once they evidently concluded discretion to be the better part of valor, the entry for January 20th being, "On the road—passed through Belknap—too lively, so kept on to the Brazos—very late." The buffalo-camps in particular were very jealous of one another, each party regarding itself as having exclusive right to the range it was the first to find; and on several occasions this feeling came near involving my brother and his companions in serious trouble.

While slowly driving the heavy wagons to the hunting-grounds they suffered the usual hardships of plains travel. The weather, as in most Texas winters, alternated between the extremes of heat and cold. There had been little rain; in consequence water was scarce. Twice they were forced to cross wild, barren wastes, where the pools had dried up, and they suffered terribly from thirst. On the first occasion the horses were in good condition, and they traveled steadily, with only occasional short halts, for over thirty-six hours, by which time they were across the waterless country. The journal reads: "January 29th.—Big hunt—no water and we left Quinn's blockhouse this morning 3 A. M.—on the go all night—hot. January 28th.—No water—hot—at seven we struck water and by eight Stinking Creek—grand 'hurrah.'" On the second occasion, the horses were weak and traveled slowly, so the party went forty-eight hours without drinking. "February 19th.—Pulled on twenty-one miles — trail bad — freezing night, no water, and wolves after our fresh meat. 20th.—Made nineteen miles over prairie; again only mud, no water, freezing hard—frightful thirst. 21st.—Thirty miles to Clear Fork, fresh water." These entries were hurriedly jotted down at the time, by a boy who deemed it unmanly to make any especial note of hardship or suffering; but every plainsman will understand the real agony implied in working hard for two nights, one day, and portions of two others, without water, even in cool weather. During the last few miles the staggering horses were only just able to drag the lightly loaded wagon,—for they had but one with them at the time,—while the men plodded along in sullen silence, their mouths so parched that they could hardly utter a word. My own hunting and ranching were done in the North where there is more water; so I have never had a similar experience. Once I took a team in thirty-six hours across a country where there was no water; but by good luck it rained heavily in the night, so that the horses had plenty of wet grass, and I caught the rain in my slicker, and so had enough water for myself. Personally, I have but once been as long as twenty-six hours without water.

The party pitched their permanent camp in a cañon of the Brazos known as Cañon Blanco. The last few days of their journey they traveled beside the river through a veritable hunter's paradise. The drought had forced all the animals to come to the larger watercourses, and the country was literally swarming with game. Every day, and all day long, the wagons traveled through the herds of antelopes that grazed on every side, while, whenever they approached the cañon brink, bands of deer started from the timber that fringed the river's course; often, even the deer wandered out on the prairie with the antelopes. Nor was the game shy; for the hunters, both red and white, followed only the buffaloes until the huge, shaggy herds were destroyed, and the smaller beasts were in consequence but little molested.

Once my brother shot five antelopes from a single stand, when the party were short of fresh venison; he was out of sight and to leeward, and the antelopes seemed confused rather than alarmed at the rifle-reports and the fall of their companions. As was to be expected where game was so plenty, wolves and coyotes also abounded. At night they surrounded the camp, wailing and howling in a kind of shrieking chorus throughout the hours of darkness; one night they came up so close that the frightened horses had to be hobbled and guarded. On another occasion a large wolf actually crept into camp, where he was seized by the dogs, and the yelling, writhing knot of combatants rolled over one of the sleepers; finally, the long-toothed prowler managed to shake himself loose, and vanished in the gloom. One evening they were almost as much startled by a visit of a different kind. They were just finishing supper when an Indian stalked suddenly and silently out of the surrounding darkness, squatted down in the circle of firelight, remarked gravely, "Me Tonk," and began helping himself from the stew. He belonged to the friendly tribe of Tonkaways, so his hosts speedily recovered their equanimity; as for him, he had never lost his, and he sat eating by the fire until there was literally nothing left to eat. The panic caused by his appearance was natural; for at that time the Comanches were a scourge to the buffalo-hunters, ambushing them and raiding their camps; and several bloody fights had taken place.

Their camp had been pitched near a deep pool or water-hole. On both sides the bluffs rose like walls, and where they had crumbled and lost their sheerness, the vast buffalo herds, passing and repassing for countless generations, had worn furrowed trails so deep that the backs of the beasts were but little above the surrounding soil. In the bottom, and in places along the crests of the cliffs that hemmed in the cañon-like valley, there were groves of tangled trees, tenanted by great flocks of wild turkeys. Once my brother made two really remarkable shots at a pair of these great birds. It was at dusk, and they were flying directly overhead from one cliff to the other. He had in his hand a thirty-eight-caliber Ballard rifle, and, as the gobblers winged their way heavily by, he brought them both down with two successive bullets. This was of course mainly a piece of mere luck; but it meant good shooting, too. The Ballard was a very accurate, handy little weapon; it belonged to me, and was the first rifle I ever owned or used. With it I had once killed a deer, the only specimen of large game I had then shot; and I presented the rifle to my brother when he went to Texas. In our happy ignorance we deemed it quite good enough for buffalo or anything else; but out on the plains my brother soon found himself forced to procure a heavier and more deadly weapon.

When camp was pitched the horses were turned loose to graze and refresh themselves after their trying journey, during which they had lost flesh wofully. They were watched and tended by the two men who were always left in camp, and, save on rare occasions, were only used to haul in the buffalo-hides. The camp-guards for the time being acted as cooks; and, though coffee and flour both ran short and finally gave out, fresh meat of every kind was abundant. The camp was never without buffalo-beef, deer and antelope venison, wild turkeys, prairie-chickens, quails, ducks, and rabbits. The birds were simply "potted," as occasion required; when the quarry was deer or antelope, the hunters took the dogs with them to run down the wounded animals. But almost the entire attention of the hunters was given to the buffalo. After an evening spent in lounging round the camp-fire, and a sound night's sleep, wrapped in robes and blankets, they would get up before daybreak, snatch a hurried breakfast, and start off in couples through the chilly dawn. The great beasts were very plentiful; in the first day's hunt, twenty were slain; but the herds were restless and ever on the move. Sometimes they would be seen right by the camp, and again it would need an all-day's tramp to find them. There was no difficulty in spying them—the chief trouble with forest game; for on the prairie a buffalo makes no effort to hide, and its black, shaggy bulk looms up as far as the eye can see. Sometimes they were found in small parties of three or four individuals, sometimes in bands of about two hundred, and again in great herds of many thousand; and solitary old bulls, expelled from the herds, were common. If on broken land, among hills and ravines, there was not much difficulty in approaching from the leeward; for, though the sense of smell in the buffalo is very acute, they do not see well at a distance through their overhanging frontlets of coarse and matted hair. If, as was generally the case, they were out on the open, rolling prairie, the stalking was far more difficult. Every hollow, every earth hummock and sage-bush had to be used as cover. The hunter wriggled through the grass flat on his face, pushing himself along for perhaps a quarter of a mile by his toes and fingers, heedless of the spiny cactus. When near enough to the huge, unconscious quarry the hunter began firing, still keeping himself carefully concealed. If the smoke was blown away by the wind, and if the buffaloes caught no glimpse of the assailant, they would often stand motionless and stupid until many of their number had been slain; the hunter being careful not to fire too high, aiming just behind the shoulder, about a third of the way up the body, that his bullet might go through the lungs. Sometimes, even after they saw the man, they would act as if confused and panic-struck, huddling up together and staring at the smoke puffs—but generally they were off at a lumbering gallop as soon as they had an idea of the point of danger. When once started, they ran for many miles before halting, and their pursuit on foot was extremely laborious.

One morning my cousin and brother had been left in camp as guards. They were sitting, idly warming themselves in the first sunbeams, when their attention was sharply drawn to four buffaloes who were coming to the pool to drink. The beasts came down a game trail, a deep rut in the bluff, fronting where they were sitting, and they did not dare stir for fear of being discovered. The buffaloes walked into the pool, and, after drinking their fill, stood for some time with the water running out of their mouths, idly lashing their sides with their short tails, enjoying the bright warmth of the early sunshine; then, with much splashing and the gurgling of soft mud, they left the pool and clambered up the bluff with unwieldy agility. As soon as they turned, my brother and cousin ran for their rifles; but before they got back the buffaloes had crossed the bluff crest. Climbing after them, the two hunters found, when they reached the summit, that their game, instead of halting, had struck straight off across the prairie at a slow lope, doubtless intending to rejoin the herd they had left. After a moment's consultation, the men went in pursuit, excitement overcoming their knowledge that they ought not, by rights, to leave the camp. They struck a steady trot, following the animals by sight until they passed over a knoll, and then trailing them. Where the grass was long, as it was for the first four or five miles, this was a work of no difficulty, and they did not break their gait, only glancing now and then at the trail. As the sun rose and the day became warm, their breathing grew quicker; and the sweat rolled off their faces as they ran across the rough prairie sward, up and down the long inclines, now and then shifting their heavy rifles from one shoulder to the other. But they were in good training, and they did not have to halt. At last they reached stretches of bare ground, sun-baked and grassless, where the trail grew dim; and here they had to go very slowly, carefully examining the faint dents and marks made in the soil by the heavy hoofs, and unraveling the trail from the mass of old foot-marks. It was tedious work, but it enabled them to completely recover their breath by the time that they again struck the grass land;

and but a few hundred yards from its edge, in a slight hollow, they saw the four buffaloes just entering a herd of fifty or sixty that were scattered out grazing. The herd paid no attention to the newcomers, and these immediately began to feed greedily. After a whispered consultation, the two hunters crept back and made a long circle that brought them well to leeward

numbers, hurry, and panic, they eventually got three more.

On another occasion, the same two hunters nearly met with a frightful death, being overtaken by a vast herd of stampeded buffaloes. All animals that go in herds are subject to these instantaneous attacks of uncontrollable terror, under the influence of which they become perfectly

A thrilling experience of life on the plains. "Splitting" a herd of stampeded buffaloes.

of the herd, in line with a slight rise in the ground. They then crawled up to this rise and, peering through the tufts of tall, rank grass, saw the unconscious beasts a hundred and twenty-five or fifty yards away. They fired together, each mortally wounding his animal, and then, rushing in as the herd halted in confusion, and following them as they ran, impeded by

mad, and rush headlong in dense masses on any form of death. Horses, and more especially cattle, often suffer from stampedes; it is a danger against which the cowboys are compelled to be perpetually on guard. A band of stampeded horses, sweeping in mad terror up a valley, will dash against a rock or tree with such violence as to leave several dead animals at its base, while the survivors race on without halting; they will overturn and destroy tents and wagons, and a man on foot caught in the rush has but a small chance for his life. A buffalo stampede is much worse—or rather was much worse, in the old days—because of the great weight and immense numbers of the beasts, who, in a fury of heedless terror, plunged over cliffs and into rivers, and bore down whatever was in their path.

Afterward they learned that another couple of hunters, four or five miles off, had fired into and stampeded a large herd. This herd, in its rush, gathered others, all thundering along together in uncontrollable and increasing panic.

The surprised hunters were far away from any broken ground or other place of refuge; while the vast herd of huge, plunging, maddened beasts was charging straight down on them not a quarter of a mile

Taking hides after a hunt

On the occasion in question, my brother and cousin were on their way homeward. They were just mounting one of the long, low swells into which the prairie was broken when they heard a low, muttering, rumbling noise, like far-off thunder. It grew steadily louder, and, not knowing what it meant, they hurried forward to the top of the rise. As they reached it, they stopped short in terror and amazement, for before them the whole prairie was black with madly rushing buffaloes.

distant. Down they came!—thousands upon thousands, their front extending a mile in breadth, while the earth shook beneath their thunderous gallop, and as they came closer, their shaggy frontlets loomed dimly through the columns of dust thrown up from the dry soil. The two hunters knew that their only hope for life was to split the herd, which, though it had so broad a front, was not very deep. If they failed they would inevitably be trampled to death.

Waiting until the beasts were in close

range, they opened a rapid fire from their heavy breech-loading rifles, yelling at the top of their voices. For a moment the result seemed doubtful. The line thundered steadily down on them; then it swayed violently, as two or three of the brutes immediately in their front fell beneath the bullets, while the neighbors made violent efforts to press off sideways. Then a narrow wedge-shaped rift appeared in the line, and widened as it came up closer, and the buffaloes, shrinking from their foes in front, strove desperately to edge away from the dangerous neighborhood; the shouts and shots were redoubled; the hunters were

almost choked by the cloud of dust through which they could see the stream of dark huge bodies passing within rifle-length on either side; and in a moment the peril was over, and the two men were left alone on the plain, unharmed, though with their nerves terribly shaken. The herd careered on toward the horizon, save five individuals who had been killed or disabled by the shots.

On another occasion, when my brother was out with one of his Irish friends, they fired at a small herd containing an old bull; the bull charged the smoke, and the whole herd followed him. Probably they were simply stampeded, and had no hostile intention; at any rate, after the death

of their leader, they rushed by without doing any damage.

But buffaloes sometimes charged with the utmost determination, and were then dangerous antagonists. My cousin, a very hardy and resolute hunter, had a narrow escape from a wounded cow which he followed up a steep bluff or sand cliff. Just as he reached the summit, he was charged, and was only saved by the sudden appearance of his dog, which distracted the cow's attention. He thus escaped with only a tumble and a few bruises.

My brother also came in for a charge, while killing the biggest bull that was slain by any of the party. He was out alone, and saw a small herd of cows and calves at some distance, with a huge bull among them, towering above them like a giant. There was no break in the ground, nor any tree nor bush near them, but by making a half-circle, my brother managed to creep up against the wind behind a slight roll in the prairie surface, until he was within seventy-five yards of the grazing and unconscious beasts. There were some cows and calves between him and the bull, and he had to wait some moments before they shifted position as the herd grazed onward and gave him a fair shot; in the interval they had moved so far forward that he was in plain view. His first bullet struck just behind the shoulder; the herd started and looked around, but the bull merely lifted his head and took a step forward, his tail curled up over his back. The next bullet likewise struck fair, nearly in the same place, telling with a loud "pack!" against the thick hide, and making the dust fly up from the matted hair. Instantly the great bull wheeled and charged in headlong anger, while the herd fled in the opposite direction. On the bare prairie, with no spot of refuge, it was useless to try to escape, and the hunter, with re-loaded rifle, waited until the bull was not far off, then drew up his weapon and fired. Either he was nervous, or the bull at the moment bounded over some obstacle, for the ball went a little wild; nevertheless, by good luck, it broke a fore leg, and the great beast came crashing to the earth, and was slain before it could struggle to its feet.

and one wagon they set out homeward. The march was hard and tedious; they lost their way and were in jeopardy from quicksands and cloudbursts; they suffered from thirst and cold, their shoes gave out and their feet were lamed by cactus spines. At last they reached Fort Sniffin in safety, and great was their ravenous rejoicing when they procured some bread—for during the final fortnight of the hunt they

A war party of Comanches "jumping" a hunter's camp

Two days after this event, a war party of Comanches swept down along the river. They "jumped" a neighboring camp, kill-ing one man and wounding two more, and at the same time ran off all but three of the horses belonging to our eight adven-turers. With the remaining three horses

had been without flour or vegetables of any kind, or even coffee, and had subsisted on fresh meat "straight." Nevertheless, it was a very healthy, as well as a very pleas-ant and exciting experience; and I doubt if any of those who took part in it will ever for-get their great buffalo-hunt on the Brazos.

HOW A STREET-CAR CAME
IN A STOCKING

by Harriet Allen

DAVID DOUGLAS wanted to be a street-car driver. That did not interfere in the least with his ambition to be a plumber with a bag of tools, or a doctor with a pocket-thermometer and a stop-watch. David was almost seven years old. He had been in love with the street-car profession for at least a year; and there was nothing he could n't tell you about that business which *can* be told to an outsider whose heart is not in it.

Yet there was nothing remarkable about David. He could read and write as well as other boys of his age, and he spelled with less originality perhaps than most. He could run as fast, jump as far, and spin tops with the best. Although David had neither brother nor sister to play with, and no nursery full of toys, he managed to have a good deal of fun, and he had a rather manly sort of character. As to play-fellows—nobody could excel his mother. She rode in his express-train, and had her ticket punched till there was nothing left of it; and when the engineer struck a broken rail, she was a passenger in the wreck, and he bandaged her up with hand-kerchiefs and old string until you would n't have known her. Then, too, she had that rare faculty of knowing, from a boy's point of view, a funny thing when she saw it—and sometimes they laughed together till the tears rolled down their cheeks.

Then there was "Jack." I nearly forgot him. He was David's beloved dog. Jack was a short-haired yellow dog without pedigree or family connections—what might be called a self-made dog. He owed his present home and success in the world to self-respecting enterprise and a kind heart. He was cheerful, fond of exercise and excitement, and always on hand.

Now, David's father had a habit of reading aloud to David's mother before breakfast, from the morning paper.

One morning, about three weeks before Christmas, David was transfixed by hearing his father read the following announcement:

CARS TO GIVE AWAY

An Offer of the Street-Car Company.

General Manager Miller, of the Citizens' Street-Railroad Company, said to-day that he had on hand thirty or forty old box street-cars which he would like to give away. The company has no further use for the cars. Mr. Miller suggests that the cars would make good play-houses for children.

Do you wonder that such a notice sent David's appetite flying?

"Oh, papa," he cried, "let us get one of those cars!" whereupon his father made big eyes of astonishment at David, and pretended to be absolutely upset by the mere suggestion of such an idea, and was in such wild haste to get out of reach of little boys who wanted to have full-grown, real street-cars for their very own, that David was unable to get in a serious word before he was gone. But David's eyes were shining and his fancy was building the most beautiful castles. He took his cap and disappeared with Jack.

Some hours later he came in glowing from the cold air, and saying enthusiastically, "Mama, I know where we can put that car, if we *should* get in—in our side yard! You can just come to the window and see! There 's plenty of room—I 've marked it out on the snow."

"My dear little boy! Did you really think we could ask for one of those cars?"

David's face flushed; he certainly had hoped so; he had spent the morning thinking about it. "I did n't know," he faltered, with a sense of bereavement tugging at his heart.

"That 's too bad! I do wish you could have one to play in, David!"

"Why can't I, mama?"

"It would cost too much, dear."

"Cost too much? Why, mama," he said, brightening up, "did n't you hear? The paper said they would give them away."

"So they will—but even a present is sometimes expensive. You see, it would cost a great deal to bring a street-car all the way over here and set it up in our yard."

"Why, mama?" and his lip trembled,—he did so want that car,—and it had looked so easy.

"Because a street-car is so large and so heavy, it would take strong horses, and a great big truck, and ever so many men to move it, and all that costs money—a great deal of money."

Very gently she convinced him that it was out of the question. If you could n't afford a thing—there you were! Yet it seemed a thousand pities—thirty or forty cars to be *given* away! It was very comforting at this point to have his mother thump him confidingly on the back, as she said that he was the bravest little man in all the world; and to be asked what he expected Santa Claus to bring him, and whether he meant to hang up Jack's stocking, too.

David had a good many Christmas wishes; a bob-sled for one thing, and skates, and a gun to shoot a dart; and he longed for a hook-and-ladder wagon, or, failing that, a police-patrol with a real gong on the front. It was quite impossible to choose, so he had sent the entire list to Santa Claus in a letter just to see what would happen.

But that night, as his mother tucked him into bed, he held her back by the hand and said hesitatingly: "Mama, why could n't they bring the car around here on the track that runs in front of our house?"

"Because those cars have no wheels."

"No wheels!"

"Not a wheel, sir! It would just be a helpless old car all the rest of its life," and she shook her hand free, gave him a little pat—a good-night kiss—and was gone.

II

Not far from David there lived a little boy whose name was Harold Wolfing; he was not quite five years old. He was a sturdy little fellow, with dark hair and eyes, and a fine red in his cheeks; and he carried his head and shoulders in quite a military fashion. He was fortunate enough to live in the same house with his grandmama and grandpapa. Whether they were equally fortunate in this arrangement is a matter I never heard discussed; but certainly they loved and petted him, and he had four aunties and three uncles—all of whom seemed really to lie awake nights thinking what they could give him next.

Harold was very fond of having David come to play, and, it is needless to say, David was very fond of going. David liked nothing better than to ride the high-headed hobby-horse, and to work the fire-engine that squirted real water through a rubber hose.

One day, not long before Christmas, David went to spend the afternoon with Harold. He found the chubby little man bending over his nursery table, busy with pencil and paper.

"Do you know what I 'm doin', David? I 'm writin' a letter!" A moment was allowed for this fact to impress the smiling David, then—"Who do you think I 'm writin' to?"

David said promptly that he could n't guess.

"Santa Claus! You can read it if you want to," added the writer condescendingly. David took the letter, which was covered with mysterious, wandering pencil-marks. He was quite embarrassed to know what to say to such a baby, who could not even print; but Harold relieved him. "Can't you read, David?" he said pityingly. "Here, I 'll read it to you." And he took the letter back into his fat little hand with an important air. After studying it very hard for a moment, he fixed David with his eye, saying: "It 's *very* long, David—but never mind, I 'll tell you what it says. It 's all about a street-car. You see, I 'm goin' to have Santa Claus bring me a street-car for Christmas." He spoke of the arrangement with such assurance that David suddenly felt very young and inexperienced.

"Yes," he went on, highly pleased with the impression he was making—"Yes, I 'm goin' to have a street-car. Perhaps you

think it 's goin' to be little, like that?" —pointing to a toy car. David did n't know.

"Well, it is n't. It is a *real* car, and as large—oh, almost as large as this house! You can come and play in it, David; and I 'll take you to ride, all the way out to the park, and clear out—clear out to the end of the world—and I 'll drive as *fast*— oh, so you can hardly hold on! Only,"— and he pulled in his fancy a little, lest David's go too far,—"you 'll be *in*-side, you know, and I 'll ring the bell when you pay me." Exciting as this picture was, David's mind flew back at once to the forty cars to be given away. Was Harold's car one of these? Hardly, he thought; since Harold looked to Santa Claus for his, and those cars belong to the Street-Railroad Company. He decided to settle the doubt. "Where will Santa Claus get a street-car?" he asked. Harold gave him a look of astonished reproach.

"Why, don't you know Santa Claus can get anything he wants, and he 'll bring it to you if you ask him, and if you 're good?"

David did know something very like this, and now on a sudden an idea flashed into his mind that made his heart jump and sent the color flushing up to his short yellow curls; it was this: You see, if Santa Claus was giving street-cars away, there was nothing to pay for hauling. No need of money at all! You just wrote the right kind of a letter—and Santa Claus did the rest! In that case he could have a car as well as Harold.

That night when his early bed-time came, he handed his mother this letter to read:

Dear Santa Claus　Harold says you are going to bring him a Street-car. Wont you please bring me one to. Not a little one but a Real one. I am trying hard to be a good boy, and I want one very much.

David Douglas.

"Why, David," his mother said, "I thought you had given up the idea of having a street-car."

"Yes, mama, I had; but you see this is different!"

"Different?"

"Of course! Don't you see?" he explained joyously—"if Santa Claus brings it, it won't cost us any money at all—not even a cent! What makes you look so sad? Don't you want me to have a car—even if Santa Claus brings it?"

"Yes, dear, of course I would like to see you have one, but—"

"But what, mama?"

"You know, David, if children ask *too* much, Santa Claus must disappoint them."

"Why?"

"Oh, for many reasons. You know mama has to say 'no' sometimes, much as she dislikes it." He began to look troubled; then, suddenly recalling Harold's assurance, he took heart and said: "Harold's grandpapa told him if he wrote and asked Santa Claus for a car, he would get it— if he was a good boy; and I 'm sure if he brings Harold one, he will give me one too; please let me ask him!"

"Will you promise not to be unhappy if it does n't come after all?" Oh, yes! He could promise that with a light heart. And next day the letter, laboriously copied in ink with high-headed "h's" and short-tailed "g's," was posted at "Harold's house" in a funny little Dutch house on the library-table. "Santa Claus comes down the chimbly and gets them," Harold explained. After that David's hopes ran sometimes high—sometimes low. In the latter state of mind he put the matter before Santa Claus again and again with

such entreaties and promises as desperate longing suggested. Here are some of the letters Santa Claus found in the little Dutch house:

Dear Santa Claus Mamma says a Street-car is too much, but I do want it so much, and I 'll be better than I ever was if you will please bring me one. David.

Dear Santa Claus You need n't bring me a Bob-sled if you will only give me a Car. I can use my old sled till next Christmas. David Douglas.

P S I will do without the Fireman's Helmet. D. D.

Dear Santa Claus Please do bring me a Street-car. If I had a Car I would n't need a hook and Ladder wagon. I will be very careful of it. Mama says I am a good boy. David Douglas.

Dear Santa Claus Mama says I must n't expect a street-car. But I want it more than Skates or Anything. If it is to much to ask for—please do bring it anyway-- and I will give up the Skates, and the Police-patrol, and everything. You can keep the gun to.

Your loving David Douglas.

P S Even if it was a little broken in some places it would do. I could mend it. I 've got a hammer and some nails. I pounded them out strate. I hope you will. Please leave it in our side yard. Good by.

David Douglas.

III

CHRISTMAS morning David woke early; every one else was fast asleep. His windows looked out on the side-yard; if he had a car it was there now. That thought was too much for him. He slid out of bed and ran to the window; he had but to raise the shade; his heart was beating so hard he could fairly hear it, and he almost made a little petition with his lips as he put out his hand. One touch—it was up! He looked out upon a smooth, shining surface of snow. There was no car! The disappointment was too terribly desolating; he drew down the shade and crept back into bed, and there, since it was dark and no one would know, he shed a few hot, unhappy tears, fighting all the time against them, and never made a sound, although he could have sobbed aloud; he remembered his mother and his promise. Then, at last, he wondered if Harold had been disappointed too. The more he thought of it the more likely it appeared. He wished Harold no ill luck— but if there had been no distribution of cars whatever, it would alter the case considerably: it would be as though he had reached for the moon. He began to make the best of it, and to wonder what Santa Claus had left in his stocking, so that later, when he came down-stairs, and his father swung him up to kiss him good-morning, saying, "Santa Claus slipped up on that car business, David,—must be he had no cars this year,—but your stocking looks pretty lumpy and tight," David was able to smile quite cheerfully. A Christmas stocking is a Christmas stocking, after all— mysterious and exciting—whatever your joys or sorrows. To Jack the queer shape was matter for suspicion, to be defied and barked at, as it divulged one secret after another; and when David tried on a fireman's helmet and new skates, with a lot of lesser treasures scattered all about, Christmas seemed pretty cheery.

Breakfast over, he and Jack set out, according to previous agreement, to see what Harold had in his Christmas stocking. They went in by the carriage-way. Just as they took the first turn in the drive,

David's heart gave a great jump and then stood still. Through the leafless lilac bushes he could see a great yellow and white street-car in the midst of a sea of snow. It was a beautiful, heart-breaking vision; and there was Harold in brown reefer, leather cap, and leggings, leaning out of the car shouting, "Hello, David! Hurry up! this car is just ready to start—hurry! You see," he cried triumphantly, as David waded through the snow, "I told you Santa Claus was goin' to bring me this car— why don't you get in?"

David stood mute beside the step, stroking Jack's head. Then for the first time the little boy remembered that David had had hopes too.

"Did you get a car?" he asked.

David's eyes filled; he tried to smile, but he could not speak, and he only shook his head as he looked from Harold to Ellen. It was seldom Harold had to think of any one but himself, but he had a kind heart, and now he be-stirred himself to make David happy. He let him work the change-slide and the doors, and gave him all coveted privileges. Then they went indoors to see the Christmas tree; the candles were lighted and all the wonderful new toys displayed for David's benefit. There was something on the tree for David, too. He flushed with pleasure and wonder when Harold's grandpapa handed down books, candy, and a dark-lantern, saying, with a twinkle in his eye, "Queer, these things were left here by mistake, David! Santa Claus must walk in his sleep."

But an hour or two later, as David went home, he was thinking that the ways of Santa Claus were very strange. His whole soul had been set upon a street-car; he was ready to give up everything else to have that one joy. Now Harold merely asked for that along with a lot of other new pleasures. Yet Santa Claus brought a car to Harold, and to David, none. It was matter to try the stoutest heart, yet he was not envious. He had pluck and good sense and he felt somehow that he ought to be as happy as he could; he tried to think about his skates and fireman's helmet. After all, a street-car was a tremendous gift to ask, even of Santa Claus. He had realized when he stood beside that dear car that it was a good deal even for Harold, and Harold had so many treasures it was not easy to surpass them. The dark-

opening into their yard. Before he could be surprised at this he came in full view of—what do you think?—a broad strong truck, two strong gray horses with heads down, looking at him from their soft eyes, and blowing a little at the snow; four or five men standing about, and—well, of course you 've guessed it! There stood a street-car large as life; a beautiful yellow and white car with No. 11 in gold figures on the side. A misty feeling swam before

"There stood a street-car large as life!"

lantern swung in his hand; it was a comfort, and he felt dimly that in a day or two he would play burglar and policeman with great effect; but it could n't keep away a very choking feeling in his throat when he remembered Harold winding up the brake. As he came around the corner near home with eyes fixed upon the slippery, trodden path, he had almost reached the house before he noticed that a part of the fence was down and wagon wheels had cut the frozen crust of snow going through this

his eyes, through which the car seemed a beautiful dream, that somehow had men in rough overcoats, gray horses, all strangely woven in it as well as his mother smiling and holding her hands tight together, watching him. Then somebody said, "Well, sir, how do you like it?" and David went forward with feet that hurried and yet seemed slow,—exactly like feet in a dream,—and somebody swung him up over the dashboard to the front platform and said, "Let me off at 116th street, please, driver." And he found a big white placard hanging to the front brake, very neatly printed in black. David could spell out the words. They said, "For David Douglas from Santa Claus." And then David really came back to earth. He laughed and kissed his mother and held his father's hand in both his own; he walked back and forth in the car, and took note of the familiar signs about no smoking and beware of pick-pockets, and to use none but Quigley's Baking Powder. There was the cash-box and the brass slide for change in the front door. The brake worked and the bell-strap rang a real bell when his father held him up to reach it. "We 'll have to let that strap out a little, driver, till you get a taller conductor." Well, it was perfect!—surpassing all dreams of joy and Christmas. Indeed, a bit of Christmas cheer had fallen to those rough-coated men who worked on Christmas day, for they were drinking coffee and eating gingerbread, and had cigars to smoke; even the horses, David noticed through his joy, had each an apple to eat. And Jack—Jack lost his head completely, and barked, and jumped on everybody with his snowy feet, and finally just tore round and round in a circle like mad.

Suddenly David's mother said, "Where is the letter, Tom?—did n't he give you a letter?"

"To be sure! I almost forgot the letter—let me see—here it is in this pocket"; and his father tore it open and began to read:

My Dear Douglas: I have taken the liberty of asking Santa Claus to deliver one of our old cars on your premises. I was growing rusty, but Santa Claus has waked me up by showing me a one-sided correspondence he 's been having with a young man by the name of David. I suddenly realized what a world of fun there was in Christmas, if you only knew how to get hold of it by the handle, as my grandfather used to say. I hope you and Mrs. Douglas will forgive me for getting my pleasure first and asking permission afterward. But when a man takes a holiday I suppose he may be allowed to take it in his own way. So please put this street-car into David's stocking! And I think this may not be a bad occasion for saying I 've never forgotten the time your mother made Christmas in my heart when I was a poor youngster with scarcely a stocking to hang. God bless you! You have a fine boy.

Very truly yours,   John Miller.

P. S. That correspondence is a confidential matter between Santa Claus and me. No questions answered at this office.

J. M.

David wondered why his mother, who had been reading the letter over his father's arm, turned suddenly, while she was smiling, and cried on his father's shoulder.

THE CITY CHILD.

Words by ALFRED TENNYSON.

Music by Mrs. ALFRED TENNYSON.

Dain-ty lit-tle maid-en, whith-er would you wan-der, Whither from this pret-ty home, the
Dain-ty lit-tle maid-en, whith-er would you wan-der, Whither from this pret-ty house, this

home where mother dwells? [OMIT...........] "Far and far away,"said the dainty lit-tle maiden;
[OMIT...............] cit-y house of ours? "Far and far away,"said the dainty lit-tle maiden;

"Far and far a-way," said the dain-ty lit-tle maid-en. "All a-mong the gar-dens, au-
"Far and far a-way," said the dain-ty lit-tle maid-en. "All a-mong the mea-dows, the

ric-u-las, an-em-o-nes, Ros-es and lil-ies, and Can-ter-bur-y bells."
clo-ver and the clem-a-tis, Dais-ies and king-cups, and hon-ey-suck-le flowers."

CHARLES DICKENS:
THE BOY OF THE LONDON STREETS

by Rupert Sargent Holland

THE little fellow who worked all day long in the tumble-down old house by the river Thames pasting oil-paper covers on boxes of blacking, fell ill one afternoon. One of the workmen, a big man named Bob Fagin, made him lie down on a pile of straw in the corner and placed blacking-bottles filled with hot water beside him to keep him warm. There he lay until it was time for the men to stop work, and then his friend Fagin, looking down upon the small boy of twelve, asked if he felt able to go home. The boy got up looking so big-eyed, white-cheeked, and thin, that the man put his arm about his shoulder.

"Never mind, Bob, I think I 'm all right now," said the boy. "Don't you wait for me; go on home."

"You ain't fit to go alone, Charley. I 'm comin' along with you."

" 'Deed I am, Bob. I 'm feelin' as spry as a cricket." The little fellow threw back his shoulders and headed for the stairs.

Fagin, however, insisted on keeping him company; and so the two, the shabbily-dressed under-sized youth, and the big strapping man came out into the murky London twilight and took their way over the Blackfriars Bridge.

"Been spendin' your money at the pastry-shops, Charley, again? That 's what was the matter with you, I take it."

The boy shook his head. "No, Bob. I 'm trying to save. When I get my week's money I put it away in a bureau drawer, wrapped in six little paper packages with a day of the week on each one. Then I know just how much I 've got to live on, and Sundays don't count. Sometimes I do get hungry, though; so hungry! Then I look in at the windows and play at being rich."

They crossed the bridge, the boy's big eyes seeming to take note of everything, the man, duller-witted, listening to his chatter. Several times the boy tried to say good night, but Fagin would not be shaken off. "I 'm goin' to see you to your door, Charley lad," he said each time.

At last they came into a little street near the Southwark Bridge. The boy stopped by the steps of a house. "Here 't 's, Bob. Good night. It was good of you to take the trouble for me."

"Good night, Charley."

The boy ran up the steps, and, as he noticed that Fagin still stopped, he pulled the door-bell. Then the man went on down the street. When the door opened the boy asked if Mr. Fagin lived there, and being told that he did not, said he must have made a mistake in the house. Turning about he saw that his friend had disappeared around a corner. With a little smile of triumph he made off in the other direction.

The door of the Marshalsea Prison stood open like a great black mouth. The boy, tired with his long tramp, was glad to

74

reach it and to run in. Climbing several long flights of stairs he entered a room on the top story where he found his family, his father, a tall pompous-looking man dressed all in black, his mother, an amiable but extremely fragile woman, and a small brother and sister seated at a table, eating supper. The room was very sparsely furnished, the only bright spot in it was a small fire in a rusty grate, flanked by two bricks to prevent burning too much fuel.

There was a vacant place at the table for Charles, and he sat down upon a stool and ate as ravenously as though he had not tasted food for months. Meanwhile the tall man at the head of the table talked solemnly to his wife at the other end, using strange long words which none of the children could understand.

Supper over, Mr. and Mrs. Dickens (for that was their name) and the two younger children sat before the tiny fire, and Mr. Dickens talked of how he might raise enough money to pay his debts, leave the prison, and start fresh in some new business. Charles had heard these same plans from his father's lips a thousand times before, and so he took from the cupboard an old book which he had bought at a little second-hand shop a few days before, a small tattered copy of "Don Quixote," and read it by the light of a tallow candle in the corner.

The lines soon blurred before the boy's tired eyes, his head nodded, and he was fast asleep. He was awakened by his father's deep voice. "Time to be leaving, Charles, my son. You have not forgotten that my pecuniary situation prevents my choosing the hour at which I shall close the door of my house. Fortunately it is a predicament which I trust will soon be obviated to our mutual satisfaction."

The small fellow stood up, shook hands solemnly with his father, kissed his mother, and took his way out of the great prison.

Open doors on various landings gave him pictures of many peculiar households; sometimes he would stop as though to consider some unusually puzzling face or figure.

Into the night again he went, and wound through a dismal labyrinth of the dark and narrow streets of old London. Some-

times a rough voice or an evil face would frighten him, and he would take to his heels and run as fast as he could. When he passed the house where he had asked for Mr. Fagin he chuckled to himself; he would not have had his friend know for worlds that his family's home was the Marshalsea Prison.

Even that room in the prison, however, was more cheerful than the small back-attic chamber where the boy fell asleep for the second time that night. He slept on a bed made up on the floor, but his slumber was no less deep on that account.

The noise of workmen in a timber-yard under his window woke Charles when it seemed much too dark to be morning. It was, however, and he was quickly dressed, and making his breakfast from the penny cottage loaf of bread, a section of cream-cheese, and small bottle of milk, which were all he could afford to buy from the man who rented him the room. Then he took the roll of paper marked with the name of the day from the drawer of his bureau and counted out the pennies into his pocket. They were not many; he had to live on seven shillings a week, and he tucked them away very carefully in a pocket lest he lose them and have to do without his lunch.

He was not yet due at the blacking factory, but he hurried away from his room and joined the crowd of early morning people already on their way to work. He went down the embankment along the Thames until he came to a place where a bench was set in a corner of a wall. This was his favorite lounging-place; London Bridge was just beyond, the river lay in front of him, and he was far enough away from people to be secure from interruption. As he sat there watching the bridge and the Thames a small girl came to join him. She was no bigger than he, perhaps a year or two older, but her face was already shrewd enough for that of a grown-up woman. She was the maid-of-all-work at a house in the neighborhood, and she had fallen into the habit of stopping to talk for a few moments with the boy on her way to work in the morning. She liked to listen to his stories. This was his hour for inventing them. He could spin wonderful tales about London Bridge, the Tower, and the wharves along the river. Sometimes he made up stories about the people who passed in front of them, and they were such astonishing stories that the girl remembered them all day as she worked

in the house. He seemed to believe them himself; his eyes would grow far away and dreamy and his words would run on and on until a neighboring clock brought him suddenly back to his own position.

"You do know a heap o' things, don't you?" said the little girl, lost in admiration. "I 'd rather have a shillin', though, than all the fairytales in the world."

"I would n't," said Charles, stoutly. "I 'd rather read books than do anything else."

"You 've got to eat, though," objected his companion; "and books won't make you food. 'T ain't common sense." She relented in an instant. "It 's fun though, Charley Dickens. Good-by till to-morrow."

Charles went on down to the old blacking factory by Hungerford Stairs, a ramshackle building almost hanging over the river, damp and overrun with rats. His place was in a recess of the counting-room on the first floor, and as he covered the bottles with the oil-paper tops and tied them on with a string, he could look from time to time through a window at the slow coal-barges swinging down the river.

There were very few boys about the place. At lunch-time he would wander off by himself, and, selecting his meal from a careful survey of several pastry-cook's windows, invest his money for the day in fancy cakes or a tart. He missed the company of friends of his own age. Even Fanny, his oldest sister, he only saw on Sundays, when she came back to the Marshalsea from the place where she worked to spend the day with her family. It was only grown-up people that he saw most of the time, and they were too busy with their own affairs to take much interest in the small shabby boy who looked just like any one of a thousand other children of the streets. In all the men at the factory it was only the big clumsy fellow named Fagin who would stop to chat with the lad. So it was that Charles was forced to make friends with whomever he could, people of any age or condition; and was driven to spend much of his spare time roaming about the streets, lounging by the river, reading stray books by a candle in the prison or in the little attic where he slept. It was not a boyhood that seemed to promise much.

In time the boy left the factory and tried being a lawyer's clerk, then a reporter, and at last wrote a book of his own. The book was "Pickwick Papers," and it was so original that people clamored for more. Then the young man took note of all the strange types of people among whom he had lived as a boy, and those days of poverty and drudgery were turned to wonderful account because he could write of such people and such scenes as he remembered them. The little maid-of-all-work became the "Marchioness" in the "Old Curiosity Shop," Bob Fagin loaned his name to "Oliver Twist," and in "David Copperfield" we read the story of the small boy who had to fight his way through London alone. Those days of his boyhood had given him a deep insight into human nature, into the humor and pathos of other people's lives; and it was that rare insight that enabled him to become in time one of the greatest of all English writers, Charles Dickens, the beloved novelist of the Anglo-Saxon people.

THE REEF

by Samuel Scoville, Jr.

LUNE-GREEN and amber, a strip of fading sky glowed across the trail of the vanished sun. Far below, the opal sea paled to mother-of-pearl. Then, over sea and sky, strode the sudden dark of the tropics and in an instant the southern stars flamed and flared through the violet night. A long, tense moment, with sea and sky waiting, and a rim of raw gold thrust itself above the horizon as the full moon of midsummer climbed toward the zenith. Rising, its light made a broad causeway across the sea clear to the dark reef which lurked in the shimmering water.

Suddenly, inked black against the moon-path, showed the lean shape of a canoe. All the way from Carib Island, a day and a night away, Jim Tom, who in his day had been a famous sponge-diver, had brought his grandson Jimmy Tom for a first visit to the reef. Both had the cinnamon-red skins of the Red Caribs, who once had ruled mightily the whole Caribbean. Jim Tom's hair was cut to an even edge all the way around his neck; his small, deep-set eyes were like glittering crumbs of black glass, and ever since a day when he dived below the twenty-five-fathom mark both of his legs had been paralyzed.

Swiftly the little craft neared the reef, and only the plash of the paddles broke the stillness. Then in an instant the molten gold of the water was shattered by a figure like a vast bat, with black wings which measured all of thirty feet from tip to tip, a spiked tail, and long antennæ streaming out beyond a huge, hooked mouth. Like a vampire from the pit, it rose into the air, blotting out the moon with its monstrous bulk, and then dropped back with a crash, raising a wave which nearly swamped the canoe. As it disappeared beneath the water, Jimmy Tom turned and looked questioningly at the old man. The latter laughed silently.

"Only a manta ray," he said at last. "They like to fly around in the moonlight and frighten untried young men," he added slyly.

For answer his grandson stretched out his paddle at full length. It showed in the air rigid and motionless as an iron bar. The old man grunted approvingly.

"You may tremble yet before you are through with the reef," was all that he said however, as he steered toward the circle of coral which separated the lagoon from the ocean, which beat against the barrier in a crashing surf. Waiting until several of the great rollers had passed, the paddlers caught the crest of a huge wave and in an instant were swept ten feet in air toward the patch of beach which showed beyond the little lagoon. Just as the wave broke, the canoe tilted and rushed down its long slope like a toboggan, clearing the rim of sharp coral and leaping into the still lagoon beyond.

All the rest of that glorious night, as the

78

moon went westering down the sky, the two slept on the rose-red, honey-brown sand, until, without any dawn, the sun suddenly rose above a heliotrope horizon. Then they breakfasted, and Jim Tom became quite talkative—for a Carib.

"We must not waste a moment of this day," he said. "Perhaps before night we may make the hundred of dollars you need for that sloop about which you have been bothering me so long. In my day," he went on severely, "boys were glad enough to have a good canoe."

Jimmy Tom grunted.

"Whoever heard," he said at last, "of making a hundred of dollars in one day?"

"It has been done—and here," returned his grandfather, positively; "but it takes good lungs and—a brave heart."

As they talked, the canoe reached a point where the reef sloped away in a series of terraces to unfathomable depths. There they stopped paddling and started down through the water which lay before them like a thick sheet of plate-glass. The great ledge over which they floated was dotted with thickets of colored corals and purple and gold seafans, among which schools of brilliant fish sped and lazed and drifted like birds in the air. Molten-silver tarpon shot through shoals of chubby cow-pilots, all green and gold and indigo, while turquoise-blue parrot-fish raced here and there, and crimson cardinal-fish crept in and out of crevices in the rocks. There were angel-fish in gorgeous robes of emerald and scarlet, and jet-black butterfly-fish with golden fins, orange gills, and vivid blue mouths, while warty purple sea-cucumbers showed among clumps of yellow sea-anemones.

"This is the treasure-ledge of the reef," said Jim Tom, suddenly. "Here too," he went on, "death hides and waits," and he paused for a moment.

Jimmy's answer was to slip out of his unbleached cotton shirt and trousers and stand poised like a red-bronze statue of speed with the long, flat muscles rippling over his lithe body and graceful limbs.

"It was here that your father died," said Jim Tom again. "I was lying watching him search among the sponges," he went on after a pause, "when before my very eyes he was gone. My only son," he went on, his voice rising as he harked back over forgotten years, "in the jaws of one of those accursed sculpins of the deep water, a *tonu* ten feet long."

"And then," asked Jimmy Tom, very softly, as the old man stopped.

"And then," went on the old man, fiercely, "everything went red around me. I gripped my spike and dove and swam, as I never swam before, down to that lurking, ugly demon. In a second I was on him and stabbed him with all my might,—once, twice, three times,—until, dying, he went off the ledge into the depths below and I followed him beyond, to where no man may dare to swim. There he died. As his hateful mouth gaped I dragged out your father by the arm and brought him back to the top; but when I climbed with him into the canoe he was dead, and I was as you see me now—dead too from the waist down. All the rest of that day and all the night beyond and the next day I paddled and paddled until we came home—my dead son and I. No, no," went on the old man, "let us try the safer side of the reef."

For answer, Jimmy Tom quickly fastened in place the outriggers on either side of the canoe, which made it firm and safe to dive from. Around his neck he slipped the "toa," the wide-mouthed bag with a drawstring into which a sponge-diver thrusts his findings. Around his neck, too, he hung the "spike," a double-pointed stick two feet long of black palmwood, hard and heavy as iron. Then, standing on the bow seat, he filled his great lungs again and again until every air-cell was opened. The old man looked at him proudly.

"You are of my blood," he said softly. "Go with God. I will watch above you and be your guard. Forget not to look up at me, and, if I signal, come back to me fast—for I cannot go to you," he finished sadly.

The young man gave a brief nod and, filling his lungs until his chest stood out like a square box, dived high into the air with that jack-knife dive which was invented by sponge-divers and, striking the water clean as the point of a dropped knife, he shot down toward the beautiful depths below. Into his lithe body rushed and pulsed the power and energy of the great swinging sea as he swam through the air-clear water toward a thicket of gorgonias, which waved against the white sand like a bed of poppies. In thirty seconds he was twenty fathoms down, where the pressure of seventy pounds to the square inch would have numbed and crippled an ordinary swimmer, but meant nothing to his steel-strong body, hardened to the depths by years of deep diving. Even as he reached the gleaming thicket he saw, with a great throb of delight, a soft, golden-brown tuft of silk sponge hidden beneath the living branches. The silk sponge is to spongers in the sea what the silver fox is to trappers on the land, and the whole year's output from all seas is only a few score.

With a quick stroke, Jimmy Tom reached the many-colored sea-shrub. The moving branches had to be parted carefully with the spike, lest they close and hide, beyond finding, the silky clump growing within their depths. Even as the boy started to slip over his head the cord from which swung the pointed stick, he looked up to see Jim Tom beckoning frantically for him to return. Yet nowhere in the near-by water could he see anything unusual, except a little fish some eight inches long marked with alternate bands of blue and gold, which came close to him and then turned and swam out to sea. Still his grandfather beckoned, his face contorted with earnestness.

The boy hesitated. An arm's length away lay a fortune. It might well be that never again could he find that exact spot if he went back to the surface now. All this passed through his mind in the same second in which he suddenly plunged his bare arm into the center of the gorgonia clump without waiting to use the spike, as all cautious sponge-divers do. Following the clue of the waving silken end, he grasped a soft mass. Even as he pulled out a silk-sponge, worth more than its weight in gold, something sharp as steel and brittle as ice pierced his hand deep, and he felt a score of spines break and rankle in his flesh like splinters of broken glass. By an ill chance he had thrust his hand against one of those chestnut-burs of the ocean, a purple-black sea-urchin, whose villainous spines, like those of a porcupine, pierce deep and break off. Setting his teeth against the pain, the boy shifted the silky clump of sponge to his other hand and swam for the canoe with all his might. As he rose he saw his grandfather mouthing the word "Hurry!" every line on his tense face set in an agony of pleading.

Even as the boy shot toward the surface, he caught sight once again of the same brilliant little fish returning from deep water. Close behind it, dim at first, but growing more and more distinct as it came, showed a sinister shape, slate-gray, with yellow-brown stripes, the dreaded tiger-shark of deep water, convoyed by that little jackal of the sea, the pilot-fish. It was fortunate for Jimmy Tom that the tiger-shark is not among the swiftest of its family and that he was half-way to the surface before the cold deadly eyes of that one caught sight of his ascending body. With a rush like a torpedo-boat, the thirty-foot shark shot toward the straining, speeding figure, and reached it just as, with a last desperate effort, Jimmy Tom broke water by the canoe. Only the fact that a shark has to be on its back to bring into play its seven rows of triangular, saw-edged teeth saved the boy's life. The tiny tick of time which the fish took in turning enabled the old man, with a tremendous heave of his powerful arms, to drag Jimmy Tom bodily over the gunwale just as the fatal jaws snapped shut below him.

For a long minute the sea-tiger circled the canoe with hungry speed. Then, seeing that his prey had escaped, he swam away, guided, as always, by the strange pilot-fish, which feeds on the scraps of the feasts which it finds for its companion.

As the shark turned toward deep water Jimmy Tom sat up from where he had been lying at the bottom of the canoe and grinned cheerfully after his disappearing foe. Then, without a word, he handed Jim Tom the clump of sponge which, throughout his almost dead-heat with death, he had held clutched tightly in his left hand. With the same motion, he stretched out his other hand, filled like a pincushion with keen, glassy spines from the sea-urchin.

"Not twice in a long lifetime," said his grandfather, "have I seen a finer silk-sponge. Already that sloop is half-paid for."

Without further words, he drew from his belt a sharp-pointed knife and began the painful process of removing one by one the embedded spines from the boy's right hand before they should begin to fester. He finished this bit of rough-and-ready surgery by washing out each deep puncture with stinging salt water. When he had entirely finished, Jimmy Tom carefully tucked away the sponge in a pocket fastened to the inside of the canoe and, slipping the wide-mouthed bag again over his neck, stood on the thwart ready for another dive.

"Try to remember with your thick head," said his grandfather, severely, "all that I have told you, and if I signal you to come back, you *come.*"

The boy nodded briefly, took several deep breaths, and again shot down through the water, directing his course toward another part of the reef, where the white sand was dotted with shells, all hyaline or clouded with exquisite colors. As he reached the bottom, the boy's swift, supple fingers searched among crystal-white, purple and rose and gold olivellas, dosinias, and tellinas which, in spite of their beauty, had no special value. Just as he was about to return to the surface empty-handed, his eye caught the gleam of several spires of the rare, sky-white coral showing among the waving water-weed. A hasty look aloft showed no signal of danger from his sentinel, and he still had nearly three minutes before water would exact her toll of oxygen from him. A swift stroke brought him to the edge of the weed-bed. Just as he was about to reach for the coral, his trained eye caught sight of a gleaming white, beautifully shaped shell nearly as large as the palm of his hand. With a quick motion, he reached under the wavering leaves and, even as his fingers closed on its corrugated surface, realized that he had found at last a perfect specimen of the royal wentle-trap, among the rarest and most beautiful of shells.

In the collections of the world, there are perhaps not six perfect specimens, and sponge-divers and shell-gathers along a thousand lonely coasts are ever on the lookout for this treasure of the sea. The pure white rounded whorls of this one were set off with wide, frilled varices, each ending in a point above, the whole forming a perfect crown of snow and crystal indescribably airy and beautiful. The sight and feeling of this treasure put every thought out of Jimmy Tom's mind save to reach the surface with it as soon as possible. The coral could wait. For that shell any one of the collectors who called at Carib Island would gladly pay him twice the hundred dollars he needed.

Suddenly, even as he turned toward the surface, from a deep crevice in the coral close to his side, shot a fierce and hideous head, like that of some monstrous snake, ridged with a fin which showed like a crest. Before the boy could move, two long jaws filled with curved teeth snapped shut on his right hand and wrist, and he realized with a dreadful pang of fear and pain that he had been gripped by one of the great conger-eels which lurk in the crevices of the reef. Eight feet in length and as large around as a man's leg, they are among the most fearsome of all the sea-folk which a diver must brave. For a second, Jimmy Tom tugged with all his strength, but with no result except that the greenish-gray body retreated deeper into its cave. Then it was that he remembered what his grandfather had told him was the only way to escape from the deadly jaws of a conger-eel. Relaxing every muscle, he allowed his hand to lie limp in the great fish's teeth. Sooner or later, if he kept quiet, the monster would open its jaws for a better grip.

As the cold, deadly eyes stared implacably into his, the beating of his laboring heart sounded in his ears like a drum of doom. If so be that the fierce fish did not relax his grip within the next thirty seconds, the boy knew that his life would go out of him in a long stream of silvery air-bubbles. By a tremendous effort of will he strove against the almost irresistible impulse to do something, to pull, to struggle, to slash with his knife at the horrid head. Yet, clinching his teeth grimly, he set himself to that hardest of all tasks—to wait and wait. His eyes, hot and dim with suffused blood, fell on the crowned shell which he held in his free hand, that shell which was to win for him the sloop, and suddenly through the luminous, gleaming water he seemed to see his cabin on far-away Carib Island and his mother's face looking into his.

As the vision faded he felt a slight shifting and loosening of the grim jaws. With a last effort of his will, dimming before the flood of unconsciousness creeping up to his brain, he allowed his body to float limp, and relaxed every straining muscle. Even as he did so, the great jaws gaped apart for an instant and the fierce head thrust itself toward him for a fresh grip. Fighting back the waves of blackness which swept across his eyes, by a quick turn and wrench he freed his imprisoned hand and, with a tremendous scissors-kick of his powerful legs, shot away just as the curved teeth struck, empty, together.

Up and up and up he sped, swimming as he had never swum before, yet seeming to himself, under the desperate urge of his tortured lungs, to move slow as the hour-hand of a clock. The sunlit surface seemed to move away and away and recede to an immeasurable distance. Just as he felt despairingly that he could no longer resist the uncontrollable desire of his anguished lungs to act, even if they drew in the waters of death, his head shot above the surface. There was a sudden roaring in his ears as the strong arms of Jim Tom pulled him into the canoe. Too weak to speak or move, he lay experiencing the utter happiness there is in breathing, which only the half-drowned may know.

All the rest of that day the boy lay in the

shade of the towering coral wall, while old Jim Tom dressed his gashed and pierced hand. As the calm weather still held, the old man decided to spend the night in the canoe just outside the sheer wall of the reef, where the water stretched away to unknown depths. Toward evening the boy's strength came back; and after eating and drinking ravenously, he showed but little effect of the strain to which he had been subjected.

"When the moon rises," said his grandfather at length, "we will start for home."

The boy shook his head obstinately.

"To-morrow, as soon as it is light," he said, "I dive again to bring up such white coral as has not been seen on Carib Island in my day."

"In your day!" exclaimed old Jim Tom, much incensed. "In your minute—for that is all you have lived. Never has any man made a better haul than you. Be satisfied. The reef is not fortunate for the greedy."

"My silk-sponge was won from the jaws of a shark and my shell from the conger-eel," returned the boy, doggedly. "I ask no favors of the reef."

The old man glanced around apprehensively, while the water seemed to chuckle as it lapped against the coral.

"It is not lucky to talk that way," he said softly. "Sleep now," he went on after a pause. "When morning comes, perhaps there will be a better spirit in you and we will go home."

A little later, while the great moon climbed the sky and the golden sea stretched away unbroken, the two slept. Hours later, Jim Tom awoke with a start. Through his sleep had penetrated the sharp sinister scent of musk, and, even before he opened his eyes, he felt some hostile living presence near him. As he raised his head above the side of the canoe, the still surface of the sea beyond was all a-writhe with what seemed a mass of white sea-snakes. Suddenly from out of the livid tangle shot toward the boat two thirty-foot tentacles larger around than a man's body, tapering to a point and covered with round, sucking discs armed with claws of black horn, sharp and curved as those of a tiger. The great white squid, the devil-fish of unknown depths, which hardly once or twice in a generation comes to the surface, was before him.

For a moment the old man stared in horror at the twisting, fatal tentacles. Then, with a hoarse cry, he roused Jimmy Tom, who started up, grasping the keen machete which always lay in a sheath at the bottom of the canoe. Even as he unsheathed the curved blade, one of the vast, pale streamers reached the canoe, flowed over its side, and licked around the waist of the old man. On the instant, red stains showed through his thin shirt where the armed discs sank deep into his flesh as the horrid arm dragged his helpless body toward the water. Just in time, the boy swung the machete over his head and severed the clutching streamer, and then, with a return stroke, cut through another that licked out toward him across the boat.

As he turned the old man stretched his arm out toward the sea with a gasp of horror. Up through the water came a vast cylindrical shape of livid flesh, many times the size of the canoe, from which long tentacles radiated like a wheel. In the middle of the shapeless mass was set a head of horror, with a vast parrot-like beak which gnashed over a mouth like a cavern. On either side of the demon jaws glared two lidless eyes, each larger than a barrel, rimmed around with white. Of an inky, unfathomable black, they stared at the boat with a malignancy which no earth-born creature could equal or endure. Unable to sustain their appalling glare, both of the Caribs thrust their arms before their faces, expecting every second to feel the deadly touch of the armed tentacles.

It was the boy who recovered himself first. Setting his teeth grimly, he suddenly raised his head to face again this demon of the lowest depths. At his exclamation of surprise, the old man forced himself to look up. The water stretched before them empty and unbroken. Only the scent of musk and grisly fragments of the death-pale tentacles in the bottom of the canoe were there to prove that the monster had not been a ghastly dream of the night. Without a word, Jimmy Tom shipped the outriggers and, gripping his paddle, took his place in the bow. All the rest of that night and far into the next day they paddled, until at last Carib Island loomed up on the horizon.

From the sale of the wentle-trap and the silk sponge Jimmy Tom bought not only his sloop and a new canoe for Jim Tom, but still had the hundred of dollars which makes a man rich on Carib Island. Yet in spite of the fortune he brought back from the reef, he has never returned to it again. When urged by friends or collectors, he only shakes his head and says oracularly, "Enough is plenty."

THE ROWENA O'TOOLE COMPANY

by Ellis Parker Butler

WHEN I was a boy, I had kept rabbits, and they burrowed into Mr. Morton's yard and ate his lettuce crop, which annoyed Mr. Morton; and I had had chickens, and they flew over the fence into Mr. Grady's yard and pecked holes in his reddest tomatoes, which displeased Mr. Grady; and so, after I had paid a boy two dollars for a goat, and then paid him fifty cents to take it back because it had eaten to desolation the gardens of both Mr. Morton and Mr. Grady, I consulted those gentlemen as to what manner of animal I had best own next.

The two gentlemen came into my father's back yard by the over-the-fence route. Mr. Grady took a seat on the sawbuck. Mr. Morton leaned against the barn door. Mr. Morton was younger than Mr. Grady, but far more serious. He was studying law, and wore his hair in a broad bang that hung over one eye; and so long as I knew him he never smiled. Mr. Grady, on the other hand, was old enough to be young again. He seemed to have no especial profession except that of veteran of two fields—Gettysburg and corn-field. He was an ex-soldier and a retired farmer, and as happy by nature as any man could possibly be. I think he lived in cycles of jokes. He would smile all day yesterday thinking of the joke he meant to tell some one; to-day he would tell the joke and smile; and to-morrow he would smile over the manner in which the joke was received. The next day he would begin the cycle again. In this way he kept himself always happy and economized his jokes.

"William," said Mr. Morton, when I had stated my indecision, "this matter is one that deserves more than usual consideration, and I must ask you to retire a few moments while Mr. Grady, my honored friend here, and I consult in private."

I knew that meant I was not wanted, and I went into the house—not especially because it was necessary to retire so far, but because there were fresh doughnuts there. When I returned their consultation was completed.

"It is the sense of the meeting," said Mr. Morton, so solemnly that I felt very important, "that, generally speaking, the confines of a city are conducive to better results in agricultural pursuits than in stock-raising."

"He means," explained Mr. Grady, "that raisin' garden truck is better than raisin' critters."

My face must have shown my disappointment, for Mr. Morton hastened to reassure me.

"However," he said, "since your nature inclines toward the animal rather than toward the vegetable kingdom, we have made proper concessions, and have decided on a fit and suitable creature upon which you may lavish your care."

"Very purty words, them," Mr. Grady asserted.

Mr. Morton wiped back his lock of hair, which had a way of falling into his eye, and proceeded.

"The animal on which we have decided," he continued, "has been known from the days of great antiquity. It is a gentle beast, —at least in its domestic state, although when wild it is considered dangerous at times,—and it adds to the food supply of the nations. While I may not call it precisely graceful, it is, in its youth, often pleasant to the eye, while with age it assumes a dignity and majesty that are suited to its rotund and weighty form."

Mr. Grady had been waiting an opportunity to speak, while I stood with my mouth open, taking in the stream of eloquence. Now Mr. Grady took his pipe from his mouth and spoke.

"Why don't you tell the lad it 's a pig?" he asked.

"A pig!" I exclaimed. "But a pig can't do anything!"

"To be sure," said Mr. Grady, "he can't fly like them chickens you had."

"Nor can I say I have ever seen one hop like a rabbit," said Mr. Morton.

"Neither can he climb a tree like a cat, nor swim like a trout; but he is a fine bit of a beast, for all that," said Mr. Grady.

"But," I suggested, "pigs cost a great deal, and all my money is gone. I used the last to buy that billy-goat."

"All of which," said Mr. Morton, "has been carefully considered; and, in view of your financial distress, Mr. Grady, my honored neighbor, and I have decided to finance the pig. In other words, we will buy him."

I hesitated.

"I don't think my father would like to have you do that," I said.

"But we do not make you a present of him," said Mr. Morton.

"Would n't he be my pig?" I asked, quite sure I should not care to own a pig that did not belong to me.

"We will make a stock company of him," said Mr. Morton. "We will divide him into three shares, of which Mr. Grady, my honored neighbor, and I shall each own one, because we supply the pig, while you shall own one, because you will have the sole care and custody of the animal."

"And when he 's sold, we divvy up fair and square," said Mr. Grady; "each of us three gettin' one half of what he sells for."

The more I considered the matter, the better I liked it. The idea that there would be something to divide when the pig was sold was pleasing; for neither my rabbits nor my chickens had produced a profit, and I considered that even should the pig prove a loss, as in my goat venture, it would be satisfactory to have two partners to help share the deficit. So I accepted the proposal.

As for the officers of the company, we made Mr. Morton president, because—well, because he was n't the sort of man you could make anything less; but, to balance the dignities, Mr. Grady and I each had two titles. Mr. Grady was made treasurer and board of directors, and I was proudly installed as secretary and general manager.

"And mind you, William," said Mr. Morton, severely, "you must keep the records of the company honestly and conscientiously." He said this with great impressiveness, while climbing the fence into the yard.

"Mr. Grady," I said to that gentleman, "how must I keep the records?"

"Well, now," said Mr. Grady, "I have n't ever kept records of a pig company myself; but I reckon you 'd best get one of these here pocket diaries an' keep it in that. It would be handiest."

So I got one. My first entry described our first meeting and the formation of the company. It ran: "Mister Morton he climbed over his fence into our yard, and Mister Grady he climbed over his fence into our yard, and we were all met together, because I did n't have to climb into our yard because I was in it," and so on. You see how conscientiously I kept the records.

To Mr. Grady, who was an expert in pigs, was intrusted the task of procuring our live stock, and it seemed to me he was long at it. At length, however, he told me he had got his eye on a remarkably fine pig, "purty as a picture, an' full o' life as an egg," which would be delivered as soon as it had a few more days' growth; for, like the wife in the song of "Billy Boy," it was still "a young thing and could not leave its mother."

But I had enough to do in the meantime. There was the sty to build, and a trough to construct, and no ordinary sty or trough would do. I soon learned the meaning of Mr. Grady's title of board of directors. I found that the general manager was a mere tool in the hands of the board of directors. Every day the smiling "board" would climb over the fence and, comfortably seated on the sawbuck, instruct the general manager.

He not only insisted on the shape and construction of the sty, but he directed me how to hold the saw and hammer, how to hit a nail, and, if I hit my thumb instead, how to tie it up. If our president had tried to direct me, I should have resented it; but Mr. Grady did it in such a good-natured manner that I enjoyed it, and his suggestions were so appropriate that I soon felt the fullest confidence in him.

At length the pig came. It was a beautiful little pink fellow, full of life and appetite, and Mr. Grady predicted that it would make a fine beast in time. I decided at once that we must call it Rowena, my favorite name; for I had just read "Ivanhoe" for the first time, and the name,

Rowena, greatly pleased my fancy. Of course I had to consult the board of directors on such an important matter, and he immediately objected.

"What sort of a name is Rowena, now?" he asked. "Be it French? Who ever heard of a French pig?"

"I don't think it is French, Mr. Grady," I said doubtfully.

"It's not Irish, anyhow," he declared; "and all my life I 've been wishing to name a pig, and there 's no name so good for man or beast as the good old Irish names. When I was a boy no bigger than you, I wanted to name a pig, but they were my father's pigs and I durst not name them. And when I grew up I had so many pigs I did n't have time to name them, let alone think of names. But now," said he, "I 've got the time, and I 've got the pig, an' I 've been layin' awake nights thinkin' over names, an' I 've decided that O'Toole is the finest name for a pig that ever was. O'Toole it is."

"I don't like O'Toole," I said, for I had set my heart on Rowena. "I don't like O'Toole."

"Then if the general manager and the board of directors disagree," said Mr. Grady, "we 'll have to call a meetin' of the stockholders an' vote on it." So a meeting was called.

Mr. Morton climbed over the fence, and when he heard our statements his face became very sober.

"Now, fellow-stockholders," he said gravely, "you have proceeded in this matter regardless of my rights. You have not consulted my preferences in the least. I shall insist that our animal shall be called Empedocles. If ever I have had a great desire, from my callow boyhood upward, it was to see a sweet, pink, porcine animal bearing the musical name of Empedocles. I shall insist on it."

"We all insist," said Mr. Grady; "an' if

we all insist, fellow-shtockholders, I see no way out of it but to fight a duel—a three-sided duel with axes."

"And then," said Mr. Morton, scornfully, "if we are all killed, the pig will be a poor outcast orphan! I propose a ballot."

I eagerly agreed to the proposal. A duel with axes did not appeal to me. So we tore up several pages of Mr. Morton's notebook and voted. The first ballot stood:

> For Empedocles 1
> For O'Toole 1
> For Rowena 1

The succeeding ballots, from the second up to the sixth, stood the same. Just when we were preparing for the next ballot a gentleman called for Mr. Morton, and this may have broken the deadlock, for we found that the seventh ballot stood:

> For O'Toole 1
> For Rowena 1
> For Rowena O'Toole 1

Mr. Morton then made a neat little speech in which he begged the Pig Company to seek harmony rather than self-interest, and suggested that we unite on Rowena O'Toole. The visiting gentleman applauded the speech, and when the eighth ballot was taken the votes stood:

> For Rowena O'Toole 3

Which settled the matter, once for all. The pig received its name with great unconcern.

As the spring advanced it became evident that we were to have a rainy season; and the ground in the pen became very soft and muddy. To my eyes, Rowena O'Toole seemed to enjoy it immensely. She unfailingly chose the softest spots, and stood leg deep in them. But Mr. Grady shook his head."

" 'T won't do," he said. "It 's all well enough for country pigs, but city pigs can't stand it. First thing we know, it will catch cold in its head, standin' in the damp, an' lose its appytite, an' a pig without an appytite is a gone pig."

"What would you advise, Mr. Grady?" I asked anxiously.

"We might get it a pair of rubber boots, now," he said thoughtfully; "an' wrap its neck in red flannel; but it would eat the boots, an' I dunno but eatin' rubber boots is worse for a pig than a cold in the head is. What I direct," he said,—and when Mr. Grady directed it was only left for me to carry out his directions,—"is that you build a pen for it in the hay-loft. Up there it would be nice and dry and comfortable."

It was not hard to build a pen in the hay-loft, but it was harder to transport Rowena O'Toole to her new home. She had grown considerably, and as Mr. Grady would do nothing but direct, I had a serious time getting the pig up the ladder. Unless you have tried it, you cannot imagine how awkward it is.

It was well along toward the next spring when Mr. Grady decided that Rowena O'Toole was fit in size to be sold, and we bargained with our butcher. He came and looked at Rowena O'Toole, and shook his head.

"She 's a thin pig for her age," he said doubtfully,—"the thinnest pig I ever see."

"She 's a proud pig," said Mr. Grady; "she lives up to her elegant name. She never was greedy like common pigs."

"Looks to me like she 'd had the fat fairly worried off her," said the butcher.

"Not having had it on her," said Mr. Grady, "it could n't be worried off. I can't imagine why she did n't put on more flesh. She 's been tended most carefully. Not a day but she 's had her bath."

"Bath!" exclaimed the butcher.

"Bath," said Mr. Grady, "every day, regular as the calendar, we 've turned the hose on her."

"Then I'll have to offer you two cents a pound below the market rates. It don't do for pigs to bathe too often. Say every other day, now, might do; but every day is a little too much. It gets them all haughty and proud and uppish, which makes them tough."

Nor could we persuade him to give the fraction of a cent a pound more.

We had to lower Rowena O'Toole from the hay-loft door by means of a block and tackle, and Mr. Grady directed me to drive her to the butcher's through the alley. I think now that he was not proud of Rowena O'Toole. She may have looked aristocratic, but she did not look over-fed.

The money we received was not a fortune, but it was, on my part at least, well earned.

When the Rowena O'Toole Company met to declare its final dividend, Mr. Grady asked me if I wished to try a pig again that year; and if not, what animal I had in mind.

I think I squirmed a little on the bench on which I sat. I know I said:

"If you don't mind, Mr. Grady, I don't think I'll try any more animals just now. I think I'll learn to grow tomatoes, if you don't mind showing me how."

"I had a serious time getting the pig up the ladder"

HOW SANTA CLAUS
FOUND THE POOR-HOUSE

by Sophie Swett

ELIOGABALUS was shoveling snow. The snow was very deep, and the path from the front door to the road was a long one, and the shovel was almost as big as Heliogabalus.

But Gobaly—as everybody called him, for short—did n't give up easily. You might have known that he would n't give up easily by one glance at his sturdy little figure, at his bright, wide-open eyes, his firm mouth, and his square, prominent chin; even the little, turned-up end of his nose looked resolute.

Besides, Mrs. Pynchum had told him to shovel out the path; and she had a switch behind the wood-shed door, to say nothing of her slipper.

Mrs. Pynchum kept the poor-farm, and Gobaly was "town's poor." The boys sometimes called him that, when he went to coast on Three-Pine Hill or to see the skating on the mill-pound; and sometimes, too, they made fun of his clothes. But it was only the boys who were a great deal bigger than he who dared to make fun of Gobaly, and some of them even ran when he doubled up his fists. But Methuselah! I don't know what would have become of Methuselah if he had not had Gobaly to defend him. For he was a delicate little fellow; "spindlin' and good for nothin'," Mrs. Pynchum called him; and he had come to her in a basket—in other words, Methuselah was a foundling.

Mrs. Pynchum "did n't think much of

children who came in a basket from nobody knew where. It did n't seem to belong to Poplarville to support him, since he did n't belong to anybody that ever lived there, and his keep and his medicine cost more than he would ever be worth to anybody."

Gobaly's mother died in the poor-house, and left him there, a baby; she had always lived in the town, and so had his father, so of course Gobaly had a perfect right there; and old Dr. Barnacle, who was very learned, had said of him that he was an uncommonly fine baby, and had named him Heliogabalus.

Besides, he was strong and willing, and did a great deal of work. Mrs. Pynchum "could put up with Gobaly." But Methuselah, she said, was "a thorn in her side." And now, after being a trial all his life, he had a hip disease, which the doctor feared was incurable, and which made him more troublesome still!

But, after all, Mrs. Pynchum was n't quite so bad as one would have thought from her talk. She must have had a soft spot somewhere in her heart, for she put plums in Methuselah's porridge, now that he was ill, and once she had let Gobaly leave his wood-chopping to draw him out on his sled.

I suppose there is a soft spot in everybody's heart, only sometimes it is n't very easy to find it; and Mrs. Pynchum might not have been so cross if she had led an easier life. There were a good many queer people in the poor-house, "flighty in their heads and wearin' in their ways," she said, and sometimes they must have been trying to the patience.

Once in a great while, indeed, Mrs. Pynchum was good-natured, and then, sometimes for a whole evening, the poor-house would seem like home. All those who lived there would then sit around the fire and roast apples; and Mrs. Pynchum would even unlock the closet under the back stairs, where there was a great bag full of nuts that Sandy Gooding and Gobaly had gathered; and Uncle Sim Perkins would tell stories.

But it happened very unfortunately that Mrs. Pynchum never had one of her good-natured days on Thanksgiving, or Christmas, or any holiday. She was sure to say on those days that she was "all tried to pieces."

And everybody was frightened and unhappy when Mrs. Pynchum was "all tried to pieces," and so that was the reason why Gobaly's heart sank as he remembered, while he was shoveling the path through the snow, that the next day was Christmas.

Some people from the village went by with a Christmas-tree, which they had cut down in the woods just beyond the poor-house; there were children in the party, and they called to Gobaly and wished him a merry Christmas, and asked him if they were going to have a Christmas-tree at his house, and expressed great surprise that he was n't going to hang up his stocking. Then one of the children suddenly exclaimed:

"Why, that 's the poor-house! It 's never Christmas there!"

Poor Gobaly's heart sank still more as he caught these words, and somehow he felt very tired, and minded the cold, as he had not thought of minding it a mo-

ment before, and the snow-bank looked as if he never could shovel through it. For though Gobaly was stout-hearted, he did n't like to be reminded that he was "town's poor," and that Christmas was nothing to him.

Just then he caught sight of Methuselah's little pinched face pressed against the window-pane. Methuselah always had, even when he was a baby, a worn and pallid face, like a little old man, and that was why they called him Methuselah. It was cold in the front room but Methuselah had wrapped himself in a piece of an old quilt and stolen into the back room and to the window, where he could see Gobaly shoveling the snow.

Methuselah never was quite happy when Gobaly was out of his sight.

Gobaly went up to the window.

"To-morrow 's Christmas, 'Thusely!" he said.

"Is it? Do you s'pose she knows it? She 'll be 'all tried to pieces,' won't she?"

("She" always meant Mrs. Pynchum in the poor-house; nobody there ever spoke of her in any other way.)

Gobaly was sadly afraid that she would, but he said, cheerfully:

"May be she won't. May be she 'll let me take you out on my sled; and one Christmas there was turkey and plum-pudding."

"Must have been a good many Christmases ago; I can't remember it!" said Methuselah. "Some folks have 'em every Christmas, Uncle Sim says, but perhaps it is n't true. Gobaly, do you believe there really is any Santa Claus, such as Uncle Sim tells about, or did he make it all up? To be sure, he showed me a picture of him."

"I know there is," said Gobaly firmly, "because I 've seen presents that he brought to boys and girls in the village."

"Then why don't he ever come here and bring us some?" said Methuselah, as if a new idea had suddenly struck him. "Do you s'pose it 's because we 're worse than any other boys in the world? She says we are, sometimes. Or may be he 's too proud to stop at the poor-house."

"Perhaps he can't find the way," said Gobaly. " 'Cause it 's a pretty crooked road, you know. Or may be he would n't think it was worth the while to come so far out of the village just for us; he would n't be going to Squire Thorndike's, because there are n't any children there, and there are n't any other houses on this road."

"I wish we lived where there was a truly Christmas, like places where Uncle Sim has been; don't you, Gobaly? May be he makes them all up, though; it seems if they must be too good to be true."

"I should n't wonder if you got lots of plums in your porridge to-morrow and perhaps a piece of mince-pie. And I 'll ask her to let me take you up to Three-Pine Hill on the sled."

Gobaly always showed the bright side of things to Methuselah and he had become so accustomed to looking for a bright side that he could find one when you would n't have thought there was any there.

And whenever he found a very big lump in his throat he swallowed it for Methuselah's sake, and pretended that he did n't see anything in the world to cry about.

He had to go back to his shoveling then, but after he had started he turned back to say:

"When I 'm a man, you shall have Christmases, 'Thusely!"

It was in that way that Gobaly often comforted Methuselah. It never seemed to occur to either of them that 'Thusely might possibly grow to be a man too.

Gobaly went to work at the snow again as if it were not a bit bigger than he was, and he soon had a rampart piled up on each side of the path so high that he thought it must look like the Chinese Wall which Uncle Sim was always telling of.

As he was digging the very last shovelful of snow out of the path, he heard the jingle of sleighbells, and saw the butcher's wagon, set upon runners and drawn by a very frisky horse, going in the direction of the village. The butcher's boy and three of his comrades occupied the seat, and as many more boys were wedged in among the joints of meat and heaps of poultry in the back of the wagon. They were evidently combining pleasure with business in the liveliest manner.

Coming in the other direction, from the village, was a large Newfoundland dog with a basket in his mouth. Gobaly liked dogs, and he was sure that he was acquainted with every one in the village. As he was on intimate terms with every big one, he knew that this must be a stranger.

The butcher's boy was driving recklessly, and seemed to think it would be fun to make a sudden turn into the drifts through which the dog was bounding. The horse, taken by surprise and somewhat frightened, made a sudden plunge; and though Gobaly could not quite see how it happened, it seemed that before the dog had time to get out of the way, the sled had gone over him, and he lay helpless and howling upon the snow!

The boys either found it impossible to stop their horse, or were too frightened to investigate the extent of the mischief they had done, for they went careering on, and left the poor dog to his fate.

Gobaly was at his side in a moment, patting his shaggy black head, calling him "poor doggie" and "good doggie," and trying to discover how badly he was hurt. He came to the conclusion, after a thorough examination, that his leg was either broken or badly sprained,—and Gobaly was a judge of such things. He had once doctored a rooster's lame leg, and though the rooster was never again able to mount a fence, and crowed with diminished energy, he was still able to cheer his heart by fighting the three other roosters all at once, and was likely to escape the dinner-pot for a long time to come, though his gait was no longer lordly. Gobaly had also successfully treated a kitten with a sprained ankle—to say nothing of one whose tail the gobbler had nipped off. And he had seen the doctor in the village set a puppy's leg, and had carefully watched the operation.

He helped the dog along toward the house—and it was well that he was a strong and sturdy little fellow or he could not have done it—and managed at last to get the poor creature, unobserved, into the wood-shed. He was very much afraid that Mrs. Pynchum, if she should see him, would order him to leave the dog in the road, and he knew it would not do to carry him in beside the kitchen fire, as he wanted to, for Mrs. Pynchum never wanted "a dirty dog in her clean house."

Gobaly found it hard to decide whether the bone was broken or only out of place, but he made a sort of a splint, such as he had seen the doctor use upon the puppy's leg, and then wound soft cloths, wet with liniment, about it, and the dog certainly seemed relieved, and licked Gobaly's hand, and looked at him with grateful eyes.

He ventured into the house after a while, and beckoned to Methuselah to come out to the woodshed.

Methuselah was convinced that Santa Claus had sent the dog to them as a Christmas present, and his delight was unbounded.

"Of course, Santa Claus must have sent him, or why would he have come down this lonely road all by himself? And you will cure him" (Methuselah thought there was little that Gobaly could n't do if he tried), "and perhaps she will let us keep him!"

But a sudden recollection had struck Gobaly. The dog had been carrying a basket in his mouth; there might be something in it that would tell where he came from.

Though the dog's appearance was mysterious, Gobaly was not so ready as Methuselah to accept the Santa Claus theory.

He ran out and found the basket, half buried in the snow, where it had fallen from the dog's mouth. There were several letters and papers in it addressed to "Dr. Carruthers, care of Richard Thorndike, Esq."

Dr. Carruthers was the famous New York physician who was visiting Squire Thorndike! Gobaly had heard the people in the village talking about him. The dog probably belonged to him, and had been sent to the post-office for his letters.

Although he had not really believed that Santa Claus sent the dog, Gobaly did feel a pang of disappointment that they must part with him so soon. But then Mrs. Pynchum would probably not have allowed them to keep him, anyhow, and she might have had him shot because his leg was hurt. That thought consoled Gobaly, and having obtained Mrs. Pynchum's permission to carry him to his master,—which was readily given, since it was the easiest way to get rid of the dog,—he put a very large box, with a bed in it made of straw and soft cloth, upon his sled, and then lifted the dog gently into the box. The dog whined with pain when he was moved, but still licked Gobaly's hand, as if he understood that he was his friend and did not mean to hurt him.

Methuselah stood in the shed door, and looked after them, weeping, sadly making up his mind that Santa Claus was proud and would never come to the poor-house.

Gobaly had never been even inside Squire Thorndike's gate before, and he went up to one of the back doors with fear and trembling; the servants at Squire Thorndike's were said to be "stuck-up," and they might not be very civil to "town's poor." But at the sight of the dog they raised a great cry, and at once ushered Gobaly into the presence of Squire Thorndike and Dr. Carruthers, that he might tell them all he knew about the accident.

Dr. Carruthers was a big, jolly-looking man, with white hair and a long white beard, just like pictures of Santa Claus. Gobaly was sure that Methuselah would think he was Santa Claus if he could see him. He evidently felt very sorry about the dog's accident, and pitied him and petted him as if he were a baby; Gobaly, who had never had so much petting in his whole life, thought the dog ought to forget all about his leg.

And then he suddenly turned to Gobaly and asked him who set the leg. Gobaly answered, modestly, that he "fixed it as well as he could because there was n't anybody else around."

"How did you know how?" asked the doctor. And Gobaly related his experiences with the rooster and the kitten and the puppy. Dr. Carruthers looked at him steadily out of a pair of eyes that were very sharp, although very kind. Then he turned to Squire Thorndike and said "an uncommon boy." Squire Thorndike answered, and they talked together in a low tone, casting an occasional glance at Gobaly.

How Gobaly's ears did burn! He wondered what Squire Thorndike knew about him, and he thought of every prank he ever had played in his life. Gobaly was an unusually good boy, but he *had* played a few pranks,—being a boy,—and he thought they were a great deal worse than they really were, because Mrs. Pynchum said so. And he imagined that Dr. Car-

ruthers was hearing all about them, and would presently turn round and say that such a bad boy had no right to touch his dog, and that such conduct was just what he should expect of "town's poor." But instead of that, after several minutes' conversation with Squire Thorndike, he turned to Gobaly, and said:

"I want an office-boy, and I think you are just the boy to suit me. How would you like to come and live with me, and perhaps, one of these days, be a doctor yourself."

Gobaly caught his breath.

To go away from Mrs. Pynchum; not to be "town's poor" any more; to learn to be a doctor! He had said once in Mrs. Pynchum's hearing that he wanted to be a doctor when he grew up, and she had said, sneeringly, that "town's poor were n't very likely to get a chance to learn to be doctors."

And now the chance had come to him! Gobaly thought it seemed too much like heaven to be anything that could happen to a mortal boy!

"Well, would you like to go?" asked the doctor again, as Gobaly could find no words to answer.

"Would I, sir? *Would n't* I!" said Gobaly, with a radiant face.

"Well, then, I will make an arrangement with the selectmen—which I have no doubt it will be easy to do—and will take you home with me to-morrow night," said the good doctor.

But the brightness had suddenly faded from Gobaly's face. He stood with his hands thrust into his trousers pockets, gazing irresolutely at the carpet.

But it was not the carpet that Gobaly saw; it might as well have been the yellow paint of the poor-house floors for all that he noticed of its luxurious pile and beautiful colors. It was 'Thusely's pale, pinched little face that he saw! It had risen before him even while the doctor was speaking. If he went away, who would take care of 'Thusely? And 'Thusely's heart would be broken.

"I can't go, sir; I forgot. No—no—I can't go!" said Gobaly.

Oh, what a lump there was in his throat! He had swallowed many a lump for 'Thusely's sake, but that was the very biggest one!

And then he turned and ran out of the house, without any ceremony. He knew it was rude, but that lump would n't stay down, and though he might be called "town's poor," he was n't going to be called a cry-baby!

And home he ran, as fast as his legs would carry him.

That night something very unusual happened. Mrs. Pynchum went to the village to a Christmas festival. She went before dark, and the spirits of everybody in the poor-house rose as soon as she was out of sight. Mr. Pynchum piled great logs upon the fire-place, till there was such a roaring fire as had not been seen there for many a long day; and he told Joe Golightly and Gobaly to go down cellar and bring up as many apples as they wanted to, and he found the key of the closet where the bag of nuts was kept! And Sandy Gooding brought out some fine pop-corn that he had saved up; and Joe Golightly brought out his violin, which, though some of its strings were broken and its voice was a little cracked and wheezy, could yet cheer one up wonderfully with "Bonnie Dundee" and "The Campbells are Coming." Everybody was merry,—although there was no Christmas-tree, and nobody had a present except 'Thusely, who had a big red peppermint-drop that Gobaly bought him with a penny hoarded for six weeks— and it would have been a very pleasant evening if there had not been one great drawback. Mrs. Pynchum had a way of

pouncing upon people when they least expected her. If a window rattled or a mouse stirred in the wall, a hush fell upon the mirth, and everybody shrank with dread. It would be so like Mrs. Pynchum to suspect that they were having a good time, and turn back to put a stop to it before she had fairly reached the festival!

Just as they had poured out a popperful of corn,—popped out so big and white that it would do you good to see it,—and Uncle Sim was clearing his throat to begin a story, there came a loud knock at the door. Everybody jumped. Mr. Pynchum and Sandy began to cram the apples into their pockets, and thrust the cornpopper into the closet, and Joe hid his violin under his coat-tails. It took them all fully two minutes to remember that Mrs. Pynchum never knocked.

Mr. Pynchum sat down again, and said, in a tone of surprise, as if he had not been in the least agitated:

"What is the matter with you all? Gobaly, open the door."

Gobaly opened the door, and who should be there but Squire Thorndike and the city doctor!

The moment 'Thusely saw Dr. Carruthers he called out "Santa Claus!" And the big doctor laughed, and took a great package of candy out of his pocket and gave it to 'Thusely.

After that it was of no use for Gobaly to whisper, "The dog gentleman!" in 'Thusely's ear; he could n't think it was anybody but Santa Claus.

"I 'm *so* glad you 've come!" he said, confidentially. "And you look just like your picture. And I don't see why you never came before, for you don't seem proud. And we are n't such very bad boys; anyway, Gobaly is n't. Don't you believe what Mrs. Pynchum tells you!—*Will* you?"

The doctor laughed, and said he was

getting to be an old fellow, and the snow was deep, and it was hard for him to get about; but he was sorry he had n't come before, for he thought they did look like good boys. Then he asked Methuselah about his lameness and the pain in his side, and said he ought to be sent to a certain hospital in New York, where he might be cured. And then he asked if he had no relatives or friends.

"I've got Gobaly," said 'Thusely.

The doctor turned and looked sharply at Gobaly.

"Is *he* the reason why you would n't go with me?" he asked.

"He 's such a little chap, and I 'm all he 's got," said Gobaly.

The doctor took out his handkerchief and said it was bad weather for colds.

"Suppose I take him, too?" said he.

This time the lump in his throat fairly got the better of Gobaly!

But 'Thusely clapped his hands for joy. He did n't understand what was to happen, only that Santa Claus was to take him somewhere with Gobaly; and one thing that 'Thusely was sure of was that he wanted to go wherever Gobaly went. And he kept saying:

"I told you that Santa Claus sent the dog,—now, did n't I, Gobaly?"

Methuselah went to the hospital and was cured, and Gobaly—well, if I should tell you his name, you might say that you had heard of him as a famous surgeon-doctor. I think it is probable that he could now make a lame rooster or a kitten with a sprained ankle just as good as new, and I am sure he would n't be above trying; for he has a heart big enough to sympathize with any creature that suffers.

There is at least one person in the world who will agree with me, and that is a gentleman who was once a miserable little cripple in a poor-house, and was called Methuselah.

TOM SAWYER AND HIS BAND

by Albert Bigelow Paine

Iɴ beginning the "Adventures of Tom Sawyer," the author says, "Most of the adventures recorded in this book really occurred," and he tells us that *Huck Finn* is drawn from life; *Tom Sawyer,* also, though not from a single individual, being a composite of three boys whom Mark Twain had known.

The three boys were himself, almost entirely, with traces of two schoolmates, John Briggs and Will Bowen. John Briggs was also the original of *Joe Harper, the Terror of the Seas.* As for *Huck Finn, the Red-Handed,* his original was a village waif named Tom Blankenship, who needed no change for his part in the story.

The Blankenship family picked up an uncertain livelihood, fishing and hunting, and lived at first under a tree in a bark shanty, but later moved into a large barn-like building, back of the Clemens home on Hill Street. There were three male members of the household: old Ben, the father, shiftless and dissolute; young Ben, the eldest son—a doubtful character, with certain good traits; and Tom—that is to say, *Huck,* who was just as he is described in the book—a ruin of rags, a river-rat, kind of heart, and accountable for his conduct to nobody in the world. He could come and go as he chose; he never had to work or go to school; he could do all the things good and bad that other boys longed to do and were forbidden. To them he was the symbol of liberty; his knowledge of fishing, trapping, signs, and of the woods and river gave value to his society, while the fact that it was forbidden made it necessary to Sam Clemens's happiness.

The Blankenships being handy to the back gate of the Hill Street house, he adopted them at sight. Their free mode of life suited him. He was likely to be there at any hour of the day, and Tom made catcall signals at night that would bring Sam out on the shed roof at the back and down a little trellis and flight of steps to the group of boon companions, which, besides Tom, usually included John Briggs, Will Pitts, and the two younger Bowen boys. They were not malicious boys, but just mischievous, fun-loving boys—youngsters of ten or twelve, rather thoughtless, being mainly bent on having a good time.

They had a wide field of action: they ranged from Holliday's Hill on the north to the cave on the south, and over the fields and through all the woods between. They explored both banks of the river, the islands, and the deep wilderness of the Illinois shore. They could run like turkeys and swim like ducks; they could handle a boat as if born in one. No orchard or melon-patch was entirely safe from them. No dog or slave patrol was so watchful that they did not sooner or later elude it. They borrowed boats with or without the owners' consent—it did not matter.

Most of their expeditions were harmless enough. They often cruised up to Turtle

Island, about two miles above Hannibal, and spent the day feasting. There were quantities of turtles and their eggs there, and mussels, and plenty of fish. Fishing and swimming were their chief pastimes, with incidental raiding, for adventure. Bear Creek was their swimming-place by day, and the river-front at nightfall, a favorite spot being where the railroad-bridge now ends. It was a good distance across to the island where, in the book, *Tom Sawyer* musters his pirate band, and where later *Huck* found *Nigger Jim,* but quite often in the evening they swam across to it, and when they had frolicked for an hour or more on the sand-bar at the head of the island, they would swim back in the dusk, breasting the strong, steady Mississippi current without exhaustion or dread. They could swim all day, those little scamps, and seemed to have no fear. Once during his boyhood, Sam Clemens swam across to the Illinois side, then turned and swam back again without landing, a distance of at least two miles, as he had to go. He was seized with a cramp on the return trip. His legs became useless, and he was obliged to make the remaining distance with his arms.

The adventures of Sam Clemens and his comrades would fill several books of the size of "Tom Sawyer." Many of them are of course forgotten now, but those still remembered show that Mark Twain had plenty of real material.

It was not easy to get money in those days, and the boys were often without it. Once "Huck" Blankenship had the skin of a coon he had captured, and offered to sell it to raise capital. At Selms's store on Wild Cat Corner the coonskin would bring ten cents. But this was not enough. The boys thought of a plan to make it bring more. Selms's back window was open, and the place where he kept his pelts was pretty handy. Huck went around

to the front door and sold the skin for ten cents to Selms, who tossed it back on the pile. Then Huck came back and, after waiting a reasonable time, crawled in the open window, got the coonskin and sold it to Selms again. The boys did this several times that afternoon, and the capital of the band grew. But at last John Pierce, Selms's clerk, said:

"Look here, Mr. Selms, there's something wrong about this. That boy has been selling us coonskins all the afternoon."

Selms went back to his pile of pelts. There were several sheepskins, but only one coonskin—the one he had that moment bought.

Selms himself, in after years, used to tell this story as a great joke.

One of the boys' occasional pastimes was to climb Holliday's Hill and roll down big stones, to frighten the people who were driving by. Holliday's Hill above the road was steep; a stone once started would go plunging downward and bound across the road with the deadly momentum of a bomb. The boys would get a stone poised, then wait until they saw a team approaching, and, calculating the distance, would give the boulder a start. Dropping behind the bushes, they would watch the sudden effect upon the party below as the great missile shot across the road a few yards before them. This was huge sport, but they carried it too far. For, at last, they planned a grand climax that would surpass anything before attempted in the stone-rolling line.

A monstrous boulder was lying up there in the right position to go down hill, once started. It would be a glorious thing to see that great stone go smashing down a hundred yards or so in front of some peaceful-minded countryman jogging along the road. Quarrymen had been getting out rock not far away and had left their picks and shovels handy. The boys borrowed the

"*The boulder sailed clear over the Negro*"

tools and went to work to undermine the big stone. They worked at it several hours. If their parents had asked them to work like that, they would have thought they were being killed.

Finally, while they were still digging, the big stone suddenly got loose and started down. They were not ready for it at all. Nobody was coming but an old colored man in a cart; their splendid stone was going to be wasted.

One could hardly call it wasted, however; they had planned for a thrilling result, and there was certainly thrill enough while it lasted. In the first place the stone nearly caught Will Bowen when it started. John Briggs had that moment quit digging and handed Will the pick. Will was about to take his turn when Sam Clemens leaped aside with a yell.

"Look out, boys, she's coming!"

She came. The huge boulder kept to the ground at first, then, gathering momentum it went bounding into the air. About half way down the hill it struck a sapling and cut it clean off. This turned its course a little and the negro in the cart, hearing the noise and seeing the great mass come crashing in his direction, made a wild effort to whip up his horse.

The boys watched their bomb with growing interest. It was headed straight for the negro, also for a cooper-shop across the road. It made longer leaps with every bound, and, wherever it struck, fragments and dust would fly. The shop happened to be empty, but the rest of the catastrophe would call for close investigation. They wanted to fly, but they could not move until they saw the rock land. It was making mighty leaps, now, and the terrified negro had managed to get exactly in its path. The boys stood holding their breath, their mouths open.

Then suddenly they could hardly believe their eyes; a little way above the road the boulder struck a projection, made one mighty leap into the air, sailed clear over the negro and his mule and landed in the soft dirt beyond the road, only a fragment striking the shop, damaging but not wrecking it. Half buried in the ground, the great stone lay there for nearly forty years; then it was broken up. It was the last rock the boys ever rolled down. Nearly sixty years later, John Briggs and Mark Twain walked across Holliday's Hill and looked down toward the river road. Mark Twain said:

"It was a mighty good thing, John, that stone acted the way it did. We might have had to pay a fancy price for that old darky —I can see him yet."

It can be no harm, now, to confess that the boy Sam Clemens—a pretty small boy, a good deal less than twelve at the time and by no means large for his years—was the leader of this unhallowed band. In any case, truth requires this admission. If the band had a leader it was Sam, just as it was *Tom Sawyer* in the book. They were always ready to listen to him—they would even stop fishing to do that—and to follow his plans. They looked to him for ideas and direction, and he gloried in being a leader and showing off, just as *Tom* did in the book. It seems almost a pity that in those far-off barefoot days he could not have looked down the years and caught a glimpse of his splendid destiny.

But of literary fame he could never have dreamed. The chief ambition—the "permanent ambition"—of every Hannibal boy was to be a pilot. The pilot in his splendid glass perch with his supreme power and princely salary was to them the noblest of all human creatures. An elder Bowen boy was already a pilot, and when he came home, as he did now and then, his person seemed almost too sacred to touch. Next to being a pilot, Sam thought he would like to be a pirate, or a bandit, or a trapper-scout—something gorgeous and awe inspiring, where his word, his nod would still be law. The river kept his river ambition always fresh, and with the cave and the forest round about helped him to imagine those other things.

The cave was the joy of his heart. It was a real cave, not merely a hole, but a marvel of deep passages and vaulted chambers that led back into the bluffs and far down into the earth, even below the river, some said. Sam Clemens never tired of the cave. He was willing any time to quit fishing, or swimming, or melon-hunting for the three-mile walk, or pull, that brought them to its mystic door. With its long corridors, its royal chambers hung with stalactites, its remote hiding-places, it was exactly suitable, Sam thought, to be the lair of an outlaw, and in it he imagined and carried out adventures which his faithful followers may not always have understood, though enjoying them none the less for that reason.

In "Tom Sawyer," *Indian Joe* dies in the cave. He did not die there in real life, but was lost there once and was half starved when they found him. He was not as bad as painted in the book, though he was dissolute and accounted dangerous; and when one night he died in reality, there came a thunder-storm so terrific that Sam Clemens at home in bed was certain that Satan had come in person for the half-breed's soul. He covered his head and said his prayers with fearful anxiety lest the evil one might decide to save another trip by taking him along then.

The treasure-digging adventure in the book had this foundation in fact: It was said that two French trappers had once buried a chest of gold about two miles above Hannibal, and that it was still there. Tom Blankenship (*Huck*) one morning said he had dreamed just where the treasure was, and that if the boys—Sam Clemens and John Briggs—would go with him and help dig, he would divide. The boys had great faith in dreams, especially in Tom's dreams. They followed him to a place with some shovels and picks, and he showed them just where to dig. Then he sat down under the shade of a pawpaw bush and gave orders.

They dug nearly all day. *Huck* did n't dig any himself, because he had done the dreaming, which was his share. They did n't find the treasure that day, and next morning they took two long iron rods to push and drive into the ground until they should strike something. They struck a number of things, but when they dug down, it was never the money they found. That night the boys said they would n't dig any more.

But *Huck* had another dream. He dreamed the gold was exactly under the little pawpaw tree. This sounded so circumstantial that they went back and dug another day. It was hot weather, too, August, and that night they were nearly dead. Even *Huck* gave it up then. He said there was something wrong about the way they dug.

This differs a good deal from the treasure incident in the book, but it shows us what respect the boys had for the gifts of the ragamuffin original of *Huck Finn*. Tom Blankenship's brother Ben was also used, and very importantly, in the creation of our beloved *Huck*. Ben was considerably older, but certainly no more reputable, than Tom. He tormented the smaller boys and they had little love for him. Yet somewhere in Ben Blankenship's nature there was a fine, generous strain of humanity that provided Mark Twain with that immortal episode—the sheltering of *Nigger Jim*. This is the real story:

A slave ran off from Monroe County, Missouri, and got across the river into Illinois. Ben used to fish and hunt over there in the swamps, and one day found him. It was considered a most worthy act in those days to return a runaway slave; in fact it was a crime not to do it. Besides, there was for this one a reward of fifty dollars—a fortune to ragged, outcast Ben Blankenship. That money and the honor he could acquire must have been tempting to the waif, but it did not outweigh his human sympathy. Instead of giving him up and claiming the reward, Ben kept the runaway over there in the marshes all summer. The negro fished, and Ben carried him scraps of other food. Then, by and by, the facts leaked out. Some woodchoppers went on a hunt for the fugitive and chased him to what was called "Bird Slough." There, trying to cross a mass of driftwood, he was drowned.

Huck's struggle in the book is between conscience and the law on one side and deep human sympathy on the other. Ben Blankenship's struggle, supposing there was one, would be between sympathy and the offered reward. Neither conscience nor law would trouble him. It was his native humanity that made him shelter the runaway, and it must have been strong and genuine to make him resist the lure of the fifty dollar prize.

Ministers and deacons did not prophesy well for Sam Clemens and his mad companions. They spoke freely of state prison and the gallows. But the boys were a disappointing lot. Will Bowen became a fine river-pilot. Will Pitts was in due time a leading merchant and bank president. John Briggs grew into a well-to-do and highly respected farmer. *Huck Finn*—which is to say, Tom Blankenship—died an honored citizen and justice of the peace in a western town.

THE TRIAL IN TOM BELCHER'S STORE

by Samuel A. Derieux

IT was a plain case of affinity between Davy Allen and Old Man Thornycroft's hound dog, Buck. Davy, hurrying home along the country road one cold winter afternoon, his mind intent on finishing his chores before dark, looked back after passing Old Man Thornycroft's house, to find Buck trying to follow him— *trying* to, because the old man, who hated to see anybody or anything but himself have his way, had chained a heavy block to him to keep him from doing what nature had intended him to do: roam the woods and poke his long nose in every brier patch after rabbits.

At the sight Davy stopped, and the dog came on, dragging behind him in the road the block of wood fastened by a chain to his collar, and trying at the same time to wag his tail. He was tan-colored, lean as a rail, long-eared, a hound every inch; and Davy was a ragged country boy who lived alone with his mother, and who had an old single-barrel shot-gun at home, and who had in his grave boy's eyes a look, clear and unmistakable, of woods and fields.

To say it was love at first sight when that hound, dragging his prison around with him, looked up into the boy's face, and when that ragged boy who loved the woods and had a gun at home looked down into the hound's eyes, would hardly be putting it strong enough. It was more than love—it was perfect understanding,

perfect comprehension. "I 'm your dog," said the hound's upraised, melancholy eyes. "I 'll jump rabbits and bring them around for you to shoot. I 'll make the frosty hills echo with music for you. I'll follow you everywhere you go. I 'm your dog if you want me—yours to the end of my days."

And Davy, looking down into those upraised, beseeching eyes, and at that heavy block of wood, and at the raw place the collar had worn on the neck, then at Old Man Thornycroft's bleak, unpainted house on the hill, with the unhomelike yard and the tumbledown fences, felt a great pity, the pity of the free for the imprisoned, and a great longing to own, not a dog, but this dog.

"Want to come along?" he grinned.

The hound sat down on his haunches, elevated his long nose, and poured out to the cold winter sky the passion and longing of his soul. Davy understood, shook his head, looked once more into the pleading eyes, then at the bleak house which this prisoner had left.

"That ol' devil!" he said. "He ain't fitten to own a dog. Oh, I wish he was mine!"

A moment he hesitated there in the road, then he turned and hurried away from temptation.

"He ain't mine," he muttered.

But temptation followed him as it has followed many a boy and man. A little way down the road was a pasture through which, by a footpath, he could cut off half a mile of the three miles that lay between him and home. Poised on top of the high rail fence that bordered the road, he looked back. The hound was still trying to follow, walking straddle-legged, head down, all entangled with the taut chain that dragged the heavy block. The boy watched the frantic efforts, pity and longing on his face; then he jumped off the fence inside the pasture and hurried on down the hill, face set straight ahead.

He had entered a pine thicket when he heard behind the frantic, choking yelps of a dog in dire distress. Knowing what had happened, he ran back. Within the pasture the hound, only his hind feet touching the ground, was struggling and pawing at the fence. He had jumped, the block had caught and was hanging him. Davy rushed to him. Breathing fast, he unclicked the chain. The block and chain fell on the other side of the fence, and the dog was free. Shrewdly the boy looked back up the road; the woods hid the old man's house from view, and no one was to be seen. With a little grin of triumph he turned and broke into a run down the pasture hill toward the pines, the wind blowing gloriously into his face, the dog galloping beside him.

Still running, the two came out into the road that led home, and suddenly Davy stopped short and his face flushed. Yonder around the bend, on his gray mare, jogged Squire Kirby toward them, his pipe in his mouth, his white beard stuck cozily inside the bosom of his big overcoat. There was no use to run, no use to try to make the dog hide, no use to try to hide himself— the old man had seen them both. Suppose he knew whose dog this was! Heart pounding, Davy waited beside the road.

Mr. Kirby drew rein opposite them and looked down with eyes that twinkled under his bushy white brows. He always stopped to ask the boy how his mother was, and how they were getting along. Davy had been to his house many a time with eggs and chickens to sell, or with a load of seasoned oak wood. Many a time he had warmed before Mr. Kirby's fire in the big living-room and bedroom combined, and eaten Mrs. Kirby's fine white cake covered with frosting. Never before had he felt ill at ease in the presence of the kindly old man.

"That's a genuine hound you got there, son, ain't it?"

"Yes, sir," said Davy.

"Good for rabbits an' 'possums an' coons, eh?"

"He shore is!"

"Well, next big fat 'possum you an' him ketch, you bring that 'possum 'round an' me an' you'll talk business. How's your ma? All right. That's good. Here—"

He reached deep down in a pocket of his enormous faded overcoat, bought out two red apples, and leaned down out of his saddle, which creaked under the strain of his weight.

"Try one of 'em yourself, an' take one of 'em home to your ma. Git up, Mag!"

He jogged on down the road, and the boy, sobered, walked on. One thing was certain, though—Mr. Kirby hadn't known whose dog this was. What difference did it make, anyhow? He hadn't stolen anything. He couldn't let a dog choke to death before his eyes. What did Old Man Thornycroft care about a dog, anyhow, the hard-hearted old skinflint!

He remembered the trouble his mother had had when his father died and Old Man Thornycroft pushed her for a note he had given. He had heard people talk about it at the time, and he remembered how white his mother's face had been. Old Man Thornycroft had refused to wait, and his mother had had to sell five acres of the best land on the little farm to pay the note. It was after the sale that Mr. Kirby, who lived five miles away, had ridden over.

"Why didn't you let me know, Mrs. Allen!" he had demanded. "I would have loaned you the money—gladly, gladly!" He had risen from the fire, and pulled on the same overcoat he wore now. It was faded then, and that was two years ago.

It was sunset when Davy reached home to find his mother out in the clean-swept yard, picking up chips in her apron. From the bedroom window of the little one-storied unpainted house came a bright red glow, and from the kitchen the smell of cooking meat. His mother straightened up from her task with a smile when with his new-found partner he entered the yard.

"Why, Davy," she asked, "where did you get him?"

"He—he just followed me, Ma."

"But whose dog is he?"

"He's mine, Ma—he just took up with me."

"Where, Davy?"

"Oh, way back down the road—in a pasture."

"He must belong to somebody."

"He's just a ol' hound dog, Ma, that's all he is. Lots of hounds don't belong to nobody—everybody knows that, Ma. Look at him, Ma. Mighty nigh starved to death. Lemme keep him. We can feed him on scraps. He can sleep under the house. Me an' him will keep you in rabbits. You won't have to kill no more chickens. Nobody don't want him but me!"

From her gaunt height she looked down into the boy's eager eyes, then at the dog beside him. "All right, son," she said. "If he don't belong to anybody."

That night Davy alternately whistled and talked to the dog beside him as he husked the corn he had raised with his own hands, and chopped the wood he had cut and hauled—for since his father's death he had kept things going. He ate supper in a sort of haze; he hurried out with a tin plate of scraps; he fed the grateful, hungry dog on the kitchen steps. He begged some vaseline from his mother and rubbed it on the sore neck. Then he got two or three empty gunny-sacks out of the corn-crib, crawled under the house to a warm place beside the chimney, and spread them out for a bed. He went into the house whistling; he didn't hear a word of the chapter his mother read out of the Bible. Before he went to bed in the shed-room, he raised the window.

"You all right, old feller?" he called.

Underneath the house he heard the responsive tap-tap of a tail in the dry dust. He climbed out of his clothes, leaving them in a pile in the middle of the floor, tumbled into bed, and pulled the covers high over him.

"Golly!" he said. "Oh, golly!"

Next day he hunted till sundown. The Christmas holidays were on and there was no thought of school. He went only now and then, anyway, for since his father's death there was too much for him to do at home. He hunted in the opposite direction from Old Man Thornycroft's. It was three miles away; barriers of woods and bottoms and hills lay between, and the old man seldom stirred beyond the boundaries of his own farm; but Davy wanted to be on the safe side.

There were moments, though, when he thought of the old man, and wondered if he had missed the dog and whether he would make any search for him. There were sober moments, too, when he thought of his mother and Mr. Kirby, and wished he had told them the truth. But then the long-drawn bay of the hound would come from the bottoms ahead, and he would hurry to the summons, his face flushed and eager. The music of the dog running, the sound of the shots, and his own triumphant yells started many an echo among the silent frosted hills that day. He came home with enough meat to last a week—six rabbits. As he hurried into the yard he held them up for the inspection of his mother, who was feeding the chickens.

"He's the finest rabbit dog ever was, Ma! Oh, golly, he can follow a trail! I never see anything like it, Ma, I never did! I'll skin 'em an' clean 'em after supper. You ought to have saw him, Ma! Golly!"

And while he chopped the wood and milked the cow and fed the mule and skinned the rabbits, he saw other days ahead like this, and whistled and sang and talked to the hound, who followed close at his heels every step he took.

THEN one afternoon, while he was patching the lot fence, with Buck sunning himself near the woodpile, came Old Man Thornycroft. Davy recognized his buggy as it turned the bend in the road. He quickly dropped his tools, called Buck to him, and got behind the house, where he could see without being seen. The buggy stopped in the road, and the old man, his hard, pinched face working, his buggy whip in his hand, came down the walk and called Mrs. Allen out on the porch.

"I just come to tell you," he cried, "that your boy Davy run off with my dog las' Friday evenin'! There ain't no use to deny it. I know all about it. I seen him when he passed in front of the house. I found the block I had chained to the dog beside the road. I heared Squire Jim Kirby talkin' to some men in Tom Belcher's sto' this very mornin'; just happened to overhear him as I come in. 'A boy an' a dog,' he says, 'is the happiest combination in nater.' Then he went on to tell about your boy an' a tan dog. He had met 'em in the road. Met 'em when? Last Friday evenin'. Oh, there ain't no use to deny it, Mrs. Allen! Your boy Davy—he stole my dog!"

"Mr. Thornycroft"—Davy could not see his mother, but he could hear her voice tremble—"he did not know whose dog it was!"

"He didn't? He didn't?" yelled the old man. "An' him a boy that knows ever' dog for ten miles around! Right in front of my house, I tell you—that's where he picked him up, that's where he tolled him off! Didn't I tell you, woman, I seen him pass? Didn't I tell you I found the block down the road? Didn't know whose dog it was? Ridiculous, ridiculous! Call him, ask him, face him with it. Likely he'll lie— but you'll see his face. Call him, that's all I ask. Call him!"

"Davy!" called Mrs. Allen. "Davy!"

Just a moment the boy hesitated. Then he went around the house. The hound stuck very close to him, eyes full of terror, tail tucked as he looked at the old man.

"There he is—with my dog!" cried the old man. "You didn't know whose dog it was, did you, son? Eh? You didn't know, now, did you?"

"Yes," cried the boy, "I knowed!"

"Hear that, Mrs. Allen? Did he know? What do you say now? He stole my dog, didn't he? That's what he done, didn't he? Answer me, woman! You come here!" he yelled, his face livid, and started, whip raised, toward boy and dog.

There were some smooth white stones the size of hen's eggs arranged around a flower bed in the yard, and Davy stood near these stones—and now, quick as a flash, he stooped down and picked one up.

"You stop!" he panted, his face very white.

His mother cried out and came running toward him, but Thornycroft had stopped. No man in his right mind wants to advance on a country boy with a rock. Goliath tried it once.

"All right!" screamed the old man. "You steal first—then you try to assault an old man! I didn't come here to raise no row. I just came here to warn you, Mrs. Allen. I'll have the law on that boy—I'll have the law on him before another sun sets!"

He turned and hurried toward the buggy. Davy dropped the rock. Mrs. Allen stood looking at the old miser, who was clambering into his buggy, with a sort of horror. Then she ran toward the boy.

"Oh, Davy, run after him! Take the dog to him! He's terrible, Davy, terrible! Run after him—anything—anything!"

But the boy looked up at her with grim mouth and hard eyes.

"I ain't a-goin' to do it, Ma!" he said.

It was after supper that very night that the summons came. Bob Kelley, rural policeman, brought it.

"Me an' Squire Kirby went to town this mornin'," he said, "to look up some things about court in the mornin'. This evenin' we run into Old Man Thornycroft on the street, lookin' for us. He was awful excited. He had been to Mr. Kirby's house, an' found out Mr. Kirby was in town, an' followed us. He wanted a warrant swore out right there. Mr. Kirby tried to argue with him, but it warn't no use. So at last Mr. Kirby turned to me. 'You go on back, Bob,' he said. 'This'll give me some more lookin' up to do. Tell my wife I'll just spend the night with Judge Fowler, an' git back in time for court in Belcher's sto' in the mornin'. An', Bob, you just stop by Mrs. Allen's—she's guardian of the boy—an' tell her I say to bring him to Belcher's sto' to-morrow mornin' at nine. You be there, too, Mr. Thornycroft—an', by the way, bring that block of wood you been talkin' about.' "

That was all the squire had said, declared the rural policeman. No, he hadn't sent any other message—just said he would read up on the case. The rural policeman went out and closed the door behind him. It had been informal, hap-hazard, like the life of the community in which they lived. But, for all that, the law had knocked at the door of the Widow Allen, and left a white-faced mother and a bewildered boy behind.

They tried to resume their usual employments. Mrs. Allen sat down beside the table, picked up her sewing, and put her glasses on, but her hands trembled when she tried to thread the needle. Davy sat on a split-bottom chair in the corner, his feet up on the rungs, and tried to be still; but his heart was pounding fast and there was a lump in his throat. Presently he got up and went out-of-doors—to get in some kindling on the back porch before it snowed, he told his mother. But he went because he couldn't sit there any longer, because he was about to explode with rage and grief and fear and bitterness.

He did not go toward the woodpile— what difference did dry kindling make now? At the side of the house he stooped down and softly called Buck. The hound came to him, wriggling along under the beams, and he leaned against the house and lovingly pulled the brier-torn ears. A long time he stayed there, feeling on his face already the fine mist of snow. To-morrow the ground would be white; it didn't snow often in that country; day after to-morrow everybody would hunt rabbits—everybody but him and Buck.

IT was still snowing when next morning he and his mother drove out of the yard and he turned the head of the reluctant old mule in the direction of Belcher's store. A bitter wind cut their faces, but it was not so bitter as the heart of the boy. Only twice on that five-mile ride did he speak. The first time was when he looked back to find Buck, whom they had left at home, thinking he would stay under the house on such a day, following very close behind the buggy.

"Might as well let him come on," said the boy.

The second time was when they came in sight of Belcher's store, dim yonder through the swirling snow. Then he looked up into his mother's face.

"Ma," he said grimly, "I ain't no thief!"

She smiled as bravely as she could with her stiffened face and with the tears so near the surface. She told him that she knew it, and that everybody knew it. But there was no answering smile on the boy's set face.

The squire's gray mare, standing huddled up in the midst of other horses and of buggies under the shed near the store, told that court had probably already convened. Hands numb, the boy hitched the old mule to the only rack left under the shed, then made Buck lie down under the buggy. Heart pounding, he went up on the store porch with his mother and pushed the door open.

There was a commotion when they entered. The men, standing about the pot-bellied stove, their overcoats steaming, made way for them. Old Man Thornycroft looked quickly and triumphantly around. In the rear of the store the squire rose from a table, in front of which was a cleared space.

"Pull up a chair nigh the stove for Mrs. Allen, Tom Belcher," he said. "I'm busy tryin' this chicken-stealin' case. When I get through, Mrs. Allen, if you're ready I'll call your case."

Davy stood beside his mother while the trial proceeded. Some of the fight had left him now, crowded down here among all these grown men, and especially in the presence of Mr. Kirby. But with growing anxiety he heard the sharp questions the magistrate asked; he saw the frown of justice, he heard the sentence, sixty days on the gang. And the man had stolen only a chicken—and he had run off with another man's dog!

"The old man's rough this mornin'," a man whispered to another above him; and he saw the furtive grin on the face of Old Man Thornycroft, who leaned against the counter, waiting.

His heart jumped into his mouth when after a silence the magistrate spoke: "Mr. Thornycroft, step forward, sir. Put your hand on the book here. Now tell us about that dog of yours that was stole."

Looking first at the magistrate, then at the crowd, as if to impress them also, the old man told, in a high-pitched, excited voice, all the details—his seeing Davy Allen pass in front of his house last Friday afternoon, his missing the dog, his finding the block of wood down the road beside the pasture fence, his overhearing the squire's talk right here in the store, his calling on Mrs. Allen, the boy's threatening him.

"I tell you," he cried, "that's a dangerous character—that boy!"

"Is that all you've got to say?" asked the squire.

"It's enough, ain't it?" demanded Thornycroft angrily.

The squire nodded. "I think so," he said quietly. "Stand aside. Davy Allen, step forward. Put your hand on the book here, son. Davy, how old are you?"

The boy gulped. "Thirteen years old, goin' on fo'teen."

"You're old enough, son, to know the nater of the oath you're about to take. For over two years you've been the mainstay an' support of your mother. You've had to carry the burdens and responsibilities of a man, Davy. The testimony you give in this case will be the truth, the whole truth an' nothin' but the truth, so help you God. What about it?"

Davy nodded, his face very white.

"All right, now. Tell us about it. Talk loud so we can hear—all of us."

The boy's eyes never left Mr. Kirby's

while he talked. Something in them held him, fascinated him, overawed him. Very large and imposing he looked there behind his little table, with his faded old overcoat on, and there was no sound in the room but the boy's clear voice.

"An' you come off an' left the dog at first?"

"Yes, sir."

"An' you didn't unfasten the chain from the block till the dog got caught in the fence?"

"No, sir, I didn't."

"Did you try to get him to follow you then?"

"No, sir, he wanted to."

"Ask him, Mr. Kirby," broke in Thornycroft angrily, "if he tried to drive him home!"

"I'll ask him whatever seems fit an' right to me, sir," said Mr. Kirby. "What did you tell your ma, Davy, when you got home?"

"I told her he followed me."

"Did you tell her whose dog he was?"

"No, sir."

"Ain't that what you ought to have done? Ain't it?"

Davy hesitated. "Yes, sir."

There was a slight shuffling movement among the men crowded about. Somebody cleared his throat. Mr. Kirby resumed:—

"This block you been tellin' about— how was it fastened to the dog?"

"Thar was a chain fastened to the block by a staple. The other end was fastened to the collar."

"How heavy do you think that block was?"

"About ten pound, I reckon."

"Five," broke in Old Man Thornycroft with a sneer.

Mr. Kirby turned to him. "You fetched it with you, didn't you? I told you to. It's evidence. Bob Kelley, go out to Mr. Thornycroft's buggy an' bring that block

of wood into court."

The room was silent while the rural policeman was gone. Davy still stood in the cleared space before Mr. Kirby, his ragged overcoat on, his tattered hat in his hand, breathing fast, afraid to look at his mother. Everybody turned when Kelley came in with the block of wood. Everybody craned his neck to watch, while at the magistrate's order Kelley weighed the block of wood on the store's scales, which he put on the magistrate's table.

"Fo'teen pounds," said Mr. Kirby. "Take the scales away."

"It had rubbed all the skin off'n the dog's neck," broke in Davy impulsively. "It was all raw an' bleedin'."

"Aw, that ain't so!" cried Thornycroft.

"Is the dog out there?" asked Mr. Kirby.

"Yes, sir, under the buggy."

"Bob Kelley, you go out an' bring that dog into court."

The rural policeman went out, and came back with the hound, who looked eagerly up from one face to the other, then, seeing Davy, came to him and stood against him, still looking around with that expression of melancholy on his face that a hound dog always wears except when he's in action.

"Bring the dog here, son!" commanded Mr. Kirby. He examined the raw place on the neck. "Any of you gentlemen care to take a look?"

"It was worse than that," declared Davy, "till I rubbed vaseleen on it."

Old Man Thornycroft pushed forward, face quivering. "What's all this got to do with the boy stealin' the dog?" he demanded. "That's what I want to know— what's it got to do?"

"Mr. Thornycroft," said Mr. Kirby, "at nine o'clock this mornin' this place ceased to be Tom Belcher's sto', an' become a court of justice. Some things are seemly in a court, some not. You stand back there!"

The old man stepped back to the counter, and stood pulling his chin, his eyes running over the crowd of faces.

"Davy Allen," spoke Mr. Kirby, "you stand back there with your ma. Tom Belcher, make way for him. And, Tom, s'pose you put another stick of wood in that stove an' poke up the fire." He took

as fur back as records go, a dog's been the friend, companion an' protector of man.

"Last night, in the libery of my old friend Judge Fowler in town, I looked up some things about this dog question. I find that there have been some queer decisions handed down by the courts, showin' that the law does recognize the fact that a dog

"Old Man Thornycroft pushed forward, face quivering. 'What's all this got to do with the boy stealin' the dog?' he demanded."

off his glasses, blew on them, polished them with his handkerchief, and readjusted them. Then, leaning back in his chair, he spoke:—

"Gentlemen, from the beginnin' of time,

is different from other four-footed critters. For instance, it has been held that a dog has a right to protect not only his life but his dignity; that where a man worries a dog beyond what would be reasonable to expect any self-respectin' critter to stand, that dog has a right to bite that man, an' that man can't collect any damages—provided the bitin' is done at the time of the worryin' an' in sudden heat an' passion. That has been held in the courts, gentlemen. The law that holds for man holds for dogs.

"Another thing: If the engineer of a railroad train sees a cow or a horse or a sheep on the track, or a hog, he must stop the train or the road is liable for any damage done 'em. But if he sees a man walkin' along the track he has a right to presume that the man, bein' a critter of more or less intelligence, will git off, an' he is not called on to stop under ordinary circumstances. The same thing holds true of a dog. The engineer has a right to presume that the dog, bein' a critter of intelligence, will get off the track. Here again the law is the same for dog an' man.

"But if the engineer has reason to believe that the man's mind is took up with some object of an engrossin' nater, he is supposed to stop the train till the man comes to himself an' looks around. The same thing holds true of a dog. If the engineer has reason to suspect that the dog's mind is occupied with some engrossin' topic, he must stop the train. That case has been tested in this very State, where a dog was on the track settin' a covey of birds in the adjoinin' field. The railroad was held responsible for the death of that dog, because the engineer ought to have known by the action of the dog that his mind was on somethin' else beside railroad trains an' locomotives."

Every one was listening so closely that the whispered sneering comment of Old Man Thornycroft to the man next to him was audible: "What's all this got to do with the case?"

"The p'int I'm gettin' to is this," went on Mr. Kirby, not paying attention to him.

"A dog is not like a cow or a horse or any four-footed critter. He's a individual, an' so the courts have held in spirit if not in actual words. Now this court of mine here in Tom Belcher's sto' ain't like other courts. I have to do the decidin' myself; I have to interpret the true spirit of the law, without technicalities an' quibbles such as becloud it in other an' higher courts. An' I hold that since a dog is *de facto* an' *de jure* an individual he has a right to life, liberty an' the pursuit of happiness.

"Therefore, gentlemen, I hold that that houn' dog, Buck, had a perfect right to follow that boy, Davy Allen, there; an' I hold that Davy Allen was not called on to drive that dog back, or interfere in any way with that dog followin' him if the dog so chose. You've heard the evidence of the boy. You know, an' I know, he has spoke the truth this day, an' there ain't no evidence to the contrary. The boy did not entice the dog. He even went down the road, leavin' him behind. He run back only when the dog was in dire need an' chokin' to death. He wasn't called on to put that block an' chain back on the dog. He couldn't help it if the dog followed him. He no more stole that dog than I stole him. He's no more a thief than I am. I dismiss this case, Mr. Thornycroft, this case you've brought against Davy Allen. I declare him innocent of the charge of theft. I set it down right here on the records of this court."

"Davy!" gasped Mrs. Allen. "Davy!"

But, face working, eyes blazing, Old Man Thornycroft started forward, and the dog, panting, shrank between boy and mother. "Jim Kirby!" cried the old man, stopping for a moment in the cleared space. "You're magistrate. What you say goes. But that dog thar—he's mine! He's my property—mine by law!" He jerked a piece of rope out of his overcoat pocket and came on toward the cowering dog. "Tom Belcher! Bob Kelley! Stop that dog! He's mine!"

"Davy!" Mrs. Allen was holding the boy. "Don't—don't say anything. You're free to go home. Your record's clear. The dog's his!"

"Hold on!" Mr. Kirby had risen from his chair. "You come back here, Mr. Thornycroft. This court's not adjourned yet. If you don't get back, I'll stick a fine to you, for contempt, you'll remember the rest of your days. You stand where you are, sir! Right there! Don't move till I'm through!"

Quivering, the old man stood where he was. Mr. Kirby sat down, face flushed, eyes blazing. "Punch up that fire, Tom Belcher," he said. "I ain't through yet."

The hound came trembling back to Davy, looked up in his face, licked his hand, then sat down at the side opposite his former master, looking around now and then at the old man, terror in his eyes. In the midst of a deathly silence the magistrate resumed:—

"What I was goin' to say, gentlemen, is this: I'm not only magistrate; I'm an officer in an organization that you country fellers likely don't know of, an organization known as the Society for the Prevention of Cruelty to Animals. As such an officer it's my duty to report an' bring to trial any man who treats a dumb brute in a cruel an' inhuman way. Mr. Thornycroft, judgin' by the looks of that houn', you ain't give him enough to eat to keep a cat alive, an' a cat, we all know, don't eat much—just messes over her victuals. You condemned that po' beast, for no fault of his own, to the life of a felon. A houn' that ain't happy, at best he's melancholy; an' a houn' that ain't allowed to run free is of all critters the wretchedest. This houn's neck is rubbed raw. God only knows what he's suffered in mind an' body. A man that would treat a dog that way ain't fitten to own one. An' I hereby notify you that, on the evidence of this boy, an' the evidence before our eyes, I will indict you for breakin' the law regardin' the treatment of animals; an' I notify you, furthermore, that as magistrate I'll put the law on you for that same thing. An' it might be interestin' to you to know, sir, that I can fine you as much as five hundred dollars, or send you to jail for one year, or both, if I see fit—an' there ain't no tellin' but what I will see fit, sir."

He looked sternly at Thornycroft.

"Now I'm goin' to make a proposition that I advise you to jump at like you never jumped at anything before. If you will give up that houn' Buck—to me, say, or to anybody I decide will be kind to him— I will let the matter drop. If you will go home like a peaceable citizen, you won't hear no more about it from me; but if you don't—"

"Git out of my way!" cried Old Man Thornycroft. "All of you! I'm goin'—I'm goin'!"

"Hold on!" said Mr. Kirby, when he had got almost to the door. "Do you, in the presence of these witnesses, turn over this dog to me, relinquishin' all claims to him, on the conditions named? Answer yes or no."

There was a moment's silence; then the old man cried out:—

"Take the old hound! He ain't wuth the salt in his victuals!"

He jerked the door open.

"Yes or no?" called Mr. Kirby inexorably.

"Yes!" yelled the old man, and slammed the door behind him.

"One minute, gentlemen," said Mr. Kirby, rising from the table and gathering his papers and records together. "Just one more thing: If anybody here has any evidence, or knows of any, tendin' to show that this boy, Davy Allen, is not the proper person to turn over a houn' dog to, I hope he will speak up." He waited a moment.

"In the absence of any objections, an' considerin' the evidence that's been given here this mornin', I think I'll just let that dog go back the way he come. Thank you, gentlemen. Court's adjourned!"

KING TRISANKU

by Henry W. Longfellow

VISWAMÍTRA the Magician,
  By his spells and incantations,
Up to Indra's realms elysian
  Raised Trisanku, king of nations.

Indra and the gods offended
  Hurled him downward, and descending
In the air he hung suspended,
  With these equal powers contending.

Thus by aspirations lifted,
  By misgivings downward driven,
Human hearts are tossed and drifted
  Midway between earth and heaven.

DANNY AND THE "MAJOR"

by Gertrude P. Greble

PAPA! Papa! The shrill, childish voice echoed sharply through the quiet house, and a small figure appeared upon the threshold of the door which led to Captain Kent's office, as if suddenly blown there by the March gale which at the same moment invaded the apartment.

"My son," said the officer in a tone of mild exasperation, laying a restraining hand upon his fluttering papers, "will you be kind enough first of all to shut the front door? And now"—when he had been obeyed with an energy which shook the house to its foundations—"take off your hat, like a gentleman."

The child snatched it off, and advanced to lay an appealing hand upon his father's arm.

"Don't make me wait for anything more, papa," he pleaded. "It is important! It is, indeed. Mackenzie begs you to come to the corral right away. The 'Major' has come back!"

"The Major! What Major?"

"Why, our Major—Captain Egerton's Major."

"Impossible!"

"But he has indeed, papa!" exclaimed the eager boy. "The herders found him up in a ravine, and he followed the horses home, and he is so lame he can hardly walk, and the corral-master says he has enough worthless brutes about now, so he is going to shoot him, and Mackenzie said to tell you to come at once, because if you did n't it might be too late—"

Two great tears overflowed from the violet eyes and rolled down the lad's cheeks, but little Dan had small reason to fear lack of attention now! Almost before his hasty explanation was completed, the cavalryman had thrown his cape about his shoulders and started for the corral at a pace satisfying even to his impatient son.

To make you understand what he found there, and what it meant, I must go back to the beginning and tell about Danny; and then—because this story is quite as much, and perhaps a little more, the Major's—about the Major too.

Danny could not remember his introduction to the frontier garrison which constituted his world, but he was never tired of hearing about it. And during the long winter evenings, when "retreat" had sounded and the soldiers had dispersed to their log barracks, the captain would seat himself beside the big stove, with his pipe between his teeth; and Danny, his sled put away, his gaiters and mittens hung up to dry by the hall fire, and his buffalo overcoat—an exact imitation of his father's big one—safe on its peg, would crawl into his father's arms and nestle close to his heart. And after a silence of greater or less length, the officer would begin and go over the details so well known to them both: of his astonishment when, on coming from "stables" one bitter winter afternoon, he had stamped the snow from his shoes and thrown aside his overcoat, to behold a stout woman with a white bundle in her arms, saying, "Will ye look at the recruit I've brought ye, Captain?"—and of how, when he had recovered from his surprise, he had examined her offering and found beneath of a lot of wrappings two tiny hands, a small face with blinking eyes, and plentiful black hair. This last never failed to impress Danny, for by the time he was old enough to notice things his hair was as yellow as the Indian maize which ripened by the river.

The years had sped swiftly after that winter evening; and if, as his father said, he had come into the world to the sound of a trumpet, he grew up to the rattle of drums and the patter of musketry in the days when Custer lived and a soldier's work was full of activity and danger. His ears became accustomed to the thrumming of the "long roll"; his odd hours were full of the excitement caused by the bustle of incoming and outgoing scouting-parties, and, at times, of watching, with far more interest than fear, those tiny specks he could just discern skirting the horizon, which he was told were "hostiles."

It was small wonder that in such an atmosphere he should develop rapidly, that he should become healthy, as a child must who spends ten hours of the twenty-four with the winds of the prairie filling his strong young lungs; that he should become honest and truth-telling as a soldier's son should be; gentle to the weaker sex, as represented by his mother and the tiny sister who bore her name; and full of an affectionate kindliness which won him the most loyal devotion from the rough troopers who shared his outdoor life.

At the time our story opens he was seven—a tall lad, whose muscles were already like fine steel threads, whose skin had tanned to a beautiful golden brown, with violet eyes, and hair which fell in tangles about his shoulders.

Those curls, heavy and girlish, had been a constant source of woe to the boy, till one never-to-be-forgotten day, when he had stood at the gate of the stockade to see the famous "Seventh" sweep by, on its way to some distant trouble. The scene had been one to remember—the smooth action of the seasoned horses, the careless swing of their riders, to whom excitement had become as the air they breathed! But of it all little Dan retained one impression only—that of the adored Custer at the column's head, his face thin, eager, resolute, and with curls, as yellow as Danny's own, falling over his shoulders!

From that hour the boy's ringlets became his most cherished possession—a connecting-link between the idolized leader of those toughened Indian-fighters and his small personality.

And now for the Major! With regard to him I confess my courage fails; for what woman's feeble pen can hope to do justice to the splendid piece of horse-flesh which answered to that name?

Two years before the March afternoon on which our story opens, an additional troop had been ordered to Fort B—— to reinforce the hard-worked garrison. The officer in command was an old friend of Captain Kent; and on the day of its arrival, shortly before sunset, Danny started off to inspect the new horses and make the acquaintance of their riders.

His intention was not carried out.

As he reached the path which led to the spot where the detachment had gone into camp for the night, he met a trooper leading a horse by the bridle, and carrying a blanket and halter over the other arm. The man's campaign dress proclaimed him a new-comer. He was tall and thin, and covered with dust from his recent ride. But neither the dust, nor the ragged stubble upon his unshaven face, could conceal the kindliness of his expression. Danny stepped aside to let him pass.

"Good evening, Corporal," he said politely, after a brief glance at the soldier's chevrons.

The trooper halted. "Gude evenin' t' yirsel', laddie," he answered in a voice whose deep tones instantly made their way to the boy's friendly heart. "I 'm after a bed for the Major; can ye show me the way tae the corral?"

Dan regarded him gravely. "I 'll show you the way to the corral with pleasure," he replied; "but you must be mistaken about a major. Papa said Captain Egerton was in command of this troop, and he is going to stay with us; so he has a bed."

For a minute the soldier looked puzzled, then he laughed.

"Hoot, laddie!" he exclaimed good-naturedly; "it 's no for anny two-legged major I 'm workin'. It 's for this vera beastie ye see at t' back, mon! And it 's a bad day he 's hed of it, and hungry an' tired he is; so stir yirsel' an' lead the way, for I heve n't a knowledge o' these pairts as yet."

Dan examined the animal critically. "He seems to be a fine horse," he remarked in the judicial tone he had heard from the officers.

The soldier smiled. "Ay," he answered briefly; "he is."

"Has he come far to-day?"

"The neighborhood o' seventy miles, aboot."

The man resumed his progress in the direction of the stables, and the little boy trotted by his side, every energy absorbed in the endeavor to keep up with his long strides. After an interval the child observed: "I don't see why you did n't put him on the picket-line with the other horses. Was n't there room for him?"

"Room for him?" repeated the trooper, disgustedly; "ay, there 'd be room and tae spare gin he wanted it, which he 'll no do while he has old John tae find him shelter. Ye 're a bit blowed, ain't ye, laddie?" he added kindly; for the first time noticing the child's breathless condition. "I 'm forgettin' t' difference in the length o' t' laigs. We 'll get over the groun' feyster gin I make the Major carry ye."

Danny looked doubtfully at the horse's dusty sides and drooping head. "Is n't he too tired?" he asked, divided between his desire for the offered ride and compassion for the evidently weary animal.

His companion regarded him with approval. "Now thet 's richt!" he said. "There ain't many little chaps 't w'u'd think o' the horse when they hed a chance tae ride. I like ye for it, lad! As for tirin' him— I w'u'dna ride him mesel', but ye 're no gret weight, an' I 'm thinkin' it 'll get him his supper the quicker."

A moment later the radiant child was seated astride the great bronze beast, and the trio pursued its way to the corral in a silence which the soldier was too weary —and Danny too happy—to break.

When Dan went home after seeing Mackenzie feed and groom his charge, he was conscious of having found a new interest in life, and of having made a new friend; and his satisfaction was complete when, on recounting his experiences at the dinner-table that evening, he was informed that the horse belonged to Captain Egerton, and that henceforth he might see him as often as he liked.

The summer days which followed were full of joy. Dan passed them for the most part in Mackenzie's company, and a very real friendship sprang up between the veteran and his small companion—a friendship that found a cementing bond in their affection for the Major. Nothing so perfect of its kind as that splendid animal had ever before come in the boy's way.

Had he been asked, it might have been difficult for him to tell which of his new friends—the human or the equine—he loved the better. But there was no question which was the more important. He trotted at Mackenzie's heels when he took his charge to and from the watering-trough; he perched himself on the cross-bar of the Major's box-stall to superintend his toilet; and he spent long hours scrubbing away with a bit of rag upon the brass mountings of the horse's saddle and bridle, on those days when the trooper was obliged to prepare for inspection—betaking himself afterward to the drill-ground to revel in the result of his labors.

And had you seen the beautiful beast as he appeared at inspection,—the brass trimmings upon which so much loving care had been expended flashing in the sunlight, his bronze coat like finest satin, his powerful limbs motionless, and with only the fire in the deep eyes and the quiver of the wide nostrils to tell how strong was the sense of duty which controlled his impatience for the command which should put in motion the troop he led,—you would not have wondered at Danny's enthusiasm —an enthusiasm which gradually increased into a great and real love, which it was easy to see the Major reciprocated in his dumb fashion.

So the weeks passed, and the long hot days grew short, and winter came and went—and with the return of summer little Dan experienced his first sorrow.

Captain Egerton's troop was ordered out on a difficult and dangerous scout; there was a battle,—a thing only too common in those wild days,—and at the end of it the gallant captain lay crippled by a gun-shot wound, and Major, swept away by the savages, had vanished as if swallowed by the treacherous quicksands which lined the river-bank.

For days after the first shock of his grief was over, the child continued to hope for the horse's return. For days he mounted to the highest point of the block-house to search for the furthest reaches of the empty prairie, confident that if the sagacious animal was alive he would find his way back. But months passed, and another winter dragged itself away, and little by little the boy abandoned hope, and settled down to the sorrowful conviction that the horse, too, had fallen a victim to the Indians.

And now he had returned! And what a home-coming!

Mackenzie and he had often talked of such a possibility—Mackenzie, who, with his beloved horse gone, and his master in the East on leave, had been even more disconsolate than Danny; together, the pair had pictured it in divers ways. Sometimes it was one of them who was to find him, sometimes the other; but in every case they had thought of it as a sort of triumphal progress, the coming of a hero who returned to claim his own. Never like this—pitiful, starved, unknown, and despised, in the very place where he had been so easily supreme! "Oh!" thought Danny, "if only the old troop had been here! Some one who loved him! Some one to remember besides Mackenzie and me!" There was a great sob in his throat as he ran by his father's side in the direction of the corral—he was half afraid of what he might find by the time that he reached it.

And when the two finally did reach it, the scene which met their gaze was so remarkable that even the officer paused in breathless amazement.

Prostrate on the earth, covered with dirt, his surly face purple, his feet kicking aimlessly in the air, lay the corral-master—a government rifle, which had evidently slipped from his grasp, on the ground beside him. And upon his chest, holding him in a grip of iron, his face white with an anger too deep for words, sat the Scotch corporal! At the left—a rusty and apparently lifeless mass—lay the Major's prostrate form. And about the group stood the employees of the stockyard.

squeeze which set him fairly gasping, and rose. "Chokin' 'u'd be tae gude for him, Capt'in," he said, as the corral-master struggled to his feet.

"What is the meaning of this performance?" inquired the officer. The trooper made no reply, and O'Reilly, emboldened, began a halting explanation.

"Wait till you are spoken to," command-

" 'What is the meaning of this performance?' inquired the officer."

The sounds which issued from the corral-master's throat made Danny think of the bellowing of those bulls which were sometimes confined in that part of the inclosure; he crept to his father's side and laid hold of his cape. The overseer's face was rapidly assuming a still deeper tint, and the captain went forward:

"You are choking that man, Mackenzie," he said sharply; "let him up at once!"

The corporal glanced up at him with an expression of relief, gave his victim a final

ed Captain Kent, sternly. He knew that Mackenzie was upon ordinary occasions the mildest and least aggressive of men.

The group about them began insensibly to melt away, excepting a few whose curiosity was sufficient to overcome their prudence.

Mackenzie pointed from the gun to the Major, with a gesture more eloquent than words.

"He tried tae steal a march on me, Capt'in," he said huskily. "I telt him tae wait till the laddie fetched ye, and I went for water for the puir beast; and when I coom back—weel, if shootin' hadna been altegither tae gude for him, he w'u'dna be here noo! Thet 's ae!"

"What have you to say to this, O'Reilly?"

"Sure I thought it would be a mercy to the poor beast to put him out of his misery," answered the man, in an injured tone. "I tried to do it unbeknownst to the corporal, knowin' how fond of him he used to be—and it 's small thanks I got for me pains! Next time I 'll leave him to settle his affairs himself. Look at the brute, Captain," he added; "it 's only a fool that would care to prolong his sufferin'." He was evidently sincere, and there seemed to be some truth in what he said.

"I 'm afraid he is right, Mackenzie," said the officer, sadly, as he followed the two men to the side of the panting animal.

Mackenzie broke down. "Ah! don't ye turn against him, too, Capt'in," he faltered. "Think o' the time he 's had gettin' here, and gi'e him a chance. He sha'n't trouble no one, and I'll work it square. If he don't show some sort o' improvement by this time to-morrow, I gi'e ye ma word I 'll make na trouble. It 's starved he is, and winded; but he 's nae deid yet, and while there 's life there 's hope!"

The captain turned away—the horse was a painful spectacle. "Very well," he said; "you may have your way for the present; but I think your labor will be wasted. I agree with O'Reilly: the most merciful thing would be to end his suffering at once."

Mackenzie moved to his side. "I 'll no forget what ye 've done for me this day," he said gratefully. "There 's ane more thing ye can do, if ye will, tae complete the gude wark. It is against orders to sell us whusky at the canteen, and whusky is what the puir beastie wants just noo. Would ye mind givin' me an order for a gallon o' the same?"

Captain Kent hesitated. "I can trust you perfectly, Mackenzie," he said (the corporal was invariably steady); "but a gallon of whisky might cause a lot of mischief."

"It 'll no," was the earnest response. "It 'll be doon the Major's throat before it hes time tae make any trouble."

The corporal's tone was a sufficient guarantee of the safety of the venture. The officer tore off the corner of an envelope, and scribbled the necessary order.

"I shall hold you responsible," he said.

Mackenzie nodded. "Yes, sir—thank ye, sir," he murmured, saluting hastily, as he started from the inclosure upon a run; and by the time Captain Kent had once more regained the garrison, he was on his way back to the corral from the trader's where the necessary liquor was kept.

No especial arguments were needed by Mackenzie to enlist the sympathies of his comrades in behalf of his fallen favorite: soldiers, as a rule, are warm-hearted men, and in the cavalry their calling fosters a love for horses. When little Dan went home at sunset, kindly hands had laid the old horse in the one box-stall the troopstable afforded, and liberal doses of whisky and water had stayed his failing strength. Through the long night the trooper tended him faithfully, watching his heaving sides by the light of a solitary lantern, and plying him, as occasion demanded, with additional draughts of the stimulant; and when morning came the change for the better was so pronounced that even O'Reilly was forced into the admission that hope was once more possible.

After the first few days the animal gained steadily. At the end of a month he was able to hobble out with the herd, the shadow of his old self. More than that he seemed likely never to become. His hoofs were cracked and torn from his long wandering over the alkali plains, his breath came rumblingly from his deep chest, and his eyes had a look of patient submission in their soft depths, which seemed to say that he understood fully the kindness which had been shown him, and would repay it to the best of his ability. The old ambition, the old fire, were things of the past. He was quite content now to browse along in rear of the herd, or to stand for hours beside little Dan perched upon a wood-pile, nudging him for the sugar which was always forthcoming, nipping lovingly at the buttons on his small trousers, or—immovable as a statue—bowing his beautiful head when the boy frolicked at his feet. And though, as time went on and the summer drills began, he would prick up his ears at the sound of the well-remembered calls, and follow the battalion with his eyes as it swept by the spot where he was picketed, it was only with a passing interest, and he would return to his grazing in placid content.

Danny never abandoned the hope of seeing him in his old place at the head of a troop. He spent hours feeding, grooming, and watering him, and when there was nothing else to be done he was quite content to perch beside him in the sunshine, and dream of the wonderful things he should do when he was once more well. If he had admired him before, he adored him now; and still the wildest flight of his imagination was not sufficient to suggest the heroic feat which this dumb friend was actually to accomplish for his sake, the great and final proof of his affection for the child who loved him, and which was to make not only the Major, but Danny too, famous!

To tell you about it, we must pass over the weeks which witnessed the horse's gradual recovery to the scorching afternoon that found him, almost his old self, saddled with Dan's own small saddle, and pawing the ground impatiently in front of Captain Kent's quarters. The loving care of the past few months had been amply rewarded. Some time before he had been pronounced fit for light work, and that afternoon Dan was to have his first ride upon the Major's back.

Mackenzie had been for several weeks suffering from a sprained wrist which prevented his doing the usual guard-duty, and in order to give him some occupation he had been detailed to superintend the herding of the quartermaster's horses—going with them to the grazing-ground in the morning, and then returning to the post until the afternoon, when he went out to assist in bringing them home.

On the present occasion, as a special favor and to celebrate the Major's recovery, Mackenzie begged that Dan might go with him. And when the child came out and prepared to mount it would be hard to say which was the happier, he or the trooper who swung him so proudly to his place.

"You are sure it is safe, Mackenzie?" said Mrs. Kent, a little anxiously, as from the porch she watched the start for the grazing-ground.

"Sure ma'am," answered the soldier, emphatically, as he made a final examination of the girths, little dreaming how much was to depend upon his care in the course of that eventful afternoon; "the beastie knows him as well as ye do yirsel'. It 's no for naething the lad has spent his time. He 'll no hurt him!"

He gathered up the reins and put them into Danny's hands as he spoke, swung himself upon his own bony gray, and they started.

In those days the summer months were always full of uneasiness and dread: the

Indians were especially restless at that time of year, and precautions were doubled; but the weeks which had gone had sped swiftly and quietly in little Dan's home. Rumors of approaching trouble had reached it from time to time; occasional false alarms had sounded, and hurried scouts had been made—only to prove the absence of any foe; and gradually the command had settled down to the conviction that for once they were to be left in peace.

On the afternoon in question nothing could have seemed more tranquil than the scene which unfolded itself before Mackenzie and his charge when, having passed through the gate of the stockade, they turned their horses' heads in the direction of the herd, which they could just discern in the distance as so many specks against the sky.

On the right the Missouri River wound like a great yellow snake from the far northern horizon; on every other side lay the rolling prairie, with only that thread of green along the river-bottom to break its level expanse. Dan had heard of the grandeur of the sea, but he sometimes wondered if anything could seem more imposing than those wide reaches of treeless, turf-covered plain.

The animals were restless and uneasy in spite of the heat, and after a short interval Mackenzie turned from the "trail" and started across the open country.

"Dinna ye go tae fast, lad," he said as the Major stretched his neck with an evident inclination to outstrip his companion. "There 's gopher-holes in plenty hereaboots, and gin ye strike one o' them our ride 's up! Ye sit yir horse like a sodger," he added admiringly; "I 'll hef ye made assistant herder yet!" Danny smiled broadly at the joke, sitting very square in his saddle, in perfect enjoyment of his new accomplishment.

After a canter of some twenty minutes the corporal reined in his horse.

"I can't think what 's happened tae O'Farrell tae let the beasties get sae far away," he muttered discontentedly. "There 's nae grass to speak of over there. I told him aboot it this mornin'. Look out, lad!"—for the Major had thrown up his head suddenly and come to a standstill, snorting, and nearly unseating his small rider.

"Why did he do that?" asked the boy in wonder, as he settled himself once more in the saddle, and got a fresh hold on the reins. "There was n't any hole there, was there?"

For a minute the corporal made no reply. His own horse was snuffing the air uneasily, and the trooper's keen glance traveled slowly along the horizon and over the herded cattle before it came back to the small figure at his side.

"Maybe there 's grass burnin'," he said, finally. "The smell o' thet always makes 'em fretty."

He put his animal to a gallop as he spoke, and the distance to the herd began to diminish rapidly.

"See how uneasy the other horses are," said Danny, as they neared the grazing-ground. "Whatever the trouble is, they know it too."

There could be no doubt of that fact. O'Farrell's apparent carelessness was explained. The animals were in almost constant motion, moving from side to side, browsing for a moment, only to pause and snuff the air in the same alarmed fashion which Danny and Mackenzie had noticed in their own horses a few minutes before. The men in charge were riding to and fro, heading off the refractory leaders, and doing their best to turn them toward the post, but without avail. Slowly but surely the herd was edging in the opposite direction along the bluff.

O'Farrell came to meet them. He was a

young Irish lad who had been in the service only a short time, and gave promise of making a most excellent soldier. On the present occasion his round, jolly face wore a troubled look.

"It 's welcome ye are, Corporal, sure!" he exclaimed, mopping his hot face. "If I 'd had any way of gettin' word to ye, ye 'd have been here long ago; but it took the two of us to kape the bastes together, and, faith, ten men could n't have done more. I can't think what 's got into them!"

He turned his horse and reined it in beside Mackenzie's gray, surveying the increasing restlessness of the animals in despair, yet conscious of inexpressible relief at the presence of a more experienced pair of shoulders on which to shift the responsibility.

"How long hef they been like this?" asked the corporal, after a silence in which his face became more and more grave.

"For the bether part of the afternoon." Mackenzie's eyes wandered once again over the empty hills. "Ye 've got a good nose, Larry," he said finally; "hef ye smelt anything in the way o' a prairie fire?"

The other shook his head. "Nothin'," he replied; "that is, nothin' to spake of. There was some smoke up there to the north this forenoon; but I have n't seen it since."

The corporal's face changed suddenly. "Steady, was it?" he queried, "or puffy, like?"

"A bit puffy. Nothin' to spake of—it died out right away."

The veteran groaned. "And ye should hef made for hame gin ye saw thet first puff;" he muttered, adding something under his breath about "the silliness o' sending babes and innocents tae do this kind o' work!"

"What 's up?" asked the young soldier, anxiously. "You don't think it 's—?"

The elder man made an imperceptible gesture toward the child.

"There 's mischief of some sort brewin'," he said gravely. "And we 'd better get out o' this, gin we want tae carry a whole skin with us. Head off those mules— they 'll stampede the lot! Laddie, coom with me!" He turned his horse in the direction of the river as he spoke, taking out his revolver and carefully examining it while he rode.

"Mackenzie," said the little boy, softly, drawing nearer to his friend's side, "do you think it is Indians?" He was not particularly alarmed at the unexpected danger which threatened them—he had the greatest faith in the corporal's ability to protect him from harm. But the face which the soldier turned slowly toward him in answer to his question was grim and set with a fear such as he had never known – nor could know—for himself! He would have given his life gladly, in the face of that deadly and too well understood peril, to have felt that little Dan was within the friendly shelter of the fort!

"I 'm no sayin' it 's Indians, lad," he said at length; "but when ye don't like the look o' things it 's better tae be prepared for the worst. There 's twa possibilities ahead o' us. One's the stampede o' the herd, which would be bad enough; the other 's that which is behind the fright o' the animals, which is far worse! Whatever happens, naething I can do will save ye, gin ye don't act like yir feyther's son and try tae help yirsel'."

He paused. While speaking he had worked his way steadily across the front of the herd, driving back such animals as he could without waste of time, but continually increasing the distance between himself and the main body of the drove. His duty as a soldier was simply to save his captain's child! By the time he had reached a point to the left of the center of the herd, experience told him that the disaster which he dreaded was not long to be delayed.

He took the last moment for a few final warning words.

"Mind one thing, laddie! Whatever comes, gie the Major his head and hold on! He 'll carry ye safe, and he can show a clean pair o' heels tae the fastest o' them! Eh! I thought as much! Get yir horse's head round, lad! Be ready!"

The avalanche was upon them!

Some seconds earlier the lead-mules of an ambulance-team on the farther side of the grazing-ground had thrown up their heads in sudden fright and caromed into the horses feeding near them, and those in turn had plunged against their neighbors, and then the whole herd, catching the infection of their terror, had bunched itself and started—a maddened, flying mass!

It seemed years to Dan, giddy and breathless from terror, before it reached him. For a brief instant he thought he saw O'Farrell and some unknown mounted figures behind it; then the air about him grew thick with dust, the noise of the beating hoofs increased to a deafening roar, and every faculty became absorbed in the effort to obey Mackenzie's instructions and to keep him in sight; for the corporal's gray, nervous and fidgety at best, had no sooner caught sight of the oncoming body than it bolted, speeding along the edge of the bluff, uncontrollable and unguidable, to plunge after a few seconds into a sandy ravine which ran up into the plain from the river-bottom—disappearing before the lad's straining gaze as completely as if swallowed by the friendly earth!

A minute or two later the Major, following almost in the footprints of his stable-mate, paused on the brink of the little gully, and then carefully, and without harm to his clinging burden, slid and floundered down its shelving sides, and stopped, quivering, at the bottom.

There was something disconcerting in the change from the recent rush and turmoil of the upper world to the gloom and stillness of the leafy covert. Danny caught his breath and peered half timidly through the underbrush. "Mackenzie," he called softly; "oh, Mackenzie!" And then with a sudden low, horrified cry he slipped from the Major's back, thrust aside the bushes, and stared, transfixed, at the spectacle before him.

Above his head, a broad swath of broken branches and uprooted reeds showed where horse and rider had crashed through the bushes to their fate. At his feet, a huddled, shapeless mass, was the runaway! And beyond lay the corporal, his blouse torn to ribbons and gray with dust, his upturned face drawn and still—a red stream trickling slowly down from a gaping wound in his forehead, to form an ever-growing stain in the sand beside him!

Little by little Dan crept to the trooper's side and gazed with wide eyes into the quiet face. Some vaguely formed protest against the injustice of fate crept through the child-mind. The peril from which he had just escaped—the possible peril even now lurking in the woods about him—was as nothing compared with this terrible stillness and helplessness of his friend!

Danny began to cry, not loudly, but with deep-drawn, shivering breaths, while the Major, with hanging, loosened reins, sniffed protestingly at the motionless body of his late comrade. There was a silence, broken only by the chirping of the sparrows in the thicket and the rustle of the leaves overhead.

Suddenly Dan looked up, and drew his sleeve across his eyes.

A deep sigh had escaped from the blue lips, and with a frown of pain Mackenzie stirred uneasily and turned his face toward the boy. Dan's first wild thrill of joy vanished at the sight of the blood which welled up afresh from the wound with the movement. Instinct told him that the flickering life could not long sustain such a loss.

The winter before he had been present while the hospital steward bound up a wound for one of the soldiers, and the attention with which he had followed the operation did him good service now.

He took out his handkerchief and measured its small length against the trooper's forehead. Then he looked about him for a more effectual bandage, and his eye fell upon the narrow leather cinch at his waist, a recent and much-prized gift from the Mexican saddler in his father's troop. It was the work of only a few seconds to unfasten it, and to make a pad of the bit of linen, after which, with much difficulty, he adjusted the strap about the corporal's head, and pulled it tight. And terrified as the child was, and tender and feeble and fluttering as his small fingers were, they did their work thoroughly, and the fatal tide at first slowly ebbed, and at length ceased.

When the task was accomplished, Danny looked about him helplessly. "What shall we do now, Major?" he said, addressing himself to his only companion.

The corporal stirred. "And ye 'll keep his head straight, lad," he murmured feebly, his half-conscious mind taking up the counsel to his charge where it had been interrupted by the stampede; "and ye 'll steer him for hame—for hame!" he repeated once again in stronger tones.

The child bent over him. "Am I to go for help, Mackenzie?" he said eagerly. "Do you mean I am to go for help?"

He waited a moment in expectant silence; but the trooper had drifted off into unconsciousness, and there was no reply. Then he rose to his feet. There seemed

nothing left but to obey. "Come, Major," he said tremulously.

He made his way slowly to the horse's side, climbed up on the stump of a fallen oak, and from that to the animal's back, and with one wistful backward glance at the grimly quiet objects at his feet bent his head over the Major's neck and wound both hands in his mane, while the sagacious beast clambered up the side of the ravine, to emerge a minute later upon the open prairie.

Away to the north a cloud of dust marked the recent passage of the herd. On every other side swept the tableland, empty and placid and smiling. And beyond, to the south, stood the fort and home. Danny took heart, settled himself in the saddle, and put the Major into a smart canter, holding the reins firmly, and trying to recall the corporal's instructions while he rode, thinking with an ever-recurring pang of his friend's condition, happy that the distance to the necessary succor was diminishing so rapidly, and totally forgetful of the anxiety which had agitated the veteran before the accident that had separated them.

Suddenly, at the end of some fifteen minutes of tranquil riding, as the Major galloped along the edge of the timber which fringed the bluff, there was a loud crackling and crashing in the bushes, and a gaily decorated war-pony scrambled through them, his rider grunting in surly surprise; while at the same moment, from the thicket beyond, three other half-naked mounted figures appeared and lined up in the path which led to safety.

The child's heart stopped beating. His frontier training told him that all that had gone before, even the tragedy which had darkened the afternoon, was as nothing compared with this new and awful danger. In a paroxysm of terror he tried to stop Major—tried with all his small strength to turn him aside toward the open plain, to check his mad plunge into the very arms of the enemy. But for the first time the horse paid attention neither to the beloved voice nor to the tiny hands pulling so desperately upon the reins.

Whether it was the sight of an old and hated foe, or whether the wise, kind heart of the animal realized the full extent of a peril of which the child was as yet only half aware, it would be hard to say. But little Dan found himself going faster than he had thought possible—and faster—and faster—till the tawny, sun-burned plain, and the pitiless smiling sky, and the nearer, greener foliage of the willows, and even the outlines of the dreaded savages themselves became as so many parts of a great rushing, whirling whole, and all his strength was absorbed in the effort to retain his seat upon the bounding horse.

And so, like some vision from their own weird legends, straight down upon the astonished Indians swept the great bronze beast with its golden-haired burden! Down upon them, and through them, and away —till by the time they had recovered from their amazement there was a good fifty yards between them and their flying prey! And that distance, hard as they might ride, was not easily to be overcome!

After that first wild rush the Major settled into a steadier pace—a smooth, even run, so easy to sit that the lad relaxed his clutch upon the animal's mane and turned his eyes to the horizon, where gathering swarms of savages showed like clusters of ants against the slope of the hillside. In his track, with shrill, singing cries, like hounds upon a trail, came his pursuers. And far to the south there was a puff of white smoke from the walls of the fort, and a moment later the first heavy, echoing boom of the alarm-gun thundered across the plains!

Within the stockaded inclosure the sunny hours wore tranquilly away. Mrs. Kent's passing uneasiness about the Major subsided, and she returned placidly to her domestic duties. Late in the afternoon, when the baby had been bathed and freshly dressed and the nurse had taken her to play in the shade of the bandstand, Mrs. Kent came out to join her husband and a group of ladies and gentlemen on the piazza.

"There must be a prairie fire somewhere," she remarked as she seated herself; "I have been smelling smoke all the afternoon."

"We were just talking about it," answered Mrs. Lane, the doctor's wife; "I am certain I saw smoke to the northward before luncheon. There is no sign of it now, but the odor is distinct!"

At that moment one of the younger lieutenants approached from the gate which led toward the corral. "Danny has gone riding, has he not, Kent?" he asked.

"Yes," replied the officer; "he went with Mackenzie."

"Have you confidence in the corporal's discretion?"

"Absolute!" was the emphatic answer. "Why do you ask?"

"Because there is some trouble with the herd. The animals are unaccountably restless, and the officer of the day has asked for a detail to go out and assist in bringing them in." He spoke in an undertone, but the captain laid a hand upon his arm and drew him away from the piazza.

"Are there signs of any other trouble?" he asked gravely.

The young fellow shook his head. "Not as yet," he replied; "but they seem to think it better to be on the safe side."

He went on to his own quarters, and the captain thoughtfully retraced his steps in the direction of the piazza. As he regained it a shot rang out—a shot that brought officers and men all over the garrison to their feet, that blanched the faces of the women, and called forth a cry of agony from Mrs. Kent.

"Indians!" she moaned. "Indians! Oh, George!—and Danny!"

Her husband caught her in his arms and carried her indoors. "Courage, dearest, courage!" he whispered, as he snatched up saber and pistols, and with a hasty farewell he left her. What he had to do must be done quickly!

The first report had been followed by another, and another, as each sentinel in turn took up and echoed the alarm. After those came the crashing bang and roar of the six-pounder, the sinister humming of the "long roll," and the shrill notes of the bugles as they sounded "boots and saddles." To an inexperienced eye the scene which resulted would have seemed like hopeless confusion.

The barracks swarmed with hastily armed men, the air was filled with the clatter of sabers and the rattle of carbines, with hurriedly shouted orders, calls, questions, till the "assembly" put a temporary check upon the uproar and the troopers departed for the stables. There saddles were flung across the horses' backs, girths were jerked tight, and, in less time than it has taken to describe the formation, the infantrymen detailed to protect the garrison were at their posts behind the stockade, and the troops of cavalry were mounted and ready for their work.

"For'rd, trot, march!" The bugles repeated the command with blatant clamor, and the troops swept through the gate of the corral and halted by one of the bastions for their orders—grimly silent, compact bodies of men, trained by long, hard years of such service as the soldiers of to-day can never know. To have seen them once in battle array is to have seen that which one can never forget! There was a quiet satisfaction on the face of the garrison commander as he regarded them, field-glass in hand, from his post of observation on top of the blockhouse. His wishes were briefly expressed: "B, to the north after the herd; K, to the west; L, in the reserve until needed."

Once again the bugles sounded, and the troops separated to their respective duties— L waiting at "place rest" on the plain beside the fort; K forming a skirmish-line at the foot of the slope some hundreds of yards to the west; and B, under Dan's own father, starting at a brisk trot along the western face of the stockade. The men were unusually grave as they rounded its last corner. There was not one among them who did not feel a pang at the thought of the tiny child practically alone and unprotected on those desolate prairies; they were full of mute sympathy for the soldier who rode with white, stern face at their head.

As they paused for a final momentary halt, the sergeant of the troop moved to the side of his commander. "There are some animals running by the timber to the left, Captain," he observed hurriedly. The officer regarded the moving figures intently, then he turned his face for a brief instant full upon his followers. "Those are mounted horsemen, lads!" he exclaimed; "and they are coming this way! Column right, gallop, march!" And the troopers, catching the subtle excitement in his tone, settled themselves in their saddles, and with a rousing cheer thundered across the plain in the direction indicated.

To Danny, as he swept along on the road to safety, the minutes which succeeded the report of the alarm-gun were full of anguish. He grew sick and giddy with the rush of his passage. The rhythmic beat of the horse's feet upon the turf mingled in a dull monotone with the roar of the wind in his ears.

The fort grew steadily nearer. In spite of his terror he began to distinguish the figures of the soldiers as they swarmed about its walls in response to the call to arms, the hurry and confusion of the preparations, and finally even the color of the black horses in his father's troop as they

glanced over his shoulder. His pursuers were close at his heels, riding low down on their unkempt ponies, their lithe, half-naked bodies gleaming like bronze statues, the red and yellow of their war-paint showing up sharply in the strong light of the afternoon.

The boy grew sick at heart, turned once more to the plains in front of him, and uttered a wailing cry of terror.

"On—on—and up into the air!"

started across the plain in his direction. With a little moan of appeal, he turned the Major toward them.

The friction of the reins had fretted the sweat upon the horse's neck into a heavy lather, he threw up his head uneasily from time to time in the effort for more air, and at length, with a spasm of dread, the child felt his smooth run slacken to a pounding gallop, while in the rear, with sinister insistence, the shrill, crooning cries of the Indians grew perceptibly louder. Danny

Before him, almost at his feet, lay a yawning gulf—one of those steep-sided arroyos which begin in a tiny crack, and increase with the storms and frosts of succeeding winters till they form impassable chasms. The one in question was fully fifteen feet in width, and the lad clutched the animal's mane, and waited, numb with horror, for the end. The savages, seeing the unexpected peril which confronted him, broke into a series of triumphant yells. At the same moment, clear and distinct in the still air, came the bugle-notes of the "charge."

The Major threw up his head at the sound; it was the well-remembered war-cry of his young, strong days; it woke an answering echo in his faithful heart, and, with a supreme and final effort of his failing strength, he responded to its command. The muscles on his extended neck grew stiff and tense with energy; his nostrils widened; he laid his small ears back, and gathered his mighty limbs under him. On —on—and up into the air! The lad closed his eyes. There was a crashing, stumbling jar, and then the horse recovered himself and galloped jerkily forward to meet his oncoming mates.

Danny was only vaguely conscious of the singing of the bullets above his head and of the cries of his baffled pursuers as they retreated before the fire of the troopers. He saw his father's face through a mist of long-delayed tears, and a significant silence fell upon the men as they closed about the staggering horse, and their leader lifted his son from the saddle and held him for a brief space against his heart.

Half an hour later, when the rattle of musketry and the crash of the Gatling guns in the sand-bag battery beside the fort had died away, the herd had been recovered, and the Indians had retreated to the shadows of the hills, a small procession wound along the edge of the timber. In the midst of it was a canvas-covered wagon with a red cross on its white sides. About that, armed and watchful, rode the soldiers of L troop. Under its shelter sat the surgeon, and at his feet lay Mackenzie, bandaged and cared for. As the sunlight faded and the evening gun sounded over the plains the little train reached the stockade, the gates opened, and the last of our heroes gained the friendly shelter of the walls.

So ends the story, and it has no moral. Only, if you had seen Danny's mother that evening, as, clinging to the Major's neck, she wept for very joy, you never could doubt the value of fidelity and courage—even in a horse.

THE PROFESSOR
AND THE PATAGONIAN GIANT

by Tudor Jenks

EARLY one morning during my third visit to Patagonia, as I was strolling upon the banks of the River Chico, keeping a sharp lookout for a choice specimen of the *Rutabaga Tremendosa*, I saw what, at the time, I supposed to be a large and isolated cliff. It looked blue, and con-

He was advancing at a run, and although not exerting himself overmuch seemed to be going at a rate of some five kilometers a minute. Much annoyed at the interruption to my researches, I paused only long enough to deposit the *Rutabaga* securely in my botany box and then broke into an

"I saw the need of taking immediate steps to save my specimens"

sequently I supposed it to be at some distance. Resuming my search for the beautiful saffron blossom which I have already named, my attention was for some moments abstracted. After pulling the plant up by the roots, however, I happened to cast my eyes again toward the supposed cliff, and you can conceive my extreme mortification and regret when I saw that it was not a cliff at all, but a giant, and, so far as I could see, one of the most virulent species.

accelerated trot. Do me the justice to acquit me of any intention of entering into a contest of speed with the pursuing monster. I am not so conceited as to imagine I can cover five or even three kilometers a minute. No; I relied, rather, on the well-established scientific probability that the giant was stupid. I expected, therefore, that my head would have an opportunity to save my heels.

It was not long before I saw the need of taking immediate steps to secure my specimens from destruction and myself from being eaten. He was certainly gaining upon me. As he foolishly ran with his mouth open, I noticed that his canine teeth were very well developed—not a proof, but strong evidence, that he was a cannibal. I redoubled my speed, keeping an eager eye upon the topography in the hope that I might find some cave or crevice into which I could creep and thus obtain time enough to elaborate a plan of escape. I had not run more than six or eight kilometers, I think (for distances are small in that part of Patagonia—or were, when I was there), when I saw a most convenient cretaceous cave.

To ensconce myself within its mineral recesses was the work of but a moment, and it was fortunate for me that it took no longer. Indeed, as I rolled myself deftly beneath a shelving rock, the giant was so near that he pulled off one of my boots.

He sat down at the entrance and breathed with astonishing force and rapidity.

"Now, if he is as stupid as one of his race normally should be," I said to myself, "he will stay there for several hours, and I shall lose a great part of this beautiful day." The thought made me restless, and I looked about to see whether my surroundings would hint a solution of the situation.

I was rewarded by discovering an outlet far above me. I could see through a cleft in the rocks portions of a cirro-cumulus cloud. Fixing my hat more firmly upon my head, I began the ascent. It did not take long. Indeed, my progress was, if anything, rather accelerated by the efforts of the attentive giant, who had secured a long and flexible switch,—a young India-rubber tree, I think, though I did not notice its foliage closely,—and was poking it with considerable violence into the cave. In fact, he lifted me some decameters at every thrust.

It may easily be understood, therefore, that I was not long upon the way. When I emerged, I was much pleased with the situation. Speaking as a military expert, it was perfect. Standing upon a commodious ledge, which seemed to have been made for the purpose, my head and shoulders projected from an opening in the cliff, which was just conveniently out of the giant's reach. As my head rose over the edge of the opening, the giant spoke:

"Aha, you 're there, are you?"

"I won't deny it," I answered.

"You think you 're safe, don't you?" he went on tauntingly.

"I know I 'm safe," I answered, with an easy confidence which was calculated to please.

"Well," he replied, "to-night I am going to eat you for supper!"

"What, then," I asked, with some curiosity, "are you going to do for dinner?"

"Oh, if that troubles you," said he, "all you have to do is to come out at dinner-time and I will eat you then."

Evidently the giant was not a witling. His answers were apt. After a moment's reflection I concluded it was worth the effort to make an appeal to his better nature—his over-soul.

"Don't you know that it is wrong to eat your fellow-beings?" I asked, with a happy mingling of austere reproach and sympathetic pain.

"Do you mean to come out soon?" asked the giant, seating himself upon an adjacent cliff, after tearing off such of the taller and stiffer trees as were in his way.

"It depends somewhat upon whether you remain where you are," I answered.

"Oh, I shall stay," said the giant, pleasantly. "Game is rare, and I have n't eaten a white man for two weeks."

This remark brought me back to my appeal to his higher being. "Then I shall remain here, too, for the present," I answered, "though I should like to get away before sunset. It 's likely to be humid here after the sun sets. But, to return to my question, have you never thought that it was immoral and selfish to eat your fellow-creatures?"

"Why, certainly," said the giant, with a hearty frankness that was truly refreshing. "That is why," he went on, "I asked you whether you were coming out soon. If not, I would be glad to while the time away by explaining to you exactly how I feel about these matters. Of course I could smoke you out" (here he showed me an enormous boulder of flint and a long steel rod, the latter evidently a propeller-shaft from some wrecked ocean-steamer), "but I make it a rule seldom to eat a fellow-mortal until he is fully convinced that, all things considered, I am justified in so doing."

The allusion to the smoking-out process convinced me that this was no hulking ignoramus of a giant, and for a moment I began to fear that my *Rutabaga Tremendosa* was lost to the world forever. But the latter part of his speech re-assured me.

"If you can convince me that I ought to be eaten," I said, willing to be reasonable, "I shall certainly offer no objection. But I confess I have little fear that you will succeed."

"I first discovered that I was a giant," he said, absently chewing the stem of the India-rubber tree, "at a very early age. I could not get enough to eat. I then lived in New York City, for I am an American, like yourself."

We bowed with mutual pleasure.

"I tried various sorts of work, but found I could not earn enough at any of them to pay my board-bills. I even exhibited myself in a museum, but found there the same trouble.

"I consulted my grandfather, who was a man of matured judgment and excellent sense. His advice was to leave the city and try for work in the country. I did so, and after some little trouble found employment upon a farm. I stayed there three days. Then I was told that it cost more to keep me than I was worth; which was true. So I left. Then I went to work on a railroad. Here I did as much as twenty men. The result was a strike, and I was discharged."

"Is there much more autobiography?" I asked as politely as I could, for I was not at all interested in this unscientific memoir.

"Very little," he answered. "I can sum it up in a few words. Wherever I tried to get work, I was discharged, because my board was too expensive. If I tried to do more work to make up for it, the other men were dissatisfied, because it took the bread out of their mouths. Now, I put it to you, what was I to do?"

"Evidently, you were forced out of civilization," I answered, "and compelled to rely upon nature for your sustenance. That is," I went on, to forestall another question, "you had to become a hunter, trapper, or fisherman,—for of course, in your case, agriculture was out of the question, as you could n't easily get down to the ground, and would crush with your feet more crops than you could raise with your hands."

His eyes sparkled with joy at being so thoroughly understood. "Exactly," he said. "But the same trouble followed me there. Wherever I settled, the inhabitants complained that what I ate would support hundreds of other people."

"Very true," I answered; "but, excuse me, could you hand me a small rock to sit upon?—it is tiresome to stand here."

"Come out," he said. "You have my word of honor, as a compatriot of George——"

"Say no more!" I broke in hastily.

I came out, and was soon, by his kind aid, perched upon the branch of a tree conveniently near.

"This argument," he said, sighing, "met me at every turn; and after much cogitation I could see no solution of the difficulty. No matter how far from the 'busy haunts of men' I proceeded, it was only to find that food grew scarcer as men were less reduced. But upon what principle do you proceed to the next step—cannibalism?"

"The greatest good to the greatest number," said he. "Whenever I eat an animal, I diminish the stock of food which supports mankind, but whenever I eat a man,

The giant and the Professor settle it amicably

numerous. At last I reached Patagonia, and after a few years I have eaten it almost bare. Now, to what conclusion am I driven?"

I thought it over. At last I said:

"I see the extremities to which you are I diminish the number to be supported. As all the wise men agree that it is the subsistence which is short, my course of action tends ultimately to the greater happiness of the race."

This seemed very reasonable and for a

moment I was staggered. Then a happy thought came to me, and I suggested that if he should allow himself to die of starvation the demand for subsistence would be still more reduced.

He shook his head sadly. "I used to hope so myself. But the experience of some years, tabulated and reduced to most accurate statistics, has convinced me beyond a doubt that I can catch and eat enough men, in a year, to more than make up for what would be saved if I should allow my own organism to cease its active exertions in the cause of humanity."

I thought very carefully over these arguments and was unable to pick a flaw in them.

"As a man of science," I said, after a pause, "I could wish that this interview might be reported to the world."

"Give yourself no uneasiness. It shall be done," said the giant.

"And I should also be glad to have the *Rutabaga Tremendosa* forwarded very soon to the Metropolitan Museum," I said thoughtfully.

"With pleasure," said the giant.

There was no excuse for further delay.

"And are you convinced?" asked the giant, speaking with much kindly consideration.

"Perfectly," I said, and kicked off the other boot.

[Note, by the giant.— In accordance with Professor Muddlehed's last wishes I have reported our full conversation verbatim. In fact, much of the foregoing account was revised by the Professor himself, before supper. He would have been glad, I have no doubt, to have gone over the paper again, but the bell rang and he was too considerate to keep the table waiting. He had many excellent tastes, and there was a flavor of originality about the man—a flavor I like. I enjoyed meeting him very much, and regret that my principles were such as to preclude a longer and less intimate acquaintance. I forwarded the specimen to the museum as directed, and received in return an invitation to visit the building in New York. Though I can not accept the kind invitation, I should find it gratifying to have the trustees at my own table.]

THE POTTED PRINCESS

by Rudyard Kipling

Now this is the true tale that was told to Punch and Judy, his sister, by their nurse, in the city of Bombay, ten thousand miles from here. They were playing in the veranda, waiting for their mother to come back from her evening drive. The big pink crane, who generally lived by himself at the bottom of the garden because he hated horses and carriages, was with them too, and the nurse, who was called the ayah, was making him dance by throwing pieces of mud at him. Pink cranes dance very prettily until they grow angry. Then they peck.

This pink crane lost his temper, opened his wings, and clattered his beak, and the ayah had to sing a song which never fails to quiet all the cranes in Bombay. It is a very old song, and it says:

> Buggle baita nuddee kinara,
> Toom-toom mushia kaye,
> Nuddee kinara kanta lugga
> Tullaka-tullaka ju jaye.

That means: A crane sat by the river-bank, eating fish *toom-toom,* and a thorn in the river-bank pricked him, and his life went away *tullaka-tullaka*—drop by drop. The ayah and Punch and Judy always talked Hindustani because they understood it better than English.

"See now," said Punch, clapping his hands. "He knows, and he is ashamed. *Tullaka-tullaka, ju jaye!* Go away!"

"*Tullaka-tullaka!*" said little Judy, who was five; and the pink crane shut up his beak and went down to the bottom of the garden to the cocoa-nut palms and the aloes and the red peppers. Punch followed, shouting *"tullaka-tullaka!"* till the crane hopped over an aloe hedge and Punch got pricked by the spikes. Then he cried, because he was only seven, and because it was so hot that he was wearing very few clothes and the aloes had pricked a great deal of him; and Judy cried too, because Punch was crying, and she knew that that meant something worth crying for.

"Ohoo!" said Punch, looking at both his fat little legs together, "I am very badly pricked by the very bad aloe. Perhaps I shall die!"

"Punch will die because he has been pricked by the very bad aloe, and then there will be only Judy," said Judy.

"No," said Punch, very quickly, putting his legs down. "Then you will sit up to dinner alone. I will not die; but, ayah, I am very badly pricked. What is good for that?"

The ayah looked down for a minute, just to see that there were two tiny pink scratches on Punch's legs. Then she looked out across the garden to the blue water of Bombay harbor, where the ships are, and said:

"Once upon a time there was a Rajah." "Rajah" means king in Hindustani, just as "ranee" means queen.

"Will Punch die, ayah?" said Judy. She too had seen the pink scratches, and they seemed very dreadful to her.

"No," said Punch. "Ayah is telling a tale. Stop crying, Judy."

"And the Rajah had a daughter," said the ayah.

"It is a new tale," said Punch. "The last Rajah had a son, and he was turned into a monkey. Hssh!"

The ayah put out her soft brown arm, picked Judy off the matting of the veranda, and tucked her into her lap. Punch sat cross-legged close by.

"That Rajah's daughter was very beautiful," the ayah went on.

"How beautiful? More beautiful than mamma? Then I do not believe this tale," said Punch.

"She was a fairy princess, Punch baba, and she was very beautiful indeed; and when she grew up the Rajah her father said that she must marry the best prince in all India."

"Where did all these things happen?" said Punch.

"In a big forest near Delhi. So it was told to me," said the ayah.

"Very good," said Punch. "When I am big I will go to Delhi. Tell the tale, ayah."

"Therefore the King made a talk with his magicians—men with white beards who do *jadoo* (magic), and make snakes come out of baskets, and grow mangos from little stones, such as you, Punch, and you, Judy baba, have seen. But in those days they did much more wonderful things: they turned men into tigers and elephants. And the magicians counted the stars under which the Princess was born."

"I—I do not understand this," said Judy, wriggling on the ayah's lap. Punch did not understand either, but he looked very wise.

The ayah hugged her close. "How should a baby understand?" she said softly. "It is in this way. When the stars are in one posi-tion when a child is born, it means well. When they are in another position, it means, perhaps, that the child may be sick or ill-tempered, or she may have to travel very far away."

"Must I travel far away?" said Judy.

"No, no. There were only good little stars in the sky on the night that Judy baba was born,—little home-keeping stars that danced up and down, they were so pleased."

"And I—I—I! What did the stars do when I was born?" said Punch.

"There was a new star that night. I saw it. A great star with a fiery tail all across the sky. Punch will travel far."

"That is true. I have been to Nassik in the railway-train. Never mind the Princess's stars. What did the magic-men do?"

"They consulted the stars, little impatient, and they said that the Princess must be shut up in such a manner that only the very best of all the princes in India could take her out. So they shut her up, when she was sixteen years old, in a big, deep grain-jar of dried clay, with a cover of plaited grass."

"I have seen them in the Bombay market," said Judy. "Was it one of the *very* big kind?" The ayah nodded, and Judy shivered, for her father had once held her up to look into the mouth of just such a grain-jar, and it was full of empty darkness.

"How did they feed her?" said Punch.

"She was a fairy. Perhaps she did not want food," the ayah began.

"All people want food. This is not a true tale. I shall go and beat the crane." Punch got up on his knees.

"No, no. I have forgotten. There was plenty of food—plantains, red and yellow ones, almond curd, boiled rice and peas, fowl stuffed with raisins and red peppers, and cakes fried in oil with coriander seeds, and sweet-meats of sugar and butter. Is that enough food? So the Princess was shut up in the grain-jar, and the Rajah made a proclamation that whoever could take her out should marry her and should govern ten provinces, sitting upon an elephant with tusks of gold. That proclamation was made through all India."

"We did not hear it, Punch and I," said Judy. "Is this a true tale, ayah?"

"It was before Punch was born. It was before even I was born, but so my mother told it to me. And when the proclamation was made, there came to Delhi hundreds and thousands of princes and rajahs and great men. The grain-jar with the cover of the plaited grass was set in the middle of all, and the Rajah said that he would allow to each man one year in which to make charms and learn great things that would open the grain-jar."

"I do not understand," said Judy again. She had been looking down the garden for her mother's return, and had lost the thread of the tale.

"The jar was a magic one, and it was to be opened by magic," said Punch. "Go on, ayah. I understand."

The ayah laughed a little. "Yes, the Rajah's magicians told all the princes that it was a magic jar, and led them three times round it, muttering under their beards, and bade them come back in a year. So the Princes, and the Subedars, and the Wazirs, and the Maliks rode away east and west and north and south, and consulted the magicians in their fathers' courts, and holy men in caves."

"Like the holy men I saw at Nassik on the mountain? They were all *nungapunga* (naked), but they showed me their little gods, and I burned stuff that smelt in a pot before them all, and they said I was a Hindu, and—" Punch stopped, out of breath.

"Yes. Those were the men. Old men smeared with ashes and yellow paint did

the princes consult, and witches and dwarfs that live in caves, and wise tigers and talking horses and learned parrots. They told all these men and all these beasts of the Princess in the grain-jar, and the holy men and the wise beasts taught them charms and spells that were very strong magic indeed. Some of the princes they advised to go out and kill giants and dragons, and cut off their heads. And some of the princes stayed for a year with the holy men in forests, learning charms that would immediately split open great mountains. There was no charm and no magic that these princes and subedars did not learn, for they knew that the Rajah's magicians were very strong magicians, and therefore they needed very, very strong charms to open the grain-jar. So they did all these things that I have told, and also cut off the tails of the little devils that live on the sand of the great desert in the north; and at last there were very few dragons and giants left, and poor people could plough without being bewitched any more.

"Only there was one prince that did not ride away with the others, for he had neither horse nor saddle, nor any men to follow him. He was a prince of low birth, for his father had married the daughter of a potter, and he was the son of his mother. So he sat down on the ground, and the little boys of the city driving the cattle to pasture threw mud at him."

"Ah!" said Punch, "mud is nice. Did they hit him?"

"I am telling the tale of the Princess, and if there are so many questions, how can I finish before bedtime? He sat on the ground, and presently his mother, the Ranee, came by, gathering sticks to cook bread, and he told her of the Princess and the grain-jar. And she said: 'Remember that a pot is a pot, and thou art the son of a potter.' Then she went away with those dry sticks, and the Potter-prince waited till the end of the year. Then the princes returned, as many of them as were left over from the fights that they had fought. They brought with them the terrible cut-off heads of the giants and the dragons, so that people fell down with fright; and the tails of all the little devils, bunch by bunch, tied up with string; and the feathers of magic birds; and their holy men and dwarfs and talking beasts came with them. And there were bullock-carts full of the locked books of magic incantations and spells. The Rajah appointed a day, and his magicians came, and the grain-jar was set in the middle of all, and the princes began, according to their birth and the age of their families, to open the grain-jar by means of their charm-work. There were very many princes, and the charms were very strong, so that as they performed the ceremonies the lightning ran about the ground as a broken egg runs over the cook-house floor, and it was thick, dark night, and the people heard the voices of devils and djinns and talking tigers, and saw them running to and fro about the grain-jar till the ground shook. But, none the less, the grain-jar did not open. And the next day the ground was split up as a log of wood is split, and great rivers flowed up and down the plain, and magic armies with banners walked in circles—so great was the strength of the charms. Snakes, too, crawled round the grain-jar and hissed, but none the less the jar did not open. When morning came the holes in the ground had closed up, and the rivers were gone away, and there was only the plain. And that was because it was all magic charm-work which cannot last."

"Aha!" said Punch, drawing a deep breath. "I am glad of that. It was only magic, Judy. Tell the tale, ayah."

"At the very last, when they were all wearied out and the holy men began to bite their nails with vexation, and the Rajah's magicians laughed, the Potter-Prince came into the plain alone, without even one little talking beast or wise bird, and all the people made jokes at him. But he walked to the grain-jar and cried, 'A pot is a pot, and I am the son of a potter!' and he put his two hands upon the grain-jar's cover and he lifted it up, and the Princess came out! Then the people said, 'This is very great magic indeed'; and they began to chase the holy men and the talking beasts up and down, meaning to kill them. But the Rajah's magicians said: 'This is no magic at all, for we did not put any charm upon the jar. It *was* a common grain-jar; and it *is* a common grain-jar such as they buy in the bazar; and a child might have lifted the cover one year ago, or on any day since that day. Ye are too wise, O Princes and Subedars, who rely on holy men and the heads of dead giants and devils' tails, but do not work with your own hands! Ye are too cunning! There was no magic, and now one man has taken it all away from you because he was not afraid. Go home, princes, or if ye will, stay to see the wedding. But remember that a pot is a pot.' "

There was a long silence at the end of the tale.

"But the charms were very strong," said Punch, doubtfully.

"They were only words, and how could they touch the pot. Could words turn you into a tiger, Punch baba?"

"No. I am Punch."

"Even so," said the ayah. "If the pot had been charmed, a charm would have opened it. But it was a common, bazar pot. What did it know of charms? It opened to a hand on the cover."

"Oh!" said Punch; and then he began to laugh, and Judy followed his example.

"Now I quite understand. I will tell it to mama."

When mama came back from her drive, the children told her the tale twice over, while she was dressing for dinner; but as they began in the middle and put the beginning first, and then began at the end and put the middle last, she became a little confused.

"Never mind," said Punch; "I will show." And he reached up to the table for the big eau-de-cologne bottle that he was strictly forbidden to touch, and pulled out the stopper and upset half the scent down the front of his dress, shouting, "A pot is a pot, and I am the son of a potter!"

THE BUTTER BETTY BOUGHT

Anonymous

BETTY BOTTA bought some butter;
"But," said she, "This butter's bitter!
If I put it in my batter
It will make my batter bitter.
But a bit o' better butter
Will but make my batter better."
So she bought a bit o' butter
Better than the bitter butter,
Made her bitter batter better.
So 'twas better Betty Botta
Bought a bit o' better butter.

THE BROWNIES' RETURN

by Palmer Cox

Once while the Brownies lay at ease
About the roots of rugged trees,
And listened to the dreary moan
Of tides around their island lone,
Said one: "My friends, unhappy here,
We spend our days from year to year.
We 're cornered in, and hardly boast
A run of twenty leagues at most.
You all remember well, I ween,
The night we reached this island green,
When flocks of fowl around us wailed,
And followed till their pinions failed.

And still our ship at every wave
To sharks a creaking promise gave,
Till half in sea, and half on rock,
She shivered like an earthen crock,
And spilled us out in breakers white,
To gain the land as best we might.
Since then, how oft we 've tried in vain
To reach our native haunts again,
Where roaming freely, unconfined,
Would better suit our roving mind.
But, hark! I have a plan will chase
The cloud of gloom from every face.

"To-night, while wandering by the sea,
A novel scheme occurred to me,
As I beheld in groups and rows
The weary fowl in deep repose.
They sat as motionless as though
The life had left them years ago.
The albatross and crane are there,
The loon, the gull, and gannet rare.

An easy task for us to creep
Around the fowl, while fast asleep,
And at a given signal spring
Aboard, before they spread a wing,
And trust to them to bear us o'er,
In safety to our native shore."
Another spoke: "I never yet
Have shunned a risk that others met,
But here uncommon dangers lie,
Suppose a fowl should seaward fly,
And never landing, course about,
And drop us, where their wings gave out?"

The first surveyed, with wondering eye,
His doubting friend, then made reply:
"To shallow schemes that will not bring
A modest risk, let cowards cling!
A Brownie to advantage shows,
The best where dangers thickest close.
But, hear me out: by sea and land,
Their habits well I understand.
When rising first they circle wide,
As though the strength of wings they tried,
Then steering straight across the bay,
To yonder coast a visit pay.

But granting they for once should be
Inclined to strike for open sea,
The breeze that now is rising fast,
Will freshen to a whistling blast,
And landward sweeping, stronger still,
Will drive the fowl against their will."

And more by vines or roots of trees,
From shelf to shelf untiring strained,
And soon the windy summit gained.
With bated breath, they gathered round.
They crawled with care along the ground.
By this, one paused, or that, one eyed;

Then no dissenting voice was raised,
But all the speaker's wisdom praised,
And at his heels, with willing feet,
They followed to the fowls' retreat.
'T was hard to scale the rugged breast
Of crags, where birds took nightly rest.
But some on hands, and some on knees,

Each chose the bird he wished to ride.
When all had done the best they could,
And waiting for the signal stood,
It hardly took a moment's space
For each to scramble to his place.
Some grabbed a neck and some a head,
And some a wing, and more a shred

Of tail, or aught that nearest lay,
To help them mount without delay.
Then rose the flaps and piercing screams,
As sudden starting from their dreams
The wondering fowl in sore dismay
Began to bring their wings in play.

Before the gale the Brownies go,
Away, away, through spray or cloud
As fancy led, or load allowed.
Some birds to poor advantage showed,
As, with an illy balanced load,
Now right or left at random cast,

Some felt the need of longer sleep,
And hardly had the strength to cheep;
While others seemed to find a store
Of screams they never found before.
It was, indeed, a daring feat
To ride on such a dubious seat.
But off like leaves or flakes of snow

They flew, the sport of every blast;
While fish below had aching eyes
With gazing upward at the prize.
They followed still from mile to mile,
Believing fortune yet would smile.
But with no common joy, indeed,
The Brownies saw the isle recede;

While plainer still before them grew
The hills and vales so well they knew.
"I see," said one, who, from his post
Between the wings, surveyed the coast,
"The lofty peaks we used to climb
To gaze upon the scene sublime."
A second cried: "And there 's the bay
From which our vessel sailed away!"
"And I," another cried, "can see
The shady grove, the very tree
We met beneath the night we planned
To build a ship and leave the land!"

Thus, while they talked, they quite forgot
The dangers of the time and spot,
Till, in confusion now at last,
The birds upon the shore were cast.
Some, crashing through the branches, fell
And spilled the load they bore so well.

Some, somersaulting to the ground,
Dispersed their riders all around;
And others, still, could barely get
To where the land and water met.
Congratulations then began,
As here and there the Brownies ran,
To learn if all had held their grip
And kept aboard throughout the trip.
"And now," said one, "that all are o'er
In safety to our native shore,
Where pleasant grove and grassy lea
In grandeur spread from sea to sea,
Such wondrous works and actions bold,
As time may bring, no tongue has told.
But see, so wasted is the night,
Orion's torch is out of sight;
And ere the lamp of Venus fades
We all must reach the forest shades."

LEONARD'S ENGLISH CHRISTMAS

by Alice Hegan Rice

OF all the lonesome people in London, I suppose Leonard Vincent was just about the lonesomest! He sat with his feet tucked under him in the stiff window-seat in Miss Meeks' stiff drawing-room, and looked down disconsolately into the wet, dreary street. Three weeks before, he and his mother had come over from America to England for a joyful holiday, and no sooner had they landed than his mother was seized with a fever and carried away to a great hospital, and he was left in charge of Miss Meeks, the strange landlady.

Miss Meeks meant to be very kind; she saw that he was properly clothed and fed, and she tried, in a way, to amuse him, but she did not know any more about little boys than she did about little lions, or little tigers, or other little wild animals.

As Leonard sat watching the raindrops trickle down the pane and thought about his mother and what a long time she had been away, he could not keep from crying a little, even if he was nine years old, and the captain of a ball team when he was at home.

"Now, Leonard," said Miss Meeks, bustling into the room, "you stop that moping this minute! Did n't I give you permission to look at the books on the table if your hands were clean?"

"Yes 'm, but I 've already looked at them."

"Would you like to cut things out with scissors?" she asked vaguely.

Leonard shook his head; he had done that two years ago, when he was seven.

"Well, you can't sit there moping all day. Why don't you go out for a walk; it is n't raining enough to matter."

"Where can I go?"

"Oh, dear, what a tiresome boy! Have n't I told you you could go as far as the park one way, and down to the Embankment the other? Just be sure to mind the crossings, and be home by five."

Leonard reluctantly put on his hat and coat and started forth. On sunny days he often went to St. James's Park and wistfully watched the children playing on the banks of the stream, or hung over the charts of water-fowls along the walk, trying to find the different names of the fat birds that waddled about in the bushes. But to-day he knew it would be cold and lonesome in the park, and even the ducks would be under cover, so he turned listlessly toward the Embankment.

The Victoria Embankment is the river-front along the Thames, and Leonard usually liked to watch the boats that came and went, and the funny two-storied street-cars, and the soldiers that sometimes marched there. But to-day he was not interested in any of these sights. There was just one thing in the world that he wanted, and that was his mother!

As he walked along blinking very hard, and trying to swallow the lump that would come in his throat, he suddenly stumbled over something on the pavement.

Looking down, he saw it was a wooden leg, and it belonged to an old man who was drawing wonderful pictures in colored chalk on the pavement.

"So sorry, sir," said the old man, hunching himself back against the wall, quite as if he were used to apologizing for being stepped on.

Leonard immediately became interested; in the first place, he had never before been called "sir," and, in the second, he had made the exciting discovery that the old man's other leg was wooden, too!

After he had stood watching for some time, the old man looked up:

"Do ye like 'em?" he asked.

For a moment Leonard did not know whether he meant the wooden legs or the pictures, but the kindly look on the old face reassured him.

" 'Course I do," he said heartily; "I think you can draw fine."

"Well, hit ain't whut ye might say high hart, but hit turns me a' honest penny."

By this time, Leonard had squatted down beside him, and was watching the magic growth of a cottage that neither Queen Anne nor any other queen would have answered for architecturally.

"Hit 's all in the knowin' 'ow," the old man continued. "You l'arn 'ow to make a 'ouse, an' ye l'arn 'ow to make a ship, an' a tree mayhap, an' then you mixes of 'em up haccordin' to yer fancy. If hit 's a sunset scene you 're haimin' at, you gives 'em a pink tint, but if hit 's moonlight, you makes 'em blue."

"How do you make the moon so round?"

"Well, some favors usin' a shilling for the purpose, but I most generally does it with a carper, that bein', as you might say, more 'andy like."

"Is this one going to be a moonlight scene?" asked Leonard.

"Yes, sir, a moonlight marine. This 'ere effect is a boat."

"I knew it!" cried Leonard, triumphantly; "why don't you put a name on the side of it?"

"I ain't awerse," said the old man, obligingly, "whut name would ye favor?"

"The U. S. A.," said Leonard; "and, if you don't mind, I think it would be awful nice to do the letters in red, white, and blue."

"Right-o!" said the old man, suiting the action to the word. "Whut might your name be, lad?"

"Leonard Vincent. What 's yours?"

"Whurtle, old Jim Whurtle. I been 'Old' Jim Whurtle for a quarter of a century."

By this time, Leonard was sitting flat on the pavement beside Mr. Whurtle, watching every movement of the chalk with flattering absorption.

"The Victoria embankment is the river-front along the Thames"

"Do you make people as good as you do boats?" he asked, almost reverently.

"Well, I can't say as I don't," replied Mr. Whurtle, modestly; "I do Mr. Gladstone, an' Lord Kitchener, an' Lloyd George."

"And not George Washington?" asked Leonard, incredulously, "or Teddy?"

"Who 's Teddy?"

"Why, Mr. Roosevelt, of course. Anybody can do him if they have a piece of chalk. I can.

The hint was not taken, and Leonard's ability as an artist was not put to the test. But he stayed on, nevertheless, watching the growth of one wonderful masterpiece after another, until Big Ben reminded him that it was time to be going home.

Big Ben is the great clock in the high tower that rises over the Houses of Parliament, and it rules the comings and goings of everybody in that part of London. It is not just as ordinary clock, for it has a wonderful set of chimes called the Westminster chimes, and every fifteen minutes all through the day and night, it sings out the passing hour.

"Well, I 'll have to be going," said Leonard, reluctantly; "will you be here to-morrow?"

Mr. Whurtle lay down his chalk and looked far off into space.

"Aye, lad," he said, "to-morrow, an' the next day, an' the day followin'."

"How early in the morning?" asked Leonard.

"Not afore noon. Mr. Minny fetches me 'ere in 'is cart on 'is second round, an' comes by fer me ag'in long about sundown."

"Who is Mr. Minny?"

"He 's the ash man that lives alongside o' me."

"And can't you go home if you want to? Not even if it 's raining like everything?"

Mr. Whurtle shook his head: "The rain ain't whut you 'd say harf bad. I ain't made o' sugar, nor yet salt, that I 'd melt in a bit of wetting. Hit 's the cold that counts."

"Anyhow," said Leonard, cheerfully, "you can't get rheumatism in your legs, can you?" And at this Mr. Whurtle laughed for the first time, a silent, fat laugh, that shook his brown waistcoat up and down and sent the wrinkles running all over his kind old face.

From this time on, Leonard ceased to be the lonesomest little boy in London; in fact, he became a very busy and interested boy, and all because he had discovered a friend. Every morning he practised with his own crayons at home, and, as soon as lunch was over, he hurried down to the Embankment to find Mr. Whurtle, and to watch the new pictures that were drawn each day on the pavement.

After the regulation moonlight effect, and snow scene, and marine view, with an occasional portrait or bunch of grapes interspersed, had been drawn, and each neatly framed in a flourishing scroll, the two would sit with their backs to the wall and wait for pennies to fall into the cap that Mr. Whurtle laid invitingly handy.

"I ain't never stooped to holdin' of hit out," he would say proudly. "I 've seen the time when the day was long, an' no supper at the end of hit, but I 'd say to meself, 'Leave the cap lay, Jim Whurtle; ye are *workin'* fer yer livin', not beggin'.' "

Yet Leonard could see that Mr. Whurtle looked rather downcast and sad on the days when the pennies failed to come.

While they waited, they discussed all sorts of interesting things, and Leonard discovered that Mr. Whurtle knew the answers to more questions than any one he had ever talked to. He never said he did not know, or told a little boy to be still. He knew where the boats on the river came from and where they were going, he knew how birds build their nests, and what makes the light in a firefly, and why policemen wear helmets; he even ventured to say where the wind went when it was not blowing, and whether or not God had a wife. Leonard asked him all the questions that had been bottled up in him since his mother went to the hospital, and each evening he thought up a lot more to ask him the following day.

The most exciting discovery he made was that Mr. Whurtle had once been a fireman and had lost his legs when a roof crashed in on a burning tenement.

"Ye would n't think now," said Mr. Whurtle, in ending the story, "that them very cobblestones there in the street has struck fire to the 'oofs of me 'orses, as I braced me two good legs ag'inst the engine an' let 'em 'ave their 'eads clean from Number Three Engine-house to the Parlymint Buildin's. Aye, lad, I was young then, an' the blood was 'ot in me veins. I can feel the wind in me face now, an' the strength in me harms, an' 'ear the poundin' of them 'orses' feet."

"Don't it make you awful sorry, Mr. Whurtle?" Leonard had asked, and then Mr. Whurtle had cleared his throat, and said:

"Per'aps it war n't so bad fer me, lad. I was young an' reckless in them days, an' my legs they carried me many a place I 'ad no right to be. Per'aps the good God seen the chanct to save me by takin' away the legs that was carryin' me to the bad."

Leonard did not tell Miss Meeks about Mr. Whurtle. Miss Meeks liked people to be very clean and proper, and he was quite sure she would not approve of a person who sat on the pavement and had no legs. Mother, of course, would understand, and he could scarcely wait for the time when he could tell her all about his new friend, and give her the many pictures he had made for her during her absence.

"There 's only one more week now to wait," Miss Meeks said to him one afternoon as he was starting off. "The nurse telephoned that your mother was sitting up a wee bit, and they hoped to let her out of the hospital by Christmas Day."

Leonard ran all the way to the Embankment. He knew Mr. Whurtle would be glad, and he was eager to share the good news with him. But, when he arrived, Mr. Whurtle was nowhere to be seen. Instead, a small crowd was gathered about an ambulance wagon, into which two men in uniform were carefully lifting a stretcher. Just as he managed to wriggle his way to the front, a policeman slammed the door of the wagon in the face of the crowd, and ordered the driver to go ahead.

"What 's the matter?" demanded Leonard, breathlessly, but, as usual, nobody noticed him. He heard something about "a runaway horse," and "an old party," and "nothing serious," and then the crowd melted away faster than it had gathered, and he was left alone gazing at a small square of carpet that lay by the wall, covered with lumps of gaily colored chalk.

Those were Mr. Whurtle's things, there was no doubt of that, but where was Mr. Whurtle? Then the truth dawned upon him: it was Mr. Whurtle that had been thrust head first into that long wagon, and it was Mr. Whurtle of whom they spoke as "the old party!"

Leonard started up to ask more questions, but nobody was left who had seen the accident, and only the chalk and the carpet lay there, mute witnesses of his friend's misfortune. His first impulse was to run home, for he was very much frightened. But what was he to do with Mr. Whurtle's things? He could n't take them to him, for he had no idea where he lived, and he could n't take them home with him, for they might be sent for any minute. It was quite a grave responsibility for a person of nine who had an exaggerated respect for artists' materials.

He decided that the only thing for him to do was to sit down and wait. He hoped he would not have to wait until Mr. Minny came at six. Big Ben chimed out the quarter past the hour, then the half-hour, then the quarter to, and still he sat with his back to the wall keeping vigilant watch over the treasure. And, as he waited, a little thought popped into his head and kept getting bigger and bigger, until there did n't seem to be room for anything else. Why could n't he make Mr. Whurtle's pictures for him? It was a sunshiny afternoon and many people were passing, and surely some of them would give a penny or two if only there were some pictures on the pavement.

His heart beat faster as he picked up a piece of chalk and began making the regulation squares. Then came the momentous decision whether his first effort should be a house and a pine-tree against a setting sun, or a boat in a storm. He decided on the former, and, stretching out his legs, just as Mr. Whurtle did his peg-sticks, he went resolutely to work. Now and then, when a shadow fell across the pavement, he knew that some one had stopped to watch him, but when one is absorbed in the engrossing business of making wreaths of blue smoke come out of red chimneys, there is no time to look up.

His first distraction came when a penny was tossed over his head. He was just beginning a new picture, and his first thought was now he would have something round to draw the moon by! His second thought was for Mr. Whurtle. He had almost forgotten the really important part of the work before him, the part that Mr. Whurtle always did first, and was most particular should n't get rubbed out. He set about to remedy his mistake at once.

He remembered the words exactly, and just how they looked on the middle square. He even remembered the exact curve of the big flourish beneath them; it was the spelling that bothered him. After several attempts which he rubbed out with his coat-sleeve, he wrote the following:

> *If wurthy of your notice*
> *Please bestow a trifel.*

The first person to read the inscription was a little girl, who carried a pail in her hand. She and Leonard eyed each other for some time in suspicious silence, then Leonard asked:

"Do you know how many pennies it takes to make a shilling?"

She was so surprised to have this strange little boy ask her a question right out of the arithmetic that she began to move away, but at a safe distance she turned and called back, "Twelve," then scampered up the street with the pail bumping against her legs.

Leonard sighed. Mr. Whurtle had told him once that unless he made a shilling a day, things went very badly with him, and here it was late in the afternoon, and only one penny collected! He sat patiently, with his back to the wall and waited, anxiously scanning each approaching figure, but nobody seemed to notice him. Of course he knew that his pictures were not so splendid as Mr. Whurtle's, but surely anybody could tell that one was a ship, and one was a house, even if he might not be certain whether the round thing in the middle was the sun or the moon!

Sitting still so long made Leonard sleepy, and by and by his head drooped, and the chalk fell out of his limp hand. The next thing he knew, somebody was shaking him gently by the shoulder, and, looking up, he saw a woman in a gray cape and with a gray veil hanging from her bonnet, leaning over him:

"Are you waiting for somebody?" she asked kindly.

For a moment, Leonard could not remember what he was doing there, then

"Sitting still so long made Leonard sleepy, and by and by his head drooped"

he rubbed his eyes and looked at the crudely drawn pictures on the pavement.

"No," he said, with dignity, "I'm 'tending to Mr. Whurtle's business while he's gone."

"Where's he gone?"

"In the ambulance."

"Oh! Do you mean the old fellow with the wooden legs who sits here every afternoon?"

Leonard's face lit up. "Yes'm, that's Mr. Whurtle. Do you know him?"

"Well, I've seen him. But who are you?"

"I'm Leonard Vincent. My mother's at the fever hospital, and we are going home just as soon as she gets well."

"Where is home?"

"In America. Don't you see my flag?" He proudly pulled out the little silk square from his breast pocket.

The woman smiled. "So you are drawing the old man's pictures for him while he's gone?"

"Yes'm, but I've only made one penny so far, and if I don't get twelve, things will go very badly with Mr. Whurtle."

The woman thought for a moment, then she stooped down suddenly, and, to Leonard's dismay, rubbed out the inscription he had so carefully lettered.

"Give me a piece of chalk," she said, and proceeded to write the following:

The wooden-legged man who usually sits here has met with an accident. This little boy is doing his work for him. Your penny is needed.

NURSE WILSON

"Now," she said, rising, "you go on making pictures. People want to see you doing it. Draw a lot. Draw them clear up to the letter-box."

"But think of the chalk it will use up!" said Leonard, eager but dubious; "I've already used up 'most all the red."

"This will pay for the chalk," she said, and dropping a shiny silver coin into his cap, she hurried on her busy way.

Leonard fell to work with enthusiasm. Now that his mind was relieved about the chalk, he let his imagination have full play. He drew houses, and boats, and bunches of grapes, and flowers, and even made so bold as to try a portrait of a gentleman with prominent teeth and eye-glasses.

As he worked, people began to stop to watch him, and to read what was written on the pavement. Some of them looked doubtful, some of them laughed, others asked questions, but sooner or later most of them tossed a penny into his cap.

When Big Ben chimed out five o'clock, Leonard glanced up anxiously. Miss Meeks allowed him to go about the neighborhood as he liked in the afternoon, provided he was at home by five. This was the first time he had disobeyed, but there was nobody to give the money to, and nobody to explain to about the chalk, and it would be a full hour before Mr. Minny came by in his cart.

Leonard had to think very hard before he decided upon a plan. He rolled the remainder of the chalk up in the square of carpet and placed it beside the cap full of pennies. Then he wrote on the pavement, below what Nurse Wilson had written:

I can't watch Mr. Whurtle's things any longer, But plese don't anyboddy take them because he has an axident and no legs.

LEONARD VINCENT

When Mr. Minny drove up an hour later in the cart in which he usually took Mr. Whurtle home, he was surprised to find the familiar figure of his old friend missing. It was strange enough to think of Mr. Whurtle getting away when he could not walk, but the most amazing thing was that the pavement was covered with strange, wild drawings that suggested he had been there, and yet did not in the least resemble the pictures he usually made.

Mr. Minny got out of the cart and read the inscriptions. Then he looked in bewilderment at the small cap overflowing with coins that had remained untouched on the pavement beside the pictures.

"Well, I 'll be blowed!" he said, and, snatching up the cap and the money, he jumped back into his cart, and went dashing off to find out what had happened to Mr. Whurtle.

At the door of the dark basement where they both lived, he paused. There were voices within, and he was almost afraid to enter.

"Whurtle?" he called anxiously.

"Still in the ring!" called out Mr. Whurtle, with a feeble attempt at cheerfulness. Then, as Mr. Minny entered, he added: "This here young gentleman, he 's a newspaper reporter."

The young man sitting beside the low couch looked up from his note-book.

"I was sent down to write up the accident," he said, "and my friend here has been telling me the story of his life."

"Being as it were n't whut you might term a haxident," began Mr. Whurtle, apologetically, but Mr. Minny interrupted impatiently:

"Any bones broken?"

"No, jes peg-sticks. Though the Lord knows it will be as 'ard fer me to get new ones as to grow new legs!"

Then Mr. Minny, unable longer to control himself, poured the money out of the cap onto the floor and proceeded to tell with great relish what had happened. By the time he had finished, the reporter was writing furiously and asking as many questions as Leonard himself.

When Christmas Day came, Leonard felt that he did not have another single thing in the world to wish for. In the first place he had his blessed mother, propped up with pillows to be sure, but bright and smiling; then he had gifts from all the old maid and old bachelor boarders at Miss Meeks's boarding-house; but most exciting of all, he had his name in the biggest newspaper in London!

One whole page of the supplement was taken up with Mr. Whurtle. It told of his early days in the fire-department, and the heroic act that had cost him his legs. It spoke of the plucky fight he had made for thirty years against poverty, supporting himself by first one thing, then another, against odds that would have discouraged the best of men. And, at the last, it gave the story of his friendship for the little American boy, who had taken his place and drawn his pictures when he could no longer draw them for himself.

The article ended thus:

Little Leonard Vincent will be going back to America soon, but old Jim Whurtle, whose picture you see below, will be doing business at the old stand in a few days, and it is predicted that the good work begun by the small American boy will be kept up by the many pedestrians on the Embankment, to whom the old man has long been a familiar figure.

DREAM MARCH
OF THE
CHILDREN.

By
James Whitcomb Riley.

Wasn't it a funny dream? —perfectly bewild'rin'!—
Last night, and night *before,* and night before *that,*
Seemed like I saw the march o' regiments o' children,
Marching to the robin's fife and cricket's rat-ta-tat!
Lily-banners overhead, with the dew upon 'em,
On flashed the little army, as with sword and flame;
Like the buzz o' bumble-wings with the honey on 'em,
Came an eerie, cheery chant, chiming as it came:

Where go the children? Traveling! Traveling!
Where go the children, traveling ahead?
Some go to kindergarten; some go to day-school;
Some go to night-school; and some go to bed!

Smooth roads or rough roads, warm or winter weather
On go the children, tow-head and brown,
Brave boys and brave girls, rank and file together,
Marching out of Babyland, over dale and down:
Some go a-gipsying out in country places—
Out through the orchards, with blossoms on the boughs
Wild, sweet, and pink and white as their own glad faces;
And some go, at evening, calling home the cows.

Where go the children? Traveling! Traveling!
  Where go the children, traveling ahead?
  Some go to foreign wars and camps by the firelight—
  Some go to glory so; and some go to bed!

Some go through grassy lanes leading to the city—
  Thinner grow the green trees and thicker grows the dust;
Ever, though, to little people any path is pretty
  So it leads to newer lands, as they know it must.
    Some go to singing less; some go to list'ning;
    Some go to thinking over ever nobler themes;
    Some go anhungered, but ever bravely whistling,
      Turning never home again only in their dreams.

Where go the children? Traveling! Traveling!
  Where go the children, traveling ahead?
  Some go to conquer things; some go to try them;
  Some go to dream them; and some go to bed!

A LITTLE CONTRABAND

by Charles McIlvaine

In 1862, my company stacked their guns one bright May evening, unslung their knapsacks, unbuckled their cartridge-belts, donned their fatigue uniforms, and, with the method of well-trained soldiers, proceeded to erect a little village of tents beside a beautiful artificial lake made by capturing the tide at its flood, as it poured from the Edisto River up a narrow sluice-way into the extensive and beautiful grounds surrounding the Seabrook mansion. The mocking-birds were in full tune among the trees, and trolling their songs from the great magnolias. Lonely palms stood stark in the glare of sunset by the side of symmetrical live-oaks and cone-shaped pines resting like enormous hay-cocks on the rim of the horizon. The gables, towers, and chimneys of the mansion rose above the mat of trees and shadow, to catch the richness of sunset tints and reflect their fire from many a dazzling dormer. Barns, cotton houses, slave-quarters, together with the multitudinous out-buildings of a Southern plantation, stood on the river bank overlooking its wide waters.

Bird-song, the hum of busy men, the thud of blows driving tent-pins, the stamping of horses as they stood in the wagon-train, the sharp, incisive orders of subaltern officers, as men moved and tents rose at their commands, were the only sounds. War had rested its palsying hand on lovely Edisto, silencing the low of herds, the happy laugh of negroes, and the joy of yonder fair and stately mansion. Everything was deserted—fields, quarters, homestead.

Dashing out of the forest line and galloping across a vast plain, with cotton rows disturbing its level like ripples on a sea of sand, rode a glittering group of officers with a train of mounted orderlies—Brigadier-General H. G. Wright and his staff. On they came, waving a passing salute to the officers of my detachment, and clattered up the broad shell-avenue to Seabrook house, there to establish brigade headquarters in its vacant halls.

The men of my company worked with a will at their canvas homes. Their hearts were light and proud that day—for had they not at grand review caught the general's eye, and by their step and keeping won his favor and the privilege of being his guard at his headquarters?

While watching the erection of my own tent, under the generous shade of a live-oak tree, I heard a shrill, childish yell, and then the shouts of the men. Turning, I saw a sight that was too much for the gravity of even a commanding officer. Down the street—newly walled off by the canvas houses—came a little darky at lightning speed. His bare black legs shone like the spokes of a rapidly revolving carriage-wheel, as they spun over the ground; his head was thrown back; his eyes stuck out until the white rings around their pupils made each look like the bull's-eye of a target; his capacious mouth was open for vociferous yelling, and the fragmentary shirt he wore was extended as far behind him as its scanty material could reach. It did not take an observant eye to see that that jet-black youngster was likely to lose his color from fright. And no wonder; for behind him was a long-legged corporal holding a bayoneted musket within reaching distance of his flying calico.

The explanation of this strange chase was not at first evident. While Corporal Russel was the jolliest of fellows in camp, and always ready for trick or joke, there was now in his gait and face a savage determination to catch that darky or run him beyond the department limits. As the youngster came closer the mystery was solved. In one hand he held a chunk of bacon, and in the other a hardtack. The little rascal had been caught stealing from the corporal's haversack.

Well knowing that the corporal would not hurt him,—for he was kindness itself the whole length of his queer, gaunt form, —the comicality of the race struck me. Naturally taking part with the weaker, I joined in the shouting with, "Go it, Sambo! You are beating him! Hold on to the bacon!"

I think this last expression of encouragement decided the little fellow, for he gave one wild, supplicating look at me, changed his course suddenly, and circled to the protection of my legs. There he clung, in terrified entreaty, much to the detriment of my uniform from his handful of grease.

"Don' you let 'im kill-er me, mas'r! Don' you let 'im kill-er me! I did n't take 'em! I 'll gib um back right away! I 's so hungry. Don' you let 'im kill-er me!"

The little fellow's cry, "I 's so hungry," touched me. I have been hungry myself, and experience makes us wonderfully

charitable. While the breathless corporal halted, shouldered his musket, and stood at "attention" before me, the perfect picture of a soldier, I did what I could to console the waif through a long and tearful outburst, which finally came to an abrupt conclusion from his choking on a piece of cracker that he had tried to swallow between his sobs.

"He is hungry, Corporal—nearly starved. He must have been left behind when the people left here, and has nothing to eat since."

In an instant Corporal Russel's face changed from embarrassment, at being so ludicrously caught, to anxious sympathy.

"Let me have him, Captain. He shall have all I 've got."

A yell from the little fellow, and a renewed grasp of his greasy fingers, admonished me that, however willing the corporal might be to feed him, I was regarded by the stray as his defender and adopted protector. Nor would he take his baconed grasp from my trousers until I had promised him that the corporal should not have him.

From that moment he believed that I had saved his life, and never afterward, on weary march, on dangerous picket, or in the heat of deadly fray, did he swerve from the fidelity born of his gratitude.

Soon the tents were pitched, the campfires were lighted, groups sat in their red glare, or lolled where the rippled lake put ruffles around the moon's reflected face (a silvery night-cap most becoming) until "taps" darkened the camp, and no sound but the bittern's cry and measured tread of sentinels disturbed the silence of the night. In a corner of my tent, well fed and sound asleep, lay little "Nigger June."

He had told me his name and his story in his own quaint way. When the Federal gunboats steamed up the Edisto River, the ignorant and terrified slaves fled to hiding-places in the swamp-forests or followed their masters from the island to the mainland; and June, whose whole family tree, so far as he knew, consisted of the one guardian he had ever had (his old "Aunt Peggy"), was, owing to the shortness of his legs and a chronic habit of going to sleep under all possible circumstances, left behind. Hunger was too much for his honesty; so, like a dog after a bone, he had sneaked into the camp and was spied by the keen-eyed corporal foraging on the provisions. He took to his new surroundings as naturally as if he had been born by a camp-fire and cradled in a drum. Like a cat left behind in a deserted home, he became a legacy to the new-comers, and he was petted and cared for accordingly.

To say anything without an enforcing emphasis, or to expect to be believed without reference to some authority of higher value than his own, was foreign to June's idea of impressive English. His lingo was that of the Carolina Sea Islands, but his laugh was cosmopolitan—there was no limit to its shades and changes. It embodied the diapason of jollity, was ready at the slightest provocation, and was as infectious as sneezes from snuff. His dancing incorporated every caper that ever was cut; his full, rich, contralto voice rang out the complete weird song-lore of his race. It was not long before he became known throughout the whole Tenth Army Corps. No picnic, coon-hunt, fishing-party, nor camp game in which the men indulged was complete without him.

He was in constant demand from all parts of the command because of the amusement he afforded, and in consequence was generally "lent out" to some one. Unlike other loans, he never failed to return. Diving for quarters in a tub of meal was his specialty. He could keep his "bullet" head under longer than any other

darky in the Department of the South,—never failing to capture the silver in his teeth and be up in time to have a laugh at his rooting, struggling competitors. Butting was a favorite pastime. With head down, shoulders up, prancing on one leg, he would issue challenge to man or boy to do battle with him, and he always scored a victory.

An immense negro, named Orchard, used to come daily into camp with a tub on his head containing shrimps, which found ready sale among the soldiers. June had repeatedly danced his war-dance around Orchard without obtaining even recognition as an enemy.

One day, after an unsuccessful challenge, he came to me disgusted and full of contempt. "See um dar, Cappin, see um, dat big niggah. Him too proud. Woffer him not butt me? Woffer him not go down on his knees an' butt me? 'Deed, I knock 'm shoo."

Being in full sympathy with my butting phenomenon, and having been his backer on many occasions, I said, "June, I will give you a quarter if you make Orchard drop that tub of shrimps."

After he had taken a roll, turned two or three somersaults, and done some dancing, to work his elation out properly, he replied:

"Mas'r, dat quartah's mine. Dat tub mighty high up. Long way up to dat tub, Mas'r Cappin. Orchard hab to git from un'er him." He dashed off in high glee, and was soon stalking beside the black shrimp merchant, with an empty cracker-box balanced on his head, imitating his big model in every action. I watched his manœuvers with keen enjoyment,—it was a contest between a pygmy and a giant. He soon attracted Orchard's attention, and the shrimp dealer came to a sudden and dignified halt.

"What you doin' dat fo', you grinnin' monkey? What you make mock ob me fo'?" asked Orchard, angrily.

"Put down you' tub, an' butt me den," was the little fellow's reply. "Ain't I ax you, ebry day, fo' to butt me? Put down you' tub."

Thus "daring" him, June laid his cracker-box upside down, a few feet in front of the irate Orchard, and backed off as if preparing for an acceptance of his challenge.

"Go 'way, chile. If I butt you, I kill you, shoo. What fo' I go buttin' sich a pickaninny like you, fo'?"

"Put down dat tub!" was all the answer he had from June, who was posturing like a goat full of fight.

"Go 'way, you sassy niggah! What fo' I put down de tub fo' de likes ob you,"

The halt and parley were what the little strategist was after. Quick as a flash he charged like a ram, leaped from the cracker-box, shot forward as from a catapult, and landed his head with the force of a solid shot fair on Orchard's waistband! If Orchard had been hinged in the middle he could not have doubled up more quickly. Down came the tub, the shrimps flew in all directions, and before the astonished giant comprehended what had happened, June was shrieking his delight and celebrating his victory behind a group of soldiers who were cheering his exploit.

The promised quarter was paid to June, and Orchard was compensated for his shrimps; but it was many a day before he forgave "dat grinnin', buttin', sassy brack monkey."

June was always the hero of his adventures, but he was not always heroic. A few days after his appearance in camp, he was despatched to fetch some water from a spring under the protecting shade of a leaning live-oak some distance away, across the plain of cotton rows. In order

that he might not have to go soon again, he determined to carry "a lazy man's load." Therefore he put a mackerel-kit on his head, took a bucket in each hand, and away he went—a walking reservoir. Pretty soon he came bounding across the field, bouncing from the cotton rows like a ricochet shot, yelling at the top of his voice, "De Debble, de Debble, de Debble!" As usual, when in trouble, he came straight to me. All he could gasp was:

"Oh, de Debble, de Debble, de Debble! Lawks-a-massy, Cappin, I see um de Debble!"

"Where?" I asked, as well as laughing would let me.

"In de watah. I stoop down to de watah ober yonder by de spring, an' jus' ez I gwine to scoop de watah in de bucket, dar wuz de Debble dar, lookin' right out de watah at me. Oh, I 'm gwine to die! De Debble's gwine to catch me, sho. Don't let um catch me, Mas'r Cappin!" He was terribly frightened—trembling, and clinging to me piteously. He had certainly seen *something*.

"Don't be afraid, June," I said consolingly. "You did not see any devil." He backed up his positive assertion to the contrary with a favorite expression. "Fo' a troof, Cappin, I *see um*. Ain't I *know* 'im when I see um? Dar wuz his two horns, an' eyes afire, an' mouf big 'nough fo' to swaller me right down kerplump,—ain't I see um?"

Nothing would convince him that he had made a mistake,—and nothing ever did.

For a moment I was frightened, too, when I went to the spring after the abandoned buckets, and to see what was the matter: for, there in the water was reflected a countenance of more than Satanic ugliness. As it quickly disappeared, a heavy thud on the ground just beside me inclined me to follow in the footsteps of

June and to confess entire adoption of his belief. An instant sufficed to show me that the supposed demon was a large Angora goat, resting in the broad crotch of the leaning tree. The goat's head and shoulders were vaguely mirrored in the spring.

June was no manner of use, so far as the performance of any duty was concerned, but in the camp he was a power which the company. His likes and dislikes for the different men were strong, and knew no compromise. Woe to the soldier who excited June's ire! His shoes would be missing, his haversack mysteriously filled with sand, his blanket with nettles, his canteen with salt-water from the lake, and his every peculiarity would be pantomined for the amusement of his comrades. He invariably

June is tried by court martial

would have been sadly missed. He was the camp Jester. From reveille to taps, his merry pranks amused the men, his laugh kept all in good humor. He was circus, clown, and side-show, combined. He could climb a tree, shake down a 'coon, and be back in time to be mixed with the pile of dogs and darkies in at the death. He could run a rabbit to earth, see a squirrel in its thickest hiding-place, throw a stone unerringly, and out-manœuver any man in appeared on dress-parade in a unique uniform. A sardine-box carried his cartridges, a bit of string answered for belt, a forked stick for a gun. No man of the company went through the parade exercises better, and, if it pleased him to imitate the commanding officer a few feet to the rear, the quivering line of muskets and red faces of the men bore testimony to the exactness of his mimicry.

He was once caught tying a pair of

wickedly clawed crabs into the coat-sleeve of one of his tormentors. The wags of the company decided to try him by court martial. The charge was "conduct prejudicial to good order and military discipline." June pleaded his own cause manfully. "What fo' you sittin' on me fo'? Mar's Cappin an' Aunt Peggy is my boss; an' Aunt Peggy ain't yere no mo'. Le' me go. Woffer you sittin' on me?"

Notwithstanding the force and logic of his defense, he was ruthlessly sentenced to a term of imprisonment within the walls of an empty and headless pork-barrel. In this predicament, he said indignantly to me, "See-um dis, Cappin! See-um dis! Cappin, fo' goodness sake, come take-er-me out. I 'll butt dat co't-ma'sh'l till um neb' go fishin' or 'coon-huntin' no mo' fo' a week!"

He kept his word. One of his persecutors narrowly escaped severe burns in the cook's fire, from being butted into the coals while lighting his pipe. Another was sent sprawling into the lake by a well-calculated blow from June's woolly head, while he was washing his platter in its waters. Another had his senses knocked out of him, being sent headlong while tying his shoes; and with all, sooner or later, the account was squared to June's complete satisfaction.

The delightful sojourn at Seabrook was only too short. One morning there was a stir at headquarters, a riding to and fro of aides-de-camp, a bustle among the orderlies, and the clerks were packing up their papers. All of these signs indicated a move.

Soon came an order to strike tents and join the main body of troops, three miles away, with my detachment. In the excitement of the move, June was in his glory. Missing articles were found as tent floors were taken up, and the secret avenues were discovered by which he obtained entrance to the tents of his enemies. "That infernal little Nigger June" was in demand throughout the camp, but he wisely shouted his derision from a safe distance.

I employed a stray contraband to carry some of the lighter and more breakable articles of my tent furniture, much to the disgust of June, and the breeding of not a little jealousy in him. Taking advantage of my being occupied away from my quarters, the little joker told the fellow that he must carry my trunk, bedding, camp-chest, and everything else that could be hung on him —load enough for a camel. Upon my return, I found June in the last contortions of a laughing convulsion. Following with my eye his pointing finger, in the direction of our march, I saw in the distance a moving object resembling a pack-mule with a huge chest on his back and side loads reaching to the ground.

"See-um, dah, Cappin? See-um dat fool niggah? 'Im don't know nuffin' no mo' dan a punken. Dah he go, totin' de chist, an' trunk, an' ebbryting. 'Deed, Cappin, guess dat niggah don't run fas' dis time, ef he hol' on to all he tote! Hi—yah!"

It was not long before it was generally known that an attack was to be made upon Charleston; that a march across John's Island to the Stono River was to be followed by a landing on James Island, under protection of the gunboats in rendezvous there.

The march commenced; not one who was in it will ever forget its miseries from its beginning to its disastrous end. Under a scorching sun, through the stench of putrid swamps filled with rotting mussels, through chaparral alive with stinging insects; across sanded plains, making the air quiver with burning reflections; amid blinding, choking, clouds of dust—batteries tugged, cavalry plunged, and infantry trod with indescribable sufferings. June, alone, seemed not to mind it. Astride a cannon, mounted on a caisson, perched behind a mounted soldier, or trotting alongside my company, his quaint songs and antics cheered the men and lightened many a step. Every haversack was open to him; every canteen was ready to quench his thirst; every hand would be outstretched to give him a lift over a difficult bit of road.

In the long days and nights that followed, of murderous work and dangerous duty, nothing could prevent June from taking part. The most positive orders would not keep him in camp; no guardhouse was tight enough to hold him. If I was doing duty with outlying pickets, on reconnaissance, or in pushing from the front a fighting skirmish-line, he would climb a chimney-flue, slip through some chink he had made or found, dash through a window or dart between the legs of his guard, and speed away with unerring scent on my track. A tiny pair of black legs moving swiftly from tree to tree, the pop of a woolly head from behind a log, a glistening of his bright eyes from some jungle, would give the first knowledge of his presence, and when detected, his laughing greeting always was, "Lor', Mas'r Cappin, what a time I 's done been hab huntin' you. Woffer you done go' way fo', an' lebe-er-me?"

He never allowed himself to be put on the defensive. No one wished to see him hurt, so all tried to care for him, but it was not possible; the little fellow, in his faithfulness, felt that it was his duty to take care of me, so all efforts to keep him away and in safety were unavailing.

One day, never to be forgotten,—June 16, 1862,—a charge was made upon the Confederate earthworks at Secessionville, South Carolina, and six hundred brave men and true were laid low in front of the defenses. At an early hour on the morning of that day, I was fastening my sword about me when June waked up where he was lying curled up like a dog in the corner of my tent. I was dressing as quietly as possible without waking him, well knowing the deadly work planned for the morning, but his watchfulness was as keen as that of a Bedouin of the desert. He surprised me with the exclamation, "Mas'r Cappin, what you gwine to do? Whar you been goin' to?"

He was told, sharply, to lie down and go to sleep, and I added, "June, if you follow me to-day, I will stand you on a barrel, with a bayonet on each side of you, and make you hold a piece of ice in each hand until it is all melted." This was the only punishment for which he cared a particle, and the threat of it usually set him to bellowing like an orphaned calf. Strange to say, on this occasion it produced no marked effect; he seemed to feel that something of more than usual importance was taking me out at that time in the morning, armed and equipped. He came to me, and in the faint light passed his hand around my sword-belt to feel whether or not my revolver was there. I seldom carried one,—never, indeed, unless there was an almost certain prospect of its need. When his hand touched its sheath, he took hold of my coat-sleeve in a pleading way, and said, "Woffer you go widout Niggah June? Leave 'im go 'long! 'Im git in de bush an' shake his shirt an' keep de Rebels from shootin' Mas'r Cappin."

With a laugh at his idea of protection, I told him that I would soon be back all right,—to stay where he was. I left him looking disconsolately after me as I went out.

Once in the heat of battle, when shells were shrieking their horrible death-songs overhead, when black balls of iron tore their way through ranks of living men, when grape and canister, shrapnel and bullets were raining death and wounds, the smoke lifted, and through the ragged branches of a hedge in front of me,—not two hundred yards from the fort,—I thought I saw a little black demon wildly waving a white flag.

"June!" I yelled; but the roar and rattle made my voice no more than the piping of a child in a storm, and a belch of smoke from the enemy's guns rolled as a mighty wall between me and the vision.

Such a battle could not last long. We were defeated, but the fort was nearly emptied of defenders.

When the wind shook out the air and cleared it of its smoke and angry trembling, heart-rending groans went up from that stricken field.

During the hurried gathering of the wounded, Corporal Russel came to me with face pale, and eyes bloodshot. "Come," said he, "over by the hedge. June wants you."

I knew what he meant; the vision came back to me. There little June lay, shot to death. In one hand he clutched his rag of a shirt; in the other was my haversack which I had left in my tent. He tried to laugh when I knelt by him, as he feebly raised the haversack toward me. "I done fotch you you' breakfas', Mas'r Cappin. Dar 's sumpin to eat an' drink in de habbersack. I done shaked my shirt an' kep de rebels from shootin' Mas'r Cappin. Don' stan' me on de bar'l, an' put col' ice in my han', dis time!"

He smiled, as he had often done before, when he knew that he had the better of me, the haversack fell to the ground, and then, with his eyes resting upon me as if waiting for an assurance of forgiveness, he died.

We laid him at the end of the long ditch where lay so many of his friends; and among those hundreds of graves was one at the head of which stood a piece of a splintered flagstaff, upon which a sincere mourner had written, "Little June."

When Thomas Takes His Pen

By Elsie Hill

Young Thomas Jones came home from
    school with sad and solemn air;
He did not kiss his mother's cheek
    nor pull his sister's hair;
He hungered not for apples, and he spoke
    in dismal tones;
'T was very clear misfortune drear had
    happened Thomas Jones.

"My precious child," his mother cried,
    "what, *what* is troubling you?
You 're hurt—you 're ill—*you 've failed in
    school!* Oh, tell us what to do!"
Then Thomas Jones made answer in a
    dull, despairing way:
"I 've got to write an essay on 'The Indian
    To-day.'"

"The more he read, the more he could not write"

His tallest sister ran to him, compassion in
her eye;
His smallest sister pitied him—nor knew
the reason why;
And all that happy family forsook its work
and play
To hunt up information on "The Indian
To-day."

They read of Hiawatha and of sad Ra-
mona's woe—
You found encyclopedias where'er they
chanced to go.
They bought a set of Cooper, and they
searched it through and through,
While Thomas Jones sat mournfully and
told them what to do.

For three whole days the library was like
a moving-van.
"Is Mr. Jones," each caller asked, "a liter-
ary man?"
And day by day more pitiful became young
Thomas' plight,

Because, alas! the more he read, the more
he could not write.
"Write what you know," his mother
begged (she stirred not from his side).
"*I do not know one single thing!*" that
wretched child replied.
"Oh, help me, *won't* you? Don't you
care?" Then when assistance came,
"Don't tell me—*don't!* It is n't *fair!*" he
pleaded just the same.

The night before the fateful day was quite
the worst of all.
Black care upon the house of Jones descended like a pall.
All pleasure paled, all comfort failed, and
laughter seemed a sin;
For "Oh, to-morrow," Thomas wailed, "it
must be handed in!"

When, lo! the voice of Great-aunt Jones
came sternly through the door:
"I cannot stand this state of things one
single minute more!

"*'Don't tell me—don't! It is n't fair!'*"

The training of a fractious child is plainly
  not my mission;
But—*Thomas Jones, go straight upstairs
  and write that composition!*"
And Thomas Jones went straight upstairs,
  and sat him down alone,
And—though I grant a stranger thing was
  surely never known—
In two short hours he returned serenely to
  display
Six neatly written pages on "The Indian
  To-day"!

His teacher read them to the class, and
  smiled a well-pleased smile;
She praised the simple language and the
  calmly flowing style;
"For while," she said, "he does not rise to
  any lofty height,
'T is wonderful how *easily* young Thomas
  Jones can write."

"*'Thomas Jones, go straight upstairs and
write that composition!'*"

BABY SYLVESTER

by Bret Harte

IT was at a little mining camp in the California Sierras that he first dawned upon me in all his grotesque sweetness.

I had arrived early in the morning, but not in time to intercept the friend who was the object of my visit. He had gone "prospecting,"—so they told me on the river—and would not probably return until late in the afternoon. They could not say what direction he had taken; they could not suggest that I would be likely to find him if I followed. But it was the general opinion that I had better wait.

I looked around me. I was standing upon the bank of the river; and, apparently, the only other human beings in the world were my interlocutors, who were even then just disappearing from my horizon down the steep bank toward the river's dry bed. I approached the edge of the bank.

Where could I wait?

O, anywhere; down with them on the river-bar, where they were working, if I liked! Or I could make myself at home in any of those cabins that I found lying round loose. Or, perhaps it would be cooler and pleasanter for me in my friend's cabin on the hill. Did I see those three large sugar-pines? And, a little to the right, a canvas roof and chimney over the bushes? Well, that was my friend's,—that was Dick Sylvester's cabin. I could stake my horse in that little hollow, and just hang round there till he came. I would find some books

in the shanty; I could amuse myself with them. Or I could play with the baby.

Do what?

But they had already gone. I leaned over the bank and called after their vanishing figures:

"What did you say I could do?"

The answer floated slowly up on the hot, sluggish air:

"Pla-a-y with the ba-by."

The lazy echoes took it up and tossed it languidly from hill to hill, until Bald Mountain opposite made some incoherent remark about the baby, and then all was still.

I must have been mistaken. My friend was not a man of family; there was not a woman within forty miles of the river camp; he never was so passionately devoted to children as to import a luxury so expensive. I must have been mistaken.

I turned my horse's head toward the hill. As we slowly climbed the narrow trail, the little settlement might have been some exhumed Pompeian suburb, so deserted and silent were its habitations. The open doors plainly disclosed each rudely-furnished interior,—the rough pine table, with the scant equipage of the morning meal still standing; the wooden bunk, with its tumbled and disheveled blankets. A golden lizard—the very genius of desolate stillness —had stopped breathless upon the threshold of one cabin; a squirrel peeped impudently into the window of another; a woodpecker, with the general flavor of undertaking which distinguishes that bird, withheld his sepulchral hammer from the coffin-lid of the roof on which he was professionally engaged, as we passed. For a moment, I half-regretted that I had not accepted the invitation to the river-bed; but, the next moment, a breeze swept up the long, dark cañon, and the waiting files of the pines beyond bent toward me in salutation. I think my horse understood as well as myself that it was the cabins that made the solitude human, and therefore unbearable, for he quickened his pace, and with a gentle trot brought me to the edge of the wood and the three pines that stood like videttes before the Sylvester outpost.

Unsaddling my horse in the little hollow, I unslung the long *riata* from the saddle-bow, and tethering him to a young sapling, turned toward the cabin. But I had gone only a few steps when I heard a quick trot behind me, and poor Pomposo, with every fibre tingling with fear, was at my heels. I looked hurriedly around. The breeze had died away, and only an occasional breath from the deep-chested woods, more like a long sigh than any articulate sound, or the dry singing of a cicala in the heated cañon, were to be heard. I examined the ground carefully for rattlesnakes, but in vain. Yet here was Pomposo shivering from his arched neck to his sensitive haunches, his very flanks pulsating with terror. I soothed him as well as I could, and then walked to the edge of the wood and peered into its dark recesses. The bright flash of a bird's wing, or the quick dart of a squirrel, was all I saw. I confess it was with something of superstitious expectation that I again turned toward the cabin. A fairy child, attended by Titania and her train, lying in an expensive cradle, would not have surprised me; a Sleeping Beauty, whose awak-

ening would have repeopled these solitudes with life and energy, I am afraid I began to confidently look for, and would have kissed without hesitation.

But I found none of these. Here was the evidence of my friend's taste and refinement in the hearth swept scrupulously clean, in the picturesque arrangement of the fur skins that covered the floor and furniture, and the striped *serápe* lying on the wooden couch. Here were the walls fancifully papered with illustrations from the *London News;* here was the wood-cut portrait of Mr. Emerson over the chimney, quaintly framed with blue jays' wings; here were his few favorite books on the swinging shelf; and here, lying upon the couch, the latest copy of *Punch.* Dear Dick! The flour-sack was sometimes empty, but the gentle satirist seldom missed his weekly visit.

I threw myself on the couch and tried to read. But I soon exhausted my interest in my friend's library, and lay there staring through the open door on the green hillside beyond. The breeze again sprang up, and a delicious coolness, mixed with the rare incense of the woods, stole through the cabin. The slumbrous droning of bumble-bees outside the canvas roof, the faint cawing of rooks on the opposite mountain, and the fatigue of my morning ride, began to droop my eyelids. I pulled the *serápe* over me, as a precaution against the freshening mountain breeze, and in a few moments was asleep.

I do not remember how long I slept. I must have been conscious, however, during my slumber, of my inability to keep myself covered by the *serápe,* for I awoke once or twice, clutching it with a despairing hand as it was disappearing over the foot of the couch. Then I became suddenly aroused to the fact that my efforts to retain it were resisted by some equally persistent force, and, letting it go, I was horrified at seeing it swiftly drawn under the couch. At this point I sat up completely awake; for immediately after, what seemed to be an exaggerated muff began to emerge from under the couch. Presently it appeared fully, dragging the *serápe* after it. There was no mistaking it now—it was a baby bear. A mere suckling, it was true,—a helpless roll of fat and fur,—but, unmistakably, a grizzly cub.

I cannot recall anything more irresistibly ludicrous than its aspect as it slowly raised its small wondering eyes to mine. It was so much taller on its haunches than its shoulders,—its fore-legs were so disproportionately small,—that in walking, its hind-feet invariably took precedence. It was perpetually pitching forward over its pointed, inoffensive nose, and recovering itself always, after these involuntary somersaults, with the gravest astonishment. To add to its preposterous appearance, one of its hind-feet was adorned by a shoe of Sylvester's, into which it had accidentally and inextricably stepped. As this somewhat impeded its first impulse to fly, it turned to me; and then, possibly recognizing in the stranger the same species as its master, it paused. Presently, it slowly raised itself on its hind-legs, and vaguely and deprecatingly waved a baby paw, fringed with little hooks of steel. I took the paw and shook it gravely. From that moment we were friends. The little affair of the *serápe* was forgotten.

Nevertheless, I was wise enough to cement our friendship by an act of delicate courtesy. Following the direction of his eyes, I had no difficulty in finding, on a shelf near the ridge-pole, the sugar-box and the square lumps of white sugar that even the poorest miner is never without. While he was eating them I had time to examine him more closely. His body was a silky, dark, but exquisitely modulated grey, deepening to black in his paws and muzzle. His fur was excessively long, thick, and soft as eider down; the cushions of flesh beneath, perfectly infantine in their texture and contour. He was so very young that the palms of his half-human feet were still tender as a baby's. Except for the bright blue, steely hooks, half-sheathed in his little toes, there was not a single harsh outline or detail in his plump figure. He was as free from angles as one of Leda's offspring. Your caressing hand sank away in his fur with dreamy languor. To look at him long was an intoxication of the senses; to pat him was a wild delirium; to embrace him, an utter demoralization of the intellectual faculties.

When he had finished the sugar, he rolled out of the door with a half-diffident, half-inviting look in his eye, as if he expected me to follow. I did so, but the sniffing and snorting of the keen-scented Pomposo in the hollow, not only revealed the cause of his former terror, but decided me to take another direction. After a moment's hesitation, he concluded to go with me, although I am satisfied, from a certain impish look in his eye, that he fully understood and rather enjoyed the fright of Pomposo. As he rolled along at my side, with a gait not unlike a drunken sailor, I discovered that his long hair concealed a leather collar around his neck, which bore for its legend the single word, "Baby!" I recalled the mysterious suggestion of the two miners. This, then, was the "baby" with whom I was to "play."

How we "played;" how Baby allowed me to roll him down hill, crawling and puffing up again each time, with perfect good humor; how he climbed a young sapling after my Panama hat, which I had "shied" into one of the topmost branches; how after getting it he refused to descend until it suited his pleasure; how when he did come down he persisted in walking about on three legs, carrying my hat, a crushed and shapeless mass, clasped to his breast with the remaining one; how I missed him at last, and finally discovered him seated on a table in one of the tenantless cabins, with a bottle of syrup between his paws, vainly endeavoring to extract its contents—these and other details of that eventful day I shall not weary the reader with now. Enough that when Dick Sylvester returned, I was pretty well fagged out, and the baby was rolled up, an immense bolster at the foot of the couch, asleep. Sylvester's first words after our greeting were:

"Is n't he delicious?"

"Perfectly. Where did you get him?"

"Lying under his dead mother, five miles from here," said Dick, lighting his pipe. "Knocked her over at fifty yards; perfectly clean shot—never moved afterwards! Baby crawled out, scared but unhurt. She must have been carrying him in her mouth, and dropped him when she faced me, for he was n't more than three days old, and not steady on his pins. He takes the only milk that comes to the settlement—brought up by Adams Express at seven o'clock every morning. They say he looks like me. Do you think so?" asked Dick, with perfect gravity, stroking his hay-colored moustachios, and evidently assuming his best expression.

I took leave of the baby early the next morning in Sylvester's cabin, and out of respect to Pomposo's feelings, rode by without any postscript of expression. But the night before I had made Sylvester solemnly swear, that in the event of any separation between himself and Baby, it should revert to me. "At the same time," he had added, "it's only fair to say that I don't think of dying just yet, old fellow, and I don't know of anything else that would part the cub and me."

Two months after this conversation, as I was turning over the morning's mail at my office in San Francisco, I noticed a letter bearing Sylvester's familiar hand. But it was post-marked "Stockton," and I opened it with some anxiety at once. Its contents were as follows:

O FRANK!—Don't you remember what we agreed upon anent the baby? Well, consider me as dead for the next six months, or gone where cubs can't follow me—East. I know you love the baby; but do you think, dear boy,—now, really, do you think you *could* be a father to it? Consider this well. You are young, thoughtless, well-meaning enough; but dare you take upon yourself the functions of guide, genius or guardian to one so young and guileless? Could you be the mentor to this Telemachus? Think of the temptations of a metropolis. Look at the question well, and let me know speedily, for I 've got him as far as this place, and he 's kicking up an awful row in the hotel-yard, and rattling his chain like a maniac. Let me know by telegraph at once.

SYLVESTER.

P. S.—Of course he 's grown a little, and does n't take things always as quietly as he did. He dropped rather heavily on two of Watson's "purps" last week, and snatched old Watson himself, bald-headed, for interfering. You remember Watson: for an intelligent man, he knows very little of California fauna. How are you fixed for bears on Montgomery street,—I mean in regard to corrals and things?

S.

P. P. S.—He's got some new tricks. The boys have been teaching him to put up his hands with them. He slings an ugly left.—S.

I am afraid that my desire to possess myself of Baby overcame all other considerations, and I telegraphed an affirmative at once to Sylvester. When I reached my lodgings late that afternoon, my landlady was awaiting me with a telegram. It was two lines from Sylvester:

All right. Baby goes down on night-boat. Be a father to him.—S.

It was due, then, at one o'clock that night. For a moment I was staggered at my own precipitation. I had as yet made no preparations,—had said nothing to my landlady about her new guest. I expected to arrange everything in time; and now, through Sylvester's indecent haste, that time had been shortened twelve hours.

Something, however, must be done at once. I turned to Mrs. Brown. I had great reliance in her maternal instincts; I had that still greater reliance, common to our sex, in the general tender-heartedness of pretty women. But I confess I was alarmed. Yet, with a feeble smile, I tried to introduce the subject with classical ease and lightness. I even said, "If Shakespeare's Athenian clown, Mrs. Brown, believed that a lion among ladies was a dreadful thing, what must——" But here I broke down, for Mrs. Brown, with the awful intuition of her sex, I saw at once was more occupied with my manner than my speech. So I tried a business *brusquerie,* and, placing the telegram in her hand, said hurriedly, "We must do something about this at once. It's perfectly absurd, but he will be here at one to-night. Beg thousand pardons, but business prevented my speaking before ——" and paused, out of breath and courage.

Mrs. Brown read the telegram gravely, lifted her pretty eyebrows, turned the paper over and looked on the other side, and then, in a remote and chilling voice, asked me if she understood me to say that the mother was coming also.

"O dear no," I exclaimed, with considerable relief; "the mother is dead, you know. Sylvester—that is my friend, who sent this —shot her when the Baby was only three days old——" But the expression of Mrs. Brown's face at this moment was so alarming, that I saw that nothing but the fullest explanation would save me. Hastily, and I fear not very coherently, I told her all.

She relaxed sweetly. She said I had frightened her with my talk about lions. Indeed, I think my picture of poor Baby— albeit a trifle highly-colored—touched her motherly heart. She was even a little vexed at what she called Sylvester's "hard-heartedness." Still, I was not without some apprehension. It was two months since I had seen him, and Sylvester's vague allusion to his "slinging an ugly left" pained me. I looked at sympathetic little Mrs. Brown, and the thought of Watson's pups covered me with guilty confusion.

Mrs. Brown had agreed to sit up with me until he arrived. One o'clock came, but no Baby. Two o'clock—three o'clock passed. It was almost four when there was a wild clatter of horses' hoofs outside, and with a jerk a wagon stopped at the door. In an instant I had opened it and confronted a stranger. Almost at the same moment, the horses attempted to run away with the wagon.

The stranger's appearance was, to say the least, disconcerting. His clothes were badly torn and frayed; his linen sack hung from his shoulders like a herald's apron; one of his hands was bandaged; his face scratched, and there was no hat on his disheveled head. To add to the general effect, he had evidently sought relief from his woes in drink, and he swayed from side to side as he clung to the door-handle; and, in a very thick voice, stated that he had "suthin" for me outside. When he had finished, the horses made another plunge.

Mrs. Brown thought they must be frightened at something.

"Frightened!" laughed the stranger, with bitter irony. "Oh no! Hossish aint frightened! On'y ran away four timesh comin' here. On no! Nobody's frightened. Everythin's all ri'. Aint it, Bill?" he said, addressing the driver. "On'y been overboard twish; knocked down a hatchway once. Thash nothin'! On'y two men unner doctor's han's at Stockton. Thash nothin'! Six hunner dollarsh cover all dammish."

I was too much disheartened to reply, but moved toward the wagon. The stranger eyed me with an astonishment that almost sobered him.

"Do you reckon to tackle that animile yourself?" he asked, as he surveyed me from head to foot.

I did not speak, but, with an appearance of boldness I was far from feeling, walked to the wagon and called "Baby!"

"All ri'. Cash loose them straps, Bill, and stan' clear."

The straps were cut loose, and Baby— the remorseless, the terrible—quietly tumbled to the ground, and rolling to my side, rubbed his foolish head against me.

I think the astonishment of the two men was beyond any vocal expression. Without a word the drunken stranger got into the wagon and drove away.

And Baby? He had grown, it is true, a trifle larger; but he was thin, and bore the marks of evident ill-usage. His beautiful coat was matted and unkempt, and his claws—those bright steel hooks—had been ruthlessly pared to the quick. His eyes were furtive and restless, and the old expression of stupid good humor had changed to one of intelligent distrust. His intercourse with mankind had evidently quickened his intellect without broadening his moral nature.

I had great difficulty in keeping Mrs. Brown from smothering him in blankets and ruining his digestion with the delicacies of her larder; but I at last got him completely rolled up in the corner of my room and asleep. I lay awake some time later with plans for his future. I finally determined to take him to Oakland, where I had built a little cottage and always spent my Sundays, the very next day. And in the midst of a rosy picture of domestic felicity, I fell asleep.

When I awoke it was broad day. My eyes at once sought the corner where Baby had been lying. But he was gone. I sprang from the bed, looked under it, searched the closet, but in vain. The door was still locked; but there were the marks of his blunted claws upon the sill of the window, that I had forgotten to close. He had evidently escaped that way,—but where? The window opened upon a balcony, to which the only other entrance was through the hall. He must be still in the house.

My hand was already upon the bell-rope, but I stayed it in time. If he had not made himself known, why should I disturb the house? I dressed myself hurriedly, and slipped into the hall. The first object that met my eyes was a boot lying upon the stairs. It bore the marks of Baby's teeth; and as I looked along the hall, I saw too plainly that the usual array of freshly-blackened boots and shoes before the lodgers' doors was not there. As I ascended the stairs I found another, but with the blacking carefully licked off. On the third floor were two or three more boots, slightly mouthed; but at this point Baby's taste for blacking had evidently palled. A little further on was a ladder, leading to an open scuttle. I mounted the ladder, and reached the flat roof, that formed a continuous level over the row of houses to the corner of the street. Behind the chimney on the very last roof something was lurking. It was the fugitive Baby. He was covered with dust and dirt and fragments of glass. But he was sitting on his hind-legs, and was eating an enormous slab of pea-nut candy, with a look of mingled guilt and infinite satisfaction. He even, I fancied, slightly stroked his stomach with his disengaged fore-paw, as I approached. He knew that I was looking for him, and the expression of his eye said plainly, "The past, at least, is secure."

I hurried him, with the evidences of his guilt, back to the scuttle, and descended on tip-toe to the floor beneath. Providence favored us; I met no one on the stairs, and his own cushioned tread was inaudible. I think he was conscious of the dangers of detection, for he even forebore to breathe, or much less chew the last mouthful he had taken; and he skulked at my side, with the syrup dropping from his motionless jaws. I think he would have silently choked to death just then, for my sake; and it was not until I had reached my room again, and threw myself panting on the sofa, that I saw how near strangulation he had been. He gulped once or twice, apologetically, and then walked to the corner of his own accord, and rolled himself up like an immense sugar-plum, sweating remorse and treacle at every pore.

I locked him in when I went to breakfast, when I found Mrs. Brown's lodgers in a state of intense excitement over certain mysterious events of the night before, and the dreadful revelations of the morning. It appeared that burglars had entered the block from the scuttles; that being suddenly alarmed, they had quitted our house without committing any depredation, dropping even the boots they had collected in the halls; but that a desperate attempt had been made to force the till in the confectioner's shop on the corner, and that the glass show-cases had been ruthlessly smashed. A courageous servant in No. 4 had seen a masked burglar, on his hands and knees, attempting to enter their scuttle; but on her shouting, "Away wid yees," he instantly fled.

I sat through this recital with cheeks that burned uncomfortably; nor was I the less embarrassed on raising my eyes to meet Mrs. Brown's fixed curiously and mischievously on mine. As soon as I could make my escape from the table, I did so; and running rapidly up stairs, sought refuge from any possible inquiry in my own room. Baby was still asleep in the corner. It would not be safe to remove him until the lodgers had gone down town; and I was revolving in my mind the expediency of keeping him until night veiled his obtrusive eccentricity from the public eye, when there came a cautious tap at my door. I opened it. Mrs. Brown slipped in quietly, closed the door softly, stood with her back against it and her hand on the knob, and beckoned me mysteriously towards her. Then she asked, in a low voice:

"Is hair-dye poisonous?"

I was too confounded to speak.

"O do! you know what I mean," she said, impatiently. "This stuff." She produced suddenly from behind her a bottle with a Greek label—so long as to run two or three times spirally around it from top to bottom. "He says it is n't a dye; it 's a vegetable preparation, for invigorating——"

"Who says?" I asked, despairingly.

"Why, Mr. Parker, of course," said Mrs. Brown, severely, with the air of having repeated the name a great many times,— "the old gentleman in the room above. The simple question I want to ask," she continued, with the calm manner of one who has just convicted another of gross ambiguity of language, "is only this: If some of this stuff were put in a saucer and left carelessly on the table, and a child or a baby or a cat, or any young animal, should come in at the window and drink it up—a whole saucer full—because it had a sweet taste, would it be likely to hurt them?"

I cast an anxious glance at Baby sleeping peacefully in the corner, and a very grateful one at Mrs. Brown, and said I did n't think it would.

"Because," said Mrs. Brown, loftily, as she opened the door, "I thought if it was poisonous, remedies might be used in time. Because," she added suddenly, abandoning her lofty manner and wildly rushing to the corner, with a frantic embrace of the unconscious Baby, "because if any nasty stuff should turn its boofull hair a horrid green or a naughty pink, it would break its own muzzer's heart, it would!"

But before I could assure Mrs. Brown of the inefficiency of hair-dye as an internal application, she had darted from the room.

That night, with the secrecy of defaulters, Baby and I decamped from Mrs. Brown's. Distrusting the too emotional nature of that noble animal, the horse, I had recourse to a hand-cart, drawn by a stout Irishman, to convey my charge to the ferry. Even then, Baby refused to go unless I walked by the cart, and at times rode in it.

"I wish," said Mrs. Brown, as she stood by the door wrapped in an immense shawl, and saw us depart, "I wish it looked less solemn—less like a pauper's funeral."

I must admit, that as I walked by the cart that night, I felt very much as if I were accompanying the remains of some humble friend to his last resting-place; and that, when I was obliged to ride in it, I never could entirely convince myself that I was not helplessly overcome by liquor, or the victim of an accident, en route to the hospital. But, at last, we reached the ferry. On the boat I think no one discovered Baby except a drunken man, who approached me to ask for a light for his cigar, but who suddenly dropped it and fled in dismay to the gentlemen's cabin,

where his incoherent ravings were luckily taken for the earlier indications of delirium tremens.

It was nearly midnight when I reached my little cottage on the outskirts of Oakland; and it was with a feeling of relief and security that I entered, locked the door, and turned him loose in the hall, satisfied that henceforward his depredations would be limited to my own property. He was very quiet that night, and after he had tried to mount the hat-rack, under the mistaken impression that it was intended for his own gymnastic exercise, and knocked all the hats off, he went peaceably to sleep on the rug.

In a week, with the exercise afforded him by the run of a large, carefully-boarded enclosure, he recovered his health, strength, spirits, and much of his former beauty. His presence was unknown to my neighbors, although it was noticeable that horses invariably "shied" in passing to the windward of my house, and that the baker and milkman had great difficulty in the delivery of their wares in the morning, and indulged in unseemly and unnecessary profanity in so doing.

At the end of the week, I determined to invite a few friends to see the Baby, and to that purpose wrote a number of formal invitations. After descanting, at some length, on the great expense and danger attending his capture and training, I offered a programme of the performances of the "Infant Phenomenon of Sierran Solitudes," drawn up into the highest professional profusion of alliteration and capital letters. A few extracts will give the reader some idea of his educational progress:

1. He will, rolled up in a Round Ball, roll down the Wood Shed, Rapidly, illustrating His manner of Escaping from His Enemy in His Native Wilds.

2. He will Ascend the Well Pole, and remove from the Very Top a Hat, and as much of the Crown and Brim thereof as May be Permitted.

3. He will perform in a pantomime, descriptive of the Conduct of the Big Bear, The Middle-Sized Bear, and The Little Bear of the Popular Nursery Legend.

4. He will shake his chain Rapidly, showing his Manner of striking Dismay and Terror in the Breasts of Wanderers in Ursine Wildernesses.

The morning of the exhibition came, but an hour before the performance the wretched Baby was missing. The Chinese cook could not indicate his whereabouts. I searched the premises thoroughly, and then, in despair, took my hat and hurried out into the narrow lane that led toward the open fields and the woods beyond. But I found no trace nor track of Baby Sylvester. I returned, after an hour's fruitless search, to find my guests already assembled on the rear verandah. I briefly recounted my disappointment, my probable loss, and begged their assistance.

"Why," said a Spanish friend, who prided himself on his accurate knowledge of English, to Barker, who seemed to be trying vainly to rise from his reclining position on the verandah, "Why do you not disengage yourself from the verandah of our friend? and why, in the name of Heaven, do you attach to yourself so much of this thing, and make to yourself such unnecessary contortion? Ah," he continued, suddenly withdrawing one of his own feet from the verandah with an evident effort, "I am myself attached! Surely it is something here!"

It evidently was. My guests were all rising with difficulty,—the floor of the verandah was covered with some glutinous substance. It was—syrup!

I saw it all in a flash. I ran to the barn; the keg of "golden syrup," purchased only the day before, lay empty upon the floor. There were sticky tracks all over the enclosure, but still no Baby.

"There's something moving the ground over there by that pile of dirt," said Barker.

He was right; the earth was shaking in one corner of the enclosure like an earthquake. I approached cautiously. I saw, what I had not before noticed, that the ground was thrown up; and there, in the middle of an immense grave-like cavity, crouched Baby Sylvester, still digging, and slowly, but surely, sinking from sight in a mass of dust and clay.

What were his intentions? Whether he was stung by remorse, and wished to hide himself from my reproachful eyes, or whether he was simply trying to dry his syrup-besmeared coat, I never shall know, for that day, alas! was his last with me.

He was pumped upon for two hours, at the end of which time he still yielded a thin treacle. He was then taken and carefully enwrapped in blankets and locked up in the store-room. The next morning he was gone! The lower portion of the window sash and pane were gone too. His successful experiments on the fragile texture of glass at the confectioner's, on the first day of his entrance to civilization, had not been lost upon him. His first essay at combining cause and effect ended in his escape.

Where he went, where he hid, who captured him if he did not succeed in reaching the foot-hills beyond Oakland, even the offer of a large reward, backed by the efforts of an intelligent police, could not discover. I never saw him again from that day until——

Did I see him? I was in a horse-car on Sixth avenue, a few days ago, when the horses suddenly became unmanageable and left the track for the sidewalk, amid the oaths and execrations of the driver. Immediately in front of the car a crowd had gathered around two performing bears and a showman. One of the animals—thin, emaciated, and the mere wreck of his native strength—attracted my attention. I endeavored to attract his. He turned a pair of bleared, sightless eyes in my direction, but there was no sign of recognition.

I leaned from the car-window and called, softly, "Baby!" But he did not heed. I closed the window. The car was just moving on, when he suddenly turned, and, either by accident or design, thrust a callous paw through the glass.

"It's worth a dollar-and-half to put in a new pane," said the conductor, "if folks will play with bears!——"

THE BLACK SHEEP'S COAT

by Cornelia Meigs

THE orange-red beam of light from the swinging ship's-lantern dipped and swayed from side to side of the narrow cabin. It showed the red coat of the soldier who sat at the table; it lit the pale face of Peter Perkins, the stoop-shouldered clerk; it shone on Granny Fletcher's clicking knitting-needles, and, in a far corner, it dropped across the white paper upon which Master John Carver's goose-quill pen was moving so busily. Once in a while, at long intervals the light swung so far, with the plunging of the ship, that it penetrated even the cranny behind the big beam where Andrew Newell was crouching, with his knees doubled up to his chin and his head bowed, to keep out of sight in the shadow.

"One more dip like that," the boy was thinking desperately, as the exploring ray seemed to seek him out of fell purpose, "and the whole company will see me. How will it fare with me then, I wonder? Will they cast me overboard?"

So far, however, the little company was quite unconscious of his presence. Master Carver laid down his pen and began to read aloud in a low voice to the two men who sat near him, David Kritchell and William Bradford.

The hidden boy could not see the first two, but he had a full view of William Bradford, who sat beyond, a young man with broad, square shoulders where the others had the stoop of scholars and clerks, whose open brow and clear, merry eyes were in contrast to the serious and stern faces of his companions.

"This *Mayflower* is a rolling ship," complained the old woman who was knitting; "it has tumbled my ball of yarn out of my lap so many times that I will even let it go where it wills for a while."

The gray ball, slowly unwinding, rolled across the cabin toward Andrew's hiding-place, but for the space of a few minutes no one noticed it. The soldier had reached the climax of the story of one of his campaigns.

"I drew my sword," he was saying, "but there were five cut-throat Spaniards all rushing upon me at once. I struck—"

"When last you told us that tale, Captain Standish, you made it only four," Granny Fletcher interrupted tartly, "three big ones and a little one; and the time before—"

"Never mind the other times, woman," returned Standish, testily. The lurching of the ship had spilled the ashes from his pipe, serving to irritate him still more, so that he added savagely, "We will all have tales to tell soon, I will wager, of Indians that burn and scalp and slay every Christian that they see."

"Heaven have mercy!" cried the granny, casting up her eyes. "Such dangers as lie before us! Perhaps those who turned back on the *Speedwell* did wisely, after all. Where is my ball of yarn?"

It was very near to Andrew, but the name of the *Speedwell* had made him wince and draw himself closer into his corner. It was on that very ship that he should have been sailing back to England, as he well knew.

His uncle, the only relative he had in the world and no very kindly one at that, had agreed to take the boy with him on this great adventure of planting a Puritan colony in the New World. But with the first day of the voyage, the worthy man's ardor had cooled and he had been glad enough to avail himself of the chance of return when the leaky *Speedwell* turned back. A hasty council had been held in the *Mayflower's* cabin as to who should go on and who should be carried back to England, at which gathering Andrew, in spite of his uncle's protests, had pushed into the front rank of those who wished to go forward.

"We are already overcrowded, and it is the able-bodied men that we need," John Carver had said.

"And those who will make solid and worthy citizens," Peter Perkins had added at his elbow, with an unfriendly glance at Andrew's shabby coat. William Bradford was the only one who had looked at him kindly, and even he had shaken his head.

"It is a great enterprise," he said, "but we must needs abide by the rule of the elders as to who is to go and who must return."

That shabby coat was now the worse for a great rent in the shoulder and a smear of tar on the sleeve, put there when Andrew had squeezed into a narrow hiding-place between two great coils of rope, instead of entering the crowded boat that put off for the other vessel. For a whole day of light winds he had waited in an agony of suspense, while they lay close to the *Speedwell,* never seeming to get so far away that he was safe from being returned to her. Toward evening, however, the breeze freshened, the two ships had drawn apart, and while the whole company was gathered in the bow to see the last of their companion vessel, Andrew had slipped below to hide in some better place than on the wet, open deck of the *Mayflower.* A footstep in the passage had alarmed him so that he had dashed into the main cabin and crawled behind a beam, for want of a better refuge. Here he still lurked, cramped, aching, and hungry, wondering how soon the lantern or the ball of yarn would be the means of betraying him.

Just as he felt sure that Granny Fletcher's sharp eye must have caught sight of his protruding elbow, there came a diversion in the sound of scurrying feet on the companionway and in the headlong entry of two excited girls, one of about fourteen years old, the other twelve.

"Oh, Father," cried the elder one, seizing David Kritchell's arm, "one of the sailors just helped me to climb up to look into the pen where the sheep and the poultry are, and what do you think! There is a little new lamb amongst them, not more than a day old!"

"Nay, my dear Drusilla," her father remonstrated, "do you not see that this is no time to speak of such matters? You are interrupting Master Carver."

"There is no harm wrought," John Carver said; "she brings good news, for surely it promises well that our flocks should already begin to increase."

"But it is a—a black sheep," Drusilla declared. "You cannot think how strange it looks among the white ones!"

"A black sheep?" cried Granny Fletcher, in shrill consternation. "There is a sign of bad luck, indeed! It is enough to send us all to the bottom. A black cat's crossing our path could not be a worse omen."

"We are scarcely in danger from the passing of any black cats," William Bradford observed, with twinkling eyes. "As for the black lamb, it shall be your very own, Mistress Drusilla, since it was you who brought us tidings of it. I think this expedition of ours is too earnest and weighty an affair to be brought to ruin by one black sheep."

"Nay, nay, we are as good as lost already," wailed the granny, so voluble in her lamenting that John Carver was forced to tell her sternly to hold her peace.

"Cobwebs and moonshine!" exclaimed Miles Standish, filling up his pipe, "There are enough straight swords and ready muskets in this company to drive away any sort of bad luck."

Granny Fletcher, much subdued, got up to fetch her yarn, which still rolled back and forth at the far end of the cabin. The crouching boy held his breath as it moved first toward him, then away, and then, with a sudden plunge of the ship, tumbled directly into his lap, so that he and the old woman stooping to grasp it were brought face to face. The poor soul's nerves were too badly shaken to withstand the shock of seeing that unexpected, tar-streaked countenance so close to her own.

"The bogy-man, the evil one himself come to destroy us all!" she screamed in such terror that all in the cabin rose to their feet.

"Come forth, whoever is there," commanded Bradford, sternly.

It was in such manner that Andrew Newell, gentleman adventurer at the age of fifteen, made his appearance as a member of the company of the Pilgrim Fathers.

There followed an uproar of questions, reproaches, and rebukes, with Granny Fletcher's shrill scolding rising high above all the rest, until John Carver struck his hand upon the table for silence.

"We must not talk of what the boy has done, but of what we are to do with him," he began. "He is amongst us, without friends—"

"And without money to pay his passage, I'll be bound," observed Peter Perkins, in an undertone. "Look at his coat; look at his dirty face! This is no company for waifs and ragamuffins. Born to die on the gallows, that is the sort he is!"

The Pilgrims, while few of them were rich, were nearly all of that thrifty class which had little patience with careless poverty. In their eyes, Andrew's ragged coat was less to be forgiven than his uninvited appearance among them.

Drusilla was tugging at her father's elbow. "Think how much he wanted to come, to dare all this for the sake of seeing the New World," she whispered.

"It is not zeal for our faith that has led him," said Peter Perkins, overhearing her, "but mere love of adventure."

"And is love of adventure so wicked a thing?" questioned Bradford, his deep, quiet voice over-riding all the buzz of excited talk. "I can understand why the boy wished to go with us and I will be responsible for him. You have, many of you, brought servants, bound to you to repay their passage by a year or two years of labor. This lad shall be bound to me in the same way and I will stand surety for him. Do you agree?" he said to Andrew; "will you serve me?"

Did he agree! Andrew felt, as he crossed the cabin to his supporter's side, that he would die for this young elder who stood among his gray-haired seniors and gave the boy the only friendly smile in all that hostile company.

"He will bring us ill luck," he heard

Granny Fletcher whisper to her neighbor. "Is not one black sheep enough for our voyage?"

"Born to die on the gallows, I know the look of them," Peter Perkins returned, wagging his head.

Through the long days of the voyage that followed, those two seemed like watchful, sharp-tongued ghosts that haunted Andrew's footsteps. Whatever went amiss, they laid the blame upon him, whatever he did was bound, in their eyes, to be wrong.

"There are always scolds in every company," Bradford told him one day, when the reproaches of his two enemies seemed past bearing. "Whether such persons wear breeches or petticoats, they are just the same, and real men must learn to close their ears to them."

Day by day Andrew grew to admire ever more this man who had befriended him. Bradford's kindness, his good sense, and the steady burning of the fire of his enthusiasm made him stand out from all the rest, since amid the depression and the deadly weariness of the long voyage he was ever cheerful, confident, and certain of their success.

"I was only of your age when I first joined the company of the dissenters, myself," he told Andrew once, "and I looked with all a boy's wonder on the ups and downs, the bickerings and complaints, the discouragements of their venture in establishing a church and in making their pilgrimage to Holland. But now I can see that it was mere human nature, and that there is real patience and courage in the heart of every one of them."

Hostility toward Andrew abated somewhat during the voyage, although, to the end, Bradford, Carver, David Kritchell, and his two daughters were the only ones who treated him with any real kindness. And that voyage, even as Bradford was always prophesying, came to an end suddenly just when they were beginning to feel that life on the high seas must last forever. Andrew and Drusilla had come on deck before the others one chill, early morning in November, a morning of light winds from the west, with the wide sea still stretching endlessly all about them. Then, "Oh, Andrew!" "Oh, Mistress Drusilla!" each cried to the other in the same breath, for each had perceived the same thing. The sharp odor of salt spray, the sting of the sea wind, had altered strangely; there came instead warm puffs of air across the water, while a line like a dark cloud stretched along the horizon. They had reached America at last!

That going ashore—how they had dreamed of it, and how unlike it was to what they had thought! They were used to a land that was green through most of the winter, so that they looked with dismay at the brown, bare woods, the unfamiliar, somber green of the pines, and the line of rolling hills in the distance.

They coasted along the shore for days, finally choosing an abiding-place merely because winter was coming close and some decision must be made. The men who landed first reported that there was high open ground, a cheerful, chattering stream of fresh water, and a good prospect over both sea and land.

"We also caught sight of four Indians and a dog," Captain Standish said, "but they stayed not for our coming and stopped only to whistle to their beast before they ran away. Yet we thought we saw them later, peeping and peering among the forest trees."

The next morning they came ashore all together, with bags and bundles and precious possessions, with the swine and the poultry and the bleating sheep from the pen amidships, Drusilla Kritchell could scarcely be separated from her beloved black lamb, but Andrew, who was to go in the boat with such of the livestock as could not swim, promised that he would take good care of it.

"And a fine pair they will make, the two black sheep of ill omen," remarked Peter Perkins, who, amid all the bustle of landing, could still find time for a bitter word.

"A goodly place," said David Kritchell, cheerily, as they stood on the beach, surveying their new home and waiting for the last of their gear to be landed. The thin sunshine lay upon the flat, wet shore and the chill wind seemed to search out the very marrow of the travelers' bones. The cries of the gulls circling above them sounded harsh and lonely. The last of the boats grated its keel on the gravel and the whole company turned their faces toward the hill. Suddenly Granny Fletcher, half hysterical, threw up her hands and lifted her voice in a long wail.

"We will perish here in this wilderness!" she cried. "God meant us to endure our persecutions in patience at home and not flee from them to a land where wild beasts and savages will soon make an end of us. What will we eat? Where will we lay our heads? Oh, England—England—!"

Her cry died away in choking sobs, while the others looked at one another. The *Mayflower* rode in the tideway, her sails, wet from last night's rain, all spread to dry, white and shining in the sun. The very wind that filled them blew full and fresh toward home. Yet, to the everlasting honor of the Pilgrims let it be said, no other face betrayed hesitation or fear. Whatever was in their hearts, men, women, and children all took up their burdens and set forth up the hill.

They found the company gathered in a circle on that spot where, later, the meeting-house was to be.

"Let us look to God in prayer," said John Carver, simply, and every head was bowed. The service was a short one, but at the end of it the anxious faces had relaxed, the women smiled again, and even Granny Fletcher dried her eyes. William Bradford, feeling a tug at his coat, turned about quickly.

"It is not true that there is naught for us to eat," Andrew told him in an excited whisper. "I was digging, just for play, in one of those round mounds of earth—look, there are a dozen of them along the shore. They must have been the savage men's treasure-houses, for see what I have found within!"

He poured into Bradford's hand a stream of something red-yellow like gold. It was not mere metal, however, but something far more precious, the round, ruddy kernels of Indian corn.

The weeks that followed were difficult and full of toil, while there arose slowly upon the hill the little huts built of logs and chinked with mud, and in their midst the square common house that was meeting-house, arsenal, and granary all in one. Winter drew in, food supplies ran low, and the settlers dipped deeper and deeper into the Indians' corn.

"We will pay the red men for it, as soon as we are given opportunity," the elders all agreed; but no one came to claim possession, and no Indians showed their faces where the white men could see.

"I would it were so that we could make payment to somebody," Bradford said more than once to Andrew, yet could offer no solution of the problem of how it was to be done. None of the men approved of taking what was not theirs; but in the face of such famine, they knew it was folly to leave the corn untouched. Andrew did not heed their talk greatly, for he was busier than the rest, being one of the few who had any skill with a fowling-piece or a fish-line. He was more shabby and ragged than ever, with clumsy patches of leather sewed where his coat had given way, and with a rude cap made of the skin of a fox. Many nights, however, when he dropped asleep on his bed of straw beside William Bradford's, he would smile to himself in the dark, knowing that he was happier than he had ever been before.

And then came the sickness.

One of the elders, Giles Peabody, was stricken first. He sat shivering by the fire before the common house at evening, he was burning with fever at midnight, and before sunrise he was dead. Three more were ill on the day that he was buried, and by the next morning there were a dozen. Soon in every family there was some one dead, some one dying; while fewer and fewer were left to go from house to house to care for the sufferers. William Bradford labored like ten men, and taught Andrew to be nearly as useful as himself. Drusilla Kritchell, although she had her mother and Granny Fletcher sick in her own house, still managed to go forth every day, with all the gravity and earnestness of a grown woman, to nurse and scrub and care for motherless children. She met Andrew at twilight one evening as both, almost too weary to set one foot before the other, were coming down the hill from the common house.

"My mother is almost well again," she told the boy as he took her basket, "and Granny Fletcher is mending, too, although she is still light-headed with the fever. But three more of the Peabody children have been taken. I have been with them the whole day."

Andrew followed Drusilla into the house to set down her basket on the table, and there discovered Granny Fletcher huddled in the big chair by the fireplace, for she had refused to stay in bed. She was alternately muttering to herself and babbling aloud.

"So we are to perish after all," she was saying. "A blight lies heavy upon us. Some wrong we must have done. Was it because we took food that was not ours and never repaid? We thought we were starving, but to die in this way is worse than to starve. God has forgotten us. He has hidden his face from us because of our sins."

She turned and saw Andrew standing by the door.

"I said you would bring us ill luck!" she cried. "It was you who broke into the red men's store-house and laid hands upon what was not ours." Her voice rose high, then dropped suddenly almost to a whisper. "For all the harm and mischief you have done, I forgive you. I will not go before the Judgment Seat thinking ill of any man, not even such as you." She closed her eyes and slipped down limply in the chair, while Drusilla ran to aid her.

"Do not heed what she says!" the girl cried over her shoulder; but the door had closed and Andrew was gone.

Inside the common house on the hill a row of stricken men lay on the straw; but some were mending and none were dying, so that William Bradford had leisure to come forth and sit down by the fire that burned before the door. Silently Andrew came through the dark and found a seat beside him, first flinging a fresh log upon the blaze. Something stirred outside the circle of ruddy light; then, as the flames leaped from the fresh fuel, there was revealed an ugly, yellowish dog that sniffed and skulked among the shadows. Andrew whistled to him, but the creature gave a strange, uncouth yelp of fear and ran away howling.

"That is no dog of ours," the boy observed wonderingly; "where could he have come from?"

"I think he is the same that we caught sight of in those days when we first landed," Bradford answered. "He was with four Indians, the only ones we ever saw."

"It is a strange thing that they never came near us again," Andrew said.

Bradford did not reply at once, so that the two sat in silence for a little. When the older man did speak at last, his voice sounded broken, weary, and listless.

"No, not strange," he remarked slowly. "The Indians fear us and they know how to hide in the forest like foxes. Do you ever think that there may be those whose eyes are always watching us, knowing how we are stricken, counting the dead and waiting—waiting until we are so few that they no longer feel afraid? That dog has waxed very bold. It may be that his masters are waxing bold also."

"We have buried the dead by night and leveled the graves so that no one could count them," declared Andrew, huskily; "and we are not quite all gone yet."

"No," said Bradford, "but we are growing perilously few." He was silent again and seemed to go on with difficulty. "I would that we had ever been able to offer payment for that corn we used. I have measured all that we were forced to take and have set a sum of money against it to be ready if the chance for paying should ever come. Perhaps you had better know that it lies in a bag in my chest, so that if— if I should be—"

"Master—Master Bradford," cried Andrew, in agony. He touched the other's hand and found it burning hot, and saw at last, by a sudden flaring of the fire, that Bradford's face was flushed and his eyes glittering with fever.

"Help me to go inside, boy," he said. "I have been trying to rise these last ten minutes and have not had the strength. It is nothing—nothing, but I think I will go within and lie down beside the others."

Half an hour later, Drusilla Kritchell was summoned from the kitchen by an un-

steady tap on the outer door. Andrew Newell stood upon the step.

"I must ask a boon of you, since there is no one else to whom I may turn," he said abruptly. "Can you prepare me food to carry on a journey? I am going into the forest to find some one whom I may pay for the grain we have taken."

"Into the forest, alone, to find the Indians?" she exclaimed. "Oh, you must not. It is certain death!"

She looked him up and down in the light of her candle and added bluntly: "You are not even properly clad; your coat is so worn and thin that you will perish with the cold. The sickness will fall upon you all alone in the wilderness."

"It does not matter," he responded indifferently. "Go I must, and if I do not succeed, I will never come back. Will you ask your father, Mistress Drusilla, to tend my master when I am gone? He is stricken with the dire sickness, too. I will come at sunrise to fetch anything you can give me to carry on my way."

He closed the door sharply and vanished into the dark.

THE sun was just coming up through the winter fog, a round red ball like a midsummer moon, when Andrew set forth next morning, the little bag of money safe beneath his coat, the scant bundle of Drusilla's provisions under his arm. A great, long-legged shadow strutted before him, seeming to mock at him and his fantastic errand. To come face to face with the lurking Indians, to explain that the white men had used their corn and wished to repay them, surely it was impossible. Yet Andrew shook his head doggedly and repeated almost aloud, "If I do not succeed, I will never come back." His devotion to William Bradford and the terrible thought of what the sickness might have wrought before his return dragged at his heart, but he turned his mind resolutely from such thoughts and trudged steadily on.

There was something about his appearance that was not quite as usual. Even the grotesque shadow ahead of him showed it, in that absence of fluttering rags and gaping elbows that had formerly marked his attire. He had a new coat, a warm substantial one, that bade defiance to all the chill morning winds that could blow.

Granny Fletcher, when she saw him in the doorway receiving his bundle of food from Drusilla, had noticed that something was changed. Her fever had abated a little, nor had it ever been great enough to quench her curiosity.

"See the lad with a whole coat to his back at last!" she exclaimed. "And what a strange color it is—rusty black! Verily, it might be the coat of your black sheep."

Drusilla flushed, said farewell hastily, and closed the door.

"You should not talk; it will bring the shaking fits upon you again," she said sternly as she adjusted the pillow in the big chair.

"You need not have been so quick in closing the door," complained the old woman; "I have no doubt that it was in no proper way that the boy came by that coat. Mercy, child, how heavy-eyed you look this morning! One would think you had not slept. But that coat, I wonder now—"

Drusilla betook herself to another room, not waiting to hear more. The secret of Andrew's new coat was no mystery to her, nor to her younger sister, sleeping profoundly upstairs after a night of intense industry. There was another who shared the secret also, a half-grown sheep, bedded tenderly in the straw of the shed, shivering and indignant at being robbed of its fleece in the dead of winter.

There had long been a story in Drusilla's family that two sisters, one of them her great-grandmother, had, when their father was called away to the wars, sheared one of their sheep, spun and woven the wool, and made him a coat all between sunset and sunrise. Drusilla's spinning-wheel and loom had come with her across the sea and stood in the corner of the room where she and her sister slept. There they had both toiled all night, as quickly and skilfully as had that great-grandmother of earlier fame.

"It is a strange color for a coat, but we had no time to dye it," Drusilla apologized, when she gave it to Andrew and bade him put it on. He, in turn, was quite overcome with surprise and gratitude and could hardly form a word of stammering thanks.

A light snow had fallen during the night, showing, as he came into the forest, the lace-like pattern of squirrel- and rabbit-tracks, and even the deep footprints here and there of larger game. Andrew scanned the ground eagerly for the marks of moccasined feet, yet knew that there was little chance of any Indian leaving a trail so plain. For want of any real direction in which to go, he followed a little stream in whose lower waters he had been used to fish for trout and whose babbling voice seemed to speak to him with cheery friendliness as it led him farther and farther into unknown country.

He ate frugally in the middle of the day, then tramped steadily on until dark. It was growing very cold when he stopped at last, built himself a rough shelter of boughs under an overhanging rock, struck a fire with his flint and steel, and kindled a cheerful blaze. But how small the fire looked in the wide, silent emptiness of the forest! The rock threw back the heat of the flame, making a warm nook where he curled up and slept comfortably until morning. Once or twice in the night he got up to replenish the fire and to listen to the unfamiliar night sounds of the wood, but he was, each time, too weary to keep long awake.

When he arose next morning it was colder than ever; his breath went up like smoke in the keen air, and the little brook was frozen solid, its friendly voice silent at last.

This second day's journey into the wilderness seemed to have brought him into a new land. The hills were higher; the great boulders towered above his head; the way was so broken that he had much difficulty in making progress at all. He still clung to the familiar stream as a guide, although it had shrunk now to a tiny thread, just a gleam of ice here and there under the slippery stones and snow-wreathed underbrush. Night found him weary and spent and utterly disheartened. In all this long journey he had not yet seen a sign of any human being.

With the greatest difficulty, he cut enough boughs for a rude tent, and got together a supply of firewood sufficient for the night. The fuel was wet, his fingers were stiff with cold, so that it was a long time before he could strike a spark and persuade the uncertain flame to creep along the leaves and set fire to the wood. Since he had not delayed his journey to hunt or fish by the way, his food was almost gone. His strength was almost gone also, as he realized when he got up from beside the fire and crawled into his shelter. He would not be able to journey much farther, yet it was his steady purpose still to go forward. Almost in the act of nestling down among the pine branches, he fell asleep.

A troubled dream aroused him many hours later. Vaguely he was conscious that he must get up and mend the fire or it would die out and leave him to freeze. It took him some minutes to summon enough resolution, but at last, with a great effort, he stirred, crawled out of his refuge, came

forth into the light, and then shrank back again with a gasp of overwhelming astonishment. For there, standing beside the glowing coals, motionless as a statue, silent as the still forest itself, was a gigantic Indian.

For a moment there was no move made, no word spoken, as Andrew crouched staring at the stranger, at the hawk-like face, at the firelight shining on the dull red of his naked arms and knees, at his misshapen shadow that danced on the snow behind him. Then at last the other, without moving his head or changing his expression, spoke quietly.

"You welcome—here," he said in slow, broken English.

Later, Andrew was to learn that many of the red men had learned English from the British sailors that manned the fishing-boats coasting along the New England shore, and that this man had even made a voyage with one of them. At that moment, however, it seemed to the boy nothing other than a miracle that here, in this far, silent wilderness, he should hear his own tongue spoken.

The Indian drew out, from somewhere in the folds of his scanty garments, a slice of dried meat and set it to broil before the fire. Andrew sniffed wistfully at the delicious odor of its cooking, but when the red man silently offered it to him, he shook his head, so firm was his determination that no Indian should know how near the white men were to starvation. The man merely nodded quietly at his refusal, brought out more meat and some dried fish, and put the whole before the fire. He looked so long and steadily at the boy that Andrew felt no detail of thin cheeks and hollow eyes was escaping that keen stare. Then the piercing glance moved onward to where the remains of Drusilla's provisions lay upon the ground, a few broken crusts of bread and a bit of cheese. The stranger made no comment, but very carefully completed his cooking, spread the feast upon a piece of bark and pushed it toward Andrew. With one lean red hand he made a gesture in the direction of the settlement.

"All hungry—starving; we know. Dying —we know that too," he said.

"You—you have seen," faltered Andrew, thrown out of his reserve by this sudden statement.

"You bury dead by night," the man nodded slowly; "you smooth graves, we count graves—morning." He thrust the food forward again and said peremptorily. "Eat."

And eat Andrew did, since there was no use for further pretense. There was a little talk between them as his strange visitor plied him with food, but it was not until the ravenous meal was ended and the boy had pushed away his bark plate that he made any attempt to speak of the errand for which he had come such a long and weary way.

"There was some corn left buried near the shore where we landed," he began. "We used it and we wish to make payment. See, I have here the proper sum of money."

He brought out from under his coat William Bradford's bag of coins.

But the Indian shook his head.

"The corn not mine," he said.

"Then to whom did it belong? Where are the men who left it there?"

"All dead," the other answered. "The great sickness—it took them all away. Only one left. He live with our tribe."

"Then take the money to him," begged Andrew. "We counted carefully and wish to pay for every measure. Look, it is all here; will you take him what should be his?"

He poured the contents of the bag into the Indian's unresponsive hand, a heap of silver and copper coins, with a few of gold. The man turned them over with little interest, letting some of them drop and disappear in the snow and the ashes. His eyes brightened, however, when he saw among them a big copper penny-piece that was new enough to shine a little still and to wink in the firelight with a pleasant glow. Andrew, seeing what attracted him, gathered up such of the fallen coin as he could find and polished them on the rough sleeve of his coat. Then he fetched a handful of sand from the tiny bank that he had noticed beside the stream and scoured the money until the silver gleamed and the copper glowed and burned in the red light of the flame. The gold did not reflect the fire and was only dulled by the scraping with sand so that, in the end, the Indian cast it aside as he received the rest of the money eagerly.

"He shall have it all, that Tisquantum —he is last of tribe, and maybe some day I bring him to you and he show you how to plant the corn for nex' year. You would not harm him."

"I will swear it," Andrew answered. "Does he really fear the white men?"

"All of us fear you. Surely you mus' know it."

"We have some brave men amongst us," Andrew said, "and a soldier who is a famous fighter to be our leader."

"Ugh, you mean round small man in red coat who go tramping through forest, musket on shoulder, breaking through the bushes and making much noise as giant moose. We could slay him many times with arrows; he mus' have known it, yet he not afraid. No, it is not this man, nor all your fighting men we fear."

"What is it, then?" Andrew asked, much puzzled.

Half by signs, half in his imperfect English, the Indian sought to explain. And so vivid were his gestures, so potent his few words, that finally Andrew began to understand.

It was the strange spirit of the English that the Indians did not comprehend. When the red men were hungry, when sickness came upon them, even when they were weary of the spot where they dwelt, they gathered up their goods and moved to some new camping-place. When the plague first fell upon the tribe that dwelt where the white men did now, they broke and scattered, carrying the same death to all who were near. Their people died in numbers past any counting; yet even now they were many more than the newcomers. But with the white man it was not the same. The men had died, and the women, but they did not run away. They went on with their daily tasks, although they were fewer and fewer. The Indians thought that the courage of those who were gone must pass into the hearts of those who still lived, and even though so many should perish that there was but one left, they would still fear him, since he would have the strength of all.

Very slowly Andrew turned this strange idea over and over in his mind.

"And we wonder at you, in our turn," the boy replied at last; "how you can find food and live in plenty in what seems to us a cruel and barren wilderness. If we could learn to be friends, white men and red men, how we could help each other in many things!"

So they made their compact of peace and friendliness there by the fire in the heart of the frozen wilderness, with the blue wood-smoke drifting above their heads and floating away over the tree-tops. Afterward, when the Indian said that they should sleep for a little to prepare for their next day's journey, they lay down side by side in the warm glow of the blaze; and since Andrew had traveled far, had eaten fully, and was quite worn out, he fell quickly asleep. He awoke, much later, with a start, to find himself alone, with the newly replenished fire crackling beside him, with a package of deer's meat and corn laid close to his hand, and with the dawn breaking behind the dark pines.

He made his way homeward more easily than he had come, for he knew the country now and could follow the stream without so much picking and choosing of the way. Although he was free from one anxiety, there was still a heavy burden upon his heart, for he could not put from him the remembrance of William Bradford,—the man who had his whole-souled devotion, —of how he had sat shivering by the fire with the shadow of the dreadful sickness already upon him. He hurried faster and faster, feeling that the dense wood hemmed him in and held him back—that he would never reach his journey's end and hear tidings of his master.

He was free of the forest at last and hastening across the stump-dotted slope to the huddle of cabins beside the stream. How few they looked! He had almost forgotten what a tiny handful of dwellings the settlement was. He was panting as he ran down the worn path, dashed through the empty street, and thundered at the door of the common house. It was growing dark; there was no light within nor any voice to answer his impatient knock. Trembling, hesitating in dread of what he might find, he opened the door and stepped over the threshold. Five men had lain on the straw the night of his departure; there was only one now. At the sound of his footstep, this one stirred as though roused from sleep, turned his head and spoke. It was William Bradford.

"Four days you were gone," Bradford said at last, after he had heard the hurried substance of Andrew's adventures. "Much can happen in such a place as this in four days. Enoch Fullerton and old Phineas

Hall have gone from us, but the others who were suffering here have got well and gone about their business. And as for me, four days were enough for the coming of the fever and its burning out, so that I shall soon be a whole man again. Now tell me that strange tale all over again; I must have not heard aright, for surely what you say is past belief."

Andrew went over his story, repeating every word of his talk in the forest with the Indian.

"They know more about us than we dreamed possible," he said, "but we need no longer fear them. And they think, poor blind savages, that, as we grow fewer, the spirit of those who have passed still dwells in those who remain."

There was a little pause, for Bradford, like Andrew, must consider this new idea carefully.

"Not so blind," he said finally; "savages and heathen, yet not so blind. Do you never think that the spirit of this adventure lies not in the elders, the older men like me, but in the young men, the youths and children—in you? We shall soon be gone, for age passes quickly; it is youth that must take up our purpose; it is on youth that the weight of it all depends. Even this errand of yours, without youth it would never have been accomplished; we should have gone on wasting our days in doubt and dread, fearing to turn our hands to the real conquering of the wilderness."

The door opened in the twilight and several men came in, John Carver and three of the elders. Bradford raised his voice that they might hear.

"This lad has succeeded in that madcap expedition from which we have all been saying that he would never come back. He has made good our debt to the Indians and has brought back good tidings and such an understanding of the red men as we could never have gained for ourselves. After this service he shall no longer be my bound servant, but a citizen of this community. Andrew Newell, whom we were calling a foolhardy boy, has shown himself to be a man."

Thereafter it was necessary for Andrew to sit down upon the straw again and tell the whole story once more, that John Carver and the elders might marvel anew at his tale. It was not until an hour later that he was suffered at last to pass out of the building and go down the little street to carry his news and his thanks to Drusilla Kritchell. The air was soft after the long days of cold; there was promise in it that this harsh country's climate held spring as well as winter.

Granny Fletcher, who was well enough now to limp out to the doorstep, was sitting on the wide stone, wrapped in Drusilla's cloak, while Peter Perkins, coming up the path, had just stopped to speak to her. Tidings of what Andrew had done seemed to have run before him, for Peter Perkins took off his broad hat and greeted him with a "Good even to you, sir."

"What is that?" Andrew heard in a shrill whisper from the old woman, who had evidently not yet learned the news; "do you call that wicked lad 'sir,' and take off your hat to him?"

"We may have been mistaken in him after all," Peter Perkins returned, in a whisper just as audible; "and it is as well to show respect to one who is now a citizen of our colony and who wears a good coat upon his back. It is little one can tell of what the future holds!"

BILLY MAYES' GREAT DISCOVERY

by Ralph Henry Barbour

CAPTAIN EZRA BLAKE, seated on the edge of the deck-house of the little schooner *Molly and Kate,* was trying to do two things at once. He was superintending the unloading of ballast by a crew of four men and a boy, and he was answering the questions of Billy Mayes, who sat beside him. Billy was twelve and Captain Ezra was almost five times twelve, but they were great cronies. The *Molly and Kate* had tied up to Forster's Wharf only last evening, and already this Saturday morning Billy was on hand to hear what wonderful adventures had befallen his friend on the latest voyage. The *Molly and Kate* carried lumber to fascinating southern ports like Charleston and Savannah and Jacksonville and even, less frequently, Havana, and never a voyage but what Captain Ezra returned with a new budget of marvelous tales for Billy's delight. Some day Billy was going to sail with the captain and see the astounding places and things with his own two very blue eyes—see Charleston and Cape Hatteras and the Sea Islands and Florida. But more especially he would visit Pirate Key, for it was on Pirate Key that the captain met with his very startlingest adventures. Billy had never been able to find Pirate Key on any map, but as the captain explained, it was n't very big and few mariners even knew of its existence. Somewhere between the Marquesas and the dry Tortugas it lay, and beyond that the cap-

tain declined to commit himself; which, under the circumstances, Billy considered quite proper, since it seemed that the natives of Pirate Key were a peculiarly sensitive people and much averse to publicity. Even the captain, with his winning personality, had had much difficulty in making friends with the inhabitants. The first time he had tried to land, many years ago, he and his crew had been fired on with poisoned arrows. Captain Ezra could still point out the scars on the old blue dory astern there.

The captain, with one mild grey eye on the crew, had just finished a soul-stirring account of the hurricane that had met them off the South Carolina coast on their northward trip, and Billy was still glowing with pride at the thought of knowing so intimately a person of such nautical skill and personal bravery,—for, although the captain had n't said so in so many words, it was very plain that only heroism and remarkable seamanship had brought the *Molly and Kate* safely through great peril, —when "Long Joe" Bowen, shoveling ballast sand near by, was conquered by a perfectly terrible spasm of coughing. Captain Ezra viewed him silently for a moment and then inquired mildly:

"Been an' swallered some o' that sand, Joe?"

"Long Joe," nodded and said, "Yes, sir," in a very husky voice.

"M—m—; well, you want to be more careful," advised the captain, most sympathetically; "'cause if you ain't, I 'm like-ly to have to swab out your throat for you, an' that 's a remarkably painful operation, Joe."

There was no response to this, but Billy could see "Long Joe's" shoulders heaving and knew that he must already be in much pain. Billy, like his friend the captain, had a very sympathetic nature. When the suf-ferer appeared to be easier Billy looked up again at the captain's seamed and ruddy countenance and asked:

"Did you get to Pirate Key this time, sir?"

"Pirate Key?" responded the captain. "Oh, yes, we was there a couple o' days. Not on business; but, you see, I 'd prom-ised the king I 'd drop in on him the next time I was down around there. Seein' as he leads a kind o' lonely life, an' him an' me bein' particular friends, as you might say, I didn't have the heart to say no to him."

"Was he quite well?" asked Billy, po-litely.

"Pretty smart for an old feller. You see, Billy, he 's—let me see—why, he must be well over a hundred now."

"A hundred!" gasped the boy.

The captain nodded gravely. "Them Pirate Key folks lives a long time. They don't go to school until they 're twenty. If they did, you see, they 'd forget all they 'd learned afore they was what you might call middle-aged."

Billy pondered that. Not going to school until one was twenty had much to be said in its favor. Still, it was revolutionary, and he decided to put it aside for further con-sideration.

"And how was the queen and the prince?" he asked interestedly.

"Well, the queen was fine; but the prince had been an' ate something as did n't agree with him. The royal physician was real worried when I got there; but I give

him a couple o' doses of kerosene oil an' it did him a power o' good."

"The—the physician?" asked Billy, doubtfully.

"No, the prince, o' course. There was n't nothing the matter with the physician." The captain sounded slightly vexed. "He 'd been an' ate some—some—what 's this now?—some hoki-moki fruit." He viewed Billy sternly. "The *prince* had."

"Really?" asked Billy. "What is hoki-moki fruit?"

"Well," replied the narrator, knocking the ashes from his pipe and thoughtfully scraping the bowl with his knife, "it 's sort o' like a orange an' sort o' like a apple."

"Oh!"

"An' it 's pizen if you eat it afore it 's ripe. Don't never touch a hoki-moki fruit till it 's purple, Billy."

Billy promised instantly. "Only," he added, "I might not know it, Captain Ezra, if I was to go to Pirate Key. Is it round? Does it grow on trees?"

"More square than round, you might say. It grows in clusters as big as that water-cask there. Hundreds of 'em to-gether. An' they grow high, because, if they did n't, the wild horses would eat 'em when they was green an' die. That 's one o' the wonders o' nature, Billy."

"Yes, sir. But I did n't know horses ate fruit."

"Ain't you ever see a horse eat a apple? Why, they 're plumb fond o' apples. Ba-nanas, too—an' watermelons. Guess the only kind o' fruit a horse won't eat is cocoanuts." The captain filled his pipe leisurely and in silence. Then: "Another peculiar thing, Billy, is what you might call the—the affinity o' the hoki-moki tree an' them wild horses. They can't keep away from 'em, the horses can't. There 's something about the—the tree itself that draws the horses; something in the wood,

they say. You don't never find any bark
on a hoki-moki tree low down, because
the wild horses keeps rubbin' themselves
against it. Seems like they just can't resist
the—the sub-tile influence. It 's extraordinary."

Billy agreed emphatically that it was.
"Are there many wild horses on the key?"
he inquired after a moment.

"Thousands. The natives catch 'em an'
train 'em. The king has more 'n three
hundred horses in his private stable, an'
the queen, she has about a hundred, an'
the prince, he 's got maybe thirty or forty."
The captain applied a lighted match to
his pipe and puffed blue smoke clouds
into the spring sunlight. "They kill 'em
for their hides, too," he went on. "They
make fine leather."

"I should n't think they 'd need leather,"
said Billy, "being just savages."

"Savages!" The captain viewed him re-
provingly. "Don't you ever let 'em hear
you say that, son! Benighted, in a manner
o' speakin', they may be, but they ain't
savages. As for leather, why, they make
saddles an' harnesses an' travelin'-bags—"

"Traveling-bags!"

"—An' trunks." The captain paid no
heed to the interruption. "An' here 's another peculiar thing. You may be able to
explain it, but I can't, an' I never heard
any one who could. Them hoki-moki trees
has just as much affinity for a horse-hide
as they has for the horse himself. Lay a
horse-hide saddle twenty feet away from
a hoki-moki tree, an' just as soon as you
lets go of it it 'll begin to move right over
to the tree and try to rub itself against it.
Now you explain that!"

"But I can't," said Billy, wide-eyed. "It
—it 's most—most extro'n'ry!"

"It surely is!" declared the captain.
"What you might call one o' the marvels
o' science. I ain't never— That the lot, Joe?
Well, I guess it 's most dinner time, ain't

it? Talkin' always gives me a powerful
appetite. Sing out to Steve to start that
galley fire an' get a hustle on him!"

BILLY's thought dwelt a good deal for the
rest of that day on Captain Ezra's interesting discourse, and when he went to sleep,
it was to dream terribly complicated things
about wild horses and hoki-moki trees and
the fascinating inhabitants of Pirate Key,
who wore the scantiest attires, but indulged
themselves in traveling-bags! Sunday was
always a hard day to live through, for
after church and Sunday-school were over
many empty hours stretched ahead. This
Sunday, however, was not so bad, for Mr.
Humbleton came to call in the afternoon
and brought Arthur with him. Arthur was
fourteen and a youth of affairs and position in the community, as became the son
of a bank treasurer. For one thing, Arthur
was captain of the Broadport Junior Baseball Team. Billy and Arthur were graciously allowed to retire from the society
of their elders to the sanctuary of the little
side porch, where the chill of an easterly
April breeze failed to penetrate. Billy was
glad of the opportunity to talk to Arthur,
for he had a request to make, and after
several false starts he managed to make it.

"I wish," he said, after swallowing hard
a couple of times, "I wish you 'd let me
play on the nine this year, Arthur."

Arthur Humbleton observed him frown-
ingly. Then he shook his head. "I don't
see how I could, Billy," he answered. "The
team 's all made up, in the first place, and
then you are n't much of a player. Maybe
next year—"

"I can play in the out-field all right,"
defended Billy, eagerly.

"Oh, most any fellow can catch a fly,"
replied the other carelessly. "There 's more
to baseball than just that, Billy. You 've
got to know how to run the bases, and bat,
and lots of things."

"I can run bases just as fast as—" Billy paused. He had been going to say, "as you can"; but diplomacy came to his aid. "As fast as Tom Wallace can," he substituted.

"Maybe, but you can't bat a little bit," responded Arthur, triumphantly. "You know you can't."

"If I had more practise—"

"No, sir; you could n't ever be a real, corking batter." Arthur was kindly but firm. "A fellow has to have the batting eye. Of course, I don't say that maybe, if you worked awfully hard this year and practised every day, you might n't be a lot better; but I don't believe you 'll ever be a real star, Billy."

The subject, engrossing to both boys, continued for some time, and in the end it was agreed that Billy should become a sort of unofficial out-field substitute, with the privilege of practising with the nine sometimes and making himself useful chasing the long flies that infrequently went over Mr. Bannerman's garden fence. As Mr. Bannerman was aged and crabbed and disliked having small boys wallow across his asparagus-bed in search of base-balls, the position assigned to Billy prom-ised as much danger as honor. But he knew himself to be fast on his feet and knew Mr. Bannerman to be slow, and he accepted gratefully. Soon after that, Arthur was summoned hurriedly by his father, so hurriedly that he left behind him an en-ticing blue paper-bound pamphlet entitled, "How to Play Baseball," which Billy hap-pened on just before supper and which he surreptitiously studied later behind the shielding pages of "Travels in the Holy Land."

But he found it difficult to understand, until he happened on a dozen pages at the end of the booklet devoted to adver-tisements. There were soul-stirring pic-tures and descriptions of mitts and gloves, bats and masks and balls. He admired and coveted, and mentally compared the prices set down against the articles with the contents of the little box in his top bureau-drawer that was his bank. The com-parison was n't encouraging. Billy sighed. And just then his eyes fell on a word that challenged attention. "Westcott's Junior League Ball," he read. "Regulation size and weight, rubber center, all-wool yarn, double cover of best quality selected *horse-hide*. Warranted to last a full game without losing elasticity or shape."

Billy read it twice. Then he became thoughtful. After that he read the descrip-tion again, and his eyes became big and round. Later, in bed, with the light from the electric lamp at the corner illumining the ceiling, he lay sleepless for a long hour, experiencing the triumph that thrills all great discoverers and inventors.

The next morning he surprised every member of the household by being down-stairs in advance of breakfast *and with his shoes tied!* His mother viewed him an-xiously and felt his face, but was unable to detect anything abnormal save, perhaps, a certain intensity of gaze and impatience of delay. There was a full half-hour be-tween breakfast and school, and Billy made the most of it. Captain Ezra was smoking his pipe on the wharf when Billy arrived, breathless, on the scene.

"Well, well!" exclaimed the captain. "Ain't you round kind o' early?"

But there was scant time for amenities, and Billy plunged directly into business. "Are you going down South again, pretty soon, sir?" he inquired anxiously. The captain allowed that he was; as soon, in fact, as the new cargo was aboard, which, if he was n't saddled with the laziest crew on record, ought to be in about four days. "And are you going to Pirate Key?" Billy continued. The captain blinked.

"Well, I might," he replied, after slight hesitation. "Why?"

"Because I want you to bring me a piece of that hoki-moki wood, sir, a piece big enough to make a bat. You see—"

"A bat? What sort of a bat?"

"Why, a baseball bat. Could you, do you think? It would have to be that long—" Billy stretched his arms—"and that big around,—" Billy formed a circle with his small fingers,—"and it ought n't to have any knots in it. Is hoki-moki very knotty, Captain Ezra?"

"Knotty? N-no, I would n't call it that. I—" He coughed and cast a troubled gaze toward the lighthouse point. "What was it you wanted it for, now?"

"A baseball bat," answered Billy, almost impatiently. "I thought if you could get me a piece big enough, I could get Jerry Williams, over at Morris's carpenter shop, to make it for me. Could you? Would it—would it be much trouble to you, sir?"

"Why, n-no, only—hm—you see I ain't plumb sure of gettin' to Pirate Key this trip, Billy." Billy's face fell, and Captain Ezra went on quickly. "But I ain't sayin' I won't, you know. Fact is, it 's more 'n likely I will. An' if I do—"

"Oh, will you, please?" cried Billy, beaming. "How much would it cost, sir? I 've only got twenty-two cents, but if you 'd take that, I 'd pay you the rest when you came back." He dug into a pocket, but the Captain waved the suggestion aside.

"Shucks!" he said; "a little piece o' wood ain't goin' to cost nothin'. Why, I guess I could bring off a whole tree, if I wanted it. I guess there ain't anything on that there island I could n't have for the askin', Billy, the king an' me bein' so friendly. Tell you what I 'll do, now. I 'll get 'em to cut a piece o' that wood an' make the bat for you right there. How 'll that be?"

Billy looked dubious. "Why, that 's awfully kind, sir, but—but do you think they 'd know how to make a baseball bat?

Bats have to be made awf'ly particular, Captain Ezra, or else they are n't much good."

"Don't you worry about that, son. They have been makin' their own bats on Pirate Key for years, an' I guess there ain't no better ones to be had."

"Why, do they play baseball *there?*" gasped the boy.

" 'Course they do! Leastways, they play what 's pretty near like it. The—the general idea 's similar. They 're plumb crazy about it, too. They got a eight-club league down there—"

But at that moment the bell in the town-hall clanged its first stroke, and Billy fled.

During the four days that the *Molly and Kate* remained at Forster's Wharf Billy and the captain met twice; and when the schooner finally sailed, the captain had full, detailed, and most explicit instructions regarding that length of straight, well-seasoned hoki-moki wood that was to be brought back either in the rough or shaped into the Pirate Key idea of a baseball bat. After that there was nothing for Billy to do save await the return of the schooner.

APRIL gave place to May, and the Broadport Juniors began to play Saturday afternoon games on the back common and to practise diligently on other days after school was over. Billy served a rigorous apprenticeship in the out-field, chasing flies that went over the heads of the regular players and several times scrambling over Mr. Bannerman's fence and recovering the ball from under the rhubarb or from between the rows of early peas. So far, fortune had attended him and he had escaped with his life. Now and then he was allowed to take his turn with the batters and stand up at the plate while Waldo Hutchins pitched his famous "slow ones." Practise is supposed to make perfect, but

Billy was still a long way from perfection as a batsman. Nor could either he or Arthur Humbleton observe any great amount of improvement. But Billy persisted, consoling himself with rosy dreams of the future. Almost any day, now, the *Molly and Kate* might return, bearing Billy's Great Discovery.

Meanwhile, the Juniors won from Scalfield Grammar School, were defeated by the West Side Reds, and were annihilated by the Downerport Eagles. And then, as it seemed to Billy, just in the nick of time to prevent a similar fate at the hands of that especial rival, the Broadport White Sox, the *Molly and Kate* tied up again at Forster's Wharf!

That was an eventful day in Billy's life —eventful from the moment he heard the glad news to the moment that he was back at the house with the precious hoki-moki bat in his possession. He had scarcely heard Captain Ezra's detailed and interesting account of the securing of the article. For once, anxious to put the bat to the test, Billy thought the captain just the least bit long-winded! But he banished the thought almost instantly, blushing for its ungraciousness, and quite overwhelmed his benefactor with thanks ere he hurried away with the bat tightly clutched and one jacket-pocket bulging with a perfectly good "genuine horse-hide" ball that had seen only two weeks' service in practise and had been acquired from Captain Humbleton for fifteen cents.

Subsiding, much out of breath, on the edge of the side porch, Billy once more examined his prize with eager eyes. As to shape it looked as fine as the best "wagon tongue" ever made. There was no doubt about it, those Pirate Key natives knew how to make a baseball bat! Billy was just a trifle disappointed about one thing, however, and that was its lack of novelty. To all appearance the bat was quite like any other bat, except that the inscription "Genoine Hoki-Moki Wood" appeared half-way along its smooth length. The words were printed in uneven characters, and evidently with pen and ink, and the ink had run with the grain of the wood. The varnish was still new and just a bit sticky; but that was to be expected, since varnish always dried slowly near salt water. Hoki-moki wood was, contrary to Billy's preconceived idea, light instead of dark, closely resembing ash. A surprising feature was the twine-wound handle. It seemed strange that the natives of Pirate Key should know of that refinement. His respect for them grew tremendously then and there!

Having examined the bat to his heart's content, he stood up and swung it experimentally. It proved the least bit heavier than he could have wished, but that was n't anything to trouble about. He had frequently heard Jack Cantrell express a preference for a heavy bat, and Jack was the hard hitter of the Broadport Juniors. Remained now the supreme test, and Billy approached it falteringly. Suppose it failed! Suppose Captain Ezra's tales of the peculiar properties of hoki-moki wood proved false! Billy feared that the disappointment would be more than he could bear! Nerving himself to the ordeal, he laid the bat at the edge of the porch, squeezed the horse-hide ball from his pocket, and deposited it with trembling fingers against the house. Seven feet separated ball and bat, and as he withdrew his fingers he gave a deep, anxious sigh. For an instant it seemed that the experiment was to fail, and Billy's heart sank sickeningly. But then, as he stepped back across the boards to the porch's edge, the miracle happened! Slowly, irresolutely, the ball moved, rolled a few inches, stopped, went on, gathered momentum, and traveled straight along a board until it bumped companionably against the hoki-moki bat!

Billy shrieked his triumph, and danced ecstatically on the mignonette bed. It was true! The Great Discovery was proved!

Again he tried the experiment, and again the ball yielded to the magic influence of the bat as the needle of a compass yields to the influence of the north pole. Thrice the experiment worked perfectly. A fourth time the ball, having been placed farther to the left, collided with the handle of the bat, jumped it, and rolled over the edge of the porch into the flower-bed. Billy waited for it to rise up and come back again, but that effort appeared beyond it. Considering that a distance of eighteen inches intervened between porch floor and flower-bed, Billy felt that it would be asking too much of the ball. Anyway, it atoned, a minute later, by rolling nicely from house wall to bat with what seemed greater alacrity. Billy was more than satisfied.

I feel that I ought to inform the reader of a fact that quite escaped Billy, which is that the outer edge of the side porch was fully an inch and a half lower than the inner, being so built that water would run off it. I doubt if Billy ever knew of this. Certainly, the slope was not perceptible to an unsuspicious vision. I make no claim that the slope had anything to do with the remarkable behavior of the ball. I am willing to believe that the ball would have rolled across to the bat had the floor been perfectly level. I only mention the fact in the interest of truth.

Later, Billy sought the back yard and tried throwing the ball in the air and hitting it with the bat. At first this experiment proved less successful than the other, but presently he found, to his great delight, that he could hit almost every time! To be sure, he did n't always hit just square, but he *hit!* That absorbing occupation came to an end when the ball went through a cellar window with a fine sound

of breaking glass. Thereupon, Billy recovered the ball and went innocently in to supper.

That night, for fear of burglary, Billy slept with the hoki-moki bat under the covers beside him.

The next day was Saturday and the day of the White Sox game. Billy spent most of the morning knocking the ball against the backyard fence, and only desisted when Aunt Julia informed him from an upstairs window that she had a headache and would go crazy if he did n't stop making all that noise. Billy stopped and went and sat on the side porch, with his feet in the mignonette and the hoki-moki bat hugged to his triumphant breast, and dreamed dreams worthy of Cæsar or Napoleon.

The Broadport Juniors wanted to win to-day's game more than they wanted to win any other contest in a long and comprehensive schedule. The White Sox team was comprised of boys who lived on the Hill. The Hill was the town's patrician quarter. Just about every one who lived up there had an automobile and a chauffeur to drive it and wore his good clothes all the time. The juvenile residents of that favored locality were, in the estimate of the down-town boys, stuck-up and snobbish, and had a fine opinion of their baseball prowess. The worst of it was that their opinion was justified, for the White Sox —the down-towners jeeringly called them the Silk Sox—beat almost every team they went up against! Last year the Juniors had played two contests with them and had been beaten decisively each time. And so Captain Arthur Humbleton and all the other boys of the Juniors and all their adherents—including mothers and brothers and sisters and an occasional father—were especially keen on a victory. And when, in the first of the sixth inning, the White Sox finally solved Waldo's delivery and made three hits, and, aided by an in-field error, sent four runs over the plate, the Juniors' bright dream faded and despondency gloomed the countenance of Captain Humbleton. The White Sox had already held a one-run lead, the score at the start of the sixth having been 12 to 11, and now, with four more tallies added, they looked to have the contest safely on ice.

Billy, his precious bat held firmly between his knees, occupied a seat on the substitute's bench, a yellow-grained settee borrowed from the High School across the common. He had twice offered his services to Arthur, and they had been twice refused, the second time with a scowl. Billy was absolutely certain that he could, if allowed to face the opposing pitcher, who had n't much but a fast ball to boast of, anyway, deliver wallops that would radically alter the history of the game. But the hoki-moki bat was no better than any little old sixty-cent stick so long as he was not allowed to use it. To his credit is the fact that he had determined, in case the White Sox held the lead at the beginning of the ninth inning, to entrust the bat to others, should Arthur still refuse his services. That was real self-denial, real patriotism. As much as Billy wanted to wield the wonderful hoki-moki bat himself, victory for the team stood first.

The friends of the Juniors clapped and cheered as "Wink" Billings went to bat in the last of the sixth, and the one who cheered the loudest was Captain Ezra Blake. The captain had come at Billy's earnest and repeated behest, and had togged himself out wonderfully in honor of the occasion. The captain did not, Billy suspected now, know a great deal about baseball, for he cheered just as loudly when a villainous White Sox rapped out a two-bagger as he did when one of the Juniors stole home from third. But it was very evi-

dent that the captain's intentions were of the best.

The last of the sixth developed no runs for the Juniors, nor did the seventh add to the score of either side. In the eighth the White Sox captain got to third with two down and tried to tally on a bunt past the pitcher's box. But short-stop ran in, scooped up the ball, and nailed him a foot from the plate. The Juniors started their inning by a safe rap that placed Cantrell on first base. Myers sacrificed neatly, and then the next man connected for a screeching liner that was too hot for the Sox second baseman, and Cantrell scored the Juniors' twelfth tally. But the score was still four runs to the advantage of the White Sox when Stone hit into a double and ended the inning.

Captain Humbleton pretended a confidence he did n't feel, and assured the team that all they had to do now was hold the Sox and then bat out a victory. It sounded easy, but Billy felt defeat impending. He tried to get a word with Arthur before that youth hurried off to his in-field position, but failed. The White Sox started by putting a runner on first in consequence of Waldo Hutchins's inability to pitch strikes. Then a bunt was mishandled by the catcher, and there were runners on first and second, and things looked very bad. The next player was thrown out, but the others moved up. The in-field crept closer. The White Sox left-fielder tried hard to slug, missed two, and finally popped up a silly little foul that dropped comfortably in the catcher's mitt, and the Junior nine's adherents cheered loudly, Captain Ezra's voice dominating all like a fog siren. There was another period of doubt and anxiety when, after knocking the ball everywhere save between the foul-lines, the Sox first baseman finally whaled out a long, arching fly. The bases emptied and the runners scuttled home, but Leo Smith arose to the occasion like a veteran—which he was not—and pulled down the ball!

"Four to tie 'em and five to win!" shouted Arthur, as he trotted in to the bench. "Come on now, fellows! Let 's get this! We can—What is it, Billy? Don't bother me now!"

"I 've got to, Arthur," said Billy, firmly, a tight clutch on the captain's arm. "You 've got to listen a minute. If you want to win this, you must let me bat, Arthur. I can't help hitting with this bat, honest, and—"

"You 're up, Waldo! Work him for a base. Get it somehow!" Arthur tugged impatiently, but Billy held like glue.

"You see, it 's a hoki-moki wood bat, Arthur, and hoki-moki wood has a—a infinity for horse-hide. All you 've got to do is just swing the bat, and the ball comes right up and hits it. It 's the greatest discovery of—"

"What are you talking about?" demanded the captain. "Let 's see your old bat. 'Hoki-moki wood', eh?" he jeered. "Where 'd you get this contraption?"

And still holding him firmly, Billy told him, and in spite of his expression of incredulity, Arthur was secretly a little bit impressed. "Oh, shucks!" he said, "I don't believe it, Billy! It ain't possible! 'Course, you might have luck—" He paused and frowned intently, and then, with a short laugh, added: "Maybe I 'll give you a chance, Billy. We 'll see."

Billy had to be content with that. Meanwhile, Waldo Hutchins had waited and walked. An attempted sacrifice, however, failed to work, and Waldo was cut off at second. The runner was safe on first. With one gone, the audience began to disperse slowly. Then the Juniors' right-fielder landed squarely and rapped past third, and hope crept back into the breasts of his team-mates. The departing onlookers

paused in their exodus. The Sox second baseman let the throw from the pitcher pass unchallenged over his head, and the runners advanced to second and third. The cheering grew frantic. The coachers shouted and danced. "Slim" Gaynor did his best, but only laid the ball down in front of the plate and was tagged out before he had taken two strides toward his base. Two on, now, and two gone.

Billy, his heart racing and jumping, watched Arthur anxiously. But Joe Ware was allowed to take his turn. Joe was an uncertain batter. The White Sox pitcher tempted him with a low one and with one on the outside, but Joe refused them. Then a fast one went as a strike, and another hit the dirt just behind the plate. The pitcher scowled and would have grooved the next offering had not the catcher signaled for a pass. So Joe walked, filling the sacks, and cheers rent the air. Arthur himself followed, and the bunt that he trickled toward first was a veritable masterpiece, for it sent a tally across the plate, moved runners from first and second, and placed him on his bag!

But three runs were still needed to tie, and four to win, and two were out. Billy arose from the bench, pale but determined. The moment of martyrdom had arrived. He would offer the hoki-moki bat to Steve Sawyer, already hurrying to the plate, and—

But as he moved toward that youth, Arthur, shaking the dust from his clothes, as first, caught sight of him and recalled his half-promise. And perhaps he had what he would have termed a "hunch." At all events, his voice sped up the base-line.

"All right, Billy Mayes!" he shouted. "Hit it out! Let Billy bat, Steve!"

And so Billy, with a choking feeling in his throat, went on to the plate and faced his fate. Mutters of surprise and disgust followed him from the bench. The White

Sox pitcher observed his small form with a frown that held bewilderment and amusement. Then, noting that the rookey was evidently nervous, he laughed his derision.

"See who 's here, Jim!' he called. "Home-run Baker, ain't it?'

"No, it 's Tris Speaker," returned the catcher. "Be good to him, Tom!"

The pitcher grinned and wound up. Billy pushed his bat far back. The runners danced and shouted, coaches yelled, the in-field jabbered. But Billy did n't hear a sound of it all. The ball was on its way now. He tried to watch it and could n't. But he swung the hoki-moki bat around just as hard as he knew how, putting every ounce of his strength into it—and something happened. There was a resounding blow, electric tingles shot up Billy's arms, he staggered, and then, still clutching the bat, he streaked for first!

Far into right-field sped the ball, just inside the base-line. In raced the runners. Billy raced, too. Pandemonium assailed his ears. As he reached the first bag he sent a final look after the ball, and his heart leaped with joy. Straight behind Mr. Bannerman's garden fence it fell, right among the early peas and bush Limas!

"Take your time, Billy!" shouted the coach at first. "It 's a home run, kid!"

THEY never did find that ball, for Mr. Bannerman appeared on the scene most inopportunely; but it did n't matter, and no one cared. The Juniors had won, 17 to 16! The hoki-moki bat had proved itself! And Billy Mayes was a hero!

There were unbelievers who denied to Billy's famous bat any special virtue, but Billy knew what he knew and had seen what he had seen, and his faith was unshaken. But, and here is the sorry part of my tale, it was several years before Billy made another home run; for although he became a regular member of the team and, as time passed, a fairly dependable hitter, the hoki-moki bat had lost its cunning. It was not the bat 's fault, however. It was due to the fact that, owing to the war, baseballs were no longer covered with horse-hide!

A RACE WITH IDAHO ROBBERS

by Joaquin Miller

Now that the President has signed the bill admitting Idaho into the Union, the forty-fourth star in our glorious constellation of States, it may not be out of place for one who, if he did not really give the name to this new State, first put that name in print, to record a page or two of its early history, and recall an incident that still makes his nerves tingle as he tells it.

Gold was first found, in that vast and trackless region now forming the new States of Washington, Idaho, and Montana, in the spring of 1860, by a small party of prospectors led by Captain Pierce on the spot where Pierce City now stands.

The writer, although not then of age, had read law and been admitted to practice under Judge Geo. H. Williams, afterwards President Grant's Attorney-General. And when news of the discovery of gold reached Oregon, I gathered up one law-book and two "six-shooters," and set out on a ride of many hundred miles through the mountains for the new placers.

But as gold was not plenty, and there was no use for the law-book, because there was no law; and as there was an opening for a good and hardy horseman to carry letters and money to and from the new mines, the writer and a young man by the name of Mossman soon had nailed up over the door of the only store as yet in all that wild region, a sign which read: "Mossman and Miller's Express."

It was two hundred miles to the nearest post-office at Walla Walla. The lover of pretty names will easily trace this Walla Walla back to its French settlers' "*Voila! Voila!*"

No man can look down from the environment of mountains on this sweet valley, with its beautiful city in the center, whose many flashing little rivers run together and make it forever green and glorious to see, without instinctively crying out *Voila! Voila!* It is another Damascus, only it is broader of girth and far, far more beautiful. In this ride of two hundred miles there was but one town, Lewiston. Get your map now, and as you follow the story of the ride, fix the geography of this new empire in your minds, for it will be a grand land.

Lewiston, you observe, is at the head of navigation on the "Shoshonee" or Snake River, by way of the Columbia River. This word Shoshonee means snake. I fancy you can almost hear the rattle of the venomous reptile as you speak this Indian word. The accent, as in nearly all Indian names, such as Dakota, Iowa, and so on, is on the middle syllable. In reading Longfellow's poems you will find he has preserved the proper pronunciation of Omaha by putting the accent where it belongs. And more than once this learned man reminded me that Idaho must be pronounced in the same soft and liquid fashion: I *da* ho.

In these long, long rides we changed

horses from five to ten times daily, and we rode at a desperate speed. We used Indian ponies only, and usually rode without escort, with pistols ready at hand. Indians were numerous, but our fear was not of them, but of white men. In fact, the Indians were by far the most peaceable people we had to deal with. They always kept our "Stations," that is, the places where we changed horses and drank a cup of coffee. These Indians were of the Nez Percé tribe. It may not be generally know that these noble Indians were nearly civilized long before the renowned Chief Joseph (who fought the whole United States for half a year not long ago) was ever heard of. These Indians, under the direction of good old Father Spaulding, published the first newspaper that was issued west of the Rocky Mountains. They also printed some portions of the Bible in their own tongue, including many Psalms. Keep these facts of history as well as the geography of this great region in mind; and we will now get to the robbers.

As before stated, we did not find gold plenty at first, and the "Express" did not pay. We two boys worked hard, took many desperate risks, and lived almost literally on horseback, with little food and with less sleep for the first few months. But suddenly gold was found, as thick as wheat on a threshing floor, far away to the east of a big black mountain which the Indians called "I-*dah*-ho," which literally means, "mountain where light comes." I happened to be in Lewiston, on my way to Pierce City with the Express, when the ragged and sunburnt leader of the party that had made the discovery beyond the Black Mountain came in. He took me into his confidence. I sent an Indian on with my Express; and branching off a hundred miles to the southeast, reached the new mines, took up "claims," and dropped an Express Office before a dozen people knew

of the discovery which was to give State after State to the Union. You will find the place on the old maps, and some of the new ones, marked "Millersburgh." But there is no town there now.

The gold lay almost in the grass-roots, in the shallow surface, like grains of wheat. It was a high bleak place, densely wooded and intensely cold as winter came on. Greater discoveries lay further on and in kindlier climes, and broad valleys and rich cities receive you there now. But our story is of the snow and the stony steeps of Mount I-dah-ho.

Returning to Lewiston with saddle-bags nearly full of gold, I wrote the first published account of the discovery; and the new mines were naturally called in that publication, as they were called by all that excited mass of people from Lewiston on their way to the mines beyond the Black Mountain, the "I*dah*ho Mines." The name, however, like that of Omah-ha, soon lost in the mouths of strangers its soft, sweet sound.

California now emptied her miners, good and bad, gamblers, robbers, desperados, right in upon our new mines and the roads thither.

My young partner, a daring and dashing boy, who, as I write, is visiting me here after thirty years, had many desperate encounters.

Suddenly, as winter came on, the rivers closed with ice, and horses could not go and steamers could not come.

I was lying ice-bound at Lewiston. Men wanted to send money below to their friends or families; merchants, anticipating the tremendous rush, must get letters through the snow to Walla Walla. Would I go? *Could* I go?

The snow was deep. The trails, over open and monotonous mountains, were drifted full. Could any living man face the drifting snow and find his way to Walla Walla?

At first the merchants had tried to hire Indians to undertake the trip and deliver their letters. Not one could be found to go. When the storm abated a little, the men who kept the ferry across the Shoshonee River scraped off the snow, and cutting down the upheaved blocks of ice made it possible to cross with a horse.

I picked out a stout little iron-gray steed, with head in the air, an eye like an eagle, and a mane that tossed and tumbled like a thunder storm. At first I meant to carry only letters. But having finally consented to take a little gold for one merchant, I soon found I should lose friends if I did not take gold for others. The result was that I had to take gold worth nearly ten thousand dollars. And ten thousand dollars of dust you must know means nearly fifty pounds!

A few muffled-up friends came down to the river bank to see me off. It was a great event. For two weeks we had not had a line from the outer world. And meantime the civil war was raging in all its terrible fury. As I set out that bleak and icy morning, after I had mounted my plunging pony I saw in the crowd several faces that I did not like. There was Dave English, who was hung on that spot with several of his followers, not forty days later; there was Boone Helm, hung in Montana; Cherokee Bob, killed in Millersburgh; and also Canada Joe. This last lived with some low Indians a little way down the river. So when he rode ahead of me I was rather glad than otherwise; for I felt that he would not go far. I kept watch of him, however. And when I saw that he skulked around under the hill, as if he were going home, and then finally got back into the trail, I knew there was trouble ahead.

But the "Rubicon" was now behind. My impetuous horse was plunging in the snow and I was soon tearing through the storm up the hill. Once fairly on my way, I looked back below. Dave English and Boone Helm were bidding good-by to two mounted cow-boys at the ferry-house. Ten minutes later, as I looked back through the blinding snow. I saw that these two desperate fellows were following me.

True, there was nothing criminal in that. The two highwaymen had a right to ride behind me if they wished. And Canada Joe had just as good a right to ride ahead of me. But to be on a horse deep in the blinding snow and loaded down with gold was bad enough. To have a desperado blocking the narrow trail before you and his two friends behind you was fearful!

I had two six-shooters close at hand under the bearskin flap of my saddle-bag where the gold was. I kept my left hand in my pocket where lay a small six-shooter warm and ready. Once, as the drifting and blinding snow broke away up the mountain, I saw Canada Joe with his head bent down in the storm still pushing on ahead of me at a safe distance. A few moments after, as I crossed and climbed the farther bank of an ugly cañon, the two robbers came close enough to hail me. One of them held up a bottle. They evidently intended to overtake me if they could, and profess to be friendly. This I must not allow. I urged my ambitious horse to his best. But, to my dismay, as I hastened up a narrow pass I found that I was not far behind Canada Joe. This low-browed black fellow was reported to be the worst man in all that country. And that was saying he was bad indeed.

I was in a tight place now, and had to think fast. My first plan was to ride forward and face this man before the others came up. But I was really afraid of him. It seemed a much easier task to turn and kill the two rear men and get back to town. But, no! No! All this was abandoned almost as soon as thought of. In those days, even the most desperate had certain rights,

"My pursuers were not a hundred yards behind me"

which their surviving friends would enforce.

I remember that I fell to wondering what the murderers would do with my body. I had a horror of being eaten by wolves. I then thought of the true and trusting men who had sent me forth on my responsible task, and I took heart.

I was now but a few hundred yards behind Canada Joe. So far as I could find out, the robbers were closing in on me. But we had ridden over the roughest part of the road and were within a few miles of the high plateau, so that the wind was tearing past in a gale, and the drifting snow almost blinded me.

Suddenly, I had a new thought. Why not take to the left, gain the plateau by a new route, and let these bloodthirsty robbers close their net without having me inside? I rose in my saddle with excitement at the idea, and striking spurs to my brave horse, I was soon climbing up the gradual slope at a gallop. Ah, but I was glad! Gallop! gallop! gallop! I seemed to hear many horses! Turning my head suddenly over my shoulder, I saw my two pursuers not a hundred yards behind me. They shouted! I was now on the high plateau and the snow was not so deep. Gallop! gallop! gallop! Canada Joe—thank Heaven!—was away to the right, and fast falling behind. Gallop! gallop! gallop! I was gaining on the robbers and they knew it. Fainter and fainter came their curses and their shouts!

And then: Whiz! Crack! Thud!

I looked back and saw that they both had thrown themselves from their saddles and were taking deliberate aim.

But to no purpose. Not one shot touched me or my horse, and I reached the first station and, finally, rode into Walla Walla, with my precious burden, safe and sound.

MAUDIE TOM, JOCKEY

by Gladys Hasty Carroll

OVERNIGHT a great white placard had appeared on the blackboard at the corner of the village street. Pictures of horses were pasted all over it, and there was printing at the bottom. Maudie Tom, crouched low on Bess's back, stared at it for a long time. Then she tugged on her rains and cantered into the bustling, crowded square.

She was a strange figure among the thronging summer guests of the little town. College-girl waitresses, off duty for a few hours, hopped on bare pink feet toward the beach, pulling off blue-and-scarlet coolie coats as they went. Ladies in soft-colored cotton dresses wandered in and out among the little gift-shops. Clean, brown children stood in sun-suits before the big show-window which revealed a gigantic candy machine in operation. Men in milk-white clothes strolled about, puffing expertly at fragrant cigars. People laughed and skipped and called across from one corner to another, and drank cloudy brown and rosy sodas from tall glasses. But Maudie Tom rode grim and dark and silent through the carnival of summer; a big, bony girl with ragged black hair, blue overalls, and a secure seat on her vicious, prancing horse.

When she attempted to draw up before the post-office, the beast flung her head about and leaped forward. Maudie Tom sawed economically but inexorably at the ugly, uplifted mouth.

"Stand, will you!" said Maudie Tom. "Hey, Bill!"

A man leaning against a building thrust his hat up from his eyes and looked at her. There was no friendliness between them—only recognition and a certain similarity of feature.

"They going to have the races again, ain't they?" called Maudie Tom, steady hands on the reins.

"Sure. What do you care?"

"When they going to have them?"

"Labor Day, of course."

"When's that?" persisted Maudie Tom. "You know I can't tell."

The man shifted his position and figured silently. Neither face had altered even faintly in expression.

"A week from Monday, that is," said the man.

Maudie Tom jerked on the reins. The horse had sagged in sleep and now awoke more irritable than ever. She reared slightly. Maudie Tom sat tight.

"How's Pa?" asked the man.

"Oh, he's all right," said Maudie Tom, laconically.

A group of girls walking with linked arms down the boardwalk watched her gallop away. "How she can ride!" one of them said.

"I always wonder what goes on inside her head," another added.

"Hasn't she a marvelous build, though!" said a third. "Sinewy as an Indian."

Maudie Tom had seen them from the corner of her eye, their crisp piqué dresses, their smooth hair knotted at their necks, but she did not know what they said of her. She only imagined, and imagining soon made her mouth grow hard with bitterness and sulking. She sat forward and urged her mount with a boot-heel sharp on a red hind quarter.

"We'll show them, you old fool of a horse," she growled, "come a week from Monday."

Fourteen years and a half ago, one December, Maudie Tom, the lighthouse keeper's daughter, had been born in the small, snugly built house on the island a half-mile off the coast. A storm raged at the time; the strip of water between the island and the mainland was too rough for doctors to cross. The mother died, but the baby lived, and was named Maudie Tom—nobody knew why.

She grew up on the island with her father and a lazy, surly brother who appeared occasionally, when no more convivial roof would shelter him. She drank goat's milk and ate hen's eggs; she ran in the sun and grew as big and strong as a boy. The room where she slept looked out on the water, across the path of the signal-light; she learned to trim the lamp herself. Fogs drifted in, storms blew out of the northeast. She heard distress signals, saw rocket flares, once made coffee for a rescued crew. Sometimes she lay all day on a shelf rock that nobody knew of but herself. Gray gulls dipped and soared; her fingers played with wet, dark-green seaweed; wind could not reach her; it grew warm, and she slept.

When she was nine, officials came to ask if she had been sent to school. She had not. The officials pursed their lips and shook their heads.

"She's got an aunt," her father said, "up to Portland. She can go up there to get her schooling. I been meaning to send her right along. A young one ain't much these days without an education."

But Maudie Tom was well past ten before she went, and then she stayed only two weeks. She did not like Portland. She could not find her way about; her aunt, and the teacher, too, had whipped her. She ran away home, and her father slapped her on the shoulder and they laughed together. When the officials came again, faintly seasick from their brief boat-ride across the choppy sea, her father said that Maudie Tom was fourteen. It was not true, but she was large for her age, and after a fourteenth birthday education was not compulsory in Maine. Maudie Tom had come back to the island, and she meant to stay. It was part of her, and she loved it as she loved no other thing.

Her father, in his glee, bought her a horse and built a stable for it beside their little boat-house on the mainland. Nearly every day when the weather was fine she rowed over, with short, rapid movements of her strong dark arms, and mounted Bess, to tear away through the village and up into the rocky, pine-covered hills, her hair blowing back in the wind, and salt water dripping off her boots. But she was not happy.

She was not happy because of the city people who came every summer. She saw perfumed women who looked to her like the brisk, neat little Portland teacher who had struck her with a ruler seven times on the hand. She saw men who lay, clean and smiling, on the sands, reading newspapers. Little children played games together— games that Maudie Tom had never played. But it seemed to her that more than half the people she saw in the village, summertimes, were girls of fourteen and fifteen. Even in the dead of winter, when storm winds rocked her bed, she could see the faces of the girls who came to the Cape in summer. Laughing, faces with small, sunburned noses and cool, appraising eyes. She could see their figures in bathing-suits, or in dresses that were sometimes rumpled but never soiled. She remembered the books and magazines old Aunt Maggie Dennis, from the fisher colony, found in their rooms when she cleaned the cottages at the end of the season. They had pictures, all of girls, and all beautiful. In the winter nights she thought of them.

"I hate them kids," thought Maudie Tom.

She did not hate them for being so different from herself, but only because of the opinion she imagined they had of her. "They ain't so much," she told herself. "I can do a lot of things they can't. I'd like to see them ride a horse like me."

Two years ago the summer people had inaugurated the Labor Day races. Horses were bought and a community stable built. It was a friendly sport. Men practised on the beach before breakfast, advising one another, admiring all the mounts. There were two girl riders among them, one in a brown leather jacket and tweed knickers, the other in a scarlet jockey-suit with an absurd little visored cap. Maudie Tom had not gone across to town on the previous Labor Days, but she had seen the horses and their riders from her steps, where she sat ominously dour.

"I could beat them," jeered Maudie Tom, "even if Bess balked, the old fool of a horse."

This year she meant to try. It had taken a tremendous amount of self-persuasion, for she feared these summer visitors as much as she envied and hated them.

The horses came, and a fine, rich scent of well-kept horse-flesh made Bess lift her upper lip and prance and neigh.

"Never mind being so friendly," scolded Maudie Tom. "You've got them all to beat in the races!"

Now the poster had appeared, spattered with the heads of handsome horses and decorated with the complete outline of a beautiful bay mare at full stride, her neck stretched out in ecstasy of effort. It was time for the trial.

"You ain't got so much looks," said Maudie Tom, buckling a strap about Bess's head, "but looks ain't everything."

Still, she trimmed the mane and tail of her mount on Labor Day morning. She brushed the straight back, rubbed down the wide, veined flanks and bulging joints, and even tied a bit of dirty ribbon on the thick black forelock. Maudie Tom herself wore a clean dress from the store—a cheap little print with the wild, glaring figures usually seen in smocks, which became her wonderfully well.

It was a cool, bright, windy day. Maudie Tom and Bess went out into the sun together, down along the coast, through the town, and up to the beach where the races were held. Men already stood about with flags and pistols; other horses had arrived, stepping high with dainty legs, twitching pleasurably with every thunderous crash of rolling breakers.

"I want to get into the races," said Maudie Tom to a man who held an open book.

"You want—"

He broke off and stepped aside to address another man. Only members of the Jockey Club were expected for the races, but Maudie Tom did not know this. Women and girls and children were approaching from all directions. The two girl jockeys, one in blue and white this year, and one in yellow leather, stared curiously.

"All right, miss," said the man of the note-book, returning. "Glad to have you. What's your name?"

"Maudie Tom."

"Maud—Well, what else?"

"I don't—Oh, Tibbetts."

"Maud Tibbetts. And the horse?"

"Huh?"

"The horse's name?"

"Bess."

"All right, Miss Tibbetts. We start the trial heats in about half an hour. I'll let you know when you're listed. Stand just over there, will you, Miss Tibbetts?"

The recurrence of "Miss Tibbetts" annoyed Maudie Tom. She sat, big and glowering, on the folded blanket which served her as a saddle. When the other two girl jockeys came up with proffered sugar, both horse and rider waited with suspicion. Maudie Tom did not speak, and Bess snapped at their fingers.

"Ouch," said the girl in blue and white. She smiled at Maudie Tom. "Unfriendly beast you have."

"Leave her alone; she's all right," growled Maudie Tom.

Inside her another prouder, more fiercely wretched voice was saying: "You can leave me alone, too. You needn't try to make out you're so much. I'm going to beat you!"

What she was thinking showed in her face. The girls drew away. "Whew!" exclaimed one. "Isn't she marvelous, though? What wouldn't Miss Kincaid make out of her if she had a chance? That girl's got stuff!" And the other said: "She's a lot of pluck to turn up here with that beast. She fascinates me." But Maudie Tom did not hear what they said. She only saw their incredulous, faintly injured faces, and the curls escaping under their caps.

A broad, white strip of hard sand, the race-track, divided the two streams of on-lookers.

Nine horses were entered. The officials divided them into three groups for the trial heats, and Bess was number two of the first. A man with snow-white hair and pink cheeks pinned a great "2" on Maudie Tom's back. She headed Bess into line, her heart pounding under the huge flowers

stamped on her dress. On one side of her was a grinning boy on a young sorrel horse, and on the other the leather-jacketed girl, riding a steed which looked as swift as ever Lochinvar's was. Both riders smiled at Maudie Tom and waved to friends on the side-lines, but Maudie Tom did not smile back and she had no friends to wave to. She crouched low on Bess's high, unlovely back.

The pistol cracked. The horses leaped forward. At the sound Bess had pawed the air in nervousness and bad temper, and set out a length behind the others. Her gait was awkward and gangling. She threw out her feet like brown spray to each side of her step. She kicked her hind left ankle with her right and left a trail of blood in the sand. The other horses ran swift and straight, tails lifted, manes flying, noses in the air. But the girl in yellow leather let her mount break from his smooth trot into a gallop, and so was disqualified. The boy who grinned so engagingly was riding for the first time in a race; he did not know where to bear his weight or when to urge his horse. Maudie Tom rode like a part of Bess—two big, bony, untamed things together, the girl's face close to the corded red neck, her voice quick with unintelligible sounds, her boot-heel a sharp, firm pressure. The red horse beat the sorrel by half a length.

"Two!" yelled the judges in good-humored amazement. What of their blooded stables now?

"Good!" cried the boy.

"Splendid!" sang out the yellow-jacketed girl, cantering up. "What *riding!* Simply magnificent!"

Clapping ran along the lines. To the summer people these races added a charming interest to their last day. Having the picturesque daughter of the lighthouse keeper entered gave new color to a familiar excitement. They rather hoped she would win the finals, and they clapped and smiled encouragement.

Maudie Tom scarcely looked at them. She was now one of the three best. She had won the first race!

"You wait. I'll show you something yet," she told them under her breath. "You think you know it all."

Her heart thumped as if it would tear through her breast. She dismounted, led Bess far up the beach, and made her walk in the salt water, to cleanse the wounded ankle. The sound of other pistol-shots and more clapping reached them. When they returned, the girl in blue and white, on a coal-black mare, and a fat, little bald-headed man on a fiery gray horse, had won the two other races. They sat waiting, a Number One and a Number Two. Some one changed Maudie Tom's number to a "3."

"You got to do it," choked Maudie Tom. "You go it, you old fool of a horse! You got to win!"

But she could not win—it was absurd! Dusky Dart was four years old, daughter of His Majesty, and had done six furlongs in 1:15 many times. Gray Skies was a three year old with a pedigree that filled a pigeonhole. Bess was twenty, if a day—badly built, untrained, and nobody had ever dreamed of recording her parentage.

The pistol cracked—they were off! Maudie Tom rode as an eagle flies; her hair blew back, and her strong body held itself as light as a feather. But Dusky Dart went past and Gray Skies' tail flicked Bess's nose. The crowd roared, the breakers boiled and foamed, the tape broke—with Dusky Dart the winner, the blue-and-white girl on her back. Gray Skies had been a three-quarter length behind. Maudie Tom let Bess into a walk twenty paces back.

The white-haired, pink-faced man tied blue ribbons on Dusky Dart's mane and tail. Blue sky, blue water, blue ribbons, and laughter. Maudie Tom thought she could not bear it.

"Get up," she breathed in Bess's ear. "Get out of here before that leg goes lame. Get up!"

They galloped off together, as if making an escape. She heard hoofs behind, and urged Bess faster.

"Go on, you!"

But again Dusky Dart proved the better horse. The girl in blue and white overtook Maudie Tom and crossed before her, so that she had to stop.

"Where are you going?" she asked. She, too, had straight hair, but it was yellow, and her cheeks were soft. "You must come back and get your ribbon."

"Ribbon?" echoed Maudie Tom dully.

"Yes, the green one. Third prize, you know. Come on."

The girl in blue and white reached for Bess's rein and turned her around. They rode back together, side by side.

"I'm Carolyn Kincaid" the girl said. "I think you're marvelous. I'd give anything in the world if I could ride the way you do."

Maudie Tom lifted her head and looked full at Carolyn. Her eyes were asking. She did not think she could have heard rightly.

"You live over at the lighthouse, don't you?" asked the other.

Maudie Tom nodded.

"Do you stay there all the time?"

Maudie Tom nodded again.

"Because I'm going to live here with my aunt until at least November. I'm supposed to stay outdoors a lot. My aunt's a teacher, but she's taking a leave of absence. I wonder—you know, you don't have to say you will—but I wonder if you'd want to teach me more about riding while I'm here. Would you?"

Maudie Tom swallowed. She wanted to

speak, but she could think of no words to use. Finally she nodded once more.

Carolyn bounced up and down in glee. "Oh, good! And listen, will you take me over to the island some time?"

This time Maudie Tom managed, "Sure!"

"Really? What fun! Do you know, I'm beginning to be *glad* I'm staying. You must come and meet my aunt. About my riding-lessons—we'll want to pay you, of course. Or—is there anything you want to learn that we could teach you?"

"Teach me?" said Maudie Tom with a comical, confidential movement of her eyebrows. "I don't know anything!"

They reached the judges, and the white-haired man replaced Bess's dirty ribbon with crisp green ones. He stroked the thin old nose and spoke gently. Bess did not snap at him, but looked up softly out of wondering, chastened eyes.

THE LITTLE ELF

by *John Kendrick Bangs*

I MET a little Elf-man, once,
  Down where the lilies blow.
I asked him why he was so small
  And why he did n't grow.

He slightly frowned, and with his eye
  He looked me through and through.
"I 'm quite as big for me," said he,
  "As you are big for you."

THE CREW OF THE CAPTAIN'S GIG

by Sophie Swett

THEY kept the light-house on Great Porpoise Island—Aunt Dorcas (nobody ever called her anything but *Darkis*), Saul and Semanthy, Nick and Little Job, and the Baby.

Job Jordan (Aunt Dorcas's brother and the children's father) was the light-house keeper, but Job was, in the language of the Porpoise Islanders, a "tarlented" man, and "dretful literary." His chief talent seemed to be for smoking and reading vividly illustrated story papers, and he devoted himself so completely to developing that talent that all the prosaic duties of the establishment fell upon Aunt Dorcas and the children. "The light-house would 'a' ben took away from him long ago, if it had n't 'a' ben for Darkis," the neighbors said.

Aunt Dorcas did seem to have the strength of ten. She and the children raised a large flock of sheep on the rocky pastures around the light-house, and, rising up early and lying down late, tilled a plot of the dry ground until it actually brought forth vegetables enough to supply the family; and they cleaned and filled and polished and trimmed the great lamp, with its curious and beautiful glass rings, which reflected the calm and steady light from so many angles that myriads of flashes went dancing out over the dark waters and dangerous rocks. Through summer and winter, storm and calm, the light on

Great Porpoise Island never was known to fail.

And they kept everything in the tower, and in the dwelling-house, as bright and shining as a new pin. So when the commissioners came to examine the light-house, their report was that "Job Jordan was a most faithful and efficient man."

What the family would have done if Job had lost the position, I don't know; though I think that Aunt Dorcas would have managed to keep their heads above water in some way. They all looked upon her as a sort of special providence; if good fortune did not come to them in the natural course of things, Aunt Dorcas would contrive to bring it.

She was very nice to look at, with smooth, shining brown hair, and pretty, soft gray eyes. She had been a beauty once—in the days when she had turned her back upon the brightness that life promised her, and shouldered the responsibilities of Job's family; but she was past thirty-five now, and years of toil and care *will* leave their traces. She still had a springy step, and laughed easily—and these are two very good things where work and care abound. It was when Mrs. Jordan died that she had come to live with them, and when the baby was only a year old.

That was four years ago, now, and the baby was still called the Baby. The reason for this was that his name was Reginald

Fitz-Eustace Montmorenci. His father named him—after a hero in one of his story papers. Aunt Dorcas scorned the name—she liked old-fashioned Bible names —and the children could n't pronounce it, so it had fallen into disuse.

He was tow-headed and sturdy—Reginald Fitz-Eustace Montmorenci—with a fabulous appetite, and totally unable to keep the peace with Little Job.

Little Job, who came next,—going up the ladder,—found life a battle. His namesake of old was not more afflicted. He had sore eyes, and his hair was "tously," and he *hated* to have it combed. He was always getting spilled out of boats, and off docks, and tumbling down steep rocks and stairs. When the tips of his fingers were not all badly scratched, his arm was broken or his ankle sprained. His clothes were always in tatters, and Aunt Dorcas sometimes made him go to bed while she mended them, and that always happened to be just when the others were going fishing. The cow swallowed the only jackknife he ever had, and when he saved up all his pennies for a year, and had bought a cannon, it would n't go off. And he always was found out. The others might commit mischief, and go scot-free, but Little Job always was found out.

And this sort of existence he had supported for nine years.

Nick was but little more than a year older than Little Job, and no larger, but he took life more easily. He was brave, and jolly, and happy-go-lucky; so full of mischief that the neighbors had christened him *"Old* Nick." Aunt Dorcas thought that he did n't deserve that, as there was never anything malicious about his mischief, but little did Nick care what they called him. He had little, bright, beady cross-eyes, which seemed to be always eagerly looking at the tip of his nose. And as the tip of his nose turned straight up to meet them, the interest appeared to be mutual.

His shock of red hair *would* stand upright, too, let Aunt Dorcas and Semanthy do what they would to make it stay down. And his ears—which were the largest ears ever seen on a small boy—would not stay down, either, but stood out on each side of his head, so that Cap'n 'Siah Hadlock (who was Aunt Dorcas's beau once, and still dropped in to see her occasionally, in the light of a friend) declared that Nick always reminded him of a vessel going wing-and-wing. Cap'n 'Siah and Nick were very good friends, notwithstanding, and now that Cap'n 'Siah had given up following the sea, and kept a flourishing store on "the main," there was no greater delight to Nick than to stand behind his counter, and sell goods; it might have been rather tame without the occasional diversion of a somersault over the counter, or a little set-to with a boy somewhat bigger than himself, but these entertainments were always forthcoming, and the store was Nick's earthly paradise.

Saul and Semanthy were twins. They were twelve, and felt all the dignity and responsibility of their position as the elders of the family. Semanthy was tow-headed and freckled, and toed-in. Saul was tow-headed and freckled, too, but he was (as Cap'n 'Siah expressed it) "a square trotter." Their tow heads and their freckles were almost the only points of resemblance between them, although they were twins. Saul had an old head and keen wits. He was very fond of mathematics, and had even been known to puzzle the schoolmaster by a knotty problem of his own making. Semanthy could do addition, if you gave her time. Saul kept his eyes continually open to all the practical details of life, and was already given to reading scientific books. Semanthy was a little absent-minded and dreamy, and as fond of stories as her father. Saul always observed the wind and the clouds, and knew when it was going to rain as well as Old Probabilities himself. And if he had been suddenly transported to an unknown country, blindfolded, he could have told you which way was north by a kind of instinct. And he heaped scorn upon Semanthy because she was n't a walking compass, too,—poor Semanthy, who never knew which way was east except when she saw the sun rise, and then could never quite remember, when she stood, with her right hand toward it, according to the geographical rule, whether the north was in front of her or behind her! Saul was a wonderful sailor, too, and had all the proper nautical terms at his tongue's end, as well as numberless wise maxims about the management of boats; if he had sailed as long as the Ancient Mariner he could n't have been more learned in sea lore. But Semanthy did n't even know what the "gaff-topsail" was, and had no more idea what "port your helm" and "hard-a-lee" meant than if it had been Sanscrit. When she was sailing, she liked to watch the sky, and fancy wonderful regions hidden by the curtain of blue ether, or build castles in the clouds which the sunset bathed in wonderful colors; she liked that much better than learning all the stupid names that they called things on a boat, or how to sail one. She was perfectly willing that Saul should do that for her. And Saul cherished a profound contempt for girls, as the lowest order of creation, and for Semanthy, in particular, as an especially inferior specimen of the sex. Semanthy had a deep admiration and affection for Saul, but still, sometimes, when he assumed very superior airs, and said very cutting things about her ignorance, she did feel, in her heart, that boys were rather a mistake.

It was about five o'clock on a sultry Saturday afternoon, in August. Aunt Dorcas was putting her last batch of huckleberry pies into the oven, and thanking her stars that they had not been troubled by any "city folks" that day; for Hadlock's Point, the nearest land on "the main," had become a popular summer resort, and troops of visitors were continually coming over to Great Porpoise Island, to explore the rocks and the lighthouse. Nick was endeavoring to promote hostilities between a huge live lobster, which he had just brought in, and which was promenading over the floor, and a much-surprised kitten. Little Job was in the throes of hair-combing, under the hands of Semanthy, and howling piteously. Suddenly they all looked up, and Little Job was surprised into ceasing his howls. A deep bass voice, just outside the door, was singing, or rather roaring, this singular ditty:

"For I am a cook, and a captain bold,
And the mate of the Nancy brig,
And a bo'sun tight, and a midshipmite,
And the crew of the captain's gig."

This was "The Yarn of the Nancy Bell," which Cap'n 'Siah Hadlock had learned from some of the summer visitors, and was never tired of singing. He had taught it to the children, too, and the experience of the "elderly naval man," who had cooked and eaten all the personages named in the rhyme, had fired Nick's soul with a desire to boil Little Job in the dinner-pot, and Little Job accordingly dwelt in terror of his life. Cap'n 'Siah was just what his voice proclaimed him—a big and jolly-looking man of forty or thereabouts, with a twinkle in his eye, and a double chin with a deep dimple in it. But what made his appearance particularly fascinating to the children was the fact that he wore ear-rings—little round hoops of gold—and had grotesque figures tattooed all over his hands, in India-ink.

All four of the children knew what he was going to say, for he always said the same thing, whether he came often or seldom.

"Gittin' ready, Darkis?"

blushing at it—such old people, too!

"Well, I kinder calkerlate that the day o' jedgment 'll get along 'thout my attendin' to it, but if ever I 'm agoin' to git a good wife, I 've got to go arter her!" said Cap'n 'Siah.

"Then p'r'aps you 'd better be agoin'," said Aunt Dorcas. Whereupon Cap'n

The Captain's gig at Great Porpoise Island

"For the day of jedgment? Yes, an' I hope you be, too," said Aunt Dorcas, trying to force a pucker upon a face that was never made for puckering. But something brought a color to her cheeks just then—perhaps the heat of the oven, as she opened the door to look after her pies.

Semanthy wondered if Cap'n 'Siah never would get tired of saying that to Aunt Dorcas, and she never would get tired of

'Siah sat down.

"I come over in the captain's gig," he said, addressing himself to the children.

They all looked bewildered, not knowing that "captains' gigs" had an existence outside of "The Yarn of the Nancy Bell."

"There 's a revenue cutter a-layin' up in the harbor; she come in last night. The cap'n he come off in his gig, and went off ridin' with some of the folks up to the hotel. He wanted some good fresh butter, an' I told him I 'd come over here an' see if I could n't git some o' the Widder Robbins, an' he said his men might row me over in the gig. So there the boat lays, down there at the shore, an' the men have gone over to the cliffs after ducks' eggs. I told 'em they need n't be in no hurry, seein' as I was n't."

The children were all out of the house in a trice, to see what kind of a boat a "captain's gig" was.

They were somewhat disappointed to find only a long, narrow row-boat; it had outriggers, and was painted black; except for those peculiarities, they might have taken it for a boat belonging to some of the summer visitors at Hadlock's Point. They all had a fancy that a "captain's gig" must bear some resemblance to a carriage.

"Cap'n 'Siah must have been fooling us; it 's nothing but a row-boat," said Nick.

Saul had been there before them, inspecting the boat, and spoke up: "That 's what they call it—the sailors said so; it 's a good boat, anyway, and I 'd like to take a row in it."

"Come on!" shouted Nick, jumping into the boat. "It 's a good mile over to the cliffs where the ducks' eggs are; the men won't be back this two hours."

"Do come, Saul," urged Semanthy, and Little Job joined his voice to the general chorus.

"I suppose they would let us take it if they were here, but I don't just like to take it without leave," said Saul, doubtfully.

"Stay home, then. We 're going, anyhow. Semanthy can row like a trooper," cried Nick.

Semanthy could row a boat if she could n't sail one, and she was proud of her accomplishment, especially as Saul always chose her as an assistant in preference to any of the boys.

"If you are all going, I suppose I shall have to go to take care of you," said Saul, jumping in. "But we must n't go so far that we can't see the sailors when they come back for their boat."

So they all went off in the "captain's gig"—Saul and Semanthy, Nick and Little Job, and the Baby.

But as soon as they were off, conscientious Saul pushed back again and sent Little Job up to the house to ask Cap'n 'Siah if it would do for them to use the "captain's gig" for a little while. And Cap'n 'Siah said that the sailors would n't be back before dark, and he would "make it all right" with them. Whether Cap'n 'Siah was anxious to get rid of the children, that he might have a better opportunity to urge Aunt Dorcas to "git ready," I cannot say, but he was certainly very willing that they should go.

Saul's mind was now at ease, and he was quite ready to enjoy himself; but I am afraid that Nick felt, in the bottom of his mischievous heart, that there was quite as much fun about it before they had anybody's permission.

"Now we can go over to the Point!" said Semanthy.

That was Semanthy's great delight, to go over to the Point and see the crowds of summer visitors, in their gay, picturesque dresses, the steamers coming in, and the flags flying. Now and then there was a band playing; and at such times Semanthy's cup of happiness ran over.

Saul did not make any objection. He liked to go over to the Point, too. Not that he cared much for crowds of people, or flags, or bands, but there was a queer, double-keeled boat, which they called a catamaran, over there, and he wanted to investigate it. The Point was nearly three miles away, but they pulled hard, Saul and Semanthy, Nick and Little Job, each taking an oar. To be sure, they had to keep an eye on Little Job, for he had an un-

Cap'n 'Siah Hadlock

pleasant way of dropping his oar into the water—if he did n't drop himself in—and of keeping the Baby in a drenched condition, which aroused all the pugnacity of his infant nature. But in spite of all drawbacks, they reached the Point in a very short space of time. And Semanthy saw a steam-boat just coming in, and it had a band on board, playing "Pinafore" selections, and some Indians had come and

pitched their tents on the shore, and hung out silvery seal-skins and beautiful, gay baskets at their tent-doors, and the little Indian children, running about, were queerer than anything out of a fairy book. And Nick had an opportunity to invest a long-cherished five-cent piece in "jaw-breakers"—a kind of candy whose merit seemed to consist in "lasting long." Little Job had time to be knocked off the wharf by a huge Newfoundland dog, and rescued dripping. Saul found the catamaran fastened to the slip, where he could inspect it to his heart's content. The owner was standing by, and noticing Saul's interest, he told him all about the boat, and ended by asking him to go sailing with him.

"Go, of course, Saul! You don't suppose we can't get home without you?" said Semanthy.

"Of course you can, but you had better go right along. You have no more than time to get home before dark," called prudent Saul, as he stepped into the catamaran with his friend.

"O my! Don't we feel big!" called out Nick, in a voice which was distinctly audible in the catamaran. "You 'd think we were the cap'n of the boat! I would n't feel big in that queer old machine—'t aint any kind of a boat, anyhow!"

And Little Job piped up, in a high, shrill voice:

"O I am a cook, and a captain bold,
And the mate of the Nancy brig,
And a bos'n tight, and a midshipmite,
And the crew of the captain's gig!"

It was clearly a relief to get rid of Saul; he was so very prudent and cautious, and kept them in such good order. "The crew of the captain's gig" meant to have a good time now!

Semanthy tried her best to make Nick pull with a will, straight for home, for it was already past six o'clock, and she had a vivid picture in her mind of the sailors all on the shore waiting for their boat, and furiously angry with those who had stolen it.

But Nick and Little Job had become hilarious, and preferred "catching crabs" and "sousing" Semanthy and the Baby, and rocking the boat from side to side to see how far it would tip without tipping over, to going peaceably along.

And all Semanthy's remonstrances were in vain, until, suddenly, she espied a black cloud swiftly climbing the sky.

"Look there boys!" she cried. *"There's a squall coming!* Now I guess you'll hurry!"

And they did. Nick and Little Job were not without sense, and they had not lived on that dangerous, rocky coast, where sudden "flaws" came down from the mountains, and squalls came up with scarcely a moment's warning, in the calmest, sunniest days, for nothing. Even the Baby understood the situation perfectly.

But there was little danger in a rowboat, unless it should grow so dark before they got home that they could not see their way, or the waves should run so high as to swamp their boat—and the "captain's gig" was not a boat to be easily swamped. Semanthy wished they were at home, but her chief anxiety was for Saul, out in a sail-boat,—and such a queer, new-fangled one, too!

"Pooh! Saul knows how to manage any sail-boat that ever was!" said Nick, scornfully, when Semanthy expressed her fears.

"And if he didn't, those fellers know how to manage their own craft," said Little Job.

The black cloud spread so quickly over the sky that is seemed as if a pall had been suddenly cast upon the light of day. The water was without a ripple, and there was a strange hush in the air. It was a relief to Semanthy when a flock of gulls flew screaming over their heads—the stillness was so oppressive.

Then the wind swooped down suddenly and fiercely upon them. On the land they could see the dust of the road torn up in a dense cloud, and the trees bent and writhing. The smooth water was broken into great, white-capped waves.

Semanthy and Nick tugged away bravely at the oars, but it was very hard work, and they made but little progress. The darkness was increasing with every moment; every ray of the setting sun had been obscured, and the sky over their heads was black. In a very few minutes they were in the midst of a thick darkness.

"Look out! You just missed that buoy!" called out Little Job. And in another moment he shouted:

"I don't b'lieve this is the way at all! I think you're goin' straight for Peaked Nose Island!"

"Well, I aint got eyes in the back o' my head, like Saul! No other fellow could tell which way to go in this darkness. Anyway, I can't tell Little Porpoise from Peaked Nose. We might just as well drift."

"Drift! I should think it was drifting, with the boat most turning a somersault every minute. Most likely we shall all be drowned," said Little Job, with the calmness of one accustomed to misfortune.

"If you say that again, I'll pitch you overboard!" said Nick. "Of course we aint going to get drowned! It will get lighter by and by, and then we'll go home."

"If night were not coming on, I should hope that it would grow lighter soon," said Semanthy; "but, as it is, I wonder why Aunt Darkis does n't light the lamp?"

But, though they strained their eyes to the utmost, peering anxiously into the darkness, there was no welcome flash from the Great Porpoise light-house. They rested on their oars, while the boat stood, now on its head and now on its feet, as the Baby said, until Nick's stock of patience was exhausted.

"I move that we pull ahead," he said. "I know this place too well to get a great ways out of my reckoning, and it 's enough to make a fellow crazy to be wabbling around here this way. We can't do any worse than to bump on a rock, and, if it 's above water, we 'll hold on to it."

Semanthy was prone to sea-sickness, and the pirouetting of the boat had caused her to begin to feel that there might be worse things even than being drowned. So she was only too glad to "pull ahead."

They did not "bump" upon any rock, but neither did they, after what seemed like hours of rowing, see any signs that they were nearing home. They were rowing against wind and tide, and could not expect to make rapid progress; but still it did seem to Nick that they ought to have got somewhere by this time, unless they had drifted out into the open sea.

"Goin' straight ter Halifax! All aboard!" shouted Little Job, whose spirits were fitful.

The wind's violence had abated somewhat, and it had begun to rain. If Semanthy had only known that the catamaran and its crew were safe, she would have felt that their woes were not beyond remedy. But the gale had come on so suddenly! Before they had time to take down their sail, the boat might have capsized, or been blown upon the rocks. Even Nick shook his head now and then, and said: "This squall 's been pretty rough on sailboats, I can tell you."

"Nick, where *can* we be that we don't see our light?"

"That must be Great Porpoise just ahead," said Nick, pointing to a spot in the distance, which looked only like darkness intensified and gathered into a small compass. "Why we can't see the light I am sure I can't tell."

As they drew nearer, the black spot grew larger, and revealed itself as land beyond a question.

"But it *can't* be Great Porpoise, Nick, because we should see the light!"

Nick looked long and earnestly, doubt growing deeper and deeper in his mind.

"Well, it *must* be Peaked Nose," he said, at last, "though it is certainly a great deal bigger than Peaked Nose ever was before."

And so they turned the boat in the direction in which Great Porpoise ought to lie, if this were Peaked Nose.

That the light on Great Porpoise might not be lighted did not occur to any one of them. For that lamp to remain unlighted after night-fall was a thing which had never happened since they were born; it would have been scarcely less extraordinary to their minds if daylight should fail to put in an appearance.

Since there was no light there, that could not be Great Porpoise Island. That was all there was about it,—so they all thought.

They rowed swiftly and in silence for a while, and another dark shape did appear ahead of them; but there was no light there!

"Oh, Nick! The Pudding Stones! I hear the breakers!" cried Semanthy, suddenly "It must be Little Porpoise!"

"Then the other was Great Porpoise!" said Nick, blankly. "What is the matter with the light?"

The Pudding Stones made Little Porpoise a terror to mariners. If the beams from Great Porpoise light-house had not fallen full upon them, they would probably have been the ruin of many a good ship. Now, where was the Great Porpoise light?

The other end of Little Porpoise was inhabited; they had friends there, and went there often, but Semanthy had never before been so near the Pudding Stones, and she was anxious only to get as far away from them as possible. They seemed to her like living monsters, with cruel teeth, eager to crush and grind helpless victims.

"Why are you going so near, Nick?" she cried, in terror.

"I want to make sure where we are. There are other rocks around besides the Pudding Stones, and it seems as if we must have got to the other side of nowhere. If we have n't, *where in creation is that light?*"

This did seem to Semanthy an almost unanswerable argument in proof of their having "got to the other side of nowhere." But still she did not feel any desire to investigate the rocks just ahead, upon which the breakers were making an almost deafening uproar. But Nick would not turn away until he had fully satisfied his mind about their position.

Suddenly, above the roar of the breakers, they heard a voice,—a shrill, despairing cry for help,—a woman's voice and not far away.

"A boat has run against the rocks, most likely," said Nick, and pulled straight on toward the breakers. "We may be in time to save somebody."

"Oh, but Nick, it is n't as if there were only you and me to think of! Here are the children. We are risking their lives!" said Semanthy.

It was Little Job who piped up then, in his high, weak little voice, and not by any means in the terror-stricken wail which might have been expected from Little Job. His courage had evidently mounted with the occasion.

"I guess we 're all the crew of the captain's gig, and we aint agoin' to let anybody get drownded if we can help it!" he said.

Nick did not reply to either Semanthy

or him, but rowed as if his own life depended upon it. Semanthy knew that he thought she was a coward, and was disgusted with her; but she was sure that, if she and Nick had been alone, she would not have hesitated.

Little Job's speech and Semanthy's thoughts occupied but a moment's space. The next moment the boat grated against a rock, and that cry, weaker and fainter, arose close beside them.

"Jehosaphat! There 's a woman clinging to this rock! Steady, Semanthy—she 's slipping off! Hold the boat tight to the rock, Little Job! Take hold here, Semanthy; she 's heavier than lead!"

Using all their force, they dragged her into the boat—a limp, drenched form, from which no sound came. The boat rocked terribly, but righted at last.

"Semanthy, she 's fainted, and she was losing her hold of the rock! If we had n't grabbed her just as we did, she 'd 'a' been drownded," said Nick, in an awed voice.

"I think she 's dead, Nick," said Semanthy, who had put her face down to the woman's lips, and felt no breath.

"Rub her hands and feet," said Nick. "We can't do anything else, but try to get out of this place, now; or we shall all be ground to bits."

"It is so dark! I can't see to do anything!" groaned Semanthy. "Oh, where is the lighthouse lamp? This all seems like a dreadful nightmare!"

"I know those were the Pudding Stones, so now I know the way home," said Nick.

"The lamp has most likely got bewitched," said Little Job, who was a reader of fairy tales.

But suddenly, like a ray of sunshine falling on the black waters, out shone the lamp!

It shone full on the white face of the unconscious and half-drowned woman, resting on Semanthy's lap.

"Aunt Darkis! Oh, Aunt Darkis!" they all cried, in concert.

"Oh, Nick, aint we dreaming?" said Semanthy, while a flood of tears fell on Aunt Dorcas's face. "How could she have come there?"

"Why, it 's plain enough. I heard Cap'n 'Siah ask her to go over to Little Porpoise with him, to see his sister, the last time he was over. They took our little sail-boat, and went over, and the squall struck 'em coming home, and drove 'em on to the rocks."

"But where is the boat, and where is— oh where is Cap'n 'Siah?"

"Can't say—p'r'aps all right!" said Nick. Semanthy and Little Job rubbed Aunt Dorcas's poor white hands, and wrung the water out of her pretty brown hair, and kissed her over and over again. And by and by they could detect a faint fluttering breath coming through her parted lips.

"But oh—oh, Nick, if we had n't been there!" Semanthy said.

Nick did n't say anything. He had too big a lump in his throat.

In a few minutes more they were carrying Aunt Dorcas tenderly and with great difficulty into the house. The sailors—the original "crew of the captain's gig"—were all there; it was one of them who had lighted the lamp. The children's father, they were told, was down at the Widow Dobbins's.

The sailors did n't scold about their boat, you may be sure, when they knew what service it had done.

Aunt Dorcas soon came to herself enough to know them, and to speak to them, but they none of them dared to ask the question that was trembling on their tongues—where was Cap'n 'Siah? And Aunt Dorcas seemed too weak to remember anything that had happened.

But while they were sitting there, looking questioningly into each other's faces, in walked a drenched and weather-beaten, and pale-faced man—Cap'n 'Siah, but ten years older, it seemed, than he had been that afternoon. But when he caught sight of Aunt Dorcas, he threw himself into a chair, and covered his face with his hands, and when he took them away they saw tears on his cheeks—great rough man as he was.

"I thought she 'd got drowned, and I 'd let her," he said. "You see, I wa' n't lookin' at the sky, as I 'd ought to 'a' ben, and that pesky little boat went over ker-slap, an' there we was, both in the water. I ketched hold o' the boat, and reached for yer Aunt Darkis, and jest missed her! Then I let go o' the boat, and tried to swim for her, but I found I was sinkin', with all my heavy toggery on, and I ketched hold o' the boat again. Then a big wave knocked me off, and I went down, and I thought I was done for, but when I came up I managed to grab the boat again. But your Aunt Darkis was gone. I could n't see nothin' of her, and in a few minutes 't was so dark I could n't see nothin' at all! By and by, after I had drifted and drifted, I heard voices, and I hollered, and that queer craft from the P'int, the catamaran, picked me up—and there was our Saul aboard of her! I did n't care much about bein' picked up, seein' your Aunt Darkis was drowned, and I 'd let her, but now I 'm obleeged to ye, Saul, for pickin' me up!"

Then Nick and Semanthy told their story, and soon Aunt Dorcas told how she had clung, for what seemed like hours, to the steep and slippery rock, from which Nick and Semanthy had rescued her just as her strength gave out.

"And yer pa he 's a-courtin' the Widder Dobbins, it appears, otherwise he might 'a' ben here to light the lamp," said Cap'n 'Siah, in a mild and meditative tone. "And yer Aunt Darkis an' me 's ben a-thinkin' that yer pa an' the Widder Dobbins an' her six might be enough here, an' so you 'd better all of you come over to the main and live with me. My house is big enough for us all, and Saul, he 'll kind of look after my boats that I keep to let, and Nick, he 'll tend in the store, when he aint to school, and Semanthy—why, of course Aunt Darkis could n't do without her; and as for Little Job and the Baby, why, they 'll kinder keep things lively."

So, not only Aunt Dorcas, but the whole "crew of the captain's gig" are "gettin' ready" now.

TABLE MANNERS

by Gelett Burgess

The Goops they lick their fingers,
And the Goops they lick their knives;
They spill their broth on the table-cloth;
Oh, they lead untidy lives.
The Goops they talk while eating,
And loud and fast they chew.
So that is why I am glad that I
Am not a Goop. Are you?

KIN TO THE WOODS

A STORY OF THE TENNESSEE CUMBERLANDS

by Maristan Chapman

DALE GILLOW did not want to go and stay at his grandfather's place on Pilot Mountain, but before he could think of a good excuse for getting out of the invitation, his mother had told him to go along and be a good boy, and watch he didn't lose his new cap; and his father had called out, "Grampa's waiting—hurry along now!" So there was nothing to do but start out.

"Can't I take my model?" he asked, lingering at the door.

"No! Your grampa will not crave you to clutter up his yard with a mess o' wheels and string. Likely it'll keep till such time as you get back."

So Dale dumped his newly built steam-engine into a box and carried it out to the tool-shed—just as he had almost got it to work, too! He went out front to make his manners to his grandfather, privately thinking that when he had a little boy he wouldn't order him around. He'd give a boy a chance to say his rathers for himself.

The grandfather, Oak Gillow, was a calm old man, and he did not see a thing out of the way in interfering with engine building, and carrying off his grandson just because he had taken a lonely notion for company.

So they trod along the road out of Glen Hazard, past the big stacks of lumber near the depôt, and up Cragg Hill, each silent with his own thoughts.

Dale was still thinking about making his escape. There wasn't any sense in going way off to Pilot, when he had his engine so nearly fixed. Yet here he was, walking along as if he didn't have right use of his legs—stride, stride, stride—keeping step with the old man, and wishing boys didn't have grandfathers.

Ordinarily he liked this grandfather of his, who never talked much, but seemed sort of friendly, and who could carve almost anything out of a pine splinter, or a peach-stone. What on earth had given the old man the notion to ask Dale to go home with him the one time Dale craved to stay in town?

At the top of Cragg Hill they met a group of boys, coming back to town from a fodder-pulling at Howard's farm; they hailed Dale: "Where you going off to, Fix-it?"

"Up to Grampa's," he said, longing to take to his heels and chase back with them. If he just ran—well, there was nothing the old man could do to stop him. Dale wavered and looked back over his shoulder.

But Oak Gillow was not an easy man to run from.

"Maybe the way is overly hard for you," he said. "You're kind of spindling for a

218

boy. Happen you feel weak, best go on home."

Dale flushed. He wasn't very sturdy, but he disliked being teased about it. He was a thin, pale boy, too tall for his strength; the kind who kept out of fights when he could, and would sooner stay in his own yard and make something than run around with the gang. But he was good at making and mending things.

He answered the old man, saying: "I'll keep on, I thank you." Because he knew, if he turned back now, there would be no end to the tale of how he was too puny to walk up a hill.

As they left the county road and took the single path down toward Fayre Jones' place, the old man went ahead, and Dale plodded on behind him.

Oak said: "There's a new squirrel family in the woodlot since you were up last."

"Yes, sir," Dale answered. Squirrels! he thought in disgust. Grampa must be taking him for a baby. He wished he'd thought about bringing his rifle. He'd have shot every squirrel on Pilot.

But directly Oak said: "There won't be a one left, nor any wild things so-ever, time they get our trees all cut."

"No, sir."

"The company has bought all but my last stand o' trees now."

They had come down the far side of Cragg Hill by now, and Dale was wondering whether, if he lagged behind, the old man would go on, unnoticing; then he could slip off, and then—

"They moved the traveling mill and saw-rig up this morning," Oak went on. "That steam-engine's powerful at eating out planks. The men that's working it hailed me coming down; said they could scarcely keep up feeding it, and did I know a handy boy to help tend it."

Dale put off running away for a while.

Suppose Grampa had thought about him for the boy? If he could get a chance to tend a real steam-engine for a week or such a matter, he would learn how to build them, and why his model wouldn't work.

Oak Gillow tramped on as if he'd used up all his words and had to make a new supply before he could open his mouth again.

The sun was lowering when they got as far as Fayre Jones' farm; and Fayre, who was cutting up wood for the supper fire, stopped long enough to ask them to stay for supper and spend the night.

Oak answered: "Not this night, kind thanks; we'd best urge on."

And when they had gained the top of the next hill he added: "There's a young feller, now, is powerful kindly to squirrels and such."

Dale said: "You talked about the steam-mill a while back."

"And liable to talk some more, time I get some supper in me," answered Oak. "And then, maybe, I'll not say another thing."

A man overtook them soon after they left Fayre Jones', and gave a hasty "Good-evening!" as they stepped off the path to let him go by.

"House afire, Lem Foster?" Oak Gillow called after him.

"Got a heap of affairs to tend," the man called back. "Me, I'm going off to New Orleans Saturday, early day."

It was getting nearly dark when they came to the trees on the near edge of Pilot. The timber was shrinking and popping in the chill of the evening after the hot day, and the whole world was full of strange chirrupings and small noises. This time of day it was a friendly thing to be there with Grampa, and Dale plodded on, with his head full of gear-wheels and piston-rods.

In fact, he was so absent-minded that he

jumped about a foot when a man walked out on them from a side path.

"Evening!" the man said.

"Fair night to you," answered Oak; and Dale nodded and tried to look as if he hadn't been scared.

"Come to your senses, I hope?" the new-comer went on, addressing the old man roughly. "We want to get to work here right away."

"I'm not over-eager for more than my share of this world, John Nolan," Oak Gillow replied quietly, "but that share I aim to keep."

John Nolan was a big man, and his lumberjack clothes, tall shoes, slouch hat, and checkered flannel shirt made him look gigantic in the twilight.

"Been down begging more store credit, and getting your folks to help you out, I guess," Nolan broke in. "Well, there's an end to that when it gets known you got nothing to pay back all you borrowed."

"I got no more help," Oak said, with the same quiet manner. "And you will see I get no more credit save you gar (*make, compel*) me cut my last left timber. Give you good night."

Dale clenched his fists as the lumber-man strode off toward town. He felt the insult in Nolan's voice, though he did not yet understand what it was all about. No-body had ever dared to talk to any Gillow iike that, and this crazy outlander was ordering Grampa around.

He said the only thing he could think of to show how he felt: "I'll not tend his old mill. I fail of craving steam-engines, anyway."

Then he felt Oak's hand on his shoulder, and they stood together, looking at the hillside of first-growth trees that sur-rounded Pilot.

"Seems like, these times, that the folks that's got money got the right in every-thing," the old man said. " 'Tis no man-ner of use me standing up to John Nolan, and he with the power to throw my debts in my face. He being manager of the company store has got power to close my credit; and he figures to starve me into selling him my last left trees. In all my days I never thought to be indebted; but for the sake of the trees I kept putting off and putting off, and lost myself at last. Hit'll make a sad bareness, time the hills is naked of trees."

Dale was going to say that steam-engine mills were made especially to cut trees, but thought he wouldn't. So he said: "Folks got to have milled lumber. Hit's what most of Glen Hazard works at—cutting out and shipping hardwood."

" 'Course they got to," his grandfather admitted. "And did they cut it right, they'd be plenty and more to come. But they leave outlanders come in, hogging in and tear-ing everything down, and flinging waste and trash. They break the new growth and spoil the land, for quick dollars. Time you are old as me," he went on, "this whole hill-country will be ruined waste-land."

Dale was torn between his loyalty to steam-engines and the wild picture made by the old man's words. His grandfather must be right—yet, old men were queer. Down in town they said: "May as well make money whilst it's offered." Or, "No call to be stubborn like Oak Gillow." And they sold off their trees without shame till already the near-by farms were bare and dismal.

Dale puzzled about things, but there was one thing he knew. He hated John Nolan.

Oak's house was an old log cabin, spread along a "bench" of the mountain, and nestled up against it so that there was no back yard at all; and the place was wrapped in trees so closely that there was just the path to the door.

When they got to the cabin, Dale gave up trying to get matters straight, and tucked into a hearty supper of bread and apple-butter and milk.

Within-doors, Oak Gillow's cabin was a homesome place. The floor was hard-packed earth, smooth and clean as concrete; for furnishing there was only a heavy table and two rough chairs that the old man had made himself, long years ago; and there was a big chest in one corner, useful to put things in. Instead of beds, there were bunks, like those on board ship, built against the wall, the lower one wide and the top one narrow, close up under the low-raftered ceiling.

After supper, Dale helped clear up, and then spent the hour till bedtime drawing sketches of his engine. Not that there was any sense in it. It was just something to do. Several times he looked up and started to ask his grandfather why he had fetched him up; but Oak was carving a twisted snake all around a new cane, and was not in a talking mood. When he was busy with his hands it was no use speaking. A person might as well expect an answer out of the fire logs.

Yet Dale began to feel glad he had come. It wasn't so bad, sitting here in this far-off cabin that smelled of pine-smoke and earthiness. And directly, it began to rain, lightly, and the new, wet air brought woodland sounds to his keen ears.

During the night the weather began to walk abroad; the rain came in sudden spatters and dashed against the side window with the rain-wind that came up from the south. This was the colding storm, that blows summer away for good and begins the chill autumn nights and frosty mornings.

Oak Gillow was up at four o'clock next morning, and had an unwilling Dale stirring before daylight. Breakfast of toasted bacon and coffee smelled too good to be re-sisted, so Dale tumbled out, washed in the big tub in the wash-house, and came in glowing and puffing from his bath, as hungry as a hunted fox.

Oak quarreled good-humoredly at him for being late and said: "You're growing to be soft as a town-fetched lass; eat a hearty meal, or you'll fail of being stout enough to feed that mill."

The house door was standing open, and while they were yet having breakfast, a fat boomer squirrel came and sat on the threshold, waiting to see if she might be welcome at the feast.

Without looking around, Oak Gillow dropped a crust of cornbread on the floor by his chair, and the squirrel lolloped cautiously in and picked it up in her fore-paws. She looked first at one of the giants, then at the other, and said, "Chit!" Then she tucked the crust into the pouch of her face, just like a monkey, and streaked out so suddenly that Dale could scarcely believe she'd been there.

"Most times," the old man said "she'll stay quite a spell. Reckon she's like the rest of folks raised in the hills—don't care to be over-free before strangers. Come on out and we'll go visiting at her house."

It was a gray day, and the thick air was being pushed through the woods by a steady wind, a "weather-breeder," the old man called it.

They went to a near-by oak tree, so big and old that its low branches were larger around than the trunks of most trees we see every day. There was a ladder against the tree, and the old man climbed up to look into the hole just above the second branch. Papa squirrel was home, too, and he skipped out of the dark hole and ran up the tree, chit-chittering like mad, while his mate, who still was busy with the corn-bread, sat near by, not at all alarmed at the human visitors, now that she was hostess in her own house. Grampa felt around in the hole, and then climbed down and sent Dale up to have a look at the family.

Cautiously, Dale put his hand way in, as far as it would go, and felt about in the darkness until he found the soft edge of the nest. Then he felt something squirming beneath his hand. Gently he grasped it, and lifted out one of the kittens—such a tiny, deformed-looking little thing, that nosed into the palm of his hand, away from the sudden light. He reached back and got the other. There they lay, helpless between his own big paws. It gave him a funny feeling.

"You got power of life and death over them things now," his grandfather said, from the bottom of the ladder. "Just drop 'em; and none would be knowen the difference."

Dale put the squirrel kittens back in the nest, and slowly came down the ladder, while the mother squirrel darted into the hole to see what damage might have been done to her twins.

"I reckon *I'd* be knowen the difference," Dale said.

"What for would you?" Oak asked him, as they started off toward the lumber-camp.

"Hit fails of being reasoned about; only it would look kind of mean to have dropped 'em down."

"Listen there!" Oak said, as the whine of the saw-mill came through the heavy air. "You'll be a man grown, directly, and likely have a steam-mill of your own, since it's in your mind to. Then you'll have power of life and death over these forests and all that lives therein. Maybe you'll think about that. There's a heap of lumber needs to be cut out; there's plenty ripe for cutting to make a man rich without he tears and wastes like a heathen and ruins the lands for the wild things. Only you got to be kin to the woods to do it rightly."

By this time they had come to the mill and Dale did not take time to answer. Already he was eager to get to work. Oak introduced him, saying to the foreman: "Here's that boy I promised you. His name is called Dale."

And the foreman answered: "He fails of being sturdy to the looks. Mr. Nolan would be more pleased did you find your way to bringing in the trees you promised."

"I never give promise of trees," Oak replied. "Moreover, I'll thank you to leave me quarrel with John Nolan my ownself and not to meddle."

"Meddle yourself," retorted the foreman, "and you bringing your grandson here to stand spy lest we cut into your last trees. Still and all, we got to have a boy. I'll try him, and I'll call him Splinter, 'cause he's a chip off the Oak."

"Better quit your plaguing Todd," one of the workers warned, as the men laughed. "Them as baits old man Gillow is liable to get in trouble."

The foreman spat contemptuously, and turning to Dale said: "Come on, Splinter, and leave me learn you about firing a boiler."

Dale stood still. "You call me by my rightful name," he said, "or there's not a hand I'll lift to this job."

"All right, *Mister* Dale Gillow," Todd corrected with mock politeness. "Happen you'll be pleased to take notice, I'll exhibit how this engine works."

Dale felt like quitting before he had started, but his eyes were on the mill. It was very tempting; and there was no sense losing a chance like this just out of temper. So he stood by in silence while Todd explained to him.

Directly he was given the job of feeding the boiler fire with the short rough slabs that are trimmed from the logs. When the fire was stoked up, he had time to look around and watch the men. He noticed that when an extra heavy log went through, the engine puffed and grunted, and when it slid out at the far end the engine raced like a mad thing. There was nobody tending the throttle, so Dale reached up, carefully watching the log-table, and as the saw got a bite into the wood he opened up, steadily, to keep the speed even, and as the end of the cut was reached and the saw ran free, he closed the throttle so that the engine idled smoothly while waiting. It was very easy. Properly handled, an engine would last a long time. Dale tried to figure out why the governor on the engine did not do this very thing; and of course forgot all about his own task.

"Get down offen there!" the foreman yelled at him. "Fire's about gone. I told you—"

But just as he was in the middle of his speech the great form of John Nolan crashed through the far side of the clearing, and all the men became busy, as if worked by steam themselves. Dale hopped back to his pile of firewood and began stoking again, keeping an eye on the big boss meanwhile.

John Nolan was an alarming man, especially when he let his anger loose on the crew, whom he had been watching as they idled away the morning. He got purple in the face as he strode about and bellowed his rage. He stamped and roared and flung his great hands about as if he would like to jump on the crew and break their several necks. He told each one just what he thought about him for a lazy scoundrel, and by the time he got down to Dale Gillow, that master-stoker was in two minds about running off like a rabbit, or shying a slab of lumber at the angry boss.

"Who's that white-faced rat you got here?" Nolan demanded of his foreman.

"I'll not have kids hired around the mill, liable to get sawed up and killed. Run him off! Boy!" Dale came forward. "Hot-foot it off from here. Move, now!"

Dale came a step nearer and shook his fist at Nolan. "I was hired fair and square," he said, "and I worked; and I'll not go saving you pay me my three hours' wages."

"Hey!" Nolan shouted, "You run off when I say run—hear me?"

"Gillows never take handily to running," Dale answered. "You pay me."

Nolan paused to take a long breath. "Well, sleep me standing up!" he said. "Where have I seen you somewhere?"

"Last night, up toward Oak Gillow's place."

"Oak Gillow's, eh? That accounts for you. I've struck that snag before to-day. The old man put you in the habit of standing against me, like as not."

"No, sir. I only want my pay, fair."

Nolan looked at him as if he saw something funny in this boy defying him, while the men he had tongue-lashed were standing around in blank surprise.

"How much do I owe you?" he asked, reaching into his pocket and drawing out a roll of bills.

"Three hours at twenty cents is sixty," replied Dale promptly.

Nolan peeled off a dollar and handed it to him. "Now you clear out."

Dale hesitated. "I got no change," he said.

"I'll forgive you that; take your dollar and go on. But I'll have no boys working around my mill—leave alone a Gillow boy," he added.

Dale walked off, miserable and disappointed. Here was his chance to work a real engine gone already. It was no fault of his that he had been turned away, yet he was ashamed to go back to his grandfather's house so early. Oak would never understand his quitting with the day only half gone.

Idly he wandered toward town, thinking about what Oak had said that morning. "The man that cuts timber in the mountains has power of life and death over all wild things, and the people besides." It was an ugly thing to think of a man like Nolan holding all Glen Hazard in his hand like that. Grandfather said the man that cut timber had to be kin to the woods. And Dale himself had wanted to grow up to be a timberman. For that matter, he had to admit to himself, he still did want to. For he knew at the bottom of his heart that his real trouble was disappointment about the engine. He walked on, getting some comfort from the homelike sounds in the woods around him. But then he remembered that pretty soon there would be no woods, if Nolan were allowed to go unhindered. It was all very puzzling.

When he got so far as Fayre Jones' house, he went in and had dinner with Fayre and Bess, and told them about his morning's adventure. Fayre and Bess were young people yet, and they might perhaps sympathize with his problem, whereas his grandfather would hold out for checking the timber-cutters.

"Hit's awkward," Fayre Jones said slowly. "Myself, I'm kin to the woods and the wild creatures; but I see where you are bound to be an engineer. Ask Bess, she's got such wits as this family owns."

"Give me your plate for more salad," Bess said. "A man can't think without he's fed right." And when she had helped him, she went on: "No reason you can't come at it both ways. There's bound to be timber-workings here, no matter who says against it. Why not you grow into a right timber-man and run off outlanders like John Nolan? Such times you can work your mill, and deal rightly with the lands and the wild folk besides."

Dale felt as if the sun had come out again. He was impatient not to have thought of this himself.

"Women like Bess," Fayre said, looking proudly at his wife, "women like Bess is able to choose both out of two things. Meanwhile, you'd best recall you owe John Nolan forty cents. Here, I'll change that bill for you, and you'll have the money handy."

"I fail of craving to pay such trash good money," Dale said. "Moreover he forgave it me."

Fayre shrugged his shoulders. "Likely then you'd sooner take a favor offen a man you hate."

Then, when they had carried the dinner dishes back to the kitchen for Bess to scour, he said: "Talking about debts, I wonder me did Lem Foster yet fail of paying what's due Oak Gillow for that stack o' ties he cut and hauled? 'Twas a sizable bill, and likely would cover Oak's credit at the store."

"No, he's not paid it," Bess said from the back room. "Reckon the old man's prideful, or maybe he's already tried for his money. Lem's not dishonest, but he's powerful careless the way he fails of his rightful debts."

Dale made kind thanks for the meal, and started happily on his way back, filled with the clever thought that he could grow up to own a mill and yet not cut the hills bare of timber. He felt nearly grown up already, and as he walked through the woods he studied the trees, looking to see which were ripe for lumber and which should be left to grow larger. Then he quickened his steps, in a grand hurry to talk over plans with his grandfather.

Oak Gillow was sitting on a rough bench outside the cabin, his eyes resting on the near trees, as though he wished the picture they made to sink deep within him. He did not look up or answer Dale's greeting, but the boy was so full of new ideas that he went ahead with his story and wound up by saying: "So I'll get to be the big timber-man and run a lot of mills, but I can run them fair and no need to harm the old dwelling trees where the wild folk live, nor the saplings that are growing more timber."

Oak Gillow considered for a long while, and then he said: "The only sound fact I see is: you owe John Nolan forty cents change. A man in debt is helpless for any business. More especially if it is to the man he aims to fight."

"Hit's only but forty cents," Dale sulked. It seemed stupid to think about that in the midst of his big schemes.

"That's just the same as if it was forty dollars, or four hundred. Pay first, and talk big afterwards."

And that's all he would say or listen to.

There wasn't much for supper. Only a small bowl of corn-meal mush and a cup of milk each. Dale did not like to ask if any more bacon and coffee was in store for breakfast.

"A man may as well starve to death as die any other way," Oak said. "But you got to leave for home to-morrow. There's no more food."

"But, Grampa, you can't be let starve just for lack of store credit. I'll ask Dad— "

"Efn I had my rathers," Oak answered, "I'd be left be. And do you ware any person about it, I'll skin you, and tan your hide for saddle-bags."

They played checkers after supper, and the old man was so absent-minded that he let Dale jump three men and get a king in one move.

"You're not playing," Dale laughed at him.

"Speaking of debts," Oak said, not paying attention at all, "speaking of debts, I give John Nolan promise to see him to-

morrow's early morning, and sign him over the trees."

"You never!"

" 'Tis the onliest way. Man as powerful as that can't be stopped with a thing save money, and that's what I fail of having."

"Maybe he can't now, but time I get a year or two older, and I'll stop him," Dale threatened. A thought struck him. "What for you make me come up here to help eat your last food?"

"Just only took a notion you'd care to say 'Farewell' to the last trees," Oak told him. "Climb you up to bed, now, and hasten that growth. These hills need such men as you will be."

Glowing with this unusual praise, Dale crawled up to his bunk and lay thinking, while he listened to the rising storm. He could see lightning flicker through the chinks in the shutters and hear the wind tearing at the trees, while sharp bursts of rain flicked on the roof and against the south wall.

His grandfather pulled the wooden shutters closer, and fastened them with a wooden pin thrust through a staple; and he planted a chair against the door lest the storm-wind break it open in the night. Then he, too, got into bed.

Dale's head was a bundle of mixed thoughts. There might be some way of taking care of the old man, if he had not been so proud; but he'd never humble himself to take help even from his own kin, so long as he had a tree of his own to sell. Yet if the trees fell to Nolan, that would be the end. A person can't handily grow more trees over night. If only Dale was bigger, or older, he would go after that man Nolan and what he would do to him would be a pity.

Suddenly an idea came to Dale, clear as another flash of lightning. Why wait to be grown? Fayre Jones that day had said that Lem Foster ought to be made to pay his rightful debts; and that would keep Grampa free of Nolan. If Grampa was too proud to ask again for his money, some one else would, and that some one would be Dale Gillow! He was kin to the woods already, and in the morning he'd go to Foster and tell him—In the morning—and Foster was going off to New Orleans early —the south-bound train left at five o'clock. Blunderhead! he should have thought of this before and gone to Foster during the long, wasted afternoon. Now it was too late.

Dale sat up in bed. It wouldn't be too late if he went over to Foster's to-night. But that was a crazy notion, with this storm growling and crashing and the woods dangerous with falling branches. He slid down again and tried to get comfortable. He flopped over uneasily on his mattress, and snuggled down into its sweet hay. It was warm, and cosy and safe. Why, he'd be liable to catch a sickness or something.

But to-morrow would be too late. Foster would be gone away; and Grampa had given John Nolan harsh promise to sign him the trees to-morrow—early.

Dale turned over again and squirmed beneath the covers. Shucks! it was only a notion, anyway, and a crazy one, moreover. And if it was not prideful for Grampa to beg for what was owing, it would be as bad for Dale. Still, it would be for Grampa—not like for himself. There were a lot of lumps in this mattress he'd never noticed before. Dale turned over once more. He was so . . . warm . . . and . . . comfortable . . . and . . . sleepy. . . . To-morrow—

"YOU OWE JOHN NOLAN FORTY CENTS!" Nobody had said it, but there it was. Fact.

Dale sat up again, swung his legs over the bunk side, and slid down cautiously to the floor. He pulled on his clothes,

shuddering a little in the new chilliness. Then, softly moving the chair away from the door, he crept out into the beating rain.

Phew! He had turned up his coat-collar and pulled down his cap, but that did no good against such a tempest. In a few minutes he could feel the cold rain trickling down through his clothes.

Luckily there was no fear of losing his way, for although it was a pitch-dark night, he had the instinct of direction that is bred in every mountain boy. Moreover, he had often gone up to the ridge behind Foster's house with the other boys, possum-hunting.

Dale thought about Nolan's disappointment and rage next morning when he learned that Oak Gillow could refuse him the trees, and in spite of the chill of the rain and the rough wind, he felt a new warmth inside him—something he had never felt before, a queer sort of anger and delight. Where would the wild things of the woods go a night like this, he wondered, if all the trees got cleaned off?

The path, so narrow that the laurel scrub brushed close against him on both sides, wound up and down till it seemed at times to be leading back the way he had come. But Dale knew its tricks and pushed on steadily till he reached the crest of Wild Cat Ridge, where his way lay along a path so narrow that it was all he could do to keep the wind from blowing him off, down the steep slope on either side.

He was cautious now, for the walk was dangerous even in daylight, and a misstep would send him rolling down into the Glen below the steep where, if he were not killed outright, he might lie broken and alone till he died. That had happened to a man from Glen Hazard last year, when he started out across the hills and none knew where he was headed. But a person can't stop walking when they start to get to a place; only Dale wished he'd had sense enough to leave notice at the cabin for his grandfather telling where he'd aimed to get.

The storm was not going to help him at all. It seemed to be getting worse, and the lightning was too close. In the middle of the noise, an unhappy thought came to Dale. Supposing Lem Foster was spending the night down in town for the sake of his early train? It would be only reasonable.

"But I'll never find out unless I keep on," Dale told himself.

Slowly he crept forward, often on all fours, waiting now and then to hold on until a vicious gust of wind had subsided. Every step was anxious. He had no time now for thinking what he should do or say when he had climbed down the ladder-like cleft that went to Foster's house.

Steadily he went on, till at last he guessed he was over above the huddle of shacks that made Lem Foster's place. But at once he felt that he had come too far. He waited for the next lightning flash that lit the world, and showed him—within a foot of where he stood—the edge of sheer rock. He had passed the down-path in the darkness and had come to the edge of Wild Cat beyond. Before him was Dead Man's Steep, a straight hundred foot drop.

Dale sat down abruptly, and from instinct. Had he stood a moment in the darkness that followed the revealing flash, he must have pitched forward into the abyss from sheer fright. Still sitting, he drew himself backwards, and at a safe distance stood up again, turned about and walked step by step, ten paces. Then he waited, "feeling for his distance" as the mountain people do, walked ten more paces and, when the lightning flared out again, found himself at the top of the rift

that led downward to Foster's. In the daylight, and to one familiar with such a path, it would have been a simple matter to step down from rock ledge to root, and from root to rock, and so arrive at the flat bench on which Foster had perched his house; but in the darkness, and tired out as he was, Dale made slow work of it. Once he slipped and grabbed at a bush for handhold, but it gave way as if he had only dreamed it, and he slithered muddily down several feet of hillside. Nearly there now! He could see a pencil of light from the tiny window. So Foster was home! Now he'd just got to tell him—The rock on which Dale was standing, loosened by the rain, tipped slowly, turned, rolled from under, and Dale went tumbling after it and landed with a tremendous wallop against some railings.

The air seemed full of feathers, and there was a frightful squawking going on. Then there came a stream of light as the door of the house was thrown open, and Foster's voice demanded, "Who's there?"

Dale picked himself up from the tangle of chicken-wire and watched the hens, into whose house he had fallen, sulkily finding roosting-places under the bushes. The birds were still only half awakened and they kept giving sad, croupy noises of distress.

Dale blinked in the light and felt silly. After he had planned to march in boldly and demand payment of the money, it was too stupid to be a tired, wet, scared boy, standing among the wreckage of hencoops!

"Time has come when I've gone and caught that thief whose been pestering my hens," Foster said, "and me thinking all the while it was a possum."

"I never!" Dale denied. 'What I mean to say is—" But he was shivering all over so he couldn't talk without his teeth chattering; and he was angry because Foster would think he was scared. This was a very bad beginning to the business.

Foster told him to come up close, where he could see him; and when Dale stepped forward, Foster let out a great roar of laughter. He took Dale by his sodden coat-collar and pulled him into the house.

"Gillows sure must be thick in the hills to spill over in these parts on such a night. Well, since you're a Gillow boy you've not come chicken-stealing. Get warm whilst you tell out to me how come you're trapesing about at this hour, and in a storm, furthermore."

Dale soaked up the grateful warmth of the big fire that crackled on the hearth, and his head began to go round and round. "I wisht for you to tell me," he said slowly, trying hard to think straight, "should I pay John Nolan forty cents."

Lem Foster paused as he was pouring boiling water from a kettle into the coffee-pot.

"Dale Gillow!" he said, "you never come way over the mountain through this storm just to ask me that! Here, drink this mug of coffee and then tell what's on your mind."

While Dale sipped the steaming coffee and felt the warmth coming back into his bones, he slowly told out the whole story. Foster stacked more wood on the fire and then sat quietly smoking his pipe until Dale finished.

"I fail of seeing where this Nolan and tree business is specially my affair," Foster said, for Dale had told his story rather in a muddle and it was not quite clear why Foster should be called in.

"Why, this way," Dale said. "Happen you pay Grampa for the ties he cut and hauled, he'd keep his trees and the wild things would have homes and—"

"All right, all right, wait a minute," Foster said. "Seemed I got you thawed out too soon. About that lumber bill; might maybe I could come it. Though a man hasn't always ready money to hand. Your old man never did pleasure me much, so I never hastened to convenience him."

Dale said: "Even did you poison-hate Grampa, that wouldn't forgive you not paying what you lawfully owe him."

"Maybe not, Mister Lawyer," Foster admitted with a smile. "But I failed of knowen the old man was so hard pressed."

He got up briskly from his chair and took a blanket from his bed.

"Skin off your wet clothing, boy, and roll up on the mat near the fire. Leave me to figure a while and I'll contrive a way to spare your trees. Hit's no harm to do a ill-turn to a man like John Nolan, either; that'll pleasure me a heap."

"Give you kind thanks," Dale said, drowsily. And then, when he felt sleep already getting the best of him, he opened one eye and added: "You're not a dangerous man, like I thought."

"No, I'm not specially dangerous," Foster owned, "saving when boys don't go to sleep. Then I'm likely to turn sour; go on now, and leave me figure."

When Dale woke up Foster has gone already, and the sun was shining as if to make up for lost time. There was half a loaf of bread on the table, some butter and jam, and a glass of milk. When he began to eat, Dale saw a piece of paper beneath the glass, with a scrawl that Foster had written: "Throw out such food as you don't eat in case of rats I will not be back until three weeks there is a check for Oak Gillow under the butter-plate and I hope the trees will be all right Lem Foster."

Dale was alarmed to see how high the sun was; it must be after six o'clock, and if he didn't hurry, Nolan would have got the tree contract signed already. He found the check, gulped some milk, and, eating a chunk of bread as he went along, started back.

It was easy to follow the path in the cheerfulness of a fine morning, but it seemed a woeful distance to run when Nolan might be there even now. Dale tried to run and eat at the same time and choked twice on crumbs before it occurred to him to throw the bread away and give his mind to getting along.

At last he could see the dark shape of Oak Gillow's cabin among its trees. It seemed a long while since he had been there; last night's journey seemed to have happened weeks ago.

As he drew closer he could see his grandfather standing outside the door— no, two figures were there; and the other was Nolan. Dale ran on faster. John Nolan was stamping about and waving a paper in the face of the old man, who stood with his hands shading his eyes looking across the hills.

Nolan's voice came booming over the hollow: "Never mind about the brat; small loss efn he did run off and lose himself. You sign here and quit wasting my time, or I'll have Sheriff Joe Marks up here!"

"You hush," Oak Gillow rebuked him, his quiet voice slicing clearly through the still air. "I thought first you'd made off with my boy; but since I see him on his way, safe on his legs, happen I'll content my mind to tend this affair."

The two men disappeared within the cabin.

Dale had waved frantically and tried to shout "Wait!" to his grandfather, but his voice was only a feeble croak. If his grand-father should sign his name to that timber contract before Dale got to the cabin, all would be useless ruin. He slid helter-skelter down the near slope, crashed down a bank, climbed the fence, and was at the cabin door.

Oak was dipping a pen into a bottle of ink, and Nolan towered over him with his hand outstretched to take the contract, as if he was afraid of losing it at this last minute, when Dale dashed through the door, panting and speechless, and grabbed a folded slip of paper from his pocket to thrust before his grandfather. Again Dale tried to speak, but only managed a rather rusty crow of excitement.

The old man sat very still, and after looking hard at Dale, as if to be sure he was actually there, he turned the check over and slowly wrote his name, and the words "Pay to John Nolan." Then he stood up and waited for Nolan to take the papers from the table.

"There's your money, John Nolan," he said. "You'll not be cutting my trees this day, nor ever, since the boy has grown to help me guard 'em. Guess I'll keep 'em until Dale gets his mill."

Nolan opened his mouth to speak. But there wasn't anything to say.

Dale was reaching for something in the bottom of his pants' pocket. He stepped up to the table and carefully put four dimes on the papers that Nolan was about to take up. "A Gillow always pays his debts," he said.

Then he turned and ran out of doors, to the big oak-tree where a gray squirrel sat chittering in the upper branches.

BASS COVE SKETCHES

by J. T. Trowbridge

Young Joe and the Ducks

ONE day, a good many years ago young Joe Scoville, of Bass Cove, went up to town to sell some wild ducks he had shot. Old Joe (that was his father) had said to him, early in the season, "When I see you come a-luggin' home a couple o' dozen ducks to oncet, then I 'll let you go and try your hand sellin' on 'em;" and young Joe, having bagged that morning his two dozen and upward, had now for the first time in his life come alone to market.

And very proud was young Joe, I assure you. He drove smartly into the Square, and cried, "Whoa!" and Here's yer nice fine ducks, gentlemen! walk up, gentlemen!" and nodded respectfully to customers, and felt and acted very much like old Joe, his father.

He thought everybody appeared greatly pleased with him. Some looked at his freckled face, long hair, and old coat that had been his father's (and had seen I don't know how many Atlantic storms), and smiled approvingly. Some appeared delighted with his manners—so fresh and natural, you know. Others regarded his little old one-horse wagon, and queer little pony,—with his unkempt mane about his face and eyes, which gave him a striking resemblance to young Joe with his long hair,—as if they had never seen anything so agreeable. "What pleasant folks these city folks be!" thought young Joe.

"Walk up, gentlemen, and take a look! Don't cost nothin' to take a look, whether ye buy or not!" he called out. "How d'e do?"

He said "How d'e do?" to about the handsomest, best-dressed, and fattest man either he or anybody else ever saw. He had a cane in his hand and a cigar in his mouth, and was altogether a nice, plump, shiny fellow, from his hat to his boots. He did not say in reply, "Pretty well, thank ye; how are you?" as Joe, who had been taught good manners at home, thought he ought to have done; but, with his hat tipped airily on one side of his head, and his cigar sticking up jauntily out of one corner of his mouth, he came along and looked carelessly into the wagon.

"Hello!" said he, when he saw the ducks. He took the cigar out of his mouth, and said "Hel-lo!" again, more emphatically than before, and looked up at young Joe. "Where did you get these?"

"Shot 'em; where d' ye s'pose?" said young Joe, proudly.

"*You* did n't shoot 'em?—a boy like *you!*" said the fat man.

"Mabby I did n't," replied Joe, indignantly; "and then, ag'in, mabby I did; and it 's a little more I did than I did n't, this time, I guess!"

"Bless my heart! if I aint surprised!"

Now the handsome and well-dressed

plump gentleman happened to be no other than Mr. Augustus Bonwig, the confectioner, whose celebrated candy-shop was well and favorably known to every good boy and girl in town. He looked almost as if he had been made of candy himself— clear white and red, and a great deal of it. There was one thing he was remarkably good at, but on which he did not pride himself at all, and that was—his business. There was another thing he was not so good at, but on which he naturally prided himself a good deal (for that is the way with some of us), and that was— gunning. He did n't care whether you praised his sweetmeats, or not; but if you happened to say, "Bonwig, people tell me you are a fine shot," that pleased Mr. Augustus Bonwig. It was this ambition of his which caused him to regard young Joe with sudden interest, and to exclaim again, very emphatically, after having examined him and the ducks once more, "Bless my heart now! I *am* surprised!"

"Do — you — want — to — buy — them —ducks?" demanded young Joe, ungrammatically, but very distinctly, beginning to distrust Mr. Bonwig. "If you don't, you need n't feel obliged to handle 'em any more, that's all."

"No, I don't care to purchase; but I 'll give something for a chance to shoot a few such birds," said Mr. Bonwig—and blessed his heart again.

"Oh! that 's it! Wal, you come down our way some time, and I 'll show ye a chance. Ye can shoot as many black ducks and coots and old wives as ye can carry away on yer back. And I wont charge ye nothin' for 't, neither. Takes gumption to git 'em, though, sometimes!" said Joe.

"I guess if *you* can get 'em *I* can, fast enough!" said the smiling Augustus. "Where do you live?"

"Bass Cove. Ask for old Joe Scoville—

that 's my father. Stage-driver 'll set ye down right by the door. Hope yo 'll bring a good gun. I ha'nt got much of a gun, nor dad ha'nt, neither;—sometimes I take mine, and sometimes I take his 'n, and sometimes I take both;—flint-locks; miss fire half the time; but we manage to make 'em do, seein' we 've got the hang o' the ducks."

This speech greatly encouraged Mr. Bonwig, who thought that if such a green youth as Joe, with an old flint-lock, could bag wild ducks at Bass Cove, surely he, Augustus the sportsman, with his fine double-barreled fowling-piece and modern accouterments, must have great success there, and astonish the natives at their own game. He named an early day for his visit, and already imagined himself shooting ducks by the dozen.

"'Arly in the mornin' 's the best time for 'em," said Joe, who accordingly advised him to come down the evening before, and stop overnight.

To this Mr. Bonwig agreed, and walked away in fine spirits, with his hat on one side, swinging his cane, and puffing his jaunty cigar. Then, having sold his ducks for a good price, and bought a new fur cap for Winter wear, and a glass of very small beer for immediate consumption, and a rattle for the baby, and a paper of brown sugar for the family, all with the duck money, young Joe turned about and drove home, with a pretty good handful of small change still jingling in his pocket.

One evening, not long after, the stage-coach rolled up to old Joe's door at the Cove, and a stout sporting gentleman got down over the wheel, from the top, and jumped to the ground. It was Mr. Augustus Bonwig, looking plumper than ever, in his short hunting-jacket, and handsomer than ever, to young Joe's fancy, in his magnificent hunting-boots (red-topped, trousers tucked into them), and with the fine double-barreled gun he carried.

"Oh, a'nt that——!" exclaimed Joe, poising the gun. He did not say *what*—no word in the language seemed adequate to express the admiration and delight with which he regarded the beautiful fowling-piece. "And what boots them are for wet walkin'! And ha'nt you got the splendidest game-bag, though! And what a huntin'-cap!—it don't seem as though a man *could* miss a bird, that wore such a cap as that! Come in," said Joe, his respect for Mr. Bonwig greatly increased, now that he had seen him in such noble sporting rig. "Father's to home. And I 'll show you our guns—old-fashioned queen's-arms, both on 'em."

"Bless my heart!" said Augustus, smiling.

"Well, now, I *am* surprised! You don't mean to say you shoot ducks with *those* things? Well, well! I *am!*"

"My boy there," said old Joe, filling his pipe and cocking his eye proudly at the youngster, "he 'd shoot ducks with 'most anything, I believe. He 'd bring 'em down with a hoe-handle, if he could n't git holt o' nothin' else. He 's got a knack, sir; it 's all in havin' a knack." And old Joe, who had been standing with his back to the fire, turned about and stooped to pick up a small live coal with the tongs. "Then ag'in,"—he pressed the coal into the bowl of his pipe, and took a puff,—"ducks is"— puff, puff—"puty plenty,"—puff,—"and puty tame on this here coast, about now." And the old man, having lighted his pipe, and replaced the tongs in the chimney-corner, stepped aside, to make room for his wife.

Mrs. Joe swung out the old-fashioned crane, hung the tea-kettle on one of the hooks, and swung it back again over the fire. Then she greased the iron spider,

placed it on the coals, and made other preparations for supper.

"Sed down, sed down," said old Joe; and Mr. Bonwig sat down. And the children crowded around him, to admire his watch-chain and his red-topped boots. And the amiable Augustus, who had come prepared for such emergencies, pulled out of one pocket one kind of candy, and another kind out of another pocket, and still a third variety from a third receptacle, and so on; for his hunting-suit seemed to be literally lined with pockets, and all his pockets to contain more or less of those celebrated sweetmeats so well and so favorably known to the good boys and girls in town. And Mr. Bonwig was pleased to observe that human nature was the same everywhere; country boys and girls were like city boys and girls, in one respect at least—all liked candy.

"O, a'nt it good!" said Maggie.

"Prime! I tell ye!" said Joe, who had his share, of course.

"Goodie, good!" said Molly.

"Goo, goo!" crowed the baby.

"Oh, my!" said Tottie.

And they all sucked and crunched, with cheeks sticking out and eyes glistening, just like so many children in town, for all the world. And Augustus was happy, thinking just then, I imagine, of three or four plump little darlings at home, of whom he was very fond, and whom he never left for a single night, if he could help it, unless it was to go on some such glorious hunting frolic as this.

It was a poor man's kitchen. I don't think there was a carpet or a table-napkin in the house; the ceiling was low, the windows were small, the walls smoky, and everything was as plain and old-fashioned as could be. But Mr. Bonwig, nice gentleman as he was, appeared delighted. He prided himself on his sportsmanlike habits, and so the rougher he found life down on the coast, the better. He admired the little smoky kitchen, he liked the fried perch and cold wild duck for supper, and he was charmed with the homely talk of gunning and fishing, and storms and wrecks, which took up the evening, and with the bed of wild fowls' feathers on which he passed the night.

The next morning young Joe came to his bedside, candle in hand, and awoke him, before dawn.

"Hello!" said Mr. Bonwig, rubbing his eyes open. "Hel-lo! I *am* surprised! I was having such a splendid time! I thought I was hunting ducks, and I had got a whole flock in range of my two barrels, and was waiting for a few more to light; but I was just going to shoot, when you woke me. I wish I had fired before!"

"Wal, you come with me, and mabby your dream 'll come to pass," said young Joe, leaving him the candle to dress by.

Mrs. Scoville was already cooking their breakfast, "For, like as not," she said, "they would n't be back till noon, and they must have a bite of something to start with."

Mr. Bonwig was sorry she had given herself so much trouble; but he afterward, as we shall see, had good reason to be thankful that he had taken that "bite."

At daylight they set out, Mr. Bonwig with his fine, stub-twist, two-barreled fowling-piece, and young Joe with both the old queen's-arms, his own and his father's.

Mr. Bonwig wished to know what the boy expected to do with two guns.

"They may come handy; they 'most alluz does," said Joe.

"But I 've *my* gun this time," said Augustus; "and I shall want you to carry the birds."

That was a somewhat startling suggestion; but Joe thought he would take both guns, nevertheless.

"I a'nt goin' to come in the way of your shootin'; but I 'll jest take what you leave —though I don't suppose that will be much," said he.

It was a cool Autumn morning. The air was crisp and exhilarating. The morning light was breaking, through dim clouds, over land and sea. Joe led the way over the short wet grass, and rocks and ledges, of a rough hill back of the Cove. At last he pulled the eager Augustus by the jacket, and said:

"Be sly now, climbin' around them rocks yender! There 's a beach t' other side, and a little stream o' water runnin' acrost it. Black ducks can't git along, as some kinds can, with salt water alone—they alluz have to go to fresh water to drink, and we 're apt to find 'em around Beach Brook here, 'fore folks are stirrin'. 'T was on this beach father shot the twenty-five, to one shot, he told ye about last night."

"Was that a true story, Joe?" Augustus asked, growing excited.

"True as guns," said Joe. "Ye see, they all gether in a huddle along by the brook, and you 've only to git in range of 'em, and let fly jest at the right minute; sometimes there 'll be a flock of a hundred, like as any way, and ye can't miss 'em all if ye try."

"I should think not!" said Mr. Bonwig, taking long, noiseless strides in his hunting-boots, and holding his gun in the approved fashion. "Only show me such a chance!"

"I 'll wait here in the hollow," said Joe. "You crawl over the rocks, and look right down on the beach before ye, and——By sixty! there 's a flock lightin' now!—see 'em?"

"Bless my heart!" said Bonwig, in no little trepidation.

He took the route Joe pointed out, and soon disappeared behind the ledges. Then all was silence for several minutes, while Joe waited to hear the double report of the destructive fowling-piece, and to see the frightened flock of ducks—or such as were left of them after Mr. Bonwig's shots—fly up again.

Bonwig in the meantime crept along behind a pile of rocks Joe had described to him, and, looking through an opening, saw a wonderful sight. Before him spread the broad, smooth beach, washed by the surf. There must have been a high wind off the coast during the night, for the sea was rough, and long, heavy breakers came curling and plunging magnificently along the shore. The morning clouds were reddening over the agitated ocean, which faintly reflected their tints.

But the sight which most interested Mr. Augustus Bonwig was the game that awaited him. The brook, which cut out afresh its channel across the beach, as often as the tide, which filled it with sand twice in the twenty-four hours, receded,—the little brook, from the rocks to the surf (it was now half tide), was alive with ducks, and more were alighting.

Mr. Bonwig silently blessed his heart two or three times—and well he might, for it was beating with very unsportsman-like rapidity at that exciting moment. His hand shook so that it was well that Joe, if he was to retain his high respect for him as a gunner, did not see them. In fact, Mr. Bonwig, who fancied himself a sportsman because he had been sometimes successful in firing at a mark, found this a very different business. He hardly knew whether he took aim or not. That one barrel went off prematurely in the air is quite certain. At the report,—the like of which ducks on that coast had made acquaintance with before, and knew that it meant mischief, —the entire flock of a hundred or more flew up at once, with a sudden noise of wings which could be heard above the roaring of the breakers. Then the other barrel went off. Then young Joe came running up in high glee, to offer his congratulations and to help pick up the dead birds. He looked, expecting to see the beach strewn with them.

There was n't a bird on the beach, dead or alive!

In utter amazement, Joe turned and looked at Mr. Bonwig. That gentleman stood with his portly form erect, his head thrown back, and his mouth and eyes open, staring at the sky, into which his fine covey of ducks were rapidly vanishing.

"Well, well!" said he. "Now, now! If I *aint* surprised! Who ever saw anything happen like that? BLESS—MY—HEART!"

"Not a darned duck!" said Joe.

"O, I must have wounded some! I must have wounded about twenty!" Augustus declared. He looked critically at his gun; then he turned his gaze once more at the sky; then he looked at young Joe, who was beginning to grin. "I think my shot must be too fine," said Mr. Bonwig.

Joe asked to see his lead.

" 'T aint no finer 'n what *I* use. Feathers on a loon's breast are so thick them shot would n't go through 'em; have to fire at a loon's head, when he 's facin' ye. But I don't see how ye could let fly into a flock o' loons even without knockin' over a few."

"It 's a very remarkable circumstance!—very singular!—*very* surprising!" observed Mr. Bonwig, wounded in his tenderest point,—his pride as a sportsman,—and betraying a good deal of chagrin and agitation. He was very much flushed. He took off his cap and wiped his forehead. "Just let me try that thing over again, that 's all!"

"Best way now will be to go off to the island," said Joe. "That 's our dory. Jest help me shove it off, and we 'll have some fun yet!"

"Yes, yes—so we will!" said Bonwig.

And so they did.

Off to the Island

"BLESS my heart!" said Mr. Bonwig, amazed at the huge rollers that came tumbling in. "How are we ever going to get a boat outside of them without swamping her?"

"I 'll show ye," said Joe.

The dory was dragged down to the edge of the surf. Then Joe put in the guns. Then he gave the skiff another gentle shove, into a receding wave. Then he told Mr. Bonwig to get aboard.

"I 've a wife and children at home!" murmured that affectionate husband and father. "If anything should happen!"

"What in sixty ye think is goin' to happen?" cried Joe, impatiently.

"I am very heavy!" said Augustus.

"So much the better; you 'll make splendid ballast," grinned Joe.

"You are going, too?"

"Of course I am; I ha'nt got no wife and children—not much!"

There was something in Joe that inspired confidence, and Mr. Bonwig resolved to stand the risk. He seated himself in the boat. Joe stood on the beach, holding the bow, and waiting. The waves were out.

"You never can shove me off in the world!" said Mr. Bonwig, painfully conscious of his own corpulence.

"You 'll see," said Joe. The next moment the waves were in. A heavy swell lifted the dory, ballast and all. The ballast uttered a scream, and made a motion as if to jump overboard. "Keep yer seat. All right!" screamed Joe, pushing off. As the next breaker lifted the stern, he gave another shove, and jumped aboard. Before the third breaker came, he had the oars in his hands, ready to meet it.

"Well, well!" said Mr. Bonwig. "I *am* surprised!" And well he might be; for, you see, this embarking in the breakers is a business that calls for no little skill and experience; you must take advantage of them, and see that they don't get the advantage of you. They have no mercy; and if they ever strike your skiff sideways, over she goes in an instant, and there she rolls to and fro in the foaming jaws until they crunch her to pieces, unless some strong hand at the right moment seizes and drags her out.

Young Joe, first by skillfully pushing off, then by prompt management of the oars, kept the dory straight across the rollers, and soon had her safe outside of them. Then he commenced rowing strongly and steadily toward a rocky island, two or three miles off, over the ends of which the sea was dashing high and white.

Mr. Bonwig was seated in the stern, which he freighted so heavily that the bow stuck up ludicrously high out of the water. He had now quite recovered his equanimity.

"Well! I enjoy this!" said he, and lighted a cigar. "How easy this boat rows!"

"It does, to look on," said Joe.

"I *am* surprised!" said Mr. Bonwig. "I 'd no idea one of these little skiffs pulled so easy!" and he smoked complacently.

"How good that cigar tastes!" said Joe, with a grin. "I had no idee cigars tasted so good!"

"Young man," replied Augustus, laughing, "I see the force of your remark. Perhaps you think I might offer to row. But I want to keep my nerves steady for the ducks. I 'll row coming back, and that will be a good deal harder, for we shall have a load of game, you know."

"All right," said Joe. "No, I thank ye"—as Bonwig offered him a cigar. "But if you happen to have any more of that 'ere sweet stuff about ye——"

"Oh, to be sure!" and Augustus had the pleasure of filling the young man's mouth with candy. "What sort of ducks do we get at the island?"

"Coots and black ducks, mostly," said Joe (and I wish I could make the words sound as sweet on paper as they did coming from his candied lips). "Black ducks go along the shore to feed, when the tide is low. They find all sorts of little live things on the rocks and in the moss, and in them little basins the tide leaves in holler places. They never dive deep; they only jest tip up, like common ducks. But coots will feed where the water is thirty feet deep; they go to the bottom, and pick up all sorts of insects and little critters. They pick young mussels off the rocks, and swaller 'em whole, shell and all, and grind 'em up in their gizzards."

"Do they catch fish?"

"No; loons ketch fish, but ducks and coots don't. A loon has got short wings that help him swim under water,—or fly under water, for that 's what it is. He 'll go faster 'n some fishes. But he can't walk; and he can't rise on the wing very well. He has to flop along the water, against the wind, a little while, 'fore he can rise. He can't rise goin' *with* the wind, any more 'n a kite can; and sometimes, when he lights in a small pond, he 's pestered to git out at all. I ketched one in Bemis's pond last Spring. He was just as well and spry as any loon ye ever see, but there was n't room for him to git a good start, and no wind to help him; and he could n't run on the land, nor fly up from the land; and there was n't any good chance to dive. A loon 'll go down in deep water, and like as not ye won't see anything more of him till by-'m-by he comes up a quarter of a mile off, or mabby ye wont never see him agin,—for he can swim with jest a little speck of his body out of water, so that it takes a perty sharp eye to git sight of him. But this loon in Bemis's pond could n't come none o' them tricks, and I jest stoned him till he could n't dive, than I in arter him, and ketched him. He was a fat feller, I tell ye!"

"That 's a good loon story," observed Mr. Bonwig.

"I can tell ye a better one than that," said Joe. "My father went a-fishin' off the end of that island once, and as the fish would n't bite, and the sea was calm, he jest put his lines out and laid down in the bottom of the dory, and spread a tarpaulin over him, and thought he 'd go to sleep. That 's a nice way to sleep,—have your boat at anchor, and it 'll rock ye like a cradle, only ye must be careful a storm don't come up all of a sudden and rock ye over. Ye can wind yer line around yer wrist, so's't if a cod does come and give it a yank, you 'll wake up. That 's the way my father did. And he 'd had a nice long nap, when all at oncet—yank! suthin' had holt. Off went the tarpaulin, and up he jumped, and he thought he 'd got a whopper, by the way it run off with his line. But before he 'd begun to pull, the line slacked, as if nothin' was on it; and the next minute up come a loon close alongside the boat, and looked at him, and my father looked at the loon, and thought he noticed suthin' queer hanging' out of his bill. Then the loon dove, and then my father felt a whopper on his line ag'in, and he began to pull, and, by sixty! if he did n't pull up that loon and bring him into the boat! He had dove I don't know how many fathom for the bait, and got hooked jest like a fish."

"That *is* a good story!" said Mr. Bonwig, who had a sportsman's relish for such things. "What makes folks say *crazy as a loon?*"

"I d'n' know," Joe replied, "without it 's 'cause they holler so. Did n't ye never hear a loon holler? Yo 'd think 't was a crazy feller, if ye did n't know. I s'pose *loonatics* are named after 'em."

"Not exactly," said Mr. Bonwig. *"Lunatics* are named after *Luna;* that 's the Latin name for the moon, which affects people's brains, sometimes."

"I would n't give much for such brains!" said Joe, contemptuously. "Moon never hurt mine none!" Hence he argued that his own were of a superior quality. "You must have been to school to learn so much Latin!" he said, regarding Mr. Bonwig with fresh admiration.

Augustus nodded with dignity.

"What 's the Latin for *dory?*" Joe asked, thinking he would begin at once to acquire that useful language.

Augustus was obliged to own that he did n't know. Thereupon Joe's admiration changed to contempt.

"What 's the use of Latin," said he, "if ye can't tell the Latin for dory?" And Mr. Bonwig was sorry he had not said *doribus,* and so have still retained a hold upon Joe's respect.

"Why do folks say *silly coot?*" he asked, to change the subject.

"Wal, a coot *is* a silly bird—jest like some folks," said Joe. "Sometimes you may shoot one out of a flock, and the rest will fly right up to you, or jest stay right around, till you 've killed 'em all." Augustus thought he would like to fall in with such a flock. "There 's some now!" said Joe. "They 're goin' to the island. The sea runs

so, we can't shoot very well from the boat, and I guess we 'd better land."

Landing was easy under the lee of the island, and the boat was hauled up on the beach. Then Joe set out to guide his friend to the best point for getting a shot.

"There!" said he, stopping suddenly near the summit of a ledge, "ye can see 'em down there, about three rods from shore. Don't stir, for if they see us we shall lose 'em."

"But we must get nearer than this!" said Mr. Bonwig, "for even *my* gun wont do execution at this distance."

"Don't you know?" Joe said. "They 're feedin'. When you come acrost a flock of coots feedin' like that, you 'll notice they all dive together, and stay under water as much as a minute; then they all come up to breathe agin. Now, when they dive, do as I do. There goes one down! there they all go! Now!" cried Joe.

He clambered over the ledge as nimbly as a lad could very well do, with an old "Queen's-arm" in each hand, and ran down rapidly toward the shore, off which the water-fowl were feeding. He was light of foot, and familiar with every rock. Not so Mr. Augustus Bonwig: he was very heavy of foot, and unacquainted with the rocks.

"Bl-e-hess m-y-hy hea-ah-rt!" he exclaimed, jolting his voice terribly, as he followed Joe down the steep, rough way.

"Here! quick!" cried Joe, dropping behind another ledge.

Poor Mr. Bonwig plunged like a porpoise, and tumbled with a groan at the boy's side.

"Flat! flat!" whispered Joe.

"I can't make myself any flatter!" panted Augustus, pressing his corpulence close to the ground. "I 've scraped off two buttons, and skinned my shins, already."

"You *a'nt* quite so flat as a flapjack, *be*

ye?" said Joe. "Never mind. We 're all right." He peeped cautiously over the ledge, cap in hand. "There comes one of 'em up agin! There they all come! Now look; be careful!" Bonwig put up his head. "Next time they go down we 'll run for them big rocks close by the shore; then we shall be near enough."

"Is that the way you do? Well, I *am* surprised!" said Bonwig. "As your father said, it requires a knack."

"There they go!" cried Joe, and started to run. Augustus started too, but stumbled on some stones and fell. When with difficulty he had regained his feet, Joe was safe in the shelter of the rocks, and the birds were coming to the surface again. It required no very fine eyesight to see Mr. Bonwig; he was, in fact, a quite conspicuous object, clumsily running down the craggy slope, with both arms extended,—the better to preserve his balance, I suppose, although they gave him the appearance of a man making unwieldy and futile efforts to fly. The coots saw him, and rose at once upon the wing.

"Bang!" "Bang!" spoke Joe's old flintlocks, one after the other; for, having fired the first as the flock started, he dropped that and leveled and fired the second, almost before the last bird had cleared the surface of the water.

"Bang! bang!" answered Bonwig's smart two-barreled piece from the hillside; and the startled Joe had the pleasure of hearing a shower of shot rattle on the rocks all around him. The enthusiastic sportsman, seeing the coots rise and Joe fire, and thinking this his only chance at them, had let off his barrel at a dozen rods, as he would very likely have done at a quarter of a mile, so great was his excitement on the occasion.

He came running down to the shore. "Hello! *hel-lo!*" said he, "I 've saved these! look there!" And he pointed triumphantly at some birds which, sure enough, had been left behind out of the flock.

"By sixty!" grumbled Joe, "you come perty nigh *savin'* me! Your shot peppered these rocks—I could hear 'em scatter like peas!"

"Do you mean to say," cried Bonwig, "that I did n't kill those ducks?"

"All I mean to say is, they are the ones I fired at," said Joe, "and I seen 'em turn and drop 'fore ever you fired. Your gun did n't carry to the water at all. I'll show ye."

Joe began to hunt, and had soon picked up a number of shots of the size used by his friend Bonwig.

"Bless my heart! Now I *am* surprised! The wind must have blown them back!" said Augustus.

"If that 's the case," muttered Joe, "I shall look out how I git 'tween you and the wind another time! By sixty! ye might have filled me as full of holes as a nutmeg-grater! And I rather guess there 's nicer sounds in the world than to have two big charges o' shot come rattlin' about your ears that fashion!" And he rubbed his ears, as if to make sure that they were all right.

"Well, well, well!" said the wondering Augustus, picking up more shot. "I *am*—surprised aint the word; I 'm astonished! Well, well, well!"

"You wait here," said Joe, "while I hurry and pick up them coots. There 's an eddy of wind takin' 'em right out to sea."

He disappeared, and soon Mr. Bonwig saw him paddling around the curve of the shore in his dory. Having taken the coots out of the water, he brought them to land, and showed them to the admiring Augustus.

"Now which way?" said the sportsman, filled with fresh zeal, "for I 'm bound to have luck next time."

"We 'll haul the dory up here, and go

over on the other side of the island, and see what we can find there," said Joe.

"What a desolate place this is!" said Mr. Bonwig, as they crossed the bleak ledges. "All rocks and stones; not a tree, not a bush even; only here and there a little patch of grass!" He struck a schoolboy's attitude, on one of the topmost ledges, and began to declaim:

" 'I'm monarch of all I survey,
    My right there is none to dispute;
From the center all round to the sea,
    I 'm lord of the——'

Plenty of fowls, but there don't seem to be any brutes here," he commented, as he came down from his elevation.

"Guess ye learnt that to school, too, did n't ye?" said Joe.

"Young friend, I did," said Augustus. And he proceeded to apostrophize the salt water:

" 'Roll on, thou deep and dark blue ocean, roll!
    Ten thousand——'

Thunder and blazes! who 'd have thought that rock was so slippery?" he said, finding himself suddenly and quite unexpectedly in a sitting posture. "Speaking of fleets, what are all those sails, Joe?"

"Fishermen. Sometimes for days you won't see scarcely one; then there 'll come a mornin' with a fair wind, like this, and they 'll all put out of port together."

"Hello! *hel-lo!*" said Augustus. "Who ever expected to see a house on this island? What little building is that?"

"It 's one of the Humane Society's houses; house of refuge they call it. They have 'em scattered along the coast where ships are most likely to be wrecked and there 's no other shelter handy."

"Nobody lives in it, of course?"

"I guess not, if they can help it," said Joe. "But more 'n one good ship has gone to pieces on this island. I remember one that struck here eight year ago. She struck in the night, and the next mornin' we could see her, bows up, on the reef yender, where the tide had left her; but the sea was so rough there was no gittin' at her in boats, and the next night she broke up, and the day after nary spar of her was to be seen, except the pieces of the wreck that begun to come ashore to the mainland, along 'ith the dead bodies. About half the crew was drowned; the rest managed to git to the island, but there wa' n't no house here then, and they 'most froze to death, for it was Winter, and awful cold. Since then this little hut has been tucked in here among the rocks, where the wind can't very well git at it, to blow it away; and come when ye will, Summer or Winter, you 'll always find straw in the bunks, and wood in the box, and matches in a tin case, and a barrel of hard bread, and a cask of fresh water. Only the wood and hard bread are apt to git used up perty close, sometimes. You see, fellers that come off here a-fishin' know about it, and so when they git hungry, they pull ashore with their fish, and come to the house to make a chowder. But I would n't," said Joe, assuming a highly moral tone, "without there was a barrel chock full of crackers! For, s'pose a ship should be wrecked, and the crew and passengers should git ashore here, wet and hungry and cold, and should find the house, and the box where the wood should be, and the barrel where the crackers should be, and there should n't be neither wood nor crackers, on account of some plaguy fellers and their chowder! No, by sixty!" said Joe, "I would n't be so mean!"

"It looks naked and gloomy enough in here!" said Augustus, as they entered.

"It would n't seem so bad, though, to wet and hungry sailors, some wild night in Janewary, after they 'd been cast away," said Joe. "Just imagine 'em crawlin' in here out of the rain and cold, and startin' up a good, nice fire in the chimbly, and settin' down afore it, eatin' the crackers!"

"How are the provisions supplied?"

"Oh, one of the Humane Society's boats comes around here once in a while, and leaves things. I don't believe but what it would be fun to live here," Joe added, romantically, "like Robinson Crusoe and his Man Friday."

"Suppose we try it?" said Mr. Bonwig.

"I 'll be Crusoe, and you may be t' other fellow."

"And we 'll shoot ducks for a livin'!" said Friday. "Come on, Mr. Crusoe!"

They left the hut, and went in pursuit of game, little thinking that accident might soon compel them to commence living the life that was so pleasant to joke about, more in earnest than either dreamed of doing now.

FLAPJACK

by Carter Hamilton

HE turned one clean half-somersault from nowhere, and landed plunk on his back at my feet. I said, "Flapjacks!" That 's how he got his name. He was only an Indian's cur, the forelornest little waif of a lost puppy, with the most beautiful dogs' eyes I have ever seen. He scrambled to his feet and used his eyes—that settled it for us. Without further introduction, we offered him the remains of our dinner. He accepted it with three gulps and then stood wagging his poor little tail, asking for more.

We were camping and trailing out in the Wind River Mountains—Brandt and I—back of the Shoshone Indian Reservation, and we had halted for dinner in a small cañon in the shade of the rock wall from whose summit Flapjack had tried his little acrobatic stunt. Whether he came from an Indian encampment near by, which we had not seen, or was just plain lost and fending for himself alone in the wilderness, we did not know. He told us about fending for one's self while he ate his dinner, an' that it was "an *awful*" hard life and sometimes "*very*" discouraging." After dinner he told us that our scraps were the very best food he had ever eaten; that our outfit, our horses, and mule, the finest he had ever seen; that we ourselves were gods, wise and very great; that he loved the ground we trod on, and only asked to stay with us forever. So he stayed.

Jinny, the mule, returned his compliments unopened, and told him what she thought of him by showing the under side of her off hind hoof and putting back her ears. But then, Jinny was the only aristocratic person in camp, in her own opinion, and you may take that for what it is worth. She did n't prejudice us against Flapjack. Still, Brandt and I happened not to share Jinny's opinion of herself. Brandt was in the habit of remarking on seventeen separate and several occasions each day that "even fer a mule, Jinny is the lowdowndest one I ever set eyes on."

At the sight of her hoof, Flapjack made a ludicrous little duck with his head and came back to us, volubly explaining that, "Of course, the mule being *yours,* don't you know? she simply must be the very finest, sweetest-tempered animal in the world, don't you know? and altogether above reproach, don't you know?" That won us completely.

And he never once reproached her for anything she did—even when she kicked him into the river. He treated her with distant courtesy always, without so much as a *yap* in her direction. And it was n't

241

because he was afraid of mules, either—
Brandt and I will deny that imputation
against his valor to our dying day. Let a
strange mule or horse get in among ours,
and Flapjack was a very lion of ferocity
until he had *yapped* him out of sight.

"Think we 'd better look for their
camp?" I asked, putting the dishes into
Jinny's pack.

"What, the purp's Injuns? Not *much!*"
answered Brandt. "If they have n't seen
us, let 'em alone. An' if they have—why,
we 've got to wait proper introductions. I
move we *hike.*"

So we hiked, and Flapjack hiked with
us.

We kept on our trail, if such it could be
called: a trail which probably no white
man but ourselves had ever set foot upon.
We were bound for a little lake that we
knew, crammed with the most innocent
fish on earth. No; I am not going to tell
you where. There are some things you
must find out for yourself, if you are
game for it, just as we did; otherwise, you
don't deserve to know.

After some ten days we arrived, without either adventure or misadventure, at
our happy fishing-ground, and made camp
on a little precipice at whose foot a deep,
dark pool lured monster and luscious
rarities.

In spite of his hard journey, little Flapjack had improved amazingly as to health,
not as to manners: for from the first day
we knew him, he had better manners
than any other dog I ever met. If you
flung him a crust, he so appreciated it—
it was the very nicest crust, the daintiest
morsel, one could have; just as everything
we did was simply perfect in his eyes.
And he was n't servile about it, either.
He simply *approved* of everything we did,
and told us so in an eloquent, dumb way
of his own.

We made camp for a two weeks' stay;

felled a tree for backlog, and fixed things
generally to be comfortable, all under his
supervising eye. And when it was done,
and the friendship fire lighted, he lay
down before it as one of us and said, "This
is *home."*

So we fished and were happy; and we
fished some more and were happier; and
we fished more and more and were happier and happier every day. Do you understand that feeling? If you have known
Wyoming camp-fires, you do.

Sometimes we tramped to distant shores
of the lake, "so 's not to git our own fish
too eddicated," Brandt explained, though
generally we fished at our camp from a
fallen forest monarch lying out over our
deep hole. We used much craft and almost any kind of bait, and drew up monsters I do not dare to describe in cold print.
Brandt used to say, "Them fish is so biame
innercent, y' could ketch um with a shoe-
button on a button-hook, if y' had it
handy"—which I did n't. And thus we
lived one blessed week of glorious days between heavenly sleeps—that is, until the
day of the Great Catch.

"Somethin' comin'," said Brandt one
day, as he looked at the Great Catch laid
in a row in front of our tent.

"Supper!" I yelled.

"I don't mean that. I mean *somethin','*"
replied Brandt, meditatively. "Jevver notice that whenever y' strike the Great
Catch somethin' comes right bang top of it
to take y' down? Every time an' *every*
time it 's so. That 's what I mean. I bet it 's
Injuns—seem to sense it that way—Injuns."

"I seem to sense it that we 've got to
clean those fish before it gets dark, *and* fry
them, *and* eat them," I said. "Do we pack
the water up or the fish down?"

"Water up, I *guess,*" said Brandt, proudly looking on the Great Catch. "A blame'
sight less to pack, er I 'm a sinner. Hang

um on a string an' souse um off the log, after."

So Brandt with one canvas bucket and the agate kettle, and I with the other bucket and the coffee-pot, meandered down our little trail to the water's edge, and dipped our household supply. We were gone, all told, twenty minutes. Brandt was in the lead, Flapjack at my

At the word Brandt's canvas bucket hurtled through the air and landed *quush!* on a big, "silver-tip" grizzly's nose.

The grizzly said, *"Woofsh-spshpts!"* very loud.

The bucket was Flapjack's cue to go on with his part, and he did. He went after the bucket with a wild *"Yee-ap!"* and a flying leap, and landed somewhere in the

"The grizzly disappeared into the brush squealing, with Flapjack yee-ap-yapping at his heels!

heel, for he superintended all the camp operations, meal-time being his great opportunity.

There were two high rock-steps at the end of our path that brought us up to our level. Flapjack ran around through the brush by a trail of his own to meet us at the top. Brandt stepped over; I followed.

"Jumpin' giraffes!" Brandt exclaimed.

At that instant I saw our last fish disappear into a great red mouth in one end of a brush-pile, and the mouth said, *"Woof!"*

neighborhood of the spot just vacated by the bucket.

The grizzly emitted something between a shriek and a groan, bounded up like a rubber-ball, cleared the top level at one jump, and disappeared into the brush squealing, with Flapjack *yee-ap-yapping* at his heels!

We heard the bushes crackle and crash while old Silver Tip ran and squealed. We heard little Flapjack *yee-ap-yapping* his views on bear in general and big ones in particular. The echoes ceased and the sounds frew fainter, and fainter—and fainter—and were swallowed up by the great silences.

"Well, I never!" groaned Brandt at last, looking ruefully at the revolver in his hand. "*Such* a chance spoilt by a purp—a plain, stump-tail Injun purp!"

"Plucky, though, was n't it?"

"Plucky! If y' call it plucky to run after a thing when y' don't know what it is an' jest throw yerself at its head till y' find out! But he won out, all the same!" added Brandt. "Yes, siree, he *won out*—on sheer pluck! What 'd I tell y'? 'T was n't Injuns, but it sure was something—the whole catch o' fish is gone—we 'll have pork fer supper."

"I 'm thinking of Flapjack," I said. " 'Fraid he 's done for by this, poor little fellow."

"Oh, he 'll be back to supper," replied Brandt, confidently; and an hour later, tongue lolling, tail erect, Flapjack sauntered into camp.

Proud of himself? Well, rather! So were we, and we told him so. He went from one to the other of us, offering his congratulations on our having such a speedy dog in camp with us: "Bears? Pooh! What are grizzly bears? You don't have to be such a very brave dog to drive *them* off! Pooh! Do it again any time you say!" —that sort of talk, you know. For a few minutes we were just a bit afraid he was looking down on us for a couple of softies —*we* had n't jumped at a grizzly and boxed his ears! But no; he was much too fine a gentleman for that. We had fed him when he was hungry, and we were just as good as he was—oh, every whit!— even if we had n't driven old Silver Tip across the landscape squealing like a pig! He made us feel perfectly at ease with him, and when supper-time came he quietly laid aside his glory with a "let 's forget it" air and ate with us like an equal and the campfire brother that he was.

"Silver Tip 'll be back to-morrow," I remarked.

"*No*-py," replied Brandt. "Don't you guess it. This time to-morrow mornin' he 'll strike Yallastone Park, an' this time to-morrow night he 'll be over in Montana visitin' his aunt in the country. If y' want *him* you 'll have to take an express-train—an' y' won't ketch him then. He 'll hike over three States 'fore he stops. I know bears—they ain't coyotes. Flappie, what d' ye think about it?"

Flapjack replied that he agreed with Brandt absolutely, that he, too, knew bears "tremenjous well," and he did a great deal of tail-wagging to prove it.

So I took their word for it—two against one—and smoked in silence, pondering the great event. For it was an event to me at that time—my first sight of Silver Tip in his native wilderness. Those were the early days of Wyoming camp-fires for me, and I had then seen very little of the larger game.

But—even though two against one—they were wrong, and in this wise it all happened five days later.

We had gone to our second pool three miles up-shore, and had made a good catch—mine was very good. It was my turn to do chores, and Brandt was after "one great whale." I have noticed that Brandt always is after "one great whale" whenever my catch is better than his. So he stayed out and I went back to camp, personally conducted by Flapjack, a string of lesser whales in my hand.

And I almost ran into Silver Tip before I saw him—for Silver Tip was in the tent! He had already munched the camera and a few other trifles of like sort, and was at the moment supping on my last film (all the views of the trip!), which hung out of his mouth and curled about like a live ribbon while he clawed it.

Silver Tip said, "*Wo-o-of!*" and struck out with his paw—at the film, probably, though I thought he was striking at me. Anyhow, he struck out—I saw that. I struck out with the fish in my hand, and hit him *swat* on the side of the head! That started it—he knew what I was.

I dropped the fish I was carrying and jumped, pulling my six-shooter. With one bound he was out of the tent after me. The next instant I found myself playing hide-and-seek with him around a big tree, to the tune of "*Woof-woof!*"—and of "*Yap-yap-yap-yee-ap!*" from Flapjack.

I am not sure but at this stage of the game Silver Tip thought he was as much pursued as pursuing, and that if I had given him time and a fair chance, he would have changed his mind about me, and decided I was n't worth it. But I did n't. Something kept saying in my ear, "Shoot! Shoot!"

I had a dim sort of realization that I could n't shoot over my head or behind my back or under my feet, and take flying leaps at the same time about a tree. So I bolted for the next tree, meaning to turn there and shoot. As I did so, Flapjack dashed from behind Bruin and nipped him in the flank. That distraction gave me one extra second and my chance. I fired and struck him amidships. Bruin turned and snapped viciously at his wound. On that, Flapjack nipped his ear. I fired a second time, but only grazed him.

He rushed me then so that I bolted to the next tree, then across the open space to the third. I gained time by this; I knew what I was going to do, and Bruin did n't. I say time—it was probably three seconds. As he came at me, Flapjack dashed back and forth between us, yapping and pirouetting just out of reach. Bruin felt annoyed,

dropped me to settle Flapjack, and I fired my third shot. It ripped along his muzzle, and bedded itself in his jaw. The roar he gave frightened me so that it literally fired my revolver! That bullet became part of the landscape.

"Two shots more!" flashed across my mind; "and two more *such* shots and it 's pussy-in-the-corner till I die."

Bruin was crazy, now, with rage and pain. Self-control was not one of his virtues. For two seconds Flapjack held the field. I repeated my triangle trick in that two seconds and with a quick start, ran between two trees, bolted for the open, and turned.

But I had miscalculated the bear's distance, or his speed. As I turned to shoot he rose to his feet almost over me, a mountain of sudden death.

And then little Flapjack did his great act—took one wild, flying leap plump into Bruin's chest, and fell flat on his own back. He recovered in a second—but a second too late. The mountain dropped on all-fours; a huge paw swung out, and little Flapjack went through the air like a shuttlecock.

That one second saved my life. The bear, with head down, faced me. I fired. The shot took him clean between the eyes. His great hulk lurched forward and literally fell on my feet.

I have no idea how long I stood there afterward, stock-still, turned to stone. I seemed to be waiting for Flapjack to do his act again—take a flying leap and sing, "*Yee-ap-ap!*" I listened and listened for the "*yee-ap-yap,*" but heard only a muffled *thud, thud, thud, thud*—my own heart. I wondered why, and why, and *why* he did n't come to congratulate me on the victory—*our* victory. Around me lay the soft silence of the forest, at my feet the huge prowler that had just meant death.

Then, on a sudden, I heard a piteous little moan, and I came to myself—and I understood everything.

I found him at the foot of a giant pine, twenty feet away.

I fell on my knees beside him.

"Flapjack, little dog!" I cried out.

And his beautiful, pain-filled eyes looked into mine and said, "If you 're all right, that 's all I care for!" and his little tongue feebly lapped my hand.

"Oh, dear little dog," I said; "you have given your life for mine. Bravest, truest heart in all the world! You saved your friend; do you know it? You won out!"

He tried to rise, but he was past rising ever again.

"Good-by, brave heart!" I said.

———

If, some day, you should find a promontory by a lonely Wyoming lake; find a giant pine-tree and a pile of stone beneath; find on the great trunk a smooth-cut slab, and read the burnt-in letters,

FLAPJACK, Aug. 9, 1897,

don't laugh, please; you 'll know what it means.

KEEPING HOUSE

by Laura Ingalls Wilder

FOR a week Father and Mother were getting ready to go, and every day they thought of new things that must not be forgotten while they were away. At last the day came when they were going, and everyone was up early.

Mother flew around faster than ever and Father moved more deliberately. They were both excited, and so were the children, although Eliza Jane and Royal, being older, did not scurry about as much as Alice and Almanzo, who could hardly swallow breakfast. And after that there were so many last things to do that it seemed Father and Mother never would get away.

But just as the sun was rising Father drove to the door in the buggy, and Royal put the bag under the seat and Mother climbed in, talking all the while.

"Be sure you gather the eggs every night," she said, "and I depend on you, Eliza Jane, to take care of the churning. Don't salt the butter too much, pack it

"Don't eat up all the sugar,"
Mother called back

in the small tub and be sure you keep it covered. Remember not to pick the peas and beans on those plants I'm saving for seed. Now you all be good while we're gone—"

She was tucking her hoopskirts in between the seat and the dashboard. Father spread the laprobe. "—and mind what Eliza Jane tells you. Be careful of fires; don't you leave the house alone while the fire's in the cookstove, and don't you get to scuffling with lighted candles, whatever you do, and—"

Father tightened the reins and the horses started.

"Don't eat up all the sugar!" Mother called back.

The buggy went through the gate and turned into the road. The horses began to trot. For a little while the sound of the buggy wheels came back, growing fainter and fainter. Father and Mother were gone.

It was ten miles to Uncle Andrew's house. Father and Mother would be ten miles away for a whole week.

The yard and the house and the barns and the fields suddenly seemed very big and empty. A week was a long time. All that space, and all those days, were Almanzo's. He could do anything he wanted to do. He threw his straw hat in the air and yelled.

Alice clapped her hands and cried, "What'll we do first?"

"We'll do the dishes and make the beds and sweep," Eliza Jane said.

"I'll tell you" Royal said, "let's make ice cream!"

Eliza Jane hesitated, then she said, "Well, you boys get the ice."

Royal and Almanzo hurried to the ice house. They dug a block of ice out of the sawdust and put it in a grain sack. They laid the sack on the back porch and pounded it with hatchets till the ice was crushed into little pieces. Alice sat on the steps, whipping the eggs on a platter. Eliza Jane measured milk and cream, and dipped cupfuls of white sugar from the barrel in the pantry. It was not the common, everyday maple sugar, but the precious white sugar bought from the store —the sugar Mother saved for ice cream and frostings, and to put on the table when company came. Eliza Jane dipped six large cupfuls, then she smoothed over the top of the sugar that was left, and you would hardly have missed any. She cooked the yellow custard, poured it into a milk pail, and set it in a tub on the back porch, packing the snowy crushed ice around it, with handfuls of salt, and covering it all with a blanket. Every few minutes Eliza Jane took off the blanket and the cover of the pail, and stirred the freezing ice cream with a long handled spoon, and they all tasted it.

While they were waiting, Alice brought saucers and spoons, and Almanzo brought out a cake and the bread knife. He cut enormous big pieces of cake and they all ate some. Then Eliza Jane said the ice cream was ready. She heaped the saucers and they all ate ice cream. They could eat all they wanted, there was no one to stop them. And they ate up *all* the cake— every last bit of it.

At noon there was only a little ice cream left in the bottom of the pail. Eliza Jane said it was time to get dinner, but the others said they didn't want any dinner. Almanzo lay on his stomach on the cool porch and kicked up his heels. He said,

"Let's get a watermelon and put it to cool."

Eliza Jane said they had to do the breakfast dishes, but Alice said she didn't care, she was going with the boys. Then Eliza Jane put on her sun-bonnet and came, too.

Out in the melon field the green melons lay rounded above the flat leaves of their vines. With their middle fingers Royal and Almanzo thumped the melons, and listened. If a melon sounded green, it *was* green, and if it sounded ripe, it *was* ripe. But some melons that the boys thought sounded ripe, Eliza Jane said sounded green. And Alice wanted a funny fat one, with its stem curled like a pig's tail.

So they each picked a big, hot melon, and holding them clutched against their middles they came down from the melon field, and they put those four melons to cool in the ice house.

That afternoon they lay on the grass in the shade of the balsam tree in front of the house. Royal plunged the butcher knife into the dewy green rinds of the melons, and every melon was so ripe that the rind cracked in front of the knife.

They all bit large mouthfuls out of the thick, red slices. They swallowed the sweet, cold juice, and they spit out the black seeds. They ate till they could eat no more. Then they just lay on the grass.

If you lie in the grass on a summer afternoon, you see the little ants going about their business. When they come to a grass blade they do not go around it. A grass blade is taller than a tree to them, but they try to climb all the way up it, dragging with them burdens larger than they are. Then you lie on your back and see the rainbows in your eyelashes. When your eyes are almost shut, and you look at the blue sky, every one of your lashes has a rainbow beside it.

Almanzo sat up and slowly ate the last slice of melon. Then he said,

"I'm going to fetch Amy here to eat up these rinds."

Amy was his own little Chester White pig. Almanzo had bought her from Mr. Webb with the half dollar Father gave him on the Fourth of July.

"You will not!" Eliza Jane said. "The idea! That dirty old pig in the front yard!"

"She is not either a dirty old pig!" said Almanzo. "Amy's a little, young, clean, white pig, and pigs are the cleanest animals there are. You just ought to see the way Amy keeps her bed clean, and turns it and airs it and makes it up. Horses won't do that, nor cows, nor sheep, nor anything. Pigs—"

"I guess I know that! I guess I know as much about pigs as you do!" Eliza Jane said.

"Then don't you call Amy dirty! She's just as clean as you!"

"Anyway, Mother told you to obey me," Eliza Jane answered. "And I'm not going to waste watermelon rinds on a pig. I'm going to make pickles of them and surprise Mother when she comes back."

Almanzo said no more, but that night when he did the chores he let Amy out of her pen. The little pig was as white as a lamb, and she had a funny little curled tail that quirked when she saw Almanzo coming. She followed him to the house and stayed outside squealing for him till Eliza Jane said she could not hear herself think.

After supper Almanzo took some scraps and fed them to Amy. He sat on the back steps in the star-light and scratched the little pig along her prickly back. Pigs like that. In the kitchen Eliza Jane and Royal were arguing. Royal wanted to have a candy pull. Eliza Jane said candy pulls were only for winter evenings, but Royal said he didn't know why candy wouldn't be just as good in the summer as it is in the winter. Alice thought it would be, too, and Almanzo went in and sided with them.

So Alice and Eliza Jane mixed sugar and molasses and water, and boiled them. When the candy had boiled long enough, they poured it on buttered platters and set it on the porch to cool. They all kept feeling the hot candy with their fingertips, and when they thought it would not burn them, they rolled up their sleeves and buttered their hands, and were ready to pull the candy.

Almanzo was ready first. He took a big wad of the brown, warm candy off the platter, and just then Amy came squealing. Almanzo thought his little pig should have some candy, too. Quickly, before Eliza Jane could catch him, he dropped the wad of candy over the edge of the porch to Amy, and Amy gobbled it up.

Then they all pulled candy. They pulled it into long strands, and doubled the strands and pulled again. The candy turned from dark brown to light brown, and from light brown to cream, and every time they doubled it, they bit off a little.

It was very sticky. It stuck their teeth together, and it stuck to their fingers, and somehow it got on their faces and stuck, and when Almanzo dropped the end of his piece on the floor, it stuck there.

It should have become hard and brittle, if they pulled it long enough. But it didn't. They pulled and they pulled, and still it was limp and sticky. So they got tired, and they put it on the platters and set it on the porch again.

"Anyway, it's past bedtime," Eliza Jane said.

Next morning when he went out to do the chores, Almanzo saw Amy going across the yard. Her tail did not quirk, and she did not squeal. Her tail hung limp and her head hung down. She shook her head sadly from side to side, and wrinkled her nose.

When she wrinkled her nose Almanzo saw, where her teeth should have been, a smooth, brown streak.

Amy's teeth were stuck together by that wad of candy! She could not eat, she could not drink, she could not even squeal. Worst of all, she would not let Almanzo catch her and help her.

Almanzo yelled for Royal, and Royal came. They chased Amy all around the house, in and out under the snowball bushes and the lilacs, and back and forth across the garden. Amy whirled and dodged and ducked and ran like anything. All the time she didn't make a sound; she couldn't. Her mouth was full of candy.

She ran between Royal's legs and knocked him down. Almanzo almost grabbed her, and went sprawling on the ground. She tore through the rows of peas, and squashed the ripe tomatoes, and upset the green, round cabbages. At last they cornered her. She made a dash, and Almanzo fell on her and clutched her in his arms. She kicked, and tore a long hole right down the front of his blouse.

Almanzo lay on top of her and held her down. Alice held her kicking hind legs. Royal pried her mouth open, and scraped out most of the candy. *Then* how she squealed! She squealed all the squeals that had been in her all night, and all the squeals she couldn't squeal while they were chasing her, and she ran away to her pen, shaking her head.

That day they made ice cream again. All the cake was gone that day, but Alice said she knew how to make a poundcake. "I'm going to do that first," she said. "And then I'm going to go sit in the parlor, like company."

Almanzo didn't think that would be any fun. But Eliza Jane said that Alice couldn't do it. The more Almanzo thought about it, the more he thought that Alice could sit in the parlor if she wanted to. It wasn't Eliza Jane's house, and Mother hadn't said that Alice couldn't sit in the parlor.

That afternoon Almanzo came into the kitchen just when Alice was taking the poundcake out of the oven. It smelled so good that Almanzo broke a piece off the corner, and then they cut a slice to hide the broken place, and then they cut two more slices and ate them with the last of the ice cream.

"I can make more ice cream," Alice said. Eliza Jane was upstairs, and Almanzo said,

"Come on, let's go into the parlor."

They opened the parlor door without making a sound, and they tiptoed in. There wasn't much light because all the blinds were down, but the parlor was beautiful. The walls were covered with white-and-gold wall paper, and the carpet was almost too fine to step on. Mother had woven it all by herself of the finest woollen rags, last winter.

In the middle of the room was the marble-topped center table, with the tall parlor lamp on it. The lamp had a white china shade, covered with pink-painted roses. By the lamp lay a photograph album, with covers of red velvet and mother-of-pearl.

All around the walls the black horsehair chairs stood solemnly, and George Washington's face looked sternly at Almanzo and Alice from the picture frame between the windows.

Alice hitched up her hoops behind, and sat on the horsehair sofa. The slippery haircloth slid her right off the sofa's hard, humped seat onto the floor. She didn't dare laugh, for fear Eliza Jane would hear and know they were in the parlor. But she sat on the sofa again, and slid off again. Then Almanzo sat on a chair and slid off.

When company came they had to sit up properly on the parlor furniture and push with their toes on the floor to keep from sliding off. But now they could slide off. They slid off every chair and also the sofa.

They looked at the shells and the coral and little china figures on the shelves of the whatnot in the corner, though they didn't touch anything. They looked at the stove. On the parlor side, even the stove was dressed up. The dining room side

stuck into that room, and it had doors and dampers, but the parlor side was flat with the white-and-gold wall, and it was covered all over with flowers, and leaves, and scrolls, all made in the iron and polished black.

They heard Eliza Jane on the stairs, and they ran tiptoe out of the parlor and shut the door without a sound. Eliza Jane didn't catch them.

It seemed that the week would last forever, and then suddenly it was gone. One morning at breakfast Eliza Jane said,

"Father and Mother will be here tomorrow."

They all stopped eating and stared at her. The garden had not been weeded, the peas and beans had not been properly picked and the vines were ripening too soon. The horses had not been combed and curried every day. The henhouse had not been whitewashed.

"This is churning day," Eliza Jane said. "And Alice and I have to clean house. But what am I going to tell Mother? The sugar is all gone."

"There's *some* left," Alice said. "Mother only said, 'Don't eat *all* the sugar'."

All day they worked as fast as they could. Royal and Almanzo weeded and hoed the garden, they whitewashed the henhouse, they curried the surprised horses in the middle of the afternoon, and rubbed them till they glistened. In the house Eliza Jane and Alice were sweeping and scrubbing. Almanzo turned the churn till the butter came, and Eliza Jane's hands flew like Mother's while she washed and salted the butter and packed it in the tub. There was only bread and butter and jam for dinner.

"Now, Almanzo, you polish the heater," Eliza Jane said.

Almanzo hated to polish stoves, but he hoped Eliza Jane would not tell that he had wasted candy on his pig. He got the stove blackening and the brush, and went to work. Eliza Jane was hurrying and scurrying around, and nagging Almanzo.

"Be careful! Don't spill the polish," she said, busily dusting.

Almanzo didn't need her to tell him not to spill the polish. But he didn't say anything.

"Use less water, Almanzo. Mercy! You'll have to rub harder than that!" Almanzo did not say anything.

Eliza Jane went into the parlor and began to dust in there. After a while she called,

"Almanzo! That stove done yet?"

"No," Almanzo said.

"Well, don't dawdle."

"Whose boss are you?" Almanzo muttered.

Eliza came to the door. "What's that you say?"

"I say, *whose boss are you?*"

Eliza Jane said he was an idle, impudent boy. "You just wait! You just wait till I tell Mother—"

Almanzo didn't really mean to do it. The blackening brush flew from his hand at Eliza Jane before he knew it. She dodged. The brush flew into the parlor and hit, smack; against the white-and-gold wall paper. A great, black splotch was smeared on the white and gold.

Almanzo's eyes shut. Alice screamed. Eliza Jane cried out,

"Wicked, wicked boy!"

Almanzo turned around and ran. He ran and hid in the haymow. He crawled far back between the hay and the Big Barn's eaves, and lay there and did not cry. A big boy going on ten years old could not cry. But he wished he could stay there hidden forever. He had spoiled the beautiful parlor.

After while he came down from the haymow, and he cleaned all the mangers and stalls and did almost all the chores

himself, more carefully than usual. But he did not feel much better, and right after supper he went to bed.

Father and Mother drove into the yard the next day. Royal and Eliza Jane and Alice went out to meet them, and Almanzo had to go, too.

"Been getting along all right?" Father asked.

"Yes, Father," Royal said.

Mother hurried about the house, looking at everything. "I must say, Eliza Jane and Alice, you've kept everything as well as if I'd been here."

"Mother," Alice said in a small voice, "Mother, you told us not to eat *all* the sugar. We didn't, but Mother—we ate 'most all of it."

Mother laughed. "You've all been so good, I won't scold about the sugar," she said.

She did not know about the black splotch on the parlor wall. She did not know that day, nor all the next day. The parlor door was shut.

That evening Mr. and Mrs. Webb drove into the yard. They had come to hear all about the visit to Uncle Andrew's. Father and Mother met them at the dining room door, and Mother said,

"Come right into the parlor!"

Almanzo could not move. He could not speak. He could not do anything to keep Mother from opening the parlor door. This was worse than anything he had imagined. Mother was so proud of her beautiful parlor, and she was taking Mr. and Mrs. Webb to see that big black splotch on the white-and-gold wall.

Mother opened the door. She went in with a candle. Mr. and Mrs. Webb went in, and then Father. Almanzo could hear Mother lighting the big parlor lamp.

Almanzo could not believe his eyes. He looked at the place where the blacking brush had hit the wall, and he saw the white paper with the beautiful gold scrolls on it. There was no black spot.

He crept to the door. Father and Mother and Mr. and Mrs. Webb were sitting on the black horsehair chairs, talking about the visit to Uncle Andrew's. The walls were white and gold all around the room. There was no black spot anywhere.

"Come in, Almanzo," Mother said.

Almanzo went in. He sat up straight and stiff with his toes pushing against the floor to keep him from sliding off the slippery horsehair, and he looked and looked at the place where the blacking brush had hit the wall paper. He minded his manners and did not say a word except when he was spoken to.

Next day when no one was looking he stole into the parlor. He climbed on the sofa and held the window shade to let a crack of light in, and he looked closely at the place where the black splotch had been. The wall paper was patched. The patch had been cut out so carefully, all around the gold scrolls, and the pattern was fitted so perfectly, and the edges of the patch had been scraped so thin, that he could hardly see it.

Almanzo waited till he could speak to Eliza Jane by herself, and then he asked if she had patched the parlor wall paper for him.

"Alice and I did," she said. "We went to the attic and got the scraps that were saved when the parlor was papered, and we cut out the patch and made flour paste, and pasted the patch over the black spot while you were out in the barn."

Almanzo said gruffly.

"Eliza Jane, I'm sorry I threw that brush at you."

"Well, I guess I'm provoking sometimes," she said. "You make me mad, too. But you're the only little brother I've got."

They never, never told, and Mother never knew.

PINKEY PERKINS
"Just a Boy"

by Captain Harold Hammond, U. S. A.

*HOW "PINKEY" ACHIEVED
HIS HEART'S DESIRE*

"VALENTINE DAY" was fast approaching, and "Pinkey" Perkins was daily growing more and more despondent. He was deeply in love, and how to secure a suitable offering to lay on the altar of his devotion was what puzzled him. His own finances aggregated exactly sixteen cents, and he shrank from enlisting his mother's aid, because of his hesitation in admitting to any one the infatuation he had fostered for weeks.

Pinkey could not bear to think of some other boy sending Hattie Warren a bigger and a costlier valentine than he did—or, in fact, sending her any valentine at all. If another suitor did send her one, she would very likely learn his name by finding his initials discreetly concealed in some obvious place on the valentine, or by some broad hint spoken in her presence. Pinkey was very formal in his ideas of propriety, and heartily disapproved of such methods as being contrary to the rules of valentine etiquette.

Pinkey's school-teacher, Miss Vance,—or "Red Feather," as she was universally known among her pupils,—had consented, after days of persuasion by the girls, to allow a "valentine-box" in school on that important day. The pupils could deposit their anonymous love-tokens in the box at any time during recreation hours, and there would be a distribution of the same just before dismissal time, both at noon and at four o'clock.

It was on this occasion that Pinkey hoped to show the affection he cherished for his Affinity, by sending her a valentine which should be, beyond question, the most elegant of all.

The prettiest valentines in town were to be found at the "Post Office Book Store," owned and conducted by Mrs. Betts, a widow to whom an economical postmaster rented a part of the large room used as post-office.

The valentine upon which Pinkey had set his heart was a large, fancy, lace-paper creation, over a foot square and nearly two inches thick. It was composed of several layers, held apart by narrow accordion-like paper strips. In the center were two large embossed hearts, one overlapping the other and both pierced by arrows fired from the bows of half a dozen cupids distributed around the border. At each corner and at the top and bottom were profusely decorated scrolls, on which were printed, "I adore thee," "Wilt thou be mine?" and other touching phrases. The light upper part was hinged to the heavier back, on which, in fancy type, were these lines:

"Pinkey remained to gaze long at the coveted prize"

If you but knew the pleasure
  And the joy 't would bring to me
If my own and onliest treasure
  Forever you would be,
All your doubt and vain misgiving
  Would be changed to love like mine,
And our lives would be worth living,
  For you 'd be my VALENTINE.

This valentine was easily the handsomest one in town, and, besides, it expressed Pinkey's sentiments so perfectly that it drove him to the depths of despair to think that he could not buy it for his Affinity. It cost a whole dollar, and having, as he did, but sixteen cents, and lacking the assurance to ask credit for the remainder, he felt doomed to disappointment.

If Pinkey had been in the book-store once to see that valentine, he had been there twenty times. He came ostensibly to inquire for the mail, but invariably remained to gaze long and fondly into the show-case at the coveted prize, and to picture to himself the joy it would bring to the heart of his Affinity to receive it. Not even to "Bunny" Morris, his bosom friend, did he confide his burning desire to buy it. He felt it would not be doing right to *her* if he should trespass on the sacred ground of his infatuation by talking about it.

Do not think that Pinkey was the only one who saw and admired the valentine. Others of his age, and perhaps older, had longed to buy it; but the price was beyond the reach of all.

Whenever any one of Pinkey's schoolfellows came into the store while he was there, he would edge aimlessly away from the show-case toward the counter where the comic valentines were displayed. Three times, to his knowledge, within the week preceding Valentine Day, his Affinity had stopped before the show-case where reposed the large lace offering and had openly admired it. Pinkey was, of course, apparently oblivious to all this, but who can say that his Affinity's hopes were not realized as her comments fell on alert ears? Once Pinkey had heard her actually price it, and his heart gave one great bound, then stood still. If she *should* purchase it, would she send it to him? Oh, what joy! But suppose Eddie Lewis, his hated rival for her affections, should be the favored one! That thought almost suffocated him.

Going home from school on the afternoon before Valentine Day, Pinkey, as usual, stopped at the post-office to inquire for the mail and to take one last look at the unattainable. He had given up all hopes of purchasing the large valentine, and had decided to invest his slender means in one of the smaller and, for him, very unsatisfactory substitutes.

There were several people in the store, most of them children bent on the same errand as Pinkey. He looked at all the valentines whose prices were within the limits of his funds, and at last selected one that seemed to him the best he could do for the money.

As he stood there, waiting to make his purchase, he saw a boy, older and larger than himself, pick up from the floor a fountain-pen which had fallen from a card on which several were displayed, glance furtively about him, and then drop it into his overcoat pocket and deliberately walk out of the door. Mrs. Betts had her back turned at the time, and so knew nothing of the occurrence.

Pinkey was much disturbed by what he had seen. His first impulse was to tell Mrs. Betts; but, before he had a chance to do so, he dropped that suggestion of his conscience as being decidedly unwise. Pinkey had no desire to become a party to the deed by keeping mum; but he was only a boy, and he did have a wholesome regard for his own bodily welfare. He knew that if he told on the culprit the latter would "lay for" him, as Pinkey said to himself, and he also knew only too well how he should fare in the result.

While he was studying over the matter another idea struck him, which, while it involved a deal of uncertainty, would, if it succeeded, accomplish the same result and at the same time be of benefit to himself. Pinkey pondered long and hard over the matter. He counted his pennies over and over, and at length decided to try his scheme, though it meant the postponement of his purchase until noon the next day and might prevent it altogether.

So, without even spending the one penny he had set aside for a "comic" to send to Red Feather, he left the book-store and went home.

Next morning he felt rather guilty as he went with the crowd to school, being one of a very few who were not carrying one or more jealously guarded envelopes to be deposited in the box.

When Pinkey reached the school-house he immediately instituted a search for the boy with the fountain-pen. It was Pinkey's intention to procure the pen, if possible, and return it to Mrs. Betts, having in view its restoration to the rightful owner as well as the possibility of reward—which reward, Pinkey hoped, might take the form of the long-wished-for valentine. If it did not, he would endeavor, by neat diplomacy, to secure the return of his purchase-money, at any rate.

Pinkey soon located a group of boys in the basement, and rightfully surmised they were "trading." He approached the group, and there, sure enough, among the participants in the arguments attending exchange, was the boy he was seeking. He was engaged in a discussion of the relative values of the fountain-pen, in its present empty state, and a four-bladed, bone-handled, "I X L" knife. The owner of the knife argued that "I X L" was a solemn guaranty of "razor-steel," while the boy with the pen declared that "X L N T" were the mystic letters that denoted that quality.

Not desiring to betray special interest in the pen, Pinkey devoted a few moments of his attention to other bargains that were being driven with all the arts known to the juvenile tradesman. Some boys were "dropping knives." "Whole blade or no trade," and "Red leather, trade forever," were the usual iron-clad agreements that made the exchange binding.

Presently Pinkey turned his attention to the unsettled argument concerning the knife and pen. It was plain that harmony of opinion was out of the question, and Pinkey felt this a good opportunity to make the effort to procure the pen.

"What 'll you take for her, Jimmy?" he inquired, assuming an indifferent air.

Jimmy did n't know just exactly what he desired most, and asked Pinkey what he had to trade.

"Ain't got nothin' much here to trade, but I 'll give you ten cents for her if you want to sell 'er."

This put new life into the transaction—cash, owing to its chronic scarcity, being invariably above par. But Jimmy must not appear anxious and ruin his chances for a rise.

"Aw," he argued, "she's worth more 'n that. She 's worth a quarter, anyhow."

"Ain't got a quarter; give you twelve cents," said Pinkey, knowing he must bargain closely, and not daring to name his limit too rapidly.

"Naw; gimme twenty cents—that 's cheap," pleaded Jimmy.

Pinkey protested that the pen would not write as it was, and that it might be no good even if it *was* filled.

This was a damaging possibility; so, after the necessary final arguments, Pinkey finally secured the coveted pen for the munificent sum of fifteen cents and' a jews'-harp "to boot." After he had concluded his bargain he retired from the market, and no amount of temptation could induce him to part with it.

The morning seemed interminable as Pinkey restlessly awaited the dismissal time, when he could return the pen to Mrs. Betts. When noon at last came, and Red Feather was distributing the valentines, Pinkey, without even waiting to see if there were any for him, hurried off to the post-office, tightly clutching in his hand the fountain-pen. He was filled with a mixture of satisfaction at the success that had so far attended his efforts, and concern as to the ultimate outcome.

Rushing in the door, he fairly thrust the pen into the hands of the astonished Mrs. Betts, saying: "I saw a boy pick this pen up off the floor yesterday and carry it away with him, and to-day I traded him out of it and brought it back." It was some moments before Mrs. Betts could definitely grasp the meaning of Pinkey's burst of speech. When she did recover from her surprise, she began to question him as to the boy's identity, but Pinkey stoutly declined to divulge it. He gave as his reason that the boy was bigger than he and would "lick him" the first time he caught him out.

In spite of Pinkey's reticence, Mrs. Betts knew him too well to attach any suspicion whatever to him. She pressed him with reasons why he should tell her for her own protection, and he was finally persuaded to whisper in her ear the boy's name.

(It may be stated here that this information caused her to be on the lookout whenever Jimmy was in the store, and resulted in eventually bringing him to the bar of parental justice.)

Not desiring to allow such apparently artless honesty to go unencouraged, Mrs. Betts began to look about for some tangible reward. While doing so, she remembered how, during the holidays nearly two months previous, Pinkey's sole desire in life had been to receive an air-gun outfit for Christmas. Day after day he had come in and fondled the precious rifle and hoped it might fall to his lot; but his hopes had not been realized, and he had been heartbroken for weeks afterward. So she decided that would be about the most acceptable gift she could bestow.

Taking from the shelf the bright-colored box containing the entire outfit,—gun, target, arrows, and all,—she turned to Pinkey, saying: "Pinkey, here is the air-gun you wanted so badly last Christmas. I want you to acept it from me as a remembrance for returning the pen."

When Pinkey heard this he was between two fires. His former desire for the air-

gun, which could now be his, returned with all its old-time fervor, and yet his more recent longing for the valentine was unabated. A dozen times, during the five minutes he had been in the store, his eyes had wandered irresistibly to the show-case where it still lay unpurchased.

Twice, while Mrs. Betts was wrapping the box in heavy paper for him to carry home, he attempted to ask that the valentine be substituted for the air-gun, and twice the words refused to come. As she placed the box in Pinkey's arms, he gave one hopeless look at the valentine, muttered some unintelligible thanks, and started for the door.

Pinkey gets the valentine

But love for his Affinity finally prevailed, and, turning resolutely about, he marched back to the counter and laid the box down, saying: "Mrs. Betts, if you 'll let me, I 'd like to trade this air-gun for that big valentine over there. It don't cost near as much as this, but I 'd lots rather have it."

To say that Mrs. Betts was surprised would be putting it mildly; but since Pinkey was the one to be satisfied, she was perfectly willing that he should choose what suited him best, especially as the valentine, from her point of view, was much the less valuable article.

When the exchange was effected, Pinkey was surprised to find how happy he felt, and he ran all the way home to show the valentine to his mother. He was bursting with exuberance and must unburden himself to some one, so he naturally chose her. He told her how he had longed for the valentine, but hated to ask her for the money to buy it, fearing she would think him foolish to want to send such an expensive one. He told her all about the fountain-pen and the air-gun, and how he had induced Mrs. Betts to exchange the latter for the valentine.

He was too happy to detect a misty look in his mother's eyes as he concluded his story by asking her to address the valentine for him—"because," he bashfully admitted, "she 'd know my writin'."

Pinkey could scarcely eat his dinner, so anxious was he to get back to school and deposit his valentine in the box before anybody saw him. It was such a large affair that, if it were once seen, it would attract immediate attention and be recognized later.

As his Affinity entered the room, just before the study-hours began, Pinkey thought he noted a serious expression on her face. He had not remained to see whether she received a valentine at noon, and down deep in his heart he hoped she had not, and that this might be the cause of her despondency.

Throughout the long afternoon she seemed very much depressed, and not once, to Pinkey's knowledge, did she even glance in his direction. But her solemnity could not temper his elation as he thought of the great, beautiful valentine peacefully reposing at the bottom of the box.

When school was dismissed and Red Feather, with unbending dignity, began distributing the valentines, Pinkey felt his heart beating away like a steam-hammer. At last his name was called, and he marched boldly up to the platform. He opened the envelop, and found, to his disgust, that he had received a "comic," a terrible caricature of an artist, no doubt suggested to the donor by Pinkey's habit of drawing pictures on his slate.

This raised his ire to the boiling-point. He was thinking deep threats of revenge, if he ever found out who sent it, when his name was called a second time.

This time he received a real valentine. It was a very small edition of the kind he had mailed to his Affinity! He studied the address critically. It had been printed by an unpractised hand, and at first he could obtain no clue whatever to the sender. Then he recognized the "J." Nobody on earth but his Affinity could make a "J" like that. Instantly he forgot his "comic" and the thoughts it had aroused in him, and a feeling of peace and general good will prevaded his entire being.

When Red Feather announced that the last valentine had been distributed, Pinkey's heart sank in him like a stone. What had become of the offering for his Affinity? He turned and whispered savagely to Bunny Morris, who was standing beside him and the only person there whom he would dare take into his confidence: "Go up 'n' tell her to look in the box again. Tell her you know there 's another 'n' in there."

Bunny did as he was bid. Red Feather searched the box carefully, and there, snugly filling the whole bottom, was the large, flat package which, in the shadows, she had overlooked.

" 'Miss Harriet Warren,' " she read; and

as Pinkey saw his Affinity's face brighten as she looked squarely at him and blushingly approached the platform, he felt repaid one hundred times over for the sacrifice of the air-gun.

Hattie Warren was at once surrounded by all the girls in the room, whose curiosity, getting the better of their envy, stimulated the desire to inspect at close range the valentine they all had admired in the show-case.

"Who sent it?" "Who sent it?" was the cry that came from all sides.

"Look at the wrapper," suggested one. "Whose writing is it?" They looked, but it was familiar to no one.

"Look on the inside of the box," "Look on the back of it," were some of the further suggestions from the curious ones.

After inspecting it all over, one of the girls detected some letters and figures on the back of the valentine, written diagonally across one corner. These were at once investigated, as possibly furnishing a clue to the giver's identity.

"E. L.," shouted one of the girls. "Eddie Lewis sent it, and it cost a dollar!"

This announcement staggered Pinkey. He thought it must be a joke, until one after another verified the telltale letters. He could in no way account for the initials of his rival being on the back of the valentine, for it had not been out of his possession after he received it until he placed it in the box. He was beside himself with indignation and perplexity. He hoped Eddie Lewis would speak up and deny sending it; but, instead of so doing, Eddie assumed a knowing, mysterious look, and said nothing.

All this was too much for Bunny Morris's sense of justice; and, without waiting to see what Pinkey was going to do, he blurted out: "Pinkey Perkins sent that valentine. Eddie Lewis did n't have anything to do with it."

Every one looked at Eddie, to see what he would do. Instead of defending himself against Bunny's accusation, as they expected, he shifted uneasily from one foot to the other, and said evasively, "I never *said* I sent it." A minute later, when attention became centered on Pinkey, Eddie silently opened the door and left the room.

Pinkey tried to look unconcerned, but he made a dismal failure. He tried to assume a vexed air, but he only grinned and blushed to the roots of his hair.

But what could the letters "E. L." signify, if not Eddie Lewis? No one else in school had the same initials. As a last resort, Red Feather, who was by this time ready to depart from the noisy throng, was consulted. She saw through the mystery at once.

" 'E. L.,' " said she, "is the cost-mark. It is n't anybody's initials."

If there were any possible remaining doubts as to who sent the valentine, Pinkey forever dispelled them by chasing Bunny Morris madly around the room, and out of the door into the yard, shouting as he ran, "Bunny Morris, if you ever tell on me again, I 'll—"

The threat was lost in the distance.

A GOURD FIDDLE

by Grace MacGowan Cooke

HE was the sole, orphaned remainder of a long line of fiddlers. I do not know upon what instrument his remote ancestor may have played for some savage mid-African chief's wild revel or fantastic pagan rite; but from the time his people were brought, slaves, to this country, the men of the family had been masters of the violin, able to earn, from music-loving owners, special indulgence by the stroke of the bow, the cry of the strings.

They had belonged to the Fithian family ever since anybody could remember, and, grandfather, father, and son, from generation to generation, they had furnished the plantation fiddlers. Not only that, but they had been sent for on state occasions to play at the "great house," when there were guests and merrymakings.

Little Orphy's grandfather, Adonis, had gone to Paris with his young master—that was in the time of Colonel Steptoe Fithian, and the family was very wealthy then—and had studied the violin under good teachers. It is true that he was never able to make much sense out of the little black dots and lines, the crotchets and quavers, and rests and ties, and many other things with long, hard names, which, he was told, went to make up the music in the "chune-books." However, if his teacher would only play over the most difficult arias, Adonis could give them back to him like an echo, and rendered with a soft, pleasing coloring of his own.

But the time of valets and Parisian sojournings for the young Fithians was long past. Indeed, there had been no young Fithians these twenty years. The old, home-staying line, white and black, had declined together. It was long since there had been only the old mistress—very old—and Miss Patrice at the great house; and of the army of Negroes who had borne the name, there was left to wait upon the two ladies only little Orpheus, without father or mother, kith or kin.

Mortgages had been, for years, eating up the big plantation, and the greedy, lawless Mississippi had been gnawing away its best fields, as a rude boy might take bites at a sugar-cake.

It seemed to Orphy that all the good things had happened before he was born and none were left for his times. He had lived his twelve years on the ruinous old plantation, and he had been Miss Patrice's house-boy for three years when the old mistress died.

Miss Patrice was his godmother. He had a fine, sweet, boy's soprano, and she taught him to sing the chants and anthems in the service of the little church where he was baptized.

She let him play on the old colonel's fine violin, and he was to have it for his own when he was twenty-one, or, if she were to die before that time, it was to be left to him in her will.

Miss Patrice was a good musician. To teach the child with her voice new airs for his violin, and, when he had learned them, to accompany him on her piano, was the solace of many lonely days to the gentle, faded little lady.

When she went away to a great Northern city, for the operation that was to save her life or end it, she parted from Orpheus very sadly.

He was to tend the house just as when she was there—to watch the hens' nests, sell all the eggs he could in the village, and give the money to Aunt Nutty, the cook.

She trusted him, too, to see that the little church altar had its Saturday supply of fresh flowers, a duty she had not failed to perform weekly for fifteen years; and she wished, if the operation should be unsuccessful, that he might sing "Lead, Kindly Light" at her funeral.

Orpheus considered that the worst which could happen to a boy had happened when Miss Patrice went away, and left him with nobody except grim, sour Aunty Nutty, who was not a Fithian Negro at all, but only a hired cook. But when those strangers who held the various mortgages on the place had foreclosed them, when the house was full of curious, loud-talking people, examining, pricing, buying, and packing the precious old Fithian possessions, and there was nobody to speak for his ownership of the colonel's violin,— when Miss Patrice was brought home, indeed, to lie in the Fithian burying-ground, and he had to see her hastily put by with a mere ordinary service, and nobody even knew of him, or that he was to have sung "Lead, Kindly Light" over the face of his last friend,—then he knew—the poor, forlorn little shadow, slipping silently in to sit in a back pew—that truly the worst had come to him.

The great house, vacant and stripped, had been locked and boarded and nailed up at every possible entrance by its new owners, since, in that impoverished village, there was nobody to rent such a mansion. Aunt Nutty, failing, for the same reason, to find a place, had gone ten miles up the river to stay with her son, Garland.

Orpheus, without any relative in the world to whom he could go, felt that when your home was broken up, and every one who belonged to it was dead or gone away, when the earth had opened and swallowed all your present life, its belongings and its possibilities, why, you went away somewhere, quite far—and there was a place there for you.

The great, strong, muddy stream which runs swiftly past these little river towns and the big plantations, showing its superiority to and contempt for the puny plans of humankind by every toss of its swirling, tawny mane, and the big boats it bears upward and downward upon its mighty breast, furnish the romance, the song and legend of the dwellers upon its banks, and weave themselves, finally, into most of the affairs of their lives.

So when Orphy first began to dream of going away, it was to the river, of course, that his thoughts turned.

All day he went about his task of collecting his small possessions, and bidding good-by to the different localities of the old place and that painfully new grave in the burial-plot, singing hopefully, almost joyously:

"Oh, de *Clindyburg* am a mighty fahn boat,
　An' a mighty fahn cap'n, too;
An' he sets up yendeh on de haycane-deck,
　An' keeps his eye on de crew.

Oh, Loozy-anner, I 's boun' ter leave dis
    town;
Take my duds an' tote 'em on my back,
    when de *Clindyburg* comes down."

Then, with his little bundle, he waited
patiently, day and night, upon the village
landing for the advent of a certain small,
dingy stern-wheel boat upon which he had

garding their magnificence through
ecstatically narrowed eyes. "I betcher thass
er fahn place whey them boats comes fum.
I betcher iss boun' ter be er fahn place
whey they 's a-goin' at."

"Whut dat ter you, how fahn dey is?"
sneered Aunt Melie's boy, who was always
asleep on the levee, or kicking his idle
heels against it, while he "feeshed" or

"The big Mississippi River floating palaces never stop at Spartanburg"

a friend in the person of a good-natured
deck-hand, of whom he was sure he could
beg a ride—up or down; it did not matter which, so it was away.

The big Mississippi River floating palaces never stop at Spartanburg. They
churn the whole river into little waves that
slap the levee insultingly as the great boats
steam contemptuously past.

"Um-*umph!*" exclaimed Orpheus, re-

watched the steamers. "Reck'n somebod'
gwine mek you er gif' outen some o' dat ar
fahnness?"

"I's 'bleege' ter b'lieve," murmured
Orpheus, more in reflection than in reply,
"dat whey dey comes fum an' whey dey
goes at, dey 's plenty wuyck for er lakly
house-boy, dest er-shinin' up de brasses an'
'poligisin' de silbeh."

And so it happened that, some days later,

there walked in among the Negro cabins of a big commercially managed plantation, thirty miles below Spartanburg, a timid and anxious-looking little yellow boy, asking in a shy and unaccustomed manner for "er jawb."

It was cotton-picking time, when everything that could work was pressed into service. There were no questions as to his qualifications and antecedents. He was asked if he could pick cotton; he answered that he "reck'ned so,"—he "nev' tried,"—received a basket, and was sent with a gang into the field.

Cotton-picking is hard, back-breaking work, and Orpheus had been literally, as the Negro phrase runs, "raised a pet." He had never labored all day in the burning sun, slept in a hut on a pallet, and fared upon corn-pone, side-meat, and the greens called collards. He had never lived or associated with common Negroes—fieldhands.

The gibes of the rough, coarse, cotton-picking boys at his slowness and incompetence angered him. He thought how they would not be permitted to touch with their awkward horny hands the work he could do so skilfully; and it was only the diplomacy of that blood which is inferior and has been enslaved that made him remain silent when they laughed at him, and stick doggedly to his work.

He found some relief in turning his back upon his detractors and muttering to himself: "Miss Patrice 'ould n' had none sich ez you gap-mouf, splay-foot, tah-baby, fiel'-han' niggahs foh a house-boy. She 'ould n' 'a' had one o' you in huh dahnin'-room. She 'ould n' 'a' let you step yo' foot on huh po'ch."

One morning Uncle Mose, who was picking in the row next Orpheus, asked him if he had seen the visitor at the great house.

Orphy had noticed him,—a slender, clean-shaven young man with glasses and rather long hair, going about among the Negroes up at the cabins, asking them some questions and writing their answers down in a little book he carried,—and Orphy said so.

Uncle Mose was old and garrulous, fonder of talking than of working. "He 's er-gittin' up er bain," he said, leaning on his basket.

"Er whut?" queried Orphy, absently, picking away industriously.

"W'y, er bain, ter play music," replied Uncle Mose. "He got 'im up one hyer las' ye'r, an' tuck hit ter de Worl's Fa'r."

At the word "music" Orphy was all alert. "Boys 'at c'd play de fiddle?" he asked anxiously.

"Er-r-r-uh-h!" answered Uncle Mose, rather contemptuously, "singin' niggahs, an' banjer-pickin' niggahs, an' fiddlin' niggahs, an' whut nut. I don' have no truck wid sich trash mos'ly."

"Did he take 'em somewhuz on de big boat?" asked Orphy, breathlessly.

Uncle Mose brightened at his interest.

"Well, yas," he admitted, mollified; "he tuck 'em, an' he gun 'em good wagers whilst dey 's wid 'im—an' dey' rashions."

"Is he gittin' mo' now t' take on de boat?"

"Yas," answered Uncle Mose, with a discouraged and discouraging shake of the head; "but I boun' y' he don' tek a-minny dish yer time. Boys ez no 'count now. W'y, in my day an' time"—and he embarked upon a long story which lasted to the end of that row and turned the next.

But Orphy heard none of it; his head was too full to allow any new ideas to come in by way of his ears. Somebody wanted boys that played the fiddle—some white person who would take them and give them a chance to live "like folks." Oh, if he only had the colonel's violin!

He fancied himself, washed clean and with his hair neatly combed as he had been taught, making his bow as he used to do, tucking the colonel's violin under his chin, playing his very best, and being found acceptable.

For hours that night his tired little body tossed from side to side of his uncomfortable pallet among the snoring field-hands, and his mind ran the gamut of every scheme or plan by which he might get a violin to play in the band, for that he must get the violin in order to join the band he never thought to doubt.

No money had been offered him, and he was too ignorant of such matters to know that his wages, such as they were, waited for him at the office. He had not a friend on the plantation to whom he felt he could go. Indeed, his gentlemanly ways, and evident shrinking from the coarser features of this life, had singled him out as an object of bullying by the worse element of his fellow-workers.

Toward morning a soothing thought dropped down upon his worry, and sent him off contentedly to sleep. He remembered a curious-looking object which used to hang upon the wall of the cabin at home. It was a fiddle, and it could be played upon. His father had made it out of a gourd.

It was the first instrument he was allowed to play, and he knew its every peg and joint, and just how the stretched sheepskin was held over the front, and the well-seasoned bit of bois d'arc or bow-wood let into the neck. Oh, he was sure he could make one like it, if Aunt Cindy, the laundress, would give him one of her big soap-gourds, and somebody would let him have the skin, and somebody else lent him a bow and strings, for he had a sharp knife, and there was plenty of bois d'arc down near the swamp! And on this slender footing of hope he fell happily asleep.

PART II

THINGS looked much more gloomy in the morning. Aunt Cindy was one of the church-going Negroes who considered fiddling and dancing deadly sins. The thought of asking for one of her cherished soap-gourds to make a fiddle sent chills down Orphy's back.

Big Mitch, the plantation fiddler, was the only one who had strings or bow, and his eldest boy, Little Mitch—nearly six feet tall, and head and shoulders above his wizened black father—was one of Orphy's chief enemies and tormentors. But, in the face of it all, the boy persisted.

"Yaller boy," said Aunt Cindy, accusingly, when he humbly pleaded for the gourd, and stated for what use it was wanted, "how you luhn ter play de fiddle?"

Orphy mumbled something, in a conciliatory tone, about "allers knowed—pappy showed me, an' Miss Patrice she teached me."

"Don' y' try wuk off none dat talk on me," snorted Aunt Cindy, contemptuously. "Y' pappy! Y' Miss P'trice! I knows how no-'count niggah trash luhns de fiddle,—an' you knows, too,—s'posin' y' really kin play hit."

"How does dey l'arn?" said Orpheus, with very round eyes.

"Dar, now," replied Aunt Cindy, expanding into a mollified grin, "I knowed li'l' boy lak you had n' been er-mixin' an' er-mommuxin' wid no sich—I knowed y' could n' play none. W'y, honey, dey jes practyzez on er Sunday,—on de good Lawd's day, w'en He say nobod' sha'n' wuk,—an' de Ol' Boy whuls in an' he'ps 'em. Yas! 'S trufe! 'N' ef he don' come de fus' time, er-tryin' ter show 'em de chunes, an' de quirly-gigs, dey crosses dey foots (dat 's a *shore* black chawm) an' scrapes de bow er few, an he comes er-floppin'!"

Orphy's evident horror over these statements was exceedingly flattering to the old woman, who was coming to expect that her wisdom would be laughed at by the rising generation.

"Dar, now," she said, "go 'long, an' don' try tellin' me sich tales 'bout mekin' fiddles, an' playin' fiddles. I gwine give y' de bes' gobe I got, 'ca'se you 's a nice li'l' gemman ter he'p me w'en I axes y'." And she did.

Orpheus worked on his fiddle at night, after the picking was over, leaving himself scarcely time to eat or sleep. He cut away the front of his gourd with the greatest care, fearing to crack the frail shell and spoil the tone of his instrument.

Meantime he had snared a rabbit, tried to cure its skin, found it too tender, and been reduced to trading his one silk handkerchief to Yellow Bob, the plantation butcher, for a bit of soft-tanned sheepskin to stretch over the opening.

The bois d'arc was found, neck and pegs shaped and in place, and he had come to the despairing point where he was ready for the strings and bow, when the foreman asked him kindly, one evening, if he knew that he could get money, or an order on the store, for the wages due him above his board.

He found that the store kept strings, and the storekeeper was willing to order a bow for him. It seemed no hardship to Orphy to do without the clothing he needed for the sake of these things he longed for.

When the curious, mandolin-shaped instrument was complete, when he had, with infinite patience and skill, brought the strings into tune, drawn his bow across them, and heard the tunes answer his call,—somewhat queer and "throaty," but real tunes,—such bliss rolled over Orphy's soul as nobody who merely *buys* a violin will ever know.

In the ardors of his work he had almost forgotten the object of it. He had been so long getting ready that the young man had made what he called his first trial, and had gone on now to another plantation, some miles below, before Orphy's homemade fiddle was done.

They said he was coming back, as he had done the year before, for a final trial, and to take away with him the boys whom he selected.

Orphy did n't believe he was coming again. Little Mitch said so, but then, Little Mitch always had things wrong. And Orphy scarcely cared whether he came or not. He had little hope of acceptance. So much fun had been made of his plan of fiddle-building that he was growing very doubtful about showing the fiddle to anybody, and the joy of its companionship was so great as to dwarf any minor misfortunes.

He was very shy of subjecting his new and dear companion to the indignity of being laughed at. "Yo' des lak ol' mis' use ter say 'bout Miss Patrice, honey," he would whisper, as he laid his chin lovingly against the sheepskin front; "y' ain' rightly purty, but you 's *mighty* sweet."

When his one holiday came, he usually carried his treasure, carefully wrapped, to a little grove down near the swamp, where people seldom passed, because it had the reputation of being "snaky." There, perched in the crotch of a water-oak, he would croon to his fiddle, and his fiddle would answer in familiar accents, all the long, warm Sunday afternoons. "Ain' no snek gwine tek de trubbl' climbin' atter sich er bone ez me!" he would chuckle gleefully, as he settled himself for hours of uninterrupted enjoyment.

But one day some of the more friendly boys surprised him there, and while he was proudly playing at their request, Little

Mitch, his tall form decked in a suit of Sunday clothes, and with shoes on his big feet, happened past.

His appearance of astonishment at the fiddle and the fiddler was so natural that no one would have guessed that one of his friends, who knew he was "layin' fer dat yaller boy," had run to call him.

"What y' got dar?" he called out, as he came in sight.

"Fiddle," replied Orphy, ceasing to play.

"Fiddle?"—drawing nearer, and reaching out his hand for the instrument. "Look ter me consid'ble lak er soap-gode."

Orphy scrambled to the ground, and held his beloved fiddle behind him.

"Le' me see her," said his tormentor, sternly.

Orphy retreated, and held the fiddle, ready for flight or fight at the slightest demonstration threatening it. He had been tenderly brought up, and had never been in a fight in his life, but at this danger to his fiddle, he felt something rising in his heart which entirely overshadowed his natural fear of Little Mitch.

But Mitch made no warlike demonstration whatever. Instead, he threw himself back with a roar of laughter which made poor Orphy's ears tingle.

"Whoopee!" he howled. "Looky dat, now! Dat w'at dish yer boy name er fiddle. Oh, my lan'! 'F dass put un'neath er daw-step f'r er hoodoo, hit 'd put er change on de bigges' man in Bayou pa'ish"—and so on with uncouth grimaces and bellows of mirth, till Orphy, consumed with mortification, began wrapping up his pet for departure.

As his victim seemed about to escape, Mitch stopped short in the middle of a guffaw. "Mek 'er play," he commanded.

Sullenly, and on the verge of tears, of which he was desperately ashamed, Orphy complied. At the first sound Mitch fell, apparently, into a great state of astonishment.

"Gre't day in de mawnin'!" he cried in pretended surprise. "Dish yer boy got er po' li'l' cat fas'n' up in dat ar gode!"

Orphy lowered his fiddle angrily, and began again to wrap it up; but Mitch had picked up a stone.

"Po' li'l' cat," he said, advancing. "Kitty kitty, kitty! I gwine bus' dat gode an' let de po' li'l' cat out."

At the word poor Orphy leaped as though stung. Dropping his fiddle behind him, he sprang blindly at Little Mitch, and, using his bare hands, fought with such passion and fury as he had never known before.

Little Mitch was, after all, only a big, cowardly bully, and resistance was the last thing he expected. The stone dropped grazing his own shin, and bringing a yap of pain, and he turned his entire attention to ridding himself of his small assailant, who seemed, like an angry cat, all teeth and claws.

The next thing Orphy knew, he was sitting on the ground, somewhat jarred and shaken, but otherwise unhurt, holding his beloved fiddle; and Little Mitch, at an extremely respectful distance, was wiping blood from his face on the cuff of his shirt, and muttering, "Nee' n' ter mek sich er fuss 'bout er joke! Nobod' ain' gwine troubl' you an' y' ol' gode fiddle."

After that Orphy knew that his fiddle was marked for destruction. He hid it during the daytime, when he was at his picking, with all the cunning of which he was master, and slept with it clutched fast every night.

The night the young man with the glasses—who had returned in spite of the fact that Little Mitch had said he would, and whose name, as Orphy had learned, was Professor Josef Blum—gathered the

boys in the big shed to make a final examination and choice, Orphy made himself
as neat as possible, and took his fiddle in
his hand with many misgivings.

Since the fight, it and its owner had become, mainly through Little Mitch's
agency, objects of much ridicule on the
plantation, and Orphy shrank sensitively
from taking it where it would excite further contempt.

Yet there was always a chance, and he
tuned it and brushed it free from dust,
polishing its bulging sides till they shone
again.

As he neared the open, lighted doorway
of the big shed, he caught sight of Little
Mitch within, and his heart failed him.

Little Mitch was one of those whom
Uncle Mose called the "banjer-pickin'
niggahs." His father had vainly tried to
teach him the violin; but he had a smooth,
powerful bass voice, which it was hoped
would recommend him.

The thought of taking his poor fiddle
in to face Mitch's scornful laughter, and
the possible amusement and derision of
the white people, was too much for Orphy.
He looked about for a hiding-place, and,
laying the fiddle in behind some cotton-
baskets by the shed wall, tucked the old
cloth over it as a mother would tuck the
covers over a little child, whispering to
it: "I ain' gwine tek you in dar ter be
made fun er. Nev' you min', honey; *I*
loves you, ef nobod' else don'!"

When in his examination Professor
Blum came to Orpheus, he put his large
white hand under the boy's chin, and
turned his eager, plaintive little yellow
face up to the light. "Well, young man,"
he said, in his pleasant voice, with its
slight foreign accent, "what can you
do?"

"I c'n sing er right fa'r soprano, suh,"
answered Orphy, modestly.

"What 's that?" said the professor,
struck by the boy's use of the proper and
technical word.

But there came a snicker from the
bench where Little Mitch sat among those
culled out for a second trial, and Mitch,
overblown with a sense of importance at
being among the chosen, called out:

"He play de fiddle. He got one whut
he brung erlong an' lef' outside."

"Is that so?" said the professor. "Why
don't you bring it in?"

"Yas," breathed Orphy, shifting from
one foot to the other in an agony of embarrassment; "but I heap rutheh try ter
sing foh y', suh. Hit ain' rightly er fiddle.
Hit 's er—hit 's er—"

"Hit 's er ol' gode fiddle," supplemented
Mitch, in malicious enjoyment of his
misery.

"A goat fiddle?" queried the young professor. "And what is that?"

At the roar of laughter which shook the
benches on which the negroes sat, and
even found an echo among the white folks
from the great house, who had come down
to see the fun, and were curiously watching this little scene, Orphy wished the
earth might open for him.

"Hit 's er gode fiddle," he said faintly.

"A goad fiddle?" asked the puzzled professor, thinking of those long sticks used
to prod oxen. "Go and get it, and play
for us, that we may see what it is."

Orphy looked appealingly around the
room. Was there no help? His glance fell
upon Little Mitch, leering triumphantly,
and the hot tears of mortification dried in
his eyes.

He would show them, he thought, that
he was a Fithian, that he had had better
raising than these corn-field darkies. It was
no sin to make a fiddle for yourself out of
a gourd—if you could not do any better.
He turned and marched out of the room

like a soldier, looking neither to the right nor to the left.

But once outside, with the fiddle in his hands, the temptation not to return was strong. The professor, he could see through the window, was busy with another boy. Should he go back to be laughed at by everybody there?

Nobody who cannot remember it can realize how agonizing to a child is the thought of being an object of universal ridicule.

The longing to run away into the cool, friendly dark, just to take his despised fiddle and run on and on till he reached the river, and could go away to a new place, was hardly to be resisted.

But he conquered it. Fiddle in hand, he returned as he had gone, without looking at any one, and so preoccupied with the effort he was making that he failed to see the professor's outstretched hand or to hear his request to see the instrument.

Tucking its bulge into the angle of his shoulder, he tuned it, and began upon the odd, uncertain quavers of "Shortening-bread."

Once he played the quaint little melody through without variation; then again, with little turns and embellishments of his own worked upon it; then, the third time through, he added his fresh young voice:

"I so glad de ol' hog dead—
  Mammy gwine mek some shawtnin'-
     bread.
Oh, mammy's baby loves shawtnin',
  Oh, mammy's baby loves shawtnin'-
     bread."

When he had finished, the professor again stretched out his hand, and Orphy put the fiddle in it.

"Well," said the professor, "this is great! Where did you get it? Why, it 's home-made! Who made it?"

"I did," said Orphy, relieved, but still somewhat apprehensive of the inevitable laugh he thought must follow.

"Oh, no," said the professor, "how could you have made it? Who showed you how?"

"Nobod' did n'," said Orphy. "My paw had one like hit; he made hit—er my gran'paw did, I dunno which. It 's de fus' kin' er fiddle I played on; but I c'n play er heap bettah on dat kin'," looking wistfully at the table, where he now saw the professor's violin lying.

"I don't want you to play better," exclaimed the professor, enthusiastically. "I want you to play this. Don't you see what a card this will be for me?" he asked, turning to Colonel Murchison, the proprietor of the plantation. "Here is the plantation musician and the plantation instrument! It will be the greatest attraction of my chorus in England and Germany. I will make him a soloist," he was going on enthusiastically, when Colonel Murchison's energetic signals caused him to halt and consult that gentleman aside for several minutes. During their conversation one of the young ladies from the great house handed Orpheus the violin, with an encouraging word, and he began an anthem of Bach's which he had often played in the little church at home.

The professor wheeled upon him at the sound. "What 's this?" he said. "Classic music? Can you read notes?"

"No, suh. Dass er chune Miss Patrice teached me faw ter play in de chu'ch. I knows er heap er dem chunes. She use ter play 'em on huh pianny, er sing 'em, 'n' I 'd ketch 'em." And tears stood in his eyes at the remembrance of those good days.

"See here," said the professor, speaking evidently upon a sudden impulse, and with a quick, piercing look at the boy's face. "The colonel, here, says I ought not to tell you that you 'll be valuable to me—you know what that word 'valuable' means, don't you?"

Orphy nodded a bewildered nod.

"Well, he says if I give you an idea that I want you pretty bad, you 'll be running off and trying to hire to some one else. Will you?"

The professor had judged his boy aright. Tears, of which he was too happy to be ashamed, ran down Orphy's cheeks as he answered stoutly; "No, suh. Dey ain' none er de Fithians tricky dat way in tradin'! I 's mighty glad that somebody wants me."

The young professor heard the home-sick boy's heart speak in that last sentence, and he patted him kindly on the shoulder.

"Well, now," he said, "that 's all right. Somebody wants you now. You sha'n't lose by it. I 'll pay you more than I can afford to pay such boys as those"—with a not too flattering wave of his hand toward the bench where Little Mitch and his fellows sat, open-mouthed and astounded. "I can pay you more, because you 're worth more."

"Yes, suh," said Orphy, respectfully; "I 'll try ter be."

It was the one fling he permitted himself at his dumbfounded and vanquished adversaries, and, delivered with demure meekness, it told in a little snicker from the benches where their elders sat, and a smile on the faces of the "white folks."

"You see," said the professor to his host, when he was leaving some days later, and Orphy, new dressed from top to toe, the happy possessor of a violin finer even than the colonel's, was going with him, out into a life bright with possibilities—"you see, nobody with a heart in him could cheat that little chap. He 's so faithful and

so trusting, and he tries so hard to please."

"Certainly," said the colonel, "you ought to give him what is justly due him; but I know Negro nature better than you, and I say better not make too much of him."

"Well," said the professor, seriously, as was his way, "I can afford to give him enough to pay good teachers to carry on his musical education, and to let him lay by a little, month by month, to give him his start when he is a man. There 's no telling what he may attain. I find he is a hereditary musician; and, for my part, I had rather come of a musical line than a noble line."

The colonel smiled indulgently. "He 'll sell you out to the first man who offers him more," he said.

"That he never will," replied the professor; "and as for keeping him in the dark about what he is worth to me, I could n't do it, if I would. He 's bound to take well abroad, and he 's bound to know it, and with such a boy I 'll take my chances on the result."

Little Mitch had finally to be dropped from the chorus. He proved too thickheaded to take any instruction.

As the boys waited on the landing—Orphy pinching himself surreptitiously now and then to be sure it was not an all-too-blissful dream—for the big boat which was to take them all to "Noo 'Leans," they could see Little Mitch in the cotton-field below, his tall form bent over as he pretended to be too busy picking to notice them.

Out of the abundance of his joy and satisfaction Orphy found time to be sorry for him.

" 'Pears lak I jes' could n' go back ter dat ar," he muttered reflectively. "Well, suh! I reck'n hit about all he 's fitten fer."

THE STORY OF A PROVERB

by Sidney Lanier

ONCE upon a time,—if my memory serves me correctly, it was in the year 6⅞,—His intensely-Serene-and-Altogether-Perfectly-Astounding Highness the King of Nimporte was reclining in his royal palace. The casual observer (though it must be said that casual observers were as rigidly excluded from the palace of Nimporte as if they had been tramps) might easily have noticed that his majesty was displeased.

The fact is, if his majesty had been a little boy, he would have been whipped and sent to bed for the sulks; but even during this early period of which I am writing, the strangeness of things had reached such a pitch, that in the very moment at which this story opens the King of Nimporte arose from his couch, seized by the shoulders his grand vizier (who was not at all in the sulks, but was endeavoring, as best he could, to smile from the crown of his head to the soles of his feet), and kicked him down-stairs.

As the grand vizier reached the lowest step in the course of his tumble, a courier covered with dust was in the act of putting his foot upon the same. But the force of the grand vizier's fall was such as to knock both the courier's legs from under him; and as, in the meantime, the grand vizier had wildly clasped his arms around the courier's body, to arrest his own descent, the result was such a miscellaneous rolling of the two men, that for a moment no one was able to distinguish which legs belonged to the grand vizier and which to the courier.

"Has she arrived?" asked the grand vizier, as soon as his breath came.

"Yes," said the courier, already hastening up the stairs.

At this magic word, the grand vizier again threw his arms around the courier, kissed him, released him, whirled himself about like a teetotum, leaped into the air and cracked his heels thrice before again touching the earth, and said:

"Allah be praised! Perhaps now we shall have some peace in the palace."

In truth, the King of Nimporte had been waiting two hours for his bride, whom he had never seen; for, according to custom, one of his great lords had been sent to the court of the bride's father, where he had married her by proxy for his royal master, and whence he was now conducting her to the palace. For two hours the King of Nimporte had been waiting for a courier to arrive and announce to him that the cavalcade was on its last day's march over the plain, and was fast approaching the city.

As soon as the courier had delivered his message, the king kicked him down-stairs (for not arriving sooner, his majesty incidentally remarked), and ordered the grand vizier to cause that a strip of velvet carpet should be laid from the front door of the grand palace, extending a half-mile down the street in the direction of the road by which the cavalcade was aproaching; adding that it was his royal intention to walk this distance, for the purpose of giving his bride a more honorable reception than any bride of any king of Nimporte had ever before received.

The grand vizier lost no time in carrying out his instructions, and in a short time the king appeared stepping along the carpet in the stateliest manner, followed by a vast and glittering retinue of courtiers, and encompassed by multitudes of citizens who had crowded to see the pageant.

As the king, bareheaded and barefooted (for at this time everybody went barefoot in Nimporte), approached the end of the carpet, he caught sight of his bride, who was but a few yards distant on her milk-white palfrey.

Her appearance was so ravishingly beautiful, that the king seemed at first dazed, like a man who has looked at the sun; but, quickly recovering his wits, he threw himself forward, in the ardor of his admiration, with the intention of running to his bride and dropping on one knee at her stirrup, while he would gaze into her face with adoring humility. And as the king rushed forward with this impulse, the populace cheered with the wildest enthusiasm at finding him thus capable of the feelings of an ordinary man.

But in an instant a scene of the wildest commotion ensued. At the very first step which the king took beyond the end of the carpet, his face grew suddenly white, and, with a loud cry of pain, he fell fainting to the earth. He was immediately surrounded by the anxious courtiers; and the court physician, after feeling his pulse for several minutes, and inquiring very carefully of the grand vizier whether his majesty had

on that day eaten any green fruit, was in the act of announcing that it was a violent attack of a very Greek disease indeed, when the bride (who has dismounted and run to her royal lord with wifely devotion) called the attention of the excited courtiers to his majesty's left great toe. It was immediately discovered that, in his first precipitate step from off the carpet to the bare ground, his majesty had set his foot upon a very rugged pebble, the effect of which upon tender feet accustomed to nothing but velvet, had caused him to swoon with pain.

Something happens to his majesty

As soon as the King of Nimporte opened his eyes in his own palace, where he had been quickly conveyed and ministered to by the bride, he called his trembling grand vizier and inquired to whom belonged the houses at that portion of the street where his unfortunate accident had occurred. Upon learning the names of these unhappy property-owners, he instantly ordered that they and their entire kindred should be beheaded, and the adjacent houses burned for the length of a quarter of a mile.

The king further instructed the grand vizier that he should instantly convene the cabinet of councilors and devise with them some means of covering the whole earth with leather, in order that all possibility of such accidents to the kings of Nimporte might be completely prevented,—adding, that if the cabinet should fail, not only in devising the plan, but in actually carrying it out within the next three days, then the whole body of councilors should be executed on the very spot where the king's foot was bruised.

Then the king kissed his bride, and was very happy.

The vizier imparts the king's decree

But the grand vizier, having communicated these instructions to his colleagues of the cabinet,—namely, the postmaster-general, the prætor, the sachem, and the three Scribes and-Pharisees,—proceeded to his own home, and consulted his wife, whose advice he was accustomed to follow with the utmost faithfulness. After thinking steadily for two days and nights, on the morning of the third day the grand vizier's wife advised him to pluck out his beard, to tear up his garments, and to make his will; declaring that she could not, upon the most mature deliberation, conceive of any course more appropriate to the circumstances.

The grand vizier was in the act of separating his last pair of bag-trousers into very minute strips indeed, when a knocking at the door arrested his hand, and in a moment afterward the footman ushered in a young man of very sickly complexion, attired in the seediest possible manner. The grand vizier immediately recognized him as a person well known about Nimporte for a sort of loafer, given to mooning about the clover-fields, and to meditating upon things in general, but not commonly regarded as ever likely to set a river on fire.

"O grand vizier!" said this young person (the inhabitants of Nimporte usually pronounced this word much like the French *personne,* which means nobody), "I have come to say that if you will procure the attendance of the king and court to-morrow morning at eleven o'clock in front of the palace, I will cover the whole earth with leather for his majesty in five minutes."

Then the grand vizier arose in the quietest possible manner, and kicked the young person down the back-stairs; and when he had reached the bottom stair, the grand vizier tenderly lifted him in his arms and carried him back to the upper landing, and then kicked him down the front-stairs,—in fact, quite out of the front gate.

Having accomplished these matters satisfactorily, the grand vizier returned with a much lighter heart, and completed a draft of his last will and testament for his lawyer, who was to call at eleven.

Punctually at the appointed time—being exactly three days from the hour when the grand vizier received his instructions— the King of Nimporte and all his court, together with a great mass of citizens, assembled at the scene of the accident to witness the decapitation of the entire cabinet. The headsman had previously arranged his apparatus; and presently the six unfortunate wise men were seen standing with hands tied behind, and with heads bent forward meekly over the six blocks in a row.

The executioner advanced and lifted a long and glittering sword. He was in the act of bringing it down with terrific force upon the neck of the grand vizier, when a stir was observed in the crowd, which quickly increased to a commotion so great that the king raised his hand and bade the executioner wait until he could ascertain the cause of the disturbance.

In a moment more, the young person appeared in the open space which had been reserved for the court, and with a mingled air of proud self-confidence and of shrinking reserve, made his obeisance before the king.

"O king of the whole earth!" he said, "if within the next five minutes I shall have covered the whole earth with leather for your majesty, will your gracious highness remit the sentence which has been pronounced upon the wise men of the cabinet?"

It was impossible for the king to refuse.

"Will your majesty then be kind enough to advance your right foot?"

The young person knelt, and drawing a bundle from his bosom, for a moment manipulated the king's right foot in a manner which the courtiers could not very well understand.

"Will your majesty now advance your majesty's left foot?" said the young person again; and again he manipulated.

"Will your majesty now walk forth upon the stones?" said the young person; and his majesty walked forth upon the stones.

"Will your majesty now answer: If your majesty should walk over the entire globe, would not your majesty's feet find leather between them and the earth the whole way?"

"It is true," said his majesty.

"Will your majesty further answer: Is

not the whole earth, so far as your majesty is concerned, now covered with leather?"

"It is true," said his majesty.

"O king of the whole earth, what is it?" cried the whole court in one breath.

"In fact, my lords and gentlemen," said the king, "I have on, what has never been known in the whole, great kingdom of

"His Majesty walked forth upon the stones."

Nimporte until this moment, a pair of— of——"

And here the king looked inquiringly at the young person.

"Let us call them—shoes," said the young person.

Then the king, walking to and fro over the pebbles with the greatest comfort and security, looked inquiringly at him. "Who are you?" asked his majesty.

"I belong," said the young person, "to the tribe of the poets—who make the earth tolerable for the feet of man."

Then the king turned to his cabinet, and pacing along in front of the six blocks, pointed to his feet, and inquired:

"What do you think of this invention?"

"I do not like it; I cannot understand it: I think the part of wisdom is always to reject the unintelligible; I therefore advise your majesty to refuse it," said the grand vizier, who was really so piqued, that he would much rather have been beheaded than live to see the triumph of the young person whom he had kicked down both pairs of stairs.

It is worthy of note, however, that when the grand vizier found himself in his own apartments, alive and safe, he gave a great leap into the air and whirled himself with joy as on a former occasion.

The postmaster-general also signified his disapproval. "I do not like it," said he; "they are not rights and lefts; I therefore advise your majesty to refuse the invention."

The prætor was like minded. "It will not do," he said; "It is clearly obnoxious to the overwhelming objection that there is absolutely nothing objectionable about it; in my judgment, this should be sufficient to authorize your majesty's prompt refusal of the expedient and the decapitation of the inventor."

"Moreover," added the sachem, "if your majesty once wears them, then every man, woman, and child, will desire to have his, her and its whole earth covered with leather; which will create such a demand for hides, that there will shortly be not a bullock or a cow in your majesty's dominions: if your majesty will but con-template the state of this kingdom without beef and butter!—there seems no more room for argument!"

"But these objections," cried the three Scribes-and-Pharisees, "although powerful enough in themselves, O king of the whole earth, have not yet touched the most heinous fault of this inventor, and that is, that there is no reserved force about this invention; the young person has actually done the very best he could in the most candid manner; this is clearly in violation of the rules of art,—witness the artistic restraint of our own behavior in this matter!"

Then the King of Nimporte said: "O wise men of my former cabinet, your wisdom seems folly; I will rather betake me to the counsels of the poet, and he shall be my sole adviser for the future; as for you, live—but live in shame for the littleness of your souls!" And he dismissed them from his presence in disgrace.

It was then that the King of Nimporte uttered that proverb which has since become so famous among the Persians; for, turning away to his palace, with his bride on one arm and the young person on the other, he said:

"To him who wears a shoe, it is as if the whole earth was covered with leather."

RUMPTY-DUDGET'S TOWER

(*A FAIRY TALE*)

by *Julian Hawthorne*

Long ago, before the sun caught fire, before the moon froze up, and before you were born, a Queen had three children, whose names were Princess Hilda, Prince Frank, and Prince Henry. Princess Hilda, who was the eldest, had blue eyes and golden hair; Prince Henry, who was the youngest, had black eyes and black hair; and Prince Frank, who was neither the youngest nor the eldest, had hazel eyes and brown hair. They were the best children in the world, and the prettiest, and the cleverest of their age: they lived in the most beautiful palace ever built, and the garden they played in was the loveliest that ever was seen.

This castle stood on the borders of a great forest, on the other side of which was Fairy Land. But there was only one window in the palace that looked out upon the forest, and that was the round window of the room in which Princess Hilda, Prince Frank, and Prince Henry slept. And since this window was never open except at night, after the three children had been put to bed, they knew very little about how the forest looked, or what kind of flowers grew there, or what kind of birds sang in the branches of the trees. Sometimes, however, as they lay with their heads on their little pillows, and their eyes open, waiting for sleep to come and fasten down the eyelids, they saw

stars, white, blue, and red, twinkling in the sky overhead; and below amongst the tree-trunks, other yellow stars, which danced about, and flitted to and fro. These flitting stars were called, by grown-up people, will-o'-the-wisps, jack-o'-lanterns,

Looking through the round window

fire-flies, and such like names; but the children knew them to be the torches carried by the elves, as they ran hither and thither about their affairs. They often wished that one of these elves would come through the round window of their chamber, and make them a visit; but if this ever happened, it was not until after the children had fallen asleep, and could know nothing of it.

The garden was on the opposite side of the palace to the forest, and was full of flowers, and birds, and fountains, in the basins of which goldfishes swam. In the center of the garden, was a broad green lawn for the children to play on; and on the further edge of this lawn was a high hedge, with only one round opening in the middle of it. But through this opening no one was allowed to pass; for the land on the other side belonged to a dwarf, whose name was Rumpty-Dudget, and whose only pleasure was in doing mischief. He was an ugly little dwarf, about as high as your knee, and all gray from head to foot. He wore a broad-brimmed gray hat, and a gray beard, and a gray cloak, that was so much too long for him that it dragged on the ground as he walked; and on his back was a small gray hump, that made him look even shorter than he was. He lived in a gray tower, whose battlements could be seen from the palace windows. In this tower was a room with a thousand and one corners in it. In each of these corners stood a little child, with its face to the wall, and its hands behind its back. They were children that Rumpty-Dudget had caught trespassing on his grounds, and had carried off with him to his tower. In this way he had filled up one corner after another, until only one corner was left unfilled; and if he could catch a child to put in that corner, then Rumpty-Dudget would become master of the whole country, and the beautiful palace would disappear, and the lovely garden would be changed into a desert, covered with gray stones and brambles. You may be sure, therefore, that Rumpty-Dudget tried very hard to get hold of a child to put in the thousand and first corner; but all the mothers were so careful, and all the children so obedient, that for a long time that thousand and first corner had remained empty.

II. TOM, THE FAITHFUL GUARDIAN

WHEN Princess Hilda and her two little brothers, Prince Frank and Prince Henry, were still very little, indeed, the Queen, their mother, was obliged to make a long journey to a distant country, and to leave the children behind her. They were not entirely alone, however; for there was their fairy aunt to keep guard over them at night, and a large cat, with yellow eyes and a thick tail, to see that no harm came to them during the day. The cat was named Tom, and was with them from the time they got up in the morning until they went to bed again; but from the time they went to bed until they got up, the cat disappeared and the fairy aunt took his place. The children had never seen their fairy aunt except in dreams, because she only came after sleep had fastened down their eyelids for the night. Then she would fly in through the round window, and sit on the edge of their bed, and whisper in their ears all manner of charming stories about Fairy Land, and the wonderful things that were seen and done there. Then, just before they awoke, she would kiss their eyelids and fly out of the round window again; and the cat, with his yellow eyes and his thick tail, would come purring in at the door.

One day, the unluckiest day in the whole year, Princess Hilda, Prince Frank and Prince Henry were playing together on the broad lawn in the center of the garden. It was Rumpty-Dudget's birthday, and the only day in which he had power to creep through the round hole in the hedge and prowl about the Queen's grounds. As ill-fortune would have it, moreover, the cat was forced to be away on this day from sunrise to sunset; so that during all that time the three children had no one to take care of them. But they did not know there was any danger, for they had never yet heard of Rumpty-Dudget; and they went on playing together very affection-ately, for up to this time they had never quarreled. The only thing that troubled them was that Tom, the cat, was not there to play with them; he had been away ever since sunrise, and they all longed to see his yellow eyes and his thick tail, and to stroke his smooth back, and to hear his com-fortable purr. However, it was now very near sunset, so he must soon be back. The sun, like a great red ball, hung a little way above the edge of the world, and was tak-ing a parting look at the children before bidding them good-night.

All at once, Princess Hilda looked up and saw a strange little dwarf standing close beside her, all gray from head to foot. He wore a gray hat and beard, and a long gray cloak that dragged on the ground, and on his back was a little gray hump that made him seem even shorter than he was, though, after all, he was no taller than your knee. Princess Hilda was not fright-ened, for nobody had ever done her any harm; and besides, this strange little gray man, though he was very ugly, smiled at her from ear to ear, and seemed to be the most good-natured dwarf in the world. So she called to Prince Frank and Prince Henry, and they looked up too, and were no more frightened than Hilda; and as the dwarf kept on smiling from ear to ear, the three children smiled back at him. Meanwhile, the great red ball of the sun was slowly going down, and now his lower edge was just resting on the edge of the world.

Now, you have heard of Rumpty-Dudget before, and therefore you know that this strange little gray dwarf was none other than he, and that, although he smiled so good-naturedly from ear to ear, he was really wishing to do the children harm, and even to carry one of them off to his tower, to stand in the thousand and first corner. But he had no power to do this so long as the children stayed on their side of the hedge; he must first tempt them to creep through the round opening, and then he could carry them whither he pleased. So he held out his hand and said:

"Come with me, Princess Hilda, Prince Frank and Prince Henry. I am very fond of little children; and if you will creep through that round opening in the hedge, I will show you something you never saw before."

The three children thought it would be very pleasant to see something they never saw before; for if that part of the world which they had already seen was so beauti-ful, it was likely that the part they had not seen would be more beautiful still. So they stood up, and Rumpty-Dudget took Prince Frank by one hand, and Prince Henry by the other, and Princess Hilda followed be-hind, and thus they all set off across the lawn toward the round opening in the hedge. But they could not go very fast, be-cause the children were hardly old enough to walk yet; and, meanwhile, the great red ball of the sun kept going down slowly, and now his lower half was out of sight beneath the edge of the world. However, at last they came to the round opening, and Rumpty-Dudget took hold of Prince Henry to lift him through it.

But just at that moment the last bit of the sun disappeared beneath the edge of the world, and instantly there was a great sound of miauing and spitting, and Tom, the cat, came springing across the lawn, his great yellow eyes flashing, and his back bristling, and every hair upon his tail stand-ing straight out, until it was as big round as your leg. And he flew at Rumpty-Dudget, and jumped upon his hump, and bit and scratched him soundly. At that Rumpty-Dudget screamed with and Prince Henry, who till then had been the other of the two best little boys in the world, began to wish to do what he was told not to do, and not to do what he was told to do. Such was the effect of the three black drops of mud.

pain, and dropped little Prince Henry, and vanished through the opening of the hedge in the twinkling of an eye.

But from the other side of the hedge he threw a handful of black mud at the three children; a drop of it fell upon the forehead of Princess Hilda, and another upon Prince Frank's nose, and a third upon little Prince Henry's chin; and each drop made a little black spot, which all the washing and scrubbing in the world would not take away. And immediately Princess Hilda, who had till then been the best little girl in the world, began to wish to order everybody about, and make them do what she pleased, whether they liked it or not; and Prince Frank, who till then had been one of the two best little boys in the world, began to want all the good and pretty things that belonged to other people, in addition to what already belonged to him;

The cat drives Rumpty-Dudget away

III. THE WAYS OF THE WIND

ALTHOUGH the Princess Hilda and her two little brothers were no longer the best children in the world, they were pretty good children as the world goes, and got along tolerably well together on the whole. But whenever the wind blew from the north, where Rumpty-Dudget's tower stood, Princess Hilda ordered her brothers about, and tried to make them do what she pleased, whether they liked it or not; and Prince Frank wanted some of the good and pretty things that belonged to his brother and sister, in addition to what were already his; and Prince Henry would not do what he was told to do, and would do what he was told not to do. And then, too, the spot on Princess Hilda's forehead, and on Prince Frank's nose, and on Prince Henry's chin, became blacker and blacker, and hotter and hotter, until at last the children were ready to cry from pain and vexation. But as soon as the wind blew from the south, where Fairy Land was, the spots began to grow dim, and the heat to lessen, until at last the children hardly felt or noticed them any more. Yet they never disappeared altogether; and neither the cat nor the fairy aunt could do anything to drive them away. But the cat used to warn Princess Hilda and her two brothers that unless they could make the wind blow always from the south, the thousand and first corner in Rumpty-Dudget's tower would be filled at last. And when, at night, their fairy aunt flew in through the round window and sat on their bedside, and whispered stories about Fairy Land into their ears, and they would ask her in their sleep to take them all three in her arms and carry them over the tops of the forest-trees to her beautiful home far away on the other side, she would shake her head and say:

"As long as those spots are on your faces, I cannot carry you to my home, for a part of each of you belongs to Rumpty-Dudget, and he will hold on to it in spite of all I can do. But when Hilda becomes a horse, and Frank a stick of fire-wood, and Henry a violin, then Rumpty-Dudget will lose his power over you, and the spots will vanish, and I will take you all three in my arms, and fly with you over the tops of the trees to Fairy Land, where we will live happily forever after."

When the three children heard this, they were puzzled to know what to do; for how could a little princess become a horse, or two little princes a stick of fire-wood and a violin? But that their fairy aunt would not tell them.

"It can only happen when the wind blows always from the south, as the cat told you," said she.

"But how can we make the wind blow always from the south?" asked they.

At that, the fairy aunt touched each of them on the heart, and smiled, and shook her head; and no other answer would she give; so they were no wiser than before.

Thus time went steadily on, to-morrow going before to-day, and yesterday following behind, until a year was past, and Rumpty-Dudget's birthday came round once more.

"I must leave you alone to-morrow," said the cat the day before, "from sunrise to sunset; but if you are careful to do as I tell you, all will be well. Do not go into the garden; do not touch the black ball that lies on the table in the nursery; and do not jump against the north wind."

Just as he finished saying these things, he sprang out of the room and disappeared.

All the next morning the children remembered what Tom, the cat, had told them; they played quietly in the palace, and did not touch the black ball that lay on the nursery table. But when the afternoon came, Princess Hilda began to be tired of staying shut up so long, when out in the garden it was warm and pleasant, and the wind blew from the south. And Prince Frank began to be tired of his own playthings, and to wish that he might have the pretty, black ball, to toss up in the air and catch again. And Prince Henry began to be tired of doing what he was told, and wished the wind would blow from the north, so that he might jump against it. At last they could bear it no longer; so Princess Hilda stood up and said:

"Frank and Henry, I order you to come out with me into the garden!" And out they went; and as they passed through the nursery, Prince Henry knocked the black ball off the table, and Prince Frank picked it up and put it in his pocket. But by the time they got to the broad lawn in the center of the garden, the three spots on their faces were blacker than ink and hotter than pepper; and, strange to say, the wind, which hitherto had blown from the south, now changed about and came from the north, where Rumpty-Dudget's tower stood. Nevertheless, the children ran about the grass, tossing the black ball from one to another, and did not notice that every time it fell to the ground, it struck a little nearer the hedge which divided Rumpty-Dudget's land from the Queen's garden. At last Prince Frank got the ball, and kept tossing it up in the air, and catching it again all by himself, without letting the others take their turns. But they ran after him to get it away, and all three raced to and fro, without noticing that at every turn they were nearer and nearer to the high hedge, and to the round opening that led into Rumpty-Dudget's ground. After a long chase, Princess Hilda and Prince Henry caught up with Prince

Frank, and would have taken the black ball away from him; but he gave it a great toss upward, and it flew clear over the high hedge and came down bounce upon the other side. Just then the great red ball of the sun dropped out of a gray cloud, and rested on the edge of the world. It wanted three minutes to sunset.

IV

THE three children were a good deal frightened when they saw where the ball had gone, and well they might be; for it was Rumpty-Dudget's ball, and Rumpty-Dudget himself was hiding on the other side of the hedge.

"It is your fault," said Princess Hilda to Prince Frank; "you threw it over."

"No, it 's your fault," answered Prince Frank; "I should n't have thrown it over if you and Henry had not chased me."

"You will be punished when Tom the cat comes home," said Princess Hilda, "and that will be in one minute, when the sun sets." For they had spent one minute in being frightened, and another minute in disputing.

Now, all this time, Prince Henry had been standing directly in front of the round opening in the hedge, looking through it to the other side, where he thought he could see the black ball lying beside a bush. The north wind blew so strongly as almost to take his breath away, and the spot on his chin burnt him so that he was ready to cry with pain and vexation. Still for all that, he longed so much to do what he had been told not to do, that by and by he could stand it no longer; but, just as the last bit of sun sank out of sight beneath the edge of the world, he jumped through the round opening against the north wind, and ran to pick up the ball. At the same moment, Tom the cat came springing across the lawn, his yellow eyes flashing, his back bristling, and the hairs sticking straight out on his tail until it was as big round as your leg. But this time he came too late. For, as soon as Prince Henry jumped through the hedge against the north wind and ran to pick up the black ball, out rushed Rumpty-Dudget from behind the bush, and caught him by the chin, and carried him away to the thousand and first corner in the gray tower. As soon as the corner was filled, the north wind rose to a hurricane and blew away the beautiful palace and the lovely garden, and nothing was left but a desert covered with gray stones and brambles. The mischievous Rumpty-Dudget was now master of the whole country.

Meanwhile, Princess Hilda and Prince Frank were sitting on a heap of rubbish, crying as if their hearts would break, and the cat stood beside them wiping its great yellow eyes with its paw and looking very sorrowful.

"Crying will do no good, however," said the cat at last; "we must try to get poor little Henry back again."

"Oh, where is our fairy aunt?" cried Princess Hilda and Prince Frank. "She will tell us how to find him."

"You will not see your fairy aunt," replied Tom, "until you have taken Henry out of the gray tower, where he is standing in the thousand and first corner with his face to the wall and his hands behind his back."

"But how are we to do it," said Princess Hilda and Prince Frank, beginning to cry again, "without our fairy aunt to help us?"

"Listen to me," replied the cat, "and do what I tell you, and all may yet be well. But first take hold of my tail, and follow me out of this desert to the borders of the great forest; there we can lay our plans without being disturbed."

With these words, Tom arose and held his tail straight out like the handle of a saucepan; the two children took hold of it, off they all went, and in less time than it takes to tell it, they were on the borders of the great forest, at the foot of an immensely tall pine-tree. The cat made Princess Hilda and Prince Frank sit down on the moss that covered the ground, and sat down in front of them with his tail curled round his toes.

"The first thing to be done," said he, "is to get the Golden Ivy-seed and the Diamond Water-drop. After that, the rest is easy."

"But where are the Golden Ivy-seed and the Diamond Water-drop to be found?" asked the two children.

"One of you will have to go down to the kingdom of the Gnomes, in the center of the earth, to find out where the Golden Ivy-seed is," replied the cat; "and up to the kingdom of the Air-Spirits, above the clouds, to find out where the Diamond Water-drop is."

"But how are we to get up to the Air-Spirits, or down to the Gnomes?" asked the children, disconsolately.

"I may be able to help you about that," answered the cat. "But while one of you is gone, the other must stay here and mind the magic fire which I shall kindle before we start; for if the fire goes out, Rumpty-Dudget will take the burnt logs and blacken Henry's face all over with them, and then we should never be able to get him back. Do you two children run about and pick up all the dried sticks you can find, and pile them up in a heap, while I get the touch-wood ready."

In a very few minutes, a large heap of fagots had been gathered together, as high as the top of Princess Hilda's head. Meanwhile, the cat had drawn a large circle on the ground with the tip of his tail, and in the center of the circle was the heap of fagots. It had now become quite dark, but the cat's eyes burned as brightly as if two yellow lamps had been set in his head.

"Come inside the circle, children," said he, "while I light the touch-wood."

In they came accordingly, and the cat put the touch-wood on the ground and sat down in front of it with his nose resting against it, and stared at it with his flaming yellow eyes; and by and by it began to smoke and smolder, and at last it caught fire and burned famously.

"That will do nicely," said the cat; "now put some sticks upon it." So this was done, and the fire was fairly started, and burned blue, red and yellow.

"And now there is no time to be lost," said the cat. "Prince Frank, you will stay beside this fire and keep it burning, until I come back with Princess Hilda from the kingdoms of the Gnomes and Air-Spirits. Remember that, if you let it go out, all will be lost; nevertheless, you must on no account go outside the circle to gather more fagots, if those that are already here get used up. You may, perhaps, be tempted to do otherwise; but if you yield to the temptation, all will go wrong; and the only way your brother Henry can be saved will be for you to get into the fire yourself, in place of the fagots."

Though Prince Frank did not much like the idea of being left alone in the woods all night, still, since it was for his brother's sake, he consented; but he made up his mind to be very careful not to use up the fagots too fast, or to go outside the ring. So Princess Hilda and Tom the cat bid him farewell, and then the cat stretched out his tail as straight as the handle of a saucepan. Princess Hilda took hold of it, and away! right up the tall pine-tree they

went, and were out of sight in the twinkling of an eye.

V

AFTER climbing upward for a long time, they came at last to the tiptop of the pine-tree, which was on a level with the clouds. The cat waited until a large cloud sailed along pretty near them, and then, bidding Princess Hilda hold on tight, they made a spring together, and alighted very cleverly on the cloud's edge. Off sailed the cloud with them on its back, and soon brought them to the kingdom of the Air-Spirits.

"Now, Princess Hilda," said the cat, "you must go the rest of the way alone. Ask the first Spirit you meet to show you the way to the place where the Queen sits; and when you have found her, ask here where the Diamond Water-drop is. But be careful not to sit down, however much you may be tempted to do so; for if you do, your brother Henry never can be saved."

Though Princess Hilda did not much like the idea of going on alone, still, since it was for her brother's sake, she consented; only she made up her mind on no account to sit down, no matter what happened. So she bid the cat farewell, and walked off. Pretty soon, she met an Air-Spirit, carrying its nose in the air, as all Air-Spirits do.

"Can you tell me the way to the place where the Queen sits?" asked Princess Hilda.

"What do you want of her?" asked the Air-Spirit.

"I want to ask her where the Diamond Water-drop is," answered Princess Hilda.

"She sits on the top of that large star up yonder," said the Air-Spirit; "but unless you can carry your nose more in the air than you do, I don't believe you will get her to tell you anything."

Princess Hilda, however, did not feel so much like carrying her nose in the air as she had felt at any time since the black spot came upon her forehead; and she set out to climb toward the Queen's star very sorrowfully; and all the Spirits who met her said:

"See how she hangs her head! She will never come to anything."

But at last she arrived at the gates of the star, and walked in; and there was the Queen of the Air-Spirits sitting in the midst of it. As soon as she saw Princess Hilda, she said:

"You have come a long way, and you look very tired. Come here and sit down beside me."

"No, your Majesty," replied Princess Hilda, though she was really so tired that she could hardly stand, "there is no time to be lost; where is the Diamond Water-drop?"

"That is a foolish thing to come after," said the Queen. "However, sit down here and let us talk about it. I have been expecting you."

But Princess Hilda shook her head.

"Listen to me," said the Queen. "I know that you like to order people about, and to make them do what you please, whether they like it or not. Now, if you will sit down here, I will let you be Queen of the Air-Spirits instead of me; you shall carry your nose in the air, and everybody shall do what you please, whether they like it or not."

When Princess Hilda heard this, she felt for a moment very much tempted to do as the Queen asked her. But the next moment she remembered her poor little brother Henry, standing in the thousand and first corner of Rumpty-Dudget's tower, with his face to the wall and his hands behind his back. So she cried, and said:

"Oh, Queen of the Air-Spirits, I am so sorry for my little brother that I do not care any longer to carry my nose in the air, or to make people mind me, whether they like it or not; I only want the Diamond Water-drop, so that Henry may be saved from Rumpty-Dudget's tower. Can you tell me where it is?"

Then the Queen smiled upon her, and said:

"It is on your own cheek!"

Princess Hilda was so astonished that she could only look at the Queen without speaking.

"Yes," continued the Queen, kindly, "you might have searched throughout all the kingdoms of the earth and air, and yet never have found that precious Drop, had you not loved your little brother Henry more than to be Queen. That tear upon your cheek, which you shed for love of him, is the Diamond Water-drop, Hilda; keep it in this little crystal bottle; be prudent and resolute, and sooner or later Henry will be free again."

As she spoke, she held out a little crystal bottle, and the tear from Princess Hilda's cheek fell into it, and the Queen hung it about her neck by a coral chain, and kissed her, and bid her farewell. And as Princess Hilda went away, she fancied she had somewhere heard a voice like this Queen's before; but where or when she could not tell.

It was not long before she arrived at the cloud which had brought her to the kingdom of the Air-Spirits, and there she found Tom the cat awaiting her. He got up and stretched himself as she approached, and when he saw the little crystal bottle hanging round her neck by its coral chain, he said:

"So far, all has gone well; but we have still to find the Golden Ivy-seed. There is no time to be lost, so catch hold of my tail and let us be off."

With that, he stretched out his tail as straight as the handle of a saucepan. Princess Hilda took hold of it; they sprang off the cloud and away! down they went till it seemed to her as if they never would be done falling. At last, however, they alighted softly on the top of a hay-mow, and in another moment were safe on the earth again.

Close beside the hay-mow was a field-mouse's hole, and the cat began scratching at it with his two fore-paws, throwing up the dirt in a great heap behind, till in a few minutes a great passage was made through to the center of the earth.

"Keep hold of my tail," said the cat, and into the passage they went.

It was quite dark inside, and if it had not been for the cat's eyes, which shone like two yellow lamps, they might have missed their way. As it was, however, they got along famously, and pretty soon arrived at the center of the earth, where was the Kingdom of the Gnomes.

"Now, Princess Hilda," said the cat, "you must go the rest of the way alone. Ask the first Gnome you meet to show you the place where the King works; and when you have found him, ask him where the Golden Ivy-seed is. But be careful to do everything that he bids you, no matter how little you may like it; for, if you do not, your brother Henry never can be saved."

Though Princess Hilda did not much like the idea of going on alone, still, since it was for her brother's sake, she consented; only she made up her mind to do everything the King bade her, whatever happened. Pretty soon she met a Gnome, who was running along on all-fours.

"Can you show me the place where the King works?" asked Princess Hilda.

"What do you want with him?" asked the Gnome.

"I want to ask him where the Golden Ivy-seed is," answered Princess Hilda.

"He works in that great field over yonder," said the Gnome; "but unless you can walk on all-fours better than you do, I don't believe he will tell you anything."

Princess Hilda had never walked on all-fours since the black spot came on her forehead; so she went onward just as she was, and all the Gnomes who met her said:

"See how upright she walks! She will never come to anything."

But at last she arrived at the gate of the field, and walked in; and there was the King on all-fours in the midst of it. As soon as he saw Princess Hilda, he said:

"Get down on all-fours this instant! How dare you come into my kingdom walking upright?"

"Oh, your majesty," said Hilda, though she was a good deal frightened at the way the King spoke, "there is no time to be lost; where is the Golden Ivy-seed?"

"The Golden Ivy-seed is not given to people with stiff necks," replied the King. "Get down on all-fours at once, or else go about your business!"

Then Princess Hilda remembered what the cat had told her, and got down on all-fours without a word.

"Now listen to me," said the King. "I shall harness you to that plow in the place of my horse, and you must draw it up and down over this field until the whole is plowed, while I follow behind with the whip. Come! There is no time to lose."

When Princess Hilda heard this, she felt tempted for a moment to refuse; but the next moment she remembered her poor little brother Henry standing in the thousand and first corner of Rumpty-Dudget's tower, with his face to the wall and his hands behind his back; so she said:

"O King of the Gnomes! I am so sorry for my little brother that I will do as you bid me, and all I ask in return is that you will give me the Golden Ivy-seed, so that

Henry may be saved from Rumpty-Dudget's tower."

The King said nothing, but harnessed Hilda to the plow, and she drew it up and down over the field until the whole was plowed, while he followed behind with the whip. Then he freed her from her trappings, and told her to go about her business.

"Put your hand over your heart, Hilda, and see what you find there."

Princess Hilda was so surprised that she could say nothing; but she put her hand over her heart, and felt something fall into the palm of her hand, and when she looked at it, behold! it was the Golden Ivy-seed.

"Yes," said the King, kindly; "you might

"But where is the Golden Ivy-seed?" asked she, piteously.

"I have no Golden Ivy-seed," answered the King; "ask yourself where it is!"

Then poor Princess Hilda's heart was broken, and she sank down on the ground and sobbed out, quite in despair:

"Oh, what shall I do to save my little brother!"

But at that the King smiled upon her and said:

have searched through all the kingdoms of the earth and air, and yet never have found that precious seed, had you not loved your brother so much as to let yourself be driven like a horse in the plow for his sake. Keep the Golden Ivy-seed in this little pearl box; be humble, gentle and patient, and sooner or later your brother will be free."

As he spoke, he fastened a little pearl box to her girdle with a jeweled clasp, and kissed her, and bade her farewell. And as Princess Hilda went away, she fancied she had somewhere heard a voice like this King's before; but where or when she could not tell.

It was not long before she arrived at the mouth of the passage by which she had descended to the kingdom of the Gnomes, and there she found Tom the cat awaiting her. He got up and stretched himself as she approached, and when he saw the pearl box at her girdle, he said:

"So far, all goes well; but now we must see whether or not Prince Frank has kept the fire going; there is no time to be lost, so catch hold of my tail and let us be off."

With that, he stretched out his tail as straight as the handle of a saucepan; Princess Hilda took hold of it, and away they went back through the passage again, and were out at the other end in the twinkling of an eye.

VI

Now, after Prince Frank had seen Princess Hilda and the cat disappear up the trunk of the tall pine-tree, he had sat down rather disconsolately beside the fire, which blazed away famously, blue, red, and yellow. Every once in a while he took a fagot from the pile and put it in the flame, lest it should go out; but he was very careful not to step outside the circle which the cat had drawn with the tip of his tail. So things went on for a very long time, and Prince Frank began to get very sleepy, for never before had he sat up so late; but still Princess Hilda and the cat did not return, and he knew that if he were to lie down to take a nap, the fire might go out before he waked up again, and then Rumpty-Dudget would have blackened Henry's face all over with one of the burnt logs, and he never could be saved. He kept on putting fresh fagots in the flame, therefore, though it was all he could do to keep his eyes open; and the fire kept on burning red, blue and yellow.

But after another very long time had gone by, and there were still no Princess Hilda and the cat, Prince Frank, when he went to take a fresh fagot from the pile, found that there was only that one fagot left of all that he and Hilda had gathered together. At this he was very much frightened, and knew not what to do; for when that fagot was burned up, as it soon would be, what was he to do to keep the fire going? There were no more sticks inside the ring, and the cat had told him that if he went outside of it, all would be lost.

In order to make the fagot last as long as possible, he took it apart, and only put one stick in the flame at a time; but after a while, all but the last stick was gone, and when he had put that in, Prince Frank sat down quite in despair, and cried with all his might. Just then, however, he heard a voice calling him, and, looking up, he saw a little gray man standing just outside the circle, with a great bundle of fagots in his arms. Prince Frank's eyes were so full of tears that he did not see that the little gray man was Rumpty-Dudget.

"What are you crying for, my dear little boy?" asked the gray dwarf, smiling from ear to ear.

"Because I have used up all my fagots," answered Prince Frank; "and if the fire goes out, my brother Henry cannot be saved."

"That would be too bad, surely," said the dwarf; "luckily, I have got an armful, and when these are gone, I will get you some more."

"Oh, thank you—how kind you are!" cried Prince Frank, jumping up in great joy, and going to the edge of the circle.

"Give them to me, quick, for there is no time to be lost; the fire is just going out."

"I can't bring them in," replied the dwarf; "I have carried them already from the other end of the forest, and that is far enough; surely you can come the rest of the way yourself."

"Oh, but I must not come outside the circle," said Prince Frank; "for the cat told me that if I did, all would go wrong."

"Pshaw! what does the cat know about it?" asked the dwarf. "At all events, your fire will not burn one minute longer; and you know what will happen then."

When Prince Frank heard this, he knew not what to do; but anything seemed better than to let the fire go out; so he put one foot outside of the circle and stretched out his hand for the fagots. But immediately the dwarf gave a loud laugh, and threw the fagots away as far as he could; and rushing into the circle, he began to stamp out with his feet the little of the fire that was left.

Then Prince Frank remembered what the cat had told him; he turned and rushed back also into the circle; and as the last bit of flame flickered at the end of the stick, he laid himself down upon it like a bit of fire-wood. And immediately Rumpty-Dudget gave a loud cry and disappeared; and the fire blazed up famously, yellow, blue and red, with poor little Prince Frank in the midst of it!

VII

Just then, and not one moment too soon, there was a noise of hurrying and scurrying, and along came Tom the cat through the forest, with Princess Hilda holding on to his tail. As soon as they were within the circle, Tom dug a little

hole in the ground with his two fore-paws, throwing up the dirt behind, and then said: "Give me the Golden Ivy-seed, Princess Hilda; but make haste; for Frank is burning for Henry's sake!"

So she made haste to give him the Seed; and he planted it quickly in the little hole, and covered the earth over it, and then said: "Give me the Diamond Water-drop; but make haste; for Frank is burning for Henry's sake!"

So she made haste to give him the Drop; and he poured half of it on the fire, and the other half on the place where the Seed was planted. And immediately the fire was put out, and there lay Prince Frank all alive and well; but the mark of Rumpty-Dudget's mud on his nose was burned away, and his hair and eyes, which before had been brown and hazel, were now quite black. So up he jumped, and he and Princess Hilda and Tom all kissed each other heartily; and then Prince Frank said:

"Why, Hilda! the black spot that you had on your forehead has gone away, too."

"Yes," said the cat; "that happened when the King of the Gnomes kissed her. But now make yourselves ready, children; for we are going to take a ride to Rumpty-Dudget's tower!"

The two children were very much surprised when they heard this, and looked about to see what they were to ride on. But behold! the Golden Ivy-seed, watered with the Diamond Water-drop, was already growing and sprouting, and a strong stem with bright golden leaves had pushed itself out of the earth, and was creeping along the ground in the direction of Rumpty-Dudget's tower. The cat put Princess Hilda and Prince Frank on the two largest leaves, and got on the stem himself, and so away they went merrily, and in a very short time the Ivy had carried them to the tower gates.

"Now jump down," said the cat.

Down they all jumped accordingly; but the Golden Ivy kept on, and climbed over the gate, and crept up the stairs, and along the narrow passageway, until, in less time than it takes to write it, the Ivy had reached the room, with the thousand and one corners, in the midst of which Rumpty-Dudget was standing; and all around were the poor little children whom he had caught, standing with their faces to the wall and their hands behind their backs. When Rumpty-Dudget saw the Golden Ivy creeping toward him, he was very much frightened, as well he might be, and he tried to run away; but the Ivy caught him, and twined around him, and squeezed him tighter and tighter and tighter, until all the mischief was squeezed out of him; but since Rumpty-Dudget was made of mischief, of course when all the mischief was squeezed out of him, there was no Rumpty-Dudget left. He was gone forever.

Instantly, all the children that he had kept in the thousand and one corners were free, and came racing and shouting out of the gray tower, with Prince Henry at their head. And when he saw his brother and sister, and they saw him, they all three hugged and kissed one another as if they were crazy. At last Princess Hilda said: "Why, Henry, the spot that was on your chin has gone away, too! And your hair and eyes are brown and hazel instead of being black."

"Yes," said a voice, which Hilda fancied she had somewhere heard before; "while he stood in the corner his chin rubbed against the wall, until the spot was gone; so now he no longer wishes to do what he is told not to do, or not to do what he is told to do; and when he is spoken to,

he answers sweetly and obediently, as a violin answers to the bow when it touches the strings."

Then the children looked around, and there stood a beautiful lady, with a golden crown on her head, and a loving smile in her eyes. It was their fairy aunt, whom they had never seen before except in their dreams.

"Oh," said Princess Hilda, "you look like our mamma, who went away to a distant country, and left us behind. And your

"And now you shall come with me to Fairy Land!"

voice is like the voice of the Queen of the Air-Spirits; and of——"

"Yes, my darlings," said the beautiful lady, taking the three children in her arms; "I am the Queen, your mother, though, by Rumpty-Dudget's enchantments, I was obliged to leave you, and only be seen by you at night in your dreams. And I was the Queen of the Air-Spirits, Hilda, whose voice you had heard before; and I was the King of the Gnomes, though I seemed so harsh and stern at first. But my love has been with you always, and has followed you everywhere. And now you shall come with me to our home in Fairy Land. Are you all ready?"

"Oh, but where is Tom the cat?" cried all the three children together. "We cannot go and be happy in Fairy Land without him!"

Then the Queen laughed, and kissed them, and said: "I am Tom the cat, too!"

When the children heard this, they were perfectly contented; and they clung about her neck, and she folded her arms around them, and flew with them over the tops of the forest trees to their beautiful home in Fairy Land; and there they are all living happily to this very day. But Princess Hilda's eyes are blue, and her hair is golden, still.

THE OLD LADY FROM DOVER

by Carolyn Wells

THERE was an old lady of Dover
Who baked a fine apple turnover.
   But the cat came that way,
   And she watched with dismay
The overturn of her turnover.

"Ring a ring o' roses"
Painted for St. Nicholas by Arthur Rackham

"Bye, Baby Bunting"
Painted for St. Nicholas by Arthur Rackham

"The Little People's Market"
Painted for St. Nicholas by Arthur Rackham

"Rain, rain, go away!"
Painted for St. Nicholas by Arthur Rackham

"Hark, hark, the dogs do bark!"
Painted for St. Nicholas by Arthur Rackham

Jack Sprat and his wife
Painted for St. Nicholas by Arthur Rackham

"There was an old woman lived under a hill"
Painted for St. Nicholas by Arthur Rackham

THANKSGIVING SNOW-SHOES

by Ben Ames Williams

THIS was before the day of town water-works in Forestville. Most folks relied for water upon a cistern in the back yard, or a well lined with moss-covered stone. Dick Hart's father, when he built their new home, looked ahead a few years, however, and saw that town water would come; and so the house was piped for that day. In the meantime, the water was to come from a lead-lined tank in the attic, which supplied the faucets by gravity; and to fill this tank there was a pump in the kitchen.

Dick hated that pump the first time he saw it. It stood higher than he did, with a great long iron handle like a cudgel; and it was painted red and black, so that it had a sinister and wicked air about it. Dick hated the pump still more when they were in the new house; for it devolved upon him to keep the tank filled.

"That 's your job, Dick," his father told him. "I leave it to you to look out for it."

Dick looked dubiously from the pump to his father. "All right, Dad," he agreed. "Here goes. I 'll fill it up for a starter, anyway."

Even then he had a pretty good idea that it would be quite a job to fill that tank; and it was. That first day he pumped endlessly, first pulling upward the heavy iron handle, and then pushing it down with all his strength. At first it came easily, but after ten minutes or so it was moving more and more stiffly, and there was a blister on Dick's palm. He wrapped a handkerchief around it to ease the smart, and worked on.

A little pipe, opening into the sink, served as telltale. When the tank in the attic was filled, water would trickle from this pipe. Dick stuck to it till the first trickle came, but he was so stiff and sore that night that even his fatigue could not make him sleep. And he dreamed about that red-and-black pump.

In later days he discovered that when the tank in the attic was empty, it required just fifteen hundred strokes to fill it. Thereafter he counted them laboriously, and when the goal was nearly reached, watched the telltale pipe eagerly for the first drops of water. He became so expert that his ear could catch the faint puff of air from the little pipe that told him the water had begun its trickling progress down from the attic, and that meant his task was done.

Dick's mother did most of her own housework; but her washing was done by a woman who "came in by the day." This woman's name was Attson—Mrs. Attson. She was a tall, gaunt woman, with a face that reminded Dick of Abraham Lincoln's, so raw-boned it was, and so lined with the burdens she had borne. Her husband was dead, Dick knew; and she had two children, little girls, each as thin and gaunt

298

as their mother. To support them she did washing, scrubbing, and kindred odd jobs, toiling from dawn to dark at her own home or at the houses of those for whom she worked.

Dick did not like her the first time he saw her. She was too ugly, somehow. There was a fierce repulsion in him at her ugliness. He had an instinctive sense that a woman should be graceful, and smooth of contour, and agreeable to the eye, as was his mother. But as he grew to know the washerwoman better, he was not so sure that she was ugly, after all. There was something about her face—well, to watch it, and to see how it changed when she smiled, and to notice the kindly light in her tired eyes,—it sort of made a fellow choke up, somehow.

Dick saw a good deal of her, too, for that infernal pump kept him in the kitchen no inconsiderable part of the day. He used to toil and toil at the red-and-black handle, while Mrs. Attson bent above the wash-tubs, her shoulders moving up and down, while she scrubbed, as regularly as the walking-beam on a river steamer. Dick wondered how she could keep going so steadily. She never seemed to tire, while he himself found his back aching and his sides nigh splitting with grinding pain after he had wrestled with that pump for a while.

One day—a hot day, it was, in late September—Dick counted from one stroke up to five hundred, knew his task was but a third done, and flung back from the pump and dropped in a chair, panting and hot. He glared at that grim iron thing, and suddenly saw red with rage. He threw himself at it and whipped the handle up and down like mad for a moment. Mrs. Attson looked up from her tubs, and wiped her sudsy hands on her apron.

"That don't do no good, Dickie," she said gently.

Her voice quieted him, somehow, and he dropped the pump-handle and sat down again.

"I know it," he said sullenly. "The old thing kicks like a steer if you work it fast, and not so much water goes up, either. I 've counted, and I know."

"Lemme try it a spell," she said; and stepping across to the pump she laid hold of the handle. Dick flushed and got to his feet and pushed in front of her.

"No, no!" he protested, ashamed. "It—it ain't work for a woman."

She chuckled softly, her grim old face wrinkling comfortably. "Shucks, Dickie!" she said. "It hain't work fer me, it 's play—changin' from the tubs fer a spell."

She thrust him aside, and he submitted. Then Mrs. Attson, with the same tireless motion of her shoulders with which she bent above her tubs, manipulated the pump-handle for a while. Dick was dead tired. He just sat there and watched, and automatically he counted the strokes. Suddenly he realized that she had passed the five-hundred mark. At that he leaped up again.

"Here!" he said gruffly, gratitude choking him, "I guess you 've done enough of that. I can do the rest."

She relinquished the pump-handle to him. "It does hit you in the back some, don't it?" she agreed.

Dick finished filling the tank, and, when it was done, searched guiltily around till he found the coal-bucket, which he usually left Mrs. Attson to fill for herself. He filled it for her, without ostentation, and left it behind the stove.

And thereafter a sort of partnership was struck up between the two. On the days when Mrs. Attson was at the house, Dick took particular pains to see that the coal and other things she needed were ready to her hand; and she, in her turn, helped him out when he was tired at the pump. And so, without much being said on either side, Dick got better acquainted with the gaunt, tired, hard-working woman every day.

Dick's elder brother had gone away to college the year before—to a college in the New Hampshire hills. When he came home in the summer for the long vacation, he brought with him, among others of his various belongings, a pair of snow-shoes. Dick had read of such things, but he had never seen them. Forestville had an occasional snow of a foot or so, but it never stayed long, and there was little use for snow-shoes thereabouts. Nevertheless, when Dick saw them, he wanted a pair. He kept the ambition to himself, for the older folks would no doubt laugh at such a desire.

"I could use them sometimes," he told himself. "And anyway, when I go to college, I 'd have them all ready. Or I might go to Canada some time—or some-thing."

He asked his brother, casually, what they cost, and was told they could be pur-chased for six dollars—a good pair, long and narrow, on the woods model, built to glide easily through thick brush, where the broader, more familiar shape would knock against every tree.

"I 'm going to get them," Dick resolved, and said to his brother, "If I send you the money, will you get me a pair?"

"What use have you got for snow-shoes?" his brother asked.

"We-ell, I just want some," Dick pro-tested, flushing. "I guess I can hang 'em on the wall of my room till I go to college, can't I?"

His brother chuckled. "Sure! I 'll get you a pair, all right, if you 'll send the money. But where are you going to raise it?"

"Oh, I 'll get it!" Dick promised.

And thereupon his ambition took more definite form, and he set about the task of amassing a fortune—six dollars.

It seems comparatively little. But to a boy of Dick's age it is wealth. Dick had no particular earning capacity. He could cut lawns, and carry coal, and empty ashes,

"He asked his brother what they cost"

and that was about all. He began experi-ments, and found a surprising number of folks willing to let him cut their grass "for fifteen cents."

Dick got his father's permission to bor-row the lawn-mower, and began his busi-ness career. He tackled a little lawn first, and finished the job, as he thought, before demanding payment. But his employer was a sharp-eyed little old lady, who came out on her veranda and pointed accusingly to the rough edges of the grass around her flower-beds and along her walks.

"You must trim that up," she told him. "The job is n't finished till you do."

Dick had forgotten that part of the task. He hurried home to get a sickle and set to work. Using a sickle had seemed easy enough when others did it, but Dick found it far from that. The blade seemed to slide through the grass without making the slightest impression, and more than once it darted around alarmingly near his ankles. He was reduced, at length, to picking the rough grass off with his fingers, or to holding a bunch with his hand while he sawed it loose with the sickle.

He got the job done at last. It took two of his afternoons after school, and, by that time, half of his other prospective customers had found some one else to do the work for them. He asked his first client if he should come again the following week.

"Oh, no," she told him, "it 's so late in the fall that I 'm sure it won't need cutting again this year."

Dick pocketed his fifteen cents gloomily. He had earned his money, but his occupation was gone. Within the week he had cut two more lawns. One was terraced, and the strain of running the lawn-mower along the slanting surface of the terraces was all but too much for him. He literally chewed that grass off. It took him all Saturday morning, and when it was done, the man who owned the lawn came out and looked sternly at the finished product and said:

"Young man, that is n't a good clean job! I don't want to refuse you your money, but it will be a lesson to you to do things properly. I can't pay you unless you go over the lawn again."

Dick looked at those terraces. "We-ell," he said doubtfully, "I—guess I 'd rather let the fifteen cents go."

That cured Dick of the lawn business. He realized there was no money in it, and set about to find new sources of revenue. He found them; but in them all, he discovered, money came hard. He began to have a new respect for money. Heretofore, he had felt somewhat injured at his father's occasional refusal of a request for a coin. Now he began to wonder whether his father had to work as hard as this for the money he earned. It gave him a new outlook on many things.

His mother discovered Dick's new desire for income, and, watching him for a few days, saw that it persisted. She decided to encourage it.

"Dick," she said one day, "I think you ought to have a chance to earn money regularly, don't you?"

Dick look at her in surprise. His mother had a curious habit, it seemed, of reading his heart and his thoughts. *"Uh-huh,"* he said doubtfully. "Yes, I think so."

"Well, I 'll tell you," she suggested. "I believe I will put you on a salary."

"Salary?" he repeated.

"Yes, salary. I think I 'll pay you twenty-five cents a week for your chores around the house, and, say, a cent a hundred strokes for the pumping you do."

She watched him, and Dick's eyes grew glassy with the mental effort of computation; then his face lighted eagerly.

"All right," he said soberly. "I—guess that 'd be fine."

The tank in the attic needed to be filled about three times a week. That meant about forty-five hundred strokes—forty-five cents a week besides the quarter for chores. Seventy cents a week! Riches! He went to his room and laboriously added up. He would have the six dollars, he decided, by the third week in November—by Thanksgiving!

"Golly!" he thought. "And I 'll bet there 'll come a big snow then, too. There 's pretty near always snow Thanksgiving."

A little later his mother heard the pump in the kitchen working desperately, and she smiled to herself. That night Dick, of his own accord, took a bath. Next night he did the same. She smiled again and told Dick's father what she had done.

"The boy 's making a market for his own work; he 's using up the water so the tank will have to be filled oftener," she explained.

"Hope it 'll last!" his father retorted.

THANKSGIVING that year came on the twenty-fourth of November. On the seventeenth Dick counted his money. He had five dollars and thirty cents. His goal, those snowshoes, was in sight!

On the Sunday before Thanksgiving, Dick's mother told his father, "I 've ordered our turkey again this year from Mr. Aiken out in the country."

"Good!" his father agreed. "He sent us a fine fat one last year."

"And I think," Mrs. Hart added, "that we 're going to have the finest pumpkin pie you ever saw. Mr. Aiken says he has a big yellow pumpkin all picked out for us."

Dick's mouth fairly watered. Next morning Mrs. Attson came to do the washing, as usual. She and Dick were the best of friends now, though Dick, as he had begun to earn wages by his efforts, had the conscience to do his own pumping. Dick toiled at the pump while she toiled above the tubs. He watched her over his shoulder, and it seemed that she was even more gaunt than she had been in the summer. She looked worried, too, he thought.

By and by he was sure of it, for she began to tell him what it was that was worrying her. One of her daughters was sick, "just sort of pindling away," Mrs. Attson said. Did n't seem to feel right, no matter what happened; had n't any appetite hardly at all. Did n't he think even little girls ought to have good appetites for their "vittles"?

Dick did. "I don't see how she can enjoy Thanksgiving without a good appetite," he said, chuckling to himself at thought of the good things his mother was planning.

Mrs. Attson smiled also. "I 'm plannin' a right nice Thanksgiving dinner for her, too," she declared. "If it don't make her hungry, I don't know what will."

Dick labored away at the pump.

"What are you going to have?" he asked.

Mrs. Attson beamed proudly. "Why," she said, "I 'm plannin' a right nice dinner, even if we do have to piece out afterwards for a spell." She soused one of Dick's shirts in the soapy water, and scrubbed it up and down, and soused it again. "I 'm going to git a nice piece of meat, not chuck like we has Sundays sometimes, but a right nice piece. Rump steak, maybe. And she 's going to have the best part of it. And some rice and potatoes—sweet potatoes fried in sugar the way she likes 'em. And I 'm going to make some apple fritters from some apples I got, too."

Dick pumped his hardest, but he could n't look at Mrs. Attson. Her voice was so proud! And Dick was horrified. He had supposed every one had turkey for Thanksgiving. He did n't know there was such a thing as Thanksgiving without turkey. Why it would n't *be* Thanksgiving without turkey, that 's all!

He pumped harder than ever; and then Mrs. Attson asked, as proudly as before, "Don't you think that ought to wake up her appetite a lot?"

"I—sure do," Dick choked hurriedly. Then he growled something at himself under his breath. What the deuce was he crying for, anyhow? Guess it must be the steam in this kitchen—or something.

He decided not to finish his pumping that day. He turned around without a word and scurried past Mrs. Attson and up to his room. After a little while he heard the pump going steadily. She was filling the tank for him! He got up and started downstairs to stop her—but he could not face her. She was so proud of that Thanksgiving she had planned. Rump steak!

"Mother, is—rump steak cheap?" he asked that night.

"Why yes, dear," his mother answered. "Why in the world—"

But she did not pursue the question.

Before he went to bed, Dick counted his money again. Somehow he felt guilty at having so much.

Tuesday morning, when he woke up, it was snowing. It snowed all day. There were ten inches of snow on the ground when Dick's father came home that night. Dick looked out of his window before he went to bed. It had stopped snowing. But before the dawn, the flakes were falling again, a thin, driving snow, the kind that keeps coming.

Dick had had an uncomfortable Tuesday; he had done some hard thinking Tuesday night; and Wednesday morning he got out his money—he kept in a drawer in his bureau—and counted it again. Then he did some more thinking, then put the money away again and thrust the drawer shut with extra emphasis. And forthwith he seemed to see the tall, gaunt figure of a woman with a face curiously like that of Lincoln, and she was laboring with something, her shoulders rising and falling. She was working the red-and-black handle of a red-and-black pump—

Then Dick could see nothing, for the mistiness of his eyes. But he could hear a cracked, tired voice, filled with infinite

pride, saying, "Rump steak, maybe, and some rice and potatoes."

"Oh—oh—oh, doggone it!" Dick exclaimed savagely; and he jerked open that drawer and picked up his money, coin by coin.

"WHAT are you buying a turkey for?" Mr. Holman, the fat grocer, asked quizzically when Dick made his purchase.

"Oh—I'm just getting one—for somebody," Dick explained lamely. "And—I want some cranberries, too. And a pumpkin. A big one."

MRS. ATTSON lived in a ramshackle little house, unpainted, with a sway-backed roof, down near the railroad tracks. Dick had hauled the washing down there once or twice when his mother did not wish the work done at their home. He trudged down that way through the deep snow in the early dusk of that Wednesday afternoon, with a heavily loaded basket on his arm. It had been snowing all day. There must be a foot and a half or two feet of snow on the ground, a record-breaker for Forestville.

Dick didn't mind—so much. "I prob'ly could n't walk on them if I had 'em," he said to himself.

Nobody saw him, he felt sure. It was almost dark. There was a light in the window of Mrs. Attson's house, so he knew some one was at home. He laid the basket gently in the deep snow by the door, and then slipped out to the street, where, from behind a telephone-pole, he threw snowballs at the door till he caught the click of the latch. Some one was going to open it.

Then he put down his head and fled.

HIS father had not come home when he arrived, but his mother was reading a letter from the older brother at college. "Jim says they 're having snow up there, too," she said. "He 's been snow-shoeing. And Dick—he says you said something about buying some snow-shoes. Did you?"

Dick flushed painfully. "Why—yes 'm," he confessed.

She looked at him thoughtfully. "Dickie," she exclaimed suddenly, "was that why you 've been working so hard, and saving your money? I knew you were n't spending any, and I wondered!"

"Uh-huh," Dick admitted, gulping hard.

"That 's fine, boy!" she told him proudly. "How much have you saved? Perhaps I can make up what you need."

Dick hesitated and kicked at a chair and threw his hat out into the hall. "I—I—it 's gone!" he said gruffly.

"Gone!—what?" she asked, puzzled.

"The money," he said.

"But—but—where?"

Dick suddenly flared at her. "If I knowed where it was would n't I go get it?" he demanded. And then, quite suddenly, he knew he was going to blubber, and so he turned and stumbled at a run up the stairs to his room.

His mother was still staring out into the hall when his father came home. She rose to help Mr. Hart off with his coat.

"Oh, by the way," said that gentleman, when their greetings were over, "Holman told me Dick bought a turkey and all the fixings there today. Why was that? Did n't Aiken's bird come?"

"Why—yes!" said Mrs. Hart in a puzzled tone. "I don't know what it was for."

"Is he here?" Mr. Hart asked; then called: "Hey! Dick!"

Dick opened his door upstairs. "What?" he growled.

"Who was it you were buying a turkey for, Dick?" his father asked.

Mr. and Mrs. Hart looked up to the darkened upper hall, but Dick did not ap-

pear at the banisters. Presently—the pause was curious—the boy answered slowly:

"Oh—I was just doing an errand for Mrs. Thompson. She forgot to do hers—till to-day—to do her shopping."

They heard his door close.

"That sounds funny!" Mr. Hart remarked after a minute. "Suppose you call up Mrs. Thompson and ask her about it."

Dick's mother smiled and stepped to the telephone.

She had just finished talking to Mrs. Thompson when the bell rang again. She answered, and spoke softly for a moment before she rejoined her husband in the living-room. There were happy tears in her eyes.

"Mrs. Attson just called up," she said gently. "She wanted to thank us. Some one left a Thanksgiving basket at their door to-day—to-night. Mrs. Hughes, across the road, saw the boy. It was Dickie. Mrs. Attson thought we had sent him with it."

Mr. Hart's eyes widened ludicrously. "Great fishes!" he cried. "But—where did that boy get the money?"

Mrs. Hart told him, then, of the little hoard Dick had said was "gone."

"The—darned little scamp!" Mr. Hart exclaimed. "Telling you a lie like that. *Huh!*"

"Not exactly," declared Mrs. Hart. "And he really *did* do a small errand at Holman's for Mrs. Thompson, she told me."

Thereafter they sat for a little space, staring into the fire. And then Mr. Hart rose suddenly and went to the telephone in the hall. "Telegraph office," he directed the operator.

WHEN Dick came down to supper, his parents smiled at him knowingly. He looked—

and felt—sheepish; and he felt more so when, without preamble, his father said, in what he evidently intended to be an offhand manner:

"By the way, Dick—thought you might want to have some fun with this snow. So I telegraphed to Chicago just now. They 're to send the best pair of snow-shoes in town—by express. Be here by Saturday."

Dick looked at his father, and then he looked at his mother. Mr. Hart coughed gruffly. His mother smiled happily through her tears. Dick choked, and grinned; his eyes were glowing—and wet.

"*Huh*—thanks, Dad!" he said.

THE GRANDILOQUENT GOAT

by Carolyn Wells

A very grandiloquent goat
  Sat down to a gay table d'hote;
    He ate all the corks,
    The knives and the forks,
Remarking; "On these things I dote."

Then before his repast he began,
  While pausing the menu to scan,
    He said: "Corn, if you please,
    And tomatoes and pease,
I'd like to have served in the can."

"BRIN"

by Dr. Wilfred T. Grenfell

WE were a hundred miles from hospital, on the west coast of the long promontory of north Newfoundland that lies between two branches of the polar current. A fortnight since, we had left our harbor of St. Anthony. As things had been quiet there, my new associate had decided to accompany me, in order that he might become familiar with the country which, next winter, he would have to travel alone. We were out giving our dogs an extra feed overnight, preparatory to starting back on the morrow.

It takes all the attention of two men to feed a team of husky dogs, if you wish to make sure that they share anywhere near alike. For not only is there a master dog, who takes all he wants anyhow, but eacn single dog knows exactly which of the others he can bully. It does n't in the least matter how good a piece may fall to him, if he sees another with apparently a better, he will immediately fly at him. The result often is that before they have settled the dispute, both pieces have vanished to their mates, and only fresh assaults and batteries will save the two contestants from going supperless.

Thus it happened our minds were so oc-cupied that the approach of a large team of dogs from the north escaped our notice. Stimulated by the well-recognized signs of a meal, the new arrivals, turning deaf ears to the cries of the man who was driving them, and who was now clinging to the sledge with both hands for dear life, simply leaped into the middle of the fracas. Before a word could be said, the sledge was capsized, the driver was sprawling beneath it, and heaving, writhing, yelping masses of fur were enjoying the one attraction superior to a meal—a good, straight fight, quite regardless of the fact that the champions of one side were still tied to their sledge, and were rapidly snarling up themselves and everything else in an utterly inextricable tangle. It went greatly against the grain to have to whip our dogs off, but under the circumstances there was no alternative. Worse still, it left the victors in possession of the supper, when our sympathies were entirely with our own team.

This irritating incident had not materially helped us to appreciate the message that Joe, the driver of the new arrivals, blurted out as soon as the dogs were quieted.

"They is wanting you in Island Harbor, Doctor. They does n't know what t' sickness be."

"Oh, that 's it—eh? How long since you left?"

"Only two days, Doctor. I got as far as the Green Ridge tilt (or shelter-hut) first night."

"Why, you came all around by the coast, did n't you?"

"Only as far as Caplin Cove Tickle. None of us had ever been straight across the Cloudy Hills. There be no track, and it 's nigh impossible to find t' cut path through t' big woods from there out here unless you know every inch of it."

Now it could n't be more than sixty or seventy miles across country to the place we wanted to reach, and it would be nearly twice that distance to go around. We could count on covering the former distance in a day, if only we could follow the trail. But that was just where the rub came. If you once lost it, it would be an endless task getting a team of dogs through the dense, stunted spruce forests with their windfalls of ages, which make them like one huge battle stockade, and with countless pitfalls, too, hidden under light snow coverings between the logs where you only crawl over one to fall into the next. We had had more than one experience of that kind, and had had to abandon our sledges and exhausted dogs while, foot-sore and frozen, we struggled on without them.

It was a great dilemma. For not only did every sporting instinct cry out, "Have a fling at the cross-country route!" but success in the venture also meant that we should reach our desired haven a day sooner. *Could* we keep the trail?

Naturally, it was the topic of the evening as soon as our pipes were lit, and just as naturally half our friends were on one side and half on the other. But soon the crackling sound of footsteps on the crisp snow outside warned us of the approach of a new-comer.

The door was opened with the assurance of an old acquaintance, and a hearty chorus of welcome greeted the muffled figure that stopped to beat the snow off itself in the porch.

"Harry," said one, "you 've just struck it right this time. Here 's t' doctor wants to cross the country to-morrow. Can you help him?"

We found Harry had come in a hurry to get help to bring out two stags he had killed, and as he had not "scaffolded" them out of the reach of animals, he had to go right back in the morning.

"I 'll tell you what I 'll do, Doctor," he suddenly volunteered; "I won't see you left. If it *is* a bit of a round, I 'll come with you as far as the big white marsh, and then if you 'se don't get t'rough before dark, you 'll surely find one of the Gray Cove men's tilts." And I saw his keen black eyes fixed on mine as if the sudden inspiration had relieved him of a burden.

"Thank you, Harry. That settles it, indeed, and try it we will, whatever comes of it."

It was unfortunate that my fellow-doctor and I had decided to leave our usual driver at home on this trip for he had crossed this very route the year previous. When we left, we had intended to return by the well-worn coast trail, in which case a driver's room would have been better than his weight on the sledges. We had left him, moreover, our good team of dogs, as there were a number of logs to be hauled home from the woods, more, indeed than we could expect to handle before the going broke up. The result was, that of all our last year's team, we had only one dog with us, a yellowish brown dog with queer black-striped markings somewhat like a Bengal tiger. These lent to his sinister face the suggestion that he was eternally grinning—an impression intensified by an odd way he had of turning up the corners of his mouth when he caught one's eye. He went by the name of "Brin."

I had reared this dog myself, and run him his second winter as my leader, though he was then little better than a pup. On several occasions he had displayed unusual instinct for direction. Very soon after his first promotion, I had been compelled to run eighteen miles, mostly over sea ice, without seeing any intervening house, in a blizzard of snow and a head wind. It was quite impossible to do any steering, as the driving snow, with no wind-break, made seeing to windward out of the question. But the pup had proved his mettle by coming up without a hitch at the door of the house we wished to find, as it marked the spot where the shore trail turned to cross the neck of land. Thus, of all the party, Brin alone had ever seen the trail we were now proposing to take, and he had only crossed it once. It had, moreover, been very bad weather all the way. No one could say, of course, how much his memory could be counted on, but, personally, I was prepared to bank a good deal on it.

An hour or so more was spent in discussing the way. Indeed, I traced out a rough map of the trail according to Harry's ideas of it. Begining with our present position, I drew in ponds, barrens, marshes, woods as he called them out, and arranged them in order as he said the road led next to the right or left. It was a weird-looking picture when we finished it.

When it had received the final verdict, "It 's as good as us can do," the company began to break up, and we lost no time in turning in, as we would have to be on foot before daylight if we hoped to "reach over" before dark.

The sky was overcast, and it was cold

and still dark as we collected our dogs next morning for the long run across country. But they were well trained to respond to our call, and though hidden away in every conceivable corner, or under houses, or often buried in the snow, they were soon rubbing their noses against our hands.

Harry and his comrade, with a large team of their own that knew that section of the country like a book, made the running all morning, and as we were climbing most of the time, it was just as well for our teams that we had only one man on each sledge. Of course we had had to bring along our medical stores and food supplies.

Nothing of any particular interest transpired till we broke out from the woods by the Hanging Marsh about ten in the morning. Indeed, nothing well could, for the path was broken for us by our pilots. However, here they had to leave us, and we halted under some large spruce-trees to boil a "mug of tea," while we received our final instructions. "It is all easy enough if you know it," were Harry's last words, as he bade us good-by.

The main thing that interested me, however, while he was talking, was the fact that there was n't a mark of any kind on the face of the Hanging Marsh. I had noticed that even the blazes on the trees near the houses, which were far more numerous and fresher than any we could hope to find for many miles to come, were so obscured by glitter, that is, ice frozen on the tree stems, that had we been without our pilots, we should have lost our way a dozen times already. As we chatted over a cup of hot tea and a pork bun, that most delectable invention, as it won't freeze, however cold the day may be, we dragged out the map which we had made the night before.

Having pointed out that the direction in which we must steer across the marsh was toward a tall spruce that towered up in solitary state above the rest of the trees, our good-natured guides returned on their tracks. It was already obvious to both of us doctors that we had not the slightest chance of finding the trail. Our only assets were our pocket-compasses giving us the general direction, our axes to clear a path when we should get stogged, a hopeful disposition which never spoiled for troubles till they came along, and—Brin.

Whether he knew his importance or not at the moment, I never could tell. But a light seemed to dance in his eyes, and his queer face assumed a fairly impish aspect as he strutted about at the end of his long leading trace. I remember he kept looking back and grinning at us as he waited for the word "go."

"Don't say a word," shouted my chum from the sledge behind. "Let 's see if he 'll head right,—across the marsh anyhow."

"All right," I called back. "Mum 's the word.—GO!"

And we simultaneously cut the lines holding the sledges back to keep the excited dogs from running away before we were ready.

Prosaic as it may seem to others, it was a moment of real excitement to us when Brin led off at a stretch gallop in an absolute line for the tall lone spruce. As we whisked by it, I can almost swear he looked back at me and winked, and although twelve fathoms away, I fancied I caught the sound of an unearthly chuckle from him.

The snow surface on these highlands was splendid, and the dogs were in a mood to go. So we just "sat tight" and let them. For the trail now led through wooded country, and we were Indians enough from years of experience to notice that we were keeping to the old cut path, in spite of having to circumvent many snags in it. Shortly, however, we struck more open country,

and as the trees were now scattered like those in an orchard, the path might have been anywhere. We could only watch the dog, who, though he had slackened somewhat, was still trotting along merrily, and as unconcerned as if he had n't yet discovered there was any problem to be solved. Somewhere about ten miles from the marsh, in just such a setting as we were now passing through, we had marked on our map that a forked juniper-tree was standing by itself in the middle of a long lead. The top boughs had been stripped from it, and the skull and antlers of an old caribou fixed in the cleft.

The utter inaccuracy of the map had led me to forget this landmark, and I was more than surprised to hear my chum suddenly shout out, "There she is!"

"There 's what?" I exclaimed.

"Why, the skull in the tree," he responded.

As we use no reins to guide the dogs, we rely entirely on our voices to swing them to the right or left. A good leader obeys instinctively even at top speed, without apparently taking notice otherwise. On this occasion we both thought Brin looked around and laughed. But even if he did n't, we did, for our spirits went up with a bound as we realized we were still all right, and another ten miles lay behind us.

A little later we passed the top ridge of the Cloudy Hills. Here the going was good, because there were no longer even scrub trees to worry us. Moreover, there could be no doubt of the right direction, as there was only one gap through which we could well go.

From the outlet of the gorge we should have seen the sea some twenty miles below us. But the shadows of evening were already drawn too close, and the sky was still overcast. There seemed to lie between us and our goal nothing but endless miles of rolling forest. It appeared folly to ex-

pect to get through before morning. Yet if
we were going to camp at all, now was the
time to get a shelter built while we could
still see.

How much longer could we trust Brin?
He had swung off almost at right angles
after emerging from the pass, and was now
guiding his followers along the upper edge
of the woods. It seemed at last as if he were
seeking something and was uncertain
where to enter. But he showed no doubt
about what to do a minute later, for, without even slackening speed, he dashed into
the forest. I looked back and caught the
eye of my companion, and I saw he also
had noticed a half-covered blaze on the
trunk of a birch to the side of us. Down—
down—down we went, the cut path every
now and again obscured by growing saplings or blocked by windfalls which had to
be carefully negotiated. But they counted
for nothing beside the fact that every minute was shortening the distance, and we
were obviously still on the track.

Time passes quickly steering a loaded
sledge down through woods. You want
all your skill and strength to steer clear
of stumps and snags. Every now and again,
even with the best of teams, some dog
will turn the wrong side of an obstruction,
and the whole team is suddenly brought
up "standing." As a rule it is not a very
long matter to haul back the prodigal, and
sling him round after the others, though
when he finds he is being dragged back,
he just hauls for all he is worth, thinking
he is going to be whipped. The presence
of a new dog in the team, named Snowball, added a new and very definite element
of trouble. For a sudden check would fling
the dogs all together in a heap, and they
seemed invariably to associate him with
the cause of their last night's trouble, which
they greatly resented. The unfortunate
Snowball was, of course, forced to defend
himself, and the process of separating the

contestants often enough drove several
more dogs around tree trunks. So that the
fracas had to end by clearing them all out
and making an entirely new start.

At the foot of the first range, the valley
contained a long lake onto which we ran
out squarely at right angles. Facing us
was a steep bluff, and the lake seemed to
end below in a narrow defile through
which we guessed the river escaped, and
toward which we, of course, expected to
turn. But no such notion apparently entered Brin's head. He made exactly for
the opposite direction, and then, crossing a
narrow portion of the lake, started to climb
the hill in front of us. The excellent en-
gineering of this move only became apparent when, after a few moments, we
were once more through a pass and discovered that we were at the head of a
second valley that led in exactly the opposite way. No marks of any kind
were visible, and it was now a long while
since we had seen any indications that
we were following a trail. We had hoped
before this to see at least snowshoe marks
of hunters from the coast. But nothing of
that kind either was discernible. However,
Brin continued to gallop down the sloping hillside, and there was nothing for
us to do but "sit tight and look on."

As we swung around a big drift of snow,
over an unusually large boulder, a very
fresh fox track ran directly down "the
bluff." Without once looking back, Brin
jumped right into it, his unquestioning
comrades following him only too gladly.
The pace at once increased, and it seemed
as if we were being made mere fools of,
while the dogs had a good time hunting.
It was mighty hard not to "butt in" and
tell a "mere dog" which way to go. But
then we did n't know which way we *did*
want to go! I looked round, however, to
see whether my comrade had noticed the
turn of events. "It 's a case of walking by

faith, I reckon," he shouted. "Do you suppose Brin knows what he 's after?" The sound of his name evidently apprized the dog that we were discussing him, for even at the pace at which we were now going, he found time to fling his impish head around and fairly grin in our faces.

I never would have believed that an ordinary fox trail could cause so much worry for a man. But when we were still following that unspeakable beast's footsteps after a full mile had elapsed, it became almost impossible not to interfere. For the likelihood that a fox was really heading for the village we were seeking seemed absurd. All of a sudden this idea was apparently proven correct beyond the possibility of doubt, for we crossed the tracks of a man's snow-shoes at right angles to our path. It was too much for us, so we halted the dogs, and, donning our own shoes, we followed the marks each way to see if they gave any clue as to how to proceed. Luckily for us, we soon found signs that the man was hunting, for his trail doubled on itself twice, and we knew he at least was not going in or out of the country.

"What 's the best thing to do, John? There 's still time to make a camp before dark. That fiend of a dog seems cock-sure of his way. But I don't know if the devil is n't in the beast. Look at his face. He looks possessed, if ever a dog did."

Brin was sitting bolt upright on his haunches and was staring directly at us—for all the world as if he understood exactly what we were saying. As he caught my eye, he put his head on one side and actually poked out his tongue. It was surely quite unnecessary to begin to pant just at that moment. But he maintained so inscrutable a mien, without even a blink, that though I half unconsciously picked up my whip as if to teach him to "quit fooling," I had n't the heart to flick it.

It was getting late, and I felt we really ought to do something at once. "What do you say to blindfolding him? Perhaps then he 'll leave this miserable fox track," I suggested.

"I 'm for giving him another chance," was the trustful reply.

"All right, then, 'Barkis is willing,'" and I threw myself onto the sledge with a "Hist" to the dogs to go "just where they jolly well liked!" Bother, if they did n't again start off at a trot along that unspeakable fox track! But at last we came out onto the bed of the river, and I saw the fox tracks disappear into the willows.

It was with real relief that we proceeded to follow the river for a time. The low banks had allowed the wind to blow the snow away, and the resulting good ice surface, together with the drop of the stream, made it easy to cover the miles at our leisure. Moreover, we knew the river must lead to the sea some time. Our hopes rose so high that we positively took the time to warm up the kettle and get our second "mug of tea" for the day. When we again started, the valley narrowed, and the river-bed was blocked with snow, while every here and there were great chasms that revealed the rushing water beneath. Worse still, the river ended abruptly in a huge lake with, at least, one large island in it. Nor was there the faintest indication now as to whether we should turn to the north, south, east, or west.

It seemed possible, however, to leave the east out of our reckoning, because in that direction we could see, across the lake, a high range of hills rising. Yet without hesitation Brin headed straight for them! On—on—on—till at last we came to the woods flanking the lake. The dogs instantly went straight into the forest, and in half a minute were on opposite sides of a dozen trees.

"That settles it, John. The sooner we

make a shelter for the night the better," I said, as I started to find a dry tree with which to light a fire.

John stood ruefully looking at the dogs. Apparently, he had counted even more on Brin than I had, and he said afterward he felt as if the bottom had fallen out of his faith in everything. The dogs, glad of a rest, lay down where they were and started chewing the icicles out of their fur. Brin alone, who was at the end of the longest trace, had it stretched out to its full length, and so he was nearly hidden by the bushes. But I could see he was standing up and looking back as he used to when the team slacked and he was accustomed to come back and snap at them. His odd manner influenced me enough to start off in his direction after I had turned over the sledge. To my amazement I found he was standing in a well-cut path which ran at an acute angle up the side of the hill! He had tried a short cut into it, about ten yards before it opened onto the lake!

There was no trouble after this. Once over the hill, we struck the wood path of the Gray Cove men, and by eight P.M. had brought up outside my patient's house. We were both able to tell "what t' sickness was," and to be of some service.

Before turning in, I went out to see what the night was like, and to make sure that Snowball was safely fastened up. For I knew he would steal home again the moment he got the chance. Everything was all right, however, and the tired dogs were stowed away somewhere asleep. My hand was on the latch of the cottage door, and I was about to reënter and turn in, when something warm and furry rubbed gently against my leg. By the light that streamed out of the open door, I found myself looking right down into Brin's eyes. They were asking, in as plain English as could be written, "How did I please you to-day, Master?" I could n't help putting my arms around his neck and hugging him! Then we both went off to our beds the happier for it.

CASPERL

by H. C. Bunner

CASPERL was a wood-chopper, and the son of a wood-chopper, and although he was only eighteen when his father died, he was so strong and active that he went on chopping and hauling wood for the whole neighborhood, and people said he did it quite as well as his father, while he was certainly a great deal more pleasant in his manner and much more willing to oblige others.

It was a poor country, however, for it was right in the heart of the Black Forest, and there were more witches and fairies and goblins there than healthy human beings. So Casperl scarcely made a living, for all he worked hard and rose up early in the morning, summer and winter. His friends often advised him to go to some better place, where he could earn more money; but he only shook his head and said that the place was good enough for him.

He never told any one, though, why he loved his poor hut in the depths of the dark forest, because it was a secret which he did not wish to share with strangers. For he had discovered, a mile or two from his home, in the very blackest part of the woods, an enchanted mountain. It was a high mountain, covered with trees and rocks and thick, tangled undergrowth, except at the very top, where there stood a castle surrounded by smooth, green lawns and beautiful gardens, which were always kept in the neatest possible order, although no gardener was ever seen.

This enchanted mountain had been under a spell for nearly two hundred years. The lovely Princess who lived there had once ruled the whole country. But a powerful and wicked magician disguised himself as a prince, and made love to her. At first the Princess loved her false suitor; but one day she found out that he was not what he pretended to be, and she told him to leave her and never to come near her again.

"For you are not a prince," she said. "You are an impostor, and I will never wed any but a true prince."

"Very well," said the magician, in a rage. "You shall wait for your true prince, if there is such a thing as a true prince; and you shall marry no one till he comes."

And then the magician cast a spell upon the beautiful castle on the top of the mountain, and the terrible forest sprang up about it. Rocks rose up out of the earth and piled themselves in great heaps among the tree-trunks. Saplings and brush and twisted, poisonous vines came to fill up every crack and crevice, so that no mortal man could possibly go to the summit, except by one path, which was purposely left clear. And in that path there was a gate that the strongest man could not open, it was so heavy. Farther up the mountain-slope, the trunk of a tree lay

313

right across the way,—a magic tree, that no one could climb over or crawl under or cut through. And beyond the gate and the tree was a dragon with green eyes that frightened away every man that looked at it.

And there the beautiful Princess was doomed to live until the true prince should arrive and overcome these three obstacles.

Now, although none of the people in the forest, except Casperl, knew of the mountain or the Princess, the story had been told in many distant countries, and year after year young princes came from all parts of the earth to try to rescue the lovely captive and win her for a bride. But, one after the other, they all tried and failed,—the best of them could not so much as open the gate.

And so there the Princess remained, as the years went on. But she did not grow any older, or any less beautiful, for she was still waiting for the True Prince, and she believed that some day he would come.

This was what kept Casperl from leaving the Black Forest. He was sorry for the Princess, and he hoped some day to see her rescued and wedded to the True Prince.

Every evening, when his work was done, he would walk to the foot of the mountain, and sit down on a great stone, and look up to the top, where the Princess was walking in her garden. And as it was an enchanted mountain, he could see her clearly, although she was so far away. Yes, he could see her face as well as though she were close by him, and he thought it was truly the loveliest face in the world.

There he would sit and sadly watch the princes who tried to climb the hill. There was scarcely a day that some prince from a far country did not come to make the attempt. One after another, they would arrive with gorgeous trains of followers, mounted on fine horses, and dressed in costumes so magnificent that a plain cloth-of-gold suit looked shabby among them. They would look up to the mountain-top and see the Princess walking there, and they would praise her beauty so warmly that Casperl, when he heard them, felt sure he was quite right in thinking her the loveliest woman in the world.

But every prince had to make the trial by himself. That was one of the conditions which the magician made when he laid the spell upon the castle; although Casperl did not know it.

And each prince would throw off his cloak, and shoulder a silver or gold-handled ax, and fasten his sword by his side, and set out to climb the hill, and open the gate, and cut through the fallen tree, and slay the dragon, and wed the Princess.

Up he would go, bright and hopeful, and tug away at the gate until he found that he could do nothing with it, and then he would plunge into the tangled thickets of underbrush, and try his best to fight his way through to the summit.

But every one of them came back, after a while, with his fine clothes torn and his soft skin scratched, all tired and disheartened and worn out. And then he would look spitefully up at the mountain, and say he did n't care so much about wedding the Princess, after all; that she was only a common enchanted princess, just like any other enchanted princess, and really not worth so much trouble.

This would grieve Casperl, for he could n't help thinking that it was impossible that any other woman could be as lovely as *his* Princess. You see, he called her *his* Princess, because he took such an interest in her, and he did n't think there could be any harm in speaking of her in that way, just to himself. For he never supposed she could even know that there was such a humble creature as poor young

Casperl, the wood-chopper, who sat at the foot of the hill and looked up at her.

And so the days went on, and the unlucky princes came and went, and Casperl watched them all. Sometimes he saw his Princess look down from over the castle parapets, and eagerly follow with her lovely eyes the struggles of some brave suitor through the thickets, until the poor Prince gave up the job in despair. Then she would look sad and turn away. But generally she paid no attention to the attempts that were made to reach her. That kind of thing had been going on so long that she was quite used to it.

By and by, one summer evening, as Casperl sat watching, there came a little prince with a small train of attendants. He was rather undersized for a prince; he did n't look strong, and he did look as though he slept too much in the morning and too little at night. He slipped off his coat, however, and climbed up the road, and began to push and pull at the gate.

Casperl watched him carelessly for a while, and then, happening to look up, he saw that the Princess was gazing sadly down on the poor little Prince as he tugged and toiled.

And then a bold idea came to Casperl. Why should n't he help the Prince? He was young and strong; he had often thought that, if he were a prince, a gate like that should not keep him away from the Princess. Why, indeed, should he not give his strength to help to free the Princess? And he felt a great pity for the poor little Prince, too.

So he walked modestly up the hill and offered his services to the Prince.

"Your Royal Highness," he said, "I am only a wood-chopper; but, if you please, I am a strong wood-chopper, and perhaps I can be of use to you."

"But why should you take the trouble to help me?" inquired the Prince. "What good will it do you?"

"Oh, well!" said Casperl, "it 's helping the Princess, too, don't you know?"

"No, I don't know," said the Prince. "However, you may try what you can do. Here, put your shoulder to this end of the gate, and I will stand right behind you."

Now, Casperl did not know that it was forbidden to any suitor to have help in his attempt to climb the hill. The Prince knew it, though, but he said to himself, "When I am through with this wood-chopper I will dismiss him, and no one will know anything about it. I can never lift this gate by myself. I will let him do it for me, and thus I shall get the Princess, and he will be just as well satisfied, for he is only a wood-chopper."

So Casperl put his broad shoulder to the gate and pushed with all his might. It was very heavy, but after a while it began to move a little.

"Courage, your Royal Highness!" said Casperl. "We 'll move it, after all." But if he had looked over his shoulder, he would have seen that the little Prince was not pushing at all, but that he had put on his cloak, and was standing idly by, laughing to himself at the way he was making a wood-chopper do his work for him.

After a long struggle, the gate gave way, and swung open just wide enough to let them through. It was a close squeeze for the Prince; but Casperl held the gate open until he slipped through.

"Dear me," said the Prince, "you 're quite a strong fellow. You really were of some assistance to me. Let me see, I think the stories say something about a tree, or some such thing, farther up the road. As you are a wood-chopper, and as you have your ax with you, perhaps you might walk up a bit and see if you can't make yourself useful."

Casperl was quite willing, for he began to feel that he was doing something for the Princess, and it pleased him to think that even a wood-chopper could do her a service.

So they walked up until they came to the tree. And then the Prince drew out his silver ax, and sharpened it carefully on the sole of his shoe, while Casperl picked up a stone and whetted his old iron ax, which was all he had.

"Now," said the Prince, "let 's see what we can do."

But he really did n't do anything. It was Casperl who swung his ax and chopped hard at the magic tree. Every blow made the chips fly; but the wood grew instantly over every cut, just as though he had been cutting into water.

For a little while the Prince amused himself by trying first to climb over the tree, and then to crawl under it. But he soon found that whichever way he went, the tree grew up or down so fast that he was shut off. Finally he gave it up, and went and lay down on his back on the grass, and watched Casperl working.

And Casperl worked hard. The tree grew fast; but he chopped faster. His forehead was wet and his arms were tired, but he worked away and made the chips fly in a cloud. He was too busy to take the time to look over his shoulder, so he did not see the Prince lying on the grass. But every now and then he spoke cheerily, saying, "We 'll do it, your Royal Highness!"

And he did it, in the end. After a long, long while, he got the better of the magic tree, for he chopped quicker than it could grow, and at last he had cut a gap right across the trunk.

The Prince jumped up from the grass and leaped nimbly through, and Casperl followed him slowly and sadly, for he was tired, and it began to occur to him that the Prince had n't said anything about the Princess, which made him wonder if he were the True Prince, after all. "I 'm afraid," he thought, "the Princess won't thank me if I bring her a prince who does n't love her. And it really is very strange that this Prince has n't said a word about her."

So he ventured to remark, very meekly: "Your Royal Highness will be glad to see the Princess."

"Oh, no doubt," said the Prince.

"And the Princess will be very glad to see your Royal Highness," went on Casperl.

"Oh, of course!" said the Prince.

"And your Royal Highness will be very good to the Princess," said Casperl further, by way of a hint.

"I think," said the Prince, "that you are talking altogether too much about the Princess. I don't believe I need you any more. Perhaps you would better go home. I 'm much obliged to you for your assistance. I can't reward you just now, but if you will come to see me after I have married the Princess, I may be able to do something for you."

Casperl turned away, somewhat disappointed, and was going down the hill, when the Prince called him back.

"Oh, by the way!" he said; "there 's a dragon, I understand, a little farther on. Perhaps you 'd like to come along and see me kill him?"

Casperl thought he would like to see the Prince do something for the Princess, so he followed meekly on. Very soon they came to the top of the mountain, and saw the green lawns and beautiful gardens of the enchanted castle,—and there was the dragon waiting for them.

The dragon reared itself on its dreadful tail, and flapped its black wings; and its great green, shining, scaly body swelled and twisted, and it roared in a terrible way.

The little Prince drew his jeweled sword and walked slowly up to the monster. And then the great beast opened its red mouth and blew out one awful breath, that caught the Prince up as if he were a feather, and whisked him clear off the mountain and over the tops of the trees in the valley, and that was the last any one ever saw of him.

Then Casperl grasped his old ax and leaped forward to meet the dragon, never stopping to think how poor his weapon was. But all of a sudden the dragon vanished and disappeared and was gone, and there was no trace of it anywhere; but the beautiful Princess stood in its place and smiled and held out her white hand to Casperl.

"My Prince!" she said, "so you have come at last!"

"I beg your gracious Highness's pardon," said Casperl; "but I am no Prince."

"Oh, yes, you are!" said the Princess; "how did you come here, if you are not my True Prince? Did n't you come through the gate and across the tree, and have n't you driven the dragon away?"

"I only helped——" began Casperl.

"You did it all," said the Princess, "for I saw you. Please don't contradict a lady."

"But I don't see how I could——" Casperl began again.

"People who are helping others," said the Princess, "often have a strength beyond their own. But perhaps you did n't come here to help me, after all?"

"Oh, your gracious Highness," cried Casperl, "there 's nothing I would n't do to help you. But I 'm sure I 'm not a Prince."

"And I am sure you are," said the Princess, and she led him to a fountain near by, and when he looked at his reflection in the water, he saw that he was dressed more magnificently than any prince who ever yet had come to the enchanted mountain.

And just then the wedding-bells began to ring, and that is all I know of the fairy story, for Casperl and the Princess lived so happily ever after in the castle on top of the mountain, that they never came down to tell the rest of it.

AMONG THE BUFFALOES

by Noah Brooks

WHILE the wagon was yet heavily loaded, the boys spared the oxen, and so, seldom rode. At first, the member of the party who drove the team was permitted to sit in the wagon part of the time. But the roads were now very hard for the cattle, and so all hands walked. Old Jim's back was sore; he could not be saddled, and he was left to follow the team, which he did with great docility. The boys hardened the muscles of their legs, but they complained bitterly of sore feet. Much walking and poorly made boots had lamed them. The moccasins which they wore at times were more uncomfortable than the cow-hide boots they had brought from home.

"Confounded Indians!" complained Tom,—"they don't put no heels to their moccasins; they tire a feller's feet awful."

"Sprinkle some whisky in your boots; that's all the use the stuff can be to us; and whisky is good to toughen your feet." This was Mont's advice.

"But why don't the Indians put heels on their moccasins? That's what I'd like to know."

"Why, Tom it is n't natural. Those Sioux that we saw down at Buffalo Creek can out-run and out-jump any white man you ever knew. They could n't do it if they had been brought up with heels on their moccasins."

"But for all that, them moccasins are powerful weak in the sole," grumbled Hi.

" 'Pears to me, sometimes, as if my feet was all of a blister, after traveling all day in the dod-rotted things. Hang Indian shoe-makers, anyhow!"—and Hiram contemplated his chafed feet with great discontent.

"Then there 's old Bally," chimed in Arty. "He 's gone and got lame. He don't wear moccasins, though."

"But," said Mont, "we may be obliged to put moccasins on him—or, at least, on his sore foot."

"What for?"

"Well, we've fixed his foot now two or three times, and he gets no better of his lameness. We might put a leather shoe, like a moccasin, filled with tar, on his foot. That's good for the foot-rot, or whatever it is."

"Gosh!" said Hi. "How much that feller does know!"

"Well," laughed Mont, "I picked that up the other day. Those Adair County men said that if Bally did n't get better, tar would be healing; and they said to bind it on with a shoe made from an old boot-leg."

"Lucky I picked up those boot-legs you thought were of no use, Barney Crogan," said Arthur. "They 'll be just the things for Bally's moccasins."

The boys had put up with many discomforts. Sometimes they had no water for drinking or cooking except what they found in sloughs and swampy places by the track. Often even this poor supply was so mixed with dead grass and weeds that it was necessary to strain it before using it. Then, again, in the long stretch which they were now traveling between Fort Kearny and Fort Laramie, fuel was scarce. Not a tree nor shrub was in sight; buffalo chips were seldom to be found, and the only stuff from which a fire could be made was the dry grass and grease-weed found in sterile spots among the bluffs above the road. They were having hard times. Along the valley of the Platte heavy rain-storms are frequent in the summer-time; and, more than once, all hands were obliged to get up in the night and stand by the tent, in a pelting rain, to keep it from blowing away. One night, indeed, after bracing the tent all around outside with extra lines, they were forced to stand on bundles and boxes inside and hold up the ridge-pole, which bent in the force of the gale and threatened to snap in twain. And then the mosquitoes!

But here was a serious trouble. Bally was a surly animal, but he was a powerful fellow and the best traveler in the team. He had gone lame these four days, and was getting worse instead of better. The boys had passed many cattle, left behind on account of their lameness by those who had gone before. They did not like to think of turning out old Bally to die by the roadside. Matters were not so serious as that. But Mont had said, almost under his breath: "If we should have to leave Bally——"

Serious remedies were now to be tried. The tar-bucket was taken out from under the wagon, and a shoe made from one of provident Arty's boot-legs. With the assistance of Bush, Messer, and one or two neighbors at the camp, poor Bally was cast by suddenly pulling on ropes attached to one hind-foot and one fore-foot. The big beast fell over on his side with a thump

that made Arty's heart jump. Then each person held that part of the animal to which he had previously been assigned. Nance, whose father was now with them for a time, looked on with profound interest.

The struggling animal subsided, after awhile, into an angry quiet, his eyes rolling wildly at Arty and Johnny, who sat on his head to keep him down.

"Set onto him heavy, boys," said Bush. " 'S long 's he can't lift you, he can't lift his head; and 's long 's he can't lift his head, he 's got to lay still."

But he did not lie still. When the shoe, full of soft tar, was fairly on, but not tied, Bally wiggled his tail animatedly, cuffed Bush on the side of his head with the lame foot, which he suddenly jerked out of the hands of the operators, and, with one mighty effort, threw up his head, angrily brandishing his horns the while. Arthur and Johnny flew into the air, one to the right and one to the left, as Bally's head swung in either direction. Struggling to his feet, the worried beast shuffled off a few paces, his shoe half-sticking to his foot in slip-shod fashion; then he stopped and regarded the whole party with profound disfavor.

"Wal, I allow you are a nice creeter, you are!" said Hi, with disgust. "Don't know yer best friends, you don't, when they 're tryin' to cure ye up."

"Why, he 's as spry as a cat and as strong as an ox," cried Bush. "But them boys is spryer. See 'em go? Tore yer shirt, did n't it, Arty?"

"My belt saved me," said the boy, bravely, exhibiting a huge rent in his flannel shirt, and a long red streak on the white skin of his chest, where Bally's sharp horn had plunged under his belt and sharply along his "hide," as Bush called it. Johnny had turned a somersault, lighting on his shoulders, but without serious damage.

"Well, we've got it all to do over again," was Mont's philosophic comment; and, under his leadership, Bally was once more thrown and held down until the shoe was firmly fixed on his foot. He walked off, with a limp, evidently very much puzzled with his first experiment in wearing leather shoes.

"Looks like a bear in moccasins," said Hi, grimly. "Leastways, he looks as I allow a bear would look in moccasins, or with one of 'em onto him. Next time you are sot on a steer's head, Arty, you git where he can't h'ist you higher 'n a kite when he tries to git up."

"I sat where I was told, Hi; but I did n't weigh enough. That 's what was the matter."

The lame ox did not keep his shoe on more than a day or two at a time, and the boys soon had the disagreeable task of replacing it quite often. It was a troublesome affair; but they were now obliged to face the more troublesome question of supplying his place, in case it became necessary to leave him behind. Bally's mate was like him—a large and powerful ox; Tige and Molly, the leaders, were lighter. With these three and their horse, Old Jim, they might go on; but the prospect was gloomy.

"Pity we can't hitch up some of these buffaloes that are running around loose," said Barnard, with a personal sense of the wastefulness of so many cattle going wild, while they needed only one draught animal. "Could we catch one of these critters and put him into the yoke, I wonder?"

"You catch one, and I will agree to yoke him," laughed Mont.

It was not surprising that Barney grumbled at the waste of animal power, and that a wild notion that some of it ought to be made useful crossed his mind. The country was now covered with vast herds of buffaloes, moving to the north. One day, Mont and Arty ascended a steep bluff, to the right of the road, while the wagon-train kept slowly on below them. As far as the eye could reach northward, the undulating country was literally black with the slow-moving herds. Here and there, on some conspicuous eminence, a solitary, shaggy old fellow stood relieved against the sky—a sentinel over the flowing streams of dark brown animals below. They moved in battalions, in single files, by platoons, and in disorderly masses, stretching out in vast dark patches and covering the green earth. Before them was grass and herbage; behind them was a trampled, earthy paste.

Occasionally, these migratory herds, coming to a stream, rushed in thirstily, each rank crowding hard upon another. When the foremost struck the water, galloping along with thundering tread, the fury of their charge sent the spray high in the air, like a fountain. In an instant, the crystal current was yellow and turbid with the disturbed soil; then a dense mass of black heads, with snorting muzzles, crowded the surface from bank to bank.

"See! see!" cried Arthur. "How those big fellows run on ahead, lie down and roll, and then jump up and dash on again. Why, they 're spryer than old Bally was, the other day, when he pitched me sky-high."

"Yes, and if you watch, you will see that all the buffaloes on the side of that bluff drop in the same place, roll and skip on again, almost like a lot of cats."

"Why do they do that, Mont?"

"Well, you know that most hairy animals like to roll; I suppose it answers for a scratching-post. If you ever come to a tree in this part of the country, you will find it all worn smooth and tufted with loose hair, where the buffaloes have rubbed themselves against it."

"But, somehow, these chaps all seem to drop in the same place and then canter on again. I should think each buffalo would want a clean spot."

"O no! that place is worn to the soil now, and is a better one to rub the hide of the creature in than a grassy place would be. For years after this, if we were to come along here, we should find a big patch right there where the buffaloes are rolling as they trot along. The grass won't grow there again for a great while. That is what the plains men call a buffalo-wallow,—though a 'waller,' I believe, is the correct plains expression."

"I like you, Mont," said Arty, looking frankly into Morse's brown face, "because you know everything."

"O no, Arty, not everything. You are a partial friend. I 'm only a greenhorn. But look at that! My! But is n't that a sight?"

As he spoke, a vast crowd of animals, moving from the eastward, came surging up over a swale in the undulating surface. There seemed to be hundreds of thousands. The ground disappeared from sight, and in its place, as if it had swallowed it, was a flood of dark animal life. There was no longer any individuality; it was a sea. It did n't gallop; it moved onward in one slow-flowing stream. There was no noise; but a confused murmur, like the rote of the distant sea before a storm, floated on the air. There was no confusion; in one mighty torrent the countless creatures drifted on, up the hills and down the horizon.

"Jingo!" exclaimed Arty. "I don't wonder Barney grumbles because there is so much cattle-power running to waste. Don't I wish we could hitch up four or five yoke of those old chaps! We 'd go to California, just 'fluking,' as Bush would say."

"If I had my way about it, my boy, I 'd have some of that good, nice, buffalo-beef that is running about loose here, cut up and sent to poor folks in Boston."

"Well, there are poor folks in other cities besides Boston, Monty, you know."

"To be sure; only I think of them first, because I know them. And wherever they are, some of those same poor folks don't get fresh meat very often. And here's millions and millions of pounds going to waste. It seems to me that there 's a screw loose somewhere that this should be so."

Arthur regarded this wonderful cattle show with great soberness and with new interest.

"Why can't some rich man have these buffaloes killed and the fresh meat sent to the poor who starve in cities?"

"Perhaps a more sensible plan would be to bring the poor out here."

"Sure enough," responded the lad, "I never thought of that. But if next year's emigrants kill the buffaloes like they do now, there will be none left when the settlers come. Why, I counted twenty-seven dead ones on the cut-off, yesterday, when Johnny and I took that trail back of Ash Hollow."

"And even the animals that are cut into are not used much for food," added Mont. "We have all the buffalo meat we want; and while you were off, yesterday, I passed a place where some party had camped, and I saw where they had kindled a fire from an old, used-up wagon, and had heaped up two or three carcasses of buffaloes to burn. Great waste of fuel and meat too, I call that. But I greased my boots by the marrow frying out of the bones."

Mont and Arty descended the bluff, and, reaching the rolling plain behind it, moved to the north and west, keeping the general course of the road, but leaving the bluff between it and them.

"We have nothing but our pistols to shoot with," said Mont, "and I would n't

shoot one if I could. But we may as well
see how near we can get to them."

They walked rapidly toward the moving
mass of buffaloes. Here and there were
grazing herds, but most of them seemed
to be slowly traveling without stopping
to eat. Mont advised that they should
creep up a bushy ravine which led into a
gap in the hills, and was blackened on its
edges with buffaloes. Cautiously moving
up this depression, they emerged at the
further end and found themselves in a
throng of animals, just out of gun-shot
range. Some were standing still, others
were moving away, but all regarded the
strangers with mild curiosity.

"Why, I though I should be afraid,"
confessed Arthur.

"No," whispered Mont. "As long as they
are not maddened by a long chase, or
driven into a corner, they are as harmless
as so many cows."

Passing out between the hills, the young
fellows found themselves on a nearly level
plain. Here, too, was a dense throng of
buffaloes, stretching off to the undulating
horizon. As the two explorers walked on,
a wide lane seemed to open in the mighty
herds before them. Insensibly, and without any hurry, the creatures drifted away
to the right and left, browsing or staring,
but continually moving. Looking back,
they saw that the buffaloes had closed up
their ranks on the trail which they had
just pursued; while before, and on either
hand, was a wall of animals.

"We are surrounded!" almost whispered
Arthur, with some alarm.

"Never mind, my boy. We can walk
out, just as the children of Israel did from
the Red Sea. Only we have waves of buffaloes, instead of water, to close behind
and open before and be a wall on each
side. See!"

And, as they kept on, the mass before

them melted away in some mysterious
fashion, always at the same distance from
them.

"See! We move in a vacant space that
travels with us wherever we go, Arty."

"Yes," said the lad. "It seems just as
if we were a candle in the dark. The open
ground around us is the light we shed;
the buffaloes are the darkness outside."

"A good figure of speech, that, my laddie. I must remember it. But we are getting out of the wilderness."

They had now come to a sharp rise of
ground, broken by a rocky ledge, which
turned the herds more to the northward.
Ascending this, they were out of the buffaloes for the time, but beyond them were
thousands more. Turning southward, they

struck across the country for the wagon-track, quite well satisfied with their ex-plorations.

Between two long divides, or ridges, they came upon a single wagon, canvas-covered, in which were two little children. Two boys—one about seven and the other eleven years old—were playing near by, and four oxen were grazing by a spring.

In reply to Mont's surprised question as to how they came off the trail, and why they were here alone, they said that their father and uncle had come up after buf-faloes, and were out with their guns. Their mother was over on the bluff—point-ing to a little rocky mass which rose like an island in the middle of the valley. She had gone to hunt for "sarvice-berries." They were left to mind the cattle and the children.

"Pretty careless business, I should say," murmured Mont. "Well, youngster," he added, "keep by the wagon; if your cattle stray off, they may get carried away by the buffaloes. Mind that!"

They went on down the valley, looking behind them at the helpless little family alone in the wilderness.

"A man ought to be licked for leaving his young ones here in such a lonely place," said Mont.

Suddenly, over the southern wall of the valley, like a thunder-cloud, rose a vast and fleeing herd of buffaloes. They were not only running, they were rushing like a mighty flood.

"A stampede! a stampede!" cried Mont; and, flying back to the unconscious group of children, followed by Arthur, he said: "Run for your lives, youngsters! Make for the bluff!"

Seizing one of the little ones, and bid-ding Arthur take the other, he started the boys ahead for the island-bluff, which was some way down the valley. There was not

a moment to lose. Behind them, like a rising tide, flowed the buffaloes in surges. A confused murmur filled the air; the ground resounded with the hurried beat of countless hoofs, and the earth seemed to be disappearing in the advancing torrent. Close behind the flying fugitives the angry, panic-stricken herd tumbled and tossed. Its labored breathing sighed like a breeze, and the warmth of its pulsations seemed to stifle the air.

"To the left! to the left!" screamed Arthur, seeing the bewildered boys, who fled like deer, making directly for the steepest part of the bluff. Thus warned, the lads bounded up the little island, grasp-ing the underbrush as they climbed. Hard behind them came Arty, pale, his features drawn and rigid, and bearing in his arms a little girl. Mont brought up the rear with a stout boy on his shoulder, and breathless with excitement and the laborious run.

Up the steep side they scrambled, fall-ing and recovering themselves, but up at last. Secure on a bare rock, they saw a heaving tide of wild creatures pour tumul-tuously over the edge and fill the valley. It leaped from ledge to ledge, tumbled and broke, rallied again and swept on, black and silent save for the rumbling thunder of many hoofs and the panting breath of the innumerable multitude. On it rolled over every obstacle. The wagon disappeared in a twinkling, its white cover going down in the black tide like a sinking ship at sea. Past the island-like bluff, where a little group stood spell-bound, the herd swept, the rushing tide separating at the rocky point, against which it beat and parted to the right and left. Looking down, they saw the stream flow by, on and up the valley. It was gone, and the green turf was brown where it had been. The spring was choked, and the wagon was trampled in a flat ruin.

Fascinated by the sight, Mont and

Arthur never took their eyes from it until it was over. Then returning to their young charges, they saw a tall, gaunt woman, with a horror-stricken face, gathering the whole group in her arms. It was the mother.

"I don't know who you be, young men, but I thank you from the bottom of my heart," she said. "Yes, I thank you from the bottom of my heart—and, oh! I thank God, too!" And she burst into tears.

Arthur, at loss what else to say, remarked: "Your wagon is all smashed."

"I don't care—don't care," said the woman, hysterically rocking herself to and fro where she sat with her children clasped to her bosom. "So 's the young ones are safe, the rest may go to wrack."

As she spoke, a couple of horsemen, carrying rifles, came madly galloping down the valley, far in the wake of the flying herd. They paused, thunderstruck, at the fragments of their wagon trampled in the torn soil. Then, seeing the group on the rock, they hastened on, dismounted, and climbed the little eminence.

"Great powers above, Jemimy! we stampeded the buffaloes!" said the elder of the pair of hunters.

Arty expected to hear her say that she was thankful so long as they were all alive.

"Yes, and a nice mess you 've made of it." This was all her comment.

"Whar 's the cattle, Zeph?" asked the father of this flock.

"Gone off with the buffaloes, I reckon, dad," was the response of his son Zephaniah.

The man looked up and down the valley with a bewildered air. His wagon had been mashed and crushed into the ground. His cattle were swept out into space by the resistless flood, and were nowhere in sight. He found words at last:

"Well, this is perfectly rediclus."

THE DICKEY BOY

by Mary E. Wilkins

I SHOULD think it was about time for him
to be comin'," said Mrs. Rose.

"So should I," assented Miss Elvira
Grayson. She peered around the corner of
the front door. Her face was thin and anxious, and her voice was so like it that it was
unmistakably her own note. One would
as soon expect a crow to chick-a-dee as Miss
Elvira to talk in any other way. She was
tall, and there was a sort of dainty angu-
larity about her narrow shoulders. She
wore an old black silk, which was a great
deal of dress for afternoon. She had considerable money in the bank and could
afford to dress well. She wore also some
white lace around her long neck, and it
was fastened with a handsome gold and jet
brooch. She was knitting some blue
worsted, and she sat back in the front
entry, out of the draft. She considered herself rather delicate.

Mrs. Rose sat boldly out in the yard in
the full range of the breeze, sewing upon
a blue-and-white gingham waist for her
son, Willy. She was a large, pretty-faced
woman in a stiffly starched purple muslin,
which spread widely around her.

"He's been gone 'most an hour," she
went on; "I hope there's nothin' happened."

"I wonder if there's snakes in that
meadow?" ruminated Miss Elvira.

"I don't know; I'm gettin' ruther uneasy."

"I know one thing—I should n't let

him go off so, without somebody older
with him, if he was my boy."

"Well, I don't know what I can do," returned Mrs. Rose uneasily. "There ain't
anybody to go with him. I can't go diggin'
sassafras-root, and you can't, and his uncle
Hiram 's too busy, and grandfather is too
stiff. And he is so crazy to go after sassafras-root, it does seem a pity to tell him
he sha'n't. I never saw a child so possessed
after the root and sassafras-tea, as he is,
in my life. I s'pose it 's good for him. I
hate to deny him when he takes so much
comfort goin'. There he is now!"

Little Willy Rose crossed the road, and
toiled up the stone steps. The front yard
was terraced, and two flights of stone steps
led up to the front door. He was quite
breathless when he stood on the top step;
his round, sweet face was pink, his fair
hair plastered in flat locks to his wet forehead. His little trousers and his shoes were
muddy, and he carried a great scraggy
mass of sassafras-roots. "I see you a-settin'
out here," he panted softly.

"You ought not to have stayed so
long. We began to be worried about you,"
said his mother in a fond voice. "Now go
and take your muddy shoes right off, and
put on your slippers; then you can sit
down at the back door and clean your
sassafras, if you want to."

"I got lots," said Willy, smiling sweetly
and wiping his forehead. "Look-a-there,
Miss Elviry."

325

"So you did," returned Miss Elvira. "I suppose now you think you 'll have some sassafras-tea."

"Yes, ma'am."

"I guess I 'll steep him a little for supper, he 's so crazy for it," said Mrs. Rose when Willy had disappeared smilingly around the corner.

"Yes, I would. It 's real wholesome for him. Who 's that comin'?"

Mrs. Rose stared down at the road. A white horse with an open buggy was just turning into the driveway, around the south side of the terraces. "Why, it 's brother Hiram," said she, "and he 's got a boy with him. I wonder who 't is."

The buggy drew up with a grating noise in the driveway. Presently a man appeared around the corner. After him tagged a small white-headed boy, and after the boy Willy Rose, with a sassafras-root and an old shoe-knife in his hands.

The man, who was Mr. Hiram Fairbanks, Mrs. Rose's brother, had a somewhat doubtful expression. When he stopped, the white-headed boy stopped, keeping a little behind him in his shadow.

"What boy is that, Hiram?" asked Mrs. Rose. Miss Elvira peered around the door. Mr. Fairbanks was tall and stiff-looking. He had a sunburned, sober face. "His name is Dickey," he replied.

"One of those Dickeys?" Mrs. Rose said "Dickeys" as if it were a synonym for "outcasts" or "rascals."

Mr. Fairbanks nodded. He 'glanced at the boy in his wake, then at Willy. "Willy, s'pose you take this little boy 'round and show him your rabbits," he said in an embarrassed voice.

"Willy Rose!" cried his mother, "you have n't changed those muddy shoes! Go right in this minute, 'round by the kitchen door, and take this boy 'round with you; he can sit down on the door-step and help you clean your sassafras-root."

Willy disappeared lingeringly around the house, and the other boy, on being further bidden by Mr. Fairbanks, followed him. "Willy," his mother cried after him, "mind you sit down on the door-step and

The Dickey boy

tie your shoes! I ain't goin' to have that Dickey boy left alone; his folks are nothin' but a pack of thieves," she remarked in a lower tone. "What are you doing with him, Hiram?"

Hiram hesitated. "Well, 'Mandy, you was sayin' the other day that you wished you had a boy to run errands, and split up kindlin's, and be kind of company for Willy."

"You ain't brought that Dickey boy?"

"Now, look here, 'Mandy—"

"I ain't going to have him in the house."

"Jest look here a minute, 'Mandy, till I tell you how it happened, and then you can do jest as you 're a mind to about it. I was up by the Ruggles's this afternoon, and Mis' Ruggles, she come out to the gate, and hailed me. She wanted to know if I did n't want a boy. Seems the Dickey woman died last week; you know the father died two year ago. Well, there was six children, and the oldest boy 's skipped, nobody knows where, and the oldest girl has just got married, and this boy is the oldest of the four that 's left. They took the three little ones to the poorhouse, and Mis' Ruggles she took this boy in, and she wanted to keep him, but her own boy is big enough to do all the chores, and she did n't feel as if she could afford to. She says he 's a real nice little fellow, and his mother wa' n't a bad woman; she was jest kind of sickly and shiftless. I guess old Dickey wa' n't much, but he 's dead. Mis' Ruggles says this little chap hates awful to go to the poorhouse, and it ain't no kind of risk to take him, and she 'd ought to know. She 's lived right there next door to the Dickeys ever since she was married. I knew you wanted a boy to do chores round, long as Willy was n't strong enough, so I thought I 'd fetch him along. But you can do jest as you 're a mind to."

"Now, Hiram Fairbanks, you know the name those Dickeys have always had. S'pose I took that boy, and he stole?"

"Mis' Ruggles says she 'd trust him with anything."

"She ain't got so much as I have to lose. There I 've got two dozen solid silver teaspoons, and four table-spoons, and my mother's silver creamer, and Willy's silver napkin-ring. Elviry 's got her gold watch, too."

"I 've got other things I would n't lose for anything," chimed in Miss Elvira.

"Well, of course, I don't want you to lose anything," said Mr. Fairbanks helplessly, "but Mis' Ruggles, she said he was perfectly safe."

"I s'pose I could lock up the silver spoons and use the old pewter ones, and Elviry could keep her watch out of sight for a while," ruminated Mrs. Rose.

"Yes, I could," assented Miss Elvira, "and my breast-pin."

"I s'pose he could draw the water, and split up the kindlin'-wood, and weed the flower-garden," said Mrs. Rose. "I set Willy to weedin' this morning, and it gave him the headache. I tell you one thing, Hiram Fairbanks, if I do take this boy, you 've got to stand ready to take him back again the first minute I see anything out of the way with him."

"Yes, I will, 'Mandy; I promise you I will," said Mr. Fairbanks eagerly. He hurried out to the buggy, and fumbled under the seat; then he returned with a bundle and a small wooden box.

"Here 's his clothes. I guess he ain't got much," said he.

Mrs. Rose took the newspaper bundle; then she eyed the box suspiciously. It was a wooden salt-box, and the sliding cover was nailed on.

"What 's in this?" said she.

"Oh, I don't know," replied Mr. Fairbanks; "some truck or other—I guess it ain't worth much."

He put the box down on the bank, and trudged heavily and quickly out to the buggy. He was anxious to be off; he shook the reins, shouted "ge lang" to the white horse, and wheeled swiftly around the corner.

"I 'd like to know what 's in that box," said Mrs. Rose to Miss Elvira.

"I hope he ain't got an old pistol or anything of that kind in it," returned Miss Elvira. "Oh, 'Mandy, I would n't shake it, if I were you!" For Mrs. Rose was shaking the wooden box, and listening with her ear at it.

"Something rattles in it," said she, desisting; "I hope it ain't a pistol." Then she entered with the newspaper-bundle and the box, and went through the house with Miss Elvira following. She set the bundle and box on the kitchen table, and looked out of the door. There on the top step sat the Dickey boy cleaning the sassafras-roots with great industry, while Willy Rose sat on the lower one chewing some.

"I do believe he 's goin' to take right hold, Elviry," whispered Mrs. Rose.

"Well, maybe he is," returned Miss Elvira.

Mrs. Rose stowed away the boy's belongings in the little bedroom off the kitchen where she meant him to sleep; then she kindled the fire and got supper. She made sassafras-tea, and the new boy, sitting beside Willy, had a cup poured for him. But he did not drink much, nor eat much, although there were hot biscuits, and berries, and custards. He hung his forlorn head with its shock of white hair, and only gave fleeting glances at anything with his wild blue eyes. He was a thin boy, smaller than Willy, but he looked wiry and full of motion, like a wild rabbit.

After supper Mrs. Rose sent him for a pail of water; then he split up a little pile of kindling-wood. After that he sat down on the kitchen door-step in the soft twilight, and was silent.

Willy went into the sitting-room, where his mother and Miss Elvira were. "He' s settin' out there on the door-step, not speakin' a word," said he, in a confidential whisper.

"Well, you had better sit down here with us, and read your Sunday-school book," said his mother. She and Miss Elvira had agreed that it was wiser that Willy should not be too much with the Dickey boy until they knew him better.

When it was nine o'clock Mrs. Rose showed the Dickey boy his bedroom. She looked at him sharply; his small pale face showed red stains in the lamplight. She thought to herself that he had been crying, and she spoke to him as kindly as she could—she had not a caressing manner with anybody but Willy. "I guess there 's clothes enough on the bed," said she. She looked curiously at the bundle and the wooden box. Then she unfastened the bundle. "I guess I 'll see what you 've got for clothes," said she, and her tone was as motherly as she could make it toward this outcast Dickey boy. She laid out his pitiful little wardrobe, and examined the small ragged shirt or two and the fragmentary stockings. "I guess I shall have to buy you some things if you are a good boy," said she. "What have you got in that box?"—the boy hung his head—"I hope you ain't got a pistol?"

"No, marm."

"You ain't got any powder, nor anything of that kind?"

"No, marm." The boy was blushing confusedly.

"I hope you 're tellin' me the truth," Mrs. Rose said, and her tone was full of severe admonition.

"Yes, marm." The tears rolled down the boy's cheeks, and Mrs. Rose said no more. She told him she would call him in the morning, and to be careful about his lamp. Then she left him. The Dickey boy lay awake, and cried an hour; then he went to sleep, and slept as soundly as Willy Rose in his snug little bedroom, leading out of his mother's room. Miss Elvira and Mrs. Rose locked their doors that night, through distrust of that little boy downstairs who came of a thieving family. Miss Elvira put her gold watch, and her breast-pin, and her pocket-book with seventeen dollars in it, under the feather-bed; and Mrs. Rose carried the silver teaspoons up-stairs, and hid them under hers. The Dickey boy was not supposed to know they were in the house, —the pewter ones had been used for supper,—but that did not signify; she thought it best to be on the safe side. She kept the silver spoons under the feather-bed for many a day, and they all ate with the pewter ones, but finally suspicion was allayed if not destroyed. The Dickey boy had shown himself trustworthy in several instances. Once he was sent on a test errand to the store, and came home promptly with the right change. The silver spoons glittered in the spoon-holder on the table, and Miss Elvira wore her gold watch and her gold breast-pin.

"I begin to take a good deal more stock in that boy," Mrs. Rose told her brother Hiram. "He ain't very lively, but he works real smart; he ain't saucy, and I ain't known of his layin' hands on a thing."

But the Dickey boy, although he had won some confidence and good opinions, was, as Mrs. Rose said, not very lively. His face, as he did his little tasks, was as sober and serious as an old man's. Everybody was kind to him, but this poor little alien felt like a chimney-sweep in a queen's palace. Mrs. Rose, to a Dickey boy, was almost as impressive as a queen. He watched with admiration and awe this handsome, energetic woman moving about the house in her wide skirts. He was overcome with the magnificence of Miss Elvira's afternoon silk, and gold watch; and dainty little Willy Rose seemed to him like a small prince. Either the Dickey boy, born in a republican country, had the original instincts of the peasantry in him, and himself defined his place so clearly that it made him unhappy, or his patrons did it

for him. Mrs. Rose and Miss Elvira tried to treat him as well as they treated Willy. They dressed him in Willy's old clothes, they gave him just as much to eat; when autumn came, he was sent to school as warmly clad and as well provided with luncheon; but they could never forget that he was a Dickey boy. He seemed in truth to them like an animal of another species, in spite of all they could do, and they regarded his virtues in the light of uncertain tricks. Mrs. Rose never thought at any time of leaving him in the house alone without hiding the spoons, and Miss Elvira never left her gold watch unguarded.

Nobody knew whether the Dickey boy was aware of these lurking suspicions or not; he was so subdued that it was impossible to tell how much he observed. Nobody knew how homesick he was, but he went about every day full of fierce hunger for his miserable old home. Miserable as it had been, there had been in it a certain element of shiftless ease and happiness. The Dickey boy's sickly mother had never chided him; she had not cared if he tracked mud into the house. How anxiously he scraped his feet before entering the Rose kitchen. The Dickey boy's dissipated father had been gentle and maudlin, but never violent. All the Dickey children had done as they chose, and they had agreed well. They were not a quarrelsome family. Their principal faults were idleness and a general laxity of morals which was quite removed from active wickedness. "All the Dickeys needed was to be bolstered up," one woman in the village said; and the Dickey boy was being bolstered up in the Rose family.

They called him Dickey, using his last name for his first, which was Willy. Mrs. Rose straightened herself unconsciously when she found that out. "We can't have two Willies in the family, anyhow," said she; "we 'll have to call you Dickey."

Once the Dickey boy's married sister came to see him, and Mrs. Rose treated her with such stiff politeness that the girl, who was fair and pretty and gaudily dressed, told her husband when she got home that she would never go into *that* woman's house again. Occasionally Mrs. Rose, who felt a duty in the matter, took Dickey to visit his little brothers and sisters at the almshouse. She even bought some peppermint-candy for him to take them. He really had many a little extra kindness shown him; sometimes Miss Elvira gave him a penny, and once Mr. Hiram Fairbanks gave him a sweet-apple tree—that was really quite a magnificent gift. Mrs. Rose could hardly believe it when Willy told her. "Well, I must say I never thought Hiram would do such a thing as that, close as he is," said she. "I was terribly taken aback when he gave that tree to Willy, but this beats all. Why, odd years it might bring in twenty dollars!"

"Uncle Hiram gave it to him," Willy repeated. "I was a-shown' Dickey my apple-tree, and Uncle Hiram he picked out another one, and he gave it to him."

"Well, I would n't have believed it," said Mrs. Rose.

Nobody else would have believed that Hiram Fairbanks, careful old bachelor that he was, would have been so touched by the Dickey boy's innocent, wistful face staring up at the bough of Willy's apple-tree. It was fall, and the apples had all been harvested. Dickey would get no practical benefit from his tree until next season, but there was no calculating the comfort he took with it from the minute it came into his possession. Every minute he could get, at first, he hurried off to the orchard and sat down under its boughs.

He felt as if he were literally under his own roof-tree. In the winter, when it was heavy with snow, he did not forsake it. There would be a circle of little tracks around the trunk.

Mrs. Rose told her brother that the boy was perfectly crazy about that apple-tree, and Hiram grinned shamefacedly.

All winter Dickey went with Willy to the district school, and split wood and brought water between times. Sometimes of an evening he sat soberly down with Willy and played checkers, but Willy always won. "He don't try to beat," Willy said. Sometimes they had popcorn, and Dickey always shook the popper. Dickey said he was n't tired, if they asked him. All winter the silver spoons appeared on the table, and Dickey was treated with a fair show of confidence. It was not until spring that the sleeping suspicion of him awoke. Then one day Mrs. Rose counted her silver spoons, and found only twenty-three teaspoons. She stood at her kitchen table, and counted them over and over. Then she opened the kitchen door. "Elviry!" she called out, "Elviry, come here a minute! Look here," she said in a hushed voice, when Miss Elvira's inquiring face had appeared at the door. Miss Elvira approached the table tremblingly.

"Count those spoons," said Mrs. Rose.

Miss Elvira's long slim fingers handled the jingling spoons. "There ain't but twenty-three," she said finally, in a scared voice.

"I expected it," said Mrs. Rose. "Do you s'pose he took it?"

"Who else took it, I 'd like to know?"

It was a beautiful May morning; the appletrees were all in blossom. The Dickey boy had stolen over to look at his. It was a round hill of pink-and-white bloom. It was the apple year. Willy came to the stone wall and called him. "Dickey," he cried,

"Mother wants you"; and Dickey obeyed. Willy had run on ahead. He found Mrs. Rose, Miss Elvira, Willy, and the twenty-three teaspoons awaiting him in the kitchen. He shook his head to every question they asked him about the missing spoon. He turned quite pale; once in a while he whimpered; the tears streamed down his cheeks, but he only shook his head in that mute denial.

"It won't make it any easier for you, holding out this way," said Mrs. Rose, harshly. "Stop cryin' and go out and split up some kindlin'-wood."

Dickey went out, his little convulsed form bent almost double. Willy, staring at him with his great, wondering blue eyes, stood aside to let him pass. Then he also was sent on an errand, while his mother and Miss Elvira had a long consultation in the kitchen.

It was a half hour before Mrs. Rose went out to the shed where she had sent the Dickey boy to split kindlings. There lay a nice little pile of kindlings, but the boy had disappeared.

"Dickey, Dickey!" she called. But he did not come.

"I guess he 's gone, spoon and all," she told Miss Elvira when she went in; but she did not really think he had. When one came to think of it, he was really too small and timid a boy to run away with one silver spoon. It did not seem reasonable. What they did think, as time went on and he did not appear, was that he was hiding to escape a whipping. They searched everywhere. Miss Elvira stood in the shed by the wood-pile, calling in her thin voice, "Come out, Dickey; we won't whip you if you *did* take it," but there was not a stir.

Toward night they grew uneasy. Mr. Fairbanks came, and they talked matters over.

"Maybe he did n't take the spoon," said Mr. Fairbanks uncomfortably. "Anyhow, he 's too young a chap to be set adrift this way. I wish you 'd let me talk to him, 'Mandy."

"*You*," said Mrs. Rose. Then she started up. "I know one thing," said she; "I 'm goin' to see what 's in that wooden box. I don't believe but what that spoon 's in there. There 's no knowin' how long it 's been gone."

It was quite a while before Mrs. Rose returned with the wooden box. She had to search for it, and found it under the bed. The Dickey boy also had hidden his treasures. She got the hammer and Hiram pried off the lid, which was quite securely nailed. "I 'd ought to have had it opened before," said she. "He had n't no business to have a nailed-up box round. Don't joggle it so, Hiram. There 's no knowin' what 's in it. There may be a pistol."

Miss Elvira stood farther off. Mr. Fairbanks took the lid entirely off. They all peered into the box. There lay an old clay pipe and a roll of faded calico. Mr. Fairbanks took up the roll and shook it out. "It 's an apron," said he. "It 's his father's pipe, and his mother's apron—I—swan!"

Miss Elvira began to cry. "I had n't any idea of anything of that kind," said Mrs. Rose huskily. "Willy Rose, what *have* you got there?"

For Willy, looking quite pale and guilty, was coming in, holding a muddy silver teaspoon. "Where did you get that spoon? Answer me this minute," cried his mother.

"I—took it out to—dig in my garden with the—other day. I—forgot—"

"Oh, you naughty boy!" cried his mother. Then she too began to weep. Mr. Fairbanks started up. "Something 's got to be done," said he. "The wind 's changed, and the May storm is comin' on. That boy has got to be found before night."

But all Mr. Fairbanks's efforts, and the

neighbors' who came to his assistance, could not find the Dickey boy before night or before the next morning. The long cold May storm began, the flowering apple-trees bent under it, and the wind drove the rain against the windows. Mrs. Rose and Miss Elvira kept the kitchen fire all night, and hot water and blankets ready. But the day had fairly dawned before they found the Dickey boy, and then only by the merest chance. Mr. Fairbanks, hurrying across his orchard for a short cut, and passing Dickey's tree, happened to glance up at it, with a sharp pang of memory. He stopped short. There, among the blossoming branches, clung the Dickey boy, like a little drenched, storm-beaten bird. He had flown to his one solitary possession for a refuge. He was almost exhausted; his little hands grasped a branch like steel claws. Mr. Fairbanks took him down and carried him home. "He was up in his tree," he told his sister brokenly, when he entered the kitchen. "He 's 'most gone."

But the Dickey boy revived after he had lain awhile before a fire and been rolled in hot blankets and swallowed some hot drink. He looked with a wondering smile at Mrs. Rose when she bent over him and kissed him just as she kissed Willy. Miss Elvira loosened her gold watch with its splendid long gold chain and put it in his hand. "There, hold it awhile," said she, "and listen to it tick." Mr. Fairbanks fumbled in his pocket-book and drew out a great silver dollar. "There," said he, "you can have that to spend when you get well."

Willy pulled his mother's skirt. "Mother," he whispered.

"What say?"

"Can't I pop some corn for him?"

"By and by." Mrs. Rose smoothed the Dickey boy's hair; then she bent down and kissed him again. She had fairly made room for him in her stanch, narrow New England heart.

A GREAT SPECULATION

by Rossiter Johnson

YOUNG Tommy Baker's uncle, who was a great reader and traveler, came to his nephew's home one day for a short visit, and during his stay he talked a good deal about the Mammoth Cave in Kentucky, which he had recently been to see, describing minutely the approach to the cave, the winding passages, the mysterious rivers, the eyeless fish, and the crystals and stalactites. Tommy was lost in admiration.

Wishing to teach him as much as possible, and to have him remember what he had learned, his father, after his uncle had gone, continued the subject, telling him about other celebrated caves—Wier's Cave and Madison's Cave, in Virginia; Franconia, in Germany; Kirkdale, in England; and Fingal's, in Staffa. Then he told him about celebrated artificial excavations—the catacombs of Paris, Rome, Syracuse, and Palermo; and, finally, he described some of the discoveries at Herculaneum and Pompeii, and in the mounds of our Western States. When he had fully awakened Tommy's interest and curiosity, he told him in what books he could find more information on these subjects, and then left him to study them up for himself.

Tommy and I were, one day, in his father's yard at the point where the sward began to slope toward the brook, a tributary to Rocky Creek. We sat on a large bowlder, with our feet hanging over the edge, looking down into the little valley of the brook, and he repeated what his father and his uncle had told him about the caves and the catacombs and Herculaneum and the mounds.

"I wish," said he, "that the mouth of one of 'em was in our yard."

"Yes," said I, "that would be nice. Then we could go in and see all the curiosities and get as many crystals and vases and arrows and hatchets as we wanted."

My fancy included the products of all the different kinds of caves and excavations in the one which was to be in Tommy's yard; but perhaps it was just as well, —certainly it was all the more enjoyable.

"But that would n't be the best of it," said he.

"Why, what would?" I asked.

"We could put up a gate, and charge folks for going in," he answered, and his eyes twinkled over his imaginary profits.

"Could we?" said I, incredulously.

"Of course I could," said he, and the singular pronoun signified to me that he was growing avaricious, and no longer wanted me for a partner in the business.

I began to wish that the cave had been located in our yard, instead of in theirs. I thought if it had been, I would teach Tommy a lesson of magnanimous liberality by dividing the money with him every Saturday night.

"You always have to pay to go into such places," he continued; "and it 's the easiest way to get rich there is. You just put up a little sign that says: 'This way to the Cave!' and a hand pointing. And then it 's a long distance, and the path is crooked and real hard to walk on, and you leave all the stones and bushes and old rubbish in it. And when the people get to the end of it, there you are, sitting by a little table with a box on it for the money; and they 've got to pay you twenty-five cents, or fifty perhaps, before they can go in, because the cave 's on your land. And some of 'em say they wont give it; and then they think about the hard, stony path, and they say it 's too bad to come over all that for nothing, and then they pay the money and go in. And you have some little books on the table, that tell all about it, and you sell 'em one of them for ten cents, or else they can't understand it; and there you make some more money."

Tommy was growing very enthusiastic on the subject, and I was catching a little of the same spirit.

"I wish we had a cave," said I.

"Yes," said the speculative Tommy, "I could sit at the little table and take the money, and you could go with the folks to show 'em the way and tell 'em about things. Some of 'em have rivers in 'em, that have fish in 'em without any eyes; and you have to row the people across in a boat, and you charge 'em extra for that."

I had an idea. "Suppose we *make* a cave?"

"Could we?" said Tommy.

"We could try," said I, remembering that somebody or other had once given that as a very heroic answer, which had made him famous. And now, what if the same answer, given in the same spirit, should make Tommy and me rich!

"How should we do it?" he asked.

"Oh, dig it!" said I, as confidently as if I had been a journeyman cave-maker half my life, and were ready to take Tommy for my apprentice.

"Where would we have it?" said he, looking around.

"I don't know! let 's look for a good place," said I, and I slid down the face of the rock, followed by the little fortune-hunter.

We surveyed the whole yard, and very quickly concluded that the entrance must be somewhere along the bank of the creek. At a certain point a few yards below, in the direction of down stream, the bank, instead of descending in a grassy slope, fell off suddenly, and presented an almost perpendicular face of clay, on which no grass grew. It was evident that this was the place to begin operations, if we were to make a cave. We had nothing to do but dig straight in at the base of the cliff; and we could throw the dirt into the stream, and the water would wash it away out of sight about as fast as we two boys could dig it. This would prevent the work from being discovered, unless some one should happen to go down the bank and approach closely to the mouth of the proposed cave.

I asked Tommy what he thought his father would say as to the cave.

"I guess," said he, "he would n't want me to do it, if he knew. But when he sees the money, he 'll say it 's all right."

"It can't hurt anything, at any rate," said I, beginning to fear that if he thought too much about what his father would say, he might give up the project.

"No," said he, "it can't hurt anything. We can throw the dirt over into the brook, and not make a bit of muss. And then it 'll be all underground, and the ground on top 'll be just as good for a garden or anything as ever 't was."

"And then," I pursued, "when we get a hundred dollars, we can make our

fathers and mothers a present of half of it"
—for I still have a vague fear that, in
some unsuspected manner, the cave *might*
interfere with some of Mr. Baker's plans.

But Tommy did n't know about making any such munificent presents. It was n't
the way people usually did when they got
rich. He promised, however, to think about
it.

One thing was certain. We must keep
the whole matter a profound secret—that
was agreed upon. And we would begin
operations the very next day—that also
was agreed upon. I stood before the face
of the clay cliff, and with a sharp stick
marked the arched outline of the entrance
to the cave that was to be.

We got together again in the evening,
alone in Mrs. Baker's kitchen, and used
up several sheets of paper in drawing
plans for the cave.

"We must have some parts of it very
crooked," said I.

"Yes, and in one place there must be
quite a large room, with stalakites hanging
down from the top," said Tommy.

"O yes! *stalactites*," said I, intending to
correct him very gently.

"It 's *stalakites*," said he; "my Uncle
Charles said so."

I was sure I was right, and was not inclined to let it go so. We came very near
falling into a serious quarrel on the subject, and giving up the project. At length
we agreed to leave it to the dictionary,
which the confident Tommy brought, and
looked out the word.

"Well, *stalactites*," said he, "if you must
have it so;" and then he hurried on to
the consideration of other parts of the
plan. "If we could strike a stream of water
underground it would be nice," he continued. "There 's one runs right through
the bottom of our well."

"Perhaps we can dig a pond and pour
some water into it," I suggested, "and

catch some fish in Rocky Creek to put into
it."

"Put their eyes out first?" asked Tommy.

"No," said I, "that would be cruel. Besides, after they 've been there awhile their
eyes will go away, and their little fishes
will be born blind."

Tommy saw that I considered the subject from a lofty point, both in morals
and in science, and he was much impressed.

"What *I* want," said he, after musing a
few minutes on these weighty questions,
"is a few skulls, so it 'll look like the catacombs. And that 'll scare the boys, and
make 'em not try to get in when we aint
there."

"There 's a horse's skull on the common," I suggested.

"I suppose we can't get human skulls,"
said he.

"I suppose not."

"Then may be, if we put the horse's skull
pretty high up, and stick the long nosepart deep into the wall, it 'll look like a
human skull, and we can make 'em think
't is."

"May be so."

"But then," said he, "the teeth ought
to show. The teeth are the scariest part of
a skull."

"That 's so," said I, emphatically; and I
immediately gave my whole mind to the
solution of the problem how to make a
horse's skull look like a human skull, and
yet have the teeth show. I solved it at last.
"I have it! I have it! provided we can
get two horses' skulls," and I stopped in
doubt on that question.

"O yes," said Tommy; "we can get two
easy enough."

"Well, then, we 'll fix one as you say,
with the long-nose part in the wall, and
close to it we 'll fix the other so that it
will be all buried up in the wall except the
mouth, which will stick out and show its

teeth. The first one will make folks think they 're human, and the other will scare 'em—a little; we don't want to scare 'em too much." Thus we agreed to arrange it.

Tommy put the finishing touches to the last plan we had drawn, and made quite conspicuous the table at the entrance, with the money-box on it.

Then I went home, and we both went to bed,—not so much to sleep as to lie awake and think about the cave and its profits.

Early next morning, with a shovel and a hoe and a light crowbar, we went to work. With an old nail-keg to stand on while working at the upper part of the arch, we got along very well. Before school-time we had dug more than a foot into the bank, and thrown the dirt, a shovelful at a time, into the brook. We were tired enough to be perfectly willing to leave off work in good season for school. But our enthusiasm was growing, and we longed for vacation to come, that we might give our whole time to the task.

After school we worked again until supper-time; and the close of that first day saw the completion of the first two feet of the tunnel.

"How much shall we charge?" said I, as we took a last look at the hollow arch, before going home to our well-earned rest.

"I never heard of a cave that you could go into, and all through, for less than twenty-five cents," said Tommy.

"That ought to be cheap enough, certainly," said I.

"Yes," said he, "we must charge a quarter of a dollar; and no half-price for children, and no free passes to anybody."

"No," said I, "no free passes. But shall we admit children at all? They 'll meddle with things, and may be break something. They 're awful troublesome."

"Admit 'em if they pay," said the busi-ness-like Tommy. This seemed to settle the matter, and we walked away in silence.

"But," said I, when we had reached the top of the bank, "not many of the boys that we know have got twenty-five cents. They never have so much, except on Fourth of July."

"Then let 'em sell something and raise the money," he answered, knowing that he had the monopoly of the cave market.

"But," I suggested, "what if they won't?"

Tommy took a few minutes to consider that question. It put the matter in a new light. He began to realize that the boys were under no obligation, and might not be at all anxious, to pay tribute to the money-box on the little table where he already imagined himself sitting at the receipt of custom.

"I guess," said he, slowly, "we shall have to let them in for about five cents apiece."

"I think that will be the best way," I answered; and then we parted for the night.

The next day was Saturday, and we gave the whole time to the work. In order to lose as little as possible, we brought our dinners; but long before noon we became fiercely hungry and ate all our provisions, and two hours later we went home for more.

By tea-time, Saturday, we had penetrated two yards into the bank, rounding the arch out completely all the way, and throwing all the dirt over into the brook, which was here pretty swift and swept it away. We saw that our progress would necessarily be slower and slower, as we had farther and farther to carry the dirt. But we thought we had done well so far, and were very much encouraged.

Thus we dug away, mornings, after-noons, and Saturdays, until we reached a point about fifteen feet from the entrance. And now it was very slow work, because every shovelful had to travel over those five yards. We began to realize that we had taken a pretty large contract. None of the winding passages had been attempted yet. It was just a straight tunnel. We sat down and discussed the situation.

"If we carry out the whole plan, it will take all Summer," said Tommy.

"Yes," said I, "and, when the Fall rains come, this wont be a pleasant place to stay in."

"No," said he; "a fellow might take an awful cold—consumption, may be—sitting here all day making change when the equinoctial was going on."

"Let's finish it up right here," said I.

"I think we 'd better," said Tommy. "We can dig some way at the sides here and make one room, and that 'll do. One room 's enough, if they 're only going to pay five cents. We can put all the skulls and things in here."

"And if it pays pretty well," said I, "we can dig it farther next year, and put in more things, and then the boys will want to come in again."

"It 's a good idea," said Tommy; "it will be most profitable that way."

So we went to work with a will, and dug away a few yards of earth on each side of the inner end of the tunnel, until we had made a small room. Then we scooped a good deal off from the ceiling of this room, until it was considerably higher than the tunnel.

"That 'll do first-rate," said Tommy; "that 's plenty dark enough."

"Now for the things," said I. "How are we going to make the stalactites?"

"Let 's go and see what we can find," said Tommy.

We went on a voyage of discovery around the house and barn. Behind the barn, leaning up against it, was a section of an old white picket-fence, that had been torn up to make room for a new one somewhere.

"I think those would do nicely," said I, and we knocked off seven or eight of the pickets, sawed them short, and carried them to the cave, where we stuck them into the ceiling, points down.

"That 's splendid!" said Tommy. "That looks just like the Mammoth Cave. Now for the skulls."

I thought it would be better not to go for the skull until evening, as somebody might see us in the day-time. Tommy agreed to that; and then we went over to our house, to see what we could find.

I stole into the front room and brought out two flint arrow-heads and a stone hatchet, which were among other curiosities on a little stand in the corner. In the wood-shed we found a broken preserve-jar and an old iron dumb-bell.

All these we carried to the cave, and arranged them around the sides.

"Those," said Tommy, "make it look like an Indian mound."

We employed the little remaining time before supper in sweeping and smoothing the floor, and discussing the management of the show.

"I wish there was a door to it, so we could lock it up," said Tommy. "I 'm afraid when a few of the boys learn the way, they 'll bring the others when we aint here."

This was a very serious consideration. But presently I thought I saw the remedy.

"We can't make a door," said I; "but we must n't let them learn the way here."

"How can we help it?" said Tommy.

"We must take them one at a time, and blindfold them at your father's gate, and then lead them down here by some real crooked, roundabout way."

Tommy was delighted with the idea.

"And that," said he, "will do instead of a winding passage."

In the evening we went to the common and got the horse's skull. Then we scoured the whole common to find another one, but we were not successful.

"Never mind," said Tommy, "I guess we can make this one do."

We carried it home and deposited it in the woodshed.

Early next morning Tommy came over to our house in high spirits.

"I 've found just the thing, in our garret," said he.

"What is it?" said I, eagerly.

"Come and see!"

I went with him over to their woodshed, and, after shutting the door and locking it, he went to a barrel in one corner, and carefully lifted out one of those plaster models of the human head which the phrenologists use, with little paper labels pasted on the bumps all over it.

"That 's splendid! That 's lucky!" said I, in unfeigned admiration.

"That 'll make it look like Herculaneum," said he.

Tommy wrapped it in an old piece of carpet, and I put a newspaper around the horse's skull, and we hurried them to the cave.

The keg we had stood on for the high work was still there. We placed it in one corner, threw the piece of carpet over it, and set the bust on it. Then we scooped a hole in the wall, and put in the skull so that it stuck about half-way out. We tamped the dirt close around it, making it look as if it had been buried there before the cave was formed.

Tommy surveyed it and pronounced it perfectly satisfactory.

"That," said he, "looks just like the catacombs."

We were now ready for customers, and we agreed upon the route over which they must travel. We thought we 'd light it up with a candle or two after school, and then bring the boys in.

If we made rather poor recitations that day, you may readily guess the reason. We hurried home after school, and got a stub of a candle and carried it to the cave, where we lighted it and placed it on a shingle driven into the wall, and then went to the front gate to look for customers.

The first boy that came along was Charlie Garnett.

"Hello, Charlie!"

"Hello!"

"We 've found a cave," said Tommy.

"A cave!" said Charlie, wonderingly.

"Yes, a cave; and it 's full of curiosities. Stalactites, and statues, and skulls, and stone tomahawks, and arrows, and lots of things. Like Herculaneum and the Mammoth Cave, you know."

"You 're foolin'," said Charlie.

"No foolin'," said Tommy, solemnly. "We 'll take you all through it for five cents."

"Honest true?"

"Honest true! Aint it?" and he turned to me for confirmation.

"Yes," said I, "it 's a splendid cave."

"But I haint got five cents," said Charlie.

"How much *have* you got?" said Tommy.

"Only three."

Tommy consulted with me. He thought it was better to let him in for three cents than not to have him visit it at all. I assented.

"We 'll let *you* in for three," said Tommy, graciously.

"All right! Where 's your cave?" said Charlie.

"We 'll blindfold you and lead you there," said Tommy.

"No you don't! I know your tricks," said Charlie.

"No trick about it," said Tommy; "is there?" and again he appealed to me.

"There is n't any trick in it," said I "It 's

a real cave. But we don't want anybody to know where to find it. And besides, it 's more fun to go blindfolded. It makes it seem like the dark winding passages of the Mammoth Cave."

Charlie concluded he 'd try it. Tommy took his three cents, and then we tied a handkerchief tightly over his eyes. We led him through the gate, three times around the house, once around the barn, once around Mrs. Baker's flower-beds, then to the bowlder and on top of it.

"Now," said I, "jump down about four feet with me."

We jumped, and at the same time Tommy rattled an iron chain against the stone, "to make it seem dungeony," he said. Then we took him down the bank to the brook, and up the other side, and three times around a tree, and over a big flat stump, and down to the brook again, and up the bank, and along the narrow path to the cave. We went to the center of the interior before we unblindfolded him.

"One, two, three!" said Tommy, and jerked off the bandage.

Charlie was lost in amazement. He looked around in perfect awe and wonder, and was speechless as a mummy—until he saw the skull. He walked up close to that, which was near the candle, and looked at it steadily a minute or two.

"That was my father's horse," said he, turning round and facing us. "You 've got to pay me for that."

"I aint agoing to pay for no dead horses," said Tommy, excitedly, his business principles getting the better of his grammar. "What 's throwed out on the common," he continued, "is anybody's that wants it."

Charlie was not ready to admit this proposition, and a serious debate seemed likely to ensue; but just here certain events which had been happening above ground came to a crisis.

Mrs. Baker had several ladies visiting her that afternoon, and they all walked out to see her flower-garden. As they stood admiring a bed of lilies-of-the-valley, six of them, including Mrs. Baker, suddenly found themselves moving in a direct line toward China.

At the same instant, we heard a cracking and crumbling overhead; and as the lumps of dirt and stalactites began to fall, Tommy cried out: "It's cavin' in! run!" and we hurriedly adjourned the debate, and fled out of the cavern in mortal terror.

We were none to quick. Six unprofitable visitors, who had not paid anything, and had no free passes, and were not blindfolded, were suddenly introduced into the midst of all the wonders of the Mammoth Cave, the Indian mounds, the catacombs, and Herculaneum. And they brought daylight with them, before which the glory and the mystery of those wonders vanished forever.

The screaming and the consternation that ensued may be imagined. Daddy Blake, who was working in a garden two doors off, came promptly to the rescue. He wasted no time in approaching the cave by the winding passage, but got the long step-ladder, let it down from the top, and helped the ladies out.

Fortunately no one was seriously hurt, but there was a terrible rumpling of toilets. Old Mrs. Simmons came out looking as if the sharpest of the Indian weapons had been deftly wielded about her scalp. Perhaps her wig reposes to this day on the bald bumps of the phrenologist's model. Miss Moore's muslin dress was badly torn on the stalactites; and Mrs. Baker's shoes, like the tiger's visitors in the fable, made no tracks away from that dread cave. If the loss of them could have saved her son from punishment, he at least would have been entirely satisfied.

As for Tommy and me, we did n't exactly want the hills to cover us—that we

could have had by standing still. But we
felt the desirability of immediate emigra-
tion. We ran down the gorge of the brook,
and escaped to the woods, not venturing
home until night-fall.

The next day, Tommy came over. He
did not come into the house, but stole
around to the woodshed, and gave a low
whistle. I went out, and we sat down on
a large billet of wood. "Old Burke was at
our house this morning," said he.

"What did he want?" said I, a little
nervously, apprehending some new peril.

"He wanted to see father. He said he 'd
wondered what made the water that comes
into his house so muddy these two or three
weeks back. And yesterday the hydraulic
ram stopped working, and he went and
found it clogged up with dirt. And then
he traced the muddy water up to the brook,
until he came to where we threw the dirt
over from the cave. That 's what he wanted
to see father about."

"What did your father say?"

"He said he was very sorry, and then he
told him all about it. Then he said he was
going to have the cave filled up, and not
have any more such works. He 's going
to send me away to boarding-school next
week."

Here Tommy looked very doleful, and a
long pause ensued.

This would necessarily wind up the
cave business, and dissolve the partnership. Tommy said nothing about dividing
the profits, and I deliberately reminded
him that there must be a little cash in the
treasury.

"There 's only three cents," said he.

"Yes," said I, "three cents."

"And that can't be divided evenly," said
he.

"That 's so," said I.

"And the cave was on our land," said
he.

"Yes," said I, "it was on your land"—
and I added silently, "I 'm glad it was."

"And, besides, *I* had to take a lickin',"
he added, ruefully.

"Did you? That 's too bad," said I,
with genuine sympathy.

Tommy handed me one cent.

"That 's fair," said I.

Charlie's eyes are unbandaged

A RUNAWAY TRAIN

by F. Lovell Coombs

"HURRY in, Al, or the lamp will blow out!" Alex Ward closed the station door behind him and laughingly flicked his rain-soaked cap toward the day operator, whom he had just come to relieve. He had been at Foothills, his first permanent station, three months.

"Is it raining that hard? You look like the proverbial drowned rat," said Saunders, as he prepared to depart.

"Wait until you are out in it, and you won't laugh. It 's the worst storm this spring," said Alex, throwing off his dripping coat.

"And you wait until you see the fun you have with the wire. The heavy rain has had it out of commission to the east for an hour. Have n't had a dot from the despatcher since six o'clock."

"There is some one now," said Alex, as the instruments suddenly began clicking.

"It 's somebody west—IC, I think. Yes; Indian Canyon," said Saunders, pausing as he turned toward the door. "But he certainly can't make himself heard by X if we can't."

"X, X, X," rapidly ticked the sounder, calling Exeter, the despatching office. "X, X! Qk! Qk!"

Alex and Saunders turned toward one another with a start. Several times the operator at Indian Canyon repeated the call, more urgently, then as hurriedly began calling Imken, the next station east of him.

"There 's something wrong!" said Alex, stepping to the instrument-table. Saunders followed.

"IM, IM, IM! Qk! Qk!" clicked the sounder.

"I, I, IM," came the response. The two operators at Foothills leaned forward expectantly.

"A wild string of loaded ore-cars just passed here," the instruments were saying. "They 're going forty miles an hour! They 'll be down there in no time! If there is anything on the main line, for heaven's sake get it off! I can't raise X for orders!"

Alex and Saunders exchanged glances of alarm and anxiously awaited Imken's reply. For a moment the instruments made a succession of inarticulate dots, then clicked excitedly, "Yes, yes! OK! OK!" and closed.

"What do you suppose he meant by that?" said Saunders. "That there was something on the main track there?"

A minute the wire remained silent, then again snapped open and whirred: "I got it off—the yard engine! Just in time! Here they come now! Ten of them! All loaded! Going like an avalanche! Thank goodness we got—"

Sharply the operator at IC cut in to as hurriedly call Terryville, the next station east.

"But the runaway won't pass Terryville, will they?" exclaimed Alex, with a new

341

anxiety. "Won't the grades between there and Imken stop them?"

Saunders shook his head. "Ten loaded ore-cars traveling at that rate would climb a stiff grade."

"Then they 'll be down here in twenty or twenty-five minutes! And there 's the accommodation coming east, and we can't reach any one to stop her!"

"Well, what *can* we do?" said Saunders, hopelessly.

Terryville answered, and breathlessly they awaited his report.

"Yes, they are coming! They are going past now," he added a moment after. "They 're past!"

"They 'll reach us! What shall we do?" gasped Saunders.

Alex turned from the instrument-table, and, as IC hastily called Jakes Creek, the last station intervening, began striding up and down the room, thinking rapidly.

"If they only had more battery—could make the current in the wire stronger!" Instantly he recalled the emergency battery he had made at Watson Siding, and with an ejaculation spun about toward the water-cooler. But only to utter an exclamation of disappointment. This cooler was of tin—of course useless for such a purpose.

Hastily he began casting about for a substitute. "Billy, think of something we can make a big battery of," he cried. "To strengthen the wire!"

"A battery? But what would you do for bluestone? I used the last yesterday," said Saunders.

Alex returned to the table and threw himself into the chair.

"Say, perhaps one of the other fellows on the wire has some, and could make the battery."

With a shout of "That 's it!" Alex seized the telegraph key, broke in, and called

Indian Canyon. "Have you any extra battery material there?" he sent quickly.

"Why . . . no. Why?"

Abruptly Alex cut him off and called Imken. He also responded in the negative. But from Terryville came a prompt "Yes. Why—"

"Have you a big stoneware water-cooler?"

"Yes; but wh—"

"Do you know how to make a battery?"

"No."

"Well, listen—"

Suddenly the instruments failed to respond. A minute passed, and another. Five went by, and Alex sank back in the chair in despair. Undoubtedly the wire had been broken somewhere.

"Everything is against us," he exclaimed bitterly. "And the runaways will be down here now in fifteen or twenty minutes. What can we do?"

"The only thing I can think of is throwing the west switch and trying to run them onto the siding," said Saunders. "But there 's not one chance in ten of their making it—probably they 'd only pile up in an awful smash."

"If there was any way of getting aboard the runaways—" Alex broke off sharply. Would it not be possible to board them as he and Jack Orr had boarded the engine the day of the forest fire? Say from a hand-car?

He started to his feet, and exclaiming, "Billy, get me a lantern, quick!" ran for his coat and hat.

"I 'm going to run for the section boss and see if we can't board that wildcat from the hand-car," he explained, struggling into the coat. "I did that once at Bixton—boarded an engine."

"Board it? And what then?"

"Why, put on the brakes and bring it to

a stop, of course; then run ahead and flag 18!"

Saunders hastened for the lantern, and quickly lighting it, Alex dashed for the door, out across the platform, and off up the tracks toward the lights of the section foreman's house. Darting through the gate, he ran about to the kitchen door and without ceremony flung it open. The foreman was at table, at his tea. He sprang to his feet.

"Joe, there is a wild ore-train coming down from the Canyon," said Alex, breathlessly, "and the wire has failed east, so we can't clear the line. Can't we get the hand-car out and board the runaways by letting them catch us?"

An instant the section boss stared, then, with the promptness of the old railroader, seized his cap, and exclaiming, "Go ahead!" dashed out after Alex, in the direction of the tool-shed.

"Where did they start from? How many cars?" he asked as they ran.

"Indian Canyon. Ten, and all loaded."

The sectionman whistled. "They 'll be going twenty-five or thirty miles an hour. We 'll be taking a big chance. But if we can catch them just over the grade beyond the sand-pits, I guess we can do it. That will have slackened them."

"Here we are."

As they halted before the section-house door, the foreman uttered a cry. "I have n't the key!"

Alex swung the lantern about and discovered a pile of ties. "Smash it in," he said, dropping the lantern; and, one on either side, they caught up a tie, swung back, and hurled it forward; there was a crash, and the door was open.

Catching up the lantern, they ran in, threw from the car its collection of tools, placed the light upon it, and seizing it on either side, staggered out with it to the rails.

"Do you hear them?" asked Alex, as he threw off his coat.

The foreman dropped to his knees and placed his ear to the rails, listened a moment, and sprang to his feet. "Yes; they are coming. Come on!"

"Run her a little first!" They pushed the little car ahead, quickly had it on the run, and springing aboard, seized the handles, one at either end, and began pumping up and down with all their strength.

As they flew toward the station, the door opened, and Saunders ran to the edge of the platform and shouted: "I cut off the west, and just heard Z pass 18. He reported the superintendent's—"

They whirled by, and the rest was lost.

"Did you catch it?" shouted Alex to the foreman above the roar of the wheels.

"I think he meant . . . the 'old man's' car . . . attached to the accommodation," shouted the sectionman, as his head flew up and down. "Heard he was coming . . . worse for us . . . we need every minute . . . Old Jerry, the engineer . . . will be breaking his neck . . . to bring the accommodation . . . through on time!"

"Do you hear . . . the runaways yet?"

"No," shouted Alex.

On they rushed through the darkness, bobbing up and down like demon jumping-jacks, the little car screaming and screeching, and bounding forward like a live thing.

The terrific and unaccustomed strain began to tell on Alex. The perspiration stood out on his brow, his muscles lagged and his breath shortened.

"How much farther?" he called hoarsely.

"Here 's the grade now! Half a mile to the top!"

As they felt the resistance of the incline, Alex began to weaken and gasp for breath. But grimly he clenched his teeth and fought on; and at last the section boss suddenly ceased pumping, peered aside into the darkness, and announced: "Here we are! Let up!" And with a gasp of relief Alex dropped down to a sitting position.

A moment after, he straightened up and listened. From the west came a sound as of distant thunder.

"It 's coming! How long before it 'll be here?" he panted.

"Five minutes, perhaps. And now," said the sectionman, "just how are we going to work it?"

"Well," said Alex, getting his breath, "when we boarded the engine at Bixton, we simply waited at the top of a grade until she was within about two hundreds yards of us, then lit out as hard as we could go, and just as she bumped us we jumped."

"All right. We 'll do the same."

As the foreman spoke, the rain, which had decreased to a drizzle, suddenly ceased, and the moon appeared. Instantly he and Alex glanced toward the station and uttered a common exclamation. Just beyond was a long black snake-like object, shooting along the rails toward them.

The runaway!

On it swept over the glistening irons, the rumble quickly increasing to a roar. With an echoing crash it flashed by the station, and on.

Nearer it came, the cars leaping and writhing; roaring, pounding, screeching.

"Ready!" said the foreman, springing to the ground behind the hand-car. Alex joined him, and peering back over their shoulder, watching, they braced themselves for the shove.

The runaways reached the incline; swept on upward. Anxiously they gazed. Would the grade materially check them?

"Are they slowing?" asked Alex, nervously.

"Some, I think. But it will tell most near the head of the grade," said the foreman.

"But get ready! We can't wait to see!

"Go!" he cried, and rushing the car forward, they leaped aboard, seized the handles, and quickly were again pumping madly.

For a few moments the roar behind them seemed to decrease. Then suddenly it broke on them afresh, and the head of the train swept over the rise behind them.

"Now pull yourself together for an extra spurt when I say," shouted the foreman, who manned the forward handles and faced the rear, "then turn about and get ready to jump."

Roaring, screaming, clanking, the runaways thundered down upon them.

"Hit it up!" cried the sectionman. With every muscle tense, they whirled the handles up and down like madmen. "Let go! Turn!"

Alex sprang back from the whirling handles and faced about. The foreman edged by them and joined him. Nearer, towering over them, rushed the leading car. "Now be sure and jump high and grab hard," shouted the foreman.

"Ready! JUMP!"

With a bound they went into the air, and the great car flung itself against them. Their outstretched hands reached the top of the end-board, and momentarily they hung, clutching desperately, while the car leaped and bounded beneath them. Getting their feet on the brake-beam, they struggled upward. And in another moment, tumbling headlong within, they were safely aboard.

Alex sank down on the rough ore, utterly exhausted, gasping; but the seasoned foreman immediately got to his feet, seized the near-by brake-wheel, quickly tightened it, and scrambling back over the bounding train, one by one put on the remaining brakes.

Soon the pressure on the wheels began

to tell, and ten minutes later, screeching and groaning protestingly, the runaways came finally to a stop.

Another ten minutes later, when a quarter-mile distant, the engineer aboard the flying accommodation suddenly "threw on his air," as he discovered a lantern between the rails ahead of him. His train came to a stand, and he was greeted by a shout from the foreman.

"And I say, Jerry," added the latter, humorously, as he went forward, "you 're not good enough for a passenger run. You 're to push ore-cars. There 's a string just ahead of you."

When he explained, the engineer stepped down from his cab, wiping the cold moisture from his forehead, and on catching sight of Alex he sprang forward to grasp his hand.

"Oh, it was more the foreman than I," said Alex, modestly. "I could n't have worked it at all without him."

At that moment the division superintendent himself appeared.

"Why, let me see!" he exclaimed. "Are you not the lad I helped fix up an emergency battery at Watson Siding last spring? and who has engineered two or three other similar clever affairs?

"Well, my boy, young as you are, if I don't give you a try-out at the division office before the month is out, my name 's not Cameron. We need men there with heads like yours."

SNAGGLE-TOOTH OF SUNKEN LAKE

by David M. Newell

FAR back in the big cypress marsh, where the frogs drone an endless chorus and the owls call gutturally on cloudy days, lies Sunken Lake. It is an eery, dismal place, surrounded by dark jungles and ghostly gray cypresses. Few are the visitors to Sunken Lake. Occasionally, a passing deer will stop to drink or a flight of ducks swing down at twilight. But rarely do these visitors fail to pay the price. With the coming of day, the ducks resume their flight,—always a smaller flock,—and often the unwary deer does not leave at all. For in the dark depths of Sunken Lake there lurks sudden, silent death. Snaggle-tooth exacts his toll.

He is old,—older than all the other creatures,—and he is wise in the way of man and beast. Many, many years ago, a rival invaded his domain. The resulting battle had been a terrible thing to see. Only the old owls remembered that fight. For three hours the giant reptiles had thrashed and churned the quiet waters of Sunken Lake. It was a fierce and bloody fight, and not until Snaggle-tooth had locked his great jaws in a deadly throat-hold was the issue decided. After the battle, Snaggle-tooth drifted into a quiet lagoon and nursed his injured jaws. Three of his big tusks had been broken completely off. But that was many, many years ago.

In a little sawmill town on the north edge of the big swamp, three or four men were talking about alligators. Back in the shadows, a youngster of fourteen was sitting on the porch rail listening with all his ears. His name was Ross Allen, and he has a great deal to do with this story. Like the great majority of boys, Ross Allen loved the out of doors. He loved to go on long jaunts after school with his two proudest possessions—"Old Tom" and "Long Tom." Old Tom was an ancient pointer dog, and Long Tom was a twelve-gage single-shot gun with a barrel of most astonishing length. With Long Tom, Ross was wont to blast away at whatever Old Tom put up, and Old Tom stopped at nothing. He pointed quail like a champion, and the next minute ran rabbits with all his heart. Occasionally, he would tree a possum for variety's sake, and once he had put a big coon up a pine. Long Tom attended to the coon, and Ross and Old Tom proudly tacked his hide where all could see. So, for his age, Ross was considered quite a hunter. Furthermore, he had been one of the few visitors to Sunken Lake.

And so when Major Jim said: "All this talk about big alligators makes me tired. I've never seen one over twelve feet long in twenty years' hunting over the State," Ross Allen's eyes sparkled and he started to speak. He had seen something that misty day on Sunken Lake. But Major Jim went on talking before Ross could say anything. Major Jim was a very "big" man, Ross's father had said, and had lots of money; so, of course, Ross did n't dare to interrupt. He waited his time. Major Jim continued:

"I 'll just wager five hundred dollars that none of you fellows ever saw a 'gator thirteen feet long. I 'll do better than that. I 'll give anybody five hundred dollars for a hide that measures thirteen feet or over."

Ross Allen's breath came fast. "Please, sir, I have seen a 'gator that looked 'bout twenty feet long."

Major Jim peered into the shadows, and laughed. "They all *look* big in the water, son, but when the tape is put on them they seem to shrink."

Ross answered earnestly, "Yes, sir, but I 've lived all my life 'round where there were big ol' 'gators."

The major laughed again as he replied, "All your life has n't been such a terribly long time at that, has it, son?"

"Fo'teen years," answered Ross, proudly.

"Where did you see this enormous alligator, son?" queried the major. Ross flushed and looked down at the floor. Major Jim nodded. "That 's all right. Keep it to yourself, lad, and if you bring him in and he goes thirteen or over, the money 's yours."

Ross Allen went home thinking hard. His father was a poor man with a large family, and five hundred dollars was a sum to dream about. Before going to bed Ross walked up to his father, who was reading before the fire. Big George Allen looked up:

"Well, what 's on your mind, Ross— want to stay home from school to-morrow and go rabbit hunting?"

"No, sir," grinned Ross, "I was jes' wonderin' if I could borrow your big rifle next Saturday."

George Allen laid down his paper. For a minute he could only gasp. Then he said: "No, Ross. That ain't no gun for you

to be a-playin' with. Why, you might shoot somebody over in Putnam County."

"Please, Dad!" begged Ross. "Maybe I can make five hundred dollars."

George Allen laughed. "What are you fixin' to do, son—capture a wild man for a circus?"

"No, sir," answered Ross, gravely. "Major Jim said he would pay five hundred dollars for a 'gator thirteen feet long, an' I know a place where there 's an awful big 'gator."

His father rose and walked to a corner of the room. Then he reached up and took down a long-barreled Winchester from a pair of deer horns and returned to Ross.

"Son," said he, "this here 's a .45—70. It ain't no pop-gun. You go ahead and kill that 'gator. Be careful where you 're shootin'. That 's all I 've got to say."

SATURDAY dawned still and cloudy. Down in the swamp the alligators were making the ground tremble with their bellowing. An ideal day, thought Ross, as he took the dim trail that led toward Sunken Lake. At home, Old Tom howled long and mournfully at being left. Down at the south end of Sunken Lake, Snaggle-tooth drifted silently toward a flock of ducks.

It was nearly noon when Ross reached the saw-grass marsh that edged the big lake. Carefully he worked his way out through the marsh until he neared the edge of the open water. Then, climbing upon a great cypress log, he scanned the lake. His heart missed a beat. There, within fifty feet, where the ducks and, rapidly nearing them, was Snaggle-tooth. Ross knew it was the king of Sunken Lake as soon as he saw him. The boy was only fourteen years old, it is true, but he had seen many a big alligator. But never had he seen the like of Snaggle-tooth. Only the monster's eyes and nostrils showed above

"Straight up out of the water he reared—fully half his length"

water, but Ross filled in the rest with his imagination. Why, from its eyes to its nose was fully two feet! The boy raised the old Winchester to his shoulder. His heart pounded against his ribs and his breath came fast with excitement. A great deal depended on that shot.

With the roar of the .45—70, the ducks got up frantically and the huge 'gator thrashed the water with his tail as he dove. Ross watched breathlessly. Gradually the ripples subsided and the placid surface of Sunken Lake remained undisturbed. The tears burned Ross's eyes. He had missed! But along the mossy lake-bottom, Snaggle-tooth swam with long, powerful strokes. There was a burning pain over his left eye, and for once he was afraid. His head still rocked from the terrific impact of the soft-nose bullet on the water. The actual wound was merely a glancing one that had scraped his thick skull and broken the skin. Snaggle-tooth did not venture near the surface until he had crossed the lake and was safely hidden in one of the many little bayous that opened into the swamp.

Ross Allen went home bitterly disappointed. That night he told Old Tom all about it, and Old Tom sympathized. Had he been able to talk, he would probably have said:

"Ross, I 'm mighty sorry, but what could you expect when I was left at home. Of course, I have never hunted alligators, but then I am a pretty old dog and know lots of tricks."

But being just a dog, he only wagged his tail and whined softly as he licked Ross's ear. And Ross, being a boy that hated to give up, and perhaps knowing just what Old Tom meant, untied the old dog the following Saturday morning and again took the Sunken Lake trail. This time he started long before daylight, so that when the east began to turn pink behind the cypresses he and Old Tom were safely settled behind a clump of saw-grass on the west shore of the lake. This morning there were no ducks on the lake. Everything was strangely still. There was not even a breath of wind, and the gray moss hung in straight, long streamers from the cypresses. An hour passed. Old Tom began to grow restless. This was a new kind of hunting to him. Ross raised the rifle and sighted it carefully at an imaginary target. Old Tom whined eagerly.

Now it so happened that Snaggle-tooth was very, very hungry. For five days he had had nothing to eat. True, it was his own fault for he had missed several easy catches. Perhaps his experience with a .45—70 bullet had made him a little too wary. At any rate, he was hungry. Furthermore, he happened to be floating along the edge of the lake when Old Tom whined. Now, several years before, Snaggle-tooth had had a very pleasant meal. The memory of that meal came to him now. He had heard a strange sound—the far-off baying of hounds. The strange sound had come nearer and nearer. Suddenly, a big buck had leaped into the lake and started across. Snaggle-tooth had made a great effort to get that deer, but had arrived too late. Immediately following the deer had come the dogs—three of them. The giant alligator had never seen a dog before, but he had decided that they would be very good eating. The result had been highly satisfactory. So now when Snaggle-tooth heard Old Tom whine, he licked his huge tusks in anticipation and swam rapidly toward the sound.

Ross had just about given up hope when he saw what looked like a great black log drift around a little point of saw-grass. Could it be Snaggle-tooth? He half raised his rifle. Old Tom knew what that meant and he again whined loudly. Straight for the sound came the alligator, and Ross crouched lower and held his breath. At this juncture, Old Tom slipped off into the water with quite a splash. Ross gave a little gasp, for he feared that the noise would scare away the giant alligator. But Snaggle-tooth heard that splash, and he swam with all his might toward Ross and Old Tom. He was swimming high, for he was in a great hurry. He was afraid that that dog might get away. Forgotten were all thoughts of men and guns. Snaggle-tooth was hungry.

When Ross saw the great ridged back and the long flat head he raised his rifle. The barrel trembled a little as he sighted it. The huge alligator was a scant twenty feet away when Ross pressed the trigger. With the shot, Snaggle-tooth gave a great lunge. Straight up out of the water he reared—fully half his length. Ross held his rifle ready, but there was no need for a second shot. The king of Sunken Lake floated under side up with a bullet in his evil brain!

For a few minutes the youngster crouched motionless behind the little clump of saw-grass. Then, realizing that Snaggle-tooth was really dead, Ross seized a near-by limb and, after several unsuccessful attempts, managed to bring the big alligator within reach. After an hour's work he succeeded in getting Snaggle-tooth into shallow water, and then gave a low whistle when he saw the reptile's real size. He had not quite realized just how large old Snaggle-tooth was. Old Tom bristled and growled. This sort of game was something out of his line and was too large a creature to take any chances with! But when Ross took out his knife and prepared to skin the great alligator, Old Tom lay down beside him with a very proud air indeed.

Ross laughed, "Tom, I guess you knew a little bit about 'gator huntin' after all."

It was nearly dark when Ross finished skinning old Snaggle-tooth and, to his dismay, he found that he could not lift the hide. He had not reckoned on this and naturally was disappointed, for he could hardly wait to take it in and measure it. He was afraid even to guess at its true length, although he knew that he had a trophy that would make Major Jim open his eyes. Finally, he decided on a plan and, calling Old Tom, set out for home. That night he again approached his father.

"Dad," he said, "I want to take old Jinny a while to-morrow."

Ross and his father were rather close friends, and after a long look into his son's eyes, big George Allen grinned. "So you got him, did you, Ross,"

"Yes, sir," answered the youngster, proudly.

"How many shots?"

"Two—I missed him last Saturday."

"How big is he, son?"

"I 'm scared to say, Dad."

"Well," grunted George, "I 'll go down with you to-morrow and help you skin him."

"He 's done skinned, Dad," answered Ross, "but I just could n't tote the hide."

His father whistled, and said: "All right. Take old Jinny—but I don't think she 'll let you pack a 'gator hide on her."

THE following morning, Ross took the trail with a singing heart. Jinny, the old mule, made good time and by eight o'clock Ross arrived at his prize. Jinny snorted and refused to be led anywhere near the hide. Finally, Ross blindfolded her and, after a good deal of trouble, managed to get Snaggle-tooth's hide across the saddle. When he reached home his father met him at the gate. For a full minute George Allen stared without saying a word. Then he said:

"Mother, come out here and see the 'gator our Ross has got. I 've seen 'em big, but this here one 's the great, great grand-daddy of all the 'gators."

The two parents surveyed old Snaggle-tooth from the great jaws to the tip of the long ridged tail. Mrs. Allen shuddered. To think that her boy had killed such a creature, and killed him in his own lair, made her a bit proud, but also just a little bit faint.

Ross, however, had other matters in mind. He was thinking of the night on the hotel porch and of words spoken by Major Jim.

"I 'll be back directly," he said, turning

to his father. "I 'm goin' over now and get this here 'gator measured."

Major Jim was on the hotel porch when Ross and old Jinny arrived. His eyes bulged at the sight of the great black hide that dragged along the ground on both sides of the old mule.

"Great jumping bullfrogs!" he roared, "Where on earth did you get *that?*"

Ross grinned. "Down on Sunken Lake."

"Well," bellowed the major, "I never heard of the place. I am beginning to think that there are several things I did n't know about. You wait here, lad, while I go after a tape-measure—and I think it might be a good idea to get my check-book too!"

Ross Allen's heart swelled in his breast. When the major came out, Ross had spread old Snaggle-tooth on the ground, and an admiring crowd was standing around. Major Jim stretched the tape. Then he stood up and, looking around, drew a long breath.

"Folks," he said in a queer voice, "this alligator hide is *fifteen feet, three inches* in length!" Then, turning to Ross: "Son, here 's your check. I wrote it when I went after the tape. I knew when I saw the hide hanging over that old mule that I was whipped. After this if a man tells me he has seen a flying-squirrel six times as big as a horse, I shall have nothing whatever to say. And, what is more, I hereby offer you one hundred dollars for that 'gator hide. What do you say?"

"Yes, sir," grinned Ross. "There it is!"

THE WRONG COAT

by Rose Terry Cooke

"FIRE! Fire!"

Jack Parry rubbed his eyes, as he sprang out of his cot-bed in the loft, and instinctively hurried on his trousers. His father's head rose above the ladder, just as he shuffled on his shoes, shouting: "Hurry up, I tell ye! woods afire! Comin' this way quicker 'n scat!"

Jack scrambled down the ladder without stopping for his jacket. He knew what that news meant—he had heard about forest fires before. His father had always thought that the creek which ran in front of their house would guard them, but now the air was dark with smoke, and he could hear the roar and crash of the forest falling before its mighty foe, while sharp gusts of wind swept ashes far and wide over the grain-fields of the farm. But the fire was still on the other side of that slow, narrow stream: could it, would it keep the enemy from their house and barns?

It would not do to run the risk. Jack, at a word, went off to harness the horses, and put them to the big wagon, while his father helped his mother to gather a few wraps and valuables together, and dress the frightened, screaming baby.

When the Parrys moved to Michigan, Grandpa Dibble, who always objected to everything, said to his son-in-law:

"But how 'll ye edicate the childern, John?"

"I don't know, Father," said John Parry. "Sary 'll teach 'm to read an' write, prob'ly, and I 'll insure they 'll learn to mind an' be honest. I take it that these two things will have to underlay any edication that 's good for shucks: we must risk the rest."

Obedience and honesty Jack had indeed been thoroughly taught. He had never harnessed the horses alone before, but at his father's order he went to work manfully, and was all ready when the others came to the house-door.

"Oh, Jack! no coat on?" said the delicate, trembling little mother.

"Can't stop for it now," said John Parry. "It 's life or death, Sary! There goes a big white-wood smash acrost the crick! Run the critters, Jack—the fire 's after us!"

In another moment they were beyond the house, but not an instant too soon, for a burning branch, whirled on by the fierce wind, swept through the air and lit on the roof, which blazed like paper beneath it.

Jack lashed the terrified horses into a run, while his father, on the back seat, held the sick baby in one arm, and put the other about his wife to steady her.

The air grew heavier and hotter; the roads were rough, the wagon-springs hard. Blinded with smoke and frightened at the nearing roar of storm and flame, the horses flew on beyond the power of any guiding hand. There was a sudden lurch, the wheels tilted on a log by the wayside, and the back seat pitched out behind, with all its occupants! Jack clung to the reins instinctively, but he could no more stop the horses than he could arrest the whirlwind and fire behind him. Father, mother, sister, all were tossed into the track of the fire like dry leaves, and never again did he see one of them. Their fate was certain: he could only hope it had been sudden and sure death.

Carried on by a force he could not control or resist, Jack whirled along, the flames nearing him every moment, till, just as he felt their hot breath on his neck, the maddened horses reached the lake-shore, and plunged headlong into its waters. But he, at least, was safe, for the shock threw him out on the sand.

Poor Jack! In the morning he was a hearty, happy boy, asleep in a good home; at night a homeless, penniless orphan, with scarce clothes to cover him. Days passed over his head in a sort of blank misery. A few others, escaped also from the devouring flames, shared with him their scanty food; a kindly woman gave him an old woolen sack she ill knew how to spare to cover his ragged shirt, and he found a pair of India-rubbers lying on the shore, which concealed his worn shoes; but a more desolate, helpless creature than the poor boy can hardly be imagined.

After a week or two, he begged his way to Pompo,—a settlement farther up the lake, which had not been touched by the great fire,—and heard there that good people at the East had sent on clothes to be distributed among those who had lost theirs. He soon got a chance to ride over on a lumber-wagon to the nearest place where these things were given out,—a town ten miles beyond Pompo,—and there the agent gave him a couple of shirts, a warm vest, a pair of half-worn black trousers, and a very good coat of mixed cloth, that until then had proved too small for the men who had applied for clothes. But

as Jack was fifteen, and large for his age, it just fitted him, and once more clothed, neat, and clean, he went back to Pompo, where he had found a place to work on a farm, happier than he had been for a long time.

It was night when he returned to the farm, and quite bed-time; so he ate some bread and milk Mrs. Smith had saved for him, and went up to his garret chamber. As he took off his new coat to hang it up, with a boy's curiosity he explored all its pockets. In one he found a half-soiled handkerchief, just as if the owner had taken the coat down from the closet peg and sent it off without a thought, for the garment was almost new. But underneath the handkerchief, lying loose in the bottom of the pocket, were two twenty-dollar bills!

Jack's heart gave a great bound; here was a windfall indeed, and he began to think what he should do with this small fortune. But perhaps there was something else in the other pocket—yes here was a letter directed, sealed, and stamped, all ready to mail; and in a small inner breast-pocket he found three horse-car tickets, a cigarette, and a three-cent piece. In the other breast-pocket were a gray kid glove, and a card with the name, "James Agard, Jr." He looked at the letter again; on one corner was printed: "Return to James Agard & Co., Deerford, Conn., if not delivered in ten days." Jack was not a dull boy, and it flashed across him at once that this coat had been put into the box by mistake; it must have belonged to James Agard, Jr. He looked again at the handkerchief, and found that name on the corner.

What should he do? The coat had been given to him—why not keep it? He sat down on his bed to think. His short end of tallow candle had gone out, but the late-risen moon poured a flood of mellow light through his window and seemed to look him in the face. While he thinks the thing out at the West, let us take up the Eastern end of the story.

Just three days after the great fires, certain prompt young people in a New England church congregation came together in the parlors of that church to receive and pack clothing for the burnt-out sufferers; and for a week contributions poured in upon them, and gave them work for both head and hands. Into this busy crowd one day hurried a slight, active young man, dressed in gray business suit.

"Hallo!" he called out, cheerily. "I 've come to help the old-clo' boxes along. Give me work at once, Mrs. Brooks—anything but sewing."

Mrs. Brooks laughed.

"Can you pack a barrel, Mr. Agard?"

"Yes, indeed; just pile on the things," and he went to work with an alacrity that showed he knew how to do his work. This energetic little man packed more than one barrel before night, and, in order to work better, threw his coat aside, as the rooms were warm. When evening came, he drew himself up with a laugh, exclaiming:

"There! I can 'go West, young man,' and earn my living as a pork-packer, if you 'll only recommend me, Mrs. Brooks."

"That I will," said she, "and others, too. We have sent off ten barrels since you came in, Mr. Agard; we had to hurry, for the freight train left at four o'clock."

Just then he turned to look for his coat. It was not where he left it. He searched the room in vain, and at last called out:

"Has anybody seen my coat?"

"Where did you leave it?" asked George Bruce, a young man who had also been packing very busily.

"On the back of that chair."

"Was it a gray mixed sack?"

"Yes."

"Well, sir, it 's gone off to the sufferers, then. I saw it on the chair, thought it was a contribution, packed it, headed up the barrel, and sent it to the train."

"What! You 're a nice fellow, Bruce— sent my coat off! How am I to get home?"

"It is too bad," said Mrs. Brooks. "I 'll take you home in the carriage, Mr. Agard."

"Thank you, kindly; but that is n't all. I had forty dollars in one pocket, and a letter to be mailed with a thousand-dollar check in it. I must hurry home and have that check stopped; the bills will go for an involuntary contribution, I suppose. Bruce, I feel like choking you!"

"And I 'm willing to let you, Jim, if it 'll relieve your mind. It was outrageously careless of me. I don't suppose there 's the slightest chance of tracing it."

"No more than a dropped penny in Broadway. Miss Van Ness wont have her Jacqueminot roses for the german, though, and I 'll tell her it was your fault—I can't throw away any more dollars on nonsense. But I 'm not sure the money is lost as much as it might have been, old fellow. Mrs. Brooks, I 'm ready."

And so James Agard went home, stopped payment of the check by a telegram, and sent an excuse to Miss Van Ness for not attending her german. The roses were to have been a surprise to her, so she did not miss them.

We left Jack sitting in the moonlight, doubting and distressed. But he did not sit there long, for suddenly there came to him a recollection of what his father had said concerning his education to Grandpa Dibble; his mother had repeated it to him so often that it was fixed in his memory. He hid his face in his hands, for it grew hot with shame, to think he had not seen at once that he must send the coat back to its owner. Jack did not hesitate—the right thing must be done quickly. He folded the coat as well as he knew how, replacing everything in the pockets, except the three-cent piece, for which he had a use. Then, quite sure that Mr. Smith, who had hired him, was not the man to understand or approve his action, he made up his mind not to wait till the morning, but to go directly back to Dayton, where he had received his clothes, and where the nearest express office was stationed. He could not return the coat to the agent, for he had distributed all the clothes destined for that point, Jack being one of the last applicants, and had gone on farther with the rest; so he rolled it in a newspaper and slipped downstairs with his shoes in his hand, putting on over his vest the old red sack he had worn before, and set out for Dayton.

He had to beg his breakfast when he reached the town; then he bought a sheet of brown paper, a string, and a postal card with the three-cent piece, and, sitting down on the sunny side of a lumber pile, made the coat into a neat bundle, firmly tied.

He asked the use of pen and ink at the express office, directed his package and wrote his postal as follows, for he could write well, though a little uncertain as to his spelling:

Dayton,——
"Dear Sir: I send you by express to Day a coat which i got in the close sent to burned out fokes here, i doant believe it ought to hev come, so i send it to the name onto the leter, all things Within except 3 sents used for paper, string, and kard.
"Jack Parry."

Jack felt a great weight off his mind when the bundle was fairly out of his hands. It was hard to send away help he needed so much—harder for a homeless, penniless boy than you know, dear Tom and Harry—you who have never been hungry, ragged, and orphaned.

And he not only lost his coat, but his place, for he knew very well, when he left the farm-house, that Mr. Smith, who was a hard and mean man, would never take back a boy who ran away the first night of his service, especially if he knew it was to return a good coat with money in the pocket.

Still he felt that his father and mother would have thought it was dishonest to keep it, and, with the courage of a resolute boy, he felt sure he could find work in Dayton. But he did not. There were plenty of boys, and men, too, already asking for work, and nobody knew him, nor had he any recommendations. For several nights he slept in an empty freight-car near the railway station, doing a little porter's work to pay for this shelter; then he did some things about the tavern stable for his board, sleeping in the shed, or on the hay-mow; and once in a while he caught himself wishing he had that forty dollars to get back to Connecticut, where he had distant relatives. But the quick thought "What would Mother say?" repressed the wish at once.

At last he found steady work on a farm out of town, with small wages. But he had a loft and a bed to himself, and his chief work was to drive a team into Dayton and back with produce, or to fetch lumber, coal, and feed for his employer and the neighbors.

One day, about a month after he went to this place, as he was driving a load of coal past the express office, walking his horses, for the load was heavy and the mud deep, the clerk saw him, and, running to the door, called out:

"Say, young fellow! D' you know anybody name of Jack Parry?"

"I guess so," said Jack, with a smile; "that 's my name. What 's to pay?"

"Nothin'—it 's prepaid. I had a faint reklektion that a fellow about your size left a package here a while ago directed to James Agard. I was n't real sure 't was you, for you are n't rigged out so fancy as you was. What have you done with that red jacket, sonny? Haw! haw! haw!"

Jack colored; he had on an old overcoat of the farmer's, but the red sack was under it, for he had no other coat.

"Well, anyhow, here 's a bundle for Jack Parry, and I reckon that 's for you, since nobody else has called for it; and it 's got a kind of a label on to the tag, same as letters have: 'Return to James Agard & Co., Deerford, Conn., if not called for in one month.' And the month 's a'most up, too,—it 's a nigh thing for you."

Jack did not know what to think or say. He signed a receipt for the bundle, put it up on the coal, and hastily went on his way.

He did not get home till after dark, and when supper was over and all his work done he could only go to bed and wait for morning, as he never was allowed a light in his loft, and he did not want to open the package till he was alone. But with the first dawning light he sprang up eagerly and untied the string. There lay the gray coat, and with it the rest of the suit, a set of warm underclothing, and, on top of all, a letter running thus:

"Deerford, Conn.

"Jack Parry: I am glad there is such an honest boy in Dayton. I wish there were more here, but we want you for another, anyway. If you are out of work, and I think perhaps you are, for I know how it is round the burnt districts, you will find money in the breast-pocket of your coat to buy a ticket for this place. James Agard & Co. want a boy in their store, and want an honest one. Come promptly, and bring this letter to identify yourself.

James Agard, Jr."

"Oh, if Mother only knew it!" was the quick thought that glistened in Jack's happy eyes, and choked him for a moment, as he laid down the letter.

Perhaps she did.

He is in Agard & Co.'s great wholesale store on the Deerford wharves now, and does credit to James Agard, Jr.'s, recommendation.

And it all came of sending the wrong coat!

RICHARD CARR'S BABY

by Richard H. Davis

A FEW years ago, all boys living in the town of Princeton who were of that age when it is easy to remember the fall, winter, spring, and summer as the foot-ball, coasting, swimming, and base-ball seasons, regarded Richard Carr as embodying their ideal of human greatness.

When they read in the history primers how George Washington became the Father of his Country, they felt sure that with a like opportunity Richard Carr would come to the front and be at least the Stepfather of his Country.

They lay in wait for him at the post-office, and as soon as he came in sight would ask for his mail and run to give it to him; they would go ahead of him on the other side of the street, cross over and meet him with a very important "How do you do, Mr. Carr?" and were quite satisfied if he gave them an amused "Hello, youngster!" in return.

Their efforts to imitate his straight, military walk, with shoulders squared and head erect, were of great benefit to their lungs and personal appearance.

Those ragged hangers-on of the college, too, who picked up odd dimes from the students by carrying baggage and chasing tennis balls, waited on Richard Carr, and shouted "Hurrah for you, Carr!" whenever that worthy walked by.

Those who have not already guessed the position which Richard Carr held in the college will be surprised to learn that he was the captain of the college foot-ball team, and those who can not understand the admiration that Arthur Waller, and Willie Beck, and the rest of the small fry of Princeton felt for this young man would better stop here—for neither will they understand this story.

Among all these young hero-worshipers, Richard Carr's most devoted follower was Arthur Waller—"Arty," as his friends called him; for, while the other boys, looking upon Carr as their ideal, hoped that in time they might themselves be even as great as he, Arthur felt that to him at least this glorious possibility must be denied. Arthur was neither strong nor sturdy, and could, he knew, never hope to be like the captain of the foot-ball team, whose strength and physique seemed therefore all the grander to him.

He never ran after Carr, nor tried to draw his attention as the others did; he was content to watch and form his own ideas about his hero from a distance. Richard Carr was more than the captain of the team to him. He was the one person who, above all others, had that which Arthur lacked—strength; and so Arthur did not merely envy him,—he worshiped him.

Although Arthur Waller was somewhat older in his way of thinking than his friends, he enjoyed the same games they enjoyed, and would have liked to play them, if he had been able; but, as he was not, the boys usually asked him to keep the score, or to referee the matches they played on the cow pasture with one of the college's cast-off foot-balls. On the whole, the boys were very good to Arthur.

It was the first part of the last half of the Yale-Princeton foot-ball match, played on the Princeton grounds. The modest grand stand was filled with young ladies and college boys, while townspeople of all sorts and conditions, ages, and sizes covered the fences and carriages, and crowded closely on the whitewashed lines, cheering and howling at the twenty-two very dirty, very determined, and very cool young men who ran, rushed, dodged, and tackled in the open space before them,— the most interested and least excited individuals on the grounds.

Arthur Waller had crept between the spectators until he had reached the very front of the crowd, and had stood through the first half of the game with bated breath, his finger-nails pressed into his palms, and his eyes following only one of the players. He was entirely too much excited to shout or call as the others did; he was perfectly silent except for the little gasps of fear that he gave involuntarily when Richard Carr struck the ground with more than the usual number of men on top of him.

Suddenly, Mr. Hobbes, of Yale, kicked the ball, but kicked it sidewise; and so, instead of going straight down the field, it turned and whirled over the heads of the crowd and settled among the carriages. A panting little Yale man tore wildly after it, beseeching Mr. Hobbes, in agonizing tones, to put him "on side." Mr. Hobbes ran past the spot where the ball would strike, and the Yale man dashed after it through the crowd. Behind him, his hair flying, his eyes fixed on the ball over his head, every muscle on a strain, came Richard Carr. He went at the crowd, who tumbled over one another like a flock of sheep, in their efforts to clear the way for him. With his head in the air, he did not see Arthur striving to get out of his way; he only heard a faint cry of pain when he stumbled for an instant, and, looking back, saw the crowd closing around a little boy who was lying very still and white, but who was not crying. Richard Carr stopped as he ran back, and setting Arthur on his feet, asked, "Are you hurt, youngster?" But, as Arthur only stared at him and said nothing, the champion hurried on again into the midst of the fray.

"There is one thing we must have before the next match," said the manager of the team, as the players were gathered in the dressing-rooms after the game, "and that is a rope to keep the people back. They *will* crowd on the field, and get in the way of the half-backs, and, besides, it is not safe for them to stand so near. Carr knocked over a little kid this afternoon, and hurt him quite badly, I believe."

"What's that?" said Richard Carr, turning from the group of substitutes who were explaining how they would have played the game and tendering congratulations.

"I was saying," continued the manager, "that we ought to have a rope to keep the people off the field; they interfere with the game; and they say that you hurt a little fellow when you ran into the crowd during the last half."

"Those boys should n't be allowed to stand in front there," said Richard Carr; "but I did n't know I hurt the little fellow. Who was he? where does he live? Do you know?"

"It was the widow Waller's son, sah," volunteered Sam, the colored attendant.

"That 's her house with the trees around it; you can see the roof from here. I think that 's where they took him."

"Took him!" exclaimed Richard Carr, catching up his great-coat. "Was he so badly hurt? You must wait until I come back, Sam."

Sam looked after him in astonishment as he ran on a jog-trot toward the gate. "That 's a nice example to set a team," growled Sam. "Running off to sick chillun without changin' his clothes or rubbin' down. He should n' be capt'n ef he don't know any better dan dat."

A pale, gentle-faced woman, who looked as if she had been crying, came to the door when Richard Carr rang the bell of the cottage which had been pointed out to him from the athletic grounds. When she saw his foot-ball costume, the look of welcome on her face died out very suddenly.

"Does the little boy live here who was hurt on the athletic grounds?" asked Richard Carr, wondering if it could have been the doctor she was expecting.

"Yes, sir," answered the lady coldly.

"I came to see how he was; I am the man who ran against him. I wish to explain to you how it happened—I suppose you are Mrs. Waller?" (Richard Carr hesitated, and bowed, but the lady only bowed her head in return, and said nothing.) "It was accidental, of course," continued Carr. "He was in the crowd when I ran in after the ball; it was flying over our heads, and I was looking up at it and did n't see him. I hope he is all right now." Before the lady could answer, Richard Carr's eyes wandered from her face and caught sight of a little figure lying on the sofa in the wide hall. Stepping across the floor as lightly as he could in his heavy shoes, Carr sat down beside Arthur on the sofa. "Well, old man," he said, taking Arthur's hands in his, "I hope I did n't hurt you much. No bones broken,—are there? You were very plucky not to cry, let me tell you. It was a very hard fall, and I 'm very, very, sorry; but I did n't see you, you know."

"Oh, no, sir," said Arthur quickly, with his eyes fixed on Richard Carr's face. "I knew you did n't see me, and I thought maybe you would come when you heard I was hurt. I don't mind it a bit, from you. Because Willie Beck says—he is the captain of our team, you know—that you would n't hurt any one if you could help it; he says you never hit a man on the field unless he 's playing foul or trying to hurt some of your team."

Richard Carr doubted whether this recital of his virtues would appeal as strongly to Mrs. Waller as it did to Arthur, so he said, "And who is Willie Beck?"

"Willie Beck! Why, don't you know Willie Beck?" exclaimed Arthur, who was rapidly losing his awe of Richard Carr. "He says he knows you; he is the boy who holds your coat for you during the practice games."

Richard Carr saw he was running a risk of hurting some young admirer's feelings, so he said, "Oh, yes, the boy who holds my coat for me. And he is the captain of your team, is he? Well, the next time you play, you wear this cap and tell Willie Beck and the rest of the boys that I gave it to you because you were so plucky when I knocked you down."

With these words he pressed his black and orange cap into Arthur's hand and rose to go, but Arthur looked so wistfully at him, and then at the captain's cap, that he stopped.

"I 'd like to wear it, Mr. Carr," he said slowly. "I 'd like to ever so much, Mamma," he added, turning his eyes to where Mrs. Waller stood looking out at the twilight and weeping softly,—"but you see, sir, I don't play myself. I generally referee.

I 'm not very strong, sir, not at present; but I will be some day,—wont I, Mamma? And the doctor says I must keep quiet until I am older, and not play games that are rough. For he says if I got a shock or a fall I might not get over it, or it might put me back—and I do so want to get well just as soon as I can. You see, sir, it 's my spine——"

At this the tender-hearted giant gave a gasp of sympathy and remorse, and, sinking on his knees beside the sofa, he took Arthur in his arms, feeling very guilty and very miserable.

For a moment, Arthur only looked startled and distressed, and patted Richard Carr's broad back with an idea of comforting him; but then he cried:

"Oh, but I did n't mean to blame *you*, Mr. Carr! I know you did n't see me. Don't you worry about me, Mr. Carr. I 'm going to get well some day. Indeed I am, sir!"

Whether it was that the doctor whom Richard Carr's father sent on from New York knew more about Arthur's trouble than the other doctors did, or whether it was that Richard Carr saw that Arthur had many medicines, pleasant and unpleasant, which his mother had been unable to get for him, I do not know,—but I do know that Arthur got better day by day.

And day after day, Richard Carr stopped on his way to the field, and on his way back again, to see his "Baby," as he called him, and to answer the numerous questions put to him by Arthur's companions. They always assembled at the hour of Richard Carr's arrival in order to share some of the glory that had fallen on their comrade, and to cherish and carry away whatever precious thoughts Richard Carr happened to let drop concerning football, the weather, or any other vital subject of college life.

"Richard Carr heard one shrill little voice, which called to him above all the others"

As soon as the doctor said Arthur could be moved, Richard Carr used to stop for him in a two-seated carriage and drive him in state to the foot-ball field. And after he had drawn up the carriage where Arthur could get a good view of the game, he would hand over the reins to one of those vulture-like individuals who hover around the field of battle, waiting for some one to be hurt, and who are known as "substitutes." In his black and orange uniform, one of these fellows made a very gorgeous coachman indeed.

And though the students might yell, and the townspeople shout ever so loudly, Richard Carr only heard one shrill little voice, which called to him above all the others; and as that voice got stronger day by day, Richard Carr got back his old spirit and interest in the game, which, since the Yale match, he seemed to have lost.

The team said Richard Carr's "Baby" brought them luck, and they called him their "Mascot," and presented him with a flag of the college colors; and when the weather grew colder they used to smother him in their white woolen jerseys, so that he looked like a fat polar bear.

It was a very pretty sight, indeed, to see how Richard Carr and the rest of the team, whenever they had scored or had made a good play, would turn first for their commendation to where Arthur sat perched above the crowd, waving his flag, his cheeks all aglow, and the substitute's arm around him to keep him from falling over in his excitement. And the other teams who came to play at Princeton soon learned about the captain's "Baby," and inquired if he were on the field; and if he was, they would go up and gravely shake hands with him, as with some celebrated individual holding a public reception.

Richard Carr is out West now at the head of a great sheep ranch, and Arthur Waller enters Princeton next year. I do not know whether he will be on the team, though he is strong enough; but I am sure he will help to hand down the fame of Richard Carr, and that he will do it in such a way that his hero will be remembered as the possessor of certain qualities, perhaps not so highly prized, but quite as excellent, as were those which fitted him to be the captain of the team.

CHRONICLES OF THE MOLBOS

There is a peculiar class of people, living in Jutland, called the Molbos, of whom a great number of tales are told. From the earliest days, these people have been known for their ingenuity and simplicity, and hence many remarkable things are told about them. Two of the stories about their curious actions are given below.

THE STORK AND THE HERDER

ONCE, in the summer, when the corn stood high, a stork was often seen in the fields belonging to the Molbos, stalking up and down in the grain-patches to catch frogs. This annoyed the Molbos greatly, for they thought the long-legged bird trod down a vast deal of grain. They therefore consulted how to drive the animal away, and the conclusion was, that the herder of their village should go into

The herder is carried on a gate

362

the fields and chase the bird out. But as he went in for the stork, they noticed that his feet were very large and broad, and it occurred to them that the herder would trample down more grain than the stork. Then they again puzzled their brains what to do and how to get rid of the stork. But one of the party spoke up at last with the sensible advice that they might carry the herder through the grain, so that he should not tread it down. This idea was approved by all. They therefore went forth and took one of the fence-gates off its hinges, made the herder sit down on it, and eight men lifted the gate to their shoulders and carried the herder through the corn where the stork was, so that he might drive it away. Thus the herder was kept from trampling down the grain with his big feet.

THE CHURCH BELL

THE Molbos were once greatly scared by a report that the enemy intended to invade their country, and they de-termined to save what they could from falling into the hands of the invaders. What they prized most, and would save first of all, was their church bell. After a great deal of trouble, they succeeded in getting it down from the belfry; but it was still harder to determine how and where it should be hid away, so that the enemy should not find it. At last, they agreed to sink it in the deep ocean. They therefore dragged the bell down to their big boat, rowed far out on the ocean, and threw the bell overboard. After it had dis-appeared, the good Molbos began to re-flect, and said to each other: "The bell is now truly safe from the enemy, but how are we to find it again when the enemy has left us?" One of them, who thought himself wiser than the rest, sprang up and cried: "That is easy enough; all we have to do is to cut a mark where we dropped it!" He snatched a knife from his pocket and cut a deep notch in that side of the boat where the bell had been thrown over-board, and said: "It was here we threw it out!" This done, they rowed back, fully assured they would be able to find the bell again by the mark.

FO'C'SLE AND WIGWAM

by Henry Morton Robinson

NEARLY a century ago, two delicately bred young men laid aside the tight dress-coats, silk caps, and kid gloves of the Harvard undergraduate, made two immortal journeys, and recorded their perilous adventures in two imperishable books. Both young men—they were scarcely more than boys—were members of old Boston families; both were taking enforced vacations from Harvard because of defective eyesight; and both had a rare talent for describing their excursions into remote and uncivilized quarters of the globe. Richard Henry Dana, barely nineteen, was to double the Horn in a two years' cruise; Francis Parkman, scarcely a year older, was to strike across the American wilderness. Unconsciously, and merely as a by-product of their travels, these lads were to provide our literature with a brace of classics: Dana with his "Two Years Before the Mast," and Parkman with that first Wild West thriller "The Oregon Trail."

Both books were written in a changing age, when the actors and institutions of an earlier period were fast slipping into tradition. Scarcely a dozen years after Dana rounded the Horn, steam was displacing canvas as the motive power for the marine commerce of the world. Dana could not have written his book even a decade later. And Parkman was certainly the last observer of the Indian in his wildly primi-tive condition. Both are recorders of scenes that have passed away forever. But in addition to being priceless histories of the early American scene, "Two Years Before the Mast" and "The Oregon Trail" are the heart-quickening hazards of two city-nurtured youths who grappled with elemental dangers, underwent harsh privations, and then transformed their adventures into clear literature.

Richard Henry Dana was born at Cambridge, Massachusetts, on August 1, 1815. He was sent to private schools in the vicinity of Boston, and was duly flogged by his masters in accordance with the best ideas of discipline then prevailing. His habit of keeping a note-book was begun early in life, and he has left in his early diaries an account of his life at Mr. Barrett's Academy—an ear-pulling, cane-brandishing institution somewhat like Dotheboys Hall in "Nicholas Nickleby." In his fifteenth year Dana entered Harvard, was rusticated (suspended) in his sophomore year for taking part in an undergraduate rebellion; and on returning to college, managed to contract a case of measles. This disease left his eyes in a weakened condition, making study or reading impossible. For a year Dana was at loose ends. His eyes showed no improvement, and finally he decided that such a serious malady needed heroic treatment. So he determined to ship before the mast as an ordinary seaman. With his family influence he could easily have secured a light berth in the cabin of some great Indiaman in the Boston-Calcutta trade. But his own good judgment told him that the hard labor, the coarse food, and the vigorous outdoor life of a seaman would strengthen him physically and thus permanently cure his weakened eyes. He was right. He went away a pallid stripling and came back "as long as a spare topmast, strong enough to knock down an ox and hearty enough to eat it."

Young Dana sailed from Boston in August, 1834, on the now famous brig *Pilgrim,* bound for California with a mixed cargo of manufactured goods and foodstuffs, to be exchanged for cowhides along the coast of California. The *Pilgrim* was commanded by the cruel and incompetent Captain Frank Thompson, whose brutal inhumanity was an exception even in those days of tyrannical skippers. Dana was absolutely ignorant of seamanship, but he refused to claim exemption from the rigorous duties and hard diet of his shipmates. Indeed, no exemption would have been granted. Common humanity, as we now reckon it, was unknown on sailing-ships doubling the Horn in the thirties. Only by the constant exercise of physical and moral courage could the newcomer gain the respect of his shipmates. To be cowardly or weak was fatal, and Dana knew it. On the foam-washed deck, in the icy rigging, and in the leaky fo'c'sle of the *Pilgrim* Richard Dana fulfilled every stern requirement of the sailor's code. In a one hundred and forty foot ship, "not much better than a bathing-machine," he made his first trip around Cape Horn, and his courageous seamanship soon won him the respect of the mate and the confidence of his companions.

For weeks at a time Dana's clothes were drenched with salt water and frozen to his body. With mittenless fingers he knotted ice-coated cordage, reefed sails as stiff as sheet-iron, and clung to perilous spars in the teeth of a constant gale howling straight up from the Pole. After a solitary watch in the antarctic night he would fling himself into his soaking berth, knowing that he might hear at any moment the cry "All hands on deck" and that he would have to furl, in the face of a squall, the very sails he had so painfully unfurled an hour before. The *Pilgrim,* like all ships of its class, was terribly undermanned; illness, death, and desertion crippled the crew from the beginning, and Dana was often obliged to do the work of three men. Fatigued and hungry, he saw many a cold sun rise out of the ocean, knowing that he could expect no sleep for eighteen hours to come. Once he knew the agony of lying in his bunk for a week with a tooth so abscessed and swollen that he could not open his mouth to take food. He went in vain to the medicine-chest; it contained only a few drops of laudanum, "which," the captain said, "could not be spared." Seeing Dana's condition, the mate asked the captain for a few spoonfuls of boiled rice in his behalf. "Let him eat salt beef and hard bread like the rest of them," was the captain's only answer.

But worse than physical pain was the spiritual anguish Dana suffered when he saw two of his shipmates spread-eagled (trussed up to a mast by ropes) and flogged to ribbons by the passion-crazed captain. Hearing the groans of the suffering victims, Dana vowed that "if God should ever give me the means, I will do something to redress the grievances and relieve the sufferings of this class of beings with whom my lot has been cast." He lived to bring about many major reforms in marine usage, and during his long career as a lawyer he defended without pay the rights of many sailors who applied to him for counsel.

Arriving in California, Dana was set to the man-killing labor of curing and carrying hides. After a solid year of what amounted to penal servitude, he was obliged to fight for his passage home on the ship *Alert,* to which he had been transferred by order of the ship-owners. Captain Thompson, who was to command the *Alert* on the homeward voyage, opposed the transfer; but with characteristic fearlessness Dana outfaced the bully in his own cabin and won his passage home. Although the *Alert* was a tighter ship than the *Pilgrim,* the homeward voyage around the Horn was almost fatal. Thompson's wretched navigation took the *Alert* seventeen hundred miles out of her course and nearly wrecked her on ice-floes drifting up from the Pole. Dana's account of those midwinter hurricanes off Staten Land, with a sullen incompetent captain and a disabled crew, is one of the great records of human endurance. "We were mere animals," writes Dana, "and if this life had lasted a year instead of a month, we should have been little better than the ropes on the ship."

But the bleakness of low longitudes, where the sun rose at nine and set at three, was finally relieved by the first rays of good weather in the Atlantic. The *Alert,* hearing the cry "Northward Ho," made four thousand miles in twenty-seven days, tearing along at such a rate that the crew swore "the Boston girls were pulling the tow-rope." The crew was set to painting ship, but scurvy—that dreaded disease of the fo'c'sle—broke out while there were yet a thousand miles to go, and many of the sailors were entirely disabled. The disease was checked, however, by a mess of fresh onions secured from a passing ship. Speaking of this medicinal vegetable, Dana says: "We were ravenous after them. An onion was like the scent of blood to a hound. We ate them at every meal by the dozen, and filled our pockets with them to eat during our watch on deck."

Finally, after having spent nearly a thousand hours at the helm, Dana saw the low sand-hills of Cape Cod rising over the port quarter, and the next day the *Alert* was safely anchored in Boston Harbor. With a face as dark and sunburned as an Indian's—and with his eyes completely cured—Dana stepped upon home soil for the first time in twenty-five months. His seaman's trunk, which contained the written account of his voyage, was left in care of a relative—who promptly lost it. But luckily Dana had kept upon his person the original journal in which he had made daily entries, and from this notebook "Two Years Before the Mast" was written.

In a state of intellectual famine Dana now returned to Harvard, and on graduating in 1837 stood first in his class, with the highest marks ever given out in every branch of study. He then entered law school, and became instructor of elocution in Harvard College. It was during this period that he wrote his famous book. The next year Dana began to practise law, and the remainder of his life was devoted, not to literature, as many had hoped and expected, but to an honorable career as a barrister. The greater part of his practice was among poor and ignorant sailors, and also in defense of fugitive slaves. Since neither the slaves nor the sailors ever had any money, Dana never became a rich man. And although his book was immediately recognized as a classic, and thousands of copies were sold in England and America, his royalties for the first twenty-eight years were only two hundred and fifty dollars.

It is probable that Richard Henry Dana aspired to the chief judgeship of Massachusetts, and that at one time he believed himself destined for the United States Senate. But neither of these ambitions was ever realized. In 1876 President Grant nominated him as Ambassador to England, but Dana's political enemies in the Senate refused to confirm the nomination. Dana was in Europe preparing a treatise on international law when he died at Rome on January 6, 1882.

"I AM a locomotive built of indifferent material, under a head of steam too great for its strength, hissing at a score of crevices yet rushing with accelerating speed to the inevitable smash."

Parkman's own description of himself is calmly uttered—and terribly true. From childhood he suffered from an assortment of ills that would have driven a weaker character to the edge of despair, and made a life of literary activity impossible; his career offers the greatest instance in history of man's triumph over the severe limitations of his bodily equipment. The three chief ailments that he laughingly refers to as "the enemy" were an almost total blindness, a defective digestion, and a mysterious nervous malady which constantly threatened his sanity. His minor afflictions were enough to ruin most lives, and included acute arthritis, which made him dependent on a wheel-chair or crutches during a large part of his life; chronic insomnia, which deprived him of the blessing of sleep; and terrific pains in the head whenever he attempted to read or write. Parkman's physician warned him many times that half an hour of reading would be suicide. At no period in his life could he read or write for more than five minutes at a time, and his daily stint, even in his healthiest seasons, was limited to two hours a day, with frequent intervals of rest.

Despite this cruel martyrdom to pain, Parkman can in no sense be called a weak man. He was possessed of tremendous mental and nervous energy; his illness only intensified his mental activity, and his fierce will-power enabled him to complete the epic task to which he had dedicated himself in his youth. From childhood he had been passionately fond of Indian stories; during his sophomore year at Harvard his ambition had crystallized, and he determined to be the historian of the American Indian. In its final development, this history included the entire struggle of the French and English for the possession of North America. Parkman is the acknowledged recorder of this struggle, which began in Europe and thrust its long tentacles into the remotest depths of the American forest.

With his head "full of Injuns," Parkman read in college all available works on Indian life. These were few and unsatisfactory, and the young historian soon came to the conclusion that the Indian character must be observed at close range, if it was to be understood and interpreted. To make these first-hand observations he undertook his famous journey over the Oregon Trail. In preparation for the journey he trained rigorously, took riding-lessons from a circus-master, and learned to shoot from all positions. He resolved not to allow any physical weakness to thwart his investigation of Indian character and customs. And he paid a fearful price in later life for his grim stubbornness in carrying out his researches.

In 1846 the Oregon Trail was the overland route taken by the thousands of emigrants seeking free government lands. The emigrant bands usually started from St. Louis, followed the Missouri northward to the Platte, then branched west through Nebraska and Wyoming, crossed the Rockies, and descended into the "Promised Land" of Oregon. When Parkman made

through such a country that Parkman, accompanied by a friend and two guides, journeyed for six months on horseback.

To make a journey of four thousand miles on horseback, living on unsalted buffalo meat, and risking one's scalp

The Oregon Trail was the overland route taken by thousands of emigrants

his trip the country was in a wildly uncivilized state. Bands of warlike Dahcotahs terrorized the emigrant parties, cutting off stragglers, shooting, burning, and scalping the white invaders. Vast herds of antelope and buffalo blackened the prairies; ruffian wolves skulked through the hollows, and the fierce grizzly disputed with a few trappers the mastery of mountain-passes. Multitudes of lizards darted over the sand, and rattlesnakes lay ambushed in every gully. Flooding storms and baking heat alternated in transforming the prairie from a mud slough to a blazing griddle. It was

among hostile Indians is an undertaking that would daunt any man in perfect health. But in addition to the dangers from without, Parkman was obliged to resist another assailant—illness—the enemy from within. Early in the journey he was stricken with dysentery, and for weeks at a time he clung to his saddle by sheer force of will. He would not turn back, realizing that this was his last chance to see the Indian in his native haunts. He also realized that the best protection against the Indians was a sturdy, self-reliant exterior, and that to show the first sign of weakness would be fatal. So with only his gun and knife for defense, and with barely enough strength to stand, he kept his illness a secret from the Indians, and was accepted by them as a mighty warrior and hunter! He lived and traveled with them, observing their customs, government, and character more closely than any white man before or since.

Hearing that a war was being fanned into flame by the Ogillallahs, he determined to be present at the council of their war-chiefs. To accomplish his purpose he had to separate himself from the rest of his party, and with only a single guide, pursue the swift Ogillallahs to their secret camp in the foot-hills of the Rockies. While on this expedition he became so weak from his illness that he could neither ride nor walk without exquisite pain. At the point of death, without medicine or suitable food, he made a bold resolution "to throw himself upon Providence for recovery, using, without regard for his disorder, any portion of strength that remained to him." His grit enabled him to push forward to the war council, but he was greatly disappointed when the chiefs, after many powwows, decided to drop the war for a time. Parkman was somewhat repaid, however, by a series of buffalo hunts, "puppy feasts," and other festivities, which he records with vigor and interest. As usual, he choked down his portion of the feast, whether it was singed puppy or roast buffalo, without giving his redskin hosts any intimation of his illness.

Parkman was the first to prophesy that with the extinction of the buffalo the Indian nations would collapse, basing his prediction on their total dependence upon the buffalo for food, shelter, weapons, and household implements. He took part in several buffalo hunts, was charged by a wounded bull, and narrowly escaped with his life. Yet with typical modesty he explains that the situation was not dangerous and that although a maddened buffalo was plunging at his pony's flank, "there was no cause for alarm." It is this blithe recklessness on the very horns of death that makes "The Oregon Trail" so exciting, and fills the reader with admiration for the plucky boy-explorer who never knew when to admit defeat.

"The Oregon Trail" originally appeared in the "Knickerbocker Magazine" for 1847. Parkman, unable to use his eyes for writing, dictated the story to his faithful traveling-companion, Quincy Adams Shaw. The book was immediately popular, and gave Parkman an encouragement he sorely needed in the midst of his physical ills. Blindness and the old nervous ailment did not prevent Parkman from writing the whole story of the French and Indian wars, of which "The Oregon Trail" was merely a preparatory essay. Five times he went to Europe to collect documents necessary for his great works on "Montcalm and Wolfe," "The Jesuits in North America," and "Pioneers of France in the New World." The greater part of his fortune, which was not large, was spent on secretaries whom Parkman employed to read the endless documents in the European archives. Work which he could have completed in a day with his own eyes, thus took months. Critical illness during his middle life cut ten years off his researches, but these years Parkman devoted to horticulture, originating several new varieties of lilies and roses. As he grew older his eyesight improved a little, and during the last years of his life he was able to scrawl out in pencil, on orange paper, the entire manuscript of "Fifty Years of Conflict."

The stoical courage of Francis Parkman, facing his ghastly misfortunes with grim forbearance, must always be ranked among the great examples of moral courage in

American history. He had but one purpose—to write an accurate and complete
history of a great period, and he succeeded
so well that he is ranked to-day among the
first of American historians. Parkman's
work, viewed as a whole, deserves a place
on the shelf of world history, along with
Gibbon, Herodotus, and Thucydides. But
great as was his work, the man was im-
measurably greater. In calm courage and
sustained valor he is the peer of Pontiac,
Montcalm, and the host of other noble
heroes who tread his shining pages.

"Parkman should have been a knight
of the Round Table," says Charles Haight
Farnum, in his excellent life of the historian. "Few men would have surpassed
him in skill at arms, in courage, in mighty
deeds, in gallant courtesy, in fidelity,
friendship, and service. In fancy, he liked
to return to the times when his own manly
nature would have found free exercise in
chivalrous accomplishments and martial
achievements. This chivalrous turn of
mind was shown in his school days, when
he turned into verse the tournament
scene in 'Ivanhoe.' But, born in the nine-
teenth century, he contented himself with
choosing for a literary theme the most ad-
venturous epoch of American history, and

living by his imaginative sympathy in those
experiences."

If the comparison between Parkman and
Dana seems striking and inevitable, the
contrast is all the more marked and
melancholy. Dana, quickened into robust
health by the sea, threw off his eye trouble
forever, and pursued an active legal career
for over forty years. But Parkman had
permanently injured his health by the exertions of the Oregon journey, and never
during the remainder of his life did he
enjoy a single hour's relief from pain. Yet
he achieved his self-imposed task of writing the story of the Franco-English struggle in America, while Dana, after a long
career of distinguished public service, could
only say, in an hour of despondency, "My
life has been a failure." Possibly he
realized, too late, that he should have been
a modern voyageur, a circumnavigator of
unexplored continents. But Dana's name
is held fast in a golden parenthesis of fame,
bracketed by his two immortal years before
the mast. Both he and Parkman are death-
less youths; somehow we never think of
them except as eager boys, storming the
highest peaks of adventure, and winning
to their goal in the early morning of their
lives.

A FUNNY LITTLE SCHOOL

by Ruth McEnery Stuart

WHEN little Louizy-Lou began teaching her grandfather his letters, she had no idea of opening school on the plantation. It all came about in this way. When the little girl would come home from school in the long afternoons, while all the rest of the family were working in the fields, she would take her book out in the yard where old Uncle Sol, her grandfather, sat, and go over the day's lesson with him—he obediently following her guiding finger with delighted eyes.

It had never occurred to either of them that the old man would himself begin to learn, until one day, when she was spelling her words as usual, he stopped her. "H-h-hold on, honey," he began, and his voice choked up so that he could hardly speak; "hold on. I knowed dat word befo' you called it out. Dat 's c-a-t, cat; an' here 's mo' cats all up an' down de page." And with trembling fingers he really found the word wherever it occurred in the lesson. He was very much excited. "Why, honey," he cried, "learnin' 's openin' up to me, sho 's you born."

The old man was so much elated that he made Louizy-Lou bring her book to the table in the cabin that night after supper, while he proved to the rest of the family that he was really "a-ketchin' on to education."

In a few days he knew not only *cats* at sight, but *bats* and *rats,* even when Louizy-Lou covered the pictures over with her hand, which was a very important test. But when he had learned these three words, and several smaller ones, such as o-n, on, u-p, up, he began to complain a little. "Why, Louizy-Lou, baby," he said one evening as he took off his spectacles and began wiping them slowly, "when is we gwine to study about some other sort o' creation? Look to me like de ups an' downs o' cats an' bats an' rats is mighty po' readin' for a Christian—dat is, to *keep on wid it.* An' dat readin'-lesson I heerd you read about 'de pup bit de cow on de lip,' I would n't read it no mo', baby. I nuver knowed no little puppy to do sech a thing; an' even ef dis heah book-pup done it, I no doubt de cow she pestered him into it. But seem to me dat 's a mighty po' sort o' puppy to pick out to put in a book, when dey so many cunnin' ones roun' dis plantation wid manners an' sense. But for de cats an' rats, of co'se I ain't got nothin' ag'in' 'em, *in dey places;* but I 'm tired of 'em."

The little girl was very thoughtful for a moment.

"What sort o' words would you like to spell, gran'daddy?" she asked at length.

"Well, I ain't partic'lar; but, *ef I could,* I 'd like to spell Moses-leadin'-de-chillen-o'-Isrul-in-de-wilderness. But, of co'se, dat mought be too hard. I know de wilderness is a bewilderin' place. But ef you has to

371

start on dumb beas'es, I 'd be mightily tickled to spell out my ole dorg here, or my mule. See ef you can't find no Rovers or Nebuchadnezzars in de book, honey. Dat ole mule, Nebuchadnezzar, he 's dead an' gone, I know; but I loved dat mule. For seven yeahs I follered him wid de plow, an' ef I could see how he 'd look on de page, I 'd be mighty glad. A man loves a' ole beas' dat he walk beside so long."

They looked all through the primer, but there was no mule to be found, much less one named Nebuchadnezzar. They did presently find a plow, though, and after three nights of loving pursuit, the old man could spell "p-l-o-w, plow," and recognize the word anywhere.

Learning that he could learn was a most delightful discovery, and the learning itself, that was joy. The little grandchild learned much faster than the old man, and before the season was over she could read long lessons from beginning to end. And pieces? She could stand up before the fireplace and recite "with motions," "The Boy stood on the Burning Deck" and "Mary had a Little Lamb," And although Uncle Sol had n't gotten so far as The-Chillen-o'-Isrul-in-de-wilderness, he had learned a few words that were dear to his old heart. There was "Ann," for instance. Ann was the name of his old wife, who had been for ten long years waiting for him in heaven. When he first stumbled on her name, he was so much affected that he could not find his voice; but, raising his finger, he said, "Sh-h-h!" and he would not let the little teacher say another word. For a long time he sat pointing to it, just thinking; and then he whispered softly to himself, "A-n-n, Ann—A-n-n, Ann;" over and over again. And presently he said, "Dat 's yo' gran'ma's name, baby: 'A-n-n, Ann.' An', somehow, when I sets an' studies over it, it sort o' looks like my ole 'oman—yas, it do. She was a short, thick-

set little 'oman, Ann was—A-n-n, Ann. An' dat big A, it favors her consider'ble, de way she used to tie her head-hankcher up in a little p'int, an' walk so biggity. Yo' gran'mammy was a neat little 'oman, Louizy-Lou, honey. An' sometimes, when I looks at you an' see how nice you ties up yo' hair wid dem purty bows of a Sunday, I 'low you tooken it arter yo' gran'ma. Of co'se she raised yo' mammy, an' she 's a-raisin' you; an' dat 's de on'ies' way nice genteel ways has to be passed along."

It was in the second season of Louizy's schooling,—when she was twelve years old, though she was so small that she seemed hardly ten,—as she and her grandfather were reading a very difficult lesson aloud to some old men who came to sit and talk at old Sol's door, that Daddy Conrad said, "Look heah, Louizy-Lou. What 's de reason you can't pass around some o' yo' book-learnin' to de rest of us, I like to know? Ef Br'er Sol kin learn, I'm sho' I kin."

"Dat 's what I say," put in Uncle Jake. "Ef Louizy-Lou kin learn Br'er Sol, she kin learn de rest of us. What you say, Unc' Mathusalem?"

"Don't you call me 'Mathusalem,'" answered old Nimrod, chuckling. He was the oldest of the lot, and had n't a tooth in his head, and his voice was thin and high, as he added, "I bet you, ef I turns my secon' sight on a book, I 'll find out what it 's got to say des as quick as de rest o' you ignunt know-nothin's; an' ef Louizy-Lou is gwine open school, she kin put my name on de books." He shook his old head decidedly as he spoke.

Daddy Conrad had proposed the school only in fun, but now he spoke in all seriousness:

"Sho' 'nough, now, Louizy-Lou is des give out dat she gwine quit school an' go in de field to pick cotton, an' I say, 'stid o' dat, she better open school for we-all. How much cotton kin you pick in a day, any-how, gal?"

"I don't know, sir; but I 'm sho' I could pick right smart, an' dey payin' sixty cents a hund'ed, now."

Sixty cents for every hundred pounds picked was a good price, and many chil-dren even smaller than Louizy were al-ready in the fields.

"Sixty cents a hund'ed," repeated Uncle Nimrod. "Well, now, listen to what I got to say. S'pos'n we-all was to pay Louizy-Lou sixty cents a hund'ed for all de book-words she 'd learn us, how about dat?"

At this the little girl shook her head. "No, sir-ee," she laughed. "Don't ketch me dat-a-way. You-all too slow-minded." They all screamed with laughter at this.

"But s'posin' we is slow-minded," said Uncle Steve, who up to this time had kept quite still, "you 'd be teachin' a lot of us at oncet; an' even ef you picks cotton wid bofe hands, you can't pick but des *so much;* and ef we-all learns a word, you 'll collect on every one for de same word. See? Every time you calls out a word, it 'll have fo', five, six chances to find a lodgmint."

There was a good deal of fun over this proposition, and old Nimrod said, "I declar', Steve, you ought to be a jedge in de co't-house. You argufies wiser 'n ole Solomon hisself. Huc-come you sets still an' let ole slim-shank Steve out-talk you in wisdom, Unc' Solomon?"

He turned to Sol.

"You forgits dat Br'er Sol is de gran'-daddy o' de teacher," said Uncle Jake. "He done passed his wisdom on to de secon' gineration."

"Dat 's so," said Nimrod, "an' I 's proud to salute it." Lifting his brimless hat, he turned and made a low bow to the little girl sitting in their midst; and then, one by one, they all followed suit.

It was a funny little school—six old men

and a white-haired woman, with a twelve-year-old girl for teacher. Old Susan was seventy, and was spoken of on the place as "child-minded"; but when she heard of the school she wanted to come in, and there was no one to hinder her. She had always been an early riser; but after she began going to school she got up every morning before day, and would wash her slate and sharpen her pencil until it seemed that they would be washed and sharpened away. Then, dressed in her best, with her slate under her arm, she would walk up and down before her cabin until Uncle Jake would come by, and she would join him. Jake was lame, but he always "al-lowed for it," and was very early. Then, presently, the others would hobble along; and last, old Solomon, looking very grave and important, with the trig little teacher beside him. She always carried the big brass bell in her hand, holding its tongue securely until she reached the church steps, when she would ring it loudly, al-though all her pupils were sitting on the steps waiting for her. She had to take the bell home to keep mischievous boys from ringing it between times.

School was held in the little room back of the church, commonly called the "mo'ners' room." They took this because, as all but Susan and the teacher were officers in the church, there was no permis-sion to ask and no rent to pay.

If the little teacher was young, she made up for it in being strict and dignified. She had been to school herself, and she knew a thing or two.

When she first called the school to order she rose from her seat and made a little speech:

"Arms folded. Heads up. Foots down," she began, pausing for obedience after each order. And then when the long-limbed pupils on the low benches had scrambled into order, she went on to say,

"Schools is made out o' three things—teachers an' scholars an' rules. An' rules is for teachers to make, an' for scholars to mind. An' I gwine give you des a few rules to begin wid. De fust rule is:

"No talkin' in school—widout commission." She meant permission, and they all understood it so.

"Secon' rule: No gum-chewin' in class."

"Third rule: No sassin' back—no time."

There were several drawbacks to the little school at first, such as, for instance, the scarcity of books. Louizy-Lou had her own primer. Steve bought a new one; but then Steve was rich—that is, he and his eighty-year-old mother had a pension of twelve dollars a month between them, left her by her old mistress. Uncle Tom had a flower-catalogue with a bright frontispiece of impossible pansies; but old Susan embarrassed him so, looking over his shoulder at it, that he finally tore it out and gave it to her. Susan had no book and no money to buy one. Indeed, there was absolutely no way for her to pay for her schooling; but as only those who learned should pay, this was not so serious a matter as it may seem. And her slate and her picture were very dear to her.

It was Tom's idea for all hands to collect letters from the advertising-placards along the roads, and for Louizy-Lou to show them how to paste them in order on the wall, and they very soon had a full alphabet in this way. And it was a most interesting one. The "T" printed on a scarlet tomato was pretty to look at and easy to remember, and there was scarcely a letter but had some beauty all its own that it could spare and still be itself.

To learn to repeat the alphabet by heart, with backs turned to the wall—this was Louizy-Lou's idea of a first step in the way of learning; and she had spent several days on this drill when she suddenly realized that she could not afford it. Only spelled words were to be paid for. But there was one thing she could do: she could hurry the class into spelling. Instead of saying A and B, why not say A-b, ab, and collect on it? This was the first exercise she gave them, and she was just beginning to rejoice that several of them were learning it, when Susan asked—though of course, she could not know how clever the question was: "What *is* abs, anyhow? I ain't nuver seen no abs in my life."

"Dat what I say," said Steve, quickly.

"An' me, too," added the others.

Louizy was puzzled, just for a minute. It happened that she could n't think of any abs in real life, either. But she quickly recovered herself.

"Well," she answered, "ef you-all ain't seen no abs, maybe you can spell b-a, ba. You know what a bay horse is, I reckon." And so b-a, ba, was the first word put down on the school bill; and when it was found that five of the six had it on their lists,—all kept by the teacher, of course,—she felt much encouraged. The fact that old Nimrod insisted on saying, "B-a, bay horse," did n't matter. If he took more than he paid for, that was his lookout. But when Susan said, "A-b, bay mule," it would n't do, though Susan could n't see why.

In a month there was quite a fine showing. All but Susan had a number of words charged against them. If some were only pieces of words like *ba*, which was made to do duty for *bay*, nobody knew it, and no account was disputed. As she had no reading-chart, Louizy-Lou taught most words orally, not even finding the letters until the scholars could repeat the words by rote. So, one day, she was saying, "A-l-e, ale; p-a-l-e, pale; b-a-l-e, bale; d-a-l-e, dale," when she added, "Stee-a-l-e, stale," and at this Steve stopped her.

"Hold on dar, teacher!" he cried;

"hold on! Spell dat last word over ag'in, please."

Louizy repeated, "Stee-a-l-e, stale."

"Well, I wants to know whar you gits dat letter *stee*." Steve was shaking his head emphatically. "I been heerd a heap o' white folks spell, an' I ain't nuver heerd no sich letter as dat."

"Neither me," said old Susan.

This was trying. The little teacher spelled the word over to herself; but she could n't get out of it. "Stee-a-l-e," seemed the only way to spell "stale"; and yet, when she came to think about it, she did n't know about "stees" either. There seemed to be nothing to do about it but to make the scholars keep still and talk less. She took her ruler and rapped loudly on the desk.

"Ef you-all knowed all yo' a-b-c's befo' you come to school, I don't see no use in comin'," she began.

"Dat 's so," her grandfather interrupted, kindly; "an' yit, 'stee' *is* got a furrin soun' to it. S'pose you was to p'int it out to us in de line, baby."

"I 'clare, gran'daddy, you-all ain't got a bit o' patience. You 'spec' to know everything befo' you knows yo' a-b, abs, sca'cely." There was real distress in the little girl's voice.

"Dat 's so, of co'se, honey; but yit, I ricollec' you say dis letter 'stee' b'longs in 'stale'; an' ef dat 's all it b'longs in, I ain't gwine bother wid it. I nuver is had no use for no stale things, nohow. Don't it b'long to nothin' else?"

"Of co'se, gran'daddy, I see some'h'n' it b'longs in right now. Stee, double e, p-l-e, ple, steeple. See de church steeple?"

The old men looked at each other.

"Dat sho' has got de sound to it," said Uncle Nimrod; and then, turning to Steve, he added, "an' here 's old Steve. Ef my ear 's right, I s'picion it 's in him."

"Stee, double e, v-e, Steve," Louizy spelled in a twinkling. "Co'se it 's in 'Steve.' "

At this Steve grew very much excited, and shook his finger at Louizy.

"Ef it 's in me, you p'int it out on de line!" he screamed. "I done tooken notice dat Tom an' Sol been spelt a week ago, an' it 's a' outrage dat I ain't been spelt long ago."

Louizy was greatly tried; but she was very courageous.

"Uncle Steve," she said firmly, "Tom an' Sol is easy names, an' I 'm a-learnin' you dese words by de hund'ed, an' I can't fool wid sech big names as Stephen tell you-all comes to 'em nachel. Wait tell you knows yo' a-b, abs, good, den I 'll learn you yo' punctuation-p'ints, an' so-fo'ths, an' stees, an' all dat. An' ricollec' dat when you ask questions, you shows yo' ignunce. Questions is for teachers, an' answers is for scholars."

This seemed good reasoning, and the irate Steve, on thinking it over, even reluctantly consented to bide his time to be spelled.

"I knowed my name wa'n't no common name," he muttered to himself.

There was much that was trying in this sort of school-teaching besides the sad fact that, thus far, there had been very little money in it for the teacher. But there were perquisites. The old men brought presents of one sort or another to the little teacher nearly every day. The fact is that although they liked to argue with her, and did not always show the proper amount of "respect," they were very proud and fond of her, and they thought her a wonder. Even Steve, the difficult, loved to whittle out things for her. Indeed, it was he who made the cat-o'-nine tails that hung beside her desk; and before he presented it to her, he had agreed with the others that if the time should come when any one of them should need it, the rest would stand by the teacher while she laid it on. Whipping was an important factor in their ideas of a school, and they were not to be defrauded of any needed discipline simply because the teacher was young —and little.

Steve himself was a giant in size, and although he was over sixty years old, he walked with a firm tread, and could, if occasion required, whip out the whole lot. He would have been at work in the field but for his mother's income.

But Steve was troublesome. He would talk out of turn, and he would n't hush when he was told. Louizy-Lou had long ago found out the secret of the "stee,"— that it was only s-t pronounced quickly,— and she would explain it in her own time. But Steve kept bringing it up; and finally it went so far that Louizy threatened to *make* him hush. This was pretty brave in a girl of twelve, and small of her age, to a man who stood six feet two in his bare feet. Her very bravery ought to have touched the old man, but it only angered him. Then he began to "sass back." For one thing, he called her a "little chit of a gal," and threatened her with a spanking.

This would never do, and neither would it do for Uncle Sol to interfere, he thought. And so he sat still, and Steve kept answering back.

Finally old Nimrod spoke up: " 'Scuse me talkin' out o' turn, teacher," he said; "but ef you 'll take Steve's own cat-o'-nine-tails to 'im, we-all 'll stan' by you."

"Yas, we will," answered the others, every one.

But the little teacher had her own ideas. "Nem you mind, Unc' Nimrod," she said bravely. "I done listened to too much Scripture-readin' to fool wid you baldheads long as dey shootin' bears in dese up-country woods. I ain't dat anxious to be e't up! But ef dat sassy ole long-leg, long-tongue Steve wants to find out who 's boss in dis school, him or me, *I'll show him!* Unc' Nimrod, you be monitor tell I come back."

While she spoke, she had risen from her seat, and before they knew it she had started across the field at a brisk pace, toward the quarters. The old men looked at each other as they watched her trim little figure moving away, but not a word was spoken. Even Steve only grunted his displeasure, but he looked grimly defiant, and did not turn his head.

Presently, however, those who watched his face saw a change come over it, and following the direction of his glance, they saw two figures approaching—Louizy-Lou's and another, which they instantly recognized as Steve's mother. She was a tiny little woman, very thin and almost doubled with age, but she carried herself as one who was sure.

When she reached the door, she walked to the center of the room and looked at her son, while Steve sank in his seat until he seemed scarcely half his size.

She did not speak for fully a minute, and then she said: "I want to know ef you gwine hush when you told?"

Steve slid down until he seemed in danger of getting quite off the bench; but he did not answer.

"Open yo' mouf, an' talk," she continued. "Is you gwine hush when you spoke to, or is I bound to whup you befo' de school?"

Steve seemed unable to speak.

"Talk, I say!" she insisted. "Is you gwine hush?"

"Yas, 'm," he answered at last; "I gwine hush." And then he added desperately, "Please, mammy, go home, *for Gord sake!* I 'll be good."

This seems irreverent, perhaps; but when the old man said it, he did not mean it so, and the others understood, and they were very serious. A man who did n't honor his mother had little respect on the plantation; and, besides, old Granny Nancy, who lived on her income, who wore white aprons on week-days,—Granny Nancy who was always inquired for when any of the old people came to visit the plantation, and who could afford to send her sixty-three-year-old son to school, and

School lasted the rest of the season; but the old people did n't learn much. Silly Susan insisted that she had learned "I-go-up," which, indeed, she could say in the approved, measured way; but as she said it as well from one page as another, Louizy-Lou refused to make out a bill

" 'Is you gwine hush when you spoke to, or is I bound to whup you befo' de school?' "

to buy a new book for him,—was the first dignitary on the place, and he would be a brave man who would defy her.

When she had said her say, she turned, and before they realized it, she had disappeared; and looking out, they saw her slim, bent figure crossing the field.

There was no trouble with Steve after this. Indeed, the little teacher had so impressed all her pupils with her fearlessness and dignity that they obeyed her as if she had been a queen.

for it. Solomon declared that he would n't take anything for the little "insight" he had gotten, even though he had only learned a few names that it pleased his old eyes to ponder over.

On the last day, just before closing, Louizy rose from her seat and made a short parting speech, which she closed by saying: "When school is dismissed, I wants all de scholars to keep dey seats. I got some'h'n to say." And then she immediately added: "School is dismissed."

And now, after first stepping down from her platform, she said:

"School is out an' done, now; an' we ain't no mo' teacher an' scholars. I ain't nothin' but des Louizy-Lou, a little gal what you-all been knowin' all yo life. An' you-all is five ole gentlemen—an' one ole lady," she added, looking at Susan; "an' I know dat, for a little gal o' my size, I is sometimes talked mighty sassy to you-all, an' I des want to tell you dat I did n't mean no harm by it." Her voice trembled so that she had to stop a minute; but she soon recovered herself, and went on: "An' I want to tell you, Unc' Steve, dat when I called you a long-leg, long-tongued, ole wo'e-out some'h'n' 'nother, you—you—you pervoked me to it; an' I did n't mean no onrespect. I ain't been raised to sass ole folks."

At this, she broke down completely, and had to raise her little apron to wipe her tears away. Old Solomon grunted, and looked at Steve. Then Tom grunted, and looked at the others. And then Daddy Conrad grunted, and shook his head; and Uncle Nimrod grunted, and shook *his* head, and said: "I sesso, too. It 's a *shame, dat* what is it, to pester de child de way we done; an' she doin' all she kin to open up education to us. It 's a plumb shame!"

And the heads all shook, and everybody grunted—all but Steve. Steve's heart was right, but he was stubborn. Finally, however, his better nature conquered. He stood up; and as he rose to his full height and looked down upon the little girl, his hand shook.

"Don't cry, honey," he began. "Don't cry. Ole Steve 's been mighty mean to you, baby; but he ain't gwine do it no mo'. You done shamed 'im out." Then, turning to his companions, he said: "An' befo' I sets down, I wants to ax pardon in de presence o' de school. I started in to pleg de little gal, des for fun; but I went too far. But you-all ain't nuver is seen nobody wuss whupped out in yo' life 'n what I was when she sprung my mammy on me!

"An' you hush cryin' now, baby. An' ef anybody ever pesters you on dis plantation, *f'om now on,* you send 'im to ole long-leg, long-tongue Steve, an' he 'll whup 'im for you. Come, shek hands all round, now."

And so, with laughter and tears and handshakings, the funny little school was over.

MALSCHICK

by Leon W. Dean

A DOG-TEAM topped the ridge and went plunging down the trail toward the river. The man who ran beside it was shouting incessantly, and whenever he dropped back to leap aboard the high-riding sledge and catch his breath, his long-lashed dog-whip hissed and snapped and whined. Snitch Donovan was in a hurry. So were his dogs. Snitch and his dogs had often been in a hurry.

Half a mile to the rear, there straggled across a valley another dog-team. He who drove it was also in a hurry. He was young. Snitch himself was not old, except as years crowded with bad living had made him old, but this second driver was scarcely more than a boy. He looked tired. His dogs looked tired. But they were good dogs—as good as those that had topped the ridge and were running for the river. The boy would have said that they were better, but there were others who might not have agreed with him. All the North Country knew Snitch and his dogs. They did not like Snitch, but they liked his dogs. They were mighty dogs. More than once had Snitch owed his salvation to their strength, speed, and endurance.

It was nothing new to Snitch to have a man upon his trail. Something stirred beneath the canvas covering of his sled, whimpering as though not at all in love with its cramped quarters. He swore aloud, and sent his dogs at the last stretch intervening between himself and the river. As

they flashed out upon the snow-covered surface of the ice, he swung them southward, bringing them to a halt.

Southward lay the village of Moosekill, with its dozen or so frame houses, its trading-post and saloons. The man stared back over the way he had come. Evidently he saw that for which he sought, for, as he smote the mittened hand against his chest to keep warm, he laughed harshly. The pursuing sled had just come in sight on the crest of the ridge that he himself had crossed some few minutes before. The outfit looked fagged. He had expected it. Ten miles more and he would be in Moosekill, and then—

Another whine came from beneath the blankets. They tossed lustily as whatever it was that was pinioned there struggled valiantly to free itself from a situation so little to its liking.

"Two thousand dollars for a pup!" muttered the man. "Two thousand dollars for a measly pup!"

From the ridge on which he was breathing his team the boy looked away over the wooded slope to the long ribbon of white where the river flowed beneath its covering of ice, and where the dark shapes of man and sledge and dogs were stretched in a smudge of contrasting color against the snowy background.

"Poor little Malschick!" he whispered softly, "Poor little Malschick!"

He leaned heavily against the handle of

his sledge. His dogs had fallen in the snow. He pitied them. A rare phenomenon in the North was Paul Kendricks, for he loved his dogs. And the big, varicolored brutes, belying their nature, loved him. Not once in all their savage, half-wild ancestry had the hand of love come to soften their fierce spirit. The whip, the burden, cold, and scant rations had been their lot. Fear, not love, had been their guiding principle. Then had come Paul Kendricks, and the miracle of change had been wrought. They were dogs of true Northern blood. Men wise in the ways of the land has scoffed and said that such dogs were not for taming, that the only power recognized by their wolfish souls was the power of a stronger brute force than their own; that to show them kindness or mercy would be perhaps to soften their bodies, but not their hearts. A team of pet dogs was not a thing for the Northland. But Paul Kendricks had stuck to his ideals. He believed that these big-framed, big-muscled fellows, with their lion hearts and trained intelligences, would make wonder dogs if but properly treated. He had gathered about him the best his money could buy. He had made companions of them rather than slaves of them. With the old dogs, suspicion had died hard; but with the younger ones—the puppies—as they began to come along, it was easier. He kept the pick of the litters, bought new dogs where he found what he wanted, and in all ways strove to perfect his breed, building for size and speed. Others commenced to take notice. A demand for dogs from the Arctic Circle Kennels made itself felt. All through the North the name of Kendricks became known as a synonym for good dogs. Men wanted the big-boned, shapely-headed fellows that came from his kennels. They found them heavier, more powerful, and at the same time swifter, than the general run. Gradually they

came to realize that the surly creatures with which they had been so long accustomed to get along were a nuisance. A manageable team was a better team. The boy's reputation spread southward across the Provinces and to the States. Orders bearing Canadian and United States postmarks began occasionally to arrive at that far-flung outpost of civilization where, within a dozen fenced-in acres, he made his home.

Then had come into the world Malschick. From the very first the boy had known him for a dog of dogs. Men who had followed the snow-trails for years without number looked upon him and marveled. Indian, white, and half-breed, it was all the same. Never before had they seen a puppy of such promise. Word of him began to travel abroad. Some one with an open eye notified some one else in the States. That some one, a man by the name of Gowan, wired a thousand dollars for him. His young owner refused. Two—three thousand? No. But who was this Gowan? Inquiries revealed him a Chicago sporting magnate. He might want the dog for anything from show purposes to breeding or fighting. Steadily the price went up. Steadily the Arctic Circle Kennels refused to part with its prize. Kendricks was fond of his dogs. He did not like what he learned of Gowan. Besides, the youngster was worth money to him right where he was. Every day of his young life he was advertising the kennels as nothing else could.

Malschick was about four weeks old when the young fancier began to suspect that mischief was afoot. One or two attempts were made to break into the building where the dogs were housed; but if the intruder was reckoning on their reputation for gentleness, his hopes were rudely shattered. They were gentle, as such dogs go, but he who ventured among them should come on lawful and timely business. The first of the attempts was made at night, and the boy was awakened by the clamor. All that his investigation disclosed to him was tracks. He was not certain of the motive of the person who had made them. The second attempt came in the daytime, when he was away. He was out hunting and had left his dogs at home. That was fortunate. Their ability as protectors was again clearly demonstrated. A few days later a stranger, looking them over, dropped a hint that Malschick was too good a six-weeks' pup to lose. Something in the man's tone caused the young owner to take notice. To his query, all the man would say, however, was that it might be well to watch him. The boy resolved to do so. His fears were crystallizing. He believed the attempts might have something to do with Malschick. There were men who would go far to get such a dog. Naturally enough, perhaps, he did not think of Gowan as having anything to do with the affair. Chicago was too far away. He ascribed it to local parties—local in that they belonged to the big North. He meant to be careful, but a message from Snitch Donovan lured him off his guard.

Snitch had one of the finest teams of dogs to be found in the country, but they were devil-dogs—dogs that would take a man's throat as quickly as crush the life from a running rabbit. They were born ferocious, and Snitch's treatment of them had made them more ferocious. A year or so before he had tried to buy a dog from the Arctic Circle Kennels, but Paul, knowing his character, had refused to let him have it. He knew the refusal had made Snitch his enemy, and he was sorry, for Snitch was a dirty fighter; but it was not to be helped. Now he received word that the man was stranded with two sick dogs at a certain cabin some dozen miles above the kennels. He wanted Paul to bring on

a dog and help him out. It was a request that in such a country could not well be refused. Paul set out with his dogs the next morning, taking two extra ones with him. That left the canine guard at the kennels rather scant.

In one way and another it was possible afterwards to piece together much of what happened while he was away. Snitch must have been watching from the wooded summit of a near-by hill and seen him go. When sure that he was safely off, he had started down. One of his dogs, catching the scent of the others that had passed, let slip a bark. A savage blow from Snitch laid him low in the snow. That blow later was to cost Snitch dear. At the kennels, he beat off the few dogs remaining and got possession of what he wanted, fighting a warlike retreat from the enclosure, so bitterly contested that he was forced to use his revolver, leaving two of the dogs dead in the yard. Then he fled, knowing that he had several hours start on his rival, and that the Arctic Circle dogs would be too tired when the trick was discovered to overtake his own fast team. That, at least, was what he thought he knew. Kendricks would be aware, of course, who was responsible for the trouble, for he had intentionally given his name to it, preferring to have the boy know that he had struck and got even. He was pretty certain of the way the affair would come out. One thing, however, he failed to take into consideration—that Paul would guess at the truth of the matter as quickly as he did.

At the cabin the boy found where a man had been, but there was no one there at the time. Sled tracks showed that he had left by a roundabout route in the direction of the kennels. It might, he knew, merely be that the dogs had become better and Snitch had gone on, or it might all have been just a revengeful joke; but something warned him that it was more. He put his nine dogs to the trail, and their going was like the going of the wind that comes down from out the vast ocean spaces of ice and snow. Before reaching the kennels he saw where a sledge had come in on the trail after his passing. A mile further on, the home clearing, with its snow-splotched log-cabin and outbuildings for the dogs, grew out from among the trees. He brought his panting team to a halt. By some freak of circumstance he had hoped to be in time, but he was not. Signs of the struggle greeted him. Malschick was gone. Two of the dogs—mothers of his puppies, that he had thought a great deal of—lay dead in the trampled snow where they had fallen in service to him. He examined their wounds, and his blood surged hot at the thought of the brutal heart and hand that had wrought them. They had been more demonstrative in their affection for him, they had more quickly responded to his advances. It was about them that he had founded the kennels. Vengeance as men know it in the North flamed within him. He could hardly breathe, so fast pounded his heart at the thought of Snitch Donovan.

At the kennels he had two fresh dogs that could be substituted for tired ones. He made the change and was soon on the trail once more. His string numbered nine. Snitch's numbered eight—reckoned as eight of the best in the North, and with such a tremendous lead as seemingly to prevent all chances of being overtaken. The most loyal supporters of the Arctic Circle Kennels would not have said otherwise. But the unexpected happened. A just fate intervened to even matters a little. As before, the boy could decipher the signs in the snow when he came to them. As the strain of the pace began to make itself felt, the dog that Snitch had knocked down for barking commenced to go groggy. No amount of beating could keep him to the trail and on his legs. Raging, the man had finally brought the team to a stop. At least an hour must have elapsed before the dog was fit to move on again, and even then the one who had struck him dared not travel as fast as he had been doing, for fear of another collapse.

All this Paul in due time read on the broad, clear page of the arctic white. He was driving his own team hard at the time—harder than he should have driven. He knew it; but what must be, must be. Always, except on the steepest up-grades, the dogs went at a run, halting only now and then as he permitted them a moment's rest and a chance to breathe. They were strong with plentiful food and the work he had made a practice of giving them. He ran ahead, breaking trail, or to the rear. When necessity demanded, he rode, but not until his own breath came short and he could keep the pace no longer. It was a light load he carried, containing only a day's supplies for himself and dogs—not an ounce of superfluous weight, not even a gun. When he came to the place where the one he was pursuing had been forced to stop, he took heart. To that extent at least had fortune favored him.

Far into the night he followed the ghostly trail. The ethereal light of the great northern regions showed him the way. The silent fir woods rose about him. Long after Snitch in all probability had made camp, he was traveling—on and on, ever lessening the distance between them. When he called his final halt the dogs dropped exhausted in their traces, burying their noses in the snow and gulping great mouthfuls to cool their parched throats.

At earliest break of day he was up and away again. He had twelve hours in which to catch the man who led him. Once more he did not spare the dogs. Nor did he spare himself. As on the day before, he traveled hard, harder decidedly than he should have traveled, but travel hard he must, or lose. He could tell that the man ahead was making better time than he had been previously. He also made better time—again, because he must. If he exacted much of his dogs to do it, he exacted much of himself. Loyally and royally they responded to every demand. The iron hearts within them drove them on. Ahead and behind, at a staggering trot, he guided them.

Snow began to fall. It fell steadily for two hours, swirling down out of a cloud-laden sky. It sifted into the coats of the dogs, lying in a ridge of white along their backs. They bowed their heads before it, as did the boy, and struggled on. As it deepened in the trail, the man and dogs ahead had to break it out. It was not of a depth to impede them much, but mile after mile of an obstruction, however slight, makes a difference. It was easier for the team behind. Filling the air, the snow would also have made excellent cover under which to approach the racing sledge ahead, but nature has her whims. After a time it ceased to fall, and the sun came out. It grew colder.

Something like an hour later the boy's heart gave a sudden leap. Outlined against a slope far in front of him was a man and a team of dogs. The country was broken and the distance great. If his vision had not been keen, he might not have seen them at all. Evidently he was gaining. He compelled the dogs and himself to maintain the pace. Just what he would do, should he overtake the man, he did not know. That must come later. The hot spirit within him made him reckless of what might happen. He asked but that the meeting might take place.

He gained slowly. The tongues of his dogs were lolling, their eyes were bloodshot, their giant muscles drugged with fatigue. But he drew closer. Screened by the uneven nature of the land, it was some time before the unsuspecting man discovered his proximity. The boy could tell when this happened. The tracks in the trail showed where he had stopped and looked back. Then the dogs had been put to a faster gait. At that, for about the first time, the boy's own whip cracked, and the final leg of the chase was on. The leading dogs were fresher; but, with whip and voice, the boy urged his own team forward, and in a desperate, heartbreaking struggle they more than held their own, more than vindicated their title of being the greatest dogs of the North, as some had claimed for them. Despite the long-bitter, fast journey at their backs, their weary limbs and spent breath, they held their distance, and even gained. The fleeing man ahead, do what he might, could not shake them off. His team, too, was tiring. When they came to the river, ten miles above Moosekill, the kennel dogs were only half a mile to the rear. The taunting yell of Snitch Donovan drifted back to them as he started his dogs forward once more.

"Hoola, Boris! Hoola!" called the boy to his leader.

Small as it was, the little village of Moosekill, with its log shacks and its store and its saloons, played its part in the life of the North—a very important part to the region it fed and clothed, whose money it counted, and whose pleasure it provided, making possible much good or much evil, according to the desires of those who came into and went forth from it. It was a river town. Just now, a small river-steamer swung at its moorings there, nearly ready to cast off. Snitch Donovan knew of this steamer, and its scheduled hour of departure. He licked his dry lips—dry not alone from the keen wind and frosty air.

"Two thousand dollars!" he panted

hoarsely. "Two thousand dollars if I get him there in time!"

In places, the snow on the river was soaked with water, particularly down under, where it lay next the ice. The boy noticed this as he swung his team toward it and headed southward behind Malschick and his captor. Where his forerunner's sled had crossed, it showed up most conspicuously, for the runners cut in, and the water filtered into the tracks they had left, quickly freezing. This condition existed only in patches, however, and was due rather to air-holes and the vagaries of the current beneath than to thin ice.

The boy's dogs could hardly keep their feet. They were completely done in. To overtake the man ahead seemed impossible. Yet the boy, too, knew of the steamer. In the endless hours of the chase he had figured it all out. He must reach the man before the man reached Moosekill. On a long stretch free from turns, Snitch faced about once more, hurling back his taunting cry. Inspiration, born of the emergency, seized the boy. He cupped his mittened hands in return, making of them a megaphone.

"Malschick!" he called. "Malschick!"— sending the words ringing down the forest-lined river. "Malschick! Malschick!"

The animated bundle of life beneath the blanket-and-canvas covering of Snitch Donovan's sled became more animated than ever as the familiar voice penetrated to its ears. All the growing puppy love in the little dog's heart responded. He was lonesome, he was frightened at the strange surroundings and treatment. He was a strong puppy. He struggled valiantly. The sledge was moving again.

"Malschick!" came the call—"Malschick!"

The struggles increased. The man at the sledge handles was cursing roundly. He brought his heavy whip down cruelly over the spot where the canvas bulged and shook from the contortions of the powerful little body beneath. Things were going wrong. The puppy was not supposed to make such a fuss. The man had underestimated the dog's strength, his sturdy, tempestuous spirit. His exertions were taking him toward the edge of the load.

"Malschick!" came the master's voice. "Ho—Malschick!"

The boy had seen that something was amiss. A sudden successful lurch brought the puppy almost free. The man sprang forward. He was too late. A tumbling bag of vigorously fighting puppyhood slipped from beneath the canvas flap and out upon the snow.

There was nothing for it but to stop. The man halted his team, unmindful that the spot was a damp one. Luckily for him, the puppy was in a sack, leaving him at liberty to work. The lashing that held the blankets and canvas in place had to be unfastened. The blankets had been to keep the puppy warm. The canvas was the usual arctic protection against storms. At night it could be used for a tent. It was bound strongly down about the load. The man worked with as much dispatch as the cold would permit, but the boy, seeing it as his last chance, was coming on fast. The dogs, too, realized that they were drawing in upon the quarry that for hours without end they had been trailing. The knowledge bore them up and sent them flying forward in a last splendid spurt that must be the end. The man's fingers tore at the knots. They trembled with haste—with fear of failure. It was a race with time against the onrushing sledge. He won. The canvas was flung back, and the puppy once more roped beneath it.

He sprang for the handles of his sledge. The charging team from the Arctic Circle Kennels was not a rod behind. Their mouths were open, their lean sides heaving, but their eagerness equalled their master's. They knew what was wanted; the game was within reach—or so it seemed. The man's whip cracked, his voice was harsh with the tenseness of the moment. He lunged heavily on the handles of his sledge to help start it. There was a ripping, splintering sound, and a runner gave way. The water, collecting about the sledge, had frozen it in. The abrupt strain, coming just right, and with all the force of a man and dogs thrown into it in their hurry to get away, had been too much for some weak spot in the wood and it had parted. Ordinarily, it might have been soon remedied enough to go on, but now—

The man whirled, revolver in hand. Down the trail, close upon him, came the boy and dashing dogs. Paul saw the flash of metal. He was not afraid. An unaccountable sense of confidence possessed him; he felt that he was going to win. The gun flashed, thundering aloud in the hushed forest. He heard the quick whine of passing lead. The space narrowed. The man fired again. The distance was measurable by yards, by feet. The man stepped back. His own dogs had swung about in their traces to face the new-comers, and were at his heels. The backward step and a third report of the gun semed simultaneous. The boy felt his arm go queer, but did not heed it. Other things were happening.

In stepping backward, the man had crushed the foot of a dog. Quick as the dart of a snake's head the animal struck, driving his fangs into the calf of the leg. The man, every faculty concentrated on something else, was taken off his guard, off his balance. He nearly fell. As he toppled, another dog leaped, and for the last time the revolver spat fire, the bullet going off harmlessly into the air. Never before had the dogs so had the man at a disadvantage. His back was toward them, he was falling—they leaped to bring him down. All their savage natures flamed up within them—the wolf natures, naturally fierce, that he had made fiercer. All their ancient grievances urged them on. The stronger brute was now the weaker. His arms went up, his revolver dropped from his grasp, the boy caught a glimpse of a face distorted with terror as he went down and under and was buried from sight beneath the fighting pack. A single shriek, filled with all the horror of a human soul in the throes of violent death, rose from its midst. Then Paul's own dogs hit.

Dog turned upon dog. There was the slash and clash of teeth, the place was a writhing mass of battling, snarling beasts. The sounds of the combat reverberated across the silent places. The boy leaped among them, shouting, striking terrific blows with the butt of his great dog-whip. Each moment he was in imminent danger of himself going down, of having the swirling packs close over him, as they had over the other. It was only because the dogs were at each other that he managed to pull the man out from beneath them. He was not dead. The turn of the battle had saved him. That and the fact that his team, when they had first attacked him, had been hampered by being still in the traces. Both teams had partially broken and cut their way out of harness by this time, but because they were still, in a measure, strung together, the boy was able somehow to get their attention and subdue and part them.

When it was all over he thought once more of his arm. He was wounded, and the dogs had mauled him somewhat in the fight, but it was Snitch who was the most badly hurt. He got him onto his sledge, and, leaving the eight dogs tethered in a clump of evergreen, went on with his own nine. It was difficult getting through, but he managed it. One of the first men he saw as he plodded into Moosekill behind his weary dogs was an officer in the uniform of the Northwest Mounted Police. He knew by this time from Snitch himself that he had not been working in his own interests alone, but in Gowan's. He and the inspector found a place where they could be by themselves.

"So you are Paul Kendricks," said the latter, when the boy's story had been told.

"Yes, sir."

Malschick, released from his prison walls of burlap, was trotting inquiringly about his new world, sniffing table-leg and corner and generally making himself interested and interesting.

"And this," continued the inspector, gingerly extending his hand as one who knows the Northern breed of dogs, "is Malschick."

"He won't snap, sir."

"No, so I understand. This is n't the first time we have heard of the Arctic Circle Kennels and Malschick. As a mat-

ter of fact, I was on my way to see you when I stopped off for the boat. One never knows what is going to happen when a boat leaves. I have with me an order for a couple of dogs. The Mounted will pay well for them. What are you going to do with Malschick?"

"Hang onto him, sir. I think too much of him to part with him. Did you see him look up when you spoke his name, sir?"

"I did that. He 's got brains as well as body. The Mounted will keep its eye on him. I have an idea that men like Snitch Donovan will show us the way no longer. The dog-show at Toronto will be coming on in a few months. Send Malschick down. I predict he will be returned a winner, and go straight through to the championships in the big Westminster Show at New York. It will be money and fame for the kennels. What do you say?"

"Yes, I believe I will. Thank you, sir."

MORE·THAN·CONQVERORS

BY
ARIADNE
GILBERT

THE TORCH-BEARER OF THE DARK CONTINENT

Mrs. Livingstone stood in the doorway looking down on her sleeping boy. With his tousled hair dark against the white pillows and his eyelashes dark against his pale cheeks, he lay there in the feeble light of the winter dawn, looking particularly small and particularly glad to dream. Indeed, the mother wished she did not have to wake her little David. He was o'er young to work! Hardly more than a bairn, after all. But it had to be done. First she called; then she touched him gently; then she put her cheek down close to his and tried by her warm Scotch love to soften the hard news—that morning had really come, and he must rub his blue eyes open, dress, and reach the factory by six o'clock. This was ninety years ago, before there was much talk about that cruel thing, child labor. The Livingstones were poor. There were many children, and David was next to the oldest. He expected to help, and his father and mother expected it of him.

The lad had to be in his place at six. Then, with a short time out to rest and eat, his little hands would tie broken threads till eight at night. Fixed to the spinning-jenny was a Latin grammar, bought with his first wages, so that while his fingers were busy with their mechanical task, his brain could keep pace with the boys at school. No doubt those boys were yawning over their verbs that very minute, and no doubt all the boys, including little David, would rather play on the banks of the singing Clyde. Its music suited a child's spirit a great deal better than the whir of wheels; and the winter wind blowing over its waters, nipping though it was, was better for a child's blood than the dust-filled air of the factory. As for sunshine, David hardly knew its flicker any more; he who had loved so much to gather shells and flowers! He would plod home by starlight or no light, as the weather decreed, so that, if the school of darkness was the best preparation for life in the "Dark Continent," his training was indeed rare.

Lives of most of the great men prove that those with the least time hold it at the highest value. It is with time as with money. The poor man, if he is wise, values five cents more than does the millionaire; David Livingstone valued a minute more than the boy of endless leisure. Free time was dear to him. But after the long factory day was over, bed was the place for a child of ten. For his golden minutes of freedom, sound sleep was the best investment. As the lad grew older, however, he felt compelled to wrench from life something besides drudgery and dreams, and so, in those precious leisure moments, he studied history, politics, and literature, puzzled out creation's secrets locked away in flowers and stones, and at nineteen had saved enough money and stored up enough knowledge to go to Glasgow and enter the university. As a boy, religious books had been hateful reading. Deacon Livingstone would fain have had his son love his catechism; but up to this time, David had taken little interest in religion. Now he made up his mind to devote his life to making men better; and accordingly, when he went to Glasgow, it was to study for the ministry. Here, as Dr. Hillis puts it, "He hired a garret, cooked his oatmeal and studied, made a little tea and studied, went forth to walk, but studied ever."

One of his first attempts at preaching was enough to make a weaker man give up preaching, for life. He was sent to Stanford to supply a sick minister's place; but no sooner had be given out his text, than something queer happened. "Midnight darkness came upon him." "My friends," he said, with his frank straightforwardness, "I have forgotten all I had to say." Then down he came from the pulpit and went out at the chapel door. We can imagine it perfectly: his young face crimson, his shoes creaking with each fatal step, and the little congregation, some laughing, some pitying, but almost all remembering the failure for years to come.

But Livingstone was not to be beaten by one defeat. Because he longed above everything else to be a missionary, he studied surgery at the medical college; he would want to heal men's bodies as well as save their souls. To his common sense, it seemed much easier to win confidence by curing pain or saving life than by preaching strange doctrines, no matter how good. If his common sense had not told him this, his Master's example, as the world's great healer, would have done it. And David Livingstone needed no better example.

As soon as he had decided on Africa as the land for his work, the whole world tried to scare him—no, not his family, and not Dr. Moffat, but most of those outside his family. When Dr. Moffat, himself an African missionary, looked into the young man's fearless eyes, he read there the courage Africa would need. But people in general did their best to frighten him. Death, they said, would meet him at every turn; between African fever, savage natives, and the merciless power of the sun, he would be cut off in the prime of his youth and hopefulness. The Missionary Board itself would not be held responsible for any such risk. If he went, he could go independently.

Despite all these threats and warnings, the strong heart was unshaken. A steamer would sail for Africa almost immediately, and on that steamer Livingstone would go. He hurried home to say good-by. It was evening before he reached the dear old door, and in the early morning he must leave again. So till midnight he and his father and mother, three understanding hearts, talked over the fears and hopes of his journey—steadfast, all three, yet finding the parting bitterly hard. When the sun flushed the sky with the light of dawn, David read, with brave simplicity, "Thou shalt not be afraid for the terror by night, nor for the arrow that flieth by day." Then, leaving his mother in the open doorway, he set out on his seven-mile walk to Glasgow. His father strode beside him till they reached the top of one of the high hills, when the good-by of their life was said.

If David Livingstone had been a cold-hearted man, the bravery needed for his African explorations would have been purely physical. Whether he was to meet fever, savages, or sunstroke, or even all three, physical bravery alone would have been enough; but he took with him into the desolation a great, warm heart pounding with love of home. I suppose the very poorness of it was dear: the old sofa; the faded carpet; the fire that had not always kept them warm; dearest of all, the faces around the fire. David Livingstone needed a great deal more than physical courage to face that life of loneliness.

Since most of us would find it tiresome to follow Livingstone's long journeys even on the map, we will pay little attention to geography. It is far better to remember that, to him, every name and every mile meant an experience—those names and miles that are too tedious for us to *read* about. As he traveled, not only was he *making* geography (seeking to discover the source of the Nile), but he was trying to rid the land of slavery, and to teach the people a happy religion. These were his three great aims. But to us his story is so full of poetry and action that it reads like a wonderful book of adventure. Sometimes, as we follow his hairbreadth escapes, we forget entirely that he was a missionary, and think he must have explored for excitement or fame. We must not do this. While he was as daring as the bravest explorer, he never faltered in his purpose; he had, above all else, the motive of redeeming Africa.

Before he could do anything for the Africans' however, he had to learn their language. This took seven months. After landing at the Cape of Good Hope, the very southern tip of Africa, he struck into the forest, and there he lived, the one white man among the half-naked black savages, learning their speech and their ways. If a man from another planet should sud-denly stand before you in the center of your city, he would not seem as queer to you as David Livingstone seemed to these black natives. We can have no idea what they thought of him, whether he was a miracle, or just a new kind of animal. But night after night he lay down to sleep among them with a fearlessness that was, in itself, power. "I trust you," his placid face would say, without speech. And without speech, armed and wondering, they would answer, "We are worthy of your trust." They were not, except as his trust had made them so. They themselves did not know why they did not kill him as he slept there among them unprotected.

He first won their confidence as a "rain-maker." By leading "runnels from the river," he taught them to irrigate; the desert changed to a fruitful valley. "He is a wizard," they said. "He brings water to dry ground." As time went on, he taught them to make gardens, raise cattle, and build houses. He taught their young people everything practical, from carpentry to taking care of the sick. After his marriage to Dr. Moffat's daughter, his wife taught the girls dressmaking. She was as brimful of bravery as her husband. She and the children spent many years in England for the children's health and education; but all the time she was in Africa, she was a strong help to the "doctor." And Livingstone's short holidays at home were very precious. With a child on each knee, he loved to turn his dangers into stories, and see the young eyes grow big with terror while all the time he and the children knew that he got away safely.

Truly the swamps and jungles, where he spent his brave life, were frightsome enough. Trees one hundred feet high, festooned with tangled vines, shut out the sun, and snakes wriggled round in the tangle. Now Livingstone was stung by nettles, now, for days together, drenched by rain. At night, his only shelter was an overturned canoe. Thirst, sunstroke, and famine, all threatened death, just as the friends in Scotland had prophesied. "A mole and two mice" do not seem, to us, like a tempting supper. One evening, Livingstone and his men were glad enough to get that. When he was starving, he wished he would not dream of "savory viands." "Took my belt up three holes to relieve hunger," reads one day's journal. His cattle died, his goods, including his precious medicines, were stolen. The rivers they swam or waded were the homes of many crocodiles. Not only was he attacked by serpents, lions, buffaloes, and hippopotami, but he was constantly harassed by tsetse-flies and ants.

"The Majestic Sneak" was Dr. Livingstone's nickname for the lion. Drawn by the smell of meat, he would come near the camp and roar.

If "lions attacked the herds in open day, or leaped into the cattle-pens by night," one had to be killed to scare off the others. Though it took tremendous courage to lead lion-hunts, Livingstone was the man who could do it. He mustered his men. Around a group of lions hiding on a wooded hill they formed a circle, but were afraid to throw their spears. Some one fired. Three animals, roaring, leaped through the line and escaped unhurt, while the panic-stricken natives huddled back into the circle. For very kinkiness, their hair could not stand upright; but their knees shook, and their eyes rolled with terror. Those who could shoot were afraid of killing their fellows. Since the whole attack seemed as useless as it was dangerous, the circle broke up, and the party was about to return to the village, when, from the other side of the hill, Livingstone made out the outline of a tawny foe. About thirty yards away, the lion crouched behind a bush.

Livingstone took good aim and "fired both barrels into it."

"He is shot! he is shot!" shouted the men.

"He has been shot by another man too; let us go to him," cried others.

"Stop a little till I load again," warned Livingstone, who saw the "lion's tail erected in anger." Then, as he "rammed down the bullets," he "heard a shout, and, looking half round, saw the lion springing upon him." "He caught me by the shoulder," reads his vivid account, "and we both came to the ground together. Growling horribly, he shook me as a terrier dog does a rat." Then a dreaminess like the effect of chloroform came over the great doctor. Though he knew what was happening, he had no "sense of pain or terror." "As he had one paw on the back of my head," the journal continues, "I turned round to relieve myself of the weight, and saw his eyes directed to Mabálue, who was aiming at him from a distance of ten or fifteen yards. His gun, which was a flint one, missed fire in both barrels. The animal immediately left me to attack him. Another man, whose life I had saved after he had been tossed by a buffalo, attempted to spear the lion, upon which he turned from Mabálue and seized this fresh foe by the shoulder. At that moment, the bullets the beast had received, took effect, and he fell dead. The whole was the work of a few moments."

In his account, Livingstone made light of his injured bones and of the deep prints in his arm of eleven sharp teeth. "I have escaped with only the inconvenience of a false joint," he says simply, and is thankful for his tartan jacket that partly protected him from those cruel teeth, and so saved his life.

This was, perhaps, his most exciting lion-fight; but the lions were familiar neighbors all the time. Livingstone could keep even for the lions a kind of understanding and friendliness. Human enough to see their point of view, he adds to his description of "dripping forests and oozing bogs," "A lion had wandered into this world of water and ant-hills, and roared night and morning, as if very much disgusted. We could sympathize with him."

He liked to watch all the different animals. In two sentences he tells of another adventure: "I killed a snake seven feet long. He reared up before me and turned to fight." Evidently bragging was not in his line.

But if it came to honoring the natives, his journal could give that generous space. "Their chief characteristic is their courage. Their hunting is the bravest thing I ever saw." Then he goes on to describe a hippopotamus-hunt. The game, if won, could be traded for maize. There were two men in each light craft. "As they guide the canoe slowly down-stream to a sleeping hippopotamus, not a single ripple is raised on the smooth water; they look as if holding in their breath, and communicate by signs only. As they come near the prey, the harpooner in the bow lays down his paddle and rises slowly up, and there he stands erect, motionless, and eager, with the long-handled weapon poised at arm's-length above his head, till, coming close to the beast, he plunges it with all his might in toward the heart." Surprised from sleep by sudden pain, the animal does not fight at once. But the instant the "enormous jaws appear, with a terrible grunt, above the water, the men must thrust a second harpoon, this time from directly above. Then comes the battle. In a flash, the paddlers shoot the canoe backward, before hippo "crunches it as easily as a pig would a bunch of asparagus, or shivers it with a kick of his hind foot." If the canoe is attacked, the men must "dive, and swim to the shore under water," playing a trick on their huge gray enemy, who will look for them on the surface. Meantime the handles, tied to the harpoons by long ropes, are floating on the stream, and from a distance other paddlers in other canoes seize them.

But there were not only lions, serpents, hippopotami, buffaloes, and other big foes, which any one would have dreaded, but there were hordes of tiny enemies: swarms of mosquitos, stinging men almost to madness; tsetse-flies, killing off in a short time "forty-three fine oxen"; pests of ants that produced a burning agony; and leeches that flew at his white skin "like furies, and refused to let go," until he gave them a "smart slap" as the natives did.

So much for the miseries of this jungle world. It had its beauties—great ones, too. Livingstone has left us a noble picture of the kingdom where animals reign. "Hundreds of buffaloes and zebras grazed on the open spaces, and there stood lordly elephants feeding majestically. . . . When we descended, we found all the animals remarkably tame. The elephants stood beneath the threes, fanning themselves with their huge ears." He wrote with affection. He gloried in the crimsons and deep blues of the African tangle, and in the flowers that made a "golden carpet." It was as if the ten-year-old Scotch laddie, cheated long ago of his sunshine, found it at last through sacrifice. No vast experience in great affairs could spoil his happiness in little things—in the songs of birds, the freshness of the morning; in everything that "God made very good." And half his heart seems at home in Scotland. There was a river "beautiful like the Clyde"; larks that did not "soar so high," or stay "so long on the wing as *ours*"; "a tree in flower brought the pleasant fragrance of hawthorn hedges back to memory." Some days the whole world seemed steeped in clear sunshine, the air filled with the hum of insects and the "courtship" of full-throated birds. Livingstone watched them "play at making little homes," or carrying nest-feathers too heavy for their strength; and often he fed them with bread-crumbs, he who had so little bread.

Into the tangled darkness of Africa, the torch-bearer carried a light; and, for the first time, eyes dull almost to blindness, saw life—clean, honest, and peaceful. Like children, the savages were quick to imitate. "From nothing I say will they learn as much as from what I am," was Livingstone's great doctrine. If the life-sermon failed, no word-sermon could win. And so, for example as well as for his own comfort, he kept himself, and everything he had, scrupulously neat. He taught them to despise a man who struck another in the back. By his own proved fearlessness and by appealing to their own bravery, he made them ashamed to be sneaks.

Livingstone offered no miracles. Still treating them as untaught children, he pleased them with music, and showed his magic-lantern pictures of his Master's life. "It is the Word from heaven," they said. But most of them grasped little except that the one who bore the Word was himself good. His genius was the genius of the heart. The natives trusted him more than they could trust father or brother; and when once their love was won, they thanked him by their faithfulness.

Of the horrors of the slave trade, it is enough to quote his own words: "The subject does not admit of exaggeration." His accounts, further than this, are only too vivid. "She is somebody's bairn," he would say pityingly, as he saw some poor chained creature. Three times Livingstone built for himself a house, only to have it destroyed by slave-traders, who hated him fiercely. After that, he was forever home-less. What Lincoln did for America, Livingstone did for Africa. The Boers, whose chief commerce was in slaves, destroyed all his possessions. "They have saved me the trouble of making a will," he said. Three times in one day he nearly lost his life, for his was the life they were seeking.

Great physical courage he needed, then, but much more. For three years, he heard no news from home; for two, the world heard nothing of him. "Oh, for one hour a day to play with my children!" he would think. Early in his African experience one of his babies had died in the wilderness. Years later, his boy Robert went to America, and there, like his father, spent himself for the slaves—he fought and fell at Gettysburg. When Livingstone was on his way home from his first journey, his father died.

"You wished so much to see David," said the old man's daughter.

"Aye, very much," with Scotch strength. "But I think I 'll know whatever is worth knowing about him. Tell him I think so when you see him."

To Dr. Livingstone's delight, his wife sailed with him back to Africa. But the dreadful fever took her away. "Oh, my Mary! my Mary! how often we have longed for a quiet home since you and I were cast adrift," he sobbed. "For the first time in my life, I feel willing to die." Yet, in his bitterest loneliness, he sustained himself with the promise, "Lo, I am with you always, even unto the end of the world." In his original way he added, "It is the word of a Gentleman of the most sacred and strictest honor, and there is an end on't."

Long before now, the London Missionary Society had given Livingstone its strong support. His home-comings were real triumphs! medals, degrees, receptions—all the honors that England showers upon her heroes. Livingstone hated such a fuss. He would rather meet a lion in the jungle than be made a lion in public. With no thought of his own glory, he set forth the commercial value of Africa: its fruits, its furs, its ivory. But his strongest appeal was for the slaves. Self-forgetful always, on his careful maps were two names of his own choosing. The beautiful cataract, de-

Death is the best he can hope for; no "good Samaritan" can possibly pass by. But suddenly, out of utter hopelessness, his faithful black man, Susi, rushed in, gasping, "An Englishman! I see him!"

Never was an American flag so dear to a Scotchman as those stars and stripes to

The meeting of Livingstone and Stanley

scribed by the natives as "Smoke that sounds," he named Victoria Falls for the "Great White Queen"; and he named a lake for his hero, Lincoln.

In September, 1865, he left England for the last time. Two years later, we find him again in the heart of Africa—a world all "froth and ooze." Again his goods have been stolen and he himself is a mere skeleton. Exhausted by exploration and sickness, with no news from home or from any one, his "forward tread" is a poor totter.

Livingstone! And never was a stage action more dramatic than Stanley's unexpected entrance—another white man in that unknown wilderness, bringing food, clothing, and medicine—everything a desolate, dying man could need. Letters? Yes, a bagful. Livingstone read two from his children; then he demanded the news. "Tell me the news. How is the world getting on? Grant, President? Good! It is two years since I have heard a word!" The story of Stanley's and Livingstone's friendship is too beautiful to miss. Every one should read it for himself. In the joy of their companionship, Livingstone grew rapidly better: his eyes brightened; his briskness and his youthfulness came back, together with that great, sweet spirit that Stanley never forgot. But when Stanley urged him to come away with him, Livingstone steadily refused. Africa might need him yet.

But his work was nearly over. During his long, wearying illness, however, he had the comfort of seeing his "boys' " faithfulness. They gave their blankets for his bed; they carried him on a litter over land; and on their shoulders through the flood. By his torch they had lighted theirs, and learned that brotherhood is true religion. Then, on a May morning, in 1873, one watcher alarmed the rest: "Come to Bwana; I am afraid. I don't know if he is alive." Susi, Chumah, and four others ran to the tent. There, by the bedside, with his face buried in the pillow, knelt their doctor, dead!

What to do they did not know; and he could not tell them any more. They wanted to keep him in Africa, but thought that his friends would want him home. And so, one of them reading the burial service, they laid his heart to rest where he had worked; but his body, cased in tree-bark and sail-cloth, they carried over a thousand miles to the ship that would bear it home. Gratitude has been called "the memory of the heart." Of all heart-memories, is there a better proof than this? The Samoans, who dug the road for Stevenson, could count on appreciation; but Livingstone's friends, with their dog-like fidelity, could never hope for a word, a look, a smile of thanks. One of the boys who made that hard journey was a slave he had freed.

England, proud to do him honor, gave him a place in Westminster Abbey, among her poets and her kings. On the black slab above him we may read:

Brought by faithful hands
Over land and sea
Here Rests
David Livingstone
Missionary, Traveler, Philanthropist
Born March 19, 1813
Died May 1, 1873

---

and on the border of the stone:

Other sheep I have which are not of this fold; them also I must bring, and they shall hear my voice.

"AS WE FORGIVE THOSE"

by T. Morris Longstreth

THE brothers Ripley were as different in nearly every way as the rapids and still pools of a mountain stream. Perhaps that is why they loved each other in a degree not usually meant by "brotherly love."

Will Ripley was the still pool. He was thoughtful to drowsiness, honest as daylight, mild-tempered, and twenty. He was up north in Pennsylvania somewhere, either alive or dead, for the date of this story is July 7th, 1863, which means, as you can read in the despatches of the time, that the terrible slaughter of Gettysburg was just over. The Ripleys, on their farm near The Soldiers' Home, outside of Washington, had not heard from him.

Although Will was no soldier at heart,—it hurt him even to stick pigs,—he had responded to Lincoln's call for more men two years before, leaving his kid brother Dan at home to help his father and mother. Dan was now fourteen, a high-strung, impetuous, outspoken lad of quick actions and hasty decisions. He was the laughing rapid. But for all his hastiness, he had a head and a heart that could be appealed to, usually. The only thing to which he could not reconcile himself was the separation from Will. Even Will's weekly letters,—which never missed their date except when the army was in retreat, and which always sent messages of love to Dan, coupled with encouragement to stay on the farm as the best way he could

aid the cause,—scarcely kept Dan from running off and hunting up his brother. Dan knew that he and his collie, Tam, were needed to look after the sheep; he knew that the President had asked the loyal to raise all the wool possible; he knew that his father was little more than an invalid since he had been hurt some time before by an accident on the farm. But to see the soldiers marching down Pennsylvania Avenue set him wild to be away with them. In fact, Tam seemed to be the anchor that held him; Dan sometimes even thought that he loved Tam next to Will.

The summer of '63 had been unbearably hot. Then there had been an increasingly ominous list of military disasters. Even the loyal were beginning to murmur against Lincoln's management of the war. Then Will's letters had ceased, and Mr. Ripley could get no satisfaction from headquarters. Even Will's uncle, a Colonel Scott, of Illinois, and a friend of Lincoln's, after repeated efforts to influence some officials at the War Department to aid him in securing news, had not been able to see the President, who was the last resort of everybody in those days of tribulation.

Dan was irritable with fatigue and his secret worry; his family, nearly sick with the heat and tension.

The climax to this state came from an unforeseen event. Tam, either crazed by the heat or some secret taste for blood, ran amuck one night, stampeded the sheep, and did grievous damage. Farmer Ripley doubtless acted on what he considered the most merciful course by having Tam done away with and buried before Dan got back from an errand to the city. But to Dan it seemed, in the first agony of his broken heart, an unforgivable thing. Weariness, worry, and now this knife-sharp woe changed the boy into a heart-sick being who flung himself on the fresh mound behind the barn and stayed there the whole day, despite the entreaties of his mother and the commands of his father.

He shed no tears; tears would have been dried up by the waves of hot anger against his father. And while he lay there, he thought and planned.

That evening his mother carried some food out to him. He did not touch it; he would not talk to her.

Sometime later, as the night wore on, he stole into the house, did up some clothes into a bundle, took the food at hand, and crept from his home. Once more he went to the grave of his slain pal. What he said there, aloud but quietly, need not be told. Sufficient it is to know that a burning resentment toward his father filled him, coupled with a sickening longing to be with his brother Will. Ill with his hasty anger, he thought that Will was the only one in the world who loved or understood him. In the wee hours of morning he left the farm, forever, as he thought, and turned down the wood-road which led to the Soldiers' Home, where he hoped to find some one who could tell him how to get to Will's regiment. The sultry, starless heat of a Washington midsummer enclosed him; the wood was very dark and breathless; his head throbbed. But he pushed on, high-tempered, unforgiving; he would show them all! Suddenly he recollected that he had not said the Lord's Prayer that

night. Dan had been strictly raised. He tried saying it, walking. But that seemed sacrilegious. He kneeled in the dark and tried. But when he got to "as we forgive those who trespass against us," he balked, for he was an honest soul. And this new gulf of mental distress was too much for him; it brought the tears.

There in the dark by the roadside, Dan lay and cried himself bitterly into an exhausted sleep.

At the same hour another worn soul, a tall, lean-faced man with eyes full of unspeakable sorrow, was pacing the chamber of the White House. The Rebellion had reached its flood tide at Gettysburg three days before; the President had stayed the flood, bearing in tireless sympathy the weight of countless responsibilities. Now, all day long, the débris of affairs had been borne down upon him—decisions that concerned not only armies, but races; not only races, but principles of human welfare. He was grief-stricken still from Willie's death, and his secretary in the room downstairs, listening unconsciously to the steady march of steps overhead, read into them the pulse-beats of human progress. Lincoln had given instructions that no one was to interrupt him. He was having one of his great spiritual battles.

Finally, shortly before dawn, the footsteps stopped, the secretary's door opened, and the gaunt, gray face looked in. "Stoddard, do you want anything more from me to-night?"

The secretary rose. "I want you in bed, sir. Mrs. Lincoln should not have gone away; you are not fair with her or us."

"Don't reproach me, Stoddard," said Lincoln, kindly; "it had to be settled, and, with God's help, it has been. Now I can sleep. But I must have a breath of air first. There's nothing?"

"Only the matter of those deserters, sir, and that can wait."

The President passed his hands over his deep-lined face. "Only!" he murmured. "Only! How wicked this war is. It leads us to consider lives by the dozen, by the bale, wholesale. How many in this batch, Stoddard?"

The secretary turned some papers. "Twenty-four, sir. You remember the interview with General Scanlon yesterday."

Lincoln hesitated, saying: "Twenty-four! Yes, I remember. Scanlon said that lenience to the few was injustice to the many. He is right, too." Lincoln held out his hand for the papers; then drew it back and looked up at Stoddard. "I can't decide," he said in a low voice, "not now. Stoddard, you see a weak man. But I want to thresh this out a little longer. I must walk. These cases are killing me; I must get out."

"Let me call an attendant, Mr. Lincoln."

"They 're all asleep. No, I 'll take my chances with God. If anybody wants to kill me, he will do it. You must go to bed, Stoddard."

The two men, each concerned for the other, shook hands in good night, and Lincoln slipped out into the dark, his long legs bearing him rapidly westward. During the heat he usually slept at the Soldiers' Home, being escorted thither by cavalry with sabers drawn. But he hated the noise of it, and, during Mrs. Lincoln's visit in New York, was playing truant to her rules. When he neared the Home he felt slightly refreshed and turned into the woods, drawn by the need of companionship with elements as calm and benignant as forest trees. The sky at his back began to lighten.

By the time dawn showed the ruts in the road, Lincoln realized that he was tired. "Abe, Abe," he said half aloud, "they

tell me you used to be a whale at splitting rails, and now a five-mile stroll before breakfast—By jings!" It was his usual "swear," that "by jings!" and this time it was occasioned by his nearly stepping on a lone youngster lying in the road. The boy raised his head from a bundle of clothes; the tall man stooped with tenderness, saying: "Hello, sonny, so you get old Mother Earth to make your bed for you! How 's the mattress?"

Dan sat up and rubbed his eyes. "What are you doin'?" he asked.

"I appear to be waking you, and making a bad job of it," said Lincoln.

"You did n't come to take me, then," said Dan, relieved. "I would n't 'a' gone," he added defiantly.

Lincoln looked at him sharply, his interest aroused by the trace of tears in the boy's eyes and the bravado in his voice. "There 's a misunderstanding here," continued Lincoln, "almost as bad a misunderstanding as Mamie and her mother had over Mr. Riggs, who was the undertaker back home." Here the gaunt man gave a preliminary chuckle. "Ever hear that story, sonny?"

Dan shook his head, wondering how such a homely man could sound so likable. Lincoln seated himself on a fallen tree trunk. "Well, it was this way. Back home there was an old chap used to drive an old rig around collecting rags. And one day when Mamie's ma was inside dusting the parlor, Mr. Riggs, whose job was undertaking, as I said, drops by for a friendly call, and Mamie sings out, country style, "Ma, here 's Mr. Riggs"; and her ma, thinking she 'd said the man for the rags, called back, "Tell him we have n't anything for him to-day."

The joke broke on Dan, after one look at his friend's face, and his quick, impetuous laugh might have disturbed the early-rising birds. Lincoln joined in, and for an instant Dan clean forgot Tam dead and home deserted; and for the same fleet instant Lincoln forgot his troubles in Dan's laugh. "Tell him we have n't anything for him to-day!" repeated the boy, "I 'll sure have to tell that to Fa—" He did n't finish the word, remembering with a pang that he was not going to see his father again.

Lincoln had caught the swift change on his face and it was his turn to wonder. He knew better than to ask questions. You can't fish for a boy's heart with question-marks, neat little fishhooks though they be. So he said, "Our sitting here when we ought to be getting back home reminds me of another story."

"Tell me," said Dan, well won already to this man, despite the gray, lined cheeks and the sadness that colored his voice. Dan did n't know yet who he was. He 'd not seen the cartoons that flooded the country during election, he was too young to go in to the inauguration, and the idea of the President of the United States sitting with him in the woods was too preposterous to cross his mind.

"You and I are pretty lazy, Son," said the kindly man; "but we are n't as lazy as the two darkies in the battle of Chancellorsville. The order came to retire, but those darkies were too lazy to move. Presently, 'Ping!' a bullet had hit one of the darkey's canteen. " 'Brother,' said the second darkey to him, 'I reckon we ought to be a-movin'.' 'I reckon we ought,' said the first; but they did n't move. And it was n't long before the hat of the second darkey was shot clean off. 'Mercy sakes! I reckon we just ought to be a-movin',' exclaimed the other darkey, and he half rose to go; but it was too much exertion, and he sank down again, saying, 'Mebbe, if we hangs aroun' a while longer, we kin git carried away.' "

When Dan had got over that story, Lincoln said, "Well, since there 's no one to carry us away, sonny, I reckon we just ought to be a-moving, don't you?" He helped the boy with his bundle.

"Are you going to the war, too?" asked Dan. "I am."

"You!" exclaimed Lincoln, "why you 're no bigger than my own Tadpole, and he 's only a wriggler yet. Does your father know?"

"I reckon he does by now," said the boy, darkly. "Father 's an early riser. You see, he killed my dog without my knowin', and so I lit out without his knowin'."

The hardness of the boy's voice hurt Lincoln, who said, "What 's your father's name, sonny?"

"William Ripley, that 's senior. Will, that 's junior, is my brother, off at the war. I 'm Dan. I 'm going to find my brother. I don't care if I never come back. I loved Tam better than—than—" His voice choked.

Lincoln put his hand on his shoulder. He was getting the situation. "Tam was your dog?" asked the big man, as gently as a mother.

"Yeh. And Father should n't 'a' killed him unbeknownst to me. I 'll never forgive him that, never!"

"Quite right," said the wise man, walking with him. "Don't you ever forgive him, Dan. Or don't ever forget it—under one certain condition."

"What 's that?" asked the boy, a trifle puzzled at the unexpected compliance of his elder with his own unforgiving mood.

"Why, that you also never forget all the kind and just things that your father has done for you. Why did he kill the dog, Dan?"

"Well—he—killed—some sheep," said the boy. He would be honest with this tall, gentle, and grave person who understood so readily.

"How old are you Dan?"

"Fourteen, going on fifteen."

"That 's quite a heap," said Lincoln, musingly, "quite a heap! In fourteen years a father can pile up a lot of good deeds. But I suppose he 's done a lot of mean ones to cancel 'em off, has he?"

"No," admitted Dan.

His frankness pleased the President. "I congratulate you, Dan. You 're honest. I want to be honest with you and tell you a story that is n't funny, for we 're both in the same boat, as I size up this proposition —yes, both in the same boat. I am in the army, in a way; at least, I 'm called Commander-in-Chief, and occasionally they let me meddle a little with things."

"Honest?" said Dan, opening his eyes very wide. He had been so absorbed in his own disasters that he had accepted this curious, friendly acquaintance, as a fellow will, without questions. But now, although the forefront of his consciousness was very active with the conversation, the misty background was trying to make him compare this man with a certain picture in the family album, with another one pasted on the dining-room-cupboard door, the same loose-hung person, only this one had a living rawness—maybe it was bigness— about him that the pictures did n't give, like a tree, perhaps. But it could n't *be* the President talking to him, Dan. If it was, what would the folks at home— And again his thought stopped. There were to be no more "folks at home" for him.

"Honest Injin, Dan. But sometimes they yell when I do meddle. There 's a case on now. Last night I pretty nearly had twenty-four men shot."

"Whew!"

"But I had n't quite decided, and that 's the reason I came out here in God's own woods. And I 'm glad I came, for you 've helped me decide."

"I have!" said Dan, astonished, "to shoot them?"

"No! Not to. You showed me the case in a new light. Here you are, deserting home, deserting your father, bringing sorrow to him and to your mother, who have sorrows enough with Will in danger and all; you 're punishing your father because he did one deed that he could n't very well help, just as if he 'd been a mean man all his life. And it 's like that with my twenty-four deserters, Dan, very like that. They 've served years, faithfully. Then, can any one thing they do be so gross, so enormously bad, as to blot out all the rest, including probably a lifetime of decent living? I think not. Is a man to blame for having a pair of legs that play coward once? I think not, Dan. I tell you what I 'll do, sonny," and the tall man stopped in the road, a new light shining in his cavernous, sad eyes, "I 'll make a bargain with you. If you 'll go home and forgive your father, I 'll go home and forgive my twenty-four deserters. Is that a bargain?"

The boy had been shaken, but it was difficult to change all at once. "It is hard to forgive," he murmured.

"Some day you 'll find it hard not to," said the great man, putting out his huge palm for the boy to shake. "Is n't that a pretty good bargain, Dan? By going home, by ceasing to be a deserter yourself, you will save the lives of twenty-four men. Won't you be merciful? Perhaps God will remember sometime and forgive you some trespass even as you forgive now."

Something of last night's horror, when he could not say the prayer, and something of the melting gentleness of the new friend before him touched the boy. He took Lincoln's hand, saying, "All right. That 's a go."

"Yes, a go home," smiled Lincoln. "I suppose I 'll have to turn, now."

" 'I 'll make a bargain with you' "

"Where 's your home?" asked the boy, knowing, yet wishing to hear the truth, to be very sure; for now he *could* tell the folks at home.

"The White House," replied Lincoln, "but I wish I were going back to the farm with you."

The boy heard him vaguely, his jaw was sagging. "Then you—are the President?"

Lincoln nodded, enjoying the boy's wonder. "And your servant, don't forget," added Lincoln. "You have been a help to me in a hard hour, Dan. Generals or no generals, I 'll spare those men. Any time that I can do anything for you, drop in, now that you know where to find me."

The boy was still speechless with his assured elation.

"But you 'd better— Wait," and Lincoln began hunting through his pockets; "you 'd better let me give you a latch-key. The man at the door 's a sort of stubborn fellow, for the folks will pester the life out of him. Here—"

And finding a card and a stub of a pencil, he wrote:

Please admit Dan'l Ripley on demand.
A. Lincoln.

"How 's that?"

"Thank you," said Dan, as proud as a cockerel. "I reckon I should 'a' guessed it was you, but those stories you told kind o' put me off."

"That 's sometimes why I tell them," and Lincoln smiled again. "It 's not a bad morning's work—twenty-four lives saved before breakfast, Dan. You and I ought to be able to stow a mighty comfortable meal. Good-bye, sonny."

And so they parted. The man strode back the way he had come; the boy stood looking, looking, and then swiftly wheeled and sped. He had been talking to the President, to Abraham Lincoln, and hearing

such talk as he never had heard before; but especially the words "You have been a help to me in a hard hour, Dan"—those words trod a regular path in his brain. He ran, eager to get to the very home he had been so eager to leave. Forgiveness was in his heart, but chiefly there was a warm and heady pride. He had been praised by Abraham Lincoln! Of this day he would talk to the end of time. Dan did not know that the major part of the day, the greatest in his life, was still to come. Certainly the dawning of it had been very beautiful.

Breathless and eye-bright with anticipation of telling his tale, he leaped the fences, ran up to the back door, and plunged into his house. The kitchen was quiet. A misgiving ran over him; were they all out in search of him? Would he have to postpone his triumph?

In the dining-room, a half-eaten meal was cooling. He explored on, and, coming out on the spacious front of the house, found them—found them in an inexplicable group around a uniformed officer. Tears were streaming down his mother's cheeks. His father, still pale from his accident, looked ashen and shriveled. They turned at Dan's approach. He expected that this scene of anguish would turn to smiles upon his discovery. He was amazed to find that his return gave them the merest flurry of relief, and alleviated their sorrow not at all.

"Danny dear, where have you been?" asked his mother.

"The Lord must have turned you about and sent you home in answer to our prayers," said his father.

And then they turned back to the officer, pleading, both talking at once, weeping. Dan felt hurt. Did his return, his forgiveness mean so little to them? He might as well have gone on. The he caught the officer's words. "Colonel Scott can do no more, Madam. The President cannot see him, and more pardons are not to be hoped for."

Mrs. Ripley turned and threw her arm across Dan's shoulders. "Danny—Danny —you are our only son now. Will was—" and she broke down completely.

"Will was found asleep while on duty, Dan, and—"

"Is to be shot?" asked the boy. "I wonder if he was one of the twenty-four." They looked at him, not understanding.

"The Lord has restored you to us. If we could only pray in sufficient faith, he could restore Will," said Farmer Ripley, devoutly. "Dear, let us go in and pray. We should release this gentleman to his duty. We can pray, dearest."

Dan realized with a sudden clearness that his brother, his beloved, was to be taken from him as Tam had been taken. It shook his brain dizzy for a moment; but he knew that he must hold on to his wits— must think. There was Abraham Lincoln, *his friend!*

"You pray," he cried to his father, shrilly, "and I 'll run."

"Run where, dear? Will is in Pennsylvania."

"To the White House, Mother. He said, 'Any time I can do anything for you, drop in.' *Any thing,* Mother. Surely he 'll—"

"Who?" cried both his parents.

"Why, the President, Mr. Lincoln!"

"But the President is busy, dear. This gentleman says that Cousin Andrew has not been able to see him, and he is a colonel, you know."

"He 'll see me—I know he will!" said Dan. "Look! We have a secret together, the President and I have." And the boy showed has card and poured out his story.

The mother saw a break in her gray heaven, saw the bright blue of hope.

"We must go at once," she said. "Father, you are not able to come with us, but pray here for us."

"Please take my horse and wagon," said the officer.

"Yes," said Dan, "let 's hurry. Oh, I 'm glad, I 'm so glad!" And the joy at his lucky turning-back shone in his face as he helped his mother into the vehicle.

"May God help you!" said the officer.

"He often does," said the boy, thinking.

It was high noon when the doorkeeper of the White House, hardened into a very stony soul by the daily onslaught of Lincoln-seekers, saw an impetuous youth leap from a light carriage and drag a woman up the portico steps toward him.

"In which room is the President?" asked Dan.

"He 's very busy," said the doorkeeper, probably for the five-hundredth time that morning. "Have you an appointment?"

"No, but he said drop in when I wanted; and what 's more, here 's my 'latch-key,' " and Dan, trembling a little with haste and pride, showed him the card "A. Lincoln" had written.

The man looked quizzically at it and at him. "In that case," he said drily, "you 'd better step into the waiting-room there."

There must have been forty or fifty people crowded into the anteroom, each on some errand urgent. Some were in uniform; all looked tired, impatient, important. Dan saw the situation and knew that Lincoln could never see them all. He whispered to his mother and put her in a chair, then went up to the door-boy and asked if the President was in the next room. The boy admitted the fact, but would not admit anything further, including Dan. The looks on the faces of the waiting-room people deepened in annoyance. "Does this urchin" (said their looks) "expect to see the President to-day, when so many more important persons (such as we) are kept waiting?"

Death has small regard for persons, and,

in this respect, boys come next to death. Dan, not caring for etiquette when his brother might be shot at any moment, slipped under the arm of the door-boy and bolted into the room.

Lincoln was standing by the window. He looked around in surprise at the noise of Dan Ripley's entry, recognized his walking partner, made a motion for the door-boy, who had one irate hand on Dan, to withdraw, and said: "Why, Dan I 'm glad to see you so soon again. You 're just in time to back me up. Let me introduce you to General Scanlon."

Dan looked into the amazed and angry eyes of a Union general who, practically ignoring the boy, went on to say: "Mr. President, I repeat, that unless these men are made an example of, the army itself may be in danger. Mercy to these twenty-four means cruelty to near a million."

The President, worn not only from his sleepless night, but from the incessant strain of things, looked grave, for the general spoke truth. He turned to Dan, "Did you go home, sonny?"

Dan nodded.

"Then I shall keep my half of the bargain. General, this boy and I each walked the woods half the night carrying similar troubles, trying to decide whether it was best to forgive. We decided that it was best, as the Bible says, even to seventy times seven. Dan, how did your folks take it?"

Dan spoke quickly. "It would 'a' killed them if I 'd run off for good, for they just got word that my brother Will—you know I told you about him—is to be shot for sleeping on watch. I just know he was tired out—he did n't go to sleep on purpose. I told my mother that you would n't let him be shot, if you knew."

Lincoln groaned audibly and turned away to the window for a moment. The general snorted.

"I brought my mother in to see you, too," said Dan, "seeing as she would n't quite believe what I said about our agreement."

Lincoln looked at the boy, and his sunken eyes glistened. "I agreed for twenty-four lives," he said; "but I don't mind throwing in an extra one for you, Dan."

And this time the general groaned.

"Stoddard," added the President, "will you see if there is a Will Ripley on file?" The secretary left the room. Lincoln turned abruptly to the general. "You have heard me," he said. "I, with the help of God and this boy, threshed out the matter to a conclusion, and we only waste time to discuss it further. If I pardon these deserters, it surely becomes a better investment for the United States than if I had them shot—twenty-four live fighters in the ranks, instead of that many corpses under ground. There are too many weeping widows now. Don't ask me to add to the number, *for I won't do it!*"

It was rarely that Lincoln was so stirred. There was a strange silence. Then the secretary entered with, "Yes, sir, a Will Ripley is to be executed to-morrow, for sleeping on duty. The case was buried in the files; it should have been brought to you earlier."

"Better for the case to be buried than the boy," said the President. "Give me the paper, Stoddard."

"Then you will!" said Dan, trembling with joy.

"I don't believe that shooting the boy will do him any good," said Lincoln, as the pen traced the letters of his name, beneath this message, "Will Ripley is not to be shot until further orders from me."

Dan looked at it. "That 's great! Oh, thank you!" he said, "Can I bring Mother in to see it—and to see you?" he asked.

The President looked down into the shining face and could not refuse. In a jiffy, Dan had dragged his mother into the presence. She was all confusion; the general was red with irritation.

She read the message; it did n't seem quite clear to her. "Is that a pardon? Does that mean that he won't be shot at all?"

"My dear Madam," replied Lincoln, kindly, "evidently you are not acquainted with me. If your son never looks on death till orders come from me to shoot him, he will live to be a great deal older than Methusaleh!"

She stretched out both her hands, crying, "I want to thank you, sir. Oh, thank you, thank you!"

"Thank Dan here," said Lincoln. "If he had not let the warmth of forgiveness soften his heart, Will Ripley would have died. And perhaps, if I had not met him in the woods at dawn, I might have gone into eternity with the blood of these twenty-four men on my hands. Dan helped me."

The boy looked as one transfigured. Lincoln went on: "And all this only confirms my notion that it is selfish, stupid, and destructive not to forgive if you 've got a loophole for forgiveness left. It reminds me of a little story. Will you excuse me another moment, General?" The pink officer bowed stiffly and Lincoln said: "One of my neighbors back home was a Quaker named Silas Greene, and he was known as a very mild and forgiving man. He was so mild-tempered that his wife could not even induce him to shoot the chickens which persisted in scratching up her garden. 'Consider, dear,' Silas used to say, 'consider the hen. Any creature that is so useful before it is born and after it is dead deserves a little consideration during its short lifetime, does n't thee think?' "

Everybody in the room laughed but the general. The president concluded: "And that 's the way I feel about these erring soldiers, Mrs. Ripley. We must consider what they have done and what they will do, as intently as we consider the wrong of the moment. Good-by, Dan, we shall both remember to-day with easy consciences."

THE waiting crowd in the anteroom could not understand, of course, why that intruder of a boy who had dragged the woman in to see the President so unceremoniously should bring her out on his arm with such conscious pride. They could not understand why the tears were rolling down her cheeks at the same time that a smile glorified her face. They did not see that the boy was walking on air, on light. But the dullest of them could see that he was radiant with a great happiness.

And if they could have looked past him and pierced the door of the inner room with their wondering glances, they could have seen a reflection of Dan's joy still shining on the somber, deep-lined face of the man who had again indulged himself in—mercy.

WHERE THE BUFFALOES BEGIN

by Olaf Baker

OVER the blazing camp-fires, when the wind moaned eerily through the thickets of juniper and fir, they spoke of it in the Indian tongue—the strange lake to the southward whose waters never rest. And Nawa, the medicine-man, who had lived such countless moons that not even the oldest brave in the tribe could remember a time when Nawa was not old, declared that, if only you arrived at the right time, on the right night, you would see the buffaloes rise out of the middle of the lake and come crowding to the shore; for there, he said, was the sacred spot where the buffaloes began. It was not only Nawa who declared that the buffaloes had their beginnings under water, and were born in the depths of the lake. The Indian legend, far older even than Nawa himself, said the same thing, and Nawa was only the voice that kept the legend walking on two feet.

And often in the winter, when the wind drove with a roar over the prairies and came thundering up the creek, making the tepees shudder and strain, Little Wolf would listen to it and think it was like the stampede of the buffaloes. And then he would snuggle warmly under the buffalo-robe that was his blanket, and be thankful for the shelter of the tepee. And sometimes he would go very far down the shadow-ways of thick sleep, and would meet the buffaloes as they came up from the lake, with the water shining on their shaggy coats and their black horns gleaming in the moon. And the buffaloes would begin by being very terrible, and shaking their great heads at him as if they fully intended to make a finish of him there and then. But afterward they would come close up to him, and smell him, and change their minds, and be companionable after all.

Little Wolf was only ten years old, but he could run faster than any other Indian boy in the tribe, and the wildest pony was not too wild for him to catch and ride. But the great thing about him was that he had no fear. He knew that an angry bull bison would gore you to death, and that if the prairie-wolves ran you down, there would be nothing left of you but your bones. Also, he was well aware that if you fell into the hands of the terrible Assiniboins, they would kill you and scalp you as neatly as could be. Yet none of these things terrified him. Only, being very wise for his age, he had a clear understanding that, for the present, it was better to keep out of their way.

But of all the thoughts that ran this way and that in his quick Indian brain, the one which galloped the hardest was the thought of the great lake to the south where the buffaloes began. And as the days lengthened and the spring began to be a thing that you could smell on the warm blowing air, the thought grew bigger and bigger in Little Wolf's brain. At last it was so very big that Little Wolf could n't bear it any longer; and so, one morning, very early, before the village was astir, he crept out of the tepee as noiselessly as his namesake, and stole along below the junipers and tall firs till he came to the spot where the ponies were hobbled.

The dawn was just beginning to break, and in the gray light the ponies looked like dark blotches along the creek; but Little Wolf's eyes were very sharp, and soon he had singled out his own pony, because it had a white fore foot, and a white patch on its left side. When he spoke, calling softly, the animal whinnied in answer, and allowed himself to be caught. Little Wolf unhobbled him, slipped on the bridle, which he had brought with him, and leaped lightly upon his back. A few minutes afterward, horse and rider had left the camp behind them, and were out upon the prairie, going due south.

When the sun rose, they were already far upon their way. Little Wolf swept his piercing gaze round the immense horizon, lest there should be any danger, moving or in ambush, which might interrupt his journey, or make him alter his course. Far off, so far as to be just on the edge of his sight, there was a dim spot on the yellowish gray of the prairie. Little Wolf reined in his pony to watch if it moved. If it did, it crept so slowly as to seem absolutely still. He decided that it was a herd of antelope feeding, and that there was nothing to fear.

On he went, hour after hour, never ceasing to watch. The prairie-grouse got up almost under his pony's feet. The larks and savanna-sparrows filled the air with their singing, and everywhere the wild roses were in bloom. It seemed as if nothing but peace would ever find its way among these singing-birds and flowers; yet Little Wolf knew well that the Assiniboins could come creeping along the

hollows of the prairie, like wolves, and that there is no moment more dangerous than the time when there is no hint of danger.

All this time he had not seen a single buffalo, but he told himself that this was because the herds had taken some other way, and that he would probably not see any until he was near the lake. He lost sight of the shadowy spot he had seen so far away. If he had known that it was a party of Assiniboins on the war-path, he might have thought twice about continuing to the lake, and would probably have returned along his trail to give warning to his tribe. But his head was too full of the singing of the birds and of the breath of the roses, and, above all, of the great thought of the buffaloes, fighting below the lake.

It was late in the afternoon when, at last, he sighted the lake. It lay, a gray sheet with a glint of silver, glimmering under the sun. He looked eagerly on all sides to see if there were any signs of buffaloes, but far and wide the prairies lay utterly deserted, very warm and still in the white shimmer of the air. As he approached nearer, however, he saw trails, many trails, all going in one direction and leading toward the lake. Antelope and coyote, wolf and buffalo; all these had left traces behind them as they went to the water and returned. But it was the buffalo trails which were most numerous and most marked, and which Little Wolf noted above all the others.

When he was quite close to the lake he dismounted, and, hobbling his pony, turned him adrift to graze. Then he himself lay down behind some tussocks of prairie-grass, above the low bank at the edge of the lake, and waited. From this position he could overlook the lake, without being seen. He gazed far over its glittering expanse, very still just now under the strong beams of the sun. It was disappointingly still. Scarcely a ripple broke upon the shore. You could not possibly imagine that the buffaloes were struggling underneath. Little Wolf asked himself where was the movement and the mysterious murmur of which Nawa had spoken? But, being of Indian blood, he had no impatience. He could afford to wait and listen for whole hours, if need be.

The time went on. Slowly the sun dipped westward, and the shadows of the grass grew longer. Yet still the lake kept its outward stillness, and nothing happened. At last the sun reached the horizon, lay there a few moments, a great ball of flame, and then sank out of sight. Twilight fell, and all over the vast wilderness crept a peculiar silence like a wild creature stealing from its lair, while far in the west there lingered long the strange orange light that belongs to the prairie skies alone when the sun is down, and the night winds sigh along the grass. And whether it was the sighing of the wind or not, Little Wolf could not tell, but there came to him along the margin of the lake a strange, low murmur that died away and rose again. As the night deepened, it grew clearer, and then he was certain that it was not the wind, but came from the center of the lake. For hours he lay and listened, but the mysterious murmur never ceased. Sometimes it was a little louder; sometimes a little softer; but always it was plain to hear —a wonderful and terrible thing in the silence of the night. And as Little Wolf lay watching under the stars, the words of Nawa kept singing in his head:

"Do you hear the noise that never ceases?
It is the Buffaloes fighting far below.
They are fighting to get out upon the
  prairie.

They are born below the Water, but are
  fighting for the Air,
In the great lake in the Southland where
  the Buffaloes begin!"

Suddenly, Little Wolf lifted himself up. He could n't tell whether he had been asleep or not, but there, in the lake, he saw a wonderful sight: the buffaloes!

There they were, hundreds and hundreds of them, risen out of the lake. He could not see the surface any more. Instead, he saw a lake of swaying bodies, and heads that shook; and on their horns and tossing heads the water gleamed in the moonlight, as he had seen it in his dreams.

Little Wolf felt the blood run along his body. He clutched at the prairie-grass, crushing it in his hot hands where the pulses throbbed. Through his staring eyeballs he drank in the great vision. And he did not only drink it with his eyes: he drank it also with his ears and with his nose; for his ears were filled with the trampling and snorting of the herd, and the flash of the water as they moved it with their feet; and his nose drank the sharp, moist smell of the great beasts as they crowded upon each other; the smell which the wolves know well when it comes dropping down the wind.

Little Wolf never knew what came to him, nor what spirit of the wild it was which whispered in his ear; but suddenly he leaped to his feet and loosed a ringing cry out of his throat. And when he cried, he flung his arms above his head; and then he cried again.

At the first cry, a shiver passed through the herd, like an electric thrill. As if they were one beast, the buffaloes threw up their heads and listened, absolutely still. They saw, in the white light of the moon, a little wild Indian boy above the margin of the lake, who made swift motions with his arms. He seemed to speak with his arms —to talk buffalo talk with the ripple of his muscles and the snatch of his fingers in the air! They had never seen such a thing before. Their little eyes fastened upon it excitedly, and shot out sparks of light. And

It was the hour when, on the lonely prairie lands, the feet of the wild folk pad softly, and sound carries to an immense distance. But the ears it might have warned —the quick ears of Assiniboin braves on the war-path—did not catch it, being too far off upon the northern trail.

"There they were, hundreds and hundreds of them, risen out of the lake"

when it cried again, there swept through the stillness of the herd a stir, a movement, a ripple which you could see. And the ripple became a wave, and the wave a billow. It was a billow of buffaloes, which, beginning on the outskirts of the herd, broke along the margin of the lake in a terrifying roar.

It was a wonderful sound, that roar of the buffaloes on the edge of a stampede. It rolled far out upon the prairie in the hollow silence of the night. Wandering wolves caught it, threw their long noses to the moon, and howled an answering cry.

On moccasins, noiseless as the padded feet of the wolves, as grim, and almost more cruel, these painted warriors were stealthily approaching the camp of Little Wolf's people, determined to wipe it out ere the dog-star faded in the dawn.

But now the buffaloes had received the strange message which the Indian boy waved to them from the margin of the lake. He himself did not understand it. He cried to the buffaloes because he could not help it; because he loved them as the creatures of his dreams. But when he saw and heard their answer; when they came surging out of the lake like a mighty flood, bellowing and stamping and tossing their heads, a wild excitement possessed him, and, for the first time in his life, he knew the meaning of fear!

Swift as one of the wolves themselves, he darted toward his pony. To unhobble it and leap upon its back took but a moment. Then he was off, riding for his life!

Behind him came the terrible sound of the buffaloes as they swept out of the lake. He threw a quick glance behind to see which way they took. He saw a dark surging mass throw itself out upon the prairie and come on at a gallop, heading due north.

Little Wolf turned his pony's head slightly westward so as to escape the middle rush of the herd. If once it surrounded him on all sides, he did not know what might happen. If his pony had been fresh, he could have easily outstripped the buffaloes, but after a long day the animal was tired, and was going at half his usual speed. Little Wolf threw a quick glance over his shoulder. The buffaloes were gaining! He cried to his pony, little, short cries that made a wild note in the night.

Soon, as they swept along, the leaders of the left flank of the herd drew so close that he could hear the snorting sound of their breath. Then they were abreast of him, and the pony and the buffaloes were galloping side by side. Yet they did nothing to him. They did not seem to have any other desire but to gallop on into the night.

Soon Little Wolf was completely surrounded by the buffaloes. In front, behind, on both sides, he saw a heaving mass of buffaloes that billowed like the sea. Again, as when he had cried beside the lake, a wild feeling of excitement seized him, and he felt the blood stir along his scalp. And once again he cried aloud, flinging his arms above his head, a long, ringing cry. And the buffaloes replied, bellowing

a wild answer that rolled like thunder far along the plains.

North the great gallop swept. Down the hollows, over the swells of the prairie, below the lonely ridges with the piles of stones where the Indians leave their dead; crashing through the alder thickets beside the creeks; through the shallow creeks themselves, churning the water into a muddy foam, the mighty herd rolled on its way, and the thunder of its coming spread terror far and wide in the hearts of all lesser prairie folk. The antelopes were off like the wind; the badgers and coyotes slunk into their holes. Even the wolves took warning, vanishing shadow-like along the hollows east and west, so as to be well out of the way.

Little Wolf was beside himself with excitement and joy. It seemed as if he, too, were a member of the herd, as if the buffaloes had adopted him and made him their own.

Suddenly he saw something ahead. He could not see very clearly, because of the buffaloes in front of him; but it looked like a band of Indians. They were not mounted, but were running swiftly on foot, as if to regain their ponies. As first, Little Wolf thought they were his own people, as he knew, by the outline of the country, that the camp could not be far off. But then he saw that they were not running toward the camp, but away from it. And then very swiftly, the thing flashed upon him. They were Assiniboins, the deadly enemies of his tribe, and they must have left their ponies some distance off, in order to approach the camp unseen through the long grass, and attack it in its sleep!

Little Wolf knew well that, unless they reached their ponies in time, the buffaloes would cut off their retreat. Once that great herd hurled itself upon them, nothing could save them from being trampled to death. He cried shrilly hoping that it would excite the buffaloes even more. He saw the Indians making desperate efforts to escape. The buffaloes seemed as if they answered to his cries. They bore down upon the fleeing Indians at a terrible gallop, and, in spite of the long distance they had come, never slackened speed. One by one the Indians were overtaken, knocked down, and trampled underfoot. The herd passed pitilessly over their prostrate bodies.

Suddenly, Little Wolf's pony went down. He leaped clear as the animal fell. Fortunately, by this time, they were on the extreme outskirts of the herd, and before Little Wolf could get to his fallen pony again, the last buffalo had passed.

OVER the blazing camp-fires, when the wind rises and moans eerily through the thickets of juniper and fir, they still speak of the great lake to the south where the buffaloes begin; but now they always add the name of Little Wolf to the legend,— the boy who led the buffaloes, and saved his tribe.

THE CROCODILE

by Oliver Herford

CROCODILE once dropped a line
To a Fox to invite him to dine;
  But the Fox wrote to say
  He was dining, that day,
With a Bird friend, and begged to decline.

She sent off at once to a Goat.
"Pray don't disappoint me," she wrote;
  But he answered too late,
  He 'd forgotten the date,
Having thoughtlessly eaten her note.

The Crocodile thought him ill-bred,
And invited two Rabbits instead;
  But the Rabbits replied,
  They were hopelessly tied
By a previous engagement, and fled.

MY GRANDMOTHER'S GRAND-
MOTHER'S CHRISTMAS CANDLE

by Hezekiah Butterworth

THERE were no Christmas celebrations in my old Puritan home in Swanzey, such as we have in all New England homes to-day. No church bells rung out in the darkening December air; there were no children's carols learned in Sunday-schools; no presents, and not even a sprig of box, ivy, or pine in any window. Yet there was one curious custom in the old town that made Christmas Eve in many homes the merriest in the year.

It was the burning of the Christmas candle; and of this old, forgotten custom of provincial towns I have an odd story to tell.

The Christmas candle? You may never have heard of it. You may fancy that it was some beautiful image in wax or like an altar-light. This was not the case. It was a candle containing a quill filled with gunpowder, and its burning excited an intense interest while we waited for the expected explosion.

I well remember Dipping Candle Day; it was a very interesting day to me in my boyhood, because it was then that the Christmas candle was dipped.

It usually came in the fall, in the short, lonesome days of November, just before the new school-master opened the winter term of the school.

My grandmother brought down from the garret her candle-rods and poles. The candle-rods were light sticks of elder, some fifty in number, and the poles were long pine bars. These poles were tied two each to two chairs, and the rods, after they had been wicked, were laid upon them at short distances apart.

Wicking the candle-rods is a term of which few people to-day know the meaning. Every country store in old times contained a large supply of balls of cotton candle-wick. This wick was to be cut, put upon the candle-rods, twisted, and tallowed or waxed, so as to be convenient for dipping.

How many times have I seen my grandmother, on the long November evenings, wicking her candle-rods! She used to do the work, sitting in her easy-chair before the great open fire. One side of the fireplace was usually hung with strings of dried or partly dried apples, and the other with strings of red peppers. Over the fireplace were a gun and the almanac; and on the hearth there were usually, in the evening, a few sweet apples roasting; and at one end of it was the dog, and at the other the cat.

Dipping candles would seem a comical sight to-day. My grandmother used to sit over a great iron kettle of melted tallow, and patiently dip the wicks on the rods into it, until they grew to the size of candles. Each rod contained about five wicks, and these were dipped together. The process was repeated perhaps fifty or more times.

A quill of powder was tied to the wick of the Christmas candle before dipping, and the wick was so divided at the lower end that the candle should have three legs. The young people took a great interest in the dipping as well as the burning of the Christmas candle.

My grandmother's candle-rods had belonged to her grandmother, who had lived in the early days of the Plymouth Colony. They had been used since the days of King Philip's war.

There was a story of the dark times of the Indian war that my grandmother used to relate on the night that we burned our Christmas candle; a story that my grandmother told of her grandmother, and of the fortunate and timely explosion of one of that old lady's Christmas candles in the last days of Philip's war, when the sight of a hostile Indian was a terror to the unarmed colonist.

"It was well that candle went off when it did," my grandmother used to say. "If it had not, I don't know where any of us would have been to-night; not here, telling riddles and roasting apples and enjoying ourselves, I imagine. I have dipped a powder-candle every season since, not that I believe much in keeping holidays, but because a powder-candle once saved the family."

She continued her story:

"My grandmother was a widow in her last years. She had two children, Benjamin and my mother, Mary. She lived at Pocassett, and the old house overlooked Mount Hope and the bay. Pocassett was an Indian province then, and its Indian queen was named Wetamoo.

"My grandmother was a great-hearted woman. She had a fair amount of property, and she used it for the good of her less fortunate neighbors. She had kept several poor old people from the town-house by giving them a home with her. Her good deeds caused her to be respected by every one.

"The Indians were friendly to her. She had done them so many acts of kindness that even the haughty Wetamoo had once called to see her and made her a present. The old house was near an easy landing-place for boats on the bay; and the Indians, as they came from their canoes, passed through the yard, and often stopped to drink from the well. It was no uncommon thing, on a hot summer's day, to find an Indian asleep in the street or under the door-yard trees.

"Among the great men of the tribe was an Indian named Squammaney; Warmmesley he was sometimes called—also Warmmesley-Squammaney. He was a giant in form, but his greatness among his people arose from his supposed magical power and his vigorous voice. It was believed that he could whoop and bellow so loud and long as to frighten away evil spirits from the sick, so that the patient would recover. All the Indians regarded old Squammaney with fear and awe, and he was very proud of his influence over them.

"When an Indian fell sick, Warmmesley-Squammaney was called to the bed-side. If old Warmmesley could not drive the evil spirits away, the patient believed that he must die.

"Squammaney did his supposed duty in such cases. He was a faithful doctor. He covered himself with dried skins, shells, and feathers, and approached the hut of the patient with as mysterious and lofty an air as one of the old-time physicians of the gig and saddle-bags. As he drew near the hut, he would rattle the dried skins, and howl. He would look cautiously into the hut, then run away from it a little distance, leap into the air, and howl. Then he would cautiously return, and if the case were a bad one, he would again run away, leap into the air, and howl. At last he would enter the hut, examine the sick man or woman, and utter mysterious cries. He would fix the mind of the sufferer entirely upon himself by a kind of mesmeric influence; then he would begin to move in a circle around the patient, shaking the dried skins and beads, bobbing his plumes, and chanting an Indian ditty. Gradually his movements would become more swift; he would howl and leap, his voice rising higher at every bound; he would continue this performance until he fell down all in a heap, like a tent of dried skins. But by this time the mind of the patient was usually so withdrawn from his sufferings as to quite forget them; and consequently it often happened that the invalid and old Warmmesley-Squammaney rose up together, and indulged in hand-shaking, thus concluding an exhibition of some of the remarkable effects of mesmeric influence, which were possible in those old times as well as now.

"In his peculiar way, old Warmmesley once cured of rheumatism a Puritan deacon who rewarded him by calling him a 'pagan.' The deacon had been confined to his room for weeks. Some Indians called to see him, and, pitying his condition, set off in great haste for Warmmesley. The latter came, in his dried skins, with his head bristling with horns and feathers. The astonished deacon forgot his infirmities at the first sight of the terrible object; and as soon as Warmmesley began to leap and howl, and shake his beads, shells, and dried skins, the white man leaped from his bed, and, running to the barn, knelt down and began to pray. There his wife found him.

" 'It is old Warmmesley,' said she.

" 'The old pagan!' said he, rising up.

'What was it, Ruth, that was the matter with me?'

"My grandmother had caught the spirit of Eliot, the Indian apostle, and she used to hold in the old kitchen a religious meeting, each week, for the instruction of the 'praying Indians' of the town. The Indians who became Christians were called 'praying Indians' by their own people, and came to be so called by the English. Among the Indians who came out of curiosity, was the beautiful Princess Amie, the youngest daughter of the great chief Massasoit, who protected Plymouth Colony for nearly forty years.

"Warmmesley came once to my grandmother's meetings, and tried to sing. He wished to outsing the rest, and he did, repeating over and over again:

" 'He lub poor Indian in de wood,
    An' me lub God, and dat be good;
    I 'll praise him two times mo'!'

"Just before the beginning of the Indian war, my grandmother offended Warmmesley. The English had taught him bad habits, and he had become a cider drinker. He used to wander about the country, going from farm-house to farm-house, begging for 'hard' cider, as old cider was called.

"One day my grandmother found him lying intoxicated under a tree in the yard, and she forbade the giving of Warmmesley any more cider from the cellar. A few days afterward, he landed from his canoe in front of the grounds, and came to the workmen for cider. The workmen sent him to my grandmother.

" 'No, Warmmesley, no more,' said she firmly. 'Steal your wits. Wicked!'

"Warmmesley begged for one porringer —just one.

" 'Me sick,' he pleaded.

" 'No, Warmmesley. Never. Wrong.'

"'Me pay you!' said he, with an evil look in his eye. 'Me pay you!'

"Just then a flock of crows flew past. Warmmesley pointed to them and said:

"'It 's coming—fight—look up there! Ugh, ugh!'—pointing to the crows. 'Fight English. Look over'—pointing to the bay— 'fight, fight—me pay you! Ugh! Ugh!'

"My grandmother pointed up to the blue sky, as much as to say that her trust was in a higher power than man's.

"Warmmesley turned away reluctantly, looking back with a half-threatening, half-questioning look, and saying 'Ugh! Ugh!' He evidently hoped that my grandmother would call him back, but she was firm.

"The upper windows of the old house overlooked the bay.

"It was fall. The maples flamed and the oak-leaves turned to gold and dust. The flocks of birds gathered and went their unknown way. The evenings were long. It was harvest time. The full moon rose in the twilight, and the harvesters continued their labors into the night.

"Philip, or Pometacom, was now at Mount Hope, and Wetamoo had taken up her residence on the high shores of Pocasset. The hills of Pocassett were in full view of Mount Hope, and between lay the quiet, sheltered waters of the bay. Philip had cherished a strong friendship for Wetamoo, who was the widow of his brother Alexander.

"Night after night the harvesters had noticed canoes crossing and recrossing the bay, moving like shadows silently to and fro. The moon waned; the nights became dark and cloudy; the movement across the water went on; the boats carried torches now, and the dark bay became picturesque as the mysterious lines of light were drawn across it.

"From time to time a great fire would blaze up near the high rocks at Mount Hope, burn a few hours, and then fade.

"It was whispered about among the English that Philip was holding war-dances, and that Wetamoo and her warriors were attending them. Yet Philip had just concluded a treaty of peace with the English, and Wetamoo professed to be a friend to the Colony.

"War came on the following summer, stealthily at first. Englishmen were found murdered mysteriously in the towns near Mount Hope. Then came the killing of the people in Swanzey as they were going home from church, about which all the histories of the Colonies tell; then the open war.

"Philip flashed like a meteor from place to place, murdering the people and burning their houses. No one could tell where he would next appear, or who would be his next victim. Every colonist during the year 1675, wherever he might be, lived in terror of lurking foes. There were dreadful cruelties everywhere, and towns and farm-houses vanished in smoke.

"Wetamoo joined Philip. She had some six hundred warriors. Philip had made her believe that the English had poisoned her husband Alexander, who was also his brother, and who had succeeded the good Massasoit. Alexander had died suddenly while returning from Plymouth, on the Taunton river. The mysterious lights on the bay were now explained.

"Before Wetamoo joined Philip, one of her captains had sent word to my grandmother that, as she had been a friend to the Indians, she should be protected.

"'I have only one fear,' said my grandmother often, during that year of terror,— 'Warmmesley.'

"Warmmesley-Squammaney had gone away with Philip's braves under Wetamoo. He was one of Wetamoo's captains. Wetamoo herself had joined Philip like a true warrior queen.

"The sultry August of 1676 brought a

sense of relief to the Colonies. The warriors of Philip were defeated on every hand. His wife and son were captured, and, broken-hearted, he returned to Mount Hope—the burial-ground of his race for unknown generations—to die. Wetamoo, too, became a fugitive, and was drowned in attempting to cross to the lovely hills of Pocassett on a raft.

"The war ended. Where was Warmmesley-Squammaney? No one knew. Annawon, Philip's great captain, had been captured, and nearly all the principal leaders of the war were executed; but old Squammaney had mysteriously disappeared.

"Peace came. October flamed, as Octobers flame, and November faded, as Novembers fade, and the snows of December fell. The Colonies were full of joy and thanksgivings.

" 'I am thankful for one thing more than all others,' said my grandmother on Thanksgiving Day; 'and that is that I am now sure that old Squammaney is gone where he will never trouble us again. I shall never forget his evil eye as he said, "I will pay you!" It has troubled me night and day.'

"That fall, when my grandmother was dipping candles, she chanced to recall the old custom of the English town from which she had come, of making a powder-candle for Christmas. The spirit of merry-making was abroad upon the return of peace, and she prepared one of these curious candles, and told her family that they might invite the neighbors' children on Christmas Eve to see it burn and explode. The village school-master, Silas Sloan, was living at the old house, and he took the liberty to invite the school, which consisted of some ten boys and girls.

"Christmas Eve came, a clear, still night, with a white earth and shining sky. Some twenty or more people, young and old,

gathered in the great kitchen to see the Christmas candle 'go off.' During the early part of the evening 'Si' Sloan entertained the company with riddles. Then my grandmother brought in the Christmas candle, an odd-looking object, and set it down on its three legs. She lighted it, blew out the other candles, and asked Silas to tell a story.

"Silas was glad of the opportunity to entertain such an audience. The story that he selected for this novel occasion was awful in the extreme, such as were usually told in those times before the great kitchen fires.

"Silas—'Si,' as he was called—was relating an account of a so-called haunted house, where, according to his silly narrative, the ghost of an Indian used to appear at the foot of an old woman's bed; and some superstitious people declared that the old lady one night, on awaking and finding the ghostly Indian present, put out her foot to push him away, and pushed her foot directly *through him*. What a brave old lady she must have been, and how uncomfortable it must have been for the ghost!—But, at this point of Silas's foolish story, the dog suddenly started up and began to howl.

"The children, who were so highly excited over Si's narrative that they hardly dared to breathe, clung to one another with trembling hands as the dog sent up his piercing cry. Even Si himself started. The dog seemed listening.

"The candle was burning well. The children now watched it in dead silence.

"A half-hour passed. The candle was burning within an inch of the quill, and all eyes were bent upon it. If the candle 'sputtered,' the excitement became intense. 'I think it will go off in ten minutes now,' said my grandmother.

"There was a noise in the yard. All heard it distinctly. The dog dashed round the room, howled, and stopped to listen at the door.

"People who relate so-called ghost stories are often cowardly, and it is usually a cowardly nature that seeks to frighten children. 'Si' Sloan was no exception to the rule.

"The excitement of the dog at once affected Silas. His tall, thin form moved about the room cautiously and mysteriously. He had a way of spreading apart his fingers when he was frightened, and his fingers were well apart now.

"A noise in the yard at night was not an uncommon thing, but the peculiar cry of the dog and the excited state of the company caused this to be noticed. My grandmother arose at last, and, amid dead silence, opened the shutter.

" 'I think that there is some one in the cider mill,' said she.

"She looked toward the candle, and, feeling confident that some minutes would elapse before the explosion, she left the room, and went upstairs, and there looked from the window.

From the window she could see in the moonlight, Mount Hope, where Philip had so recently been killed, and also the arm of the bay, where Wetamoo had perished. She could see the bay itself, and must have remembered the lights that a year before had so often danced over it at night. She lingered there a moment. Then she called:

" 'Silas—Silas Sloan!'

"Silas hurried up the stairs.

"They both came down in a few minutes. Silas's face was as white as the snow.

" 'What is it?' the children whispered.

"There was another painful silence. Grandmother seemed to have forgotten the candle. All eyes were turned to her face.

"Then followed a sound that sent the blood from every face. It was as if a log

had been dashed against the door. The door flew open, and in stalked two Indians. One of them was Warmmesley-Squammaney.

" 'Ugh!' said Warmmesley.

" 'What do you want?' demanded my grandmother.

" 'Me pay you now!—Old Squammaney pay you. Cider!'

"He sat down by the fire, close to the candle. The other Indian stood by his chair, as though awaiting his orders. The young children began to cry, and Silas shook like a man with the palsy.

" 'Me pay you!—Me remember! Ugh!' said Squammaney. 'Braves all gone. Me have revenge—old Squammaney die hard. Ugh! Ugh!'

"The door was still partly open, and the wind blew into the room. It caused the candle to flare up and to burn rapidly.

"Squammaney warmed his hands. Occasionally he would turn his head, slowly, with an evil look in his black eye, as it swept the company.

"The candle was forgotten. The only thought of each one was what Squammaney intended to do.

"All the tragedies of the war just ended were recalled by the older members of the company. Were there other Indians outside?

"No one dared to rise to close the door, or to attempt to escape.

"Suddenly Squammaney turned to my grandmother.

" 'White squaw get cider. Go—go!'

"The Indians threw open their blankets. They were armed.

"The sight of these armed warriors caused Silas to shake in a strange manner, and his fear and agitation became so contagious that the children began to tremble and sob. When the sound of distress became violent, Squammaney would sweep the company with his dark eyes, and awe it into a brief silence.

"My grandmother alone was calm.

"She rose, and walked around the room, followed by the eyes of the two Indians.

"As soon as the attention of the Indians, attracted for a moment by the falling of a burnt stick on the hearth, was diverted from her, she whispered to Silas:

" 'Go call the men.'

"The attitude of Silas on receiving this direction, as she recalled it afterward, was comical indeed. His hands were spread out by his side, and his eyes grew white and wild. He attempted to reply in a whisper, but he could only say:

" 'Ba-b-b-ba!'

"Squammaney's eyes again swept the room. Then he bent forward to push back some coals that had rolled out upon the floor.

" 'Go call the men," again whispered my grandmother to Silas; this time sharply.

" 'Ba—b—b—b—ba!' His mouth looked like a sheep's. His hands again opened, and his eyes fairly protruded. His form was tall and thin, and he really looked like one of the imaginary specters about whom he delighted to tell stories on less perilous occasions.

"Squammaney heard Grandmother's whisper, and became suspicious. He rose, his dark form towering in the light of the fire. He put his hand on the table where burned the candle. He turned, and faced my grandmother with an expression of hate and scorn.

"What he intended to do was never known, for just at that moment there was a fearful explosion. It was the powder-candle.

"A stream of fire shot up to the ceiling. Then the room was filled with the smoke of gunpowder. The candle went out. The room was dark.

" 'White man come! Run!' my grandmother heard one of the Indians say. There was a sound of scuffling feet; then the door closed with a bang. As the smoke lifted, the light of the fire gradually revealed that the Indians had gone. They evidently thought that they had been discovered, pursued, and that the house was surrounded by soldiers.

"At last my grandmother took a candle from the shelf and lighted it. Silas, too, was gone. Whither? Had the Indians carried him away?

"Late in the evening the neighbors began to come for their children, and were told what had happened. The men of the town were soon under arms. But old Warmmesley-Squammaney was never seen in that neighborhood again, nor was his fate ever known to the town's-people. That was the last fright of the Indian war.

"Silas returned to the school-room the next day, but he never visited the old house again. Whatever may have been his real belief in regard to people of the air, he had resolved never again to put himself under a roof where he would be likely to meet Warmmesley-Squammaney.

"After this strange event, two generations of grandmothers continued to burn on each Christmas Eve, the old powder-candle."

TO REPEL BOARDERS

by Jack London

No; honest, now, Bob, I 'm sure I was born too late. The twentieth century 's no place for me. If I 'd had my way—"

"You 'd have been born in the sixteenth," I broke in, laughing, "with Drake and Hawkins and Raleigh and the rest of the sea-kings."

"You 're right!" Paul affirmed. He rolled over upon his back on the little after-deck, with a long sigh of dissatisfaction.

It was a little past midnight, and, with the wind nearly astern, we were running down Lower San Francisco Bay to Bay Farm Island. Paul Fairfax and I went to the same school, lived next door to each other, and "chummed it" together. By saving money, by earning more, and by each of us foregoing a bicycle on his birthday, we had collected the purchase-price of the *Mist,* a beamy twenty-eight-footer, sloop-rigged, with baby topsail and centerboard. Paul's father was a yachtsman himself, and he had conducted the business for us, poking around, overhauling, sticking his pen-knife into the timbers, and testing the planks with the greatest care. In fact, it was on his schooner the *Whim* that Paul and I had picked up what we knew about boat-sailing, and now that the *Mist* was ours, we were hard at work adding to our knowledge.

The *Mist,* being broad of beam, was comfortable and roomy. A man could stand upright in the cabin, and what with the stove, right into the timbers, and testing the cooking-utensils, and bunks, we were good for trips in her of a week at a time. And we were just starting out on the first of such trips, and it was because it was the first trip that we were sailing by night. Early in the evening we had beaten out from Oakland, and we were now off the mouth of Alameda Creek, a large salt-water estuary which fills and empties San Leandro Bay.

"Men lived in those days," Paul said, so suddenly as to startle me from my own thoughts. "In the days of the sea-kings, I mean," he explained.

I said "Oh!" sympathetically, and began to whistle "Captain Kidd."

"Now, I 've my ideas about things," Paul went on. "They talk about romance and adventure and all that, but I say romance and adventure are dead. We 're too civilized. We don't have adventures in the twentieth century. We go to the circus—"

"But—" I strove to interrupt, though he would not listen to me.

"You look here, Bob," he said. "In all the time you and I 've gone together what adventures have we had? True, we were out in the hills once, and did n't get back till late at night, and we were good and hungry, but we were n't even lost. We knew where we were all the time. It was only a case of walk. What I mean is, we 've never had to fight for our lives. Understand? We 've never had a pistol fired at us, or a cannon, or a sword waving over our heads, or—or anything.

"You 'd better slack away three or four feet of that main-sheet," he said in a hopeless sort of way, as though it did not matter much anyway. "The wind 's still veering around.

"Why, in the old times the sea was one constant glorious adventure," he continued. "A boy left school and became a midshipman, and in a few weeks was cruising after Spanish galleons or locking yard-arms with a French privateer, or—doing lots of things."

"Well,—there *are* adventures to-day," I objected.

But Paul went on as though I had not spoken:

"And to-day we go from school to high school, and from high school to college, and then we go into the office or become doctors and things, and the only adventures we know about are the ones we read in books. Why, just as sure as I 'm sitting here on the stern of the sloop *Mist,* just so sure am I that we would n't know what to do if a real adventure came along. Now, would we?"

"Oh, I don't know," I answered noncommittally.

"Well, you would n't be a coward, would you?" he demanded.

I was sure I would n't, and said so.

"But you don't have to be a coward to lose your head, do you?"

I agreed that brave men might get excited.

"Well, then," Paul summed up, with a note of regret in his voice, "the chances are that we 'd spoil the adventure. So it 's a shame, and that 's all I can say about it."

"The adventure has n't come yet," I answered, not caring to see him down in the mouth over nothing. You see, Paul was a peculiar fellow in some things, and I knew him pretty well. He read a good

deal, and had a quick imagination, and once in a while he 'd get into moods like this one. So I said, "The adventure has n't come yet, so there 's no use worrying about its being spoiled. For all we know, it might turn out splendidly."

Paul did n't say anything for some time, and I was thinking he was out of the mood, when he spoke suddenly:

"Just imagine, Bob Kellogg, as we 're sailing along now, just as we are, and never mind what for, that a boat should bear down upon us with armed men in it, what would you do to repel boarders? Think you could rise to it?"

"What would *you* do?" I asked pointedly. "Remember, we have n't even a single shot-gun aboard."

"You would surrender, then?" he demanded angrily. "But suppose they were going to kill you?"

"I 'm not saying what I 'd do," I answered stiffly, beginning to get a little angry myself. "I 'm asking what you 'd do, without weapons of any sort?"

"I 'd find something," he replied—rather shortly, I thought.

I began to chuckle. "Then the adventure would n't be spoiled, would it? And you 've been talking rubbish."

Paul struck a match, looked at his watch, and remarked that it was nearly one o'clock—a way he had when the argument went against him. Besides, this was the nearest we ever came to quarreling now, though our share of squabbles had fallen to us in the earlier days of our friendship. I had just seen a little white light ahead when Paul spoke again.

"Anchor-light," he said. "Funny place for people to drop the hook. It may be a scow-schooner with a dinky astern, so you 'd better go wide."

I eased the *Mist* several points, and, the wind puffing up, we went plowing along at a pretty fair speed, passing the light so wide that we could not make out what manner of craft it marked. Suddenly the *Mist* slacked up in a slow and easy way, as though running upon soft mud. We were both startled. The wind was blowing stronger than ever, and yet we were almost at a standstill.

"Mud-flats out here! Never heard of such a thing!"

So Paul exclaimed with a snort of unbelief, and, seizing an oar, shoved it down over the side. And straight down it went till the water wet his hand. There was no bottom! Then we were dumbfounded. The wind was whistling by, and still the Mist was moving ahead at a snail's pace. There seemed something dead about her, and it was all I could do at the tiller to keep her from swinging up into the wind.

"Listen!" I laid my hand on Paul's arm. We could hear the sound of rowlocks, and saw the little white light bobbing up and down and now very close to us. "There's your armed boat," I whispered in fun. "Beat the crew to quarters and stand by to repel boarders!"

We both laughed, and were still laughing when a wild scream of rage came out of the darkness, and the approaching boat shot under our stern. By the light of the lantern it carried we could see the two men in it distinctly. They were foreign-looking fellows with sun-bronzed faces, and with knitted tam-o'-shanters perched seaman fashion on their heads. Bright-colored woolen sashes were around their waists, and long sea-boots covered their legs. I remember yet the cold chill which passed along my back-bone as I noted the tiny gold ear-rings in the ears of one. For all the world they were like pirates stepped out of the pages of romance. And, to make the picture complete, their faces were distorted with anger, and each flourished a long knife. They were both shouting, in

high-pitched voices, some foreign jargon we could not understand.

One of them, the smaller of the two, and if anything the more vicious-looking, put his hands on the rail of the *Mist* and started to come aboard. Quick as a flash Paul placed the end of the oar against the man's chest and shoved him back into his boat. He fell in a heap, but scrambled to his feet, waving the knife and shrieking:

"You break-a my net-a! You break-a my net-a!"

And he held forth in the jargon again, his companion joining him, and both preparing to make another dash to come aboard the *Mist*.

"They 're Italian fishermen," I cried, the facts of the case breaking in upon me. "We 've run over their smelt-net, and it 's slipped along the keel and fouled our rudder. We 're anchored to it."

"Yes, and they 're murderous chaps, too," Paul said, sparring at them with the oar to make them keep their distance.

"Say, you fellows!" he called to them. "Give us a chance and we 'll get it clear for you! We did n't know your net was there. We did n't mean to do it, you know!"

"You won't lose anything!" I added. "We 'll pay the damages!"

But they could not understand what we were saying, or did not care to understand.

"You break-a my net-a! You break-a my net-a!" the smaller man, the one with the ear-rings, screamed back, making furious gestures. "I fix-a you! You-a see, I fix-a you!"

This time, when Paul thrust him back, he seized the oar in his hands, and his companion jumped aboard. I put my back against the tiller, and no sooner had be landed, and before he had caught his balance, than I met him with another oar, and he fell heavily backward into the boat. It was getting serious, and when he arose and caught my oar, and I realized his strength, I confess that I felt a goodly tinge of fear. But though he was stronger than I, instead of dragging me overboard when he wrenched on the oar, he merely pulled his boat in closer; and when I shoved, the boat was forced away. Besides, the knife, still in his right hand, made him awkward and somewhat counterbalanced the advantage his superior strength gave him. Paul and his enemy were in the same situation—a sort of deadlock, which continued for several seconds, but which could not last. Several times I shouted that we would pay for whatever damage their net had suffered, but my words seemed to be without effect.

Then my man began to tuck the oar under his arm, and to come up along it, slowly, hand over hand. The small man did the same with Paul. Moment by moment they came closer, and closer, and we knew that the end was only a question of time.

"Hard up, Bob!" Paul called softly to me.

I gave him a quick glance, and caught an instant's glimpse of what I took to be a very pale face and a very set jaw.

"Oh, Bob," he pleaded, "hard up your helm! Hard up your helm, Bob!"

And his meaning dawned upon me. Still holding to my end of the oar, I shoved the tiller over with my back, and even bent my body to keep it over. As it was the Mist was nearly dead before the wind, and this manœuvre was bound to force her to jibe her mainsail from one side to the other. I could tell by the "feel" when the wind spilled out of the canvas and the boom tilted up. Paul's man had now gained a footing on the little deck, and my man was just scrambling up.

"Look out!" I shouted to Paul. "Here she comes!"

Both he and I let go the oars and tumbled into the cockpit. The next instant the big boom and the heavy blocks swept over our heads, the main-sheet whipping past like a great coiling snake and the Mist heeling over with a violent jar. Both men had jumped for it, but in some way the little man either got his knife-hand jammed or fell upon it, for the first sight we caught of him, he was standing in his boat, his bleeding fingers clasped close between his knees and his face all twisted with pain and helpless rage.

"Now 's our chance!" Paul whispered. "Over with you!"

And on either side of the rudder we lowered ourselves into the water, pressing the net down with our feet, till, with a jerk, it went clear. Then it was up and in, Paul at the main-sheet and I at the tiller, the Mist plunging ahead with freedom in her motion, and the little white light astern growing small and smaller.

"Now that you 've had your adventure, do you feel any better?" I remember asking when we had changed our clothes and were sitting dry and comfortable again in the cockpit.

"Well, if I don't have the nightmare for a week to come"—Paul paused and puckered his brows in judicial fashion—"it will be because I can't sleep, that 's one thing sure!"

THE THREE BRASS PENNIES

by *Augusta Huiell Seaman*

I T is in the good old-fashioned way that this fairy-story begins—as all such stories should,—Once upon a time. And a very long time ago it was, in the far-away city of Wang Po, in that far-away country, China.

Within this city lived a young man, Ah Fo, by name, who was poor in worldly goods, but of a rarely studious and thoughtful turn of mind.

One fine day it chanced that he was walking through the forest outside of the city, thinking deeply on existence and the universe in general, when he came suddenly face to face with a huge spider-web stretched across the path, in whose silky meshes a bee was wound and struggling vainly to be free, while an ugly spider sat in the center and watched its fruitless efforts.

Many might have dodged the web and sauntered on, leaving the hapless bee to its fate; but Ah Fo was not of this nature. He could not pass a helpless creature in trouble, if it was in his power to assist. Gingerly, therefore, he took an end of his cotton robe, extracted the bee from the web, and then, not daring to leave it near its enemy, so exhausted was it, he carried it to his home in the city.

There he placed it on his writing-table to recover, while he himself sat down to resume his interrupted thoughts on philosophy. While he was so occupied, the bee slowly regained its strength, crawled to a cake of wet India ink, which the Chinese use for their writing instead of our liquid variety. There it remained standing for a moment, perfectly still. Then it lit on a sheet of blank paper. After that, it spread its wings and flew out of the window, quite unperceived by the dreaming Ah Fo.

It was when that young student awoke from his reverie, however, that a surprise awaited him. Looking about for the lately rescued bee, he could perceive no sign of him. But there before him, on a sheet of white paper, directly in the center where the bee had stood, was printed in fresh ink the Chinese character representing the word Gratitude!

It was an astonishing moment for Ah Fo. How the symbol had come there, he could not imagine; yet he could not but attribute it in some manner to the lately rescued insect. He spent the remainder of the day cogitating upon the question, and lay awake half the night bewildered by the mystery. Early next morning, however, a solution arrived, for a note was conveyed to him which read:

There is a reward awaiting you, Ah Fo for mercy to a tiny creature in desperate plight, if you will call to-day at the fourth house in the Street of the Purple Lantern.

Naturally, Ah Fo let no grass grow under his heels in seeking out the street and house designated. Here he found an old, old man, living in the utmost simplicity who shook hands with himself within his voluminous sleeves as is the Chinese custom of greeting) and bade Ah Fo to enter and be seated. When the young student had done so, the old man seated himself opposite and began:

"I know that you are bewildered by the affair which happened yesterday; but I will at once dispel the mystery. I am a magician. Through all these many years, I have devoted my power to the relief of suffering and the betterment of humanity. Long have I been pursued, however, by a fellow-magician, more subtle than I and entirely unscrupulous, who would rid the city of me because I have been accustomed to undo much of his evil by my merciful arts. It has been well understood that, should he ever lure me into his clutches, my life would be forfeit, unless some kindly soul effected a rescue. In that case, his power over me would eternally vanish. Yesterday I changed myself into a bee, in order to fly quickly to some distant city where I was needed. He must have been spying upon me, for he changed himself into a huge spider, and in the forest, where I settled to rest awhile, he caught me in his wicked web. It was the first and only time this had ever happened, and I gave myself up for lost—when you appeared, and broke his spell over me forever.

"Now, I have little in worldly goods with which the reward you; but I have the power to make you rich and successful, provided you use my gift properly and with discretion. Here are three brass pennies. They do not look any different from our ordinary money" (and indeed they did not, being simply the brass Chinese "cash" with a square hole in the middle of each), "but they are magic pennies, and he who possesses them may have a wish for each. This wish he may enjoy just so long as he retains the penny in his possession, but he loses it, should he part with the coin. Only by mentioning these wishes to me, however, may they be attained."

Then the magician spread out the three pennies before him on the table and stared thoughtfully at Ah Fo through his great, square, horn-rimmed spectacles. "Let us now see," he began. "You will desire, no doubt, an unlimited supply of gold and jewels, a huge castle in the best part of the town, and the beautiful daughter of the ruling potentate for your wife?"

He was about to touch the first penny with his forefinger, when Ah Fo raised his hand.

"A moment, I pray you!" began the student. "This is too serious a matter to be decided so speedily. I feel that the possessions you suggest might not be an unmitigated joy. Allow me, if you will, to go home and think on this matter over night. To-morrow, after due consideration, I may be better able to come to a decision."

The magician smiled a benevolent and delighted smile. "I have not seen so much discretion and forethought in many a long day!" he exclaimed. "Go and consider the matter, by all means, and may Confucius guide your meditations!"

And Ah Fo took his departure.

The next morning he was early at the magician's house. "I have carefully considered the matter, O wise and generous one!" he announced.

"And what might your decision be?" asked the magician, as he spread out the three brass pennies before him.

"I would ask first," went on Ah Fo, "for the power to read accurately the thoughts of others; secondly, for the power to foretell my own future at least a month in advance of any given moment; third, for the power to acquire all learning without any effort!"

When he had finished, the magician sat back with a gasp, took off his spectacles and wiped them, put them on once more, and stared at Ah Fo in astonishment and not a little dismay. "This is most unusual," he stammered, "not to say somewhat dangerous! Have you duly considered, my son, the extent of all you ask?"

"I have duly considered," replied Ah Fo, "and I feel that nothing but these demands can satisfy me, if you intend to be so good as to grant any wishes. I have no others."

"Very well, then," agreed the magician, reluctantly, and he touched each penny before him, murmuring something in a language unknown to Ah Fo. Then he handed them to the young man, bidding him fasten each securely about his neck and touch the proper one of them when he made any of the three wishes. And he carefully indicated the wish represented by each penny, for they all bore slightly different markings.

"And now may I inquire what you intend to do?" asked the old man, curiously.

"I intend to go out and see all the world, acquire all wisdom and possibly, at the end, overthrow this dynasty and become ruler of the Celestial Kingdom myself!" announced Ah Fo, grandly.

"You are perfectly equipped to do so. I wish you all success!" smiled the magician. But he gazed after the young man somewhat sadly as Ah Fo walked away. "Come back and see me, I beg, when you have attained your purpose!" he called after him.

WHEN Ah Fo reached his home, elated by his rare fortune, he packed up his small belongings, preparatory to starting out on his tour of the world. He had decided that he would see his own country, before going on to others, so he planned to cross the great river below the city and penetrate into the southern part of China.

But first, in order to test the power of his pennies, he touched the one enabling him to see into the future, in order that he might ascertain the wisdom of this plan. To his horror, he beheld himself in a small boat, or sampan, on the river in the midst of a violent storm. The sampan was suddenly upset, he saw himself struggling in the waves and finally disappearing beneath the black water!

"This will never, never do!" he cried, trembling at a fate so terrible. "I was fortunate to have thought of looking the matter up before I started. Evidently the southern route is not safe. I will investigate the northern one, though I would have preferred the other." He consulted his penny, but only to behold himself traveling through the mountains, beset by bandits and left dying by the roadside.

Hurriedly he changed his plans again, with the thought of a western route across the country, this time to discover himself lost in a burning desert, parched with thirst, stricken with a fever, and perishing alone under the pitiless sun. In a frenzy, he turned to the last expedient, crying, "I will cross the seas out of this wretched country and see the rest of the world first!" But again his prophetic penny revealed to him a vision of himself captured by Chinese pirates and set to work at the galleys.

Pale with fright at the calamities he had so narrowly escaped, Ah Fo sat down to consider the matter.

"It is plain that fate does not intend me to carry out this part of my program at present," he meditated. "Perhaps it is because I am not yet sufficiently equipped. Possibly it might be a better plan to acquire all wisdom first, and I will then be better prepared to conquer this kingdom when the time comes. Study was ever a pleasure to me, and there are some knotty problems that have baffled me of late. With my newly acquired power, it will be quite delightful to wrestle with them!"

So he put his house in order once more,

got out his books, and prepared for a tussle with a difficult mathematical problem. And as this was plainly the time to try out the qualities of another of his magic pennies, he touched the proper one hopefully. To his delighted astonishment, he read in his mind the working out of the problem and its answer as plainly as though it were written out in the book before him.

"Now *this* is truly wonderful!" he cried. "It has not taken me one moment to solve what I have been puzzling over for the past month. At this rate, I shall acquire all wisdom in a short week or so. Let us try another!"

He worked feverishly for a little less than an hour, at the end of which he found he had solved every problem in every branch of higher mathematics that had ever puzzled either himself or any of the great mathematicians of the land. But, strangely enough, the delight and elation of the feat had somehow vanished.

"It is almost too easy!" he sighed. "It is like reading it out of a book, instead of achieving it after hours of painstaking and unsuccessful work. However, mathematics was never my favorite study. Let us try how it will work with other branches."

All that day he spent over his studies, with the assistance of the magic penny, discovering that the difficulties of each became as simple to him as the reading of a child's primer would seem to an old man. And more and more did the zest for the achievement of wisdom and learning, under these conditions, slip away from him. At length he closed his books with a dissatisfied exclamation.

"This power may prove to be very useful later," he mused, "but it has taken all the joy from study for me at the present time. Since the acquiring of wisdom is so easy, I need spend little time over it, I perceive. Perhaps it would be just as well, for my next move, to go about the city and visit my friends and try to ascertain just what they think of me, so that I can judge whom I may count upon as supporters when the time comes for me to overthrow the dynasty and assume my place as monarch."

Forthwith he set out to visit his friend Tuan See, anxious to put to the test the powers of the last magic penny. He found his friend with his family, seated at the evening meal, and was cordially invited by Tuan See to join them at the repast. Ah Fo, was about to comply with real pleasure, for he enjoyed a well-spread table and congenial company, when his fingers accidentally touched the third penny.

Plainly, as if it had been written on the wall before him, could he read the real, inner thoughts of Tuan See—thoughts which ran very much like this: "I hope that he has to go quickly! I hope that he cannot accept! There is so little of that dish of delicious bamboo-tips, I do not want to share it! And I am weary to-night. I do not wish to talk. He will probably stay till midnight, and I am ready to drop with sleep!"

It was as if Ah Fo had been struck a blow in the face. He could not have imagined such duplicity in the heretofore absolutely cordial and devoted friend. And yet, quick on its heels, came the memory that he had not infrequently felt the same way himself. This reading of other people's minds certainly had its inconveniences!

He hastily refused the invitation to dine, saying he had just dropped in to sit a few moments and must hurry on. Then, all the while fingering his third penny, he began to detail to his friend how easily he had solved that day some of the intricate problems they had often mused over unsuccessfully together. And he could not help but feel that Tuan See must be delighted and admire his success.

Tuan See certainly lavished upon him,

in words, all the praise he had hoped for; yet the telltale penny kept revealing those horridly candid inner thoughts; "What a conceited coxcomb Ah Fo is getting to be! I always realized that he could be tiresome, but he was never so much so as now. What do I care how many problems he has solved? I am only interested now in my work and my family. I wish he would go. I wish he would go! I wish he would *go!*"

Ah Fo rose and bade his friend a good-by that was almost a sob. Out in the street, tears so blinded his eyes that he could scarcely see his way home. Once there, however, he shut his door and sat himself down to think it over, longing for guidance as he clutched the penny that was to show him all wisdom. Scene after scene flashed through his brain, detailing to him where he had felt precisely the same toward certain friends, Tuan See among them, when courtesy had demanded that he appear most cordial. Had they been able to read his heart, they would have discovered the same thoughts.

"After all, we are but human!" he mused. "Tuan See is no worse than I. But what am I to do now?" He spent the night in considering the question, and in the early morning sought once more the magician in the Street of the Purple Lantern.

"Kind old man," he said, "I beg you to take back these brass pennies. They have brought me nothing but woe, and I quite realize that it was all through my own silly choosing. I desire only to be as I was before!"

The old man looked at him with an understanding twinkle in his eye. "I rather thought it would be somewhat like this," he answered. "I felt that you were overreaching yourself in your desire for power. Better to have chosen the gold and jewels, the stately castle in the best part of town, and the beautiful daughter of our potentate. And, by the way, these can all still be yours, if you care to have me change the power of the pennies!"

"No, no, no!" cried Ah Fo, wildly. "With all gratitude to you, I desire none of these

"The magician walked to the river and hurled them far into its deep"

things,—less now than ever. If you would grant me three wishes, let them, I pray you, be these. Allow me to forget all that I have learned through the agency of these terrible pennies; give me a contented mind; and lastly, allow me to return to my studies with a new zest and the determination to rise by my own honest effort above all obstacles. It is all I would ask!"

"It shall be as you say," smiled the magician, tapping him lightly on the forehead. "And for that you do not need the pennies. I can see that they would not have brought you happiness, in any case, since that attribute lies within yourself. You had it before ever I met you, and lost it for a time in seeking after less desirable things. Farewell!"

Ah Fo went out into the street, a contented and happy man once more. And the magician, after thoughtfully considering the brass pennies for a time, took them in his hand, walked out to the bank of the river, and hurled them far into its deep, engulfing tide!

PUZZLED

by Carolyn Wells

THERE lived in ancient Scribbletown a wise
    old writer-man
Whose name was Homer Cicero Demos-
    thenes McCann.
He 'd written treatises and themes till "For
    a change," he said,
"I think I 'll write a children's book before
    I go to bed."

He pulled down all his musty tomes in
    Latin and in Greek;
Consulted cyclopedias and manuscripts
    antique,
Essays in Anthropology, studies in counter-
    poise—
"For these," he said, "are useful lore for
    little girls and boys."

He scribbled hard, and scribbled fast, he
    burned the midnight oil,
And when he reached "The End" he felt
    rewarded for his toil;
He said, "This charming Children's Book
    is greatly to my credit."
And now he 's sorely puzzled that no
    child has ever read it.

WITH THE BLACK PRINCE

by William O. Stoddard

THE GREAT DAY OF CRÉCY

'TIS yet an hour before the tide will be out, but I believe that horsemen might cross now."

The speaker was a clownish-looking man wearing the wooden shoes and coarse blouse of a French peasant. He stood at the stirrup of a knight in black armor, whose questions he was answering.

"Sir William of Wakeham," the Prince said, "send in thy men-at-arms. Post thy archers on the bank, right and left. We shall soon see if Godemar du Fay can bar the Somme against us."

"The archers are already posted," replied Sir William: "Neville and his Warwickshire men hold the right. The men of Suffolk and Kent are on the left."

"Forward, in the King's name!" commanded the young general, for his royal father had given him charge of the advance.

It was a critical moment, for if the ford of Blanche Taque should not be forced, the entire English army would be hemmed in between the river Somme and the hosts of France. It was but little after sunrise and Edward had sent orders to all his captains to move forward.

The river Somme was wider here than in its deeper channels, above and below. The opposite bank was held by a force that was evidently strong, but its numbers were of less account at the outset. Only a few from either side could contend for the passage of Blanche Taque.

Therefore these were the chosen knights of all England who now rode into the water, finding it nearly up to their horse-girths.

Forward from the other shore rode in the men-at-arms of Godemar du Fay to hold the ford for Philip of Valois.

"Now is our time!" shouted Richard to his archers. "Guy the Bow, let every archer draw his arrow to the head!"

Ill fared it then for the French riders when among them, aimed at horses rather than at men, flew the fatal messengers of the marksmen from the forest of Arden. Lances were fiercely thrust, maces and swords rang heavily upon helm and shield; but soon, the French column fell into confusion. Its front rank failed of support and was driven steadily back. It was almost as if the English champions went on without pausing; and in a few minutes they were pushing forward and widening their front upon the land.

Blanche Taque was taken, for of Godemar du Fay's twelve thousand, only a thousand were men-at-arms. When the regular ranks of these were broken, his ill-disciplined infantry took to flight and the battle was over. All the while the tide was running out.

"Stand fast, O'Rourke!" called Richard, to the impatient Irish chieftain, who was striding angrily back and forth in front of his line of axmen.

"Ay, but, my lord of Wartmont," returned the O'Rourke, "there is fighting and we are not in the battle. Hark!"

"Neville, advance! Thou and all thine to the front, seeking Wakeham. In the King's name, forward!"

A knight in bright armor had drawn rein at a little distance, and he pointed toward the ford as he spoke. It was crowded still by Sir Thomas Gifford's men-at-arms, but the battle on the other shore had drifted far away.

"Forward, O'Rourke!" shouted Richard. "Forward, Guy the Bow! Forward, David Griffith! Good fortune is with us! We are to be under the Prince's own command!"

Loud cheers replied, and with much laughter and full of courage Richard's force waded into the shallow Somme.

It was easy crossing now for all, with none to hinder. Then, as the last flags of the English rear guard fluttered upon the left bank of the Somme, good eyes might have discovered on the horizon the banners of the foremost horsemen of King Philip. He had marched fast and far that morning, and once more the English army seemed barely to have escaped him.

"A cunning hunter is our good lord the King," remarked Ben o' Coventry, to his fellows as they pushed on.

"Thou art ever malapert," said Guy the Bow. "What knowest thou of the thoughts of thy betters?"

"He who runs may read," said Ben. "Can a Frenchman live without eating?"

"I trow not," responded Guy. "What is thy riddle?"

"Did we not waste the land as we came?" said Ben. "Hath not Philip, these three days, marched through the waste? I tell thee that when he is over the Somme he must fight or starve. Well for us, and thanks to the King, that we are to meet a host that is both footsore and half famished. I can put down a hungry man, any day."

Deep, indeed, had been the wisdom of the King, and his army encamped that Thursday night, without fear of an attack, and the next morning they again went on.

Edward himself rode forward in the advance, after the noontide of Friday, and during the whole march he seemed to be searching the land with his eyes.

"Sir John of Chandos," he exclaimed, at last; "see yon windmill on the hill. This is the place, I sought. Ride thou with me." The hill was not not very high, and its sides sloped away gently. The King dismounted at the door of the mill, and gazed in all directions.

"They will come from the west," he said, "with the sun in their eyes. Yon is our battlefield. Here we will bide their onset. Chandos, knowest thou that I am to fight Philip of Valois on mine own land?"

"The village over there is called Crécy," replied Sir John. "Truly, the crown of France is thine, rather than Philip's."

"Ay, so," said Edward, "whether or no he can keep it from me; but this broad vale and the village and the chateaux are my inheritance from my grandmother. Seest thou that ditch, to the right, with its fellow on the left? I trust they have good depth. 'T is a field prepared!"

After that he rode slowly, with his son and a gallant company, throughout the camps, talking kindly and familiarly with high and low alike, and bidding all to trust God and be sure of victory. Brave men were they and well did they love their King, but it was good for their courage that they should see his face and hear his voice and assure their hearts that they had a great captain for their commander.

In number, they were about as many as had sailed at the first from England, small losses by the way, and the absence of those left as garrisons of strongholds captured in Normandy, having been made good by later arrivals.

This first duty done, the King went to his quarters in the neighboring castle of La Broye, and here he gave a grand entertainment to all his captains and gentlemen of note. There was much music at the royal feast, and every man was inspired to do his best on the morrow. All the instruments sounded together loudly, at the close, when the warriors, who were so soon to fight to the death, arose to their feet and stood thus in silence, while the King and the Prince turned away and walked out of the hall together, no man following.

"Whither go they?' whispered the Earl of Hereford to Sir John Chandos.

"As it doth well become our King at this hour," replied Sir John. "They go to the chapel of La Broye to pray for victory. 'T will do our men no harm to be told that the King and the Prince are on their knees."

"Verily, my men shall know," said Richard Neville to Sir Thomas Gifford.

All of Edward's army, save the watchers and sentries, slept soundly that night. It was wonderful how little uncertainty they had about the result of the battle.

The morning came, but there were clouds in the sky, and the air was sultry. It was Saturday, the 26th of August, 1346.

Edward the King posted himself at the windmill. On the slope and below it were a third of his men-at-arms and a strong body of footmen. This was the reserve. In front thereof, the remainder of the army was placed in the form of a great harrow, with its point—a blunt one enough—toward the hill, and its beams marked by the ditch lines.

The right beam of this English harrow was commanded by the Black Prince in person, and with him were the Earls of Warwick and Hereford, Geoffrey of Harcourt, and Sir John Chandos, with many another famous knight. This force was less

than a thousand men-at-arms, with Irish and Welsh, but they were especially strong in bowmen, for the King retained few archers with him.

But little less was the strength of the left beam of the harrow, commanded by the Earls of Northampton and Arundel.

"Fortune has favored us!" exclaimed one of the men-at-arms to his young commander; "we are well placed here at the right. We shall be among the first to face the French!"

"Here cometh the Prince," responded Richard, "with his Red Dragon banner of Wales. The royal standard is with the King at the mill."

Reviewing the lines with care, and giving many orders as he came, the Prince rode up, clad in his plain black armor and wearing the helmet of a simple esquire.

"Richard Neville," he said, as he drew near, "see that thou dost thy devoir, this day."

Richard's head bowed low as the Prince wheeled away; as he again sat erect upon his war-horse, a voice near him muttered: "Ho! Seest thou? The French are coming!"

Richard looked, and in the distance he could see a glittering and a flag, but after a long gaze he replied:

"It is too soon. Those are but a band of skirmishers."

So it proved; and the long, hot hours went slowly by. At length the King ordered that every man should be supplied with food and drink, that they might not fight fasting.

Darker grew the clouds until they hung low over all the sky. Blue flashes of lightning were followed by deafening thunder-peals, and then there fell a deluge of warm rain.

The English archers were posted in the front ranks, among the harrow beams, but the rain harmed not their bows. Every bowstring was as yet in its case, with its hard spun-silk securely dry.

"Harken well, all," said Richard, addressing his men. "The Prince orders that there shall not be shouting. Fight with shut lips, and send forth no shaft without a sure mark."

"We are to bite and not to bark," said Ben o' Coventry in a low voice. Then he added aloud: "Yon marshy level is better for the rain. A horse might sink to his pasterns."

"The ditch runs full," said Richard. "The King chose his battleground wisely."

"We are put behind the archery, now," said David Griffith to his Welshmen. "So are the Irish; but our time to fight will come soon enough."

Most of the men-at-arms belonging to each beam of the harrow were drawn up at the inner end, ready to mount and ride, but wasting no effort, now, of horse or man.

"The very rain has fought for England," remarked the Prince to his knights, as at the front they wheeled for their return. "There will be hard marching for the host of Philip of Valois."

"They must come through deep mud and tangled country, my lord the Prince," replied the Earl of Warwick. "His huge rabble of horse and foot will be sore crowded and well wearied."

Moreover, there was much free speech among the knights concerning the difference between the opposing armies as to their training and discipline.

King Philip willed to begin the fight with an advance of his Genoese crossbowmen, fifteen thousand strong. It was bolts against arrows. The Genoese might have done better on another day, for their fame was great; but at this hour they were at the end of a forced march of six leagues, each man carrying his cumbrous weapon with its sheaf of bolts. This had weakened their muscles and diminished their ardor; besides, the sudden rain had soaked their bowstrings. The cords stretched when the strain of the winding winch was put upon them, and had lost their spring, so that they would not throw with good force. Their captains nevertheless drove them forward, at the French king's command.

From his post at the mill-foot the royal general of England surveyed the field.

"The day waneth," he said to his earls; "but the waiting is over. The sun is low and sends the stronger glare into their eyes. Mark you how closely packed is that hedge of men-at-arms and lances behind the Genoese? Philip is mad!"

On pushed the crossbowmen, until they were well within the beams of the broad harrow, but there they halted, to do somewhat with their bolts, if they could; and they sent up a great shout. No answer came, for the English archers stood silent, holding each a clothyard arrow ready for the string.

Small harm was done by the feebly shot crossbow-bolts, and the Genoese were ordered to go nearer. They made a threatening rush, indeed; but then of their own accord they halted again and shouted, thinking perhaps to terrify the English army.

Steady as statues stood the archers until the Earl of Hereford, at a word from the Prince, rode out to where he could be seen by all and waved his truncheon.

Up came the bows, along the serried lines, while each man chose his mark as if he were shooting for a prize upon a holiday in Merry England.

Those of the enemy who escaped to tell the tale said afterward that then it seemed as if it snowed arrows, so swiftly twanged the strings and sped the white shafts.

With yells of terror, the stricken Genoese broke and fled; for by reason of Edward's order of battle they were in a cross-fire from the two beams of the harrow, and few shots failed of a target among them.

Some of them even cut the damp strings of their useless crossbows as they went, lest they should be bidden to turn and fight again. They were now, however, only a pell-mell mob, and it was impossible to command them.

Behind the advance of the Genoese had been the splendid array of King Philip's men-at-arms, a forest of lances. In a fair field, and handled well, they were numerous enough to ride down the entire force of King Edward. Against such an attack the English king had cunningly provided. At no great distance in the view of his knights rode Philip himself, with kings and princes for his company; and fierce was his wrath over the unexpected discomfiture of his luckless crossbowmen.

"Slay me these cowardly scoundrels!" he shouted to his knights. "Charge through them, smiting as ye go!"

Forward rode the thousands of the chivalry of France and Germany and Bohemia, every mailed warrior among them being full of contempt for the thin barrier of English foot-soldiers. All they now needed, it seemed to them, was to disentangle their panoplied war-horses from that crowd of panic-stricken Genoese. It would also be well if they could pass the wet ground, and avoid plunging against one another in the hurly-burly.

But now was to be noted another proof of the wise forethought of the English king. He had had prepared, and the Prince had placed at short intervals along the battle-line a number of the new machines called "bombards." These were short, hollow tubes, made either of thick oaken staves, bound together with strong straps of iron, or (as was said of some of them), the staves themselves were bars of iron. Before this day, none knew exactly when, there had been discovered by the alchemists a curious compound that, packed into the bombards, would explode with force when touched by fire, and hurl an iron ball to a great distance. It would hurt whatever thing it might alight upon; but the King's thought was rather that the loud explosions and the flying missiles might affright the mettled horses of the French men-at-arms.

Soon the air was full of the roaring of these bombards; and they served somewhat the King's purpose. But so little was then thought of this use of gunpowder at Crécy that some who chronicled the battle, not having been there to see and hear, failed even to mention it.

The fine array of the gallant knights was now confused indeed. They vainly sought to restore their broken order. Not only the manner of the flight of the Genoese, and the greater force and longer line of the right beam of the English harrow invited them to urge their steeds in that direction, but there also floated the Red Dragon banner of the Prince of Wales. Well did each good knight know that there was beating the heart of the great battle.

Worse than the noisy wrath of bombards came now at the command of the Prince. To right and left, plying their bows as they went, wheeled orderly sections of the archery lines, that through those gaps might pass the fierce rush of the wild Welshmen. They were ordered forward, not to contend with knights in armor of proof, but to slay the horses with their javelins.

Terrible was the work they did, darting lightly to and fro; and it was pitiful to see so many gallant knights rolled helplessly upon the ground, encumbered by their armor. Nevertheless, many kept their saddles, and broke through the Welsh to find themselves forced to draw rein in front of the deep ditches that guarded the archery, who were ever plying their deadly bows.

"Down lances!" shouted the Black Prince to his men-at-arms, at the head of the harrow. "For England! For the King! St. George! Charge!"

More than two thousand mailed horsemen, of England's best, struck their spurs deep as the royal trumpet sounded. Riders and horses were fresh and unwearied.

There was the thunder of many hoofs, a crash of splintering lances, and they were hand-to-hand with King Philip's disordered chivalry. Well for him and his if he had then sounded a recall, so that his shattered forces might be rearranged; but instead he poured forward his reserves, thereby increasing the pressure and the tumult, while the English archers ever plied their bows with deadly effect.

It was then that the blind King of Bohemia, the ally of Philip in this war, was told how the day was going. At his side rode several of his nobles, and he said to them:

"I pray and beseech you that you lead me so far into the fight that I may strike one blow with this sword of mine."

He had been accounted a knight of worth in his youth, and the spirit of battle was yet strong upon him, neither did there yet seem to be good reason why his request should not be granted. Therefore his friends, on either hand, fastened the bridle-bits of their horses on a line with his own, and they rode bravely forward together.

Right hard was the strife that now went on, especially between the beams of the harrow and toward the right. In the midst of it floated the Red Dragon flag, and here the Prince and his companions-in-arms were contending against the greater numbers of their assailants. Here was the center toward which all were pressing, and here, it was seen, the fate of the battle was to be decided. For this very reason, the pressure was less upon the left beam of the harrow, and its captains could the better observe the

marvelous passage at arms around the Prince.

"Sir Thomas Norwich," spoke the Earl of Northampton, "we must all go forward and do our best. Ride thou to the King, and crave of him that he send help with speed. We fear it is full time for the reserves to move, if it be not even now too late."

Then the Earl of Arundel and other knights lowered their lances and setting spurs to their horses charged into the thickest press.

Away spurred the knight of Norwich, and, ere many minutes had elapsed, he gave the message to the King at the foot of the windmill. For there had the King been standing all the while watching the course of the battle with better perception than could be had by any of those who were in it. He could, therefore, discern in what manner Philip of Valois was defeating himself, crushing his own forces.

"Is my son dead, or unhorsed, or so wounded that he cannot help himself?" he calmly inquired of the messenger.

"No, sire," responded Norwich; "but he is in a hard passage at arms, and sorely needs your help."

"Return thou, Sir Thomas, to those who sent thee," said the King, "and bid them not to send to me so long as my son lives. Let the boy win his spurs; for, if God so order it, I will that the day may be his, and that the honor may be with him and with them to whom I gave it in charge."

No more could the good knight say, and back he rode without company.

There were those who thought it hard of the King, but better it was that he should hold his reserves for utter need.

Nevertheless, the aspect seemed to be growing darker to the true English hearts that were fighting in the press. They saw not, as the King did, that owing to his cunning plan of battle, more in number of the

English than of the enemy were at any instant actually smiting, save at the center, around the Prince himself.

Dark as was the seeming, the heart of none was failing.

"To the Prince! To the Prince!" shouted Richard Neville, as the space in front of him was cleared somewhat of foemen. "Follow me!" Forward he went, and loudly rang out behind him the battle-shouts of his men. They were fewer than at the beginning; but boldly and loyally they had closed up shoulder to shoulder.

Richard's horse was slain under him, by a thrust from a German pike; but the rider was lifted to his feet in time to meet the rush of the King of Bohemia and his friends. Their horses were sadly hampered by that hitching together of bridles, and were rearing, plunging, unmanageable. More than one blow had the old, blind hero given that day, as he had willed. None knew now by whose arrows his horse and those of his comrades went down, but after they were unhorsed the wild tide of the battle passed over them, for none of them rose again.

"To the Prince!" shouted Richard, fiercely. "I saw his crest go down!"

The arrows and darts flew fast as the young hero of Wartmont fought his way in amid the crash of swords and lances.

"Now, Heaven be praised!" he cried out. "I see the Prince! He lives!"

He said no more, for before him stood a tall knight with a golden wing upon his helmet, and wielding a battle-ax.

Clang, clang, followed blow on blow between those twain. It had been harder for Richard, but that his foe was wearied with the heat and the long combat. Well and valorously did each hold his own, but a blow from another blade fell upon Richard's bosom, cleaving his breastplate. Then, even as he sank, across him strode what

seemed some giant, and a wild cry in the Irish tongue went up as the O'Rourke's pole-ax fell upon the shoulder of the knight of the golden wing.

"On!" shouted the furious chief. "On, men of the fens! Forward, Connaught and Ulster! Vengeance for our young lord!" Down with the French!"

Hundreds of strong Irish had followed their leader, and timely indeed was their coming, for the sun was sinking and need was to win the victory speedily.

"Alas!" said Guy the Bow, as he bent over Richard. "I pray thee, tell me, art thou deadly hurt, my lord?"

"Lift me!" gasped Richard. "Put me upon my feet. I would fight on and fall with the Prince."

Quickly they lifted him, but he staggered faintly and leaned upon Guy the Bow.

"I fear he is sore hurt," muttered Guy.

But at that moment there arose a great shouting. It began among the reserves who were with the King on the slope of the hill.

"They fly! The foe are breaking! The day is ours! The field is won! God and St. George for England, and for the King!"

It was true, for the army of the king of France could bear no more. All things were against them. They could neither fight in ranks nor flee from the clothyard shafts.

The Prince came near the group around Richard, and pausing from giving swift orders to his knights he stepped forward.

" 'T is Richard of Wartmont!" he exclaimed. "Is he dying?"

Straight up stood Richard, raising his visor. He was ghastly pale, but his voice had partly come back to him.

"I think not, Prince Edward," he faltered. "But I thank Heaven that thou art safe!"

"Courage," said the Prince. "The field is ours, and thou hast won honor this day. Bear him with me to the King."

Here and there, brave fragments of what

had been the mighty host of France held out and still fought on; but they were not enough. All others sought to save themselves as best they might from the pitiless following of the English. Those in the rear who fled at once were safe enough, and the sunset and the evening shadows were good friends to many more of the French. Most fortunate were such horsemen as had not been able to get into the harrow, for only about twelve hundred knights were slain. With them, however, fell eleven princes and the King of Bohemia, and thirty thousand footmen. The King of France himself was a fugitive that night, seeking where he might hide his head.

From his place on the hill, King Edward of England watched the closing of the great day of Crécy, and now before him stood a strange array. Shorn plumes, cloven crests or none, battered and bloody armor, broken swords, shivered lances, battle-worn faces, lighted somewhat by pride of victory, were arrayed before him. All were on foot and each man bowed the knee.

Few, but weighty and noble with thanks and honor, were the words of the King.

More he would say, he told them, when he should better know each man's meed of praise.

At length the Black Prince came forward, and he knelt before his father, to rise a knight, for he had won his spurs.

"Richard of Wartmont!" cheerily spoke the King. "Come thou!"

"Sore wounded, sire," said Sir Henry of Wakeham; "but I will aid."

"Not so," exclaimed the Prince, "I will bring him myself."

When Richard was brought before King Edward, he heard but faintly the words that made him a knight:

"Arise, Sir Richard of Wartmont!"

All strength and life that were yet in Richard had helped him to lean upon the Prince's arm, to kneel, to rise again, and to hear, almost without hearing, the good words of the King. Then he stepped backward, and Guy the Bow put an arm around him and said lovingly:

"Sir Richard of Wartmont! Proud will thy lady mother be. I trow the war is over. When thy wounds are well healed, we will take thee home to her."

SARA CREWE

OR,

WHAT HAPPENED AT MISS MINCHIN'S

by Frances Hodgson Burnett

I N the first place, Miss Minchin lived in London. Her home was a large, dull, tall one, in a large, dull square, where all the houses were alike, and all the sparrows were alike, and where all the door-knockers made the same heavy sound, and on still days—and nearly all the days were still—seemed to resound through the entire row in which the knock was knocked. On Miss Minchin's door there was a brass plate. On the brass plate there was inscribed in black letters.

> ### MISS MINCHIN'S
> SELECT SEMINARY FOR YOUNG LADIES

Little Sara Crewe never went in or out of the house without reading that door-plate and reflecting upon it. By the time she was twelve, she had decided that all her trouble arose because, in the first place, she was not "Select," and in the second, she was not a "Young Lady." When she was eight years old, she had been brought to Miss Minchin as a pupil, and left with her. Her papa had brought her all the way from India. Her mamma had died when she was a baby, and her papa had kept her with him as long as he could. And then, finding the hot climate was making her very delicate, he had brought her to England and left her with Miss Minchin, to be part of the Select Seminary for Young Ladies. Sara, who had always been a sharp little child, who remem-

bered things, recollected hearing him say that he had not a relative in the world whom he knew of, and so he was obliged to place her at a boarding-school, and he had heard Miss Minchin's establishment spoken of very highly. The same day, he took Sara out and bought her a great many beautiful clothes,—clothes so grand and rich that only a very young and inexperienced man would have bought them for a mite of a child who was to be brought up in a boarding-school. But the fact was that he was a rash, innocent young man, and very sad at the thought of parting with his little girl, who was all he had left to remind him of her beautiful mother, whom he had dearly loved. And he wished her to have everything the most fortunate little girl could have; and so, when the polite sales-women in the shops said, "Here is our very latest thing in hats, the plumes are exactly the same as those we sold to Lady Diana Sinclair yesterday," he immediately bought what was offered to him, and paid whatever was asked. The consequence was that Sara had a most extraordinary wardrobe. Her dresses were silk and velvet and India cashmere, her hats and bonnets were covered with bows and plumes, her small undergarments were adorned with real lace, and she returned in the cab to Miss Minchin's with a doll almost as large as herself, dressed quite as grandly as herself, too.

Then her papa gave Miss Minchin some

money and went away, and for several days Sara would neither touch the doll, nor her breakfast, nor her dinner, nor her tea, and would do nothing but crouch in a small corner by the window and cry. She cried so much, indeed, that she made herself ill. She was a queer little child, with old-fashioned ways and strong feelings, and she had adored her papa, and could not be made to think that India and an interesting bungalow were not better for her than London and Miss Minchin's Select Seminary. The instant she had entered the house, she had begun promptly to hate Miss Minchin, and to think little of Miss Amelia Minchin, who was smooth and dumpy, and lisped, and was evidently afraid of her older sister. Miss Minchin was tall, and had large, cold, fishy eyes, and large, cold hands, which seemed fishy, too, because they were damp and made chills run down Sara's back when they touched her, as Miss Minchin pushed her hair off her forehead and said:

"A most beautiful and promising little girl, Captain Crewe. She will be a favorite pupil; *quite* a favorite pupil, I see."

For the first year she was a favorite pupil; at least she was indulged a great deal more than was good for her. And when the Select Seminary went walking, two by two, she was always decked out in her grandest clothes, and led by the hand, at the head of the genteel procession, by Miss Minchin herself. And when the parents of any of the pupils came, she was always dressed and called into the parlor with her doll; and she used to hear Miss Minchin say that her father was a distinguished Indian officer, and she would be heiress to a great fortune. That her father had inherited a great deal of money, Sara had heard before; and also that some day it would be hers, and that he would not remain long in the army, but would come to live in London. And every time a letter came, she hoped it would say

he was coming, and they were to live together again.

But about the middle of the third year a letter came bringing very different news. Because he was not a business man himself, her papa had given his affairs into the hands of a friend he trusted. The friend had deceived and robbed him. All the money was gone, no one knew exactly where, and the shock was so great to the poor, rash young officer, that, being attacked by jungle fever shortly afterward, he had no strength to rally, and so died, leaving Sara with no one to take care of her.

Miss Minchin's cold and fishy eyes had never looked so cold and fishy as they did when Sara went into the parlor, on being sent for, a few days after the letter was received.

No one had said anything to the child about mourning, so, in her old-fashioned way, she had decided to find a black dress for herself, and had picked out a black velvet she had outgrown, and came into the room in it, looking the queerest little figure in the world, and a sad little figure, too. The dress was too short and too tight, her face was white, her eyes had dark rings around them, and her doll, wrapped in a piece of old black crape, was held under her arm. She was not a pretty child. She was thin, and had a weird, interesting little face, short black hair, and very large green-gray eyes fringed all around with heavy black lashes.

"I am the ugliest child in the school," she had said once, after staring at herself in the glass for some minutes.

But there had been a clever, good-natured little French teacher who had said to the music-master:

"Zat leetle Crewe. Vat a child! A so ogly beauty! Ze so large eyes; ze so little spirituelle face. Waid till she grow up. You shall see!"

"She slowly advanced into the parlor, clutching her doll"

This morning, however, in the tight, small black frock, she looked thinner and odder than ever, and her eyes were fixed on Miss Minchin with a queer steadiness as she slowly advanced into the parlor, clutching her doll.

"Put your doll down!" said Miss Minchin.

"No," said the child, "I won't put her down; I want her with me. She is all I have. She has stayed with me all the time since my papa died."

She had never been an obedient child. She had had her own way ever since she was born, and there was about her an air of silent determination under which Miss Minchin had always felt secretly uncomfortable. And that lady felt even now that perhaps it would be as well not to insist on her point. So she looked at her as severely as possible.

"You will have no time for dolls in future," she said; "you will have to work and improve yourself, and make yourself useful."

Sara kept the big odd eyes fixed on her teacher and said nothing.

"Everything will be very different now," Miss Minchin went on, "I sent for you to talk to you and make you understand. Your father is dead. You have no friends. You have no money. You have no home and no one to take care of you."

The little pale olive face twitched nervously, but the green-gray eyes did not move from Miss Minchin's, and still Sara said nothing.

"What are you staring at?" demanded Miss Minchin sharply. "Are you so stupid you don't understand what I mean? I tell you that you are quite alone in the world, and have no one to do anything for you, unless I choose to keep you here."

The truth was, Miss Minchin was in her worst mood. To be suddenly deprived of a large sum of money yearly and a show pupil, and to find herself with a little beggar on her hands, was more than she could bear with any degree of calmness.

"Now listen to me," she went on, "and remember what I say. If you work hard and prepare to make yourself useful in a few years, I shall let you stay here. You are only a child, but you are a sharp child, and you pick up things almost without being taught. You speak French very well, and in a year or so you can begin to help with the younger pupils. By the time you are fifteen

you ought to be able do that much at least."

"I can speak French better than you, now," said Sara; "I always spoke it with my papa in India." Which was not at all polite, but was painfully true; because Miss Minchin could not speak French at all, and, indeed, was not in the least a clever person. But she was a hard, grasping business woman, and, after the first shock of disappointment, had seen that at very little expense to herself she might prepare this clever, determined child to be very useful to her and save her the necessity of paying large salaries to teachers of languages.

"Don't be impudent, or you will be punished," she said. "You will have to improve your manners if you expect to earn your bread. You are not a parlor boarder now. Remember, that if you don't please me, and I send you away, you have no home but the street. You can go now."

Sara turned away.

"Stay," commanded Miss Minchin, "don't you intend to thank me?"

Sara turned toward her. The nervous twitch was to be seen again in her face, and she seemed to be trying to control it.

"What for?" she said.

"For my kindness to you," replied Miss Minchin. "For my kindness in giving you a home."

Sara went two or three steps nearer to her. Her thin little chest was heaving up and down, and she spoke in a strange, unchildish voice.

"You are not kind," she said. "You are not kind." And she turned again and went out of the room, leaving Miss Minchin staring after her strange, small figure in stony anger.

The child walked up the staircase, holding tightly to her doll; she meant to go to her bedroom, but at the door she was met by Miss Amelia.

"You are not to go in there," she said. "That is not your room now."

"Where is my room?" asked Sara.

"You are to sleep in the attic next to the cook."

Sara walked on. She mounted two flights more, and reached the door of the attic room, opened it and went in, shutting it behind her. She stood against it and looked about her. The room was slanting-roofed and white-washed; there was a rusty grate, an iron bedstead, and some odd articles of furniture, sent up from better rooms below, where they had been used until they were considered to be worn out. Under the skylight in the roof, which showed nothing but an oblong piece of dull gray sky, there was a battered old red footstool.

Sara went to it and sat down. She was a queer child, as I have said before, and quite unlike other children. She seldom cried. She did not cry now. She laid her doll, Emily, across her knees and put her face down upon her, and her arms around her, and sat there, her little black head resting on the black crape, not saying one word, not making one sound.

From that day her life changed entirely. Sometimes she used to feel as if it must be another life altogether, the life of some other child. She was a little drudge and outcast; she was given her lessons at odd times and expected to learn without being taught; she was sent on errands by Miss Minchin, Miss Amelia, and the cook. Nobody took any notice of her except when they ordered her about. She was often kept busy all day and then sent into the deserted school-room with a pile of books to learn her lessons or practice at night. She had never been intimate with the other pupils, and soon she became so shabby that, taking her queer clothes together with her queer little ways, they began to look upon her as a being of another world than their own. The fact was that, as a rule, Miss Minchin's pupils were rather dull, matter-of-fact young people, accustomed to being rich and comfortable; and Sara, with her elfish cleverness, her desolate life, and her odd habit of fixing her eyes upon them and staring them out of countenance, was too much for them.

"She always looks as if she was finding you out," said one girl, who was sly and given to making mischief. "I am," said Sara, promptly, when she heard of it. "That's what I look at them for. I like to know about people. I think them over afterward."

She never made any mischief herself or interfered with any one. She talked very little, did as she was told, and thought a great deal. Nobody knew, and in fact nobody cared, whether she was unhappy or happy, unless, perhaps, it was Emily, who lived in the attic and slept on the iron bedstead at night. Sara thought Emily understood her feelings, though she was only wax and had a habit of staring herself. Sara used to talk to her at night.

"You are the only friend I have in the world" she would say to her. "Why don't you say something? Why don't you speak? Sometimes I'm sure you could, if you would try. It ought to make you try, to know you are the only thing I have. If I were you, I should try. Why don't you try?"

It really was a very strange feeling she had about Emily. It arose from her being so desolate. She did not like to own to herself that her only friend, her only companion, could feel and hear nothing. She wanted to believe, or to pretend to believe, that Emily understood and sympathized with her, that she heard her even though she did not speak in answer. She used to put her in a chair sometimes and sit opposite to her on the old red footstool, and stare at her and think and pretend about her until her own eyes would grow large with something which was almost like fear, particularly at night when the garret was so still, when the only sound that was to be heard was the occasional squeak and skurry of rats in the wainscot. There were rat-holes in the garret and Sara detested rats, and was always glad Emily was with her when she heard their hateful squeak and rush and scratching. One of her "pretends" was that Emily was a kind of good witch and could protect her. Poor little Sara! everything was "pretend" with her. She had a strong imagination; there was almost more imagination than there was Sara, and her whole forlorn, uncared-for child-life was made up of imaginings. She imagined and pretended things until she almost believed them and she would scarcely have been surprised at any remarkable thing that could have happened. So she insisted to herself that Emily understood all about her troubles and was really her friend.

"As to answering," she used to say, "I don't answer very often. I never answer when I can help it. When people are insulting you, there is nothing so good for them as not to say a word—just to look at them and *think*. Miss Minchin turns pale with rage when I do it, Miss Amelia looks frightened, so do the girls. They know you are stronger than they are, because you are strong enough to hold in your rage and they are not, and they say stupid things they wish they had n't said, afterward. There 's nothing so strong as rage, except what makes you hold it in—that 's stronger. It 's a good thing not to answer your enemies. I scarcely ever do. Perhaps Emily is more like me than I am like myself. Perhaps she would rather not answer her friends, even. She keeps it all in her heart."

But though she tried to satisfy herself with these arguments, Sara did not find it easy. When, after a long, hard day, in which she had been sent here and there, sometimes on long errands, through wind and cold and rain; and, when she came in wet and hungry, had been sent out again because nobody chose to remember that she was only a child, and that her thin little legs might be tired, and her small body, clad in its forlorn too small finery, all too short and too tight, might be chilled; when she had been given only harsh words and cold, slighting looks for thanks; when the cook had been vulgar and insolent; when Miss Minchin had been in her worst moods, and when she had seen the girls sneering at her among themselves and making fun of her poor, outgrown clothes,—then Sara did not find Emily quite all that her sore, proud, desolate little heart needed as the doll sat in her old chair and stared.

One of these nights, when she came up to the garret cold, hungry, tired, and with a tempest raging in her small breast, Emily's stare seemed so vacant, her sawdust legs and arms so limp and inexpressive, that Sara lost all control over herself.

"I shall die presently!" she said at first.

Emily stared.

"I can't bear this!" said the poor child, trembling. "I know I shall die. I 'm cold, I 'm wet, I 'm starving to death. I 've walked a thousand miles to-day, and they have done nothing but scold me from morning until night. And because I could not find that last thing they sent me for, they would not give me any supper. Some men laughed at me because my old shoes made me slip down in the mud. I 'm covered with mud now. And they laughed! Do you *hear?*"

She looked at the staring glass eyes and complacent wax face, and suddenly a sort of heart-broken rage seized her. She lifted her little savage hand and knocked Emily off the chair, bursting into a passion of sobbing.

"You are nothing but a Doll!" she cried. "Nothing but a Doll—Doll—Doll! You care for nothing. You are stuffed with sawdust. You never had a heart. Nothing could ever make you feel. You are a *Doll!*" Emily lay upon the floor, with her legs ignominiously doubled up over her head, and a new flat place on the end of her nose; but she was still calm, even dignified.

Sara hid her face on her arms and sobbed. Some rats in the wall began to fight and bite each other, and squeak and scramble. But, as I have already intimated, Sara was not in the habit of crying. After a while she stopped, and when she stopped, she looked at Emily, who seemed to be gazing at her around the side of one ankle, and actually with a kind of glassy-eyed sympathy. Sara bent and picked her up. Remorse overtook her.

"You can't help being a doll," she said, with a resigned sigh, "any more than those girls downstairs can help not having any sense. We are not all alike. Perhaps you do your sawdust best."

None of Miss Minchin's young ladies were very remarkable for being brilliant; they were Select, but some of them were very dull, and some of them were fond of applying themselves to their lessons. Sara, who snatched her lessons at all sorts of untimely hours from tattered and discarded books, and who had a hungry craving for everything readable, was often severe upon them in her small mind. They had books they never read; she had no books at all. If she had always had something to read, she would not have been so lonely. She liked romances and history and poetry; she would read anything. There was a sentimental house-maid in the establishment who bought weekly penny papers, and subscribed to a circulating library, from which she got greasy volumes containing stories of marquises and dukes who invariably fell in love with orange-girls and gypsies and servant-maids, and made them the proud brides of coronets; and Sara often did parts of this maid's work, so that she might earn the privilege of reading these romantic histories. There was also a fat, dull pupil, whose name was Ermengarde St. John, who was one of her resources. Ermengarde had an intellectual father who, in his despairing desire to encourage his daughter, constantly sent her valuable and interesting books, which were a continual source of grief to her. Sara had once actually found her crying over a big package of them.

"What is the matter with you?" she asked her, perhaps rather disdainfully.

And it is just possible she would not have spoken to her, if she had not seen the books. The sight of books always gave Sara a hungry feeling, and she could not help drawing near to them if only to read their titles.

"What is the matter with you?" she asked.

"My papa has sent me some more books," answered Ermengarde wofully, "and he expects me to read them.

"Don't you like reading?" said Sara.

"I hate it!" replied Miss Ermengarde St. John. "And he will ask me questions when he sees me; he will want to know how much I remember! how would *you* like to have to read all those?"

"I'd like it better than anything else in the world," said Sara.

Ermengarde wiped her eyes to look at such a prodigy.

"Oh, gracious!" she exclaimed.

Sara returned the look with interest. A sudden plan formed itself in her sharp mind.

"Look here!" she said. "If you'll lend me those books, I'll read them and tell you everything that's in them afterward, and I'll tell it to you so that you will remember it. I know I can. The A B C children always remember what I tell them."

"Oh, goodness!" said Ermengarde. "Do you think you could?"

"I know I could," answered Sara. "I like to read, and I always remember. I 'll take care of the books, too; they will look just as new as they do now, when I give them back to you."

Ermengarde put her handkerchief in her pocket.

"If you 'll do that," she said, "and if you 'll make me remember, I 'll give you—I 'll give you some money."

"I don't want your money," said Sara, "I want your books—I want them." And her eyes grew big and queer, and her chest heaved once.

"Take them, then," said Ermengarde; "I wish I wanted them, but I am not clever, and my father is, and he thinks I ought to be."

Sara picked up the books and marched off with them. But when she was at the door, she stopped and turned around.

"What are you going to tell your father?" she asked.

"Oh," said Ermengarde, "he need n't know; he 'll think I 've read them."

Sara looked down at the books; her heart really began to beat fast.

"I won't do it," she said rather slowly, "if you are going to tell him lies about it—I don't like lies. Why can't you tell him I read them and then told you about them?"

"But he wants me to read them," said Ermengarde.

"He wants you to know what is in them," said Sara; "and if I can tell it to you in an easy way and make you remember, I should think he would like that."

"He would like it better if I read them myself," replied Ermengarde.

"He will like it, I dare say, if you learn anything in any way," said Sara. "I should, if I were your father."

And though this was not a flattering way of stating the case, Ermengarde was obliged to admit it was true, and, after a little more argument, gave in. And so she used afterward always to hand over her books to Sara, and Sara would carry them to her garret and devour them; and after she had read each volume, she would return it and tell Ermengarde about it in a way of her own. She had a gift for making things interesting. Her imagination helped her to make everything rather like a story, and she managed this matter so well that Miss St. John gained more information from her books than she would have gained if she had read them three times over by her poor stupid little self. When Sara sat down by her and began to tell some story of travel or history, she made the travelers and historical people seem real; and Ermengarde used to sit and regard her dramatic gesticulations, her thin little flushed cheeks and her shining odd eyes, with amazement.

"It sounds nicer than it seems in the book," she would say. I never cared about Mary, Queen of Scots, before, and I always hated the French Revolution, but you make it seem like a story."

"It is a story," Sara would answer. "They are all stories. Everything is a story—everything in this world. You are a story—I am a story—Miss Minchin is a story. You can make a story out of anything."

"I can't," said Ermengarde.

Sara stared at her a minute reflectively.

"No," she said at last. "I suppose you could n't. You are a little like Emily."

"Who is Emily?"

Sara recollected herself. She knew she was sometimes rather impolite in the candor of her remarks, and she did not want to be impolite to a girl who was not unkind —only stupid. Notwithstanding all her sharp little ways, she had the sense to wish to be just to everybody. In the hours she spent alone, she used to argue out a great many curious questions with herself. One thing she had decided upon was, that a person who was clever ought to be clever enough not to be unjust or deliberately unkind to any one. Miss Minchin was unjust and cruel, Miss Amelia was unkind and spiteful, the cook was malicious and hastytempered—they all were stupid, and made her despise them, and she desired to be as unlike them as possible. So she would be as polite as she could to people who in the least deserved politeness.

"Emily is—a person—I know," she replied.

"Do you like her?" asked Ermengarde.

"Yes, I do," said Sara.

Ermengarde examined her queer little face and figure again. She did look odd. She had on, that day, a faded blue plush skirt, which barely covered her knees, a brown cloth sacque, and a pair of olivegreen stockings which Miss Minchin had made her piece out with black ones, so that they would be long enough to be kept on. And yet Ermengarde was beginning slowly to admire her. Such a forlorn, thin, neglected little thing as that, who could read and read and remember and tell you things so that they did not tire you all out! A child who could speak French, and who had learned German, no one knew how! One could not help staring at her and feeling interested, particularly one to whom the simplest lesson was a trouble and a woe.

"Do you like me?" said Ermengarde, finally, at the end of her scrutiny.

Sara hesitated one second, then she answered:

"I like you because you are not ill-natured —I like you for letting me read your books —I like you because you don't make spiteful fun of me for what I can't help. It 's not your fault that——"

She pulled herself up quickly. She had been going to say, "that you are stupid."

"That what?" asked Ermengarde.

"That you can't learn things quickly. If you can't, you can't. If I can, why, I can— that 's all." She paused a minute, looking at the plump face before her, and then, rather slowly, one of her wise, oldfashioned thoughts came to her.

"Perhaps," she said, "to be able to learn things quickly, is n't everything. To be kind is worth a good deal to other people. If Miss Minchin knew everything on earth, which she does n't, and if she was like what she is now, she 'd still be a detestable thing, and everybody would hate her. Lots of clever people have done harm and been wicked. Look at Robespierre——"

She stopped again, and examined her companion's countenance.

"Do you remember about him?" she demanded. "I believe you 've forgotten."

"Well, I don't remember all of it," admitted Ermengarde.

"Well," said Sara with courage and determination, "I 'll tell it to you over again."

And she plunged once more into the gory records of the French Revolution, and told such stories of it, and made such vivid pictures of its horrors, that Miss St. John was afraid to go to bed afterward, and hid her head under the blankets when she did go, and shivered until she fell asleep. But afterward she preserved lively recollections of the character of Robespierre, and did not even forget Marie Antoinette and the Princess de Lamballe.

"You know they put her head on a pike and danced around it," Sara had said; "and she had beautiful blonde hair; and when I think of her, I never see her head on her body, but always on a pike, with those furious people dancing and howling."

Yes, it was true, to this imaginative child everything was a story; and the more books she read the more imaginative she became. One of her chief entertainments was to sit in her garret, or walk about it, and "suppose" things. On a cold night, when she had not had enough to eat, she would draw the red footstool up before the empty grate, and say in the most intense voice:

"Suppose there was a great, wide steel grate here, and a great glowing fire—a *glowing* fire—with beds of red-hot coal and lots of little dancing, flickering flames. Suppose there was a soft, deep rug, and this was a comfortable chair, all cushions and crimson velvet; and suppose I had a crimson velvet frock on, and a deep lace collar, like a child in a picture; and suppose all the rest of the room was furnished in lovely colors, and there were book-shelves full of books, which changed by magic as soon as you had read them; and suppose there was a little table here, with a snow-white cover on it, and little silver dishes, and in one there was hot, hot soup, and in another a roast chicken, and in another some raspberry-jam tarts with criss-cross on them, and in another some grapes; and suppose Emily could speak, and we could sit and eat our supper, and then talk and read; and then suppose there was a soft, warm bed in the corner, and when we were tired, we could go to sleep, and sleep as long as we liked."

Sometimes, after she had supposed things like these for half an hour, she would feel almost warm, and would creep into bed with Emily and fall asleep with a smile on her face.

"What large, downy pillows!" she would whisper. "What white sheets and fleecy blankets!" And she almost forgot that her real pillows had scarcely any feathers in them at all, and smelled musty, and that her blankets and coverlid were thin and full of holes.

At another time she would "suppose" she was a princess, and then she would go about the house with an expression on her face which was a source of great secret annoyance to Miss Minchin, because it seemed as if the child scarcely heard the spiteful, insulting things said to her, or, if she heard them, did not care for them at all. Sometimes, while she was in the midst of some harsh and cruel speech, Miss Minchin would find the odd, unchildish eyes fixed upon her with something like a proud smile in them. At such times she did not know that Sara was saying to herself:

"You don't know that you are saying these things to a princess, and that if I chose, I could wave my hand and order you to execution. I only spare you because I *am* a princess, and you are a poor, stupid, old, vulgar thing, and don't know any better."

This used to please and amuse her more than anything else; and, queer and fanciful as it was, she found comfort in it, and it was not a bad thing for her. It really kept her from being made rude and malicious by the rudeness and malice of those about her.

"A princess must be polite," she said to herself. And so when the servants, who took their tone from their mistress, were insolent and ordered her about, she would hold her head erect, and reply to them sometimes in a way which made them stare at her, it was so quaintly civil.

"I am a princess in rags and tatters," she would think, "but I am a princess, inside. It would be easy to be a princess if I were dressed in cloth-of-gold; it is a great deal more of a triumph to be one all the time when no one knows it. There was Marie Antoinette: when she was in prison, and her throne was gone and she had only a black gown on, and her hair was white, and they insulted her and called her the Widow Capet,—she was a great deal more like a queen then than when she was so gay and had everything grand. I like her best then. Those howling mobs of people did not frighten her. She was stronger than they were, even when they cut her head off."

Once when such thoughts were passing through her mind, the look in her eyes so enraged Miss Minchin that she flew at Sara and boxed her ears.

Sara wakened from her dream, started a little, and then broke into a laugh.

"What are you laughing at, you bold, impudent child!" exclaimed Miss Minchin.

It took Sara a few seconds to remember she was a princess. Her cheeks were red and smarting from the blows she had received.

"I was thinking," she said.

"Beg my pardon immediately," said Miss Minchin.

"I will beg your pardon for laughing, if it was rude," said Sara; "but I won't beg your pardon for thinking."

"What were you thinking?" demanded Miss Minchin. "How dare you think? What were you thinking?"

This occurred in the school-room, and all the girls looked up from their books to listen. It always interested them when Miss Minchin flew at Sara, because Sara always said something queer, and never seemed in the least frightened. She was not in the least frightened now, though her boxed ears were scarlet, and her eyes were as bright as stars.

"I was thinking," she answered gravely and quite politely, "that you did not know what you were doing."

"That I did not know what I was doing!" Miss Minchin fairly gasped.

"Yes," said Sara, "and I was thinking what would happen, if I were a princess and you boxed my ears—what I should do to you. And I was thinking that if I were one, you would never dare to do it, whatever I said or did. And I was thinking how surprised and frightened you would be if you suddenly found out——"

She had the imagined picture so clearly before her eyes, that she spoke in a manner which had an effect even on Miss Minchin. It almost seemed for the moment to her narrow unimaginative mind that there must be some real power behind this candid daring.

"What?" she exclaimed; "found out what?"

"That I really was a princess," said Sara, "and could do anything—anything I liked."

"Go to your room," cried Miss Minchin breathlessly, "this instant. Leave the school-room. Attend to your lessons, young ladies."

Sara made a little bow.

"Excuse me for laughing, if it was impolite," she said, and walked out of the room, leaving Miss Minchin in a rage and the girls whispering over their books.

"I should n't be at all surprised if she did turn out to be something," said one of them. "Suppose she should!"

PART II

THAT very afternoon Sara had an opportunity of proving to herself whether she was really a princess or not. It was a dreadful afternoon. For several days it had rained continuously, the streets were chilly and sloppy; there was mud everywhere—sticky London mud—and over everything a pall of fog and drizzle. Of course there were several long and tiresome errands to be done,—there always were on days like this,—and Sara was sent out again and again, until her shabby clothes were damp through. The absurd old feathers on her forlorn hat were more draggled and absurd than ever, and her down-trodden shoes were so wet they could not hold any more water. Added to this, she had been deprived of her dinner, because Miss Minchin wished to punish her. She was very hungry. She was so cold and hungry and tired that her little face had a pinched look, and now and then some kindhearted person passing her in the crowded street glanced at her with sympathy. But she did not know that. She hurried on, trying to comfort herself in that queer way of hers by pretending and "supposing,"—but really this time it was harder than she had ever found it, and once or twice she thought it almost made her more cold and hungry instead of less so. But she persevered obstinately. "Suppose I had dry clothes on," she thought. "Suppose I had good shoes and a long thick coat and merino stockings and a whole umbrella. And suppose—suppose, just when I was near a baker's where they sold hot buns, I should find sixpence—which belonged to nobody. Suppose, if I did, I should go into the shop and buy six of the hottest buns and should eat them all without stopping."

Some very odd things happen in this world sometimes. It certainly was an odd thing which happened to Sara. She had to cross the street just as she was saying this to herself—the mud was dreadful—she almost had to wade. She picked her way as carefully as she could, but she could not save herself much; only, in picking her way she had to look down at her feet and the mud, and in looking down—just as she reached the pavement—she saw something shining in the gutter. A piece of silver—a tiny piece trodden upon by many feet, but still with spirit enough left to shine a little. Not quite a sixpence, but the next thing to it—a four-penny piece! In one second it was in her cold, little, red and blue hand.

"Oh!" she gasped. "It is true!"

And then, if you will believe me, she looked straight before her at the shop directly facing her. And it was a baker's, and a cheerful, stout, motherly woman, with rosy cheeks, was just putting into the window a tray of delicious hot buns,—large, plump, shiny buns, with currants in them. It almost made Sara feel faint for a few

seconds—the shock and the sight of the buns and the delightful odors of warm bread floating up through the baker's cellar-window.

She knew that she need not hesitate to use the little piece of money. It had evidently been lying in the mud for some time, and its owner was completely lost in the streams of passing people who crowded and jostled each other all through the day.

"But I 'll go and ask the baker's woman if she has lost a piece of money," she said to herself, rather faintly.

So she crossed the pavement and put her wet foot on the step of the shop; and as she did so she saw something which made her stop.

It was a little figure more forlorn than her own—a little figure which was not much more than a bundle of rags, from which small, bare, red and muddy feet peeped out—only because the rags with which the wearer was trying to cover them were not long enough. Above the rags appeared a shock head of tangled hair and a dirty face, with big, hollow, hungry eyes.

Sara knew they were hungry eyes the moment she saw them, and she felt a sudden sympathy.

"This," she said to herself, with a little sigh, "is one of the Populace—and she is hungrier than I am."

The child—this "one of the Populace"—stared up at Sara, and shuffled herself aside a little, so as to give her more room. She was used to being made to give room to everybody. She knew that if a policeman chanced to see her, he would tell her to "move on."

Sara clutched her little four-penny piece, and hesitated a few seconds. Then she spoke to her.

"Are you hungry?" she asked.

The child shuffled herself and her rags a little more.

"Ain't I jist!" she said, in a hoarse voice. "Jist ain't I!"

"Have n't you had any dinner?" said Sara.

"No dinner," more hoarsely still and with more shuffling, "nor yet no bre'fast—nor yet no supper—nor nothin'."

"Since when?" asked Sara.

"Dun'no'. Never got nothin' to-day—no-where. I've axed and axed."

Just to look at her made Sara more hungry and faint. But those queer little thoughts were at work in her brain, and she was talking to herself though she was sick at heart.

"If I 'm a princess," she was saying—"if I 'm a princess——! When they were poor and driven from their thrones—they always shared—with the Populace—if they met one poorer and hungrier. They always shared. Buns are a penny each. If it had been sixpence! I could have eaten six. It won't be enough for either of us—but it will be better than nothing."

"Wait a minute," she said to the beggar-child. She went into the shop. It was warm and smelled delightfully. The woman was just going to put more hot buns in the window.

"If you please," said Sara, "have you lost fourpence—a silver fourpence?" And she held the forlorn little piece of money out to her.

The woman looked at it and at her—at her intense little face and draggled, once-fine clothes.

"Bless us—no," she answered. "Did you find it?"

"In the gutter," said Sara.

"Keep it, then," said the woman. "It may have been there a week, and goodness knows who lost it. *You* could never find out."

"I know that," said Sara, "but I thought I 'd ask you."

"Not many would," said the woman, looking puzzled and interested and good-natured all at once. "Do you want to buy something?" she added, as she saw Sara glance toward the buns.

"Four buns, if you please," said Sara; "those at a penny each."

The woman went to the window and put some in a paper bag. Sara noticed that she put in six.

"I said four, if you please," she explained. "I have only the fourpence."

"I 'll throw in two for make-weight," said the woman, with her good-natured look. "I dare say you can eat them some time. Are n't you hungry?"

A mist rose before Sara's eyes.

"Yes," she answered. "I am very hungry, and I am much obliged to you for your kindness and," she was going to add, "there is a child outside who is hungrier than I am." But just at that moment two or three customers came in at once and each one seemed in a hurry, so she could only thank the woman again and go out.

The child was still huddled up on the corner of the steps. She looked frightful in her wet and dirty rags. She was staring with a stupid look of suffering straight be-fore her, and Sara saw her suddenly draw the back of her roughened, black hand across her eyes to rub away the tears which seemed to have surprised her by forcing their way from under her lids. She was muttering to herself.

Sara opened the paper bag and took out one of the hot buns, which had already warmed her cold hands a little.

"See," she said, putting the bun on the ragged lap, "that is nice and hot. Eat it, and you will not be so hungry."

The child started and stared up at her; then she snatched up the bun and began to cram it into her mouth with great wolfish bites. "Oh, my! Oh, my!" Sara heard her say hoarsely, in wild delight.

"Oh, my!"

Sara took out three more buns and put them down.

"She is hungrier than I am," she said to herself. "She 's starving." But her hand trembled when she put down the fourth bun. "I'm not starving," she said—and she put down the fifth.

The little starving London savage was still snatching and devouring when she turned away. She was too ravenous to give any thanks, even if she had been taught politeness—which she had not. She was only a poor little wild animal.

"Good-bye," said Sara.

When she reached the other side of the street she looked back. The child had a bun in both hands, and had stopped in the middle of a bite to watch her. Sara gave her a little nod, and the child, after another stare, —a curious, longing stare,—jerked her shaggy head in response, and until Sara was out of sight she did not take another bite or even finish the one she had begun.

At that moment the baker-woman glanced out of her shop-window.

"Well, I never!" she exclaimed. "If that young 'un has n't given her buns to a beggar-child. "It was n't because she did n't want them, either—well, well, she looked hungry enough. I 'd give something to know what she did it for." She stood behind her window for a few moments and pondered. Then her curiosity got the better of her. She went to the door and spoke to the beggar-child.

"Who gave you those buns?" she asked her.

The child nodded her head toward Sara's vanishing figure.

"What did she say?" inquired the woman.

"Axed me if I was 'ungry," replied the hoarse voice.

"What did you say?"

"Said I was jist!"

"And then she came in and got buns and came out and give them to you, did she?"

The child nodded.

"How many?"

"Five."

The woman thought it over. "Left just one for herself," she said, in a low voice. "And she could have eaten the whole six—I saw it in her eyes."

She looked after the little, draggled, far-away figure, and felt more disturbed in her usually comfortable mind than she had felt for many a day.

"I wish she had n't gone so quick," she said. "I 'm blest if she should n't have had a dozen."

Then she turned to the child.

"Are you hungry, yet?" she asked.

"I 'm allus 'ungry," was the answer; "but 't ain't so bad as it was."

"Come in here," said the woman and she held open the shop-door.

The child got up and shuffled in. To be invited into a warm place full of bread seemed an incredible thing. She did not know what was going to happen; she did not care, even.

"Get yourself warm," said the woman, pointing to a fire in a tiny back room. "And,

look here,—when you 're hard up for a bit of bread, you can come here and ask for it. I 'm blest if I won't give it you for that young 'un's sake."

Sara found some comfort in her remaining bun. It was hot; and it was a great deal better than nothing. She broke off small pieces and ate them slowly to make it last longer.

"Suppose it was a magic bun," she said, "and a bit was as much as a whole dinner. I should be over-eating myself if I went on like this."

It was dark when she reached the square in which Miss Minchin's Select Seminary was situated; the lamps were lighted, and in most of the windows gleams of light were to be seen. It always interested Sara to catch glimpses of the rooms before the shutters were closed. She liked to imagine things about the people who sat before the fires in the houses, or who bent over books at the tables. There was, for instance, the Large Family opposite. She called these people the Large Family—not because they were large, for indeed most of them were little, but because there were so many of them. There were eight children in the Large Family, and a stout rosy mother, and a stout rosy father, and a stout rosy grandmamma, and any number of servants. The eight children were always either being taken out to walk, or to ride in perambulators, by comfortable nurses; or they were going to drive with their mamma; or they were flying to the door in the evening to kiss their papa and dance around him and drag off his overcoat and look for packages in the pockets of it; or they were crowding about the nursery windows and looking out and pushing each other and laughing,—in fact they were always doing something which seemed enjoyable and suited to the tastes of a large family. Sara was quite attached to them and had given them all names out of books. She called them the Montmorencys, when she did not call them the Large Family. The fat, fair baby with the lace cap was Ethelberta Beauchamp Montmorency; the next baby was Violet Cholmondely Montmorency; the little boy who could just stagger, and who had such round legs, was Sydney Cecil Vivian Montmorency; and then came Lilian Evangeline, Guy Clarence, Maud Marian, Rosalind Gladys, Veronica Eustacia, and Claude Harold Hector.

Next door to the Large Family lived the Maiden Lady, who had a companion, and two parrots, and a King Charles spaniel; but Sara was not so very fond of her, because she did nothing in particular but talk to the parrots and drive out with the spaniel. The most interesting person of all lived next door to Mrs. Minchin herself. Sara called him the Indian Gentleman. He was an elderly gentleman who was said to have lived in the East Indies, and to be immensely rich and to have something the matter with his liver,—in fact, it had been rumored that he had no liver at all, and was much inconvenienced by the fact. At any rate, he was very yellow and he did not look happy; and when he went out to his carriage, he was almost always wrapped up in shawls and overcoats, as if he were cold. He had a native servant who looked even colder than himself, and he had a monkey who looked colder than the native servant. Sara had seen the monkey sitting on a table, in the sun, in the parlor-window, and he always wore such a mournful expression that she sympathized with him deeply.

"I dare say," she used sometimes to remark to herself, "he is thinking all the time of cocoa-nut trees and of swinging by his tail under a tropical sun. He might have had a family dependent on him, too, poor thing!"

The native servant, whom she called the Lascar, looked mournful too, but he was evidently very faithful to his master.

"Perhaps he saved his master's life in the Sepoy rebellion," she thought. "They look as if they might have had all sorts of adventures. I wish I could speak to the Lascar. I remember a little Hindustani."

And one day she actually did speak to him, and his start at the sound of his own language expressed a great deal of surprise and delight. He was waiting for his master to come out to the carriage, and Sara, who was going on an errand as usual, stopped and spoke a few words. She had a special gift for languages and had remembered enough Hindustani to make herself understood by him. When his master came out, the Lascar spoke to him quickly, and the Indian Gentleman turned and looked at her curiously. And afterward the Lascar always greeted her with salaams of the most profound description. And occasionally they exchanged a few words. She learned that it was true that the Sahib was very rich—that he was ill—and also that he had no wife nor children, and that England did not agree with the monkey.

"He must be as lonely as I am," thought Sara. "Being rich does not seem to make him happy."

That evening, as she passed the windows, the Lascar was closing the shutters, and she caught a glimpse of the room inside. There was a bright fire glowing in the grate, and the Indian Gentleman was sitting before it, in a luxurious chair. The room was richly furnished and looked delightfully comfortable, but the Indian Gentleman sat with his head resting on his hand and looked as lonely and unhappy as ever.

"Poor man!" said Sara; "I wonder what *you* are 'supposing'?"

When she went into the house she met Miss Minchin in the hall.

"Where have you wasted your time?" said Miss Minchin. "You have been out for hours!"

"It was so wet and muddy," Sara answered. "It was hard to walk, because my shoes were so bad and slipped about so."

"Make no excuses," said Miss Minchin, "and tell no falsehoods."

Sara went downstairs to the kitchen.

"Why did n't you stay all night?" said the cook.

"Here are the things," said Sara, and laid her purchases on the table.

The cook looked over them, grumbling. She was in a very bad temper indeed.

"May I have something to eat?" Sara asked, rather faintly.

"Tea 's over and done with," was the answer. "Did you expect me to keep it hot for you?"

Sara was silent a second.

"I had no dinner," she said, and her voice was quite low. She made it low, because she was afraid it would tremble.

"There 's some bread in the pantry," said the cook. "That 's all you 'll get at this time of day."

Sara went and found the bread. It was old and hard and dry. The cook was in too bad a humor to give her anything to eat with it. She had just been scolded by Miss Minchin, and it was always safe and easy to vent her own spite on Sara.

Really it was hard for the child to climb the three long flights of stairs leading to her garret. She often found them long and steep when she was tired, but to-night it seemed as if she would never reach the top. Several times a lump rose in her throat, and she was obliged to stop to rest.

"I can't pretend anything more to-night," she said wearily to herself. "I 'm sure I can't. I 'll eat my bread and drink some water and then go to sleep, and perhaps a dream will come and pretend for me. I wonder what dreams are."

Yes, when she reached the top landing there were tears in her eyes, and she did not feel like a princess—only like a tired, hungry lonely, lonely child.

"If my papa had lived," she said "they would not have treated me like this. If my papa had lived, he would have taken care of me."

Then she turned the handle and opened the garret-door.

Can you imagine it—can you believe it? I find it hard to believe it myself. And Sara found it impossible; for the first few moments she thought something strange had happened to her eyes—to her mind—that the dream had come before she had had time to fall asleep.

"Oh!" she exclaimed breathlessly. "Oh! It is n't true! I know, I know it is n't true!" And she slipped into the room and closed the door and locked it, and stood with her back against it, staring straight before her.

Do you wonder? In the grate, which had been empty and rusty and cold when she left it, but which now was blackened and polished up quite respectably, there was a glowing, blazing fire. On the hob was a little brass kettle, hissing and boiling; spread upon the floor was a warm, thick rug; before the fire was a folding-chair, unfolded and with cushions on it; by the chair was a small folding-table, unfolded, covered with a white cloth, and upon it were spread small covered dishes, a cup and saucer, and a tea-pot; on the bed were new, warm coverings, a curious wadded silk robe and some books. The little, cold, miserable room seemed changed into Fairyland. It was actually warm and glowing.

"It is bewitched!" said Sara. "Or I am bewitched. I only *think* I see it all; but if I can only keep on thinking it, I don't care—I don't care,—if I can only keep it up!"

She was afraid to move, for fear it would melt away. She stood with her back against the door and looked and looked. But soon she began to feel warm, and then she moved forward.

"A fire that I only *thought* I saw surely would n't *feel* warm," she said. "It feels real—real."

She went to it and knelt before it. She touched the chair, the table; she lifted the cover of one of the dishes. There was something hot and savory in it—something delicious. The teapot had tea in it, ready for the boiling water from the little kettle; one plate had toast on it, another, muffins.

"It is real," said Sara. "The fire is real enough to warm me. I can sit in the chair; the things are real enough to eat."

It was like a fairy story come true—it was heavenly. She went to the bed and touched the blankets and the wrap. They were real too. She opened one book, and on the title-page was written in a strange hand, "The little girl in the attic."

Suddenly—was it a strange thing for her to do?—Sara put her face down on the queer foreign-looking quilted robe and burst into tears.

"I don't know who it is," she said, "but somebody cares about me a little—somebody is my friend."

Somehow that thought warmed her more than the fire. She had never had a friend since those happy, luxurious days when she had had everything; and those days had seemed such a long way off—so far away as to be only like dreams—during these last years at Miss Minchin's.

She really cried more at this strange thought of having a friend—even though an unknown one—than she had cried over many of her worst troubles.

But these tears seemed different from the others, for when she had wiped them away they did not seem to leave her eyes and her heart hot and smarting.

And then imagine, if you can, what the rest of the evening was like. The delicious comfort of taking off the damp clothes and putting on the soft, warm, quilted robe before the glowing fire—of slipping her cold feet into the luscious little wool-lined slippers she found near her chair. And then the hot tea and savory dishes, the cushioned chair and the books!

It was just like Sara, that, once having found the things real, she should give herself up to the enjoyment of them to the very utmost. She had lived such a life of imaginings, and had found her pleasure so long in improbabilities, that she was quite equal to accepting any wonderful thing that happened. After she was quite warm and had eaten her supper and enjoyed herself for an hour or so, it had almost ceased to be surprising to her, that such magical surroundings should be hers. As to finding out who had done all this, she knew that it was out of the question. She did not know a human soul by whom it could seem in the least degree probable that it could have been done.

"There is nobody," she said to herself, "nobody." She discussed the matter with Emily, it is true, but more because it was delightful to talk about it than with a view to making any discoveries.

"But we have a friend, Emily," she said; "we have a friend."

PART III

SARA could not even imagine a being charming enough to fill her grand ideal of her mysterious benefactor. If she tried to make in her mind a picture of him or her, it ended by being something glittering and strange—not at all like a real person, but bearing resemblance to a sort of Eastern magician, with long robes and a wand. And when she fell asleep, beneath the soft white blanket, she dreamed all night of this magnificent personage, and talked to him in Hindustani, and made salaams to him.

Upon one thing she was determined. She

would not speak to any one of her good fortune—it should be her own secret; in fact, she was rather inclined to think that if Miss Minchin knew, she would take her treasures from her or in some way spoil her pleasure. So when she went down the next morning she shut her door very tight and did her best to look as if nothing unusual had occurred. And yet this was rather hard, because she could not help remembering, every now and then, with a sort of start, and her heart would beat quickly every time she repeated to herself, "I have a friend!"

It was a friend who evidently meant to continue to be kind, for when she went to her garret the next night—and she opened the door, it must be confessed, with rather an excited feeling—she found that the same hands had been again at work and had done even more than before. The fire and the supper were again there, and beside them a number of other things which so altered the look of the garret that Sara quite lost her breath. A piece of bright, strange, heavy cloth covered the battered mantel, and on it some ornaments had been placed. All the bare, ugly things which could be covered with draperies had been concealed and made to look quite pretty. Some odd materials in rich colors had been fastened against the walls with fine sharp tacks—so sharp that they could be pressed into the wood without hammering. Some brilliant fans were pinned up, and there were several large cushions. A long old wooden box was covered with a rug, and some cushions lay on it, so that it wore quite the air of a sofa.

Sara simply sat down, and looked, and looked again.

"It is exactly like something fairy come true," she said; "there is n't the least difference. I feel as if I might wish for anything, —diamonds and bags of gold,—and they would appear! *That* could n't be any

stranger than this. Is this my garret? Am I the same cold, ragged, damp Sara? And to think how I used to pretend, and pretend, and wish there were fairies! The one thing I always wanted was to see a fairy story come true. I am *living* in a fairy story! I feel as if I might be a fairy myself, and be able to turn things into anything else!"

It was like a fairy story, and, what was best of all, it continued. Almost every day something new was done to the garret. Some new comfort or ornament appeared in it when Sara opened her door at night, until actually, in a short time, it was a bright little room, full of all sorts of odd and luxurious things. And the magician had taken care that the child should not be hungry, and that she should have as many books as she could read. When she left the room in the morning the remains of her supper were on the table, and when she returned in the evening, the magician had removed them, and left another nice little meal. Downstairs Miss Minchin was as cruel and insulting as ever,—Mrs. Amelia was as peevish, and the servants were as vulgar. Sara was sent on errands and scolded and driven hither and thither, but somehow it seemed as if she could bear it all. The delightful sense of romance and mystery lifted her above the cook's temper and malice. The comfort she enjoyed and could always look forward to was making her stronger. If she came home from her errands wet and tired, she knew she would soon be warm, after she had climbed the stairs. In a few weeks she began to look less thin. A little color came into her cheeks, and her eyes did not seem much too big for her face.

It was just when this was beginning to be so apparent that Miss Minchin sometimes stared at her questioningly, that another wonderful thing happened. A man came to the door and left several parcels. All were addressed (in large letters) to "the little girl in the attic." Sara herself was sent to open the door and she took them in. She laid the two largest parcels down on the hall-table and was looking at the address, when Miss Minchin came down the stairs.

"Take the things upstairs to the young lady to whom they belong," she said. "Don't stand there staring at them."

"They belong to me," answered Sara, quietly.

"To you!" exclaimed Miss Minchin. "What do you mean?"

"I don't know where they come from," said Sara, "but they 're addressed to me."

Miss Minchin came to her side and looked at them with an excited expression.

"What is in them?" she demanded.

"I don't know," said Sara.

"Open them!" she demanded, still more excitedly.

Sara did as she was told. They contained pretty and comfortable clothing,—clothing of different kinds; shoes and stockings and gloves, a warm coat, and even an umbrella. On the pocket of the coat was pinned a paper on which was written, "To be worn every day—will be replaced by others when necessary."

Miss Minchin was quite agitated. This was an incident which suggested strange things to her sordid mind. Could it be that she had made a mistake after all and that the child so neglected and so unkindly treated by her had some powerful friend in the background? It would not be very pleasant if there should be such a friend, and he or she should learn all the truth about the thin, shabby clothes, the scant food, the hard work. She felt very queer indeed and uncertain, and she gave a side-glance at Sara.

"Well," she said, in a voice such as she had never used since the day the child lost her father—"well, some one is very kind to you. As you have the things and are to have new ones when they are worn out, you may

as well go and put them on and look respectable; and after you are dressed, you may come downstairs and learn your lessons in the school-room."

So it happened that, about half an hour afterward, Sara struck the entire school-room of pupils dumb with amazement, by making her appearance in a costume such as she had never worn since the change of fortune whereby she ceased to be a show-pupil and a parlor-boarder. She scarcely seemed to be the same Sara. She was neatly dressed in a pretty gown of warm browns and reds, and even her stockings and slippers were nice and dainty.

"Perhaps some one has left her a fortune," one of the girls whispered. "I always thought something would happen to her. She is so queer."

That night, when Sara went to her room, she carried out a plan she had been devising for some time. She wrote a note to her unknown friend. It ran as follows:

"I hope you will not think it is not polite that I should write this note to you when you wish to keep yourself a secret, but I do not mean to be impolite, or to try to find out at all, only I want to thank you for being so kind to me—so beautiful kind, and making everything like a fairy story. I am so grateful to you and I am so happy! I used to be so lonely and cold and hungry and now, oh, just think what you have done for me! Please let me say just these words. It seems as if I ought to say them. *Thank you —thank you—thank you!*

The Little Girl in the Attic."

The next morning she left this on the little table, and it was taken away with the other things; so she felt sure the magician had received it, and she was happier for the thought.

A few nights later a very odd thing happened. She found something in the room which she certainly would never have expected. When she came in as usual, she saw something small and dark in her chair,—an odd, tiny figure, which turned toward her a little weird-looking, wistful face.

"Why, it 's the monkey!" she cried. "It is the Indian Gentleman's monkey! Where can he have come from!"

It *was* the monkey, sitting up and looking so like a mite of a child that it really was quite pathetic; and very soon Sara found out how he happened to be in her room. The skylight was open, and it was easy to guess that he had crept out of his master's garret-window, which was only a few feet away and perfectly easy to get in and out of, even for a climber less agile than a monkey. He had probably climbed to the garret on a tour of investigation, and, getting out upon the roof, and being attracted by the light in Sara's attic, had crept in. At all events this seemed quite reasonable, and there he was; and when Sara went to him, he actually put out his queer, elfish little hands, caught her dress, and jumped into her arms.

"Oh, you queer, poor, ugly, foreign little thing!" said Sara, caressing him. "I can't help liking you. You look like a sort of baby, but I am so glad you are not, because your mother could *not* be proud of you, and nobody would dare to say you were like any of your relations. But I do like you; you have such a forlorn little look in your face. Perhaps you are sorry you are so ugly, and it 's always on your mind. I wonder if you have a mind?"

The monkey sat and looked at her while she talked, and seemed much interested in her remarks, if one could judge by his eyes and his forehead, and the way he moved his head up and down, and held it sideways and scratched it with his little hand. He examined Sara quite seriously, and anxiously, too. He felt the stuff of her dress, touched her hands, climbed up and examined her ears, and then sat on her shoulder holding a lock of her hair, looking mournful but not at all agitated. Upon the whole, he seemed pleased with Sara.

"But I must take you back," she said to him, "though I 'm sorry to have to do it. Oh, the company you *would* be to a person!"

She lifted him from her shoulder, set him on her knee, and gave him a bit of cake. He sat and nibbled it, and then put his head on one side, looked at her, wrinkled his forehead, and then nibbled again, in the most companionable manner.

"But you must go home," said Sara at last; and she took him in her arms to carry him downstairs. Evidently he did not want to leave the room, for as they reached the door he clung to her neck and gave a little scream of anger.

"You must n't be an ungrateful monkey," said Sara. "You ought to be fondest of your own family. I am sure the Lascar is good to you."

Nobody saw her on her way out, and very soon she was standing on the Indian Gentleman's front steps, and the Lascar had opened the door for her.

"I found your monkey in my room," she said in Hindustani. "I think he got in through the window."

The man began a rapid outpouring of thanks but just as he was in the midst of them, a fretful, hollow voice was heard through the open door of the nearest room. The instant he heard it the Lascar disappeared, and left Sara still holding the monkey.

It was not many moments, however, before he came back bringing a message. His master had told him to bring Miss into the library. The Sahib was very ill, but he wished to see Missy.

Sara thought this odd, but she remembered reading stories of Indian gentlemen who, having no constitutions, were extremely cross and full of whims, and who must have their own way. So she followed the Lascar.

When she entered the room the Indian Gentleman was lying on an easy chair, propped up with pillows. He looked frightfully ill. His yellow face was thin, and his eyes were hollow. He gave Sara a rather curious look—it was as if she wakened in him some anxious interest.

"You live next door?" he said.

"Yes," answered Sara. "I live at Miss Minchin's."

"She keeps a boarding-school?"

"Yes," said Sara.

"And you are one of her pupils?"

Sara hesitated a moment.

"I don't know exactly what I am," she replied.

"Why not?" asked the Indian Gentleman. The monkey gave a tiny squeak, and Sara stroked him

"At first," she said, "I was a pupil and a parlor-boarder; but now——"

"What do you mean by 'at first'?" asked the Indian Gentleman.

"When I was first taken there by my papa."

"Well, what has happened since then?" said the invalid, staring at her and knitting his brows with a puzzled expression.

"My papa died," said Sara. "He lost all his money, and there was none left for me —and there was no one to take care of me or pay Miss Minchin, so——"

"So you were sent up into the garret, and neglected, and made into a half-starved little drudge!" put in the Indian Gentleman. "That is about it, is n't it?"

The color deepened on Sara's cheeks.

"There was no one to take care of me, and no money," she said. "I belong to nobody."

"What did your father mean by losing his money?" said the gentleman, fretfully.

The red in Sara's cheeks grew deeper,

and she fixed her odd eyes on the yellow face.

"He did not lose it himself," she said. "He had a friend he was fond of, and it was his friend who took his money. I don't know how. I don't understand. He trusted his friend too much."

She saw the invalid start—the strangest start—as if he had been suddenly frightened. Then he spoke nervously and excitedly:

"That's an old story," he said. "It happens every day; but sometimes those who are blamed—those who do the wrong— don't intend it, and are not so bad. It may happen through a mistake—a miscalculation; they may not be so bad."

"No," said Sara, "but the suffering is just as bad for the others. It killed my papa."

The Indian Gentleman pushed aside some of the gorgeous wraps that covered him.

"Come a little nearer, and let me look at you," he said.

His voice sounded very strange; it had a more nervous and excited tone than before. Sara had an odd fancy that he was half afraid to look at her. She came and stood nearer, the monkey clinging to her and watching his master anxiously over his shoulder.

The Indian Gentleman's hollow, restless eyes fixed themselves on her.

"Yes," he said at last. "Yes; I can see it. Tell me your father's name."

"His name was Ralph Crewe," said Sara. "Captain Crewe. Perhaps,"—a sudden thought flashing upon her,—"perhaps you may have heard of him? He died in India."

The Indian Gentleman sank back upon his pillows. He looked very weak, and seemed out of breath.

"Yes," he said, "I knew him. I was his friend. I meant no harm. If he had only lived he would have known. It turned out well after all. He was a fine young fellow.

I was fond of him. I will make it right. Call—call the man."

Sara thought he was going to die. But there was no need to call the Lascar. He must have been waiting at the door. He was in the room and by his master's side in an instant. He seemed to know what to do. He lifted the drooping head, and gave the invalid something in a small glass. The Indian Gentleman lay panting for a few minutes, and then he spoke in an exhausted but eager voice, addressing the Lascar in Hindustani:

"Go for Carmichael," he said. "Tell him to come here at once. Tell him I have found the child!"

When Mr. Carmichael arrived (which occurred in a very few minutes, for it turned out that he was no other than the father of the Large Family across the street), Sara went home and was allowed to take the monkey with her. She certainly did not sleep very much that night, though the monkey behaved beautifully, and did not disturb her in the least. It was not the monkey that kept her awake—it was her thoughts, and her wonders as to what the Indian Gentleman had meant when he said, "Tell him I have found the child." "What child?" Sara kept asking herself. "I was the only child there; but how had he found me, and why did he want to find me? And what is he going to do, now I am found? Is it something about my papa? Do I belong to somebody? Is he one of my relations? Is something going to happen?"

But she found out the very next day, in the morning; and it seemed that she had been living in a story even more than she had imagined. First Mr. Carmichael came and had an interview with Miss Minchin. And it appeared that Mr. Carmichael, besides occupying the important situation of father to the Large Family, was a lawyer, and had charge of the affairs of Mr. Carrisford,—which was the real name of the Indian Gentleman,—and, as Mr. Carrisford's lawyer, Mr. Carmichael had come to explain something curious to Miss Minchin regarding Sara. But, being the father of the Large Family, he had a very kind and fatherly feeling for children; and so, after seeing Miss Minchin alone, what did he do but go and bring across the square his rosy, motherly, warm-hearted wife, so that she herself might talk to the little lonely girl, and tell her everything in the best and most motherly way.

And then Sara learned that she was to be a poor little drudge and outcast no more, and that a great change had come in her fortunes; for all the lost fortune had come back to her, and a great deal had even been added to it. It was Mr. Carrisford who had been her father's friend, and who had made the investments which had caused him the apparent loss of his money; but it had so happened that after poor young Captain Crewe's death, one of the investments which had seemed at the time the very worst, had taken a sudden turn, and proved to be such a success that it had been a mine of wealth, and had more than doubled the Captain's lost fortune, as well as making a fortune for Mr. Carrisford himself. But Mr. Carrisford had been very unhappy. He had truly loved his poor, handsome, generous young friend, and the knowledge that he had caused his death had weighed upon him always, and broken both his health and spirit. The worst of it had been that, when first he thought himself and Captain Crewe ruined, he had lost courage and gone away because he was not brave enough to face the consequences of what he had done, and so he had not even known where the young soldier's little girl had been placed. When he wanted to find her, and make restitution, he could discover no trace of her; and the certainty that she was poor and friendless somewhere had made him more miserable than ever. When he had taken the house next to Miss Minchin's, he had been so ill and wretched that he had for the time given up the search. His troubles and the Indian climate had brought him almost to death's door—indeed, he had not expected to live more than a few months. And then one day the Lascar had told him about Sara's speaking Hindustani, and gradually he had begun to take a sort of interest in the forlorn child, though he had only caught a glimpse of her once or twice; and he had not connected her with the child of his friend, perhaps, because he was too languid to think much about anything. But the Lascar had found out something of Sara's unhappy little life, and about the garret. One evening he had actually crept out of his own garret-window and looked into hers, which was a very easy matter, because, as I have said, it was only a few feet away—and he had told his master what he had seen, and in a moment of compassion the Indian Gentleman had told him to take into the wretched little room such comforts as he could carry from the one window to the other. And the Lascar, who had developed an interest in and an odd fondness for the child who had spoken to him in his own tongue, had been pleased with the work; and, having the silent swiftness and agile movements of many of his race, he had made his evening journeys across the few feet of roof from garret-window to garret-window, without any trouble at all. He had watched Sara's movements until he knew exactly when she was absent from her room and when she returned to it, and so he had been able to calculate the best times for his work. Generally he had made them in the dusk of the evening, but once or twice when he had seen her go out on errands, he had dared to go over in the daytime, being quite sure that the garret was never entered by any one but herself. His pleasure in the work and his reports of the results

had added to the invalid's interest in it, and sometimes the master had found the planning gave him something to think of, which made him almost forget his weariness and pain. And at last, when Sara brought home the truant monkey, he had felt a wish to see her, and then her likeness to her father had done the rest.

"And now, my dear," said good Mrs. Carmichael, patting Sara's hand, "all your troubles are over, I am sure, and you are to come home with me and be taken care of as if you were one of my own little girls; and we are so pleased to think of having you with us until everything is settled, and Mr. Carrisford is better. The excitement of last night has made him very weak, but we really think he will get well, now that such a load is taken from his mind. And when he is stronger, I am sure he will be as kind to you as your own papa would have been. He has a very good heart, and he is fond of children—and he has no family at all. But we must make you happy and rosy, and you must learn to play and run about, as my little girls do——"

"As your little girls do?" said Sara. "I wonder if I could. I used to watch them and wonder what it was like. Shall I feel as if I belonged to somebody?"

"Ah, my love, yes!—yes!" said Mrs. Carmichael; "dear me, yes!" And her motherly blue eyes grew quite moist, and she suddenly took Sara in her arms and kissed her. That very night, before she went to sleep, Sara had made the acquaintance of the entire Large Family, and such excitement as she and the monkey had caused in that joyous circle could hardly be described. There was not a child in the nursery, from the Eton boy who was the eldest, to the baby who was the youngest, who had not laid some offering on her shrine. All the older ones knew something of her wonderful story. She had been born in India; she had been poor and lonely and unhappy, and had lived in a garret and been treated unkindly; and now she was to be rich and happy, and to be taken care of. They were so sorry for her, and so delighted and curious about her, all at once. The girls wished to be with her constantly, and the little boys wished to be told about India; the second baby, with the short round legs, simply sat and stared at her and the monkey, possibly wondering why she had not brought a hand-organ with her.

"I shall certainly wake up presently," Sara kept saying to herself. "This one must be a dream. The other one turned out to be real; but this *could n't* be. But, oh! how happy it is!"

And even when she went to bed, in the bright, pretty room not far from Mrs. Carmichael's own, and Mrs. Carmichael came and kissed her and patted her and tucked her in cozily, she was not sure that she would not wake up in the garret in the morning.

"And oh, Charles, dear," Mrs. Carmichael said to her husband, when she went downstairs to him, "we must get that lonely look out of her eyes! It is n't a child's look at all. I could n't bear to see it in one of my own children. What the poor little love must have had to bear, in that dreadful woman's house! But, surely, she will forget it in time."

But though the lonely look passed away from Sara's face, she never quite forgot the garret at Miss Minchin's; and, indeed, she always liked to remember the wonderful night when the tired Princess crept upstairs, cold and wet, and opening the door found fairy-land waiting for her. And there was no one of the many stories she was always being called upon to tell in the nursery of the Large Family, which was more popular than that particular one; and there was no one of whom the Large Family were so fond as of Sara. Mr. Carrisford did not die, but recovered, and Sara went to live

with him; and no real princess could have been better taken care of than she was. It seemed that the Indian Gentleman could not do enough to make her happy, and to repay her for the past; and the Lascar was her devoted slave. As her odd little face grew brighter, it grew so pretty and interesting that Mr Carrisford used to sit and watch it many an evening, as they sat by the fire together.

They became great friends, and they used to spend hours reading and talking together; and, in a very short time, there was no pleasanter sight to the Indian Gentleman than Sara sitting in her big chair on the opposite side of the hearth, with a book on her knee and her soft dark hair tumbling over her warm cheeks. She had a pretty habit of looking up at him suddenly, with a bright smile, and then he would often say to her:

"Are you happy, Sara?"

And then she would answer:

"I feel like a real princess, Uncle Tom."

He had told her to call him Uncle Tom.

"There does n't seem to be anything left to 'suppose,'" she added.

There was a little joke between them that he was a magician, and so could do anything he liked; and it was one of his pleasures to invent plans to surprise her with enjoyments she had not thought of. Scarcely a day passed in which he did not do something new for her. Sometimes she found new flowers in her room; sometimes a fanciful little gift tucked into some odd corner; sometimes a new book on her pillow;—once as they sat together in the evening they heard the scratch of a heavy paw on the poor of the room, and when Sara went to find out where it was, there stood a great dog—a splendid Russian boarhound with a grand silver and gold collar. Stooping to read the inscription upon the collar, Sara was delighted to read the words: "I am Boris; I serve the Princess Sara."

Then there was a sort of fairy nursery arranged for the entertainment of the juvenile members of the Large Family, who were always coming to see Sara and the Lascar and the monkey. Sara was as fond of the Large Family as they were of her. She soon felt as if she was a member of it, and the companionship of the healthy, happy children was very good for her. All the children rather looked up to her and regarded her as the cleverest and most brilliant of creatures—particularly after it was discovered that she not only knew stories of every kind, and could invent new ones at a moment's notice, but that she could help with lessons, and speak French and German and discourse with the Lascar in Hindustani.

It was rather a painful experience for Miss Minchin, to watch her ex-pupil's fortunes, as she had the daily opportunity to do, and to feel that she had made a serious mistake, from a business point of view. She had even tried to retrieve it by suggesting that Sara's education should be continued under her care, and had gone to the length of making an appeal to the child herself.

"I have always been very fond of you" she said.

Then Sara fixed her eyes upon her and gave her one of her odd looks.

"Have you?" she answered.

"Yes," said Miss Minchin. "Amelia and I have always said you were the cleverest child we had with us, and I am sure we could make you happy—as a parlor boarder."

Sara thought of the garret and the day her ears were boxed,—and of that other day, that dreadful desolate day when she had been told that she belonged to nobody; that she had no home and no friends,—and she kept her eyes fixed on Miss Minchin's face.

"You know why I would not stay with you," she said.

And it seems probable that Miss Minchin did, for after that simple answer she had not the boldness to pursue the subject. She merely sent in a bill for the expense of Sara's education and support, and she made it quite large enough. And because Mr. Carrisford thought Sara would wish it paid, it was paid. When Mr. Carmichael paid it he had a brief interview with Miss Minchin in which he expressed his opinion with much clearness and force; and it is quite certain that Miss Minchin did not enjoy the conversation.

Sara had been about a month with Mr. Carrisford, and had begun to realize that her happiness was not a dream, when one night the Indian Gentleman saw that she sat a long time with her cheek on her hand looking at the fire.

"What are you 'supposing' Sara?" he asked. Sara looked up with a bright color on her cheeks.

"I *was* 'supposing,'" she said; "I was remembering that hungry day and a child I saw."

"But there were a great many hungry days," said the Indian Gentleman with a rather sad tone in his voice. "Which hungry day was it?"

"I forgot you did n't know," said Sara. "It was the day I found the things in my garret."

And then she told him the story of the bunshop, and the fourpence, and the child who was hungrier than herself; and somehow as she told it, though she told it very simply indeed, the Indian Gentleman found it necessary to shade his eyes with his hand and look down at the floor.

"And I was 'supposing' a kind of plan," said Sara, when she had finished; "I was thinking I would like to do something."

"What is it?" said her guardian in a low tone. "You may do anything you like to do, Princess."

"I was wondering," said Sara,—"you

know you say I have a great deal of money —and I was wondering if I could go and see the bun-woman and tell her that if, when hungry children—particularly on those dreadful days—come and sit on the steps or look in at the window, she would just call them in and give them something to eat; she might send the bills to me and I would pay them—could I do that?"

"You shall do it to-morrow morning," said the Indian Gentleman.

"Thank you," said Sara; "you see I know what it is to be hungry, and it is very hard when one can't even *pretend* it away."

"Yes, yes, my dear," said the Indian Gentleman. "Yes, it must be. Try to forget it. Come and sit on this footstool near my knee, and only remember you are a princess."

"Yes," said Sara, "and I can give buns and bread to the Populace." And she went and sat on the stool and the Indian Gentleman (he used to like her to call him that, too, sometimes,—in fact, very often) drew her small dark head down upon his knee and stroked her hair.

The next morning a carriage drew up before the door of the baker's shop and a gentleman and a little girl got out—oddly enough, just as the bun-woman was putting a tray of smoking hot buns into the window. When Sara entered the shop the woman turned and looked at her, and leaving the buns, came and stood behind the counter. For a moment she looked at Sara very hard indeed, and then her good-natured face lighted up.

"I'm that sure I remember you, miss," she said. "And yet——"

"Yes," said Sara, "once you gave me six buns for fourpence, and——"

"And you gave five of 'em to a beggar-child," said the woman. "I've always remembered it. I could n't make it out at first. I beg pardon, sir, but there's not many young people that notices a hungry face in

that way, and I've thought of it many a time. Excuse the liberty, miss, but you look rosier and better than you did that day.".

"I am better, thank you," said Sara, "and —and I am happier, and I have come to ask you to do something for me."

"Me miss!" exclaimed the woman, "why, bless you, yes, miss! What can I do?"

And then Sara made her little proposal, and the woman listened to it with an astonished face.

"Why, bless me!" she said, when she had heard it all. "Yes, miss,—it 'll be a pleasure to me to do it. I am a working woman, my-self, and can't afford to do much on my own account, and there's sights of trouble on every side; but if you 'll excuse me, I 'm bound to say I 've given many a bit of bread away since that wet afternoon, just along o' thinkin' of you. An' how wet an' cold you was, an' how you looked,—an' yet you give away your hot buns as if you was a princess."

The Indian Gentleman smiled involuntarily, and Sara smiled a little too. "She looked so hungry," she said. "She was hungrier than I was." "She was starving," said the woman. "Many 's the time she 's told me of it since—how she sat there in the wet and felt as if a wolf was a-tearing at her poor young insides."

"Oh have you seen here since, then?" exclaimed Sara. "Do you know where she is?"

"I know?" said the woman. "Why, she 's in that there back room now, miss, an' has been for a month, an' a decent, well-meaning girl she 's going to turn out, an' such a help to me in the day shop, an' in the kitchen, as you 'd scare believe, knowing how she 's lived."

She stepped to the door of the little back parlor and spoke; and the next minute a girl came out and followed her behind the counter. And actually it was the beggar-child, clean and neatly clothed, and looking as if she had not been hungry for a long time. She looked shy, but she had a nice face, now that she was no longer a savage; and the wild look had gone from her eyes. And she knew Sara in an instant, and stood and looked at her as if she could never look enough.

"You see," said the woman, "I told her to come here when she was hungry, and when she 'd come I'dgive her odd jobs to do, an' I found she was willing, an' somehow I got to like her; an' the end of it was I 've given her a place an 'a home, an' she helps me, an' behaves as well, an' is as thankful as a girl can be. Her name 's Anne—she has no other."

The two children stood and looked at each other a few moments. In Sara's eyes a new thought was growing.

"I 'm glad you have such a good home," she said. "Perhaps Mrs. Brown will let you give the buns and bread to the children—perhaps you would like to do it—because you know what it is to he hungry, too."

"Yes, miss," said the girl.

And somehow Sara felt as if she understood her, though the girl said nothing more, and only stood still and looked, and looked after her as she went out of the shop and got into the carriage and drove away.

AN OLD-FASHIONED THANKSGIVING

by Louisa M. Alcott

SIXTY years ago, up among the New Hampshire hills, lived Farmer Bassett, with a houseful of sturdy sons and daughters growing up about him. They were poor in money, but rich in land and love, for the wide acres of wood, corn, and pasture land fed, warmed, and clothed the flock, while mutual patience, affection, and courage made the old farm-house a very happy home.

November had come; the crops were in, and barn, buttery, and bin were overflowing with the harvest that rewarded the summer's hard work. The big kitchen was a jolly place just now, for in the great fireplace roared a cheerful fire; on the walls hung garlands of dried apples, onions, and corn; up aloft from the beams shone crooknecked squashes, juicy hams, and dried venison—for in those days deer still haunted the deep forests, and hunters flourished. Savory smells were in the air; on the crane hung steaming kettles, and down among the red embers copper saucepans simmered, all suggestive of some approaching feast.

A white-headed baby lay in the old blue cradle that had rocked six other babies, now and then lifting his head to look out, like a round, full moon, then subsided to kick and crow contentedly and suck the rosy apple he had no teeth to bite. Two small boys sat on the wooden settle shelling corn for popping, and picking out the biggest nuts from the goodly store their own hands had gathered in October. Four young girls

stood at the long dresser, busily chopping meat, pounding spice, and slicing apples; and the tongues of Tilly, Prue, Roxy, and Rhody went as fast as their hands. Farmer Bassett, and Eph, the oldest boy, were "chorin' 'round" outside, for Thanksgiving was at hand, and all must be in order for that time-honored day.

To and fro, from table to hearth, bustled buxom Mrs. Bassett, flushed and floury, but busy and blithe as the queen bee of this busy little hive should be.

"I do like to begin seasonable and have things to my mind. Thanksgivin' dinners can't be drove, and it does take a sight of victuals to fill all these hungry stomicks," said the good woman, as she gave a vigorous stir to the great kettle of cider applesauce, and cast a glance of housewifely pride at the fine array of pies set forth on the buttery shelves.

"Only one more day and then it will be time to eat. I did n't take but one bowl of hasty pudding this morning, so I shall have plenty of room when the nice things come," confided Seth to Sol, as he cracked a large hazel-nut as easily as a squirrel.

"No need of my starvin' beforehand. I *always* have room enough, and I 'd like to have Thanksgiving every day," answered Solomon, gloating like a young ogre over the little pig that lay near by, ready for roasting.

"Sakes alive, I don't, boys! It 's a marcy it don't come but once a year. I should be worn to a thread-paper with all this extra work atop of my winter weavin' and spinnin'," laughed their mother as she plunged her plump arms into the long bread-trough and began to knead the dough as if a famine was at hand.

Tilly, the oldest girl, a red-cheeked, black-eyed lass of fourteen, was grinding briskly at the mortar, for spices were costly, and not a grain must be wasted. Prue kept time with the chopper, and the twins sliced away at the apples till their little brown arms ached, for all knew how to work, and did so now with a will.

"I think it 's real fun to have Thanksgiving at home. I 'm sorry Gran'ma is sick, so we can't go there as usual, but I like to mess 'round here, don't you, girls?" asked Tilly, pausing to take a sniff at the spicy pestle.

"It will be kind of lonesome with only our own folks." "I like to see all the cousins and aunts and have games, and sing," cried the twins, who were regular little romps, and could run, swim, coast, and shout as well as their brothers.

"I don't care a mite for all that. It will be so nice to eat dinner together, warm and comfortable at home," said quiet Prue, who loved her own cozy nooks like a cat.

"Come, girls, fly 'round and get your chores done, so we can clear away for dinner jest as soon as I clap my bread into the oven," called Mrs. Bassett presently, as she rounded off the last loaf of brown bread which was to feed the hungry mouths that seldom tasted any other.

"Here 's a man comin' up the hill lively!" "Guess it 's Gad Hopkins. Pa told him to bring a dezzen oranges, if they war n't too high!" shouted Sol and Seth, running to the door, while the girls smacked their lips at the thought of this rare treat, and Baby threw his apple overboard, as if getting ready for a new cargo.

But all were doomed to disappointment, for it was not Gad, with the much-desired

fruit. It was a stranger, who threw himself off his horse and hurried up to Mr. Bassett

"The cat sat blinking her eyes in the cheerful glow"

in the yard, with some brief message that made the farmer drop his ax and look so sober that his wife guessed at once some bad news had come; and crying, "Mother 's wuss! I know she is!" out ran the good woman, forgetful of the flour on her arms and the oven waiting for its most important batch.

The man said old Mr. Chadwick, down to Keene, stopped him as he passed, and told him to tell Mrs. Bassett her mother was failin' fast, and she 'd better come to-day. He knew no more, and having delivered his errand he rode away, saying it looked like snow and he must be jogging, or he would n't get home till night.

"We must go right off, Eldad. Hitch up, and I 'll be ready in less 'n no time," said Mrs. Bassett, wasting not a minute in tears and lamentations, but pulling off her apron as she went in, with her head in a sad jumble of bread, anxiety, turkey, sorrow, haste, and cider apple-sauce.

A few words told the story, and the children left their work to help her get ready, mingling their grief for "Gran'ma" with regrets for the lost dinner.

"I 'm dreadful sorry, dears, but it can't be helped. I could n't cook nor eat no way now, and if that blessed woman gets better sudden, as she has before, we 'll have cause for thanksgivin', and I 'll give you a dinner you wont forget in a hurry," said Mrs. Bassett, as she tied on her brown silk pumpkin-hood, with a sob for the good old mother who had made it for her.

Not a child complained after that, but ran about helpfully, bringing moccasins, heating the footstone, and getting ready for a long drive, because Gran'ma lived twenty miles away, and there were no railroads in those parts to whisk people to and fro like magic. By the time the old yellow sleigh was at the door, the bread was in the oven, and Mrs. Bassett was waiting, with her camlet cloak on, and the baby done up like a small bale of blankets.

"Now, Eph, you must look after the cattle like a man, and keep up the fires for there 's a storm brewin', and neither the children nor dumb critters must suffer," said Mr. Bassett, as he turned up the collar of his rough coat and put on his blue mittens, while the old mare shook her bells as

if she preferred a trip to Keene to hauling wood all day.

"Tilly, put extry comfortables on the beds to-night, the wind is so searchin' up chamber. Have the baked beans and Injun-puddin' for dinner, and whatever you do, don't let the boys git at the mince-pies, or you 'll have them down sick. I shall come back the minute I can leave Mother. Pa will come to-morrer anyway, so keep snug and be good. I depend on you, my darter; use your jedgment, and don't let nothin' happen while Mother 's away."

"Yes 'm, yes 'm—good-bye, good-bye!" called the children, as Mrs. Bassett was packed into the sleigh and driven away, leaving a stream of directions behind her.

Eph, the sixteen-year-old boy, immediately put on his biggest boots, assumed a sober, responsible manner, and surveyed his little responsibilities with a paternal air, drolly like his father's. Tilly tied on her mother's bunch of keys, rolled up the sleeves of her homespun gown, and began to order about the younger girls. They soon forgot poor Granny, and found it great fun to keep house all alone, for Mother seldom left home, but ruled her family in the good old-fashioned way. There were no servants, for the little daughters were Mrs. Bassett's only maids, and the stout boys helped their father, all working happily together with no wages but love; learning in the best manner the use of the heads and hands with which they were to make their own way in the world.

The few flakes that caused the farmer to predict bad weather soon increased to a regular snowstorm, with gusts of wind, for up among the hills winter came early and lingered long. But the children were busy, gay, and warm in-doors, and never minded the rising gale nor the whirling white storm outside.

Tilly got them a good dinner, and when it was over the two elder girls went to their spinning, for in the kitchen stood the big and little wheels, and baskets of wool-rolls, ready to be twisted into yarn for the winter's knitting, and each day brought its stint of work to the daughters, who hoped to be as thrifty as their mother.

Eph kept up a glorious fire, and superintended the small boys, who popped corn and whittled boats on the hearth; while Roxy and Rhody dressed corn-cob dolls in the settle corner, and Bose, the brindled mastiff, lay on the braided mat, luxuriously warming his old legs. Thus employed, they made a pretty picture, these rosy boys and girls, in their homespun suits, with the rustic toys or tasks which most children nowadays would find very poor or tiresome.

Tilly and Prue sang, as they stepped to and fro, drawing out the smoothly twisted threads to the musical hum of the great spinning-wheels. The little girls chattered like magpies over their dolls and the new bed-spread they were planning to make, all white dimity stars on a blue calico ground, as a Christmas present to Ma. The boys roared at Eph's jokes, and had rough and tumble games over Bose, who did n't mind them in the least; and so the afternoon wore pleasantly away.

At sunset the boys went out to feed the cattle, bring in heaps of wood, and lock up for the night, as the lonely farm-house seldom had visitors after dark. The girls got the simple supper of brown bread and milk, baked apples, and a doughnut all 'round as a treat. Then they sat before the fire, the sisters knitting, the brothers with books or games, for Eph loved reading, and Sol and Seth never failed to play a few games of Morris with barley corns, on the little board they had made themselves at one corner of the dresser.

"Read out a piece," said Tilly from Mother's chair, where she sat in state, finishing off the sixth woolen sock she had knit that month.

"It 's the old history book, but here 's a bit you may like, since it 's about our folks," answered Eph, turning the yellow page to look at a picture of two quaintly dressed children in some ancient castle.

"Yes, read that. I always like to hear about the Lady Matildy I was named for, and Lord Bassett, Pa's great-great-great-grandpa. He 's only a farmer now, but it 's nice to know we were somebody two or three hundred years ago," said Tilly, bridling and tossing her curly head as she fancied the Lady Matilda might have done.

"Don't read the queer words, 'cause we don't understand 'em. Tell it," commanded Roxy, from the cradle, where she was drowsily cuddled with Rhody.

"Well, a long time ago, when Charles the First was in prison, Lord Bassett was a true friend to him," began Eph, plunging into his story without delay. "The lord had some papers that would have hung a lot of people if the king's enemies got hold of 'em, so when he heard one day, all of a sudden, that soldiers were at the castle-gate to carry him off, he had just time to call his girl to him, and say: 'I may be going to my death, but I wont betray my master. There is no time to burn the papers, and I can not take them with me; they are hidden in the old leathern chair where I sit. No one knows this but you, and you must guard them till I come or send you a safe messenger to take them away. Promise me to be brave and silent, and I can go without fear.' You see, he was n't afraid to die, but he *was* to seem a traitor. Lady Matildy promised solemnly, and the words were hardly out of her mouth when the men came in, and her father was carried away a prisoner and sent off to the Tower."

"But she did n't cry; she just called her brother, and sat down in that chair, with her head leaning back on those papers, like a queen, and waited while the soldiers hunted the house over for 'em: was n't that a smart girl?" cried Tilly, beaming with pride, for she was named for this ancestress, and knew the story by heart.

"I reckon she was scared, though, when the men came swearin' in and asked her if she knew anything about it. The boy did his part then, for *he* did n't know, and fired up and stood before his sister; and he says, says he, as bold as a lion: 'If my lord had told us where the papers be, we would die before we would betray him. But we are children and know nothing, and it is cowardly of you to try to fright us with oaths and drawn swords!'"

As Eph quoted from the book, Seth planted himself before Tilly, with the long poker in his hand, saying, as he flourished it valiantly:

"Why did n't the boy take his father's sword and lay about him? I would, if any one was ha'sh to Tilly"

"You bantam! he was only a bit of a boy, and could n't do anything. Sit down and hear the rest of it," commanded Tilly, with a pat on the yellow head, and a private resolve that Seth should have the largest piece of pie at dinner next day, as reward for his chivalry.

"Well, the men went off after turning the castle out of window, but they said they should come again; so faithful Matildy was full of trouble, and hardly dared to leave the room where the chair stood. All day she sat there and at night her sleep was so full of fear about it, that she often got up and went to see that all was safe. The servants thought the fright had hurt her wits, and let her be, but Rupert, the boy, stood by her and never was afraid of her queer ways. She was 'a pious maid,' the book says, and often spent the long evenings reading the Bible, with her brother by her, all alone in the great room, with no one to help her bear her secret, and no good news of her father. At last, word came that the king was dead and his friends banished out of England. Then the poor children were in a sad plight, for they had no mother, and the servants all ran away, leaving only one faithful old man to help them."

"But the father did come?" cried Roxy, eagerly.

"You 'll see," continued Eph, half telling, half reading.

"Matilda was sure he would, so she sat on in the big chair, guarding the papers, and no one could get her away, till one day a man came with her father's ring and told her to give up the secret. She knew the ring, but would not tell until she had asked many questions, so as to be very sure, and while the man answered all about her father and the king, she looked at him sharply. Then she stood up and said, in a tremble, for there was something strange about the man: 'Sir, I doubt you in spite of the ring, and I will not answer till you pull off the false beard you wear, that I may see your face and know if you are my father's friend or foe.' Off came the disguise, and Matilda found it was my lord himself, come to take them with him out of England. He was very proud of that faithful girl, I guess, for the old chair still stands in the castle, and the name keeps in the family, Pa says, even over here, where some of the Bassetts came along with the Pilgrims."

"Our Tilly would have been as brave, I know, and she looks like the old picter down to Gran'ma's, don't she, Eph?" cried Prue, who admired her bold, bright sister very much.

"Well, I think you 'd do the settin' part best, Prue, you are so patient. Till would fight like a wild cat, but she can't hold her tongue worth a cent," answered Eph; whereat Tilly pulled his hair, and the story ended with a general frolic.

When the moon-faced clock behind the door struck nine, Tilly tucked up the children under the "extry comfortables," and having kissed them all around, as Mother did, crept into her own nest, never minding the little drifts of snow that sifted in upon her coverlet between the shingles of the roof, nor the storm that raged without.

As if he felt the need of unusual vigilance, old Bose lay down on the mat before the door, and pussy had the warm hearth all to herself. If any late wanderer had looked in at midnight, he would have seen the fire blazing up again, and in the cheerful glow the old cat blinking her yellow eyes, as she sat bolt upright beside the spinning-wheel, like some sort of household goblin, guarding the children while they slept.

When they woke, like early birds, it still snowed, but up the little Bassetts jumped, broke the ice in their jugs, and went down with cheeks glowing like winter apples, after a brisk scrub and scramble into their clothes. Eph was off to the barn, and Tilly soon had a great kettle of mush ready, which, with milk warm from the cows, made a wholesome breakfast for the seven hearty children.

"Now about dinner," said the young housekeeper, as the pewter spoons stopped clattering, and the earthen bowls stood empty.

"Ma said, have what we liked, but she did n't expect us to have a real Thanksgiving dinner, because she wont be here to cook it, and we don't know how," began Prue, doubtfully.

"I can roast a turkey and make a pudding as well as anybody, I guess. The pies are all ready, and if we can't boil vegetables and so on, we don't deserve any dinner," cried Tilly, burning to distinguish herself, and bound to enjoy to the utmost her brief authority.

"Yes, yes!" cried all the boys, "let 's have a dinner anyway; Ma wont care, and the good victuals will spoil if they aint eaten right up."

"Pa is coming to-night, so we wont have dinner till late; that will be real genteel and give us plenty of time," added Tilly, suddenly realizing the novelty of the task she had undertaken.

"Did you ever roast a turkey?" asked Roxy, with an air of deep interest.

"Should you darst to try?" said Rhody, in an awe-stricken tone.

"You will see what I can do. Ma said I was to use my judgment about things, and I 'm going to. All you children have got to do is to keep out of the way, and let Prue and me work. Eph, I wish you 'd put a fire in the best room, so the little ones can play in there. We shall want the settin'-room for the table, and I wont have them pickin' 'round when we get things fixed," commanded Tilly, bound to make her short reign a brilliant one.

"I don't know about that. Ma did n't tell us to," began cautious Eph, who felt that this invasion of the sacred best parlor was a daring step.

"Don't we always do it Sundays and Thanksgivings? Would n't Ma wish the children kept safe and warm anyhow? Can I get up a nice dinner with four rascals under my feet all the time? Come, now, if you want roast turkey and onions, plum-puddin' and mince-pie, you 'll have to do as I tell you, and be lively about it."

Tilly spoke with such spirit, and her last suggestion was so irresistible, that Eph gave in, and, laughing good-naturedly, tramped away to heat up the best room, devoutly hoping that nothing serious would happen to punish such audacity.

The young folks delightedly trooped away to destroy the order of that prim apartment with housekeeping under the black horse-hair sofa, "horseback-riders" on the arms of the best rocking-chair, and an Indian war-dance all over the well-waxed furniture. Eph, finding the society. of peaceful sheep and cows more to his mind than that of two excited sisters, lingered over his chores in the barn as long as possible, and left the girls in peace.

Now Tilly and Prue were in their glory, and as soon as the breakfast-things were out of the way, they prepared for a grand cooking-time. They were handy girls, though they had never heard of a cooking-school, never touched a piano, and knew nothing of embroidery beyond the samplers which hung framed in the parlor; one ornamented with a pink mourner under a blue weeping-willow, the other with this pleasing verse, each word being done in a different color, which gave the effect of a distracted rainbow:

"This sampler neat was worked by me,
In my twelfth year, Prudence B."

Both rolled up their sleeves, put on their largest aprons, and got out all the spoons, dishes, pots, and pans they could find, "so as to have everything handy," Prue said.

"Now, sister, we 'll have dinner at five; Pa will be here by that time, if he is coming to-night, and be so surprised to find us all ready, for he wont have had any very nice victuals if Gran'ma is so sick," said Tilly, importantly. "I shall give the children a piece at noon" (Tilly meant luncheon); "doughnuts and cheese, with apple-pie and cider, will please 'em. There 's beans for Eph; he likes cold pork, so we wont stop to warm it up, for there 's lots to do, and I don't mind saying to you I 'm dreadful dubersome about the turkey."

"It 's all ready but the stuffing, and roasting is as easy as can be. I can baste first-rate. Ma always likes to have me, I 'm so patient and stiddy, she says," answered Prue, for

the responsibility of this great undertaking did not rest upon her, so she took a cheerful view of things.

"I know, but it 's the stuffin' that troubles me," said Tilly, rubbing her round elbows as she eyed the immense fowl laid out on a platter before her. "I don't know how much I want, nor what sort of yarbs to put in, and he 's so awful big, I 'm kind of afraid of him."

"I aint! I fed him all summer, and he never gobbled at me. I feel real mean to be thinking of gobbling him, poor old chap," laughed Prue, patting her departed pet with an air of mingled affection and appetite.

"Well, I 'll get the puddin' off my mind fust, for it ought to bile all day. Put the big kettle on, and see that the spit is clean, while I get ready."

Prue obediently tugged away at the crane, with its black hooks from which hung the iron tea-kettle and three-legged pot; then she settled the long spit in the grooves made for it in the tall andirons, and put the dripping-pan underneath, for in those days meat was roasted as it should be, not baked in ovens.

Meantime Tilly attacked the plum-pudding. She felt pretty sure of coming out right, here, for she had seen her mother do it so many times, it looked very easy. So in went suet and fruit; all sorts of spice, to be sure she got the right ones, and brandy instead of wine. But she forgot both sugar and salt, and tied it in the cloth so tightly that it had no room to swell, so it would come out as heavy as lead and as hard as a cannon-ball, if the bag did not burst and spoil it all. Happily unconscious of these mistakes, Tilly popped it into the pot, and proudly watched it bobbing about before she put the cover on and left it to its fate.

"I can't remember what flavorin' Ma puts in," she said, when she had got her bread well soaked for the stuffing. "Sage and onions and applesauce go with goose, but I can't feel sure of anything but pepper and salt for a turkey."

"Ma puts in some kind of mint, I know, but I forget whether it is spearmint, peppermint, or pennyroyal," answered Prue, in a tone of doubt, but trying to show her knowledge of "yarbs," or, at least, of their names.

"Seems to me it 's sweet majoram or summer savory. I guess we 'll put both in, and then we are sure to be right. The best is up garret; you run and get some, while I mash the bread," commanded Tilly, diving into the mess.

Away trotted Prue, but in her haste she got catnip and wormwood, for the garret was darkish, and Prue's little nose was so full of the smell of the onions she had been peeling, that everything smelt of them. Eager to be of use, she pounded up the herbs and scattered the mixture with a liberal hand into the bowl.

"It does n't smell just right, but I suppose it will when it is cooked," said Tilly, as she filled the empty stomach, that seemed aching for food, and sewed it up with the blue yarn, which happened to be handy. She forgot to tie down his legs and wings, but she set him by till his hour came, well satisfied with her work.

"Shall we roast the little pig, too? I think he 'd look nice with a necklace of sausages, as Ma fixed him at Christmas," asked Prue, elated with their success.

"I could n't do it. I loved that little pig, and cried when he was killed. I should feel as if I was roasting the baby," answered Tilly, glancing toward the buttery where piggy hung, looking so pink and pretty it certainly did seem cruel to eat him.

It took a long time to get all the vegetables ready, for, as the cellar was full, the girls thought they would have every sort. Eph helped, and by noon all was ready for cooking, and the cranberry-sauce, a good deal scorched, was cooking in the lean-to.

Luncheon was a lively meal, and doughnuts and cheese vanished in such quantities that Tilly feared no one would have an appetite for her sumptuous dinner. The boys assured her they would be starving by five o'clock, and Sol mourned bitterly over the little pig that was not to be served up.

"Now you all go and coast, while Prue and I set the table and get out the best chiny," said Tilly, bent on having her dinner look well, no matter what its other failings might be.

Out came the rough sleds, on went the round hoods, old hats, red cloaks, and moccasins, and away trudged the four younger Bassetts, to disport themselves in the snow and try the ice down by the old mill, where the great wheel turned and splashed so merrily in the summer-time.

Eph took his fiddle and scraped away to his heart's content in the parlor, while the girls, after a short rest, set the table and made all ready to dish up the dinner when that exciting moment came. It was not at all the sort of table we see now, but would look very plain and countrified to us, with its green-handled knives, and two pronged steel forks; its red-and-white china, and pewter platters, scoured till they shone, with mugs and spoons to match and a brown jug for the cider. The cloth was coarse, but white as snow, and the little maids had seen the blue-eyed flax grow, out of which their mother wove the linen; they had watched and watered while it bleached in the green meadow. They had no napkins and little silver; but the best tankard and Ma's few wedding-spoons were set forth in state. Nuts and apples at the corners gave an air, and the place of honor was left in the middle for the oranges yet to come.

"Don't it look beautiful?" said Prue,

when they paused to admire the general effect.

"Pretty nice, I think. I wish Ma could see how well we can do it," began Tilly, when a loud howling startled both girls, and sent them flying to the window. The short afternoon had passed so quickly that twilight had come before they knew it, and now, as they looked out through the gathering dusk, they saw four small black figures tearing up the road, to come bursting in, all screaming at once: "The bear, the bear! Eph, get the gun! He's coming, he's coming!"

Eph had dropped his fiddle, and got down his gun before the girls could calm the children enough to tell their story, which they did in a somewhat incoherent manner. "Down in the holler, coastin', we heard a growl," began Sol, with his eyes as big as saucers. "I see him fust lookin' over the wall," roared Seth, eager to get his share of honor.

"Awful big and shaggy," quavered Roxy, clinging to Tilly while Rhody hid in Prue's skirts, and piped out: "His great paws kept clawing at us, and I was so scared my legs would hardly go."

"We ran away as fast as we could go, and he come growlin' after us. He's awful hungry, and he'll eat every one of us if he gets in," continued Sol, looking about him for a safe retreat.

"Oh, Eph, don't let him eat us," cried both little girls, flying upstairs to hide under their mother's bed, as their surest shelter.

"No danger of that, you little geese. I'll shoot him as soon as he comes. Get out of the way, boys," and Eph raised the window to get good aim.

"There he is! Fire away, and don't miss!" cried Seth hastily following Sol, who had climbed to the top of the dresser as a good perch from which to view the approaching fray.

Prue retired to the hearth as if bent on dying at her post rather than desert the turkey, now "browning beautiful," as she expressed it. But Tilly boldly stood at the open window, ready to lend a hand if the enemy proved too much for Eph.

All had seen bears, but none had ever come so near before, and even brave Eph felt that the big brown beast slowly trotting up the door-yard was an unusually formidable specimen. He was growling horribly and stopped now and then as if to rest and shake himself.

"Get the ax, Tilly, and if I should miss, stand ready to keep him off while I load again," said Eph, anxious to kill his first bear in style and alone; a girl's help did n't count.

Tilly flew for the ax, and was at her brother's side by the time the bear was near enough to be dangerous. He stood on his hind legs, and seemed to sniff with relish the savory odors that poured out of the window.

"Fire, Eph!" cried Tilly, firmly.

"Wait till he rears again. I'll get a better shot then," answered the boy, while Prue covered her ears to shut out the bang, and the small boys cheered from their dusty refuge up among the pumpkins.

But a very singular thing happened next, and all who saw it stood amazed, for suddenly Tilly threw down the ax, flung open the door, and ran straight into the arms of the bear, who stood erect to receive her, while his growlings changed to a loud "Haw, haw!" that startled the children more than the report of a gun.

"It's Gad Hopkins, tryin' to fool us!" cried Eph, much disgusted at the loss of his prey, for these hardy boys loved to hunt, and prided themselves on the number of wild animals and birds they could shoot in a year.

"Oh, Gad, how could you scare us so?" laughed Tilly, still held fast in one shaggy arm of the bear, while the other drew a dozen oranges from some deep pocket in the buffalo-skin coat, and fired them into the kitchen with such good aim that Eph ducked, Prue screamed, and Sol and Seth came down much quicker than they went up.

"Wal, you see I got upsot over yonder, and the old horse went home while I was floundering in a drift, so I tied on the buffalers to tote 'em easy, and come along till I see the children playin' in the holler. I jest meant to give 'em a little scare, but they run like partridges, and I kep' up the joke to see how Eph would like this sort of company," and Gad haw-hawed again.

"You 'd have had a warm welcome if we had n't found you out. I 'd have put a bullet through you in a jiffy, old chap," said Eph, coming out to shake hands with the young giant, who was only a year or two older than himself."

"Come in and set up to dinner with us. Prue and I have done it all ourselves, and Pa will be along soon, I reckon," cried Tilly, trying to escape.

"Could n't, no ways. My folks will think I 'm dead ef I don't get along home, sence the horse and sleigh have gone ahead empty. I 've done my arrant and had my joke; now I want my pay, Tilly," and Gad took a hearty kiss from the rosy cheeks of his "little sweetheart," as he called her. His own cheeks tingled with the smart slap she gave him as she ran away, calling out that she hated bears and would bring her ax next time.

"I aint afeared—your sharp eyes found me out; and ef you run into a bear's arms you must expect a hug," answered Gad, as he pushed back the robe and settled his fur cap more becomingly.

"I should have known you in a minute if I had n't been asleep when the girls squalled. You did it well, though, and I advise you not to try it again in a hurry, or you 'll get shot," said Eph, as they parted, he rather crestfallen and Gad in high glee.

"My sakes alive—the turkey is all burnt one side, and the kettles have biled over so the pies I put to warm are all ashes!" scolded Tilly, as the flurry subsided and she remembered her dinner.

"Well, I can't help it. I couldn't think of victuals when I expected to be eaten alive myself, could I?" pleaded poor Prue, who had tumbled into the cradle when the rain of oranges began.

Tilly laughed, and all the rest joined in, so good-humor was restored, and the spirits of the younger ones were revived by sucks from the one orange which passed from hand to hand with great rapidity while the old girls dished up the dinner. They were just struggling to get the pudding out of the cloth when Roxy called out: "Here 's Pa!"

"There 's folks with him," added Rhody.

"Lots of 'em! I see two big sleighs chock full," shouted Seth, peering through the dusk.

"It looks like a semintary. Guess Gramma 's dead and come up to be buried here," said Sol, in a solemn tone. This startling suggestion made Tilly, Prue, and Eph hasten to look out, full of dismay at such an ending of their festival.

"If that is a funeral, the mourners are uncommon jolly," said Eph, dryly as merry voices and loud laughter broke the white silence without.

"I see Aunt Cinthy, and Cousin Hetty— and there 's Mose and Amos. I do declare, Pa 's bringin' 'em all home to have some fun here," cried Prue, as she recognized one familiar face after another.

"Oh, my patience! Aint I glad I got dinner, and don't I hope it will turn out good!" exclaimed Tilly, while the twins pranced with delight, and the small boys roared:

"Hooray for Pa! Hooray for Thanksgivin'!"

The cheer was answered heartily, and in came Father, Mother, Baby, aunts, and cousins, all in great spirits, and all much surprised to find such a festive welcome awaiting them.

"Aint Gran'ma dead at all?" asked Sol, in the midst of the kissing and hand-shaking.

"Bless your heart, no! It was all a mistake of old Mr. Chadwick's. He's as deaf as an adder, and when Mrs. Brooks told him Mother was mendin' fast, and she wanted me to come down to-day, certain sure, he got the message all wrong, and give it to the fust person passin' in such a way as to scare me 'most to death, and send us down in a hurry. Mother was sittin' up as chirk as you please, and dreadful sorry you did n't all come."

"So, to keep the house quiet for her, and give you a taste of the fun, your Pa fetched us all up to spend the evenin', and we are goin' to have a jolly time on 't, to jedge by the looks of things," said Aunt Cinthy, briskly finishing the tale when Mrs. Bassett paused for want of breath.

"What in the world put it into your head we was comin', and set you to gittin' up such a supper?" asked Mr. Bassett, looking about him, well pleased and much surprised at the plentiful table.

Tilly modestly began to tell, but the others broke in and sang her praises in a sort of chorus, in which bears, pigs, pies, and oranges were oddly mixed. Great satisfaction was expressed by all, and Tilly and Prue were so elated by the commendation of Ma and the aunts, that they set forth their dinner, sure everything was perfect.

But when the eating began, which it did the moment wraps were off, then their pride got a fall; for the first person who tasted the stuffing (it was big Cousin Mose, and that made it harder to bear) nearly choked over the bitter morsel.

"Tilly Bassett, whatever made you put wormwood and catnip in your stuffin'?"

demanded Ma, trying not to be severe, for all the rest were laughing, and Tilly looked ready to cry.

"I did it," said Prue, nobly taking all the blame, which caused Pa to kiss her on the spot, and declare that it did n't do a mite of harm, for the turkey was all right.

"I never see onions cooked better. All the vegetables is well done, and the dinner a credit to you, my dears," declared Aunt Cinthy, with her mouth full of the fragrant vegetable she praised.

The pudding was an utter failure in spite of the blazing brandy in which it lay—as hard and heavy as one of the stone balls on Squire Dunkin's great gate. It was speedily whisked out of sight and all fell upon the pies, which were perfect. But Tilly and Prue were much depressed, and did n't recover their spirits till dinner was over and the evening fun well under way.

"Blind-man's bluff," "Hunt the slipper," "Come, Philander," and other lively games soon set every one bubbling over with jollity, and when Eph struck up "Money Musk" on his fiddle, old and young fell into their places for a dance. All down the long kitchen they stood, Mr. and Mrs. Bassett at the top, the twins at the bottom, and then away they went, heeling and toeing, cutting pigeon-wings, and taking their steps in a way that would convulse modern children with their new-fangled romps called dancing. Mose and Tilly covered themselves with glory by the vigor with which they kept it up, till fat Aunt Cinthy fell into a chair, breathlessly declaring that a very little of such exercise was enough for a woman of her "heft."

Apples and cider, chat and singing, finished the evening, and after a grand kissing all round, the guests drove away in the clear moonlight which came out to cheer their long drive.

When the jingle of the last bell had died away, Mr. Bassett said soberly, as they stood together on the hearth: "Children, we have special cause to be thankful that the sorrow we expected was changed into joy, so we 'll read a chapter 'fore we go to bed, and give thanks where thanks is due."

Then Tilly set out the light-stand with the big Bible on it, and a candle on each side, and all sat quietly in the fire-light, smiling as they listened with happy hearts to the sweet old words that fit all times and seasons so beautifully.

When the good-nights were over, and the children in bed, Prue put her arm round Tilly and whispered tenderly, for she felt her shake, and was sure she was crying:

"Don't mind about the old stuffin' and puddin', deary—nobody cared, and Ma said we really did do surprisin' well for such young girls."

The laughter Tilly was trying to smother broke out then, and was so infectious, Prue could not help joining her, even before she knew the cause of the merriment.

"I was mad about the mistakes, but don't care enough to cry. I 'm laughing to think how Gad fooled Eph and I found him out. I thought Mose and Amos would have died over it when I told them, it was so funny," explained Tilly, when she got her breath.

"I was so scared that when the first orange hit me, I thought it was a bullet, and scrabbled into the cradle as fast as I could. It was real mean to frighten the little ones so," laughed Prue, as Tilly gave a growl.

Here a smart rap on the wall of the next room caused a sudden lull in the fun, and Mrs. Bassett's voice was heard, saying warningly, "Girls, go to sleep immediate, or you 'll wake the baby."

"Yes 'm," answered two meek voices, and after a few irrepressible giggles, silence reigned, broken only by an occasional snore from the boys, or the soft scurry of mice in the buttery, taking their part in this old-fashioned Thanksgiving.

GRIZEL COCHRANE'S RIDE

FOUNDED ON AN INCIDENT OF THE MONMOUTH REBELLION

by Elia W. Peattie

In the midsummer of 1685, the hearts of the people of old Edinburgh were filled with trouble and excitement. King Charles the Second, of England, was dead, and his brother, the Duke of York, reigned in his stead to the dissatisfaction of a great number of the people.

The hopes of this class lay with the young Duke of Monmouth, the ambitious and disinherited son of Charles the Second, who, on account of the King's displeasure, had been living for some time at foreign courts. On hearing of the accession of his uncle, the Duke of York, to the throne, Monmouth yielded to the plans of the English and Scottish lords who favored his own pretensions, and prepared to invade England with a small but enthusiastic force of men.

The Duke of Argyle, the noblest lord of Scotland, who also was an exile, undertook to conduct the invasion at the north, while Monmouth should enter England at the west, gather the yeomanry about him and form a triumphant conjunction with Argyle in London, and force the "usurper," as they called King James the Second, from his throne.

Both landings were duly made. The power of Monmouth's name and rank rallied to his banner at first a large number of adherents; but their defeat at Sedgemoor put an end to his invasion. And the Duke of Argyle, a few days after his landing in Scotland, was met by a superior force of the King's troops. Retreating into a morass, his soldiers were scattered and dispersed. Many of his officers deserted him in a panic of fear. The brave old nobleman himself was taken prisoner, and beheaded at Edinburgh, while all he people secretly mourned. He died without betraying his friends, though the relentless King of England threatened to compel him to do so, by the torture of the thumbscrew and the rack.

Many of his officers and followers underwent the same fate; and among those imprisoned to await execution was a certain nobleman, Sir John Cochrane, who had been made famous by other political intrigues. His friends used all the influence that their high position accorded them to procure his pardon, but without success; and the unfortunate baronet, a moody and impulsive man by nature, felt that there was no escape from the terrible destiny, and prepared to meet it in a manner worthy of a follower of the brave old duke. But he had one friend on whose help he had not counted.

In an upper chamber of an irregular, many-storied mansion far down the Canongate, Grizel Cochrane, the imprisoned man's daughter sat through the dread hours waiting to learn her father's sentence. There was too little doubt as to what it would be. The King and his generals meant to make merciless examples of the leaders of the rebellion. Even the royal blood that flowed in the veins of Monmouth had not saved his head from the block. This proud prince, fleeing from the defeat of Sedgemoor, had been found hiding in a ditch, covered over with the ferns that flourished at the bottom. Grizel wept as she thought of the young duke's horrible fate. She remembered when she had last seen him about the court at Holland, where she had shared her father's exile. Gay, generous, and handsome, he seemed a creature born to live and rule. What a contrast was the abject, weeping coward covered with mud and slime, who had been carried in triumph to the grim Tower of London to meet his doom! The girl had been taught to believe in Monmouth's rights, and she walked the floor trembling with shame and impatience as she thought of his bitter defeat. She walked to the little dormer window and leaned out to look at the gray castle, far up the street, with its dull and lichen-covered walls. She knew that her father looked down from the barred windows of one of the upper apartments accorded to prisoners of state. She wondered if a thought of his little daughter crept in his mind amid his ruined hopes. The grim castle frowning at her from its rocky height filled her with dread; and shuddering, she turned from it toward the street below to let her eyes follow absently the passers-by. They whispered together as they passed the house, and when now and then some person caught a glimpse of her face in the ivy-sheltered window, she only met a look of commiseration. No one offered her a happy greeting.

"They all think him doomed," she cried to herself. "No one hath the grace to feign hope." Bitter tears filled her eyes, until suddenly through the mist she was conscious that some one below was lifting a plumed hat to her. It was a stately gentleman with a girdled vest and gorgeous coat and jeweled sword-hilt.

"Mistress Cochrane," said he, in that hushed voice we use when we wish to direct a remark to one person, which no one else shall overhear, "I have that to tell thee which is most important."

"Is it secret?" asked Grizel, in the same guarded tone that he had used.

"Yes," he replied, without looking up, and continuing slowly in his walk, as if he had merely exchanged a morning salutation.

"Then," she returned, hastily, "I will tell Mother; and we will meet thee in the twilight, at the side door under the balcony." She continued to look from the window, and the man sauntered on as if he had no care in the world but to keep the scarlet heels of his shoes from the dust. After a time Grizel arose, changed her loose robe for a more ceremonious dress, bound her brown braids into a prim gilded net, and descended into the drawing-room.

Her mother sat in mournful state at the end of the lofty apartment. About her were two ladies and several gentlemen, all conversing in low tones such as they might use, Grizel thought to herself, if her father were dead in the house. They all stopped talking as she entered, and looked at her in surprise. In those days it was thought very improper and forward for a young girl to enter a drawing-room uninvited, if guests were present. Grizel's eyes fell before the embarrassing scrutiny, and she dropped a timid courtesy, lifting her green silken skirts daintily, like a high-born little maiden, as she was. Lady Cochrane made a dignified apology to her guests and then turned to Grizel.

"Well, my daughter?" she said, questioningly.

"I pray thy pardon, Mother," said Grizel, in a trembling voice, speaking low, that only her mother might hear; "but within a few moments Sir Thomas Hanford will be secretly below the balcony, with news for us."

The lady half rose from her seat, trembling.

"Is he commissioned by the governor?" she asked.

"I can not tell," said the little girl; but here her voice broke, and regardless of the strangers, she flung herself into her mother's lap, weeping: "I am sure it is bad news of Father!" Lady Cochrane wound her arm about her daughter's waist, and, with a gesture of apology, led her from the room. Half an hour later she re-entered it hurriedly, followed by Grizel, who sank unnoticed in the deep embrasure of a window, and shivered there behind the heavy folds of the velvet hangings.

"I have just received terrible intelligence, my friends," announced Lady Cochrane, standing, tall and pale, in the midst of her guests. "The governor has been informally notified that the next post from London will bring Sir John's sentence. He is to be hanged at the Cross." There was a perfect silence in the dim room; then one of the ladies broke into loud sobbing, and a gentleman led Lady Cochrane to a chair, while the others talked apart in earnest whispers.

"Who brought the information?" asked one of the gentlemen, at length. "Is there not hope that it is a false report?"

"I am not at liberty," said Lady Cochrane, "to tell you who brought me this terrible news; but it was a friend of the governor, from whom I would not have expected a service. Oh, is it too late," she cried rising from her chair and pacing the room, "to make another attempt at intercession? Surely something can be done!"

The gentleman who had stood by her chair—a gray-headed, sober-visaged man—returned answer:

"Do not count on any remedy now dear Lady Cochrane. I know this new King. He will be relentless toward any one who has questioned his right to reign. Besides, the post has already left London several days, and will doubtless be here by to-morrow noon."

"I am sure," said a gentleman who had not yet spoken, "that if we had a few days more he might be saved. They say King James will do anything for money, and the wars have emptied his treasury. Might we not delay the post?" he suggested, in a low voice.

"No," said the gray-headed gentleman; "that is utterly impossible."

Grizel, shivering behind the curtain, listened with eager ears. Then she saw her mother throw herself into the arms of one of the ladies and break into ungoverned sobs. The poor girl could stand no more, but glided from the room unnoticed and crept up to her dark chamber, where she sat, repeating aimlessly to herself the words that by chance had fixed themselves strongest in her memory: "Delay the post—delay the post!"

The moon arose and shone in through the panes, making a wavering mosaic on the floor as it glimmered through the wind-blown ivy at the window. Like a flash, a definite resolution sprang into Grizel's mind. If by delaying the post, time for intercession with the King could be gained, and her father's life so saved, then the post *must* be delayed! But how? she had heard the gentleman say that it would be impossible. She knew that the postboy went heavily armed, to guard against the highwaymen who frequented the roads in search of plunder. This made her think of the wild stories of masked men who sprung from some secluded spot upon the postboys, and carried off the letters and money with which they were intrusted.

Suddenly she bounded from her seat, stood still a moment with her hands pressed to her head, ran from her room, and up the stairs which led to the servants' sleeping apartments. She listened at a door, and then, satisfied that the room was empty, entered, and went straight to the oaken wardrobe. By the light of the moon she selected a jacket and a pair of trousers. She looked about her for a hat and found one hanging on a peg near the window; then she searched for some time before she found a pair of boots. They were worn and coated with mud.

"They are all the better," she said to herself, and hurried on tiptoe down the corridor. She went next to the anteroom of her father's chamber. It was full of fond associations, and the hot tears sprung into her eyes as she looked about it. She took up a brace of pistols, examined them awkwardly, her hands trembling under their weight as she found at once to her delight and her terror that they were loaded. Then she hurried with them to her room.

Half an hour later, the butler saw a figure which he took to be that of Allen, the stable-boy, creeping down the back stairs, boots in hand.

"Whaur noo, me laddie?" he asked. "It's gey late for ye to gang oot the nicht."

"I hae forgot to bar the stable door," replied Grizel in a low and trembling voice, imitating as well as she could the broad dialect of the boy.

"Hech!" said the butler. "I ne'er hear ye mak sae little hammer in a' yer days."

She fled on. The great kitchen was deserted. She gathered up all the keys from their pegs by the door, let herself quietly out, and sped across the yard to the stable. With trembling hands she fitted first one key and then another to the door until she found the right one. Once inside the stable, she stood irresolute. She patted Bay Bess, her own little pony.

"Thou wouldst never do, Bess," she said. "Thou art such a lazy little creature." The round fat carriage-horses stood there.

"You are just holiday horses, too," said Grizel to them, "and would be winded after an hour of the work I want for you to-night." But in the shadow of the high stall stood Black Ronald, Sir John Cochrane's great, dark battle-horse, that riderless, covered with dust and foam, had dashed down the Canongate after the terible rout of Argyle in the bogs of Levenside, while all the people stood and stared at the familiar steed, carrying, as he did, the first silent message of disaster. Him Grizel unfastened and led out.

"Thou art a true hero," she said, rubbing his nose with the experienced touch of a horsewoman; "and I'll give thee a chance to-night to show that thou art as loyal as ever." Her hands were cold with excitement but she managed to buckle the saddle and bridle upon him, while the huge animal stood in restless expectancy anxious to be gone. She drew on the boots without any trouble and slipped the pistols into the holsters.

"I believe thou knowest what I would have of thee," said Grizel as she led the horse out into the yard and on toward the gateway. Frightened, as he half circled about her in his impatience, she undid the fastening of the great gates, but her strength was not sufficient to swing them open.

"Ronald," she said in despair, "I can not open the gates!" Ronald turned his head about and looked at her with his beautiful eyes. He seemed to be trying to say, "I can."

"All right," said Grizel, as if he had spoken. She mounted the black steed, laughed nervously as she climbed into the saddle. "Now," she said "go on!" The horse made a dash at the gates, burst them open, and leaped out into the road. He curveted about for a moment, his hoofs striking fire from the cobble-stones. Then Grizel turned his head down the Canongate, away from the castle. She knew the point at which she intended to leave the city, and toward that point she headed Black Ronald. The horse seemed to know he was doing his old master a service, as he took his monstrous strides forward. Only once did Grizel look backward, and then a little shudder, half terror, half remorse, struck her, for she saw her home ablaze with light, and heard cries of excitement borne faintly to her on the rushing night wind. They had discovered her flight. Once she thought she heard hoof-beats behind her, but she knew she could not be overtaken.

Through the streets, now narrow, now broad, now straight, now crooked, dashed Black Ronald and his mistress. Once he nearly ran down a drowsy watchman who stood nodding at a sharp corner, but horse and rider were three hundred yards away before the frightened guardian regained his composure and sprang his discordant rattle.

Now the houses grew scarcer, and presently the battlements of the town wall loomed up ahead, and Grizel's heart sank, for there were lights in the road. She heard shouts, and knew she was to be challenged. She firmly set her teeth, said a little prayer, and leaned far forward upon Black Ronald's neck. The horse gave a snort of defiance, shied violently away from a soldier who stood by the way, and then went through the gateway like a shot. Grizel clung tightly to her saddle-bow, and urged her steed on. On, on they went down the firm roadway lined on either side by rows of noble oaks—on, on, out into the country-side, where the sweet odor of the heather arose gracious and fragrant to the trembling girl. There was little chance of her taking a wrong path. The road over which the postboy came was the King's highway, always kept in a state of repair.

She gave herself no time to notice the green upland farms, or the stately residences which stood out on either hand in the moonlight. She concentrated her strength and mind on urging her horse forward. She was too excited to form a definite plan, and her only clear idea was to meet the postboy before daylight, for she knew it would not be safe to trust too much to her disguise. Now and then a feeling of terror flashed over her, and she turned sick with dread; but her firm purpose upheld her.

It was almost four in the morning, and the wind was blowing chill from the sea, when she entered the rolling woodlands about the Tweed. Grizel was shivering with the cold, and was so tired that she with difficulty kept her place in the saddle.

"We can not hold out much longer, Ronald," she said; "and if we fail, we can never hold up our heads again." Ronald, the sure-footed, stumbled and nearly fell. "It is no use," sighed Grizel; "we must rest." She dismounted, but it was some moments before her tired limbs could obey her will. Beside the roadway was a ditch filled with running water, and Grizel managed to lead Ronald down the incline to its brink, and let him drink. She scooped up a little in her hand and moistened her tongue; then, realizing that Ronald must not be allowed to stand still, she, with great difficulty, mounted upon his back again, and, heartsick, fearful, yet not daring to turn back, coaxed him gently forward.

The moon had set long before this, and in the misty east the sky began to blanch with the first gleam of morning. Suddenly, around the curve of the road where it leaves the banks of the Tweed, came a dark object. Grizel's heart leaped wildly. Thirty seconds later she saw that it was indeed a horseman. He broke into a song:

"The Lord o' Argyle cam' wi' plumes and wi' spears,
And Monmouth he landed wi' gay cavaliers!

The pibroch has caa'd every tartan the-
gither,

B'thoosans their footsteps a' pressin' the
heather;

Th' North and the Sooth sent their bravest ones out,

But a joust wi' Kirke's Lambs put them
all to the rout."

By this time, the horseman was so close
that Grizel could distinguish objects hanging upon the horse in front of the rider.
They were the mail-bags! For the first time
she realized her weakness and saw how
unlikely it was that she would be able to
cope with an armed man. The blood rushed
to her head, and a courage that was the inspiration of the moment took possession of
her. She struck Black Ronald a lash with
her whip.

"Go!" she said to him shrilly, while her
heartbeats hammered in her ears, "Go!"

The astonished and excited horse leaped
down the road. As she met the postboy, she
drew Black Ronald, with a sudden strength
that was born of the danger, back upon
his haunches. His huge body blocked the
way.

"Dismount!" she cried to the other rider.
Her voice was hoarse from fright, and
sounded strangely in her own ears. But a
wild courage nerved her, and the hand that
drew and held the pistol was as firm as a
man's. Black Ronald was rearing wildly,
and in grasping the reins tighter, her other
hand mechanically altered its position
about the pistol.

She had not meant to fire, she had only
thought to aim and threaten, but suddenly
there was a flash of light in the gray atmosphere, a dull reverberation, and to the
girl's horrified amazement she saw the
horse in front of her stagger and fall heavily to the ground. The rider, thrown from
his saddle, was pinned to the earth by his
horse and stunned by the fall. Dizzy with

pain and confused by the rapidity of the
assault, he made no effort to draw his
weapon.

The mail-bags had swung by their own
momentum quite clear of the horse in its
fall, and now lay loosely over its back,
joined by the heavy strap.

It was a painful task for the exhausted
girl to dismount, but she did so, and, lifting
the cumbersome leathern bags, she threw
them over Black Ronald's neck. It was yet
more painful to her tender heart to leave
the poor fellow she had injured lying in so
pitiable a condition, but her father's life
was in danger, and that, to her, was of more
moment than the postboy's hurts.

"Heaven forgive me," she said, bending
over him. "I pray this may not be his
death!" She clambered over the fallen horse
and mounted Ronald, who was calm again.
Then she turned his head toward Edin-
boro' Town and hurriedly urged him for-
word. But as she sped away from the scene
of the encounter, she kept looking back,
with an awe-struck face, to the fallen postboy. In the excitement of the meeting and
in her one great resolve to obtain her
father's death-warrant, she had lost all
thought of the risks she ran or of the in-
juries she might inflict; and it was with
unspeakable relief, therefore, that she at
last saw the postboy struggle to his feet, and
stand gazing after her. "Thank Heaven, he
is not killed!" she exclaimed again and
again, as she now joyfully pressed Ronald
into a gallop. Throughout the homeward
journey, Grizel made it a point to urge
him to greater speed when nearing a farm-
house, so that there would be less risk of
discovery. Once or twice she was accosted
by laborers in the field, and once by the
driver of a cart, but their remarks were lost
upon the wind as the faithful Ronald thundered on. She did not feel the need of sleep,
for she had forgotten it in all her excitement, but she was greatly exhausted and

suffering from the effects of her rough ride.

Soon the smoke in the distance showed Grizel that her native town lay an hour's journey ahead. She set her teeth and said an encouraging word to the horse. He seemed to understand, for he redoubled his energies. Now the roofs became visible, and now, grim and sullen, the turrets of the castle loomed up. Grizel felt a great lump in her throat as she thought of her father in his lonely despair.

She turned Ronald from the road again and cut through a clump of elms. She came out in a few minutes and rode more slowly toward a smaller gate than the one by which she had left the city. A stout soldier looked at her carelessly and then turned to his tankard of ale, after he had noticed the mail-bags. Grizel turned into a crooked, narrow street lined on each side with toppling, frowning buildings. She drew rein before a humble house, and slipped wearily from her saddle and knocked at the door. An old woman opened the heavy oaken door and Grizel fell into her arms.

"The bags—the mail," she gasped, and fainted. When she recovered consciousness, she found herself on a low, rough bed. The old woman was bending over her.

"Losh keep me!" said the dame. "I did na ken ye! Ma puir bairnie! Hoo cam' ye by these?" and she pointed to the clothes of Allen.

"The bags?" said Grizel, sitting bolt upright—

"Are under the hearth," said the old woman.

"And Ronald?" continued Grizel.

"Is in the byre wi' the coos," said the other with a knowing leer. "Not a soul kens it. Ne'er a body saw ye come."

Breathlessly Grizel explained all to her old nurse, and then sprung off the bed. At her request the old dame locked the door and brought her the bags. By the aid of a

sharp knife the pair slashed open the leathern covering, and the inclosed packets fell upon the floor. With trembling hands Grizel fumbled them all over, tossing one after another impatiently aside as she read the addresses. At last she came upon a large one addressed to the governor. With beating heart she hesitated a moment, and then tore the packet open with shaking fingers. She easily read the bold handwriting. Suddenly everything swam before her, and again she nearly fell into her companion's arms.

It was too true. What she read was a formal warrant of the King, signed by his majesty, and stamped and sealed with red wax. It ordered the governor to hang Sir John Cochrane of Ochiltree at the Cross in Edinburgh at ten o'clock in the morning, on the third day of the following week. She clutched the paper and hid it in her dress.

The disposition of the rest of the mail was soon decided upon. The old lady's son Jock—a wild fellow—was to put the sacks on the back of a donkey and turn it loose outside the gates, at his earliest opportunity. And then Grizel, clad in some rough garments the old lady procured, slipped out of the house, and painfully made her way toward the Canongate.

It was four o'clock in the afternoon when she reached her home. The porter at the gate could scarcely be made to understand that the uncouth figure before him was his young mistress. But a moment later her mother was embracing her, with tears of joy.

All the male friends of Sir John were hastily summoned, and Grizel related her adventure, and displayed the death-warrant of her father. The hated document was consigned to the flames, a consultation was held, and that night three of the gentlemen left for London.

The next day, the donkey and the mail-sacks were found by a sentry, and some little excitement was occasioned; but when the postboy came in later, and related how he had been attacked by six stalwart robbers, and how he had slain two of them and was then overpowered and forced to surrender the bags, all wonderment was set at rest.

The Cochrane family passed a week of great anxiety, but when it was ended, the three friends returned from London with joyful news. The King had listened to their petition, and had ordered the removal of Sir John to the Tower of London, until his case could be reconsidered. So to London Sir John went; and after a time the payment of five thousand pounds to some of the King's advisers secured an absolute pardon. His lands, which had been confiscated, were restored to him; and on his arrival at his Scottish home, he was warmly welcomed by a great concourse of his friends. He thanked them in a speech, taking care, however, not to tell who was so greatly instrumental in making his liberation possible. But we may be sure that he was secretly proud of the pluck and devotion of his daughter Grizel.

THE CROW-CHILD

by Mary Mapes Dodge

MIDWAY between a certain blue lake and a deep forest there once stood a cottage, called by its owner "The Rookery."

The forest shut out the sunlight and scowled upon the ground, breaking with shadows every ray that fell, until only a few little pieces lay scattered about. But the broad lake invited all the rays to come and rest upon her, so that sometimes she shone from shore to shore, and the sun winked and blinked above her, as though dazzled by his own reflection. The cottage, which was very small, had sunny windows and dark windows. Only from the roof could you see the mountains beyond, where the light crept up in the morning and down in the evening, turning all the brooks into living silver as it passed.

But something brighter than sunshine used often to look from the cottage into the forest, and something even more gloomy than shadows often glowered from its windows upon the sunny lake. One was the face of little Ruky Lynn; and the other was his sister's, when she felt angry or ill-tempered.

They were orphans, Cora and Ruky, living alone in the cottage with an old uncle. Cora—or "Cor," as Ruky called her—was nearly sixteen years old, but her brother had seen the forest turn yellow only four times. She was, therefore, almost mother and sister in one. The little fellow was her companion night and day. To-

gether they ate and slept, and—when Cora was not at work in the cottage—together they rambled in the wood, or floated in their little skiff upon the lake.

Ruky had dark, bright eyes, and the glossy blackness of his hair made his cheeks look even rosier than they were. He had funny ways for a boy, Cora thought. The quick, bird-like jerks of his raven-black head, his stately baby gait, and his habit of pecking at his food, as she called it, often made his sister laugh. Young as he was, the little fellow had learned to mount to the top of a low-branching tree near the cottage, though he could not always get down alone. Sometimes when, perched in the thick foliage, he would scream, "Cor! Cor! Come, help me down!" his sister would answer, as she ran out laughing, "Yes, little Crow! I 'm coming."

Perhaps it was because he reminded her of a crow that Cora often called him her birdie. This was when she was good-natured and willing to let him see how much she loved him. But in her cloudy moments, as the uncle called them, Cora was another girl. Everything seemed ugly to her, or out of tune. Even Ruky was a trial; and, instead of giving him a kind word, she would scold and grumble until he would steal from the cottage door, and, jumping lightly from the door-step, seek the shelter of his tree. Once safely perched among its branches he knew she would finish her work, forget her ill-humor, and be quite ready, when he

484

cried "Cor! Cor!" to come out laughing, "Yes, little Crow! I 'm coming I 'm coming!"

No one could help loving Ruky, with his quick, affectionate ways; and it seemed that Ruky, in turn, could not help loving every person and thing around him. He loved his silent old uncle, the bright lake, the cool forest, and even his little china cup with red berries painted upon it. But more than all, Ruky loved his golden-haired sister, and the great dog, who would plunge into the lake at the mere pointing of his chubby little finger.

Nep and Ruky often talked together, and though one used barks and the other words, there was a perfect understanding between them. Woe to the straggler that dared to cross Nep's path, and woe to the bird or rabbit that ventured too near!—those great teeth snapped at their prey without even the warning of a growl. But Ruky could safely pull Nep's ears or his tail, or climb his great shaggy back, or even snatch away the untasted bone. Still, as I said before, every one loved the child; so, of course, Nep was no exception.

One day Ruky's "Cor! Cor!" had sounded oftener than usual. His rosy face had bent saucily to kiss Cora's upturned forehead, as she raised her arms to lift him from the tree; but the sparkle in his dark eyes had seemed to kindle so much mischief in him that his sister's patience became fairly exhausted.

"Has Cor nothing to do but to wait upon *you*," she cried, "and nothing to listen to but your noise and your racket? You shall go to bed early to-day, and then I shall have some peace."

"No, no, Cor. Please let Ruky wait till the stars come. Ruky wants to see the stars."

"Hush! Ruky is bad. He shall have a whipping when Uncle comes back from town."

Nep growled.

"Ha! ha!" laughed Ruky, jerking his head saucily from side to side; "Nep says 'No!' "

Nep was shut out of the cottage for his pains, and poor Ruky was undressed, with many a hasty jerk and pull.

"You hurt, Cor!" he said, plaintively. "I 'm going to take off my shoes my own self."

"No, you 're not," cried Cor, almost shaking him; and when he cried she called him naughty, and said if he did not stop he should have no supper. This made him cry all the more, and Cora, feeling in her angry mood that he deserved severe punishment, threw away his supper and put him to bed. Then all that could be heard were Ruky's low sobs and the snappish clicks of Cora's needles, as she sat knitting, with her back to him.

He could not sleep, for his eyelids were scalded with tears, and his plaintive "Cor, Cor!" had eached his sister's ears in vain. She never once looked up from those gleaming knitting-needles, nor even gave him his good-night kiss.

It grew late. The uncle did not return. At last Cora, sulky and weary, locked the cottage door, blew out her candle, and lay down beside her brother.

The poor little fellow tried to win a forgiving word, but she was too ill-natured to grant it. In vain he whispered "Cor,—Cor!" He even touched her hand over and over again with his lips, hoping she would turn toward him, and, with a loving kiss, murmur as usual, "Good-night, little birdie."

Instead of this, she jerked her arm angrily away, saying:

"Oh, stop your pecking and go to sleep! I wish you were a crow in earnest, and then I should have some peace."

After this, Ruky was silent. His heart drooped within him as he wondered what this "peace" was that his sister wished for so often, and why he must go away before it could come to her.

Soon, Cora, who had rejoiced in the sudden calm, heard a strange fluttering. In an instant she saw by the starlight a dark object wheel once or twice in the air above

His empty place was still warm—perhaps he had slid softly from the bed. With trembling haste she lighted the candle, and peered in every corner. The boy was not to be found!

Then those fearful words rang in her ears:

"Oh, Ruky! Is this you?"

her, then dart suddenly through the open window.

Astonished that Ruky had not either shouted with delight at the strange visitor, or else clung to her neck in fear, she turned to see if he had fallen asleep.

No wonder that she started up, horror-stricken,—Ruky was not there!

"I wish you were a crow in earnest!"

Cora rushed to the door, and, with straining gaze, looked out into the still night.

"Ruky! Ruky!" she screamed.

There was a slight stir in the low-growing tree.

"Ruky, darling, come back!"

"Caw, caw!" answered a harsh voice

from the tree. Something black seemed to spin out of it, and then, in great, sweeping circles, sailed upward, until finally it settled upon one of the loftiest trees in the forest.

"Caw, caw!" it screamed, fiercely.

The girl shuddered, but, with outstretched arms, cried out:

"O Ruky, if it is *you,* come back to poor Cor!"

"Caw, caw!" mocked hundreds of voices, as a shadow like a thunder-cloud rose in the air. It was an immense flock of crows. She could distinguish them plainly in the starlight, circling higher and higher, then lower and lower, until, screaming "Caw, caw!" they sailed far off into the night.

"Answer me, Ruky!" she cried.

Nep growled, the forest trees whispered softly together, and the lake, twinkling with stars, sang a lullaby as it lifted its weary little waves upon the shore: there was no other sound.

It seemed that daylight never would come; but at last the trees turned slowly from black to green, and the lake put out its stars, one by one, and waited for the sunshine.

Cora, who had been wandering restlessly in every direction, now went weeping into the cottage. "Poor boy!" she sobbed; "he had no supper." Then she scattered breadcrumbs near the door-way, hoping that Ruky would come for them; but only a few timid little songsters hovered about, and, while Cora wept, picked up the food daintily, as though it burned their bills. When she reached forth her hand, though there were no crows among them, and called "Ruky!" they were frightened away in an instant.

Next she went to the steep-roofed barn, and, bringing out an apronful of grain, scattered it all around his favorite tree. Before long, to her great joy, a flock of crows came by. They spied the grain, and soon were busily picking it up, with their short, feathered bills. One even came near the mound where she sat. Unable to restrain herself longer, she fell upon her knees, with an imploring cry:

"Oh, Ruky! Is *this you?*"

Instantly the entire flock set up an angry "caw," and surrounding the crow who was hopping closer and closer to Cora, hurried him off until they all looked like mere specks against the summer sky.

Every day, rain or shine, she scattered the grain, trembling with dread lest Nep should leap among the hungry crows, and perhaps kill her own birdie first. But Nep knew better; he never stirred when the noisy crowd settled around the cottage, excepting once, when one of them settled upon his back. Then he started up, wagging his tail, and barked with uproarious delight. The crow flew off with a frightened "caw," and did not venture near him again.

Poor Cora felt sure that this could be no other than Ruky. Oh, if she only could have caught him then! Perhaps with kisses and prayers she might have won him back to Ruky's shape; but now the chance was lost.

There were none to help her; for the nearest neighbor dwelt miles away, and her uncle had not yet returned.

After a while she remembered the little cup, and filling it with grain, stood it upon a grassy mound. When the crows came, they fought and struggled for its contents, with many an angry cry. One of them made no effort to seize the grain. He seemed contented to peck at the berries painted upon its sides, as he hopped joyfully around it again and again. Nep lay very quiet. Only the tip of his tail twitched with an eager, wistful motion. But Cora sprang joyfully toward the bird.

"It *is* Ruky!" she cried, striving to catch it. Alas! the cup lay shattered beneath her hand, as, with a taunting "caw, caw," the crow joined its fellows and flew away.

Next, gunners came. They were looking for other game; but they hated the crows, Cora knew, and she trembled night and day. She could hear the sharp crack of fowling-pieces in the forest, and shuddered whenever Nep, pricking up his ears, darted with an angry howl in the direction of the sound. She knew, too, that her uncle had set traps for the crows, and it seemed to her that the whole world was against the poor birds, plotting their destruction.

Time flew by. The leaves seemed to flash into bright colors and fall off almost in a day. Frost and snow came. Still the uncle had not returned, or, if he had, she did not know it. Her brain was bewildered. She knew not whether she ate or slept. Only the terrible firing reached her ears, or that living black cloud came and went with its ceaseless "caw."

At last, during a terrible night of wind and storm, Cora felt that she must go forth and seek her poor bird.

"Perhaps he is freezing—dying!" she cried, springing frantically from the bed, and casting her long cloak over her night-dress.

In a moment, she was trudging bare-footed through the snow. It was so deep she could hardly walk, and the sleet was driving into her face; still she kept on, though her numbed feet seemed scarcely to belong to her. All the way she was praying in her heart, and promising never, never to be passionate again, if she only could find her birdie—not Ruky, the boy, but whatever he might be—she was willing to accept her punishment. Soon a faint cry reached her ear. With eager haste, she peered into every fold of the drifted snow. A black object caught her eye. It was a poor storm-beaten crow, lying there benumbed and stiff.

For Ruky's sake, she folded it closely to her bosom, and plodded back to the cottage. The fire cast a rosy light on its glossy wing as she entered, but the poor thing did not stir. Softly stroking and warming it, she wrapped the frozen bird in soft flannel and breathed into its open mouth. Soon, to her great relief, it revived, and even swallowed a few grains of wheat.

Cold and weary, she cast herself upon the bed, still folding the bird to her heart. "It may be Ruky! It is all I ask," she sobbed. "I dare not pray for more."

Suddenly she felt a peculiar stirring. The crow seemed to grow larger. Then, in the dim light, she felt its feathers pressing lightly against her cheek. Next, something soft and warm wound itself tenderly about her neck; and she heard a sweet voice saying:

"Don't cry, Cor,—I 'll be good."

She started up. It was, indeed, her own darling! The starlight shone into the room. Lighting her candle, she looked at the clock. It was just two hours since she had uttered those cruel words. Sobbing, she asked:

"Have I been asleep, Ruky, dear?"

"I don't know, Cor. Do people cry when they 're asleep?"

"Sometimes, Ruky," clasping him very close.

"Then you have been asleep. But, Cor, please don't let Uncle whip Ruky."

"No, no, my birdie—I mean, my brother. Good-night, darling!"

"Good-night."

THE AFFAIR OF THE "SANDPIPER"

by *Elizabeth Stuart Phelps*

AUNT JOHN, you know, is always doing something; I mean something for us fellows,—Jill and me. Perhaps you will remember Aunt John. I told about her once in the *Young Folks;* how we went down to her house one vacation and fell through the floor into the cellar and thought the Day of Judgment had come.

Jill thinks that scrape we got into at Gloucester would do to tell; he thinks it would do very well for a story. Aunt John took us to Gloucester.

We went to Eastern Point to one of the big boarding-houses. We had n't been to the beach before for some time. But we 'd always known about boats, and so forth, at home. Could swim, of course. Aunt John taught us to swim in Deepwater Brook, that runs behind her house, when I was a little shaver, only six. Aunt John can swim forwards and backwards and under water, and dive, too; she 's one of the handsomest swimmers I ever saw.

So we went to Gloucester. Gloucester is a very interesting place. At least, I thought so; Jill did n't so much, at first. I like to see them dry the mackerel on the wharves all up and down the road between the town and the Point. I know most every mackerel-dryer there is there, and sometimes I help; they lay them out on stretchers in the sun. Then there 's a tin-shop, where they have a boy to stand in a cart and catch tin pails out of a second-story window; he piles them up in a row in a cart to take off. I tried one day myself. You 'd think it would be easy; but I dropped three and banged a notch in one.

Then there 's a sail-boat ferry. The boat goes over and back between the town and the Point, and you pay four cents a trip. Two men make a living out of that ferry, but I don't see how. I spent half my allowance going over, but he would n't let me help at the sails. One day he put off some drunken fellows because they did n't quite tip the boat over. They splashed into the water, and were just as mad! Then, under the wharves I like it. The piers look like trees, long and straight, and in green rows. There 's a piece in my reading-book it makes me think of:

> "Where Alph, the sacred river, ran
>   Through caverns, measureless to man,
>   Down to a sunless sea."

But Jill says it is n't very clean (and it is n't). And he says boys have no business to quote poetry; he says girls have. One day we put under the piers in a dory, and got wedged in, and an old fisherman had to come and haul us out with a boat-hook. Then there are the boats on a dark night, with the colored lights, all sailing in, and you try to count 'em. Sometimes there 's an outside steamer in for shelter, if it 's stormy, but she makes out early next morning, before you 're up.

So we went to Gloucester, and one day we got a sail-boat. They don't have a great many sail-boats on the Point; and Jill hired this for a week of a chap in town that had gone home to see his young lady. She was a neat craft, painted black and gold. The gold was inside, and overflowing to the gunwale's edge,—Aunt John said, like an overflowing heart. Aunt John thought it was a pretty boat. Her name was the "Sandpiper." She was finished as neatly as any boat in the harbor. We got her for five dollars a week, and the moorings. We moored her off the rocks in front of the boarding-house with one of those pulley moorings, you know, in a ring, where you set her in and out, hand over hand, and tie the painter too long, and have her bang up against another man's boat, and are called away from dinner to got out and haul her all in and do it over, and find your pudding cold. Of course, you learn to tie a sailor knot. There was one girl at our house who tied a pretty sailor knot. She learned on neckties, but she had a boat. Frank Starkweather went with her. Her name was Tony Guest. But she would n't let Frank tie the boat up.

Now, there was this about having that boat. Aunt John said: "Boys! I 've found a boat in town you can have for a week." Then she said: "Now, boys! if I give you leave to come and go in that boat, free from fret and orders and questions (which she knows how boys hate—she 's 'most as good as a boy herself), I shall expect you to act with great prudence," said Aunt John. "I expect you to look out for dangers as carefully as grown men do. If I *treat* you like men, you *act* like them, and whenever you go outside the bar you must take Frank Starkweather."

Aunt John said this, and then she never said any more. She did not bother nor fuss. We just took that boat and did as we

pleased, and, I tell you it was fun. But, then, we were careful.

Friday, it came up, somehow, about going to Swampscott. Frank Starkweather said he 'd go. He said he thought it was safe, but he said he thought we might as well mention it to our aunt, or some other good sailor. But, I believe we did n't mention it at all. I can't say exactly whether we *meant* not to mention it, but, at any rate, we did n't. I wanted to go like sixty the minute it was spoken of. So did Jill. We got up early, you know, and off before anybody was up.

At least, nobody was up but Tony Guest and her older sister; for they row themselves 'most every morning. They stood on the rocks and said, "Bon voyage!" At least, the sister did, but Miss Tony said, "Good luck to you!"

Miss Tony said she 'd tell Aunt John, and we sent our good-by, and that we might n't be home till late, and that the day was just right, and no danger. Miss Tony stood on the rocks and waved her hat—a little jockey sailor hat she wears, with long streamers. And Frank was so taken up with looking at her that he steered us into Black Bess, and gave us one good soft jerk to begin with. Black Bess is a mean, pointed reef off Niles'. But no harm happened, and nothing happened of any account till we got to Swampscott. We had a stiff nor' by nor'-easter part of the way and plenty of sun, and we made a clear tack, and got in to dinner by twelve o'clock, as hungry as sharks. And Frank knew the way pretty well, or else he thought he did,—I don't know which. Frank Starkweather is seventeen.

So we went ashore for dinner, and ate two chowders apiece, and a horn button that they called a lemon pie as a pleasant exercise of the imagination, and hard cider for Frank. But we did n't. That's one thing we 've promised our Aunt John,—that we wont take drinks round with boys,—because she says half of 'em you might get drunk on, if you wanted to.

Once, when I was a mite of a chap, Aunt John looked at me with that way she has of snapping her eyes, and said she, "George Zacharias!" (but she generally calls me Jack), "George Zacharias! if you ever should get *drunk,* I should be so ashamed I should n't want to *look* at you!"

It was just like Aunt John. You know, when anybody says anything like that to you, you remember it.

So we did n't take the cider and Frank did n't laugh at us,—for he 's a gentleman, —and about one o'clock we went down and hauled the "Sandpiper" round to go home.

We meant to get home early, and surprise them if we could. I rather wanted to be home by seven or eight, because we had n't seen Aunt John nor said good-by to her.

There was an old captain down on the rocks when we hauled round, and he had a pipe in his mouth. So he took it out when he saw us, and said, "Goin' fur?"

So Frank told him. Then the captain said: "Humph!" At least, that 's the way books spell it. *I* should spell it more this way, "Enguhph!"

Now, when an old tar says that,—whichever way you spell it,—you 'd better ask him what he means, I think. So Frank did.

"Head-winds," said the captain, "and thick weather!"

But the weather was clear as a bell, and who minds a little head-wind? So we laughed, and laid the "Sandpiper" round, and started off like a bumble-bee. That boat looked more like a bumble-bee than she did like a sandpiper, anyway.

"What did the old cove mean?" asked Frank, after we 'd rounded the headland and put bravely out.

"He said them boys' mothers had better have kept 'em at home," spoke up Jill. "I heard him, to another fellow."

"Sea-captains out of business are always scarey as doves," said Frank Starkweather.

"And wise as serpents," said I,—just to say it. I did n't especially mean anything; most people don't, half the time.

It was grand on the water that day. The "Sandpiper" laid to and ran near the wind, as if she 'd been running a race with it. Frank took the ropes and I the rudder. We began not to talk much as we got farther out. You had to keep your eyes open pretty sharp, and a great many little craft were about. They all seemed to be making port, at Salem, Beverly, and different places. I wondered why; Frank said, perhaps they looked for a storm *to-morrow*. But he put "to-morrow" in italics.

To tell the truth, we did n't make very good headway after the first. The sea began to rise, and the breeze was stiff as a poker, from the east. I thought Frank looked a little solemn once or twice, when she careened clear over. Sometimes she tipped, so it was really ugly; and we were all drenched by three o'clock, by the waves. By half-past three, Frank told Jill he thought he 'd better bail a little, to keep our feet dry. But *I* thought *he* thought it was just as well we should n't carry quite so much water. But, perhaps, he did n't.

I think it was just about four o'clock. I was looking at the water, thinking; Jill was watching for boats and telling Frank their tack and kind. Frank had his sleeves rolled up and his hat off, and his eyes set sharp in his head at everything. I was leaning over the gunwale and counting how many colors I could see in the water,—for we were off shore in a weedy place,—and wondering how many more Aunt John would find than I could.

All at once, I found that I could n't see

a great many. What there were were dull
and ugly. Then I heard Frank say:

"Ah-h-h-h!" between his teeth.

I looked up. I could see just one color—
only one,—the ugliest color I think I ever
saw, or expect to see, in my life. Just grey,
—cold, crawling grey. You could n't see
the shore; you could n't see the boats making the harbor. Now we knew why.

We could just see each other's faces
and our own rigging, and a little patch of
greeny-black water round about.

You could n't realize, unless you 'd seen
it, how quick a fog comes down. A minute,
and there is n't any! A minute, and there
is n't anything else! We had n't even seen
it *crawl*. It *pounced*.

As I said, Frank Starkweather said:
"Ah-h-h-h!"

Jill said, "Ow-w-w!"

I said, "Wh-ew-w-w!"

But when we 'd made these three intellectual remarks, we did n't find ourselves
talkative. Frank jammed his head into his
hat, and took to the ropes with a jerk. I
asked him if he thought he could saw a
fog in two. But I got an extra hold of the
tiller, for I felt more comfortable. Jill but-
toned up his coat and brushed out his hair,
as if he 'd been going to a party. He looked
very nervous.

There 's no doubt about it, and we may
as well own up now. We did n't one of us
know enough to take a sail-boat from
Gloucester to Swampscott. Not one. And
we 'd no business to have come without
asking advice. But we were n't so green we
did n't know that to take a sail-boat from
Swampscott to Gloucester, in the teeth of
an east wind, and *then* to have the luck to
run into a fogbank. was no joke, anyway
you might look at it.

I asked Frank once if he thought Miss
Tony would wear mourning; but he looked
so black at me, I gave it up, and nobody
tried to make a joke after that.

So we set to, and did the best we could.

You don't enjoy it, sailing in a fog like
that. I 'd have given all I owned, if I had n't
kept thinking about Aunt John so often.
But I did. So did Jill, I guess.

We began to hear the boat-horns soon—
here and there and everywhere, up and
down. And whistles; such screeching
whistles from steamers and tugs! We passed
the "Stamford" once, on her way to Boston.
I knew *her* whistle well as I knew Jill's.
But I could n't see her. It gave you a funny
feeling, to hear so many things that you
could n't see.

Pretty soon, Frank turned slowly around
and looked at me. He looked white, I
thought.

"I thought so!" said he.

"Thought what?" said I.

"Thought we were n't, and we aint! We
aint making an inch in this confounded
fog! Not one!"

"I should like to know what we *are*
making?" said I, half mad.

"A circle," said Frank; "that's all. Just
going round and round. I think we 're off
the Manchester Rocks, but I can't say sure.
But I know that red buoy with the piece of
kelp on it. We left that buoy half-an-hour
ago. We 've turned a circle and come back
to it. If you can manage this boat, Jack, you
may, for I can't!"

I 'd never seen Frank Starkweather act
so. He just gave up, and pulled his hat over
his eyes, and I had to take his place till he
felt better; I suppose, from being so much
older and from Aunt John's trusting him,
he felt badly.

First we knew after that, it began to
grow dark. It was the last of August, and
darkened early. But we knew how late it
must be, and that we must have been going
round and round for a long time. I don't
think Frank could steer by the wind very
well, or else the wind had changed. At any
rate, he did n't know what to do.

Well, sir, we were sitting in that boat, three of the solemnest-looking boys *you* ever saw, when, all at once, Frank Starkweather just gave one jump and grabbed me around the throat, as if he 'd been getting up a first-class murder, and pulled my watch-guard off,—it was my old rubber one,—and it broke. Something rattled on the bottom of the boat, and Frank gave another leap, and at it.

"Why in the name of mercy did n't you tell a fellow that you 'd got a compass with you?" roared Frank.

"And, sure enough, he meant the little compass that Jill gave me for a charm last Christmas. It was a neat little thing—truer than most such arrangements.

You ought to have seen Frank holding on to that silly little brittle thing to see if it was true—head bent over this way, and one hand on the tiller. The hand that held the little compass shook like a rabbit.

If it had n't been for that compass, I wont pretend to say what would have happened. It was bad enough as it was. But Frank stuck to the tiny thing, and kept our bearings pretty well.

Only, there was the bother of the fog. The fog was thick as mud, and the wind had shifted to the sou'-east, and it was growing very dark.

We guessed now that we must be nearing Norman's Woe. Norman's Woe is an awful reef. It 's the one Longfellow's poetry tells of, about the skipper's daughter. I felt as if I could have written a poem myself about it, if I had n't been so frightened as we went by,—creeping that way,—feeling out into the fog, you know, to find it. The wind just *hammered* us towards the reef.

For I *was* frightened. So were we all. We huddled together. It was a dreadful feeling to go sailing on and not know but any minute you 'd strike one of the worst reefs on all the Massachusetts coast (for it 's an awful lonesome rock, and thick pine woods

around, and no houses to speak of, and all the passing craft so shy of it), and you three boys in a sail-boat by yourselves in thick weather, after dark!

I suppose it 's the way with a good many other dreadful things; but we never knew it till it was over. Frank had just said, "There 's a lift in the fog, boys," and I had said, "How dark it is!" when Jill screeched out, "We 've hit! O, we 've hit!" and there was a horrid scraping noise and a great push of the wind, and I gave such a crunch to the tiller I heard it crack, and then we sailed off in a spurt, and all looked back.

There it lay. Black, long, ugly—the ugliest thing! It ran out, like a monster's long tongue, to sea, as if it would lap up poor fellows, I could n't but think. And the lonesome pine woods were so black above, and there was such a noise of the water all about!

We had cleared it—just.

I don't know what the other fellows did, but *I* said my prayers.

There was need of it, too, may be, for we were n't home yet, by any means. And there are places I 'd rather be in than Gloucester harbor on a dark night.

You see, the fog was getting off, but the *blow* was awful, and it just beat against that western shore and its solid cliffs, there, for miles. And there is the island and half a dozen little reefs to think of; and the harbor was full of craft in for the blow, which made you steer as if you were all eyes.

The fog-bell was tolling, too, for it was still thick outside. I hate to hear it ever since that night. I wondered what Aunt John thought of it. That bell sounds like a big funeral-bell, tolled over all the poor fellows that go down on this ugly coast.

So we crawled along in, frightened to death.

Whether we could see the lights in the boarding-house parlor, I don't know. There were a great many lights, and we got confused.

We meant to steer clear east of Ten Pound Island, and then back straight as we could.

"We 're 'most there!" said Frank.

"Time we were," said I. It must be 'most eleven o'clock."

That instant there was a horrible crunching, grinding noise.

The "Sandpiper" leaped and leaped again. Then she grated up roughly, and stuck fast.

We were on the rocks. Where?

We looked up, and a great light blazed over our heads, like a great eye.

It was the light on Ten Pound Island. We had hit the little, long, narrow reef that juts out into the channel towards the sea.

The "Sandpiper" struggled as if she had been hurt, and began to settle over on her side slowly.

We lifted up our voices high and strong as we knew how, over the noise the water made.

"Help! Help!"

You can't think what a sound it has—your own voice calling that word out for the first time in your life.

We caught hold of each other,—knee-deep in the water, that came up cold as ice over the "Sandpiper's" pretty colors,—and called, and called:

"Help! *Help!* Help! Oh, HELP!"

"Help! Oh, he-*elp!*"

Our voices rang out all together. First we knew, another one rang into them. He'd been shouting, nobody knew how long, at us.

"Hold on! There in a minute! Keep up! Where are you? Keep up! Keep up!"

We knew the voice as soon as we heard it. It was the light-keeper at Ten Pound Island. It was just the jolliest, cheeriest, *helpingist* voice that ever was, we boys

thought; and he was as used to the water as a duck. The minute we heard him we felt safe.

The water was washing over us pretty strongly by that time, where the "Sandpiper" lay over on the reef. She did not move very much, but lay just pinioned there, and so kept us out of the trough of the waves. It would have been a tough swim in the dark and such a sea. May be Frank Starkweather could have made it. *Perhaps* I might myself; but I don't know about Jill. The water was so cold, and you 'd get dashed so.

The light-keeper came down on the reef with a lantern. He stood and swung it to and fro. He has grey hair and a long, grey beard, and they blew about in the wind. For all I was in such a fix, I remember thinking how his grey hair looked, and how the light overhead in the light-house tower seemed to wink over his head at us, as much as to say:

"What fools you were! Oh, what fools you were!"

The light-keeper swung his lantern twice, and put his hands to his mouth trumpetwise, and hollered out:

"What foo-oo-ools you were!" At least, it sounded like that at first, but we found it was more like this:

"Can't—do—anything without—the—boats! You're—too far—out—the reef! Can—you—keep—up—till I can—get—around?"

We hollered back that we guessed so, and he just ran! It 's some little job to get to the boathouse; that 's the other side of the island. He just put into it, I guess, for, before we knew it, the sound of oars came splashing around. Not the little, easy, quite-at-home, no-hurry kind of strokes he generally takes, but quick and sharp, like knives.

He hauled alongside, and we got in. We all shivered. Nobody said anything at first.

The light-keeper rowed around, and looked the "Sandpiper" over.

We boys looked at each other. I don't think we 'd thought about the "Sandpiper" before.

"Is she much hurt?" asked Frank.

"Oh, I hope not—hope not!" said the light-keeper, cheerily. "At any rate, you can't do much for her to-night. She 'll stay where she is till next tide, I think. I 'll just take you home, and when I come over I 'll find her anchor, and drop it till morning. You 'd better get home and see your friends quick as you can."

Now, Frank told him he was very kind, but we 'd take the other boat and row ourselves home. We would n't trouble him. But he said, "Oh, no," he 'd rather like to go, and see what the folks said.

He did n't *say* he knew we were all too scared to want to touch another boat that night, even that distance,—because we were boys,—but I suppose he thought so. And, as far as I 'm concerned, I was mighty glad to be treated like a little boy for a few minutes, and to get down in the stern and be still, and feel myself rowed through the dark by a pair of arms that knew that harbor well enough to cut it up into patchwork and sew it together again.

He and Frank talked, and Jill, some; but I did n't. I did n't feel like it.

First place, I 'd been too near drowning, I suppose. I 'd rather die 'most any way than drown, I think.

Then there was Aunt John. Then there was another thing,—*somebody* had got to be responsible for the "Sandpiper."

They were all out, when we got there, looking for us. It seemed to me as if all the Point were out—all our house, and everybody from the pretty little brown cottage, where the two hammocks are, and the tent.

Tony Guest was there, Frank said, 'way out on a slippery rock, looking and look-

ing, in her little sailor hat. I did n't see her for some time. I did n't notice anybody in particular. I don't think I could see very clearly I could n't see Aunt John anywhere.

When we got out we found we were used up, and staggered along on the rocks. Frank was white as chowder. I saw spots on Jill's face, as if he 'd rubbed it, and his hands were dirty. But I could n't see Aunt John.

So they all crowded round, and we did n't know what to say; and then I saw her. She was coming over the rocks with great shawls. She put one on me and one on Jill, and led us up to the house away from everybody. When she got us into her own room she kissed us—but not before.

She was very pale. I thought she 'd cry; I thought she 'd scold. But she did n't do either one. She only flew around and got us to bed, and got blankets and bottles and hot coffee and things. She did n't even ask a question till she saw *me* choke; then she just said, "Oh, boys, how *could* you?" That was all. Now, she never scolded nor crowed; upon my word, she did n't. The more frightened some people are about you, the more they abuse you. But Aunt John is different. She knew we felt badly enough; and when I spoke up about the "Sandpiper," though she looked troubled, she only told me to go to sleep, and we 'd see to-morrow.

So the next day we felt pretty tired, and we all went over to see the "Sandpiper." We could see her from the boarding-house window. She lay on the rock much as we had left her, only the tide was lower. She looked like the cow that the cars ran over —very much "discouraged." So we got the light-keeper and another man that knew about boats, and Aunt John, and rowed over to the island. The "Sandpiper" lay between her anchor and a rope the light-keeper 'd set to the rock. Her mast was snapped in two. We thought there seemed to be a bad leak, but could n't tell very well at first.

A lot of men had collected around,—men always go to wrecks in Gloucester just as you 'd go to fires anywhere else,—and some of 'em set to work and tried to haul her off the rocks. But they tried an hour, and gave it up. They said she looked to them pretty badly jammed.

The fellow that owned her had got back for some reason, and he came over. He looked very black. He said she was worth two hundred dollars.

Frank and Jill and I looked at each other. I don't think I ever felt so in my life.

"She 's a bad smash," said the fellow that owned her, "and somebody will be out of pocket on her. It can't be expected to be me, I suppose."

"She 'll come off when the tide serves," said the light-keeper. "We 'll see then how much she 's damaged. Perhaps it is n't such a bad job, after all."

But it was a bad job—very bad.

When the "Sandpiper" got off the reef at last, she looked like a sandpiper that had been shot on the wing—ruffled and struggling and half dead. Her mast was broken all to nothing, and there was a great gouge in her bows. The fellow that owned her had her towed into town, and said he 'd have the damages estimated and let us know. In the afternoon he came over and said it would take about seventy-five or eighty dollars to set her trim again.

Now, our people are n't very well off. They could n't afford eighty dollars to pay for a sail-boat, any way, in the world. I did n't know what on earth to do or say. I just walked around and thought of things. I had an awful headache. I could n't go to dinner. I wondered if I should have to go into a store and earn the money. I wondered if the fellow that owned her would arrest us, if we did n't pay. I thought what father and mother would think, and how

disgraced we were. I was the most miserable boy you ever knew, unless it was Jill.

I was out on the rocks in a cubby there is there, where nobody sees you, when I heard a step behind.

You 'd know Aunt John's step in a regiment, if you 'd ever heard it. It springs along, and strikes down broad. She wears great low boot-heels, like a man's, and her dresses don't drag.

"Coming in to supper?" asked Aunt John.

She bent over to look at me. She had a white shawl over her head, and she was smiling. She 's very gentle for a smart woman, my Aunt John.

I said no. I did n't want any supper.

"I 'm up such a tree about that boat!" said I.

"The boat," said Aunt John, quietly, "is paid for. You 'd better come to supper."

"Paid for? The 'Sandpiper?'" said I. "Who paid for her?"

But I knew. I knew when she shook her head and said, "No matter!" smiling. I knew she could n't afford it, and how it came out of what she 'd laid up. I felt so ashamed that I could n't speak, and I made up my mind we 'd pay her back, if it took ten years to do it. But I felt as if all Eastern Point had jumped up and rolled away off my heart. And still she never scolded nor crowed at us. Never!

And Frank Starkweather and Tony Guest said there were n't many like her, and they said if we did n't behave ourselves to pay her for it, we 'd be poor stuff, and I think so, too.

There is n't any moral to this story, that I know of,—I hate stories with morals tacked on. But I think *this:* I think a good sail-boat is something like a good friend. If you know much of anything, you won't abuse 'em—either of 'em; and if you *don't* know enough to know how to treat 'em, you 'd better go without.

FREDDY LOW TAKES THE WHEEL

by Cornelius Brett Boocock

FREDDY LOW was bow man. That is, he lay on the deck beside the mast and whenever his father called "hard-a-lee," he would cross over to the other side.

On this day the *Vigilant,* his father's boat, was sailing only a fair race and would probably finish fourth or fifth, and there was a good breeze too.

There was a time when Freddy was thrilled at the idea of sailing with his father. But that time had passed. He used to think that the *Vigilant* was the fastest cat-boat on the bay and that his father was the best racing skipper. He knew better now, because he had sailed his own fifteen-foot sneak-box in too many midweek races not to realize that his father missed many an opportunity to advance the *Vigilant.* But the *Vigilant* was a good racer still, although some of the newer boats won most of the races.

He glanced at the luff of the sail and was disgusted, but not surprised, to see a flutter of canvas as the wind hit the lee side.

"I don't know what has got into Dad," he said half aloud. "Here we are slopping along in the middle of the fleet when we ought to be up in front fighting it out for first place with the *Wampus* and *Scatt.* Just look how he's luffing! He does n't half sail the boat."

A loud laugh came from the cockpit where a group of men, friends of Mr. Low's, were sitting.

"Listen to that!" continued Freddy, to himself. "They don't know they are racing. How can a boat sail a race when she is weighted down by a lot of old men who crack jokes and talk business?"

The *Vigilant* was making the outer buoy nicely on the starboard tack. Underneath the sail, Freddy noticed the *Hummer* coming up on the port tack.

Now every one, who has ever been on the water, knows that a boat sailing on the starboard tack, that is, with the wind hitting the starboard side of the sail, has the right of way over a boat on the other tack.

Freddy called his father's attention to the approach of the *Hummer,* and then realized that he had been foolish to do this, as Mr. Low put the *Vigilant* about and gave the *Hummer* an advantage that was, by rights, his.

"Dad," called back Freddy, to his father, "you had the right of way. Why did you go about?"

"Remember the story of Irving Day, who died maintaining his right of way," replied Mr. Low, and went on talking with his friends.

Freddy was given little chance to forget the sad story of Mr. Day. On many occasions he had heard of him and wondered just why he should prevent the *Vigilant* from winning races.

"Steve Brodie may have been foolhardy when he jumped off the Brooklyn Bridge," thought Freddy, a minute later; "but he had nerve and took a chance."

That evening, when father and son were putting the boat away for the night, Freddy was not in a happy frame of mind.

"Dad," he said, "I don't think I 'll race with you any more."

"Why not, my boy?" asked his father, a bit surprised, "you used to be keen about it."

"Because I get so mad," the boy answered frankly. "You don't half sail the boat. You don't insist on your right of way and are the laughing-stock of all the captains because of it. The *Vigilant* finishes fifth or sixth. She ought to be among the first three."

Freddy glanced up as he tied a stop and, seeing that he was making an impression, went on with less strain in his voice.

"You know, you always tell me to do with all my heart whatever I am doing— to study as hard as I can when I 'm studying and to play as hard as I can when I 'm playing. But you sail a race as if you did n't give a rip whether you finish first or last. I love the *Vigilant* and I hate to see tubs like the *Hummer* and *Daisy* beat her as they did to-day. So I 'd rather not race with you any more."

Freddy did n't realize how disrespectful he had been, but his father, seeing the earnest and really pained expression on his son's face, understood and was silent. He recognized the truth in his remarks, too. When he had been younger he had raced with all his heart, but as he grew older he found that it was too fatiguing to come down from the city for a few days and work hard on his boat when he actually came for a rest. But he continued to race the *Vigilant,* more for the pleasure of the sail than for the excitement of the race. He selected his crews not for their seamanship, but for their good-fellowship and joviality.

It is not hard to see Mr. Low's point of view, but Freddy, who loved yachting, thought of a race as a race and was not satisfied with half-hearted attempts.

For several days Mr. Low thought over what Freddy had said. He did n't want to lose the respect of his son, yet he hardly felt like returning to his old racing habits.

So one day, in the middle of the week, after Freddy had sailed a beautiful race in his sneak-box, he called his son to him.

"Fred, my boy," he began, "I have decided that it is your turn to take over racing the *Vigilant*. I have done it for years, and, as you said after the last race, I don't really sail her. So from now on, you are to be her captain in the races. You get the boat in shape, select the crew, and sail her, and, if you want me to go along as advisory committee, I 'd be delighted to form part of the crew."

"That 's great!" the boy replied, "and of course I want you to come along, and perhaps together we can make the old ship step along with the best."

The race the next Saturday was perhaps the most important of the season, as it was for the celebrated Morgan Cup. This cup had been up for competition twenty years, and inscribed upon it were the names of eleven different boats. On two occasions the *Vigilant* had won it, but that was years before. Of late, the *Wampus* had won it twice, and her skipper was out to make it three in a row. In fact, the *Wampus* had an exceptional chance, as Mr. Waldron, her captain, was an excellent sailor and a good racer, while the boat itself was in fine shape. The *Scatt* was counted on to give it a good race, as she had won the two races that season which the *Wampus* had lost.

"Beat the *Scatt* and the cup is ours," Mr. Waldron had said to his crew after the last race.

Fred worked hard to put the *Vigilant* in condition. He pulled her up on a flat, with the help of some friends, and scraped her thoroughly. He stretched her sail and shifted ballast so that on the day of the race she was in fine trim. He selected his crew from his many friends and had several practice runs so that each one knew his job. Mr. Low was to 'tend sheet.

Shortly before the preliminary gun, the *Vigilant* swung away from the dock and sailed across the bay. The crew were at their stations and all waited eagerly for the starting gun. There was a fresh breeze from the southeast, which bellied out the big sail. The course required a beat into the wind for three legs, and a run free on the return.

At the start the boats grouped near the pier head and fought for the windward position. But Freddy kept out of the mess of boats, and, although in a leeward position, was free to sail without hindrance. This piece of strategy was well thought out, as he would cross the line on the starboard tack, and would thus have the right of way.

"Bang!" went the little brass cannon, and eleven boats got under way. Near the pier, there was much confusion and crowding, some minor collisions, with loud talking and yelling as ten boats tried to occupy the space of one. Alone across the bay, the *Vigilant* started unmolested and headed for the first buoy. The crew was stretched out on the deck, Mr. Low was seated on the leeward seat with the sheet rope in his hand, while his son Freddy stood at the wheel.

"Trim her a little, Dad," he directed, as he let up on the pressure of the wheel to allow the *Vigilant* to take advantage of a puff and work up to windward.

The *Vigilant* approached the other boats that were strung out in a long line with scarcely any space between them. Leading them was the *Wampus*, with the *Scatt* second. It was seen that the *Vigilant* would pass under the stern of the *Scatt*, forcing the *Hummer* about.

But the captain of the *Hummer* had no idea of going about. Of course, the *Vigilant* had the right of way, but she had had it in many previous races and had sacrificed it by going about. So Mr. Abbot, the *Hummer's* captain, only chuckled when some of the boys on the *Vigilant* called to him.

"You 'd better go about, Fred," said Mr. Low, in a rather anxious voice. "We 'll hit the *Hummer* if we don't."

"Who 's on the starboard tack, I 'd like to know?" asked Freddy, a little impatiently. "If anybody 's going about, it will be Abbot on the *Hummer*. We 've got the right of way and we are going to insist on it."

"I know, my boy," said Mr. Low, warningly, "but remember Irving Day who—"

"Irving Day is n't racing to-day," broke in the young skipper; "we 've got Steve Brodie aboard and we 're going to take a chance."

By this time the two boats were scarcely a length apart. Both captains were anxiously peering under their sails.

"Go about, Mr. Abbot," called Freddy, "or we 'll hit you."

But Mr. Abbot only smiled and looked toward the luff in his sail. Slowly, it seemed the bow of the *Hummer* crossed in front of the *Vigilant*. A collision was inevitable unless one of the skippers changed his course. But Freddy had no intention of changing his.

"I 'll teach this crowd a lesson!" he said between clenched teeth.

There was a crash and a jolt as the stay of the *Vigilant* hit the boom of the *Hummer*. The force of the blow swung the *Hummer* broadside to the wind, and she was in no position for the gust of wind that at that moment struck her sail. She keeled away over as the water washed her deck. The sheet rope could not be released, as the end of the boom was held by the *Vigilant*, and she could not head into the wind, as her stern was being pushed around. Now the water was pouring into the cockpit and her crew was climbing up on her sides. Suddenly the *Vigilant* shook herself free, and, as she did so, the end of the *Hummer's* boom dropped into the water. For a second she hesitated, then slowly the sail settled on the water, her hull was flooded, and she was over!

Fred never turned around, but you may be sure his father did, and the others of the crew, and all were relieved to see several motor-boats rushing to the rescue.

Mr. Low glanced at the immovable features of his son. He started to speak, checked himself, and took a new grip on the sheet rope.

At the first buoy the *Vigilant* passed the *Scatt,* and kept on down the bay after the leading *Wampus.* Freddy never took his eye off the luff of the sail, and time and again sent the *Vigilant* shooting forward as a puff of wind struck them. It was great sailing!

But do what he could, Freddy was unable to overtake the *Wampus,* as windward work was her strongest point.

When she reached the outer buoy, she rounded it, her sheet was allowed to run, and she started for home. A minute later the *Vigilant* did the same thing. As the center-board came up and the sheet rope burned through the blocks, the crew breathed easier, because the *Vigilant* would now be on her best run. A fair windward boat, the *Vigilant* was famous for her speed in running before the wind, so the crew had reason to be confident.

Gradually the distance that separated the two boats became less. The men on the *Wampus* kept looking around with anxiety written on their faces as the prow of the *Vigilant* came closer and closer.

"Well, boys," said Mr. Low, "take a look at her stern and read those letters, W-A-M-P-U-S, because, from now on, our friends on the other boat will be spelling out V-I-G-I-L-A-N-T."

"Don't be so sure of that, Dad," said Freddy, "because Mr. Waldron knows how to sail a race, and he 's going to give us a fight."

A minute later, Freddy's prediction was fulfilled when he shot the *Vigilant* into the wind so that he could pass the *Wampus* to windward and blanket her. But Mr. Waldron was not to be beaten so easily. As the *Vigilant* crept up, his practised hand guided his yacht to windward also, so that, although the courses of the boats had changed, their positions had not, because, sailing into the wind, the *Wampus* was the equal, if not the superior, of the *Vigilant.*

Freddy soon saw that he could not pass them that way, so he put his helm hard over and tried to pass to leeward. But the *Wampus* changed also, and, when the *Vigilant* came even with the other boat, her sail was blanketed and the *Wampus* forged ahead again.

"I said we 'd have a fight," remarked Freddy.

For a while the two boats sailed along together. The crew on the *Wampus* watched the *Vigilant* like hawks, for a sudden shift of course might mean defeat. Suddenly, Freddy put his helm over as if to pass far to leeward, and, when the *Wampus* started to follow, he shot his boat into the wind.

"Down board—trim her in, Dad," he ordered.

The bow of the *Vigilant* slid past the stern of the *Wampus* and was abreast of her. Had the moment of victory come? For several minutes the two boats, cutting through the water, hung in the same relative position. A puff struck them and they both jumped forward, but the *Wampus* began to gain. Little by little at first, and then, as her sail got the wind unobstructed, she took the lead again. Freddy kept his position, hoping against hope that a favoring gust would send them ahead.

During this luffing match, the two leaders had sailed way out of their course and would probably have gone on indefinitely had not Freddy glanced across the bay and seen the *Scatt* tearing in a straight line for home.

"Look at that *Scatt,* will you!" he ejaculated. "If we keep on this way, she 'll beat us both."

For this reason the *Vigilant* gave up her fight for first and headed for home, with the *Wampus,* as always, just ahead.

A feeling of hopelessness came over Freddy. Here he was, sailing the *Vigilant* in second place, and his ship could have passed and sailed away from the *Wampus* if he could only get the wind first and not be cut off by the other sail. He could not indulge in luffing matches now and try to pass to windward, because, if he did so, it would give the race to the *Scatt.* So he sat watchful on the wheel-box, with his head busy thinking out some plan.

The race was nearly over. Already the crowd on the pier could be seen, as the many spectators came out to see the finish.

"Dad," said Freddy, "get the rope ready on the bow, will you?"

The crew of the *Wampus* were taking matters less strenuously, as they believed the race as good as over. When Mr. Low went to the bow they were assured that all fight was good as over from the young skipper of the *Vigilant.*

"Say, Low," called Mr. Waldron, from the *Wampus,* "your boy has sailed a pretty race."

"I think he has," replied Mr. Low, good-naturedly; "but you are too old a hand to let a boy beat you."

"Now listen!" whispered Freddy, suddenly, as the two men were exchanging remarks. "Bill, you take the sheet rope, and when I give the word, trim like mad. At the same time, you, Tom, jam down the board. Then, when I give the word, pull her up, and you, Bill, let the sheet go."

The finish-line was in sight. The steward of the club had the little brass cannon ready to fire when the first boat crossed the line. There was no time to lose, for the race would be over in a minute.

"Now," gasped Fred, as he put the wheel hard over and shot his boat into the wind. Down went the board with a "plunk" and the sheet came in as fast as Bill's arms could pull it. Mr. Waldron gave a start. He had been caught asleep.

"Put down the board!" he yelled, excitedly; "trim in the sheet. Get some life!"

And he sent the *Wampus* to windward to block off the *Vigilant.* As his crew were feverishly on their jobs, Fred gave another order: "Up board, out sheet."

And, as the center-board came up, and the sheet rope sped through Bill's toughened hands, Fred whirled the wheel in the other direction, and the *Vigilant* was heading again for the finish-line as the *Wampus* still sailed out to windward. It was over in a minute. A puff of wind struck them and they dashed across the line!

"*Bang!*" The gun! The *Vigilant* had won!

The *Wampus* finished three seconds later.

"Well," said Fred, "I feel better. I knew this old boat could sail."

"She always could," replied Mr. Low, "but I took warning from Irving Day and you rather favored Mr. Brodie."

NOT SO BLACK AS HIS FEATHERS

by Dallas Lore Sharp

THIS is about Kratz's crow; but for all that I can see, Kratz's crow may be the very black rascal who pulls my corn, plugs my melons, picks my juicy pears, mocks, derides, and lords it over me by building his nest in the tallest white pine to be found on my place. *My* place? Where did I get that notion? Don't tell that to the crows. What a row there would be in *my* wood lot if this copy of ST. NICHOLAS should fall under the eye of *my* crows!

I am not certain that they can read. But I am certain that nothing goes on about Mullein Hill concerning them which they don't know. I think if they see it in the magazine they would understand. Big, black, cautious, impudent, canny, contentious, they are rather shady characters, the whole band of them, and very useful citizens.

No other word in ornithology, no other creature in my outdoors, is such a conflict of questions and answers as this word and creature—Crow. To-day I would destroy him. To-morrow I would defend him against all comers. While I am looking for him in the woods with a gun, he is helping himself to cutworms in my garden. He knows my plantings and harvestings, my uprisings and downsittings; the difference between firearms and garden tools; just how far my gun will carry; what time he can call me names, and when it is wise to treat me with respect. I don't know him

quite so well; but though he wears the colors of the pirate, I am sure his soul is rather saintly white.

Few lovers of birds will agree with me. I do not agree with myself in nesting-time, for the crow is a robber of nests. He looks guilty and acts guiltily all through May and June, sneaking and lurking about the trees, slipping silently in and out, perfectly conscious of his dirty work, and careful to avoid observation.

It is then that I sometimes snatch my gun and sally forth to destroy the crow tribe. But the news seems to go forth ahead of me. The woods are deep and wide and capable of hiding a good many crows. I have never killed a crow. Perhaps I ought to. But the birds they rob, like the robins, were more numerous this past summer than I have ever seen them in Hingham, as my cherry-trees would swear to if they could testify. Out of ten loaded cherry-trees (there was a mulberry-tree among them which I had planted especially for the birds), the robins, catbirds, and waxwings took a bushel for every quart I gathered. The crows are fond of cherries, too.

Suppose I shoot the crows because they rob the robins. Then I shall have to shoot the robins because they rob the cherry-trees. And then—I have started something, something bad, which I had far better let alone. So I let the crows plug my melons and pilfer the nests, knowing it will last but a few weeks, when, for all the months

502

to follow till the robins come again, there will be loud cawing in the empty woods and continuous warfare waged against the insect enemies encamped round about Mullein Hill besieging me.

Who would hush that raucous cawing in the winter woods? Or wish his world without this strong, black figure, and the stronger—I won't say blacker—personality cloaked in this solemn, judicial garb? No other bird looks so wise—not even the owl —or is so wise as the crow. He invests all nature with intelligence. He comes nearest of all wild things to speaking the human language.

For he is wild and intends to be. A circling hen-hawk against the sky is so distant and alien as to seem like one of the stars. The fox is hidden, furtive, a creature of legend and story-book rather than of the real, near-by woods. Down by the kitchen steps sits the hop-toad in the twilight thinking, thinking, but no one would give a penny for his thoughts. Bob-white comes up in the winter to feed with the chickens, half inclined to join the flock and leave his wild estate. Not so the crow.

Perhaps there are quail-like crows, but I have never seen them. In the dead of winter I have seen the birds down and out— dead from starvation and disease. Yet never did I see a humble crow. Bold and wary; always out, the year around, to hail you; knowing as well as you where you are going and why, he watches curiously, comes prudently close, making no bones of his intense human interest, which, however, he tempers with extraordinary good sense, the kind we call "common," but which might well be called "crow."

"Hi, you black rascals," I shout at them.

"Hi, you 're black yourself!" they shout at me in turn. "We know a thing or two you 'd like to know. Ha! Ha!" and off they go, leaving me sure that animals and men can talk together, at least that crows and

men can understand each other. And this I can prove in the case of Kratz's crow.

Kratz had brought up several crows.

So had I; and thereby made myself a general nuisance about home. But never did I inflict on my family a crow of such high craft and cunning as one that was brought up by my friend Kratz.

All house-raised crows which I have known or known about grew up as thieves. Domestication seems very bad for them. It was bright, shiny things particularly that tempted Kratz's crow. He grabbed the scissors from the sewing-basket, knives, forks, and spoons from the table, darting out of doors with them to the top of the house, thence to the top of the chimney, where he would drop them into the flue. Some one would be sure to shout at him, and he would turn on the chimney-top and squawk joyously back, giving every bit as good as he got, though sometimes it was the lady of the house who was wringing her hands and imploring him from below.

One day a pet crow we had stole Grandmother's silver-bowed spectacles. Grandmother was a Quaker. Jim, the crow, had never been to meeting. The "spirit moved" both of them, Quaker and crow, and they had a very lively time of testimony between them, one on the ridge-pole, the other by the pump in the yard.

Another peculiarity tame crows seem to have in common is their very marked preference for a certain member of the family, following that person about as faithfully as a dog. If a dog happens to be in the family, rank jealousy will be sure to develop between the two animals where this chosen person is concerned. This is not uncommon between cats and dogs, any attention, by any member of the family, paid to the cat being quite enough to make some sensitive dogs sick with jealousy.

It is a mark of unusual mental power, I take it, that such feelings can be enter-

tained by a bird. I have never known a
tame crow and the pet dog to get on
sweetly together. There is constant bicker-
ing and nagging between them.

Kratz's mother was the particular object
of his crow's affections. He went with her
everywhere and helped her with everything. On her head or shoulder, or tagging,
stiffer than a drum-major, along behind, he
would follow from sewing-room to garden,
taking a hand in all her tasks, talking a
good deal, and none too modestly, of how
indispensable he was.

You can imagine how much he helped
when he got in with both feet among the
spools and small wares, especially among
the silks, of the sewing-table. Let a long-
toed crow, with an inquisitive turn of
mind, walk into your knitting, to say nothing of the sewing, and notice what happens.

Curiously enough, I never knew a mis-
chief-maker to blame himself for the
trouble he gets into, no matter what language he blames in. Kratz's crow was always in mischief, and always blaming the
family in general for it. Instantly the thread
got tangled in his toes, he would fall to
squawking angrily, then get frightened and
flop over helplessly for some one to un-
thread his miserable feet. He was exceedingly resourceful at inventing mischief, but
most incapable at mending it.

His fondness for the mistress of the house
caused him to become a kind of shadow to
her. He attended her everywhere, but he
was especially interested in her gardening.
Old-fashioned mother that she was, she had
a way of punishing the crow for his
naughty tricks by using a small switch
across his big black wings. He could n't
have felt it, but the noise was terrible
enough, and he "would be good" instanter!
At the first swish of the rod he would
tumble down, turn over on his back, and,
crying like a booby, stick up his black

claws to ward off the blows. And this always worked. To switch him on his tender
bare feet was more than the mother of
Kratz and his crow could bear.

A fence with a swing gate ran between
the dooryard and the Kratz's vegetable
garden. One day Mrs. Kratz, with the crow
as usual on her shoulder, went into the
garden to pick snap-beans. And the crow as
usual began industriously to assist with the
picking, doing exactly as he saw Mrs.
Kratz doing. Only this time, because they
were harder to get off, possibly, the crow
would not touch the long, big beans, the
ones that were ready to pick, but insisted
upon picking the little ones.

He was told better. But crows do not
always listen to instruction. He kept on
picking little beans. Then he was well
scolded and warned. But crows do not like
scolding, and sometimes pay little heed to
warnings. He kept on picking little beans.
He just did n't hear. It was such fun picking little beans.

How eager he was! He would not put
the beans in the basket, however, but always in a separate pile on the ground close
beside it. Every time the basket was moved,
the busy crow would start a fresh pile of
his little beans. The beans were plentiful,
and his industry very touching, so he was
indulged like a spoiled child in his whim
until his mistress chanced to notice that he
was bringing not only beans, but also little
cucumbers and baby watermelons.

This would never do. It was quite terrible, really! And snatching him in the act,
she pulled a weed and began to punish
him. Over he went on his back, cawing
piteously, thrusting his sprawling feet up
to cover him.

That old trick had worked many a time.
This time the wilful bird must truly be corrected. Spare the rod and spoil the watermelon patch. No, no! He must be taught
to let the watermelons alone, or worse

things than switches would descend upon him, in harsher hands than hers. So down upon the naked feet came the swishing, stinging weed,—once, twice, three times, before the astonished crow fully grasped the situation.

He grasped it firmly then—in both tingling feet at once! With a kind of handspring from the flat of his back, he turned clear over in the air, struck out with both black wings, cleared that garden fence, and landed on the ridge-pole of the house before you could say "Kratz"! Then he turned right about and began to squall, everything he could think of and several things he never had thought of before, down at the lady.

Out West they would say, "He got his needin's." And he did n't forget them, either. He forgave his mistress, as she forgave him. He continued to attend her everywhere—except through that garden gate. Bygones were bygones up to the garden gate. Let her enter here, and he left her shoulder, taking a position upon the gate-post, where he held forth, haranguing the lady most violently the while she picked beans or worked in the garden.

I know few, if any, parallels to such conduct among birds or animals under domestication, which seems to me to indicate a very high degree of intelligence for the crow. It also speaks for a very quick sympathy for his human neighbor and a readiness to meet him at least part of the way. Once the ice is broken, the suspicions and animosities laid, the crow tribe seems ready to meet the tribe of man, making one world again of these two worlds of crows and men.

Like a crow of mine, this crow of my friend Kratz showed a strong fear for all wild crows, his own relatives, about the farm. He would cry out in plain alarm at sight of them flying about, and would always retreat until they disappeared. Most

wild things under domestication will return, if free, to the wilds for a mate. But spring came and went, and the crow, if he wanted a mate, did not seek her, though his wings were strong and free and all the sky was his.

"Taking a position upon the gate-post, he held forth, haranguing most violently"

It was the fear of death, I think, stronger in his keen consciousness than the desire for a mate, that restrained him. I have seen it several times (once in the case of a tame robin) that a bird, separated from his kind and brought up in human ways, has the mark of Cain put on him. Just what the sign is I should like to know. I have known a tamed wild duck and a tamed bluebird to return to their tribes and find mates; but such a renegade crow is the object of suspicion and fury on the part of the wild tribe. Let him try to come back, and he is set upon with violence and done to death.

An untimely accident took off Kratz's crow, leaving no opportunity to see later, when the call of the wild in his blood should be more urgent, if he would overcome his fears. We only know that to the end the sight and sound of his wild kin drove him croaking to shelter.

Here may be found a scrap of evidence, possibly, to justify that persistent old legend of crows court-martialing guilty members of their bands and picking them to death. Within a month, such a story, from an eye-witness, has come to me by way of an editor who wished to publish the tale. It was all too circumstantial, too much like a story in my first reader at school. Yet who can say that such a thing may not go on within the councils of this black, powerful band of uncanny birds, who seem more than birds, both in their solemn demeanor, and in their well-established ways.

In my neighborhood a small band of about a dozen crows live their gipsy life all winter. Spring finds them reduced to about three mated pairs, but whether reduced by death or agreement, dividing the land among them, I do not know. I hear them cawing over in the thick pines. All winter long they will be heard in loud, confident talk deep in the hollow woods. And I shall see them all winter long, when few other creatures care to stir abroad, flying strongly against the leaden sky and stalking black upon the drifted snow, their raven dress and harsh, unlovely voices just the touch, in the wintry landscape, of contrast and courage to give one heart.

Say every evil thing you can against him, then live through the winter with him as I do here on Mullein Hill. He does plug melons and pull sprouting corn. But read the Government's report of his year-round warfare in defense of farm and garden, and see what else he does. I have caught him robbing nests of smaller birds, and is not one robin of as much value as one crow? I suppose it is. And I confess that I do not know whether or not to kill the robber. But I do know that when the nesting season is over I am always glad I did not kill him; and I am sure that I could lose almost any other bird from my world out of doors and miss it less than I should miss this constant, cantakerous, dubious character, the crow.

THE FIND

by Orville W. Mosher, Jr.

THE story I am about to tell is of Indians, a battle and hidden treasure. The battle and the Indians are real, and as for the treasure—that may be real, too, for all I know, and some of the things that I tell about did happen and others might have happened.

As long as there are boys in New Richmond, St. Croix County, Wisconsin, they will tell the story of the great Find to succeeding generations of boys, and they, in turn, will pass it on again to other generations as long as there are boys in New Richmond; and I reckon that will be a long time, judging from the large crop of boys there now. You see, things just like this don't happen every day in the week, and, when they do come, they simply stagger the imagination, and I am going to tell it to you all so that you can see for yourself. But first I must begin a long way back.

In 1842 two families, working northward from Ohio in their canvas-covered wagons, halted their journey on the shore of what is now called Bass Lake, some eight miles south of New Richmond. They constructed log cabins on the prairie and proceeded to wrest a living from the wilderness. Of that little settlement of people by the lake, only one is now living, a white-haired old lady by the name of Greenborough. We boys used to gather on her back porch after she had supplied our internal cravings with a plentiful supply of ginger cookies, and then she would tell us about a battle that took place between the Chippewas and Sioux, right over there where her field of corn was waving in the breeze. She told how she, as a frightened little girl, peered between the logs of the cabin garret late one afternoon and saw a band of Chippewas, some seventy in number, sorely pressed, plunge their panting ponies into the lake from the opposite shore and swim them for a landing near her house. I remember she said some of the Indians hung by their horses' tails and let the horses pull them through the water. She told how, almost immediately following them, there appeared a band of some two hundred Sioux, on war ponies, pursuing them.

The Chippewas, their horses too exhausted to run farther, turned to fight in the unequal match and were killed to the last man. And then the Sioux stripped the bodies of the slain and all rode away "yip-yipping, and barking like coyotes," as Grandma Greenborough expressed it. They carried with them the bodies of their own dead and a great mass of plunder taken from the Chippewas.

Why the Sioux did not stop to massacre the few whites crouched fearfully in the two homes set alone on the prairie, it is hard to say, but they did not; and that night, when the moon came out and lit up the wide, level plain, the men of the family loaded their wives and children into their wagons and hurried away to Fort Snelling, near Minneapolis, to be under the protection of the United States soldiers. There they stayed through the long, terrible, anxious weeks, during which each day brought news of the massacre of settlers and destruction of emigrant trains, until the Sioux were at last corralled on their reservation and it was safe to return.

Nearly seventy years had passed away

The battle between the Chippewas and the Sioux

since that time, and now we boys sat at the feet of the white-haired, kind old lady, looked out over the battle-field, and listened. Instead of prairie and woods dotting the landscape, there were well-kept farms. It seemed as though nothing could have happened there, so calm and peaceful it looked. How little did we think or know that soon the reality of that battle would be brought home to us! You can't always tell—a mighty quiet time may contain within it the seeds of genuine excitement, for Jimmy Warrick—or, to be more exact and to give him the name read out at the Sunday-school, James Montgomery Warrick, Jr.—was there. He sat there and listened to Grandma Greenborough's stories and tucked away dozens of perfectly good cookies. He was just the same sort of boy as any of the rest of us; but he had an imagination that his mother said was like a "house afire," and that imagination ran to Indians. He was fond of Indians. He collected "Injun" arrow-heads and chummed with every Indian or half-breed who stuck his nose into New Richmond. He was so good at shooting with the bow and arrows that his Indian friends had made him that he could kill squirrels and rabbits with them, and sometimes shot the glass insulators of the telegraph-poles when the railroad men were n't looking. I was a little younger than Warrick, but I was in his "gang," and he let me go with him once in a while to hunt arrow-points or cornelians, so I know all about him and what happened. Sometimes he let me shoot with his bow, too.

Jimmy was mighty lucky because he had an uncle who was United States Indian agent at the Pine Ridge Agency. I wished I had an uncle living there, too, so that I could go and see the Indians; but my uncle was a justice of the peace, and did n't care for war and "Injuns."

It was just after school closed for the summer vacation when Jimmy got the letter from his uncle. I know because I saw it. It said:

If you want to see some real Indians, come out and visit your aunt and me during fair week. We are going to let them kill a few beeves in the old-fashioned way —riding bareback, one rawhide strand held in their teeth to guide the horse, and bow and arrows to kill the beeves with. I will have Red Horse meet you at the Lame Deer Station and drive you over to the agency.

Did Jimmy want to go! Did he? Well, would n't you?

So we all said good-by to him as he went away on the train, carrying his bow and arrows, and some colored handkerchiefs and gewgaws that he said he was going to trade. My, he looked happy!

We were most awfully lonesome after Jimmy had gone, because he was always stirring up something new, and all we did was just go swimming and wish he would hurry up and come back and tell us all about it. It was two whole months before he came back; and when he did, my, but he was loaded down with curios! He had a whole Indian suit—beaded vest, feathers, leggings, and all. We boys just looked up to him; and if he put on a few airs, we did n't mind, because anybody who had been chumming around with chiefs has a right to put on airs. He would talk about Charging Eagle, Wahitika, and Waupoose just as though he had known them for years. We boys stood around and listened with our mouths open. But most of all Jimmy talked about his friend Powless, the son of one of the Santee Sioux chiefs there, and Jimmy hinted at a visit and spoke mysteriously about something big that Powless knew. How we boys wished we could see him and tag along with him and Jimmy when they went exploring! But Jimmy said that it was something mighty important, and only they two should go together.

I was with Jimmy when he came—Powless, I mean. The boys of New Richmond know where Honey Hole and Fox Hole are, on Willow River, where we all used to go swimming. The river takes a wide bend down below Wearses, and flows smoothly on for about a mile, where it is a little broken by rocks and the bank on the right-hand side rises tall and steep. We boys liked to roll rocks down the sides and hear them splash. Beyond this, the forest thickens and boys don't go there so much, because it is marshy. Along the banks of the river are the lower fringes of the forest that, following these shores, sweeps northward to the great woods of Northern Wisconsin, with all their mysteries of lake and stream. As I was saying, the boys did n't go much beyond the high cliffs; for it was marshy and the willows lay thick and close. But Jimmy and I went there, and we knew where a break in the cliff, the entrance covered with brush, led to a small cañon where the water had washed, and there we would set up targets and shoot and cook our dinner sometimes. Nobody but just us two knew the place. We never told anybody for fear the East Enders would jump it; and I guess you know that would mean war between the east and west ends of town, sure enough.

About a month after Jimmy got back from his trip to his uncle, Jimmy and I were in there and were getting a fire ready and stopping once in a while to shoot an arrow through a barrel-hoop that we would roll across the ground, when, from somewhere, a stone dropped at our feet.

"That did n't roll down the cliff, did it?" asked Jimmy.

"I dunno," said I; "it might have; nobody knows this place; it must have just got loose and rolled down."

We did n't say anything more about it, thinking it was nothing; but about five minutes later another stone landed where the first one had fallen, and Jimmy said, "I 'm going to see about this." And he slipped through the brush. A half-hour later he came back, saying he could n't find anybody, but he was sure some one was around, for stones had dropped near him and he had heard some one calling like a screech-owl behind him. He had n't more than said this when from behind a rock, not ten feet from us, stepped an Indian boy.

"Powless!" yelled Jimmy, as he sprang toward his friend.

"How, how," said Powless, making a sign across Jimmy's right arm. My, were n't my eyes just sticking out, though, for he was dressed all up in sure-enough Indian clothes—hair tied with strips of fur and two feathers, and moccasins and fringed leggings and everything.

Jimmy and Powless talked together for a moment, making signs with their hands, and then Jimmy came to me and said: "Powless and me are going into the woods now; you go home and don't tell anybody. Promise, 'Cross your heart I hope to die.'"

So I said, "Cross my heart I hope to die," and then I went home and did n't say a thing. I hated like the dickens to go home; but I knew if I tried to tag along, they 'd run away from me and Jimmy would n't let me go with him again—I guess you know what that would mean.

The first thing we knew anything big had happened was when Jimmy staggered into town carrying a great buffalo-robe, ornamented with bead and porcupine work —the finest of its kind, said old Bill Bascomb, who had been a trapper and knew. Jimmy would disappear into the woods and come out looking mighty solemn and important, carrying with him great quivers filled with arrows, guns, tomahawks, in almost endless array, and then came ax-heads of stone, and queer-looking rocks, and finally rings and jewelry. He always went into the woods alone, and when he came out his father would meet him with the wagon and carry the findings back to the Warrick library, where they hung on the walls and began to pile on the floor—such piles of rich skins, of bead-work, of Indian weapons of war! The whole town watched and waited to see what would come next. We boys hung around the War-rick fence in crowds all day, waiting for Jimmy and his father to drive up with their load. Everybody was asking, "Where *did* that boy get those wonderful things?" Some tried to follow; but Jimmy always gave them the slip.

Then one day both newspapers in our town printed a story all about a tremendous find of Indian wealth, and, along with it, a picture of Jimmy as the finder. Jimmy tried mighty hard not to look as though he felt pretty big; but I don't see how he could help it; do you? At first it was just the home papers, but later on many other papers printed it.

Everybody in town was getting pretty excited, and I could tell it was a mighty big thing because Father asked me about it, and he does n't usually bother with such doings. Then one day it came out that the head of a great university was coming. Jimmy's father had telegraphed him, and he had wired that he was coming at once.

I was there, standing alongside of the three o'clock train, when the great man came. He was a big tall man, with white hair and kind blue eyes. Jimmy said I could come, too, and the man and Jimmy's father and Jimmy and me all went into the Warrick library. And say! do you know, it was packed pretty nearly solid from floor to ceiling with Indian things.

"Phew!" said the man when he saw it; "this certainly is a find!"

As he looked over the collection he got more and more excited. He had a note-book and checked off the different things. He would put down: "800 spear-points, all identical, probably the same maker, largest cache of its kind yet found." Once he said, "I never saw white flint ax-heads before, but here are 45 perfect ones." And then he would pick up one queer-looking stone after another, and would say to himself, "H-m-m-m, ceremonial stones, pendants, gorgets, butterfly-stones;" and then he would put them down on the list. "These skins are remarkably preserved," he said; and after he had tested some brown stains on the beaded blankets, he added: "These are blood-stains; all these blankets have been soaked with blood. Was there ever an Indian battle near here?"

"I never heard of any," said Mr. Warrick.

I could n't help piping up then with, "Yes, there was, Mister! Mrs. Greenbor-ough can tell you all about it—it was Sioux and Chippewas, right over on her farm, and she said the Sioux carried off all the Chippewas' things."

"Well, well!" said the university man, "here is the Chippewa mark on these moc-casins, and yes—this is the sign of the Sioux worked in in the beadwork on these buffalo and beaver robes. It might be—it might be—that these blankets with the blood-stains were some taken from the Chippewas at that battle."

Then Jimmy showed him some of the jewelry, and there were lots of military buttons. Most of the jewelry was old-fashioned, heavy, old gold.

"Some of this must have been taken from the white settlers; the Indians prob-ably killed the settlers or emigrants and the soldiers guarding the wagon-trains, and then cached their plunder," said the great man. "This is the greatest find of its kind I have had anything to do with in all my experience of thirty years with the university. You are to be congratulated, Jimmy," he added.

And Jimmy looked down, proud and pleased as could be.

When he had made a careful list and description of everything, he said to Jimmy, "Now let me hear just exactly how and where you found these"; and he took out his note-book to jot down what Jimmy was to say.

"Yes," said Jimmy, "I can tell you how I got these; but I can't tell where."

"Yes, you will tell where," said Jimmy's father, looking toward the barn with a look that all us boys know.

"I can't," said Jimmy, his lip trembling; " 'cause I can't find the place now. I know pretty near where it is, but I can't find it."

"Let the boy go ahead and tell his story," said the university man.

Jimmy said: "Powless and me were chums, and I told him when I was visiting my uncle on the Pine Ridge Reservation about there being a battle between the Sioux and Chippewas here, and he said his grandfather, White Elk, used to tell about it, and about a place where the Sioux hid their things in the cliffs across the St. Croix River. He said that before White Elk died he drew a picture on the sand, and showed him how to find the place in the cliff where the Sioux kept the things they captured. After I came home from my trip to my uncle, Powless slipped off the reservation and found me down at our hiding-place; did n't he?" said Jimmy, turning to me.

"I was there when he came," I spoke up.

"After we left you," went on Jimmy, "we went into the dark woods the other side of Constance Bridge and followed the Willow River for a long way—you know, it twists in and out; and then Powless left me after he had told me to wait till he came back. He came back in about a half an hour

and said he did n't want even me to know how to get to the place where the things were hid. He tore a piece from his blanket and bound it over my eyes tight, so that I could n't see anything, and then pulled me through the woods after him.

"When he finally jerked off the cloth from my eyes, we were standing on a spot like a circle on the ground, and high cliffs were all around. It was a queer-looking place, with funny-looking rocks thrown up on edge; some of them looked as though they might roll down the cliffs any minute. I did n't like the looks of it—it did n't look safe. 'Help me with this stone,' Powless said; and when we pulled at it hard together, it rolled away and there underneath was a deep black hole. It was mighty dark down there, so we lit some branches and made a torch and went down inside. It looked as though somebody had dug it out inside; there were sort of stone steps cut out, and on the inside was a long passage, with rooms and other passages leading off to the sides. Along the big passage the walls were cut into sort of long shelves, and on them lay great piles of Indian things; these things here are just a few of them that were near the hole and easy to get out; but back in there were just piles of things."

"What were in the other passages?" the university man asked.

"I don't know about most of them," said Jimmy, "but Powless went in one; and when he came out he said it was dead Indians, and I was afraid to look and see. He said he wanted me to have some of those things in the cave, so I stood up at the top of the hole and he passed them up to me; we did the same thing every day for nearly all the rest of the week, until we got all these things here out. Powless always blindfolded me when I came and went, so I never knew how we got there or went away. When I went home every day, after we had worked at the cave, he took the things that we had got and carried them away. I asked Powless what he did with them; he would n't tell me where he put them, but said he had put them away and would let me have them later. At the end of the week, that was just a month ago to-day, he said we were n't going to the cave any more—that he was going away. He did n't blindfold me, but brought me straight to a tepee he had made out of branches, and there under it was this big pile of things that we had taken out of the cave. Powless told me they were all for me. Then he made the sign of the Sioux on my right shoulder, gave me this arrow-head, and disappeared in the woods. I have n't seen him since. I wrote to Uncle Fred at the Pine Ridge Reservation, but he says Powless has gone, no one knows where. After he went away I came home and got Father to go with me and get these things. I 've tried to find the cave, but I can't do it."

"Strange, very strange!" said the great man; "this is a remarkable collection and the university needs it."

Then Jimmy turned to his father and said, "Shall I give this to the university?"

"It 's yours. Do as you like with it, Jimmy," said his father.

"All right," said Jimmy, "you can have the whole collection, except this pink arrow-head here. Powless put it into my hand just before he went into the woods."

"Let me see it," said the great man.

Jimmy held it out—such a beauty it was, a soft pink color, of wonderful shape.

"It is very precious," said the man. "I know of only one other like it."

"I want to keep it," said Jimmy, " 'cause —'cause I 'm afraid Powless is dead!" and Jimmy looked very sad.

"What makes you think that?" said his father.

"Because there was a high cliff hanging over the cave, and the rocks on it looked as though they were going to fall any minute; and about an hour after Powless left me I heard a roar way off in the woods, and it sounded as if it might be the cliff falling; and since then, when I can't find out anything about him, I 'm—I 'm afraid he went back to the cave and was killed."

That was all. The university man stayed through the week, trying, with Jimmy's help, to find the cave, but without success; then he left, carrying the collection with him. There in the university museum the collection that Jimmy got hangs to-day; but somewhere in the dark woods there is a fallen cliff, and underneath it a deep cave that holds a far more wonderful collection of the relics of many past generations of Indians.

The boys at New Richmond, Wisconsin, know that, after you cross Constance Bridge, you turn to the left along the Willow River, go across an open field that is crossed by gullies in which woodchucks have made their holes, and then, going on, you come to a dark forest that, in the springtime, is open and just a dandy place to get dog-tooth violets, but that in summer is choked deep with undergrowth. Boys don't go in there much, it is so deep and solemn.

I will tell you, as nearly as I can, how to try to find this hidden cave. First, follow that river in and out as it winds, keeping close to the shore; then, over at the right, but back a ways from the river, are low cliffs that gradually rise higher. When you come to the spot where the high cliffs on the right come right up to the river-bank, there is the one sure place that we know about. It was right there, where the cliffs and river meet, that Powless made his tepee and placed the things that Jimmy got. Somewhere farther on, where the cliffs twist and turn, or maybe back inland among the gullies, there is the cave. Where it is, I don't know; Jimmy can't find it, though we hunted for it when we were boys and often do now, when we are older. Perhaps some time some lucky boy will discover it, with all its hidden treasures of buried Indians. As nothing has ever been heard from Powless, it may be Jimmy is right, and that somewhere underneath that cliff and in the depths of the cave Powless sleeps with his fathers.

THE SENSITIVE CAT

by Alice Brown

THERE once was a sensitive cat
Who couldn't abide the word "Scat."
"If you want me to go,"
She yowled, "Say so, you know,
But don't be so rude as all that!"

YOUNG ABEL YANCEY

BY ARCHIBALD RUTLEDGE

I
F that old robber takes one of my kids,
and I can get to him, he 'll have me to
whip."

Little Abel Yancey looked skyward over
the great mountains, in whose mighty
shadow he stood, gazing at the powerful
golden eagle wheeling in indolent superiority over a solitary peak.

"He thinks he can do as he pleases; and
last week, when brother Ben was minding
these here goats, he came swooping down
and carried off a kid. If he tries that kind
of thing with me, there 's going to be a
fight right here in this pasture. He need n't
think he can feed his young ones on our
little kids."

Abel's threat to whip the great eagle,
judged in the light of the small lad's very
frail appearance, did not seem impressive.
Indeed, had the great marauding bird of
the lonely mountain decided to make one
of his fierce falls upon Abel, and had borne
him away, the thing would not have
seemed incredible. Abel was not ten; and

his singularly slight build made him appear even younger. But in his clear blue
eyes was a light that told the story of spirit
and courage and determination. Therefore
his remarks concerning the soaring eagle
formed no idle threat. Those who knew
little Abel knew well that the boy would
carry through his purpose with a skill and
an independence that did credit to the race
of hardy mountaineers from whom he
sprang.

Far away in the wild heart of those
mighty mountains that roll their blue
breakers westward from North Carolina
into Tennessee, nestled among the purple
peaks and looking down into the fair valleys,—now misty, now violet with the lights
of evening or of morning, now veiled in
thunder-storms,—there you might see the
tiny cabin of Brant Yancey, the home of
little Abel. You should not think of these
people as only mountaineers, for they belong to that great race of stalwart pioneers
who came from highland Scotland, and

515

who, in spite of the rigors of poverty, have retained admirably the pride, the haughty honesty, the high spirit of their ancestors.

Singular, indeed, was the calling of this particular mountain-man. He was a herder of goats. He had many flocks; and these he rented to neighbors who, having lumbered their land, wanted to get rid of the undergrowth. Goats can accomplish this arduous task, and the Yancey goats were known for a radius of many a long mountain mile. Usually the goats needed no attention; but in the late winter and the early spring, when the young were born, they had to be guarded. In those wild mountains were wildcats, panthers, and eagles. It was against these enemies that little Abel, eight miles from home, was watching one of the largest of the Yancey herds. He had with him no weapon save a stout hickory stick. Toward sundown he would drive this herd into the central pasture down the mountain; where his father and his brothers would bring theirs, and there the goats would spend the night, their number, their manner of herding for the dark hours, and a rude stockade making for safety. But in these high and separate pastures the watchers were responsible for the safety of the creatures under their care.

Abel, sturdy in spirit, though slight of frame, felt the full weight of this responsibility; and when he saw the great eagle wheeling as if for a fall, he was instantly aware of the menace. He knew enough of eagles to realize what his present duty was and what was the meaning of the lordly bird's peculiar manœuvers in the air.

"I believe," he said, "I 'd better take these here goats and kids down the mountain. It 's early, but I don't like that thing flying up yonder. He 's powerful quick."

Through the still mountain pasture, now shimmering in the sunlight of mid-afternoon and in the delicate greens of the first month of the springtime, the voice of Abel now sounded out. He called the goats together; his voice was high and pleading. From almost every direction they came running; the playful little kids scampered, gamboled, and jumped in frolic over the huckleberry bushes. They knew well what the call meant; and they were obeying it willingly. Up the bushy slope an old ewe walked slowly with her two kids. One was a jetty black, and the other a soft brown. They were wee things, and very appealing in their innocent beauty.

"That old Betty yonder surely is slow," said Abel, his eyes resting with affection and amusement on his favorite of the whole flock. "She thinks most as much of them two kids as Brother Ben and I do," he added with a smile.

But the smile on his boyish face changed into an expression of sudden rage. As if he had been shot out of a gun, he rushed down the mountain.

"You, there!" he cried in his shrill voice. "You black robber! You, there!"

Gasping and swinging his hickory stick in a fury, he rushed down upon the mighty golden eagle that had fallen upon the brown kid. Abel thought to reach the huge bird before it rose. It had seemed to stay on the ground a long time. He knew it was fixing its long talons in its helpless prey. But the boy was too late. The eagle's powerful wings beat the air with ponderous strength. By the time Abel reached the spot where he had been, the dark marauder was as high as the chestnut-sprouts. Gripped in his cruel talons was the pitiful victim. Near the boy, the old mother goat cowered, her other baby quaking in the shelter of her flank. She bleated mournfully. After one glance at her, Abel's eyes followed the eagle's flight. Instead of crossing the deep valley, the great bird beat steadily up the mountain-side. Far up amid the plume-like, solitary pines, there was a gray cairn of rocks, almost a mile from where the boy stood. It was upon these rocks that the eagle alighted. And from something in the eagle's behavior, visible even at that distance through the crystal mountain atmosphere, Abel could not doubt but that he was looking at the eagle's eyrie.

"That's where he has his nest," the boy said; "and I'm going up there. I don't know but maybe the brown kid will still be alive. Leastways, I can tell Ben and the others that I did something and was n't asleep. I may get the chance to fight him yet," he added, with a brightening face, as he turned his steps with quick decision toward the dim pathway leading up the wild mountain.

It was a strange sight to see the slight, barefooted lad running with agile steps up that rain-gulleyed pathway. There was no other human being within miles. Down in the pasture, all would have been safe and quiet. But he was going, on his own initiative, into certain danger. Abel Yancey, however, thought not of the danger, but of a duty he owed his father, who had trusted him to guard one great herd of the goats. Blood tells; and it tells best where there are no witnesses, no substitutes, and where the stakes may be life and death.

It took Abel scarcely ten minutes to reach the shelf of rocks that joined the beetling gray cairn to the mountain-side. There, sheltered by the gloomy pines, he looked out over the gray cliff upon which he had seen the golden eagle alight. From his position he could see no eagle, no brown kid, no eagle's eyrie. Abel wondered if he had, by mistake, come to the wrong cliff. But suddenly, even as he doubted, he saw a movement far out on the verge of the lofty cliff.

"It's the brown kid!" the boy exclaimed. "He ain't dead. I done seen him bat his ear. Where's the eagle?" he asked himself, as he climbed out from under the shadows of the mighty pines and emerged upon the

dizzy cliff that sprang outward from the mountain. He had in his hand the hickory stick.

As Abel stepped out on the high rocks that seemed suspended above the valley, he had a sense of danger. Far below him lay the pasture he had left. The cliff fell away sheerly into space, though hundreds of feet below them there were the grizzled tops of certain storm-blasted trees. The rocks on the promontory were heaped in rude confusion; and some of these gave a kind of shelter, in which the great eagles had made their nest. The male bird, bringing his prey to the cliff, had left it near the lofty brink and had crossed the space between the edge and the eyrie. He was with the young birds when Abel came upon him.

With a harsh hissing of anger and of hate, the eagle beat his way upward. Then he swooped to the point of a rock on the verge of his eyrie. The boy facing him was intent upon one thing: he meant to rescue the brown kid from its desperate position. He could see that it was still alive; once, indeed, it bleated feebly, appealingly.

"I'm going to get it," said Abel Yancey; "and that there robber, he's going to try to keep it for himself."

He had stated the problem simply and truly.

As there was no sign of the other eagle, Abel counted on the single enemy alone. Glancing about him carefully, to get his bearings, he saw the robber's nest under a shelving rock. There were young in it, and they were almost feathered. But with them the lad had nothing to do. His eye measured the distance between himself and the kid lying out on the very brink of the precipice. He wondered that the eagle should leave it there. The distance between the little goat and its rescuer was about twenty feet. The gray rocks on the cliff had been worn until they were slippery. There were great seams and cracks in them; and

Abel saw at least one gap in the cliff that appeared to have been made by a recent fall of a section of the stone face. Would the beetling brink hold his weight? As he drew nearer to the eagle's prey, would the monstrous bird attack him? Could he keep his balance with the eagle battling with him for the possession of the brown kid? These questions might have arisen in the boy's mind; but his answers to all of them might be found in what he did. Swinging his hickory stick menacingly, he shouted at the eagle, at the same time stepping forward resolutely on those perilous rocks that no human foot, except possibly that of an Indian of the ancient days, had ever trod.

The golden eagle rose on skilful wings, and swung in a great circle behind the boy. It seemed that the big bird was trying to get at Abel's back. The lad turned to face the danger. He whirled his stick and cried out defiantly at his attacker. At the same time he backed slowly toward the terrible brink of the cliff. He watched each step. He frequently paused, for the walking backward made him dizzy. Once, after a backward glance, during which his eye had caught a sight of the empty chasm over the edge of the cliff, he put out his stick to steady himself. The stick seemed not to touch anything, and Abel, to keep his balance, was forced suddenly to let it go. It dropped into the sloping crevice whose bottom it had failed to touch while the boy held it. Abel saw it slide down, then it shot away into space. Its fall showed the mountain lad how a thing looked as it left the hanging crag, and imaged to his mind the dizzy momentum of its drop. At such a moment, almost any boy, having adventured thus far, would have abandoned the attempt of rescue. But, though he now had no kind of weapon, Abel Yancey felt rising in him a determination that he would never yield a foot of space on that cliff to the eagle. Blood of an ancient, heroic race was

in his veins, making and keeping him strong.

But as Abel approached the brink of the cliff, he changed his tactics. Watching the eagle carefully, he picked his chance and stooped low; then he lay down on the rocks. The eagle, becoming bolder, swept just over his head. Though the lad did not see the motion, the mighty bird had struck at him with his curved beak. Slowly, painfully, cunningly, Abel made his way backward over the sloping cliff drawing nearer to the kid.

Evidently the little thing had sensed the attempt to rescue it. At least it knew that Abel, whose hands had petted it, was near. Once, in looking back, the lad saw the kid try to rise. It could not; and for this Abel was glad; for there was danger lest it fall over the cliff the moment it staggered to its feet. The boy had now come to a point just out of reach of the object of his rescue.

Suddenly he felt his bare feet leave the rock. He knew they were over the edge of the cliff. He must go no farther.

All this while he had been keeping the eagle off by sharp shouts and by fiercely striking at the attacking bird with his bare fists. But the wary eagle appeared to know at what a disadvantage he had his enemy —a disadvantage that increased as Abel neared the eagle's prey.

Just as the boy ceased his critical descent, the eagle, now wholly bold, alighted fairly on Abel's back, and the talons that had brought the brown kid so high and so far now raked the lad's flesh. Abel turned swiftly on his back, and the savage bird cleared himself. The boy was now almost within reach of the kid. Shouting at the eagle, he leaned forward toward the pitiful, crumpled little object. The eagle at the same moment, seeing himself about to be robbed of his prey, made a desperate swoop from behind, striking Abel at the base of the neck with his full weight and all the force of his flight. The boy was lifted from the rock—he was hurled forward, almost stunned. He clutched manfully at the brink of the gray cliff. But when he fully came to his senses, all his blood was in his head, and he was hanging partly over the awful chasm.

Dimly, in that fearful moment, he seemed to hear the voice of his father, though it was but through his memory that it sounded.

"Abel," he heard, "be a man; you got to be a man, son!"

It was what his mountaineer father had said to him a hundred times.

"I got to be a man," muttered little Abel, clutching the sharp edges of the perilous cliff. The eagle, in rising from him, had torn his back cruelly, and the sight of the blood from these wounds and of the fearful chasm into which he seemed to be dropping were enough to shake his strength. If he could turn around, he might pull himself to safety. He had tried to push back, but could make no progress that way. He *had* to turn.

The eagle, meanwhile, satisfied now that he had little to fear from the boy, was swinging back toward him. Abel set his teeth, made his muscles hard, and summoned all his strength to turn on the cairn's brink without slipping. He manœuvred with cautious skill, and at last succeeded, although a sudden blow from the eagle's powerful wings unbalanced him. For a moment his feet and legs swung violently over the cliff; but he clutched and gripped a sharp rock with one hand and wriggled his body back upon the ledge until his head was turned away from the chasm and he could no longer see the terrible spear-heads of the blasted trees hundreds of feet below.

He was near fainting, however, when the eagle whirled upon him with a savage blow. The boy struck upward with his free hand, and it came in contact with the bird's great heavy feet. A sudden thought shot like fire through the mountain lad's mind. The eagle was coming for another stroke. He would swoop down again in a moment. His circling took him out over the chasm, then back, then up over his eyrie. Abel watched this route. Holding on now with the strength of a new hope, the boy waited the eagle's return.

And soon the ponderous form swept lower, hovering above its victim. With a deft upward reach of his left arm, Abel caught the eagle fairly about its ankles. Taken by surprise, the great black robber beat its wings powerfully. Abel began to shout. The eagle strained upward, heading in the direction of his eyrie. The boy let the bird struggle. He, too, pulled with all his might, and soon his body was drawn clear away from the edge of the cliff. Then in a moment, realizing that the solid rock was once more beneath his feet, and sure of his safety, he released his hold on the eagle, and the great bird soared off in a disheveled splendor of flight. Abel for a moment sat on a boulder, breathing heavily. His eye was still upon the eagle, now high above the mountain pines.

Suddenly he heard a faint sound beside him. It was the little brown kid. Abel, with great tenderness, took the trembling animal in his arms, and started across the shelf of rocks. In another moment he was in the dim pathway leading down the mountain. He was so busily examining the hurts of the creature he was carrying that he had no thought for his own.

"Old Betty will be glad to get her baby back," he said. Then, thinking of his father, he added in his simple way: "Reckon I'll tell Pop about this, and tell him not to shoot the eagle, 'cause he helped me to keep from dropping off that there place. I did n't 'xactly whip him," he went on, "but I give him as big a scare, I reckon, as he give me. Ain't it so, you little brown kid?"

CHRISTMAS EVERY DAY

by W. D. Howells

THE little girl came into her papa's study, as she always did Saturday morning before breakfast, and asked for a story. He tried to beg off that morning, for he was very busy, but she would not let him. So he began:

"Well, once there was a little pig——"

She put her hand over his mouth and stopped him at the word. She said she had heard little pig stories till she was perfectly sick of them.

"Well, what kind of story *shall* I tell, then?"

"About Christmas. It 's getting to be the season. It 's past Thanksgiving already."

"It seems to me," argued her papa, "that I 've told as often about Christmas as I have about little pigs."

"No difference! Christmas is more interesting."

"Well!" Her papa roused himself from his writing by a great effort. "Well, then, I 'll tell you about the little girl that wanted it Christmas every day in the year. How would you like that?"

"First-rate!" said the little girl; and she nestled into comfortable shape in his lap, ready for listening.

"Very well, then, this little pig,——Oh, what are you pounding me for?"

"Because you said little pig instead of little girl."

"I should like to know what 's the difference between a little pig and a little girl that wanted it Christmas every day!"

"Papa," said the little girl, warningly, "if you don't go on, I 'll *give* it to you!" And at this her papa darted off like lightning, and began to tell the story as fast as he could.

Well, once there was a little girl who liked Christmas so much that she wanted it to be Christmas every day in the year; and as soon as Thanksgiving was over she began to send postal cards to the old Christmas Fairy to ask if she might n't have it. But the old Fairy never answered any of the postals; and, after a while, the little girl found out that the Fairy was pretty particular, and would n't notice anything but letters, not even correspondence cards in envelopes; but real letters on sheets of paper, and sealed outside with a monogram,—or your initial, any way. So, then, she began to send her letters; and in about three weeks—or just the day before Christmas, it was—she got a letter from the Fairy, saying she might have it Christmas every day for a year, and then they would see about having it longer.

The little girl was a good deal excited already, preparing for the old-fashioned, once-a-year Christmas that was coming the next day, and perhaps the Fairy's promise did n't make such an impression on her as it would have made at some other time. She just resolved to keep it to herself, and surprise everybody with it as it kept coming true; and then it slipped out of her mind altogether.

She had a splendid Christmas. She went to bed early, so as to let Santa Claus have a chance at the stockings, and in the morning she was up the first of anybody and went and felt them, and found hers all lumpy with packages of candy, and oranges and grapes, and pocket-books and rubber balls and all kinds of small presents, and her big brother's with nothing but the and snow-shovels, and photograph-frames, and little easels, and boxes of water-colors, and Turkish paste, and nougat, and candied cherries, and dolls' houses, and water-proofs,—and the big Christmas-tree, lighted and standing in a waste-basket in the middle.

She had a splendid Christmas all day. She ate so much candy that she did not

The second Christmas morning

tongs in them, and her young lady sister's with a new silk umbrella, and her papa's and mamma's with potatoes and pieces of coal wrapped up in tissue paper, just as they always had every Christmas. Then she waited around till the rest of the family were up, and she was the first to burst into the library, when the doors were opened, and look at the large presents laid out on the library-table—books, and portfolios, and boxes of stationery, and breast-pins, and dolls, and little stoves, and dozens of handkerchiefs, and ink-stands, and skates, want any breakfast; and the whole forenoon the presents kept pouring in that the expressman had not had time to deliver the night before; and she went 'round giving the presents she had got for other people, and came home and ate turkey and cranberry for dinner, and plum-pudding and nuts and raisins and oranges and more candy, and then went out and coasted and came in with a stomach-ache, crying; and her papa said he would see if his house was turned into that sort of fool's paradise another year; and they had a light supper, and pretty early everybody went to bed cross.

Here the little girl pounded her papa in the back, again.

"Well, what now? Did I say pigs?"

"You made them *act* like pigs."

"Well, did n't they?"

"No matter; you ought n't to put it into a story."

"Very well, then, I 'll take it all out."

Her father went on:

The little girl slept very heavily, and she slept very late, but she was wakened at last by the other children dancing 'round her bed with their stockings full of presents in their hands.

"What is it?" said the little girl, and she rubbed her eyes and tried to rise up in bed.

"Christmas! Christmas! Christmas!" they all shouted, and waved their stockings.

"Nonsense! It was Christmas yesterday."

Her brothers and sisters just laughed. "We don't know about that. It 's Christmas to-day, any way. You come into the library and see."

Then all at once it flashed on the little girl that the Fairy was keeping her promise, and her year of Christmases was beginning. She was dreadfully sleepy, but she sprang up like a lark—a lark that had overeaten itself and gone to bed cross—and darted into the library. There it was again! Books, and portfolios, and boxes of stationery, and breast-pins——

"You need n't go over it all, Papa; I guess I can remember just what was there," said the little girl.

Well, and there was the Christmas-tree blazing away, and the family picking out their presents, but looking pretty sleepy, and her father perfectly puzzled, and her mother ready to cry. "I 'm sure I don't see how I 'm to dispose of all these things," said her mother, and her father said it seemed to him they had had something just like it the day before, but he supposed he must have dreamed it. This struck the little girl as the best kind of a joke; and so she ate so much candy she did n't want any breakfast, and went 'round carrying presents, and had turkey and cranberry for dinner, and then went out and coasted, and came in with a——

"Papa!"

"Well, what now?"

"What did you promise, you forgetful thing?"

"Oh! oh, yes!"

Well, the next day, it was just the same thing over again, but everybody getting crosser; and at the end of a week's time so many people had lost their tempers that you could pick up lost tempers anywhere; they perfectly strewed the ground. Even when people tried to recover their tempers they usually got somebody else's, and it made the most dreadful mix.

The little girl began to get frightened, keeping the secret all to herself; she wanted to tell her mother, but she did n't dare to; and she was ashamed to ask the Fairy to take back her gift, it seemed ungrateful and ill-bred, and she thought she would try to stand it, but she hardly knew how she could, for a whole year. So it went on and on, and it was Christmas on St. Valentine's Day, and Washington's Birthday just the same as any day, and it did n't skip even the First of April, though everything was counterfeit that day, and that was some *little* relief.

After a while, coal and potatoes began to be awfully scarce, so many had been wrapped up in tissue paper to fool papas and mammas with. Turkeys got to be about a thousand dollars apiece——

"Papa!"

"Well, what?"

"You 're beginning to fib."

"Well, *two* thousand, then."

And they got to passing off almost any-thing for turkeys,—half-grown humming-birds, and even rocs out of the "Arabian Nights,"—the real turkeys were so scarce. And cranberries—well, they asked a dia-mond apiece for cranberries. All the woods and orchards were cut down for Christmas-trees, and where the woods and orchards used to be, it looked just like a stubble-field, with the stumps. After a while they had to make Christmas-trees out of rags, and stuff them with bran, like old-fash-ioned dolls; but there were plenty of rags, because people got so poor, buying presents for one another, that they could n't get any new clothes, and they just wore their old ones to tatters. They got so poor that every-body had to go to the poor-house, except the confectioners, and the fancy store-keepers, and the picture-booksellers, and the expressmen; and *they* all got so rich and proud that they would hardly wait upon a person when he came to buy; it was perfectly shameful!

Well, after it had gone on about three or four months, the little girl, whenever she came into the room in the morning and saw those great ugly lumpy stockings dangling at the fire-place, and the disgust-ing presents around everywhere, used to just sit down and burst out crying. In six months she was perfectly exhausted; she could n't even cry any more; she just lay on the lounge and rolled her eyes and panted. About the beginning of October she took to sitting down on dolls, wherever she found them,—French dolls, or any kind,—she hated the sight of them so; and by Thanksgiving she was crazy, and just slammed her presents across the room.

By that time people did n't carry pres-ents around nicely any more. They flung them over the fence, or through the win-dow, or anything; and, instead of running their tongues out and taking great pains to

Exhausted

write "For dear Papa," or "Mamma," or "Brother," or "Sister," or "Susie," or "Sam-mie," or "Billie," or "Bobby," or "Jimmie," or "Jennie," or whoever it was, and troub-ling to get the spelling right, and then signing their names, and "Xmas, 188—," they used to write in the gift-books, "Take it, you horrid old thing!" and then go and bang it against the front door. Nearly everybody had built barns to hold their presents, but pretty soon the barns over-flowed, and then they used to let them lie out in the rain, or anywhere. Sometimes the police used to come and tell them to shovel their presents off the sidewalk, or they would arrest them.

"I thought you said everybody had gone to the poor-house," interrupted the little girl.

"They did go, at first," said her papa; "but after a while the poor-houses got so full that they had to send the people back to their own houses. They tried to cry, when they got back, but they could n't make the least sound."

"Why could n't they?"

"Because they had lost their voices, saying 'Merry Christmas' so much. Did I tell
you how it was on the Fourth of July?"

"No; how was it?" And the little girl
nestled closer, in expectation of something
uncommon.

Well, the night before, the boys staid up
to celebrate, as they always do, and fell
asleep before twelve o'clock, as usual, expecting to be wakened by the bells and
cannon. But it was nearly eight o'clock before the first boy in the United States woke
up, and then he found out what the
trouble was. As soon as he could get his
clothes on, he ran out of the house and
smashed a big cannon-torpedo down on
the pavement; but it did n't make any
more noise than a damp wad of paper, and,
after he tried about twenty or thirty more,
he began to pick them up and look at
them. Every single torpedo was a big
raisin! Then he just streaked it upstairs,
and examined his fire-crackers and toy-
pistol and two-dollar collection of fire-
works, and found that they were nothing
but sugar and candy painted up to look
like fireworks! Before ten o'clock, every
boy in the United States found out that his
Fourth of July things had turned into
Christmas things; and then they just sat
down and cried,—they were so mad. There
are about twenty million boys in the United
States, and so you can imagine what a
noise they made. Some men got together
before night, with a little powder that had
n't turned into purple sugar yet, and they
said they would fire off *one* cannon, any
way. But the cannon burst into a thousand
pieces, for it was nothing but rock-candy,
and some of the men nearly got killed.
The Fourth of July orations all turned into
Christmas carols, and when anybody tried
to read the Declaration, instead of saying,
"When in the course of human events it
becomes necessary," he was sure to sing,

"God rest you, merry gentlemen." It was
perfectly awful.

The little girl drew a deep sigh of satisfaction.

"And how was it at Thanksgiving?" she
asked.

Her papa hesitated. "Well, I 'm almost
afraid to tell you. I 'm afraid you 'll think
it 's wicked."

"Well, tell, any way," said the little girl.

Well, before it came Thanksgiving, it
had leaked out who had caused all these
Christmases. The little girl had suffered so
much that she had talked about it in her
sleep; and after that, hardly anybody
would play with her. People just perfectly
despised her, because if it had not been for
her greediness, it would n't have happened; and now, when it came Thanksgiving, and she wanted them to go to
church, and have squash-pie and turkey,
and show their gratitude, they said that all
the turkeys had been eaten up for her old
Christmas dinners, and if she would stop
the Christmases, they would see about the
gratitude. Was n't it dreadful? And the
very next day the little girl began to send
letters to the Christmas Fairy, and then
telegrams, to stop it. But it did n't do any
good; and then she got to calling at the
Fairy's house, but the girl that came to the
door always said "Not at home," or "Engaged," or "At dinner," or something like
that; and so it went on till it came to the
old once-a-year Christmas Eve. The little
girl fell asleep, and when she woke up in
the morning——

"She found it was all nothing but a
dream," suggested the little girl.

"No, indeed!" said her papa. "It was all
every bit true!"

"Well, what *did* she find out then?"

"Why, that it was n't Christmas at last,

and was n't ever going to be, any more. Now it 's time for breakfast."

The little girl held her papa fast around the neck.

"You sha'n't go if you 're going to leave it *so!*"

"How do you want it left?"

"Christmas once a year."

"All right," said her papa; and he went on again.

Well, there was the greatest rejoicing all over the country, and it extended clear up into Canada. The people met together everywhere, and kissed and cried for joy. The city carts went around and gathered up all the candy and raisins and nuts, and dumped them into the river; and it made the fish perfectly sick; and the whole United States, as far out as Alaska, was one blaze of bonfires, where the children were burning up their gift-books and presents of all kinds. They had the greatest *time!*

The little girl went to thank the old Fairy because she had stopped its being Christmas, and she said she hoped she would keep her promise, and see that Christmas never, never came again. Then the Fairy frowned, and asked her if she was sure she knew what she meant; and

the little girl asked her, why not? and the old Fairy said that now she was behaving just as greedily as ever, and she 'd better look out. This made the little girl think it all over carefully again, and she said she would be willing to have it Christmas about once in a thousand years; and then she said a hundred, and then she said ten, and at last she got down to one. Then the Fairy said that was the good old way that had pleased people ever since Christmas began, and she was agreed. Then the little girl said, "What 're your shoes made of?" And the Fairy said, "Leather." And the little girl said, "Bargain 's done forever," and skipped off, and hippity-hopped the whole way home, she was so glad.

"How will that do?" asked the papa.

"First-rate!" said the little girl; but she hated to have the story stop, and was rather sober. However, her mamma put her head in at the door, and asked her papa:

"Are you never coming to breakfast? What have you been telling that child?"

"Oh, just a moral tale."

The little girl caught him around the neck again.

"*We* know! Don't you tell *what,* Papa! Don't you tell *what!*"

THE MAJOR'S BIG-TALK STORIES

by F. Blake Crofton

CHASED BY A HOOP-SNAKE

In the Yelgree forest, near our trading-post, there was a big snake that had adopted rapid transit. I saw him when he first learned it. He was chasing a small hoop-snake, when the little one put his tail in his mouth, after the manner of his kind, and rolled clean out of sight. Well, what did his big snakeship do but put his own

tail into his mouth, and begin practicing! After a few turns he grew accustomed to the thing, and in half an hour could beat the best bicycle time on record.

A few days after this I shot a deer, and was carrying its horns home. As I was passing a few hundred yards from the Yelgree forest, I saw what seemed to be a loose wheel coming out of the wood. It was the biggest wheel I ever saw. I felt almost as if the polar circle had got loose from its fixings and was making for me.

"Hoop la!" I cried, and then I shut up, for I saw it was the big revolving python.

'T was no use shooting at his head, for he was revolving at the rate of sixty miles an hour; and no use trying to escape, unless I could hire an express engine on the spot. So I just lay down to make it harder for the reptile to swallow me.

When the snake came up and noticed the deer's horns, he shivered, just as a Christian would if he saw a horned man! As I lay, they must have seemed to be growing out of my head, and the python may have mistaken me for the Old Serpent himself. Whatever his idea may have been, he had not ceased shivering before he made tracks for the forest and let me go in peace.

On my way home I reflected that horned animals are bad for the health of serpents, which swallow their prey whole, and that, time and again, imprudent pythons and boas have been found dead with deer all swallowed but the antlers.

"A snake," I said to myself, "that is smart enough to take a hint in the way of locomotion is smart enough to take a hint in the way of feeding."

Anyhow, his prudence or his fears lost him a good meal, for I was fat then. A little learning is a dangerous thing for snakes.

A SPELLING SPAT

by Nancy Byrd Turner

A GNAT came wailing to a Gnu, a most unhappy midget.

The Gnu said, "Gnat, don't do like that. You put me in a fidget."

"I'm sad," said Gnat. "No, mad—just that. To save me, I can't see why folks should call us what they do but spell us with a 'G.' "

"That's true," said Gnu. "Here's what we'll do: I'll write a note—so plain, so strong, sarcastic, full of spleen, they'll not offend again."

"Dear Friends and Neighbors:" (ran the note),

"We gneed to know quite clearly what gnovel gnotion makes you spell our gnames so very queerly. Gno other beast, gnorth, south, or east, gneed bear that gnoxious 'G'—gnocturnals, gnesters, gnibblers. Gno, and gneither, sirs, gneed we.

"It gnettles and it gnags us, but there's gnaught that we can do. A gnasty gnuisance! (That's gnot gnice, but you'd be gnaughty, too).

"Gnumbskulls and gninnies! Gnever use that G extraordinary—it's gnonsense, gneither gnatural, gnice, gnor gneat, gnor gnecessary.

"These gnamby-pamby gnicknames make us gnervous, kindly gnote, dear Gnag, and Gnightingale, and Gnewt, and gnoble Gnanny-goat."

They sent the letter off post-haste, and in a day or two received reply. 'Twas terse and dry. It ran:

"Dear Nat and Nu: We feel like naves. We scarcely new—in fact, we couldn't no —a silent letter'd have the nack of nifing people so.

"We nash our teeth, and nit our brows, and riggle on our nees, the nowledge of our retched rong so rings us. Pardon, please!"

"Something's amiss," growled Gnu,

"with this!" He scowled above the letter. "They've spelled my name right; all the same, I can't say things look better."

"Alas," mourned Gnat, "this knocks me flat. I had no idea, Gnu, that such a lot of things must change in changing me and you. Just look at all these idiot words! We thought we'd be in clover; instead we've got to learn to read and write and spell all over."

"We moved too fast," Gnu said at last.

"We might have known there're rules for spelling, Gnat. I fear we've proved a pair of precious fools."

He seized a pen and scrawled in haste: "P.S. We write to say: at length we find we do not mind the dictionary way. The silent letters aren't so bad; at least no harm they'll do.

"So, please retain. And we remain, as ever, Gnat and Gnu."

FRIENDS

By E. Vincent Millay (HONOR MEMBER, AGE 17)

May 1910

I. HE

I 'VE sat here all the afternoon, watching her
      busy fingers send
That needle in and out. How soon, I wonder,
      will she reach the end?
Embroidery! I can't see how a girl of Molly's
      common sense
Can spend her time like that! Why now—
      just look at that! I may be dense,
But, somehow, I don't see the fun in punch-
      ing lots of holes down through
A piece of cloth; and, one by one, sewing
      them up.
      But Molly 'll do
A dozen of them, right around
That shapeless bit of stuff she 's found.
A dozen of them! Just like that!
And thinks it 's sense she 's working at.
But, then, she 's just a girl (although she 's
      quite the best one of the lot!),
And I 'll just have to let her sew, whether it 's
      foolishness or not.

II. SHE

HE 's sat here all the afternoon, talking about
      an awful game;
One boy will not be out till June, and then he
      may be always lame.
Foot-ball! I 'm sure I can't see why a boy like
      Bob—so good and kind—
Wishes to see poor fellows lie hurt on the
      ground. I may be blind,

But, somehow, I don't see the fun. Some one
      calls,
      "14–16–9";
You kick the ball, and then you run and try
      to reach a white chalk line.
And Bob would sit right there all day
And talk like that, and never say
A single word of sense; or so
It seems to me. I may not know.
But Bob 's a faithful friend to me. So let him
      talk that game detested,
And I will smile and seem to be most wonder-
      fully interested!

THE DIARY OF A DRAGON

By Morris G. Bishop (Age 11)

July 1905

(HONOR MEMBER)

12689 B.C.

JUNE 1.   Ate a magician. I think I 'm getting
sick. That magician had a bottle labeled
"Sleeping Mixture." I think I 'll take it. My
old friends the Seven Sleepers said there was
nothing as refreshing as a good long nap.

1905 A.D.

JUNE 1.   I took it. I did n't remember anything else until I found an old man prod-
ding me in the ribs and saying: "Fine specimen of a Rinlobistoxatsthorus." I ate him
instantly for insulting me so. What does he
take me for? A Russian?
JUNE 7.   These people have more impudence.
I met a man to-day who tried to sell me a
sewing-machine. I threatened to eat him,

528

and he offered me a cure for indigestion. I ate his traps besides himself.

JUNE 8. Went to a museum, and there I saw the bones of my poor old mother, labeled "Shakepopidaristankoranorifitorus." I just lay down and cried. But I only cried the oil for that sewing-machine. It's my own fault. The family doctor always said such things would go to my head.

JUNE 12. Saw a lot of people getting something from a boy called a newsboy. I went up to him. He said, "Take the 'World'?" "It would be too much at one gulp," I replied. "'Sun'?" said he. "No, thanks; I don't deal in planets," said I. "Have a 'Herald'?" he said. "Yes," I answered. "Heralds have a distinct flavor and don't wear armor, which gives me indigestion." But the insolent cub only gave me a piece of paper. He tasted awfully.

JUNE 17. A dime-museum man offered me $20 per week and all his creditors for food if I would join his company. I accepted.

JUNE 18. The dime-museum man was saying, "This is the only great and original dragon," when a man said, "Aw, he's all hot air. That dragon is just two men inside a skin." I showed him I was all hot air. I scorched the people for ten rows back. And as for two men, there must have been a dozen.

(EXTRACT FROM THE "NEW YORK COURIER.")

"A dragon was found sleeping on the third rail of the subway, just above Forty-second Street. He stopped traffic for four hours, until he was blown up with dynamite. That cleared the track."

MY FAIRY-BOOK PRINCE

By Margaret Widdemer (Age 16)

(CASH PRIZE $5.00)

DEAR little prince of Fairyland,
The rose you hold in your outstretched hand
Is not half so sweet as the loving look
You bend from your page of my picture-book
On the calm little princess over the way.

Do you win her, or lose? Do you go or stay?
Ah, you wed, I know! I have but to look
Over the page of my picture-book.

Dear little prince of Fairyland,
Is the red, red rose in your tight-clasped hand
For none but your princess, cold as fair?
Surely she's many a love to spare!
She never would care if you went away!
Could you not step from your page, and stay
With a lone little maid who would love but
      you?
(And ah, little prince, I would love you true!)

Cold little prince of Fairyland!
Silently, haughtily, still you stand.
"To none but my princess," you seem to say,
"My rose and my love, though there come
      who may!"
And you'll wed the princess—the book says
      so;
And I know you lived many a year ago;
Yet—ah, little prince, if you could but look
Loving but me from my picture-book!

A PATRIOT

By Robert Hillyer (Age 13)

July 1908

(SILVER BADGE)

A HERO brave, of grandeur and renown,
   Leads forth his force to conquer and begin
   The conquest of the land he sought to win,
   To set a burdened, hopeless people free;
   And what for all his victories finds he?
A laurel crown!

But in the ranks a hero struggles brave,
   And though undaunted is his sturdy heart,
   His life is only an unnoticed part
   Of earth's great struggle to keep just and
      free;
   But what for all his industry finds he?
A lowly grave!

But, though his task seems one long hopeless
      strife,
   "Uneasy lies the head that wears a crown."

So he is fortunate without renown,
While he, himself, is honest, just, and free.
So what for all his industry finds he?
Unending life!

IN THE TWILIGHT

By Eudora Welty (Age 15)

January 1925

(GOLD BADGE. SILVER BADGE WON AUGUST, 1920)

THE daylight in glory is dying away;
The last faded colors are fast growing gray;
The sun nears the beckoning portals of night,
And leaves to the skies his long, ling'ring light.

The sunbeams have hid 'neath a sad, misty
veil,
And softened to shadows—dim, silvery, pale.
The Queen of the Night shly peeps o'er the
hill,
And reigns in her radiance—soft, cold, and
still.

A lone cypress-tree, with its feathery grace,
Casts delicate shadows, like old Spanish lace,
On the cool, trembling waters that meet the
gray sky,
And the moon rules supreme in her palace on
high.

MYSTERY

By Stephen Vincent Benét (Age 15)

February 1914

(GOLD BADGE. SILVER BADGE WON SEPTEMBER,
1912)

THE giant building towered in the night
Like a titanic hand released at last
From under cumbering mountain-ranges
vast,
Poised menacingly high, as if to smite
A silent, sudden, deadly blow at Man.

I slunk along its base; then, cowering, ran,
Feeling the while it mattered not how fast,
Since it would strike me from behind at last.

Next morning, as I passed among the hive
Of careless people, to myself I said:
"You do not fear. You 've only seen it dead.
I 've seen the thing alive!"

THE FROZEN BROOK

By Stella Benson (Age 13)

January 1906

(HONOR MEMBER)

THE frost set in and laid its icy hand
Upon the land;
It froze the brook and caused its songs to
cease;
What once was gentle murm'ring now was
peace—
Stern, silent peace.

Then the snow fell, and on the frozen stream
It laid a lovely cloak without a seam
Or blemish. Down it fell without a sound,
Cov'ring the frost-flowers traced upon the
ground,
And icicles of lovely, graceful mold
Sparking in different colors, blue and gold—
But oh, so cold

HOME, TO PENELOPE

By Bruce T. Simonds (Age 15)

Dec. 1910

(HONOR MEMBER)

ALONE and weary, I, in this my house,
Must weave my tapestry; but not too swift,
Lest I should end this welcome respite, gain'd
From those who e'en besiege me in my home.
My home! Is this a home?—what mockery!—
A prison, beautiful in strangers' sight,

But like a dungeon drear and desolate
To my poor hungry eyes. I hate these walls,
The bleak, bare chambers, empty-echoing
long,
The tall, straight pillars, gaunt and gray and
grim
In never-ending, cold, monotonous rows,
The halls in which his footsteps used to sound.
Why must I stay in this most cheerless place?
Home is not home without Odysseus.

But if once more he should come back to me,
If I should see once more that godlike form,
Then would the palace seem more beautiful
Than e'er before; the marble in the sun
Would warmly gleam; the house would then
be home;
'T is but an empty shell when friends are
gone.
So now it is; Odysseus is gone.

Athene! Strike me too, if he is dead!
For were he there, then Hades would be bliss
Beside slow, cruel death in this sad tomb.

VACATION SONG

By E. Vincent Millay (Age 15)

August 1907

(HONOR MEMBER)

SHINE on me, oh, you gold, gold sun,
    Smile on me, oh, you blue, blue skies,
Sing, birds! and rouse the lazy breeze
    That, in the shadow, sleeping lies,
Calling, "Awaken! Slothful one
    And chase the yellow butterflies."

Laugh! Sober maiden in the brook,
    Shake down your smoothly plaited hair,
Let it fall rippling on the grass
    Daring the wind to leave it there,
Dancing in all its sun-kissed folds,—
    Laughing low in the sun-kissed air.

Frown if you will, you staid old trees,
    You cannot silence the birds and me;

You will sing yourself ere we leave you in
    peace,—
    Frown if you will but we shall see.
I 'll pelt you with your own green leaves
    Till you echo the strains of our minstrelsy.

Oh, mower! All the world 's at play,—
    Leave on the grass your sickle bright;
Come, and we 'll dance a merry step
    With the birds and the leaves and the gold
    sunlight,
We 'll dance till the shadows leave the hills
    And bring to the fields the quiet night.

THE VOICE OF THE CITY

(A SYMPHONY)

By John C. Farrar (Age 17)

January 1914

(GOLD BADGE. SILVER BADGE WON FEBRUARY, 1913)

ANDANTE

BENEATH the tawny sky where the misty
    housetops lie,
The cock, with tousled feathers, gives the
    city's muezzin cry:
        "Awake! awake! The day! the day!"
Then, from their dingy hovels, come men
    with picks and shovels,
Who tramp with slow, accustomed feet upon
    the fast-awakening street,
And hear the morning knelling, with steel
    voice ever telling:
        "To work! to work! Obey! obey!"

(ALLEGRO)

From a hushed diminuendo to a gradual
    crescendo,
Comes the whirring, roaring tune of the city's
    heart at noon,
Pale faces, red faces, faces streaked with care,
Foul hearts, cunning hearts, hearts pure and
    fair,
Rushing on, rushing on, merciless and swift,
Evermore, evermore, human atoms drift.

(SCHERZO)

The tune of the night when the lights are
　　bright
Sings with gaiety and hilarity;
Filled with the sound of dancing feet,
Catching the laughter that fills the street,
Marked with the rhythm of passion's heat,
And rolling out in a human song
The wonderful battle of right and wrong.

(LARGHETTO)

Sounds of the night, sounds of deep emotion,
Strike upon the stars to capture peace;
Hush thy vain and clamorous commotion,
Hush, and with the midnight echoes, cease!

VACATION DOWN SOUTH

By E. Babette Deutsch (Age 11)

August 1907

(SILVER BADGE)

LIL' chile, lil' chile wid 'lasses on yo' nose,
Come an' kiss yo' Pappy, lil' Tipsytoes.
Now dey ain't no lessons to be leahned no mo',
Go an' make yo' mud pies by de kitchen do'.
Do yo' miss de schooldays, an' de book an'
　　slate?
Pappy 'll play de school-ma'am, "Chilluns sit
　　up straight!"
Nevah mine mah honey, don' yo' waste a teah.
Pappy an' yo mammy 'll make fun all de yeah.
Mammy 'll make prime biskits, yo' will like
　　dem, sho',
Nevah mine, mah honey, dat school don'
　　come no mo'!

GRATITUDE

By Cornelia Otis Skinner (Age 11)

February 1911

(SILVER BADGE)

I THANK thee, gentle breeze that blows,
　For all thy coolness bringing;

I thank thee, happy little bird,
　For all thy cheerful singing.

I thank you, pretty flowers that grow,
　For you carpet all the land;
I thank thee, smooth and sunny beach,
　For thy white and shimmery sand.

But should we thank these things so fair,
　For all their splendid show?
Nay! Bend our knees in gratitude
　To Him that made them so.

IN JUNE-TIME

By William R. Benét (Age 16).

June 1902

HARK, hark, to the meadow-lark
　As he swells his throat in a burst of song!
By the rippling brook sway the lilies. Look!
　They lift their heads in a surpliced throng.
The sun's bright gleam shakes the silver
　　stream
　With ripples of light that dance and play;
The fields are white with the daisies bright;
　The earth rejoices, and all is gay.
　　　It 's June-time, it 's June-time,
　　　　The sparkling ripples tell;
　　　It 's June-time, it 's June-time,
　　　　So shakes each lily bell.
The sky is smiling blue above; the streams
　　below run clear.
It 's June-time, it 's June-time, the chosen of
　　the year!
　　　It 's June-time, it 's June-time,
　　　　The daisies whispering note.
　　　It 's June-time, it 's June-time!
　　　　So swells each robin's throat.
The world is one vast Paradise, and heaven
　　shines more near.
It 's June-time, it 's June-time, the chosen of
　　the year!

WHEN SWALLOWS BUILD

By Corey H. Ford (Age 14)

October 1916

(SILVER BADGE)

"My dear, you 're getting very thin of late;
  Cod-liver oil will add much to your weight.
You know it 's good for you; why hesitate,
    When swallows build?

"Just hold your nose and soon it will be
    downed,
A few more swallows will build another
    pound.
This fact remains which you can't get
    around—
    That swallows build.

"Pretend it 's chocolate candy soft and brown;
  Just close your eyes and, smiling, gulp it
    down.
'T will do you good, therefore why sit and
    frown,
    When swallows build?"

WHERE DO THE FAIRIES MEET?

By Jessica Nelson North (Age 13).

July 1905

(HONOR MEMBER)

WHERE, oh where, do the fairies meet?
  I 've hunted the country through;
I 've looked in the heart of the violet sweet
  As it shone with its wealth of dew,
And I 've watched the crest of a cloudland fleet
  As it floated across the blue.

I 've searched the sky when the thunder
    rolled,
  By the wrestling demons riven;
And I 've watched the lights of red and gold
  As they shone in the west at even,
And the still white beams, so clear and cold,
  That fell from the moon in heaven.

I thought, as I stood on the silent hill,
  That I heard their hastening feet;
But it was the wind of midnight chill
  As it rustled the fields of wheat.
And the question remains unanswered still,—
  Where do the fairies meet?

A WINTER WALK

By Rachel Lyman Field (Age 16) ....

June 1911

(SILVER BADGE)

As soon as the little country school closed, late that winter afternoon, I hastened out-of-doors and started toward home. How beautiful it was out there with the rosy glow of sunset on the pure, glistening snow. The branches of the trees reared white arms toward the sky, and the effect of the feathery sprays against the pale yellow of the eastern sky was more wonderful than gorgeous foilage. Far off, the irregular outlines of the mountains rose, while above, faintly glimmering, hung the thin, delicate, new moon. All on one side of the road stretched fields of untrodden snow; they seemed to sweep in undulations, not unlike the waves of the sea. The only sound was the wind stirring among the branches of the pines; they seemed to be murmuring or talking in their long winter sleep.

A feeling of awe came over me, such as I had never experienced before. I felt how great and wonderful the world was, and what a small place I held in it. Overhead the stars shone faintly, and the near-by pines waved their great branches majestically to and fro. Just across the road ran the brook, a merry, laughing, shallow brook, which was my constant companion in the summer days. Now, however, its merry chatter was ceased; it was covered with ice and snow. From behind a fallen tree a wild rabbit sprang across my path. "Poor little thing," I thought, "he misses the brook too!"

At last the road made a sharp turn, and there, over the snow, shone out the lights of home. How cheerful they looked streaming across the fields. Then I realized that the best part of my magical winter walk was coming home.

A SONG OF SUMMER

By Sterling North (Age 8)

October 1915

VACATION 's come,
And in the trees
The birds are singing.
I hear the hum
Of golden bees
On daisies swinging.

By grassy stream
The long-legged crane
Is deeply wading.
In pink and cream,
Beyond the lane,
The sun is fading.

A SONG OF THE WOODS

By S. V. Benét (Age 13)

Sept. 1912

(SILVER BADGE)

There 's many a forest in the world,
  In many lands leaves fall;
But Sherwood, merry Sherwood,
  Is the fairest wood of all.

They say that on midsummer night,
If mortal eyes could see aright,
  Or mortal ears could hear,
A wanderer on Sherwood's grass
Would see the band of Robin pass,
  Still hunting of the deer.

And sometimes to his ears might come
The beating of an elfin drum,
  Where Puck, the tricksy sprite,
Would dance around a fairy ring,
With others of his gathering,
  All on midsummer night.

Queen Guinevere would ride again
With all her glittering, courtly train,
  Through Sherwood's lovely glades;
'Til dawn begins to glow near by,
And from the kingdom of the sky,
  The magic darkness fades.

· · · · · · ·

There's many a forest in the world,
In many lands leaves fall;
But Sherwood, merry Sherwood,
  Is the fairest wood of all.

By Anne L. Parrish (Age 14)

October 1903

(GOLD BADGE)

I PUT down my pencil with a sigh, and read what I had just written.

"My favorite character in fiction is Alice in Wonderland."

Then I crossed the words out, and sighed again. The fifth bad beginning in as many minutes! The task seemed hopeless.

I was just about to give up, when, to my great surprise, I heard a voice behind me.

"I heard you thinking about me, so I came to help you."

I spun around, and saw her there—Alice! The Alice of my dreams!

She stood in the open doorway, with the sunlight streaming over her, in her blue frock and little white pinafore, just as she had come to me so many times before when I had been sick or unhappy, laughing and dimpling at me, and whispering her stories in my ear, until I had laughed with her.

"Are you really going to write about *me?*" she asked. "There are a lot who thought you would choose *them*—Undine, and Ivanhoe, and Tom, out of the 'Water Babies,' you know, and—oh, lots! And since you have n't, they feel a bit cross."

"Of course I chose you," I said. "But the trouble is, I don't know what to say about you."

"I can't stay but a minute," said Alice. "I 'll help you all I can, though I 'm afraid my adventures are all in the book, are n't they?" she added regretfully.

"Yes," I said. *"Everything 's* in the book, it seems to me. But I don't think St. Nicholas wants a story, anyway. It ought to be more of an essay, you know—all about your character and your looks. What shall I say?"

"You might say that I like plum jam better than strawberry, and anything better than lessons. There's my character. As for my looks, my hair does n't curl—"

"And your eyes are dreamy and blue, and your cheeks are pink, and your mouth is laughing, and you are perfectly dear!"

"Oh!" laughed Alice. "You 're not a bit like the Caterpillar or the Queen. But I must be going. Good-by. Oh, yes! you can put in that Dinah is very well, thank you. Write the story, won't you?"

"I 'll try," I called after her.

And I have.

FOUR CHARADES

by C. P. Cranch

I

WHEN swiftly in my first you glide along,
  Naught ruffles up the temper of your
    mind;
All goes as smoothly as a summer song,
  All objects flit beside you like the wind.

But if you should be stopped in your career,
  And forced to linger when you fain
    would fly,
You 'll leave my first, and, very much I
    fear,
  Will fall into my second speedily.

Till in some snug and comfortable room
  Your friends receive you as a welcome
    guest,
You 'll own that Winter 's robbed of half
    his gloom,
  When on my whole your feet in slippers
    rest.

II

MY FIRST

I SUNDER friends, yet give to laws
A place to stand and plead their cause.
Though justice and sobriety
Still find their safest ground in me,
I spread temptation in man's way,
And rob and ruin every day.

MY SECOND

Success and power are in my name,
Men strive for me far more than fame,
One thing I am unto the wise,
But quite another in fools' eyes,
Through me the world is rich and strong,
Yet too much love of me is wrong.

MY WHOLE

My first and second when they meet,
As lawyers' fees, my whole complete.
And yet my first too oft enjoyed,
Is sure to make my second void.
My whole is good and bad by turns,
As every merchant daily learns.

III

MY first the stout Hibernian wields
On banks and streets and stubborn fields,
To earn the bread that labor yields.

My second is a name for one
Whose youth and age together run,
A leader all good people shun.

My whole in summer-time is sweet,
When youths and maids together meet
Beneath some shady grove's retreat.
(So simple is this short charade,
That I am very much afraid
You 'll guess at once, without my aid.)

IV

WHEN I was a little boy, how welcome was
    my first;
When tired of play I went to bed, my les-
    sons all rehearsed.
How soundly all the night I slept, without
    a care or sorrow,
And waked when sunshine lit the room,
    and robins sang good-morrow.

When I was a little boy, what joy it was to
    see
My second waiting at the door for Willy
    and for me;

And how we trotted off to bring ripe apples
from the farm,
And piled our bags on Nellie's back, nor
felt the least alarm.

But when I was a little boy, I had an ugly
dream,

A huge black bear was in my bed, I gave
a dreadful scream,
And roused the house; they brought in
lights, and put my whole to flight,
Since then I made a vow to eat no supper
late at night.

EIGHT CHARADES, DONE UP IN RHYME, FOR LAD AND LASS AT CANDLE-TIME

by Ralph Henry Barbour

I

MY first can trace the written word;
(Some say 't is mightier than the sword!)
My last, our cousins o'er the sea
Are proud to bend to royalty:
My whole, if borrowed or if lent,
To *us* is worth no more 'n a cent.

II

My first is you, but never me;
My last is found beside the sea,
My whole 's a number that—ahem!—
In Rome was written with an M.

III

My first 's a receptacle fashioned of tin:
We find fruits delectable often therein.
  My last 's a girl's name
  That reads just the same
No matter which end you begin it.
  A country quite near
  Is my whole—But, oh dear,
You 'll guess my charade in a minute!

IV

My first 's a speck—just such a one
As floats and dances in the sun.
My last is taken from the soil
Wherever men in mines do toil.
My whole makes power, gives us light,
And works away both day and night.

V

My first may be black or be green or be
  blue:
(Without it, my puzzle you 'd never see
  through!)
It 's open by day and it 's closed very
  tight—

Or *ought* to be closed—just as soon as it 's
  night.
My second 's a wagon, and also a car,
And likewise the front, where the smart
  people are.
My last is an implement used in all gar-
  dens;
It makes calloused hands and the muscles
  it hardens.
My whole is a story of Scottish romance
That will thrill and enthrall, engross and
  entrance.

VI

My first is a bird that farmers all scorn;
My last is in Kansas, but never in corn;
My whole is a game that is played on the
  lawn.

VII

My first is dug from out the ground;
My next on ev'ry foot is found;
My third 's a crowd disorderly;
My last is like a snake at sea!
My whole 's a thing in city street
Or country road goes fast and fleet:
It 's here and there and all about—
Dear me, here comes one now! *Look out!*

VIII

My first 's a chip, the kind we hate
To find upon the dinner-plate;
My second 's roundest of all let-
Ters in the English alphabet;
My last is something with a curl—
In short, 't is nothing but a girl;
My whole is lovable and quaint,
The last name of a dear old Saint.

thirds of the name of a Western State. 3. Close at hand. 4. Past. 5. An insect. 6. A point of the compass. 7. A light. 8. A poisonous plant. 9. A wind instrument. 10. An excrescence.

ELINOR LOTHROP DANIELS.

CROSS-WORD ENIGMA

My first is in jolly, but not in gay;
  My second 's in slumber, but not in sleep;
My third is in sunlight, but not in day;
  My fourth is in crying, but not in weep;
My fifth is in study, but not in learn;
  My sixth is in darkness, but not in night;
My seventh 's in cowslip, but not in fern;
  My eighth is in battle, but not in fight;
My ninth is in goodness, but not in wrong;
  My tenth is in majesty, not in king;
My eleventh is in carol, but not in song;
  My twelfth is in Easter, and also in
    spring.
Now, if you have guessed these rhymes
    aright,
  You will surely find the name
Of an ancient general full of might,
  And widely known to fame.

C. F. BABCOCK (Prize-winner, Nov., 1899).

ANAGRAM

TOSS, HO! REST NO PENT MEN.
(A popular author.)

DOUBLE ACROSTIC

(*Second Prize*, St. Nicholas League Competition.)

My primals spell the surname of a famous man, and my finals state what he was.

CROSS-WORDS: 1. Melted Rock. 2. Two

CONNECTED SQUARES

I. UPPER LEFT-HIND SQUARE: 1. To stow away snugly. 2. Shortly. 3. To draw near. 4. A joint.

II. UPPER RIGHT-HAND SQUARE: 1. To bridge. 2. A tree. 3. Repeatedly. 4. A small lizard.

III. CENTRAL SQUARE: 1. Hibernia. 2. To travel. 3. A notion. 4. Clean.

IV. LOWER LEFT-HAND SQUARE: 1. Drops of water. 2. A church dignitary. 3. A large bird. 4. A cozy home.

V. LOWER RIGHT-HAND SQUARE: 1. A weed. 2. An exclamation. 3. To grate. 4. To descry.

FLORENCE AND EDNA.

DIAMOND

1. In March. 2. A reticule. 3. The subject of a poem. 4. A statesman born in

March, who died in March. 5. Deep shade.
6. Amount. 7. In January.

JENNIE N. CHILD (League Member).

ILLUSTRATED PRIMAL ACROSTIC

ILLUSTRATED PRIMAL ACROSTIC.

EACH of the six small pictures may be
described by a single word. When these
words have been rightly guessed, and
placed one below another, in the order in
which they are numbered, the initial letters
will spell the name of a distinguished man.

AN "AGED" PUZZLE

Pray what 's the best age for a girl or a
boy? (Courage.)
And what is the one we 'd refuse? (Do-
tage.)
What age does an Englishman highly en-
joy? (Peerage.)
And what would all fond lovers choose?
(Marriage.)

There 's an age for the farmer (1) and one
for the clerk (2);
One shared by the doctor and thief (3);
An age for the man who directs others'
work (4),
And one that expresses belief (5).

What age is it troubles the traveler's mind
(6)?
And what is the age of the slave (7)?
The one that the soldier has often to find
(8)?
The age that the battle-field gave (9)?

And what is the age that the lame man will
please (10)?
One loved by the wild Irish lad (11)?
The age of the emigrant on the high seas
(12)?
The age that we all wish we had (13)?

Can you tell me the age of the plants (14)?
of the birds (15)?
The age that the heathen adore (16)?
The age that is heavy (17)? the one that
impairs (18)?
The one that is not less nor more (19)?

The wild age (20)? the one that the future
foretells (21)?
The one where the vessels safe ride (22)?
The snug little age where the minister
dwells (23)?
And the common one right by our side
(24)?

HELEN A. SIBLEY.

OBLIQUE RECTANGLE

1. In oblique. 2. A club. 3. Work. 4. Allured. 5. A riddle. 6. Pertaining to a certain nobleman. 7. A weapon. 8. A fruit. 9. Dressed. 10. An African. 11. A bill of exchange. 12. To tender. 13. Character. 14. A deer. 15. In rectangle.

GEORGE LINWOOD HOSEA.

THE MAGIC LETTERS

(*First Prize,* St. Nicholas League Competition.)

THE MAGIC LETTERS.

(*First Prize,* St. Nicholas League Competition

X	J	A	G	M
L	U	S	E	O
D	I	A	R	D
V	N	C	I	U
E	B	O	O	B

THE above magic letters contain the name, and a brief history, of a great man who died in March. Choosing any letter as a starting-point, and moving one square in any direction, spell out:

1. The man's first name.
2. His middle name.
3. His last name.
4. The year of his birth.
5. The name of the city in which he was born and died.
6. The name of his aunt, and of his daughter.
7. The name of a country where he gained great fame.
8. A famous saying of his.
9. The name of a river which played an important part in his life.
10. The year of his death.
11. The part of the month on which he died.

Each letter may be used more than once, if necessary.

MAURICE P. DUNLAP.

M.M.D.

by Josephine Daskam Bacon

LOVER of little ones
  Up to the end,
Everywhere children now
  Mourn for their friend.

Age could not conquer her,
  Youth ne'er forsook;
Child among children, she
  Laughed heart and book.

Long on the Lonely Road
  She 'll never roam:
Hundreds of children will
  Welcome her home!